# 戰勝 NEW TOEIC
# 新制多益
## 高分演練

### 試題本

# 戰勝
# 新制多益
## 高分演練

NEW
TOEIC

# 戰勝新制多益高分演練：
## 聽力閱讀模擬試題1200題＋中譯解析

| | |
|---|---|
| 作　者 | Kim, Lang／Park, JaEun／ NEXUS TOEIC Research Institute |
| 譯　者 | 關亭薇／蔡裴驊／蘇裕承 |
| 編　輯 | 賴祖兒 |
| 主　編 | 丁宥暄 |
| 校　對 | 黃詩韻／吳思薇 |
| 內文排版 | 謝青秀／林書玉 |
| 封面設計 | 林書玉 |
| 製程管理 | 洪巧玲 |
| 出版者 | 寂天文化事業股份有限公司 |
| 發行人 | 黃朝萍 |
| 電　話 | +886-(0)2-2365-9739 |
| 傳　真 | +886-(0)2-2365-9835 |
| 網　址 | www.icosmos.com.tw |
| 讀者服務 | onlineservice@icosmos.com.tw |
| 出版日期 | 2023 年 02 月 初版再刷（寂天雲隨身聽APP版）(0103) |

國家圖書館出版品預行編目(CIP)資料

戰勝新制多益高分演練：聽力閱讀模擬試題1200題+中譯解析 (寂天雲隨身聽APP版) / Kim, Lang, Park, JaEun等著. -- 初版. -- 臺北市：寂天文化, 2021.11
　　面；　公分
ISBN 978-626-300-083-4 (16K平裝)

1.多益測驗

805.1895　　　　　　　　　110018401

---

Original Title: 나혼자 끝내는 신(新)토익 기출 모의고사 1200제 LC + RC 6회(ISBN: 9791161655529)
written by Kim, Lang & Park, JaEun & NEXUS TOEIC Research Institute
Copyright © 2019 NEXUS Co., Ltd.
All rights reserved.

Original Korean edition published by NEXUS Co., Ltd., Seoul, Korea.
Traditional Chinese Translation Copyright © 2020 by Cosmos Culture Ltd.
This Traditional Chinese edition was published by arrangement with NEXUS Co., Ltd. through Pauline Kim Agency.

# ✒ 作者序

　　在現在這個時代，無論是就業、升遷或是轉職，都需要提供各式各樣的資格證照，當中最不可或缺的證照無疑是多益證書。多益測驗改制後，比起追求在短時間內獲取高分，更需要的是真正的英文實力。因此，接受專業的課程、或是透過具公信力的教材輔助，便顯得更為重要。

　　準備多益的方式務必要採用與個人目標分數相符的學習策略，才能有效達成目標。若考生的目標設定在800分以上，與其為了答對占全部考題一成左右的高難度題型，而備感壓力，不如確實掌握好每個月重複出現的題型，更具得分效果。

　　若是將目標分數瞄準在900分以上的人，則要比其他考生更加著重在PART 3、PART 4的「圖表整合題」、PART 6的「句子插入題」和PART 7的「多篇閱讀題」上面。

　　本書按照**最新多益命題趨勢**編寫實戰試題，並針對各大題型**標示完美解題線索**，有效幫助考生們在短時間內達成目標分數。比起繁雜的理論，更注重在考試時能即刻派上用場的重點，協助考生熟悉考試臨場感。

　　筆者精選出與每期**多益測驗難易度相當、題型相似的試題**，同時在PART 5、PART 6加入多年來授課及研究所獲得的獨門解題技巧，提供讀者詳盡又清晰的解說，讓人彷彿置身在現場聽課般。筆者身為YBM學院的多益代表講師，帶著使命感編寫出此本教材，願讀者們都能快速達成多益目標。

　　由衷感謝在撰寫本書期間，提供多方協助的NEXUS出版社。同時向對筆者的授課及研究，不吝給予協助的金宣華院長、朴友川局長、金勇哲會長、申郁華老師、姜明熹老師表達我們的謝意。

# 目錄

# 架構與特色

符合新制多益
最新趨勢的
六回實戰模擬試題

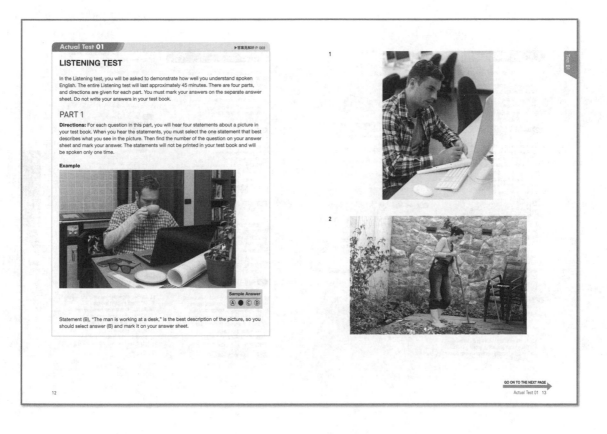

模擬試題反映**最新多益命題趨勢**，幫助學習者完整建立實戰能力。完整涵蓋**六回聽力閱讀實戰試題**，營造與實際多益測驗相同的考試環境，讓學習者以此書作為**考前最後的總複習**。

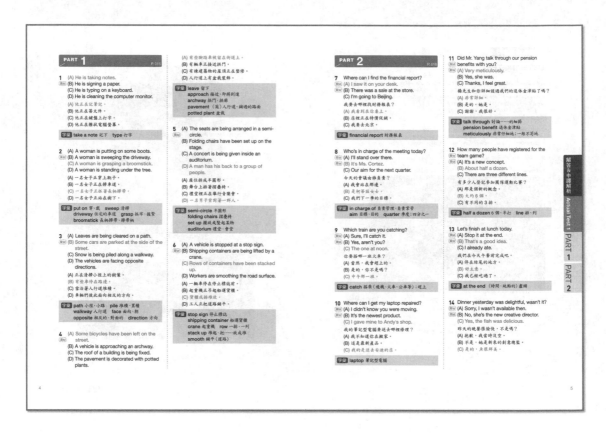

中譯解析本收錄**六回試題的詳盡中譯解析**，讓學習者作答後能**立刻確認答案**，進入**複習**的步驟。

同時標示出**答題關鍵字句**與**重點字彙**，幫助學習者輕鬆找出答案，快速理解內容。

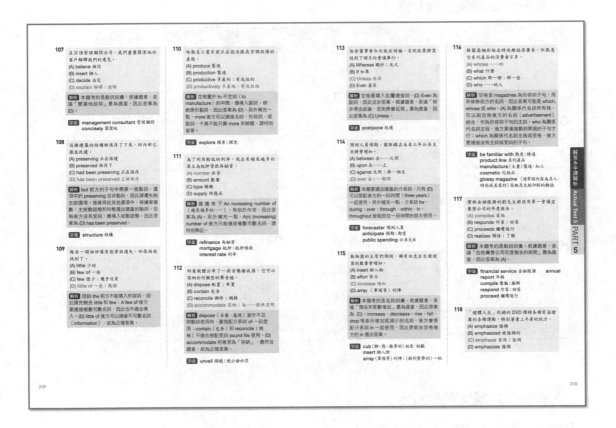

針對僅用中譯難以理解的Part 5、Part 6，更**詳加分析解題過程**，說明**選項正確理由**，釐清選項錯誤原因，完美突破解題障礙。

# 新制多益重點資訊

配合當前的英語使用環境，自2018年3月起開始實施新制多益測驗。總題數與測驗時間仍維持不變，但是各大題的題數略有變化，同時加入過去未曾出現的**圖表**、**文字簡訊**、**線上聊天**與**多篇閱讀**等新題型。

## 新制多益測驗題型介紹

| 題型 | Part | 各大題題型 | 題數 | 時間 | 分數 |
|---|---|---|---|---|---|
| **Listening Comprehension** | 1 | 照片描述 | 6 | 45分 | 495分 |
| | 2 | 應答問題 | 25 | | |
| | 3 | 簡短對話 | 39 | | |
| | 4 | 簡短獨白 | 30 | | |
| **Reading Comprehension** | 5 | 句子填空 | 30 | 75分 | 495分 |
| | 6 | 段落填空 | 16 | | |
| | 7 | 單篇閱讀 | 29 | | |
| | | 雙篇閱讀 | 10 | | |
| | | 多篇閱讀 | 15 | | |
| Total | | 7個大題 | 200題 | 120分 | 990分 |

## 新制多益題型更動部分

**Part 1**　題數從 10 題減少為 6 題

**Part 2**　題數從 30 題減少為 25 題

**Part 3**　題數從 30 題增加為 39 題，新增「三人對話」、「來回五次以上的長對話」、「掌握說話者意圖題」、「圖表資訊整合題」

**Part 4**　題數維持 30 題不變，新增「掌握說話者意圖題」、「圖表資訊整合題」

**Part 5**　題數從 40 題減少為 30 題

**Part 6**　題數從 12 題增加為 16 題，新增「句子插入題」

**Part 7**　題數從 48 題增加為 54 題，新增「文字簡訊、線上聊天文章」、「掌握意圖題、句子插入題」、「多篇閱讀題」

## 🔍 新制多益重點資訊

| | | | |
|---|---|---|---|
| **Part 3** | 掌握說話者意圖題 | 2–3 題 | 詢問說話者在對話中說出某句話的意圖 |
| | 圖表資訊整合題 | 2–3 題 | 掌握對話與圖表資訊（表格、圖形等）兩者之間的關係 |
| | 三人對話 | 1–2 篇對話 | 部分對話中出現三名以上的說話者 |
| | 來回五次以上的長對話 | | 來回超過五次以上的長篇對話題 |
| **Part 4** | 掌握說話者意圖題 | 2–3 題 | 詢問說話者在獨白中說出某句話的意圖 |
| | 圖表資訊整合題 | 2–3 題 | 掌握獨白與圖表資訊（表格、圖形等）兩者之間的關係 |
| **Part 6** | 句子插入題 | 4 題（一篇文章 1 題） | • 選出符合前後文意的句子填入空格中<br>• 必須藉由選項列出的句子掌握文意 |
| **Part 7** | 句子插入題 | 2 題（一篇文章 1 題） | 將題目列出的句子填入適當的空格中 |
| | 文字簡訊、線上聊天 | 各一篇 | 兩人對話的文字簡訊、多人進行的線上聊天 |
| | 掌握意圖題 | 2 題（一篇文章 1 題） | • 詢問說話者說出某句話的意圖<br>• 從文字簡訊、線上聊天文中出題 |
| | 多篇閱讀 | 三組文章 | 測驗是否理解三篇文章間的關係 |

# 自我學習計畫表

**目標為初級者** 具有一定的基礎,但是仍難以考到**700分以上**。

即使具有一定的基礎,仍有可能未充分練習過模擬試題。在實際進行多益測驗時,經常會有時間不夠用的狀況發生。這類考生的準備重點在於平常練習時,就要像實際測驗一樣記錄作答時間。

| 第1天 | 第2天 | 第3天 | 第4天 | 第5天 | 第6天 |
|---|---|---|---|---|---|
| Actual Test 1 解題&對答案 | Actual Test 1 確認聽力詳解&聽寫練習 | Actual Test 1 確認閱讀詳解&單字複習 | Actual Test 2 解題&對答案 | Actual Test 2 確認聽力詳解&聽寫練習 | Actual Test 2 確認閱讀詳解&單字複習 |
| 第7天 | 第8天 | 第9天 | 第10天 | 第11天 | 第12天 |
| Actual Test 3 解題&對答案 | Actual Test 3 確認聽力詳解&聽寫練習 | Actual Test 3 確認閱讀詳解&單字複習 | Actual Test 4 解題&對答案 | Actual Test 4 確認聽力詳解&聽寫練習 | Actual Test 4 確認閱讀詳解&單字複習 |
| 第13天 | 第14天 | 第15天 | 第16天 | 第17天 | 第18天 |
| Actual Test 5 解題&對答案 | Actual Test 5 確認聽力詳解&聽寫練習 | Actual Test 5 確認閱讀詳解&單字複習 | Actual Test 6 解題&對答案 | Actual Test 6 確認聽力詳解&聽寫練習 | Actual Test 6 確認閱讀詳解&單字複習 |

**目標為中級者** 已掌握考試的重點,但是分數仍徘徊在**800分上下**。

已認真準備過多益,也考過兩至三次試,但是分數仍舊停滯不前。雖然練習聽力模擬試題相當重要,但是若能以聽寫練習進行二次複習尤佳。閱讀部分的練習,請按照各大題的建議作答時間,同時檢視自己的弱點在哪裡。

| 第1天 | 第2天 | 第3天 | 第4天 | 第5天 | 第6天 |
|---|---|---|---|---|---|
| Actual Test 1 解題&對答案 | Actual Test 1 對答案及確認詳解 | Actual Test 2 解題&對答案 | Actual Test 2 對答案及確認詳解 | Actual Test 3 解題&對答案 | Actual Test 3 對答案及確認詳解 |
| 第7天 | 第8天 | 第9天 | 第10天 | 第11天 | 第12天 |
| Actual Test 4 解題&對答案 | Actual Test 4 對答案及確認詳解 | Actual Test 5 解題&對答案 | Actual Test 5 對答案及確認詳解 | Actual Test 6 解題&對答案 | Actual Test 6 對答案及確認詳解 |

**目標為高級者** 目前以**900分以上**為目標,但是仍覺得難以達成。

有時候以為自己考得不錯,卻在意料之外的地方出錯。曾經答錯的題目,極有可能會再犯同樣的錯誤,因此請務必再確認一次。

| 第1天 | 第2天 | 第3天 | 第4天 | 第5天 | 第6天 |
|---|---|---|---|---|---|
| Actual Test 1 &詳解 | Actual Test 2 &詳解 | Actual Test 3 &詳解 | Actual Test 4 &詳解 | Actual Test 5 &詳解 | Actual Test 6 &詳解 |

# 自我實力檢測

請在每回試題作答完畢後，填寫下方表格。記錄每回測驗的答對題數，並檢視自己是否有進步。

## 對答案之前

|  | 作答日期 | 作答所需時間 | 難易度感受 |
|---|---|---|---|
| **Actual Test 1** |  |  | 難　中　易 |
| **Actual Test 2** |  |  | 難　中　易 |
| **Actual Test 3** |  |  | 難　中　易 |
| **Actual Test 4** |  |  | 難　中　易 |
| **Actual Test 5** |  |  | 難　中　易 |
| **Actual Test 6** |  |  | 難　中　易 |

## 對完答案後

|  | 答對題數 | 分數換算 | 總分 |
|---|---|---|---|
| **Actual Test 1** | 聽力：<br>閱讀： |  | 分 |
| **Actual Test 2** | 聽力：<br>閱讀： |  | 分 |
| **Actual Test 3** | 聽力：<br>閱讀： |  | 分 |
| **Actual Test 4** | 聽力：<br>閱讀： |  | 分 |
| **Actual Test 5** | 聽力：<br>閱讀： |  | 分 |
| **Actual Test 6** | 聽力：<br>閱讀： |  | 分 |

＊ 請參照 p. 270 的分數換算表進行分數換算。

**慢著！**作答前請務必**確認！**

- 請當作實際考試般，將書桌收拾乾淨，做好心理準備。
- 請將手機關機，並善用時鐘或手錶計時。
- 規定作答時間為 120 分鐘，請務必遵守規定時間。
- 請盡可能按照題目順序作答，碰到難題時，切勿直接跳過。

# Actual Test

---

# 01

開始時間 ：
完成時間 ：

# LISTENING TEST

In the Listening test, you will be asked to demonstrate how well you understand spoken English. The entire Listening test will last approximately 45 minutes. There are four parts, and directions are given for each part. You must mark your answers on the separate answer sheet. Do not write your answers in your test book.

# PART 1 🎧 01

**Directions:** For each question in this part, you will hear four statements about a picture in your test book. When you hear the statements, you must select the one statement that best describes what you see in the picture. Then find the number of the question on your answer sheet and mark your answer. The statements will not be printed in your test book and will be spoken only one time.

**Example**

**Sample Answer**
Ⓐ ● Ⓒ Ⓓ

Statement (B), "The man is working at a desk," is the best description of the picture, so you should select answer (B) and mark it on your answer sheet.

1

2

3

4

5

6

# PART 2 🎧 ❨02❩

**Directions:** You will hear a question or statement and three responses spoken in English. They will not be printed in your test book and will be spoken only one time. Select the best response to the question or statement and mark the letter (A), (B), or (C) on your answer sheet.

7   Mark your answer on your answer sheet.

8   Mark your answer on your answer sheet.

9   Mark your answer on your answer sheet.

10  Mark your answer on your answer sheet.

11  Mark your answer on your answer sheet.

12  Mark your answer on your answer sheet.

13  Mark your answer on your answer sheet.

14  Mark your answer on your answer sheet.

15  Mark your answer on your answer sheet.

16  Mark your answer on your answer sheet.

17  Mark your answer on your answer sheet.

18  Mark your answer on your answer sheet.

19  Mark your answer on your answer sheet.

20  Mark your answer on your answer sheet.

21  Mark your answer on your answer sheet.

22  Mark your answer on your answer sheet.

23  Mark your answer on your answer sheet.

24  Mark your answer on your answer sheet.

25  Mark your answer on your answer sheet.

26  Mark your answer on your answer sheet.

27  Mark your answer on your answer sheet.

28  Mark your answer on your answer sheet.

29  Mark your answer on your answer sheet.

30  Mark your answer on your answer sheet.

31  Mark your answer on your answer sheet.

# PART 3 🎧03

**Directions:** You will hear some conversations between two or more people. You will be asked to answer three questions about what the speakers say in each conversation. Select the best response to each question and mark the letter (A), (B), (C), or (D) on your answer sheet. The conversations will not be printed in your test book and will be spoken only one time.

32  What does the man want to do?
- (A) Recruit an assistant
- (B) Get a degree
- (C) Have a facial
- (D) Visit a Web site

33  Why did the woman contact the college?
- (A) To locate a suitable salon
- (B) To sign up for a college course
- (C) To rent some equipment
- (D) To find trained job applicants

34  Why does the woman recommend the Health and Beauty Web site?
- (A) It features useful advice.
- (B) It is only for professionals.
- (C) It has a lot of users.
- (D) It is simple to navigate.

35  What does the man ask about?
- (A) The woman's availability
- (B) The amount of tax to be returned
- (C) The return from a vacation
- (D) The call to a client

36  What does the woman plan to do this week?
- (A) Finalize a seminar
- (B) Visit the tax office
- (C) Attend a ceremony
- (D) Provide some paperwork

37  What does the man suggest doing?
- (A) Setting up a conference call
- (B) Filling out a registration form
- (C) Submitting the required documentation
- (D) Making a phone call

38  What event does the woman want to attend?
- (A) A movie premiere
- (B) A sporting event
- (C) A book launch
- (D) A theater performance

39  What is the problem?
- (A) A phone system is not working.
- (B) A representative reserved the wrong tickets.
- (C) A credit card was stolen.
- (D) A game is sold out.

40  What information does the man request?
- (A) A reference number
- (B) A business address
- (C) The name of an event
- (D) Credit card details

41  Who most likely is the woman?
- (A) A technical director
- (B) A human resources manager
- (C) A temporary worker
- (D) A factory worker

42  Why is the man calling?
- (A) To request a reference
- (B) To submit his portfolio
- (C) To ask about employment
- (D) To explain a forthcoming training session

43  What does the man offer to send?
- (A) An extended contract
- (B) A draft design
- (C) An upgraded portfolio
- (D) An updated résumé

GO ON TO THE NEXT PAGE

**44** Where does the conversation most likely take place?

(A) At a hotel
(B) At a rental agency
(C) At a weekend retreat
(D) At a conference hall

**45** What does the woman mention about the promotion?

(A) A free bus service
(B) Details of a special offer
(C) The date of a new hotel opening
(D) Discounts at the restaurant

**46** What does the man explain to the woman?

(A) The discount applies only on certain days.
(B) There will be a two-hour delay.
(C) The hotel is closed to the public.
(D) The promotion has false information.

---

**47** What problem are the speakers discussing?

(A) Changing a menu
(B) Rescheduling an event
(C) Being understaffed
(D) Hiring employees

**48** What does the woman offer to do?

(A) Wash dishes
(B) Meet a client
(C) Move tables
(D) Serve food

**49** What does the woman mean when she says, "I don't think you have to worry about that"?

(A) She believes she can handle the task.
(B) She is able to help cooking.
(C) She is having some trouble with the customer.
(D) She thinks the men can't solve the problem.

**50** What does the woman plan to write about?

(A) Professional landscaping
(B) Farming
(C) Public transportation
(D) Fashion trends

**51** What did the man receive from the woman?

(A) A billing statement
(B) Samples of her work
(C) A rental contract
(D) References

**52** What does the woman mean when she says, "Absolutely"?

(A) She will answer some questions.
(B) She can't call at the moment.
(C) She will not be able to complete the draft by the deadline.
(D) She agrees to the man's suggestion.

---

**53** Why will Amanda be late for the meeting?

(A) She is still on site.
(B) She has to make a phone call.
(C) She is caught in traffic congestion.
(D) She has lost the keys to the office.

**54** What did Amanda ask the man to do?

(A) Fetch a hard hat
(B) Drive straight to the office
(C) Take notes at a meeting
(D) Get some keys from her desk

**55** What does the man say he will do next?

(A) Pick up some work supplies
(B) Contact a supervisor
(C) Link up his computer
(D) Call the site manager

**56** Where does the woman work?

   (A) At an educational institute
   (B) At a convention center
   (C) At a stationery store
   (D) At a staffing agency

**57** What does the man ask about the job?

   (A) The starting date
   (B) The salary
   (C) The duration
   (D) The location

**58** Why does the man say, "Not a problem"?

   (A) He doesn't have any questions at the moment.
   (B) He wants to start on a different date.
   (C) He can start working on Monday.
   (D) He can take the job right away.

---

**59** What does the woman want to do?

   (A) Request a collection service
   (B) Hold a new dance class
   (C) Alter a previous order
   (D) Have an area specially designed

**60** What does the man say he can do?

   (A) Comment on her work
   (B) Design a dance stage
   (C) Check a building guarantee
   (D) Obtain an approximate estimate

**61** What does the woman request?

   (A) Contact information
   (B) Design samples
   (C) Blueprint drawings
   (D) A stock catalog

**62** What are the speakers mainly discussing?

   (A) Factory installations
   (B) Security systems
   (C) A new brand launch
   (D) A fashion magazine

**63** What does the woman ask for?

   (A) A list of security cameras
   (B) An Internet address
   (C) A purchase order number
   (D) Details of a magazine

**64** What does the man offer to do?

   (A) Give the woman his magazine
   (B) Install a security device
   (C) Review a feature
   (D) Purchase products online

**GO ON TO THE NEXT PAGE**

| Manager's Office | Staff Room | Copy Room |
| A102 | A103 | A104 | A105 |

| Inventory | |
|---|---|
| Item | Quantity |
| Dining table | 6 |
| Stool | 5 |
| Table cloth | 2 |
| Small-sized rug | 7 |

**65** Why is the man calling?

(A) To cancel an appointment
(B) To place an order
(C) To arrange a delivery
(D) To obtain contact information

**66** Look at the graphic. Where is the LCD computer monitor supposed to go?

(A) A102
(B) A103
(C) A104
(D) A105

**67** When will the speakers most likely meet?

(A) At 2:00 P.M.
(B) At 3:00 P.M.
(C) At 4:00 P.M.
(D) At 5:30 P.M.

**68** What are the speakers discussing?

(A) The duration of a promotional event
(B) The recent inventory
(C) Sales figures of a new product
(D) Strategies for promoting the business

**69** Look at the graphic. Which item will the man order right away?

(A) Dining table
(B) Stool
(C) Table cloth
(D) Small-sized rug

**70** What does the woman say she will do in a few weeks?

(A) Make a list of items
(B) Repair a broken display
(C) Invite customers to the shop
(D) Promote an event

# PART 4 🎧04🎧

**Directions:** You will hear some talks given by a single speaker. You will be asked to answer three questions about what the speaker says in each talk. Select the best response to each question and mark the letter (A), (B), (C), or (D) on your answer sheet. The talks will not be printed in your test book and will be spoken only one time.

**71** Where does the speaker work?

(A) At an accounting firm
(B) At a construction materials supplier
(C) At an office supply store
(D) At a window replacement company

**72** Why is the speaker calling?

(A) To query an order
(B) To offer a discount
(C) To explain shipment costs
(D) To cancel a delivery

**73** What is the listener asked to do?

(A) Email a reply
(B) Return a phone call
(C) Check an estimate
(D) Provide a credit card

**74** Who most likely is the speaker?

(A) A ship employee
(B) A local singer
(C) A park attendant
(D) An entertainer

**75** According to the speaker, where will dinner be served?

(A) On the beach
(B) In the lobby
(C) In the cafeteria
(D) On the deck

**76** What will the listeners attend after dinner?

(A) A play
(B) A welcome speech
(C) A film
(D) A concert

**77** What have listeners been learning?

(A) New employee orientation
(B) Technology training
(C) First aid in the office
(D) Improving production techniques

**78** What does the speaker ask listeners to complete?

(A) A questionnaire
(B) A timetable
(C) A consent form
(D) A test

**79** Why would listeners provide an e-mail address?

(A) To receive a list of advanced classes
(B) To apply for employment opportunities
(C) To cancel a reservation
(D) To get details of trainer's notes

**80** What is being advertised?

(A) Retail opportunities
(B) Offices for hire
(C) Sports training
(D) Sales consulting

**81** What new service did the company recently add?

(A) Internet selling
(B) Web page design
(C) Facility management
(D) Mail handling

**82** What will happen next month?

(A) Prices will increase.
(B) More staff will be recruited.
(C) A new location will open.
(D) An online seminar will be offered.

GO ON TO THE NEXT PAGE

83 What kind of company does the
speaker work for?

(A) A retail store
(B) A packaging company
(C) A fitness corporation
(D) An illustration company

84 What has the company recently done?

(A) Moved to Germany
(B) Opened a new branch
(C) Signed a contract
(D) Launched a new product range

85 According to the speaker, what will
listeners do over the next few weeks?

(A) Recruit new employees
(B) Design a building
(C) Prepare work samples
(D) Join a health club

86 What products are being discussed?

(A) Solar cells
(B) Heating systems
(C) Computer programs
(D) Home insulation

87 According to the speaker, what might
surprise listeners about these products?

(A) They are cheap to install.
(B) They are selling very well.
(C) They cost little to maintain.
(D) They teach directions to use.

88 What does the speaker mean when he
says, "This is as good as it gets"?

(A) The system is in good condition.
(B) He can't make the system better.
(C) His staff is very knowledgeable.
(D) He thinks he is offering a good deal.

89 Who is the speaker?

(A) A building manager
(B) A contractor
(C) A mover
(D) An inspector

90 What does the woman mean when she
says, "that's not an option anymore"?

(A) A service is no longer available.
(B) A lease has been terminated.
(C) A building failed to pass inspection.
(D) A date needs to be changed.

91 What does the woman offer to do?

(A) Arrange a moving service
(B) Contact the listener under certain
condition
(C) Supervise an installation
(D) Give a discount

| Receipt | |
|---|---|
| Doughnut | $1.75 |
| Chocolate cake | $2.50 |
| Apple pie | $3.00 |
| Pastry | $4.25 |
| Total | $11.50 |

92 Why is the speaker calling?

(A) To cancel an order
(B) To report a missing item
(C) To arrange a delivery
(D) To request a refund

93 Look at the graphic. What is the price of
the item the speaker refers to?

(A) $1.75
(B) $2.50
(C) $3.00
(D) $4.25

94 What does the speaker want the listener
to do?

(A) Get in touch with him
(B) Give him a refund
(C) Email the list
(D) Upgrade the shipping method

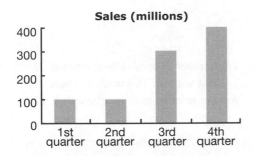

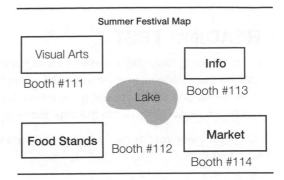

**95** Where most likely does the speaker work?

(A) At a phone company
(B) At an accounting firm
(C) At a lighting maker
(D) At an appliance manufacturer

**96** Look at the graphic. When did the company release the new products?

(A) 1st quarter
(B) 2nd quarter
(C) 3rd quarter
(D) 4th quarter

**97** What does the speaker say she will do for the listeners?

(A) Treat them to dinner
(B) Give them a financial incentive
(C) Present an award
(D) Let them take a vacation

**98** What does the speaker say about the Summer Festival?

(A) He plans to attend it.
(B) There is not much room to park cars.
(C) He will perform there.
(D) He is one of the sponsors.

**99** Look at the graphic. Where will the radio station be broadcasting from?

(A) Booth #111
(B) Booth #112
(C) Booth #113
(D) Booth #114

**100** According to the speaker, what can listeners do at the Summer Festival's Web site?

(A) Buy tickets
(B) Reserve seats
(C) Get a certificate
(D) Obtain maps

This is the end of the Listening test. Turn to Part 5 in your test book.

GO ON TO THE NEXT PAGE

# READING TEST

In the Reading test, you will read a variety of texts and answer several different types of reading comprehension questions. The entire Reading test will last 75 minutes. There are three parts, and directions are given for each part. You are encouraged to answer as many questions as possible within the time allowed.

You must mark your answers on the separate answer sheet. Do not write your answers in your test book.

# PART 5

**Directions:** A word or phrase is missing in each of the sentences below. Four answer choices are given below each sentence. Select the best answer to complete the sentence. Then mark the letter (A), (B), (C), or (D) on your answer sheet.

**101** The Amoti Management executives have decided to uphold the funding ------- of the research department team.

(A) deciding
(B) decisions
(C) decide
(D) decides

**102** To conserve energy, please switch off electrical appliances before ------- the workplace.

(A) to leave
(B) leaves
(C) leaving
(D) left

**103** The National Painting and Decorating Show features chances to listen to specific ------- from experienced craftsmen.

(A) case
(B) advice
(C) songs
(D) house

**104** The KKL Group has a vacancy ------- an experienced management accountant.

(A) across
(B) for
(C) through
(D) off

**105** Salaries are ------- to remain the same this quarter due to the plunge in domestic consumption.

(A) liked
(B) likely
(C) likened
(D) likeable

**106** Ms. Lucas forecasts that the entire regeneration program should be completed ------- the end of the month.

(A) by
(B) until
(C) of
(D) on

**107** A recent questionnaire revealed that over 50 percent of online customers plan to renew ------- broadband connection with the same company.

(A) them
(B) theirs
(C) they
(D) their

**108** To ------- to a customer service representative, please dial the number located at the bottom of this form.

(A) tell
(B) mention
(C) speak
(D) inform

109 Even though Ms. Onaissis will be unable to attend this week's seminar, -------, along with all the department managers, will be at the one next week.
(A) she
(B) her
(C) hers
(D) herself

110 The acquisition of Titan Industries should help Pacific Holdings ------- its business strategies.
(A) diversity
(B) diverse
(C) diversify
(D) diversely

111 Without updated security software, computer systems are ------- to numerous viruses.
(A) superior
(B) exemplary
(C) vulnerable
(D) cautious

112 Elias Store's security department reacted ------- to employees' concerns over a suspicious package.
(A) prompt
(B) promptly
(C) prompting
(D) promptness

113 Travelers must show appropriate identification ------- boarding any domestic flight.
(A) in addition
(B) such as
(C) although
(D) when

114 Long-distance lorry drivers are forbidden from entering Park Avenue because the road is too -------.
(A) narrow
(B) narrowly
(C) narrows
(D) narrower

115 The headquarters for Acoho International are located ------- the post office in Springhill.
(A) near
(B) besides
(C) close
(D) next

116 Since a winner has not yet been -------, the judges will have to further assess the competing entries.
(A) decided
(B) decisive
(C) deciding
(D) decision

117 If the university you have applied for is full, your name will ------- be placed on a waiting list in case someone drops out.
(A) intermittently
(B) automatically
(C) progressively
(D) considerably

118 By ------- old buses with new, more fuel-efficient models, Kennewick was able to save on maintenance and repairs.
(A) replacement
(B) replacing
(C) replace
(D) replaced

119 ------- for Artist of the Year must be received by the judging committee before 3:00 P.M. on Monday.
(A) Authorities
(B) Performances
(C) Occurrences
(D) Nominations

120 Thanks to our excellent sales records, our sales executives can ------- look forward to bonuses this month.
(A) which
(B) all
(C) another
(D) any

GO ON TO THE NEXT PAGE

**121** Richard K. Norse's mystery story *House In The Mist* has been ------- as the best novel of the decade.

(A) totaled
(B) alleviated
(C) billed
(D) consisted

**122** Most consumers, ------- given a choice between a cheap and a high-quality appliance, put product quality first.

(A) who
(B) which
(C) when
(D) what

**123** Howard Financial is pleased to ------- its loyal customers with the best consulting services available in the region.

(A) provide
(B) providing
(C) provided
(D) provider

**124** If Voks Tech had agreed to make a contract, the necessary funds -------.

(A) send
(B) would have sent
(C) were sent
(D) would have been sent

**125** By the time the fire on Birdseed Lane was reported, it ------- to the neighborhood.

(A) spreading
(B) spreads
(C) were spread
(D) had spread

**126** In August, the Connors Gallery will display a number of works by the ------- artist James McNeil.

(A) distinguished
(B) founded
(C) estimated
(D) allocated

**127** The training, ------- was scheduled to begin on June 20, was put off for three weeks.

(A) which
(B) this
(C) what
(D) that

**128** The planners of the music festival tomorrow at Jenkins Park are considering postponing the event ------- the weather clears up tonight.

(A) even if
(B) nevertheless
(C) regardless of
(D) so that

**129** Although the Clearfit water purifier was a success this summer, it has been ------- unreliable by the Quality Guidelines Association.

(A) inspected
(B) conducted
(C) deemed
(D) allowed

**130** Several tenants of the Sandrine Building reported that they frequently had to ------- a lot of noise.

(A) participate in
(B) put forth
(C) contend with
(D) aspire to

# PART 6

**Directions:** Read the texts that follow. A word, phrase, or sentence is missing in parts of each text. Four answer choices for each question are given below the text. Select the best answer to complete the text. Then mark the letter (A), (B), (C), or (D) on your answer sheet.

**Questions 131-134** refer to the following e-mail.

**To:** service@blueoceanair.com

**From:** james.gimbel@cmail.com

**Re:** Reservation Error

Hi there. My name's James Gimbel. I made a reservation on a flight from Sydney to Washington on Tuesday, July 12. I was planning to return to Washington to celebrate my 10th anniversary with my wife. My ------- number is 5774001. On the day of my departure, which was July 15,
**131.**
I arrived at the airport an hour early. I ------- went to one of Blueocean Air's check-in kiosks.
**132.**
When I entered my reservation information to the kiosk, it said that my check-in status was invalid. I rushed to one of your representatives and let her know what happened to me, presenting the printed confirmation e-mail. -------. She said I had to wait until a seat was available. I stood
**133.**
nervously next to the counter for two hours before boarding the plane at the last minute.

I was so upset and really disappointed with your system. I would like your explanation ------- this
**134.**
issue. Please call my cell phone number as soon as possible.

Thank you,

James Gimbel

131 (A) book
(B) booking
(C) booked
(D) bookable

132 (A) gradually
(B) substantially
(C) comprehensively
(D) immediately

133 (A) Therefore, I had to make an additional payment.
(B) Then, she put me on the waiting list.
(C) Unfortunately, the printer was not working.
(D) Afterward, she required me to open my luggage.

134 (A) beyond
(B) concerning
(C) along
(D) up to

GO ON TO THE NEXT PAGE

Anna Ruben
80-5 Winston Flats
2917 Woody Avenue
Riverside, CA 89723

Dear Ms. Ruben:

Thank you for your request for information regarding your bank account. The $20 fee was included in your latest statement because your August payment was received late. -------. Because of this, we are ------- the normal charge. Your account has been
     **135.**                          **136.**
revised accordingly.

To guarantee that your monthly payments are ------- on time, we advise that you sign
                      **137.**
up for our automatic debit option. With this service, you can pay the minimum amount due on a ------- amount on a regular basis. Visit www.chvasbankingservice.com/
          **138.**
payments for details.

Should you have questions or concerns, I can be contacted at d.adelaide@ chvasbankingservice.com.

Thank you for your business.

Dana Adelaide

Account Specialist

---

**135** (A) You can pay this late fee either electronically or in person.
(B) We encourage you to open a new savings account.
(C) However, we understand that you are a longtime client of good standing.
(D) You should complete necessary forms to be reimbursed by the end of the month.

**136** (A) expecting
(B) imposing
(C) waiving
(D) honoring

**137** (A) already
(B) always
(C) evenly
(D) shortly

**138** (A) specified
(B) specifying
(C) specifically
(D) specification

**Questions 139-142** refer to the following notice.

Fitness Center Closing

Most of the Acebody fitness centers will be closed starting on Monday, August 14, for

an ------- renovation. Major upgrades include the newest exercise equipment, a new
    **139.**
coat of interior paint, and new flooring and fixtures. After considering opinions from

our center -------, we will add more GX rooms and sauna facilities. As we will have
    **140.**
more GX rooms on the second floor, some of equipment such as bench presses and

treadmills will be moved to the first floor.

The closure may last several months. -------.
                      **141.**
You'll still be able to use the following branches:

- Wellers location (25 Main Blvd.)

- Paradise location (8 Brea Dr.)

- Aquatic location (110 East St.)

------- a location near you, visit www.acebodyfit.com and speak to a gym staff member
**142.**
through online chatting service.

---

139 (A) extend
    (B) extensively
    (C) extensive
    (D) extending

140 (A) candidates
    (B) patrons
    (C) pedestrians
    (D) passengers

141 (A) We expect to reopen our doors on
        December 1.
    (B) You can register for a dance class at
        www.acebodyfit.com.
    (C) Regular exercise is considered
        necessary for your health.
    (D) The gym is scheduled to open at 10
        A.M. tomorrow.

142 (A) Find
    (B) Having found
    (C) To be found
    (D) To find

GO ON TO THE NEXT PAGE

**To:** All employees
**From:** Director, HR Department
**Re:** Personnel Changes

After a ------- passed at a board meeting on February 10, Melrose System is delighted
      **143.**
to announce the following personnel changes. We believe Melrose System will continue

growing steadily under the new management.

Angela Lansbury, the senior accounting director, has been appointed as chief financial

officer. She will be ------- responsible for supervising all budget management and
       **144.**
investment strategies.

------- we are expanding our international business, the company has established a
**145.**
new position: international business director. Andy Griffith, the domestic sales manager,

has been assigned to this position, and he will oversee all of the company's global

operations.

John Walton, the senior marketing manager, has been promoted to the domestic

sales manager position. -------. He will be in charge of developing the sales strategies
      **146.**
designed to achieve short-term and long-term growth for our business in the domestic

market.

143 (A) resolves
    (B) resolved
    (C) resolving
    (D) resolution

144 (A) regularly
    (B) primarily
    (C) relatively
    (D) positively

145 (A) Now that
    (B) Rather than
    (C) During
    (D) Whether

146 (A) As of next month, he will be working
        overseas.
    (B) He will take over Andy Griffith's
        duties.
    (C) This will be an addition to his
        responsibilities as CFO.
    (D) He will take care of all of the
        company's budget estimates.

# PART 7

**Directions:** In this part you will read a selection of texts, such as magazine and newspaper articles, e-mails, and instant messages. Each text or set of texts is followed by several questions. Select the best answer for each question and mark the letter (A), (B), (C), or (D) on your answer sheet.

**Questions 147-148** refer to the following text message.

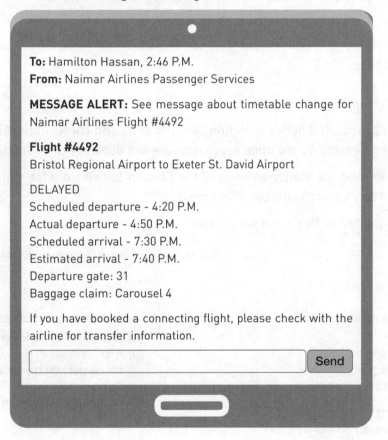

**To:** Hamilton Hassan, 2:46 P.M.
**From:** Naimar Airlines Passenger Services

**MESSAGE ALERT:** See message about timetable change for Naimar Airlines Flight #4492

**Flight #4492**
Bristol Regional Airport to Exeter St. David Airport

DELAYED
Scheduled departure - 4:20 P.M.
Actual departure - 4:50 P.M.
Scheduled arrival - 7:30 P.M.
Estimated arrival - 7:40 P.M.
Departure gate: 31
Baggage claim: Carousel 4

If you have booked a connecting flight, please check with the airline for transfer information.

Send

**147** Why was the text message sent?
(A) To confirm a flight booking
(B) To announce a change in flight status
(C) To inform a passenger of the departure gate
(D) To provide an update about connecting flights

**148** What is indicated about Mr. Hassan?
(A) He will depart from Bristol.
(B) He paid for his flight in Exeter.
(C) He checked two bags onto a flight.
(D) He lost his ticket information.

GO ON TO THE NEXT PAGE

Questions 149-151 refer to the following flyer.

Join us for the
## Grand Opening of Jackson's on April 18!

To celebrate the opening of our new store, Jackson's is offering "Buy One, Get One Half Price" over the first week of trading. So come and see our handbags and shoes. Make a choice from more than 20 brand names including:

- Yanto
- Siegried
- La Manche
- Indigo
- Peach Mama

Jackson's is located between Helton Clothing and Food For All in the Cherish Vale Shopping Center. We are open seven days a week during regular shopping hours.

Take a look at the March 30 issue of the *Cherish Vale Herald* for a profile of the new Jackson's store manager, Ellie Juno.

Offer is limited to five items per customer.

149 What is sold at Jackson's?
(A) Food
(B) Clothing
(C) Fashion accessories
(D) Sports equipment

150 According to the flyer, what can customers do on April 18-24?
(A) Receive a free copy of the *Cherish Vale Herald*
(B) Attend a press reception for the opening of a new store
(C) Purchase one item and receive another half price
(D) Present the flyer for a further discount

151 What is mentioned about Jackson's?
(A) It is advertising for employees.
(B) It is situated in a shopping mall.
(C) Its owner will be interviewed by Ellie Juno.
(D) Its opening will be on March 30.

**Questions 152-153** refer to the following notice.

# Namaski

The Namaski Group is dedicated to protecting the environment and ensures that every attempt is made to prevent our waste from being sent to a landfill. We have a policy of encouraging our customers to dispose of our products responsibly at the end of the product's lifecycle. If you buy a product from one of our Namaski stores, we will gladly deliver the appliance to you. At the same time, we will happily collect your old appliance and take it to our disposal facility. Alternatively, you can make arrangements to have your old appliance delivered to our disposal plant. Your local Namaski store can also give you a list of other disposal facilities near to you that offer similar environmentally friendly disposal methods for any-sized electrical appliance.

**152** What is the purpose of the notice?

(A) To promote a new line of electrical goods

(B) To indicate that a delivery has been postponed

(C) To alert customers to a discount offer

(D) To describe available services

**153** According to the notice, what information does Namaski offer?

(A) The names of nearby disposal centers

(B) Published client reviews of products

(C) Recent research on environmental disposal methods

(D) Descriptions of the company's production depots

GO ON TO THE NEXT PAGE

## Clearview Film Studios

686 Whale Avenue, Surrey, UK

March 30
Ms. Imogen Cranford
34 Thames Street, Clarendon Apt. 121
Surrey, UK

Dear Ms. Cranford,

Thank you for your interest in Clearview Film Studios. Our client Ian Blaine has mentioned you as a suitable candidate for the position of catering manager, and we have now received your application form.

I'd like to arrange an interview with you on Wednesday April 17, at 1:00 P.M. Please contact my assistant, Shimla Shem, as soon as possible to confirm that this is an acceptable time. She can be reached at 010-555-9234.

Also, I would be grateful if you would resend your résumé to me via e-mail. The résumé you submitted online through our Web site was corrupted and we could not view the last page of the document.

Finally, please find enclosed several mandatory forms you must complete and bring with you to the interview. We look forward to hearing from you.

Sincerely,

Edward Trent
Human Resource Manager

Enclosures

---

**154** Why does Mr. Trent write to Ms. Cranford?

(A) To arrange an appointment
(B) To ask for a recommendation
(C) To inquire about a job opening
(D) To request alterations to an online form

**155** Whom is Ms. Cranford asked to contact?

(A) Mr. Blaine
(B) The production manager
(C) The studio executive
(D) Ms. Shem

**156** What problem does Mr. Trent mention?

(A) He was unable to check some part of an electrical document.
(B) The vacancy Ms. Cranford applied for has already been filled.
(C) The person Ms. Cranford mentioned as a reference could not be contacted.
(D) The application Ms. Cranford sent was received after the deadline.

**Questions 157-158** refer to the following text message chain.

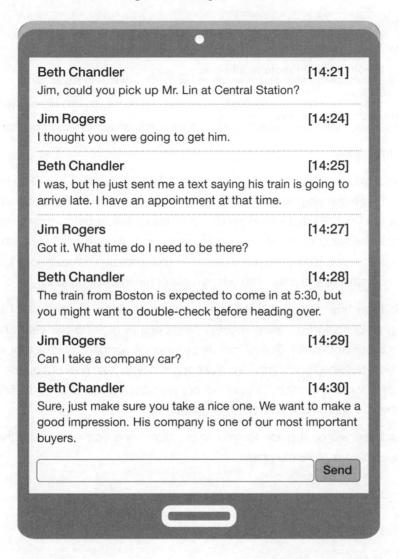

**Beth Chandler** [14:21]
Jim, could you pick up Mr. Lin at Central Station?

**Jim Rogers** [14:24]
I thought you were going to get him.

**Beth Chandler** [14:25]
I was, but he just sent me a text saying his train is going to arrive late. I have an appointment at that time.

**Jim Rogers** [14:27]
Got it. What time do I need to be there?

**Beth Chandler** [14:28]
The train from Boston is expected to come in at 5:30, but you might want to double-check before heading over.

**Jim Rogers** [14:29]
Can I take a company car?

**Beth Chandler** [14:30]
Sure, just make sure you take a nice one. We want to make a good impression. His company is one of our most important buyers.

Send

**157** What is most likely true about Mr. Lin?

(A) He rescheduled a meeting.
(B) He boarded the train late.
(C) He is Ms. Chandler's boss.
(D) He is traveling from Boston.

**158** At 14:27, what does Mr. Rogers most likely mean when he writes, "Got it"?

(A) He knows where Central Station is located.
(B) He is going to get in touch with Mr. Lin.
(C) He understands the reason for the request.
(D) He realizes that trains are sometimes late.

GO ON TO THE NEXT PAGE

**Questions 159-161** refer to the following e-mail.

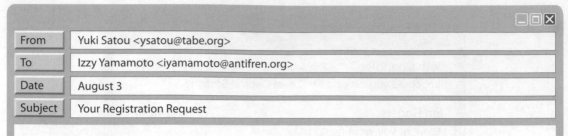

| From | Yuki Satou <ysatou@tabe.org> |
|------|------------------------------|
| To | Izzy Yamamoto <iyamamoto@antifren.org> |
| Date | August 3 |
| Subject | Your Registration Request |

Dear Mr. Yamamoto,

Thank you for your interest in our Construction Industry Update Convention planned for September 15. Regrettably, we are no longer receiving attendance requests, as the event has already sold out. Please let me know if you would like to be put on our waiting list. Should anyone already registered be unable to attend, we will offer spots to those on the list. If we are unable to offer you a place on this occasion, please note that the CIU Convention is held every quarter, with our next event planned for January.

May I also take this opportunity to invite you to become a member of the Tokyo Association of Building Engineers (TABE)? Membership is $300 per year and you will receive a number of benefits. These include inclusion in an industry directory, a discount card for a local building supply firm, and the opportunity to join us at our quarterly cocktail party. To apply for membership, please call our membership office at (440) 555-9943 or visit the relevant page on our Web site, www.tabe.org.

I hope that there will be a place for you at our upcoming convention and that you will consider becoming a TABE member.

Best regards,

Yuki Satou
Tokyo Association of Building Engineers
www.tabe.org
Tel: (440) 555-9943
Fax: (440) 555-4631

159 What is indicated about the
Construction Industry Update
Convention?

(A) It is held four times a year.
(B) It is chaired by Ms. Satou.
(C) It is a new initiative.
(D) It is relocating to a larger venue.

160 What does Ms. Satou suggest that
Mr. Yamamoto do?

(A) Request a refund
(B) Send his contact information to her
(C) Make an appointment with her
(D) Join an organization

161 What is mentioned as a benefit offered
to TABE members?

(A) A list of recommended lawyers
(B) Advance registration for seminars
(C) Reserved seating at seminars
(D) An invitation to a social event

**To:** S&L Manufacturing Group
**From:** Financial Forecast Committee
**Date:** April 14
**Re:** Analysis report

S&L has a well-established reputation for producing the highest quality packaged meals, having been involved in the mass catering industry for many years. However, we are now facing a crisis. As you may be aware, packaging costs have increased significantly by 12 percent over the last three years. We have discussed numerous options to allow us to cover these costs. The general consensus is that we increase the prices of our product lines, but a rise in prices involves the risk of losing customers.

Please bear in mind we have extremely effective business strategies. Our social media promotions are widely viewed and we receive a good response from our customers. We suggest that we keep advertising costs the same. However, we have to seek to find new and more cost-effective packaging designs. This way, we can maintain our pricing strategy without discouraging potential customers and this will help us recoup any losses.

Jane Cox

162 What is stated about S&L Manufacturing Group?
  (A) They manufacture packaging for the catering industry.
  (B) They are well regarded in their field.
  (C) They are a global company.
  (D) They have invested in new product research.

163 Why does S&L Manufacturing Group have a problem?
  (A) Production has become more expensive.
  (B) Few of their business strategies have been successful.
  (C) The quality of their products has decreased.
  (D) Their advertisements are not popular.

164 What does the committee recommend S&L Manufacturing Group do?
  (A) Increase prices universally
  (B) Invest in more economical packaging
  (C) Shut down production
  (D) Increase new product development

Questions 165-168 refer to the following article.

# Spotlight on Alexandria Businesses

The Main Square Business Association and the Supporting Alexandria Organization have amalgamated to host the first Alexandria Business Platform. –[1]–. Organized for Saturday, August 24, from 11:30 A.M. to 8:30 P.M., it will be held in the Main Square and will offer local businesses the opportunity to display their goods and services. For any business that wants to raise its profile in the community, this will be the ideal showcase.

The goal is to provide a platform for a variety of local businesses and performers in Alexandria to highlight their talents. Local shops and boutiques will be displaying their goods, and local restaurants and cafés will offer samples, some even cooking in the open air. –[2]–.

The event will be free and open to the public. Booths for interested parties are available for a rental fee of €100 for the day. As there are a limited number of booths available, vendors are encouraged to reserve theirs as soon as possible. –[3]–. Applicants should fill out an event application form and send it with a €50 non-refundable deposit to Husama Al Enani at henani@alex.org by July 3. –[4]–.

165 For whom is the article most likely intended?

(A) Husama Al Enani
(B) Local business owners
(C) Cookery professionals
(D) Employees of the Main Square Business Association

166 What is NOT mentioned as an action that interested vendors should take?

(A) Paying a sum of money up front
(B) Filling out a form
(C) Submitting a product sample
(D) Emailing details

167 What is indicated about the showcase?

(A) Two organizations are sponsoring the event.
(B) Visitors will be expected to pay to attend.
(C) There will be a surplus of stands available to rent.
(D) The event was well attended in the past.

168 In which of the positions marked [1], [2], [3], and [4] does the following sentence best belong?

"In addition, Amateur performers and artists will be performing throughout the event."

(A) [1]
(B) [2]
(C) [3]
(D) [4]

GO ON TO THE NEXT PAGE

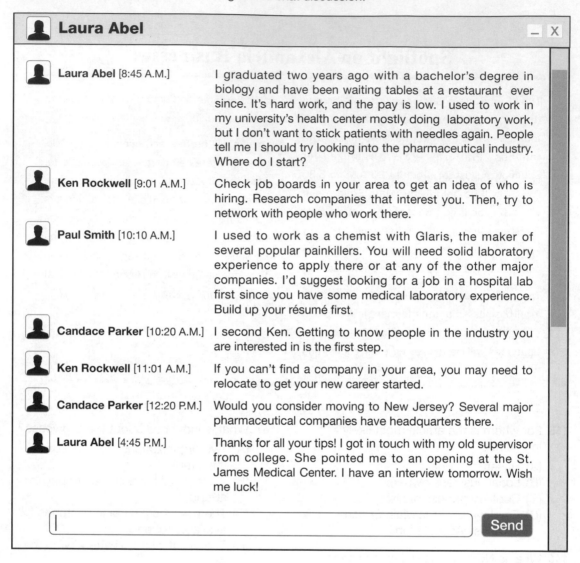

**Laura Abel**                                                              — X

**Laura Abel** [8:45 A.M.]   I graduated two years ago with a bachelor's degree in biology and have been waiting tables at a restaurant ever since. It's hard work, and the pay is low. I used to work in my university's health center mostly doing laboratory work, but I don't want to stick patients with needles again. People tell me I should try looking into the pharmaceutical industry. Where do I start?

**Ken Rockwell** [9:01 A.M.]   Check job boards in your area to get an idea of who is hiring. Research companies that interest you. Then, try to network with people who work there.

**Paul Smith** [10:10 A.M.]   I used to work as a chemist with Glaris, the maker of several popular painkillers. You will need solid laboratory experience to apply there or at any of the other major companies. I'd suggest looking for a job in a hospital lab first since you have some medical laboratory experience. Build up your résumé first.

**Candace Parker** [10:20 A.M.]   I second Ken. Getting to know people in the industry you are interested in is the first step.

**Ken Rockwell** [11:01 A.M.]   If you can't find a company in your area, you may need to relocate to get your new career started.

**Candace Parker** [12:20 P.M.]   Would you consider moving to New Jersey? Several major pharmaceutical companies have headquarters there.

**Laura Abel** [4:45 P.M.]   Thanks for all your tips! I got in touch with my old supervisor from college. She pointed me to an opening at the St. James Medical Center. I have an interview tomorrow. Wish me luck!

|                                                          | Send |

**169** What is suggested about Mr. Smith?

(A) He worked in the pharmaceutical industry.
(B) He used to manage a laboratory.
(C) He currently lives in New Jersey.
(D) His company is accepting applications.

**170** At 10:20 A.M, what does Ms. Parker most likely mean when she writes, "I second Ken"?

(A) She followed Mr. Rockwell's advice before.
(B) She thinks it is important to make connections.
(C) She currently works for a drug maker.
(D) She wants to meet new people.

**171** What is most likely true about Ms. Abel?

(A) She will return to her former employer.
(B) She recently revised her résumé.
(C) She plans to go back to school.
(D) She applied for a job at a hospital.

GO ON TO THE NEXT PAGE

```
┌─────────────────────────────────────────────────────────────────┐
│                         E-Mail Message                            │
├─────────────────────────────────────────────────────────────────┤
│  From:      hamish@dunfair.com                                    │
│  To:        lmckenzie@hotline.com                                 │
│  Subject:   Dunfair Island Food Festival                          │
│  Date:      June 2                                                │
└─────────────────────────────────────────────────────────────────┘
```

Dear Ms. McKenzie,

Thank you for inquiring about the Dunfair Island Food Festival. –[1]–. For more than five years, we have been hosting this festival held exclusively by the residents of Dunfair Island. Cakes, savories, candy, special occasion menus and main courses are some of the foodstuffs on offer, all made by local chefs. We only allow food that is freshly cooked on the day of the festival using local ingredients, and we send inspectors to check the foods; we do not allow any pre-packaged food. Prices range from £1 cookies to wedding cakes priced at £100 and upwards. –[2]–.

On the first Saturday of every month, we also hold the Dunfair Craft Evening, which features goods made by local residents and businesses, and we offer free refreshments between 4 and 6 P.M. –[3]–. This event is always very well attended and typically attracts more than 50 tourists and residents. Sales tend to be brisk, especially throughout the summer months which are the height of the tourist season.

If you would like to join the Dunfair Island Food Festival family, please email visual images of your specialized food and include a list of ingredients used. –[4]–. Also please mention any catering qualifications you have. We will contact you within seven days with further instructions.

Best regards,

Hamish Green
Administrator, Dunfair Island Food Festival

**172** What is the purpose of the e-mail?

(A) To explain how an event operates
(B) To publicize Dunfair Craft Evening
(C) To order some items to be handmade
(D) To promote a cookery competition

**173** Who most likely is Ms. McKenzie?

(A) A craftsperson
(B) A tourist
(C) A restaurant employee
(D) A chef

**174** What is indicated about all the items for sale at Dunfair Island Food Festival?

(A) Nothing is priced higher than £100.
(B) Their prices are reduced by 30% in June, July and August.
(C) They are made by Dunfair Island residents.
(D) They use ingredients from around the world.

**175** In which of the positions marked [1], [2], [3], and [4] does the following sentence best belong?

"Vendors must pay a 10% commission on the food they sell."

(A) [1]
(B) [2]
(C) [3]
(D) [4]

GO ON TO THE NEXT PAGE

---

**Wotamba Real Estate Company**

## Serving businesses in Brisbane, Cairns and the Gold Coast for more than a decade

Featured Listings

**395 Lyons Place:** 170 square meters. Office space in excellent condition in purpose-built complex. Main reception area, multiple offices, and three medium conference rooms. Parking area shared with rest of complex. Great Gold Coast location.

**229 Bayland View:** 280 square meters. Entire ground floor of Georgian building in Brisbane. Fully equipped for catering purposes. In good condition. Electrical appliances also included.

**12 Watama Avenue:** 320 square meters. Upmarket double-tiered commercial premises in the center of Brisbane's tourist district. Brand new fixtures and fittings, including a 20-meter-long marble floor with ivory inset.

**7 Adelaide Street:** 320 square meters. Fitted for restaurant or catering purposes but can be used for retail purposes. Busy location on a main street. Close to Cairns.

We have many more office and retail spaces for sale or lease!
For full listings, visit our Web site at www.wotambarealty.com or contact us by telephone at (330) 555-3593 or by e-mail at properties@wotambarealty.com.

---

## Restaurant Announces New Home

December 1 — Jasmine Palace, the popular Thai restaurant, reopened at a new venue yesterday at 211 Matin Boulevard. Local folk group, Skippy Beat, supplied musical entertainment, and owners Chai and Lan Yong provided guests with a sumptuous banquet featuring dishes typically served on special occasions in their home town of Bangkok. Guests came in hundreds, with loyal customers first on the guest list. Chai Yong gave a short speech in which he thanked the generosity and support of the local community. "Thank you to the residents of Brisbane who took us into their community when we came from Thailand and who have continued to support our restaurant ever since."

Jasmine Palace was opened seven years ago, and since then, the restaurant has become so popular that the existing premises simply could not accommodate the number of customers. "Our previous restaurant had less than 300 square meters of floor space and parking was a problem, as customers had to park in the adjacent car park," said Mr. Yong. "The sales representative at Wotamba Real Estate, who arranged for our old place to be one of his company's featured properties, was invaluable in helping us find this place with its excellent dining and catering facilities, as well as its central location in the heart of the Brisbane community."

One of the restaurant's most fervent supporting customers is Councilor James Taylor, who has struck up a close relationship with the family. He gave a short address to the guests. Replying to a question about the reopening, Councilor Taylor said, "Jasmine Palace has secured its place in the Brisbane local community. I am sure that this new location will only enhance its popularity."

176 What is suggested about Wotamba Real Estate Company?

(A) It sells properties in multiple cities.
(B) It concentrates on the rental market.
(C) It currently has only four properties for sale.
(D) It prefers to deal with vendors face to face.

177 What is the main purpose of the article?

(A) To teach traditional Thai cookery
(B) To announce the sale of a local restaurant
(C) To profile a Brisbane city official
(D) To report on an event at a business

178 According to the article, why did Jasmine Palace relocate?

(A) A new lease was refused.
(B) Its owners decided to move to Brisbane.
(C) The previous location was too small.
(D) The new premises have more modern facilities.

179 Where most likely was Jasmine Palace previously located?

(A) On Bayland View
(B) On Adelaide Street
(C) On Watama Avenue
(D) On Lyons Place

180 What is indicated about the Yongs?

(A) They are friends of Councillor Taylor.
(B) They are musical performers.
(C) They are regular customers of Jasmine Palace.
(D) They are originally from the Gold Coast.

**Questions 181-185** refer to the following e-mail and invoice.

---

**E–Mail Message**

| | |
|---|---|
| **To:** | Gita Litovic <glitovic@voicedesign.com> |
| **From:** | Sasha Timovis <stimovis@manatidesign.com> |
| **Subject:** | Design Delite |
| **Date:** | December 12 |

Dear Ms. Gita Litovic,

As a regular client of Manatidesign, you will be interested in the launch of our newly updated version Design Delite. The most advanced and efficient package of design solutions software on the market now has even more options!

Design Delite still has all of the standard features included in previous versions, such as drawing tools to create technical drawings, shapes, logos and animations. However, the latest version includes advanced options for intricate vector filter effects, colors and 3D effects. Additionally, you will be able to upgrade and add-on new features to Design Delite as the software is constantly being updated.

We are inviting you to participate in an online training session, free of charge, where the trainer will provide expert advice and demonstrations on how to use the software. Furthermore, just by taking part in this workshop, you will receive a 10% discount and free installation on any future Manatidesign product. To register, you must go to our Web site and follow the link for online registration; you can also see a list of our entire product portfolio.

Sincerely,

Sasha Timovis
Technical Services Manager

---

## INVOICE

| **From:** | Manatidesign | **To:** | Gita Litovic |
|---|---|---|---|
| | 11 Yassa Road | | Voice Design studio |
| | Dubrovnic 34963 | | 992 Mayfair Street |
| | Bulgaria | | London W11 |
| | | | United Kingdom |

**Order Date:** January 6
**Shipping date:** January 7
**Expected delivery date:** January 11

| Item | Quantity | Description | Cost |
|---|---|---|---|
| AC41 | 1 | Design Delite (business edition) | $525.00 |
| | 1 | 10 percent discount | $ -52.50 |
| | 1 | Shipping | $ 0.00 |

All sales are final. No refunds or exchanges.
For technical support, visit our Web site at www.manatidesign.com/support.

181 Why did Ms. Timovis email Ms. Litovic?

(A) To recommend a new product
(B) To offer installation advice
(C) To request feedback on a workshop
(D) To remind her to attend a meeting

182 What is true about Design Delite?

(A) It is capable of creating accounting databases.
(B) It is an updated version of a previously released product.
(C) It can only be purchased online.
(D) It is twice as efficient as similar products from competitors.

183 When did Ms. Litovic make a purchase?

(A) On January 6
(B) On January 7
(C) On January 11
(D) On January 14

184 What is indicated about Ms. Litovic?

(A) She paid for overnight delivery.
(B) She purchased the software for residential purposes.
(C) She ordered more than one copy of the same software.
(D) She participated in a training session.

185 What is mentioned about Manatidesign?

(A) It offers one-to-one training sessions.
(B) It provides refunds and exchanges for software.
(C) It provides online customer assistance.
(D) It accepts registration by mail.

GO ON TO THE NEXT PAGE

Questions 186-190 refer to the following advertisement, e-mail, and form.

# CIELO IMAGES

## A premier wedding photography and videography company

Whether it is traditional, modern, or something in between, your wedding is very special. Cielo Images can work with you to make sure it is documented in your own special way. For the past ten years, we have worked with hundreds of couples to create memorable photographs and videos. Based in Rohaton, our team of talented professionals can travel to locations within 200 kilometers. In addition to wedding ceremonies and receptions, we do bridal showers, bachelor/bachelorette parties, and post-wedding brunches. Contact us at info@cieloimages.com.

---

**To:** mjones@jmail.com
**From:** info@cieloimages.com
**Date:** January 28
**Re:** Availability
**Attachment:** Reservation Form

Dear Ms. Jones:

Thank you for expressing interest in Cielo Images. We are available on the day of your wedding. The location you mentioned works for us. If you would like to make a reservation, please complete the attached form and email it back to us to tentatively save the date. We will then contact you to set up a preliminary meeting. At the meeting, we will discuss your needs and budget. To hold the reservation, we ask that you make a $200 nonrefundable deposit at that time. About two weeks before your actual wedding date, we will set up a final appointment with you to review your plans. If you have any questions, feel free to contact me at this e-mail address or call 555-9090.

Sincerely,
Lorna Taylor

**Cielo Images**

**Name:** Marion Jones

**Phone number:** (412) 555-6736

**Date(s) needed:** Saturday, May 1

**Time(s) needed:** 2:00 P.M. – 7:00 P.M.

**Location(s):** Bickford Park, Sudbury Court Reception Center

**Description of your needs:** My fiancé and I would like you to shoot our wedding ceremony and reception. We are still discussing the possibility of having a video made as well, but we would like to discuss the costs with you first. If possible, could we see some samples of your work?

**186** What is indicated about Cielo Images?

(A) It charges an initial consultation fee.
(B) It can staff an event on May 1.
(C) It can send ten employees.
(D) It will make a video for Ms. Jones.

**187** What is most likely true about Ms. Jones?

(A) She plans to be married indoors.
(B) She is having a large wedding reception.
(C) She initially called Ms. Taylor.
(D) She will meet with Cielo in April.

**188** According to the e-mail, what must Ms. Jones do to ensure that Cielo will photograph her event?

(A) Make an initial payment
(B) Submit proper identification
(C) Contact a wedding planner
(D) Visit Ms. Taylor's office

**189** What is suggested about Bickford Park?

(A) It is an inexpensive place to rent.
(B) It hosts many weddings a year.
(C) It is capable of hosting many guests.
(D) It is within 200 km of Rohaton.

**190** In the form, the word "shoot" in line 6 is closest in meaning to

(A) attend
(B) document
(C) photograph
(D) service

| To | ALL TENANTS |
| Subject | CHILDCARE CENTER OPENING SOON |

Precious Wishes has signed a contract to open a childcare center in the Burton Building. The facility will be located on the third floor. Licensed childcare professionals will provide basic daycare services with a strong educational component for children ages three months to five years.

**Hours:** Monday through Friday, 7:00 A.M. to 6:30 P.M.

Applications are now being accepted for children of employees or tenants in the building. Space is limited. The deadline to apply is January 31.

For monthly rates, meal schedules, application forms, and more, visit www.preciouswishes.com.

---

# Precious Wishes

### Application Form

Name: *Laurie Waters*

Employer: *Jackson Consulting*

Phone (work): *(505) 555-0334*

Phone (personal): *(505) 555-2217*

E-mail: *lwaters@jacksonconsulting.com*

Number of children to be enrolled: *2*

Age(s) of children to be enrolled: *14 months, 4 years*

Days needed: *[√] Monday [√] Tuesday [√] Wednesday*
         *[√] Thursday [√] Friday*

Hours needed: *[ ] half day (5 hours or less) [√] full day (5 + hours)*

*Additional information: My daughter is allergic to peanuts.*

| To | lwaters@jacksonconsulting.com |
|---|---|
| From | poliver@preciouswishes.com |
| Subject | Your Application |
| Date | February 8 |

Dear Ms. Waters:

Thank you for applying for a space at our newest location. Interest in the facility has far exceeded our capacity. Therefore, we have been placing children in the order in which applications were received.

Although we are not able to offer you a space at this time, you have been placed on the waiting list. You are currently number seven out of forty-two. When a position opens up, you will be notified. You will then have 48 hours to decide whether to accept or reject the position.

If, at any time, you would like to be removed from the list, kindly let us know. However, we are unable to refund the $50 per child application fee submitted along with your application.

Sincerely,
Patricia Oliver

**191** What is NOT indicated about Precious Wishes?

(A) It will expand its new facility.
(B) It has multiple locations.
(C) It employs trained staff.
(D) It offers care for infants.

**192** In the notice, the word "rates" in paragraph 3, line 1, is closest in meaning to

(A) costs
(B) numbers
(C) ranks
(D) speeds

**193** What is suggested about Jackson Consulting?

(A) It is located on the third floor.
(B) It rents space in the Burton Building.
(C) Many of its employees have kids.
(D) It is Precious Wishes' landlord.

**194** Why did Ms. Oliver write to Ms. Waters?

(A) To offer her a space at a new location
(B) To request a payment for childcare
(C) To move her forward on a list
(D) To inform her of the status of her request

**195** What is most likely true about Ms. Waters?

(A) She will find another childcare provider.
(B) She works four days a week.
(C) She will cancel her application.
(D) She gave $100 to Precious Wishes.

GO ON TO THE NEXT PAGE

Questions 196-200 refer to the following article, e-mail, and notice.

DANTON (July 1) – Last weekend, thousands of Linwood residents came out to celebrate the grand opening of Sunshine Market. Occupying 5,000 square meters in the ground floor of the recently renovated six-story Lancing Building, the new grocery store offers a wide variety of fresh produce, meats, bread, and more.

While the Linwood neighborhood has seen significant growth over the past decade, one thing it has lacked is a grocery store. In fact, residents have had to travel a minimum of 5 kilometers to shop for food. The new store, located in the heart of Linwood, has 15,000 residents living within 1 kilometer.

The city purchased the Lancing Building last year as part of Mayor Justin Bendix's Downtown and Beyond plan. Since taking office two years ago, the mayor has made economic development of the downtown area and its surrounding neighborhoods his top priority.

To: Kaley Chase <kchase@sunshinemarket.com>

from: Justin Bendix <jbendix@cityofdanton.gov>

Subject: Parking Issues

Date: August 28

Dear Ms. Chase:

Thank you for contacting me with your concerns about parking on Main Street. I understand the frustration that you and your customers must be experiencing. Rest assured that the city is dedicated to remedying this situation. We are currently moving forward with the second phase of our development plan. It includes the construction of a new parking garage on the corner of 10th Avenue and Main Street, approximately 500 meters from your store. Parking will be free for your customers.

Regards,

Justin Bendix

# NOTICE

To: All Customers

We have received numerous complaints about the parking situation in front of the store. Please avoid parking there. Instead, use Coleman Street behind the store or any of the nearby side streets. If you are unable to carry your groceries to your vehicle, our staff will be more than happy to assist you.

The city has assured us that it is working hard to find a solution to this pressing issue. In the meantime, your patience and cooperation are greatly appreciated.

Sincerely,

The Management
Sunshine Market

**196** What is suggested about Linwood?

(A) City buses do not serve the area.
(B) Many of its residents work downtown.
(C) There used to be no proper grocery store before Sunshine Market.
(D) Economic growth has been limited there.

**197** What is most likely true about the Downtown and Beyond plan?

(A) It proposes to add more housing.
(B) It will be completed in two years.
(C) It was started by the former mayor.
(D) It will expand available parking.

**198** What is the purpose of the notice?

(A) To explain a situation
(B) To voice a complaint
(C) To criticize customers
(D) To propose a new service

**199** In the notice, the word "hard" in paragraph 2, line 1, is closest in meaning to

(A) strongly
(B) diligently
(C) firmly
(D) mostly

**200** What is suggested about Sunshine Market?

(A) It is located on Main Street.
(B) It has about 5,000 customers.
(C) Few customers have their own cars.
(D) It will build a new parking lot.

**Stop! This is the end of the test. If you finish before time is called, you may go back to Parts 5, 6, and 7 and check your work.**

## 慢著！作答前請務必確認！

- 請當作實際考試般，將書桌收拾乾淨，做好心理準備。
- 請將手機關機，並善用時鐘或手錶計時。
- 規定作答時間為 120 分鐘，請務必遵守規定時間。
- 請盡可能按照題目順序作答，碰到難題時，切勿直接跳過。

# Actual Test

# 02

開始時間　：
完成時間　：

# LISTENING TEST

In the Listening test, you will be asked to demonstrate how well you understand spoken English. The entire Listening test will last approximately 45 minutes. There are four parts, and directions are given for each part. You must mark your answers on the separate answer sheet. Do not write your answers in your test book.

# PART 1

**Directions:** For each question in this part, you will hear four statements about a picture in your test book. When you hear the statements, you must select the one statement that best describes what you see in the picture. Then find the number of the question on your answer sheet and mark your answer. The statements will not be printed in your test book and will be spoken only one time.

**Example**

Statement (B), "The man is working at a desk," is the best description of the picture, so you should select answer (B) and mark it on your answer sheet.

1

2

3

4

5

6

**GO ON TO THE NEXT PAGE**

# PART 2 🎧06

**Directions:** You will hear a question or statement and three responses spoken in English. They will not be printed in your test book and will be spoken only one time. Select the best response to the question or statement and mark the letter (A), (B), or (C) on your answer sheet.

**7** Mark your answer on your answer sheet.

**8** Mark your answer on your answer sheet.

**9** Mark your answer on your answer sheet.

**10** Mark your answer on your answer sheet.

**11** Mark your answer on your answer sheet.

**12** Mark your answer on your answer sheet.

**13** Mark your answer on your answer sheet.

**14** Mark your answer on your answer sheet.

**15** Mark your answer on your answer sheet.

**16** Mark your answer on your answer sheet.

**17** Mark your answer on your answer sheet.

**18** Mark your answer on your answer sheet.

**19** Mark your answer on your answer sheet.

**20** Mark your answer on your answer sheet.

**21** Mark your answer on your answer sheet.

**22** Mark your answer on your answer sheet.

**23** Mark your answer on your answer sheet.

**24** Mark your answer on your answer sheet.

**25** Mark your answer on your answer sheet.

**26** Mark your answer on your answer sheet.

**27** Mark your answer on your answer sheet.

**28** Mark your answer on your answer sheet.

**29** Mark your answer on your answer sheet.

**30** Mark your answer on your answer sheet.

**31** Mark your answer on your answer sheet.

## PART 3 🎧07

**Directions:** You will hear some conversations between two or more people. You will be asked to answer three questions about what the speakers say in each conversation. Select the best response to each question and mark the letter (A), (B), (C), or (D) on your answer sheet. The conversations will not be printed in your test book and will be spoken only one time.

32  Where are the speakers going?
   (A) To an exhibition
   (B) To a museum
   (C) To a taxi stand
   (D) To a friend's house

33  What will happen in 20 minutes?
   (A) A meeting
   (B) A bus ride
   (C) A talk
   (D) A display

34  Why does the woman suggest that she and the man walk?
   (A) There are no available taxis.
   (B) The walk would do them good.
   (C) They are close to the venue.
   (D) Buses are expensive.

35  What are the speakers mainly discussing?
   (A) Returning an item
   (B) Repairing an item of clothing
   (C) Hiring a furniture maker
   (D) Arranging a delivery

36  What day will the man be available?
   (A) Monday
   (B) Thursday
   (C) Friday
   (D) Sunday

37  According to the woman, what requires an extra fee?
   (A) An extended guarantee
   (B) Overnight shipping
   (C) A bespoke design
   (D) Removal of the existing item

38  What event does the man plan to attend?
   (A) A sports event
   (B) A concert
   (C) A theater performance
   (D) A school play

39  Why is the woman surprised?
   (A) A performance has been relocated.
   (B) An event has been cancelled.
   (C) Space is available.
   (D) Parking is charged.

40  What should the woman do by the end of the day?
   (A) Contact the booking desk
   (B) Change a schedule
   (C) Confirm her intention to attend
   (D) Issue an invitation

41  What has the woman decided to do?
   (A) Sell a building
   (B) Extend the lease
   (C) Increase the rent
   (D) Renovate a house

42  According to the woman, who will come to the unit on Saturday?
   (A) A contracting team
   (B) A vendor
   (C) A few friends
   (D) A work crew

43  What request does the man make?
   (A) That a contract be renewed
   (B) That the dates be rearranged
   (C) That the rent be reduced
   (D) That the exterior be painted

**GO ON TO THE NEXT PAGE**

44 Where does the woman work?

(A) At a travel agency
(B) At an employment agency
(C) At a fast food chain
(D) At a clothing store

45 What does the woman offer the man?

(A) An apprenticeship
(B) Some food samples
(C) Travel opportunities
(D) A franchise

46 What was the woman particularly interested in?

(A) A résumé
(B) A reference letter
(C) A portfolio
(D) A travel schedule

47 Where do the speakers most likely work?

(A) At a pharmacy
(B) At a fitness center
(C) At a copy center
(D) At a doctor's office

48 What does the man say he needs to see?

(A) A bill
(B) Medical information
(C) A billing statement
(D) A label

49 Why does the man say, "No harm done"?

(A) He is glad the bills are found.
(B) He has an idea to organize files.
(C) He is not concerned about the issue.
(D) He is satisfied with the women's performance.

50 Why is the woman calling?

(A) To return a key
(B) To change a reservation
(C) To dispute a charge
(D) To inform the man of the payday

51 What does the man say happened?

(A) A door was damaged.
(B) A reservation was cancelled.
(C) A key was lost.
(D) All pensions were already rented out.

52 What does the woman mean when she says, "I don't get it"?

(A) She was lost in the area.
(B) She never received an inspection report.
(C) She thinks the door is too expensive.
(D) She doesn't understand the reason for the fee.

53 What are the speakers mainly discussing?

(A) A construction material
(B) A bid for a contract
(C) An affected deadline
(D) A completed task

54 Why does the man say, "that's a shame"?

(A) He is not proud of what the woman did.
(B) He is expressing sympathy.
(C) He expected the result.
(D) He is excited to hear the news.

55 What does the man remind the woman about?

(A) She has gained experience.
(B) She will need his help soon.
(C) She has to put in a higher bid.
(D) She was recently hired.

**56** What position is the man applying for?

(A) Second in command
(B) Company engineer
(C) Colonel in chief
(D) Chief lieutenant

**57** What does the man say he was in charge of?

(A) Planning a campaign
(B) Training army personnel
(C) Teaching at a school
(D) Constructing a building

**58** Why did the man leave his last post?

(A) He was employed on a temporary basis.
(B) He was offered a better position.
(C) He wanted to diversify.
(D) He moved to a different city.

---

**59** Where do the speakers most likely work?

(A) In a doctor's office
(B) In a decorating shop
(C) In an employment agency
(D) At a music store

**60** What does the man ask the woman about?

(A) The location of some information
(B) The time of an interview
(C) The contact details of a painter
(D) The cost of an item

**61** What does the woman say is happening today?

(A) A business is relocating.
(B) New equipment is being installed.
(C) An office is being refurbished.
(D) A filing system is being updated.

**62** What type of work does the man most likely do?

(A) He designs products.
(B) He coordinates training sessions.
(C) He provides landscape services.
(D) He heads advertising campaigns.

**63** What are the speakers mainly discussing?

(A) Sports equipment
(B) Gardening clothing
(C) A cleaning product
(D) A wireless computer

**64** According to the man, what will happen this week?

(A) A marketing campaign will be launched.
(B) A manufacturing process will start.
(C) A product will be ready for sale.
(D) A research study will take place.

| Staff | Extension |
|---|---|
| Paul Smith | 234 |
| Ronny Hanks | 235 |
| Ginger Harrison | 236 |
| Kelly Shaffer | 237 |

| Lunch Menu | |
|---|---|
| Fresh Salad | $8 |
| Hearty Soup | $9 |
| Personal Pizza | $12 |
| Salmon Sandwich | $7 |

**65** According to the woman, what does the man have 45 days to do?

(A) Apply for a promotion
(B) Register his driving license
(C) Enroll in an insurance plan
(D) Hire a full-time employee

**66** What does the man want to obtain?

(A) An insurance card
(B) A list of entire staff
(C) A new phone number
(D) Information about specific benefits

**67** Look at the graphic. What number will the man call?

(A) 234
(B) 235
(C) 236
(D) 237

**68** What does the man say he needs to do at noon?

(A) Have a business meeting
(B) Take a bus
(C) See a friend
(D) Return to the office

**69** Look at the graphic. How much will the man pay for his food?

(A) $8
(B) $9
(C) $12
(D) $7

**70** What does the woman say she will do next?

(A) Set the man's table with dishes
(B) Return with a part of the man's order
(C) Bring the check
(D) Buy a bottle of wine

# PART 4 🔊08

**Directions:** You will hear some talks given by a single speaker. You will be asked to answer three questions about what the speaker says in each talk. Select the best response to each question and mark the letter (A), (B), (C), or (D) on your answer sheet. The talks will not be printed in your test book and will be spoken only one time.

71  What happened today at the municipal library?
(A) An extension was opened.
(B) A new curator was appointed.
(C) An exhibit space closed.
(D) Some media were invited.

72  Who is Richard Blaine?
(A) A teacher
(B) A librarian
(C) A curator
(D) An architect

73  According to the speaker, what will the library offer on Sunday?
(A) Free food and drink
(B) Free computer access
(C) Instructional videos
(D) Library vouchers

74  What kind of business did the caller reach?
(A) A department store
(B) A solicitor's firm
(C) A royal residence
(D) A governmental department

75  Why is the business closed?
(A) A national holiday is observed.
(B) Some departments have merged.
(C) A ceremony is taking place.
(D) The office has shut down.

76  When will the business reopen?
(A) After a few hours
(B) Tomorrow
(C) In two days
(D) Next week

77  What is being advertised?
(A) Appliance maintenance
(B) Residential repairs
(C) Technician training
(D) Cooking classes

78  Why are listeners asked to call?
(A) To reach an agreement
(B) To arrange an inspection
(C) To receive a new oven
(D) To sign up for discounts

79  What will happen at the beginning of the month?
(A) Payments will be collected.
(B) A program will start.
(C) A discount scheme comes into force.
(D) A report will be issued.

80  What type of event is being held?
(A) An art gallery opening
(B) An awards ceremony
(C) A conservative meeting
(D) A play preview

81  What field does Ms. Jukkin work in?
(A) Writing
(B) Teaching
(C) Catering
(D) Publishing

82  What will listeners most likely do next?
(A) Watch a video
(B) Hear a speech
(C) Eat a meal
(D) Pick up a brochure

**83** Where most likely does the speaker work?

(A) At a used car lot
(B) At a gas station
(C) At a supermarket
(D) At a vehicle repair outlet

**84** What does Mr. Ubamo want to do?

(A) Ask for a job
(B) Repair his truck
(C) Advertise a business
(D) Sell a vehicle

**85** What should Mr. Ubamo do when he returns the call?

(A) Speak to a manager
(B) Ask for an estimate
(C) Negotiate the price
(D) Provide credit card details

---

**86** Who most likely is the speaker?

(A) A guide
(B) An animal activist
(C) A fitness trainer
(D) A logger

**87** What does the man mean when he says, "No one can guarantee anything, though"?

(A) He is uncertain if they are going in the right direction.
(B) He is uncertain if the weather will be good.
(C) He cannot be sure this hike is not hard.
(D) He cannot be sure they will see any animals.

**88** What does the speaker suggest the listeners do?

(A) Wear warm cloths
(B) Bring a map
(C) Carry water
(D) Stay with a group

**89** What most likely was the topic of the seminar?

(A) Organizing a task force
(B) Cooperating with colleagues
(C) Coordinating a hiring process
(D) Arranging assignments effectively

**90** What did the speaker pass out to the listeners?

(A) A recent article
(B) A list of resources
(C) An enrollment form
(D) A list of attendees

**91** Why does the speaker say, "Make sure to go over all of these"?

(A) To celebrate a product launch
(B) To give an assignment
(C) To promote other seminars
(D) To recommend Web sites

---

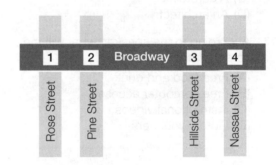

**92** What is causing traffic delays at exit number 4?

(A) A car accident
(B) A slippery road
(C) Road repair work
(D) A scheduled town event

**93** What does the Transportation Department recommend?

(A) Using detours
(B) Commuting by public transportation
(C) Not passing through downtown
(D) Avoiding a certain bridge

**94** Look at the graphic. What traffic light is NOT working?

(A) 1
(B) 2
(C) 3
(D) 4

## The amount of negative feedback

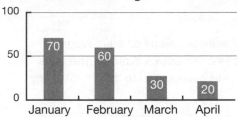

| INVOICE | |
|---|---|
| Product Number | Description |
| P365 | Soccer ball (# 3) |
| P345 | Basketball (# 2) |
| P443 | Running shoes (# 2 pairs) |
| P334 | Track Jacket (# 1) |

**95** What does the speaker say about the customer service team?

(A) It was recently transferred.
(B) It received a pay increase.
(C) Its workforce has been expanded.
(D) It still needs to improve.

**96** What was the cause of negative comments?

(A) An ambiguous policy
(B) An expensive service price
(C) Untrained staff
(D) A defective product

**97** Look at the graphic. When was the training session held?

(A) In January
(B) In February
(C) In March
(D) In April

**98** Why is the speaker calling?

(A) To cancel an order
(B) To ask a preference
(C) To ask for a payment
(D) To sell a product

**99** Look at the graphic. Which item is currently out of stock?

(A) P365
(B) P345
(C) P443
(D) P334

**100** What does the speaker offer to do?

(A) Refund some money
(B) Waive a shipping fee
(C) Upgrade a shipping method
(D) Cancel an order

This is the end of the Listening test. Turn to Part 5 in your test book.

# READING TEST

In the Reading test, you will read a variety of texts and answer several different types of reading comprehension questions. The entire Reading test will last 75 minutes. There are three parts, and directions are given for each part. You are encouraged to answer as many questions as possible within the time allowed.

You must mark your answers on the separate answer sheet. Do not write your answers in your test book.

# PART 5

**Directions:** A word or phrase is missing in each of the sentences below. Four answer choices are given below each sentence. Select the best answer to complete the sentence. Then mark the letter (A), (B), (C), or (D) on your answer sheet.

**101** Mr. Lin has handed in his expense claim, but Ms. Anker has not yet finished -------.
(A) hers
(B) her
(C) herself
(D) she

**102** HTR Company offers ------- wireless service at affordable yearly rates.
(A) reliable
(B) reliant
(C) reliably
(D) reliability

**103** Fun & Turn ------- an online newsletter that is emailed to customers.
(A) publisher
(B) publishes
(C) publish
(D) publishable

**104** ------- the Internet is an excellent place to exchange ideas, many people now join online forums.
(A) Because
(B) So
(C) Owing to
(D) After

**105** When ------- a moving company, you should ask for an accurate estimate.
(A) choice
(B) choosing
(C) chosen
(D) choose

**106** Mr. Dorson is considered a welcome ------- to the financial team because of his extensive knowledge in the area.
(A) output
(B) addition
(C) response
(D) reception

**107** Creating an impressive résumé of ------- can be easy and simple with the help of the Job-hunt program.
(A) you
(B) your own
(C) your
(D) yourself

**108** The battery life of your laptop can ------- by shutting it down when not in use.
(A) extends
(B) have extended
(C) be extended
(D) extending

109 Employees who want to access the office ------- the holiday must request permission in advance.

(A) since
(B) among
(C) during
(D) next

110 In an effort ------- compliance, auditors have to check all areas of the factory.

(A) ensures
(B) to be ensured
(C) to ensure
(D) were ensured

111 You should become thoroughly ------- with the software program before you take an online class.

(A) familiarization
(B) familiarize
(C) familiarity
(D) familiar

112 JPR Mortgage Company makes it easy to get a housing loan ------- your present financial status.

(A) depending
(B) regardless of
(C) even if
(D) as long as

113 Following a long discussion, the proposal to update the lobby furnishings was ------- accepted.

(A) finally
(B) rarely
(C) exactly
(D) immensely

114 Reservations ------- through the hotel Web site must be confirmed 12 hours before check-in.

(A) make
(B) are made
(C) made
(D) will make

115 Earlier this year, Bashir Khan interviewed several celebrities ------- have appeared on the cover of the *Star on Stage* magazine.

(A) since
(B) recently
(C) where
(D) who

116 Representatives of several local shops reported remarkable sales this year ------- the region's weak economy.

(A) even though
(B) in case
(C) provided that
(D) notwithstanding

117 Marston Breweries recruited extra staff members to ------- unprecedented demand throughout the holiday period.

(A) estimate
(B) advertise
(C) propose
(D) accommodate

118 Your questions will be given ------- attention and you will receive a phone call within three business days.

(A) prompt
(B) promptly
(C) promptness
(D) more promptly

119 Clive and Dunn's Fitness Center has ------- in boxing and martial arts for over 5 years.

(A) offered
(B) specialized
(C) maintained
(D) consisted

120 All events planned for the Three Corners Hotel ------- until damage to the main hall has been fixed.

(A) are postponing
(B) will be postponed
(C) should postpone
(D) postponing

GO ON TO THE NEXT PAGE

**121** Cinquento Limited has become more ------- focused on social media advertising over the past twelve months.

(A) narrowly
(B) narrowing
(C) narrower
(D) narrows

**122** The event venue is ------- enough to accommodate more than 1,000 people from all around the city.

(A) included
(B) overall
(C) insufficient
(D) spacious

**123** ------- Yingtan Motors begins trading in Japan is dependent on the feasibility report being undertaken by its financial consultants.

(A) Whether
(B) Although
(C) While
(D) Despite

**124** The Gourmet Best restaurant is seeking an apprentice with a strong interest in ------- the culinary art.

(A) to learn
(B) will learn
(C) learning
(D) learns

**125** Market research reports show that a hotel's level of ------- can directly affect customer satisfaction.

(A) clean
(B) cleanly
(C) cleanlier
(D) cleanliness

**126** Cough medication manufactured by Procten Limited is formulated ------- for adults and should not be given to young children.

(A) alternatively
(B) partially
(C) mutually
(D) exclusively

**127** The development of containers in specific sizes and shapes helped boost ------- across the entire shipping industry.

(A) standardize
(B) standardized
(C) more standardized
(D) standardization

**128** ------- using our online bill payment system, you must first fill in the registration form.

(A) Before
(B) So that
(C) In order
(D) According to

**129** It has been increasingly difficult to ------- authentic antique furniture from imitations.

(A) integrate
(B) suppose
(C) distinguish
(D) modify

**130** Daley Incorporated intends to hold a company picnic to ------- cooperation and teamwork among all employees.

(A) proceed
(B) facilitate
(C) retrieve
(D) convince

# PART 6

**Directions:** Read the texts that follow. A word, phrase, or sentence is missing in parts of each text. Four answer choices for each question are given below the text. Select the best answer to complete the text. Then mark the letter (A), (B), (C), or (D) on your answer sheet.

**Questions 131-134** refer to the following memo.

MEMO

**To:** All Technical Support Staff Members

**From:** Fiona Norton

**Subject:** Training Courses

Over the next two weeks, we will be offering several ------- training courses to
                                                    **131.**
employees in our department. The objective of these programs is to provide technical

support staff members with an opportunity to enhance their expertise and knowledge.

The six-hour workshops will deal with an array of topics, including addressing frequent

technical issues, satisfying particular customer needs, and improving productivity.

------- the courses are not mandatory, employees are strongly advised to participate.
**132.**

All training-related expenses ------- by the company.
                              **133.**

The courses are being organized by Joice Training (www.joicetraining.com).

-------.
**134.**

131 (A) compulsory
    (B) constant
    (C) lengthy
    (D) optional

132 (A) Due to
    (B) Even though
    (C) So that
    (D) While

133 (A) were covered
    (B) will have covered
    (C) will be covered
    (D) have covered

134 (A) We apologize for any inconvenience this may cause.
    (B) Those interested can find a schedule on the company's Web site.
    (C) Only those supervisors who have completed a course can obtain certificates.
    (D) Thank you for your help in resolving this challenging situation.

Questions 135-138 refer to the following press release.

Los Angeles — Tocom Financial has announced that it will ------- a new investment
135.
advisory service for retail clients by the end of the month. This new service will

combine the expertise of a ------- advisor with the convenience of a mobile application.
136.

Here's how it works. -------. After answering a series of questions and entering
137.
personal financial information, users will be contacted by a financial advisor who

will provide guidance customized to each unique situation. Users can chat with their

assigned advisors around the clock if they have further questions.

The cost for this service ------- to be about 0.5% of managed assets per year. Users'
138.
assets must be held in a Tocom Financial account, where several hundred investment

options are available.

135 (A) waive
(B) imitate
(C) unveil
(D) cancel

136 (A) profession
(B) professional
(C) professionally
(D) professionalism

137 (A) Users should first download an
application on their smartphones.
(B) Customers are worried about
personal information leakage.
(C) Please browse our Web site to view
additional products.
(D) Computer software has advanced
considerably recently.

138 (A) expects
(B) expected
(C) is expected
(D) has expected

**To:** Canberra Finance Department
**From:** Brett Ling
**Date:** August 12
**Subject:** Legal Filing

Dear all:

I am writing with news and updates from the Government finance department.

-------, there is a new law that requires all tax invoices and corporation documents to
**139.**
be submitted electronically.

I know some of us are already familiar with the online system at www.canberracorp/

govfiling and have found it quite complex. -------. Then enter the password, ensuring
**140.**
that you enter the correct reference number so that ------- individual details can be
**141.**
entered in the correct place.

Please contact me via e-mail with any questions about this -------.
**142.**

Yours,

Brett Ling

---

**139** (A) Additionally
(B) Initially
(C) Conversely
(D) Apparently

**140** (A) You first need to find the relevant
page for inputting information.
(B) You should print out the registration
form.
(C) You can take online courses to get
used to it.
(D) A fine may be imposed unless you
follow the tax regulation.

**141** (A) their
(B) your
(C) his
(D) my

**142** (A) procedure
(B) research
(C) report
(D) problem

**To:** Cecilia Feridino <cferidino@hmail.net>
**From:** Darcey Kerr <dkerr@homedecor.com>
**Subject:** Your submission
**Date:** June 10

Dear Ms. Feridino:

Thank you for your submission to our -------. Your article, "How to make your home
                                        **143.**
look better," ------- in the July issue of *Home Decor* with only small changes. Both of
                    **144.**
the photographs that you sent us will accompany the text. As indicated in your contract,

you will be given $300 for the work. I believe you said you would now like it deposited

directly into your checking account. -------.
                                      **145.**

It is always a pleasure to work with you. Should you have ------- ideas for future
                                                            **146.**
publication, please let me know.

Sincerely,

Darcey Kerr
Editor-in-chief
Home Decor

143 (A) publication
    (B) photographer
    (C) council
    (D) exhibition

144 (A) appeared
    (B) will appear
    (C) to appear
    (D) has appeared

145 (A) The terms of the contract can be
        renegotiated in two years.
    (B) If so, please verify your account
        information with our payroll
        department.
    (C) This is a great chance to increase
        your salary.
    (D) Therefore, we are unable to process
        your payment now.

146 (A) adding
    (B) additional
    (C) addition
    (D) additionally

# PART 7

**Directions:** In this part you will read a selection of texts, such as magazine and newspaper articles, e-mails, and instant messages. Each text or set of texts is followed by several questions. Select the best answer for each question and mark the letter (A), (B), (C), or (D) on your answer sheet.

**Questions 147-148** refer to the following information.

The following pages illustrate how to work your new Tanvak printer and how to connect it to electronic devices in your home. If any of the instructions confuse you, please call a Tanvak customer service team member during working hours. Service centers and all contact details are listed alphabetically on Page 4.

**147** Where would the information most likely appear?

(A) In an owner's manual
(B) In a product catalog
(C) In a telephone directory
(D) In an employee manual

**148** According to the information, how can a Tanvak representative help?

(A) By explaining a return policy
(B) By processing invoices
(C) By scheduling a service call
(D) By clarifying instructions

GO ON TO THE NEXT PAGE

## Lamas Heritage Center

The Lamas Heritage Center holds more than one million books, photographs, and artifacts related to the cultural history of our local areas. The center provides information and resources on historic and significant events that have shaped our traditions. Together with a comprehensive historical collection of books and letters, the center contains a selection of photographs and images from other communities and countries that have influenced our heritage. Our extensive collection of published works and archives can be accessed by local residents as well as tourists and visitors. The center's history section contains a number of ancient artifacts with a photographic display that contains thousands of images, some taken by local people. We can provide copies of any of the photographs for a small charge. Appointments and reference assistance to those wishing to use our archives are available upon request.

**149** What is the information about?

(A) A community event
(B) A research library
(C) A local photography course
(D) A tourist information center

**150** What is available for purchase?

(A) Traditional gifts
(B) Replica documents
(C) Copies of magazine articles
(D) Reprints of photographs

Questions 151-152 refer to the following text message chain.

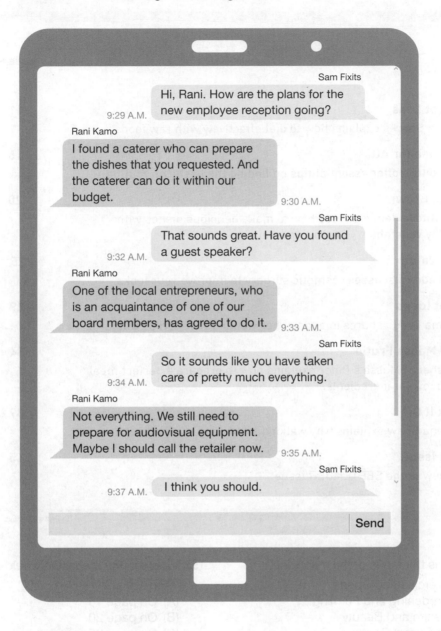

**Sam Fixits**
Hi, Rani. How are the plans for the new employee reception going?
9:29 A.M.

**Rani Kamo**
I found a caterer who can prepare the dishes that you requested. And the caterer can do it within our budget.
9:30 A.M.

**Sam Fixits**
That sounds great. Have you found a guest speaker?
9:32 A.M.

**Rani Kamo**
One of the local entrepreneurs, who is an acquaintance of one of our board members, has agreed to do it.
9:33 A.M.

**Sam Fixits**
So it sounds like you have taken care of pretty much everything.
9:34 A.M.

**Rani Kamo**
Not everything. We still need to prepare for audiovisual equipment. Maybe I should call the retailer now.
9:35 A.M.

**Sam Fixits**
I think you should.
9:37 A.M.

Send

**151** What is indicated about the reception?

(A) A board member will be the speaker.
(B) The food will not cost more than expected.
(C) The equipment has already been set up.
(D) Ms. Kamo is a new employee.

**152** At 9:37 A.M., what does Mr. Fixits mean when he writes, "I think you should"?

(A) He wants Ms. Kamo to pick up the equipment.
(B) He agrees that the reception is a good idea.
(C) He wants Ms. Kamo to contact the store.
(D) He has to end the conversation immediately.

GO ON TO THE NEXT PAGE

**Questions 153-155** refer to the following table of contents in a magazine.

## CONTENTS

Issue 613

**Weight Loss**     **11**
Amelia Sparks explains how to diet effectively with raw foods.

**Exercise for All**     **15**
Our editors offer essential tips on finding the best gym routine.

**Home Grown**     **20**
Cate Kitova demonstrates how to make delicious dishes with healthy vegetables you grow yourself.

**Face Value**     **25**
Lea Cedra discusses cosmetic surgery to improve your looks.

**Great Ideas**     **29**
Paloma Gregg shares images of her walking tour across Bulgaria.

**Chef Massa Frulio**     **34**
The chef at Massa's Diner explains how to prepare a perfect meal using low fat ingredients.

**Walk It Off**     **39**
Rowena Shaw explains why walking and hiking are the best exercise.

**Next Issue**     **45**
Preview of the SEPTEMBER issue

---

**153** What is the focus of the magazine?

(A) Exercise and Sports
(B) Gardening and Farming
(C) Health and Beauty
(D) Food and Cooking

**154** According to the table of contents, who recently traveled abroad?

(A) Ms. Gregg
(B) Ms. Kitova
(C) Ms. Massa
(D) Ms. Shaw

**155** Where in the magazine would a recipe most likely be found?

(A) On page 15
(B) On page 20
(C) On page 25
(D) On page 45

**Questions 156-158** refer to the following notice.

#  Blenratha Talent Contest

Do you have a talent other people would like to see? Then apply for a place in the Blenratha Talent Contest.

## What is the Blenratha Talent Contest?

The contest was started by Alex Balden, a resident of Blenratha, who also owns the Red Lion Public House on the High Street and was looking for an actor to perform at his venue. -[1]-.The winner of the competition will be rewarded with 100 pounds to launch their performance career. Last year's winner, for example, went on to play at sold out venues around the UK. The winner will be judged by local residents and a representative from St. Andrew's School of Musical Theater at the Blenratha Community Center on August 21. -[2]-.

## Am I eligible?

The contest is open to every Scottish national, regardless of age, status or ability. Amateur and semi-professional artists are welcome to enter. -[3]-.

## How can I apply?

Entries must be submitted either by mail or by e-mail by July 2. Application forms and entry details can be found on our Web site: www.blenratha/sc/entry_form. If you have any questions, Hamish Roscoe is your main contact at (050) 555-0258. -[4]-. If you want to put forward your name as a member of the judging panel, please contact Brenda Rhys, our evaluation coordinator, at (050) 555-0259.

---

**156** What is stated about the Red Lion?

(A) It hosts talent shows weekly.
(B) It is located outside of Blenratha.
(C) It is owned by Alex Balden.
(D) It is next to St. Andrew's School of Musical Theater.

**157** According to the notice, why would an individual contact Ms. Rhys?

(A) To request a deadline extension
(B) To volunteer to help determine the contest winner
(C) To confirm attendance
(D) To inquire about official rules

**158** In which of the positions marked [1], [2], [3], and [4] does the following sentence best belong?

"Entries are also welcomed from those who have entered the competition in previous years."

(A) [1]
(B) [2]
(C) [3]
(D) [4]

Questions 159-162 refer to the following article.

## No more anti-social behavior in the city

By Grace Galento

In an effort to ease anti-social behavior in the streets of Entebbe, the city council is planning changes to the legal drinking hours. –[1]–. "Our city is at its loudest and rowdiest at nighttime," said Aruba Challis, spokesperson for the Entebbe City Council. "That's because local people and tourists alike head to the downtown region to enjoy the entertainment available, including bars, nightclubs and casinos. When visitors come into town, they generally come by free public buses so they don't have to worry about drinking and driving. This leads to increased disruptions on the street." –[2]–.

Currently, certain bars are offering half-price drinks from 6 P.M. to 8 P.M., and some bars offer cheap drinks all through the night. "This needs to change." Ms. Challis said. "We'd like to introduce a common pricing structure as other cities do, where prices are the same in every venue." –[3]–.

If the proposed change goes into effect, it will be one of many introduced recently. In May, a new card system limits the number of drinks purchased per person from 6 P.M. to 8 P.M. –[4]–.

**159** What is suggested about Entebbe?
(A) It has too many entertainment venues.
(B) It must pay a surcharge on alcohol.
(C) It has trouble with disorderly behavior.
(D) It has a problem with drunk driving.

**160** What is the city council considering?
(A) Raising the prices of drinks
(B) Creating new parking areas
(C) Lowering the amount of people allowed in a bar
(D) Introducing security staff

**161** What has recently happened in Entebbe?
(A) Some downtown stores were damaged.
(B) It became harder to get a license to open a bar.
(C) Many more bars and clubs were opened.
(D) New monitoring measures for drinkers were introduced.

**162** In which of the positions marked [1], [2], [3], and [4] does the following sentence best belong?

"The card is given at the door and stamped upon each purchase."

(A) [1]
(B) [2]
(C) [3]
(D) [4]

Questions 163-165 refer to the following online chat discussion.

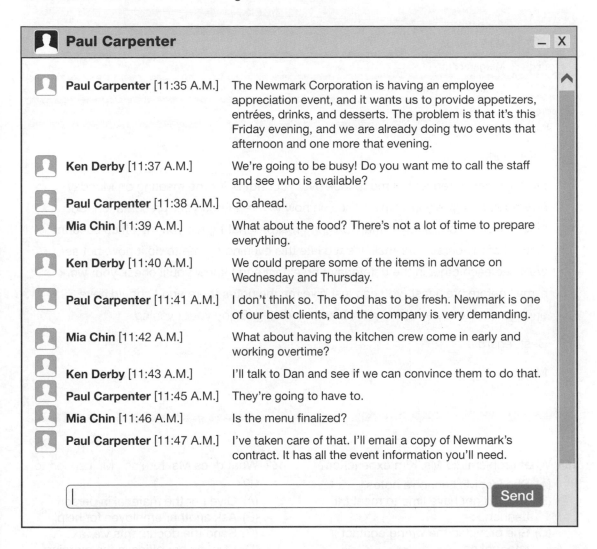

**Paul Carpenter**      — X

**Paul Carpenter** [11:35 A.M.]    The Newmark Corporation is having an employee appreciation event, and it wants us to provide appetizers, entrées, drinks, and desserts. The problem is that it's this Friday evening, and we are already doing two events that afternoon and one more that evening.

**Ken Derby** [11:37 A.M.]    We're going to be busy! Do you want me to call the staff and see who is available?

**Paul Carpenter** [11:38 A.M.]    Go ahead.

**Mia Chin** [11:39 A.M.]    What about the food? There's not a lot of time to prepare everything.

**Ken Derby** [11:40 A.M.]    We could prepare some of the items in advance on Wednesday and Thursday.

**Paul Carpenter** [11:41 A.M.]    I don't think so. The food has to be fresh. Newmark is one of our best clients, and the company is very demanding.

**Mia Chin** [11:42 A.M.]    What about having the kitchen crew come in early and working overtime?

**Ken Derby** [11:43 A.M.]    I'll talk to Dan and see if we can convince them to do that.

**Paul Carpenter** [11:45 A.M.]    They're going to have to.

**Mia Chin** [11:46 A.M.]    Is the menu finalized?

**Paul Carpenter** [11:47 A.M.]    I've taken care of that. I'll email a copy of Newmark's contract. It has all the event information you'll need.

     |                          **Send**

163 At what kind of company do the writers' most likely work?

(A) A restaurant
(B) A catering company
(C) A grocery store
(D) A hotel

164 Why do the writers need additional staff?

(A) A client demanded additional services.
(B) An order was not completed on time.
(C) An event was added to their schedule.
(D) A mistake was made with the scheduling.

165 At 11:45 A.M., what does Mr. Carpenter mean when he writes, "They're going to have to"?

(A) He is requiring the kitchen crew to work extra.
(B) He wants the clients to be treated with extra care.
(C) He doesn't have time to explain the situation to Dan.
(D) He needs the serving staff to come into work early.

GO ON TO THE NEXT PAGE

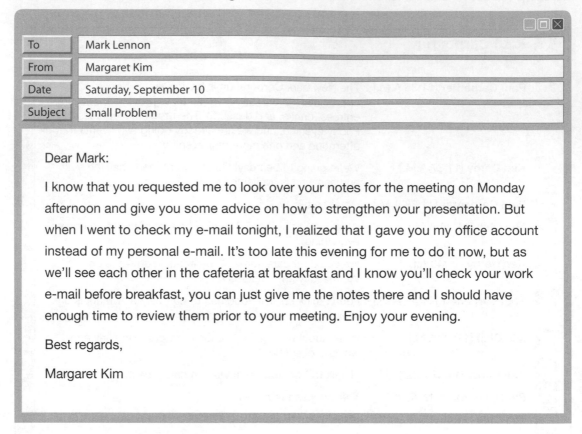

To          Mark Lennon

From        Margaret Kim

Date        Saturday, September 10

Subject     Small Problem

Dear Mark:

I know that you requested me to look over your notes for the meeting on Monday afternoon and give you some advice on how to strengthen your presentation. But when I went to check my e-mail tonight, I realized that I gave you my office account instead of my personal e-mail. It's too late this evening for me to do it now, but as we'll see each other in the cafeteria at breakfast and I know you'll check your work e-mail before breakfast, you can just give me the notes there and I should have enough time to review them prior to your meeting. Enjoy your evening.

Best regards,

Margaret Kim

**166** What problem did Ms. Kim experience?
(A) She lost Mr. Lennon's notes.
(B) She did not have time to meet Mr. Lennon.
(C) She provided the wrong contact information.
(D) She forgot to check her e-mail account.

**167** What does Ms. Kim ask Mr. Lennon to do?
(A) Give her the material in person
(B) Ask another employee for help
(C) Send the documents via fax
(D) Stop by her office in the morning

**Questions 168-171** refer to the following flyer.

Have you recently relocated to Miami?
Join our orientation: Getting Around Miami.

### Presentation Schedule

| | |
|---|---|
| **10:00 A.M.** Hitting the City — options for public transport (Room 212) | |

| | |
|---|---|
| **11:00 A.M.** Renting a condominium or house in Miami (Room 212) | **11:00 A.M.** Dealing with finance and banking (Room 206) |

| | |
|---|---|
| **12:00 P.M.** Getting to know your neighbors (Room 208) | **12:00 P.M.** Finding employment in Miami (Room 206) |

| | |
|---|---|
| **1:00 P.M.** Out and about in Miami — a round-up of local events and attractions (Room 204) | |

Please note that some of the presentations clash time-wise, so you need to decide which one to attend that will be of most value to you. The talk about public transportation and finding suitable accommodation are very popular, so in order to guarantee your seat, please arrive early.

These talks are all conducted in English, but there are translated transcripts in French, Spanish and Arabic. Food and drinks are available for purchase.

After the last presentation, you are invited to take a guided tour of the main areas of attraction. A long-term resident of Miami Beach and a member of the Orientation Committee will be leading the tour. For more details, visit www.miamiwelcoming.com.

**168** For whom is the flyer likely intended?

(A) Miami town officials
(B) Tourists visiting America
(C) Miami tourist board members
(D) Residents who are new to the area

**169** Where are the most popular presentations held?

(A) In Room 212
(B) In Room 208
(C) In Room 206
(D) In Room 204

**170** What is indicated about the Miami Orientation Committee?

(A) It provides free transport to visitors.
(B) It will soon offer a wider variety of services.
(C) It has offices in multiple locations.
(D) It provides materials in several languages.

**171** According to the flyer, what can attendees do after the presentations?

(A) Go on a tour of the city
(B) Request membership details
(C) Reserve seats to public events
(D) Enjoy a free lunch

July 15 — Axis 24, the company that provided photographic images for the acclaimed KeepActive TV campaign, has been nominated for the international Schiffer Prize, which has been rewarding excellence in published photography and graphic illustrations for more than 20 years. Chosen from more than 3,000 entrants, Axis 24 is the only Karachi-based photographic studio to ever be nominated. On the 20 August, a ceremony will be held in Cologne, Germany, where the winners of this year's Schiffer Prize will be announced.

"We are extremely proud of this nomination, which is a tribute to the high level of professionalism, expertise, and creativity within the company," said Aslam Minish, founder and CEO of the company. The Schiffer Prize judges comprise a group of six top executives from advertising agencies around the world. They commented that Axis 24 was chosen for its quality and innovation within its photographic portfolio.

"We photograph everything from wildlife to sporting activities, people and nature," continued Mr. Minish, "and we liaise with our clients to ensure the end product is better than they could possibly have imagined."

Aside from the prestige of the nomination, business has increased for Axis 24, as has its public profile. When the names of the nominees were announced, the studio was inundated with requests from interested parties wanting to commission work from them. "The only way we can meet this increased demand is to hire more professional photographers and technical staff, which is precisely what our next move will be," said Mr. Minish.

More information about Axis 24 can be found at www.axis24.co.pk. Details about the Schiffer Prize are at www.schifferprize.org.

172 What is the purpose of the article?
   (A) To highlight a company's accomplishments
   (B) To describe the work of a famous artist
   (C) To invite entrants to a photographic contest
   (D) To nominate an executive for an award

173 What is suggested about the Schiffer Prize?
   (A) It is a prestigious award with worldwide influence.
   (B) It has been won by a Karachi-based company before.
   (C) It was established by a single individual.
   (D) It was first awarded to a photographic company.

174 What is NOT mentioned as an area of Axis 24 photographs?
   (A) Sporting events
   (B) Billboards
   (C) Nature
   (D) People

175 According to the article, what does Mr. Minish plan to do?
   (A) Increase his public relations budget
   (B) Open another photographic studio
   (C) Hire additional employees
   (D) Attend a ceremony in Karachi

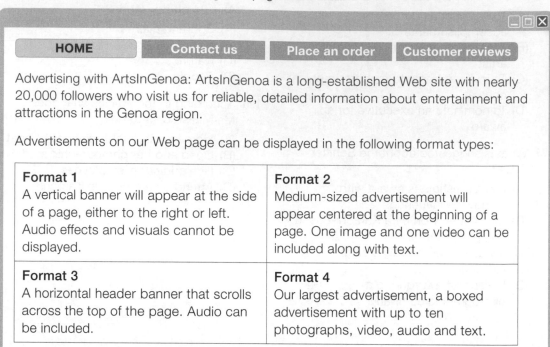

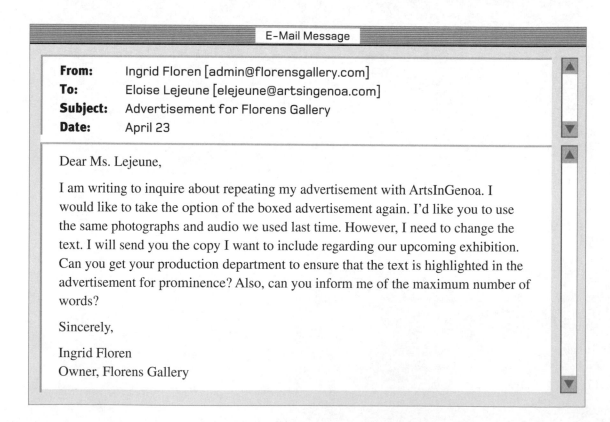

**176** Where does Ms. Lejeune work?

(A) At an advertising agency
(B) At a marketing research firm
(C) At a gallery in Genoa
(D) At an arts-related Web site

**177** What is stated about Format 1?

(A) It does not allow visuals.
(B) It is the most expensive.
(C) It can include the most text.
(D) It can be prepared quickly.

**178** In what advertisement format, is Ms. Florens most likely interested?

(A) Format 1
(B) Format 2
(C) Format 3
(D) Format 4

**179** What is suggested about Florens Gallery?

(A) It is being renovated.
(B) It recently displayed a new exhibition.
(C) It will be closed until further notice.
(D) It has advertised in ArtsInGenoa before.

**180** What does Ms. Floren ask about the text?

(A) What font size it should be
(B) What length it should be
(C) Which format is the best
(D) How much it costs to publish it

# ANISTON FRUIT GROWERS

Fruits and Vegetables
87 Wisteria Road, Somerset YL3
(013) 90 72 65 58
www.aniston.co.uk

If you want to grow your own fruits and vegetables, come to Aniston Fruit Growers. We offer a huge selection of plants and seeds from all over the world. Take a tour across our 6 acre working farm and decide which fruits and vegetables you'd like to grow. We offer four categories of products:

**Section 1:** Ground-growing fruits and vegetables
**Section 2:** Tree-growing fruits
**Section 3:** Root vegetables
**Section 4:** Exotic fruits and vegetables from around the world

Our gardeners speak many different languages and will be happy to answer any queries about the best practices for growing, nurturing and picking fruits and vegetables.

Looking for something exotic and different? At the entrance, ask for our master gardener, who will show you our international produce.

After you make your selection, Aniston Fruit Growers can ship your order anywhere in the UK.

---

## Aniston Fruit Growers Order Form

| Type | Quantity |
|---|---|
| 1. Red peppers | 100 |
| 2. Green chilies | 100 |
| 3. Fruit tree: apples | 1 |
| 4. Raspberry plants | 300 |
| 5. Strawberry plants | 200 |

**Customer Name:** Angela Stallard
**Delivery Date:** March 12
**Address:** 26 Hill Rise, Yeovil, Somerset
**Phone:** (01398) 319553

When you have completed your order form, please hand it in at the service desk. The assistant will check your order, answer questions, and confirm if the items are in stock. Customers should receive their order within a week of the original order. Damaged plants or trees must be reported within one day of their delivery to your location.

181 What is suggested about Aniston Fruit Growers?

(A) It allows customers to explore its gardens.
(B) It often ships exotic vegetables internationally.
(C) It sells most of its produce to local farms and orchards.
(D) It will replace any fruit trees that fail to flourish.

182 According to the advertisement, what information can employees give customers?

(A) Selecting the best recipes for exotic produce
(B) Geographical origins of each fruit and vegetable
(C) Pricing for discounts on large orders
(D) Advice on how to grow fruits and vegetables

183 How can customers ask for unusual plants?

(A) By speaking to a master gardener
(B) By mailing a separate application to the company
(C) By visiting the Fruit Growers' Web site
(D) By handing an order form to a gardening expert

184 Where will the Fruit Growers employees find most of Ms. Stallard's order?

(A) In section 1
(B) In section 2
(C) In section 3
(D) In section 4

185 According to the form, what must Ms. Stallard do by March 13?

(A) Inform the company of any problems with her purchase
(B) Pay for her fruit tree order plus the delivery charge
(C) Return any extra plants that were delivered in error
(D) Plant the items that she has purchased

http://www.sandeventcontest.com

**Event Name:** Summer Sand Sculpture Contest
**Location:** Marquise Beach, Nova Scotia
**Dates:** August 15-18
**Contact:** Jeremy Chan

**About:** This annual event, now in its fifth year, brings in over 80 professional and amateur contestants from around the world and includes both solo and team categories with about 12,000 visitors in attendance in the preceding year. The contest has become one of the most popular beach events in Nova Scotia. Marquise Beach, one of the largest sandy beaches in this part of Canada, is located about 40 minutes from Halifax. In addition to sculpting, the four-day festival boasts music performances, an array of food vendors, and sand-sculpting classes for visitors. Admission is free, but there is a $10 charge for parking.

## The Winners of the Fifth Annual Summer Sand Sculpture Contest

\* Solo Category

| Placement | Name | Country | The title |
|---|---|---|---|
| First Prize | Rachel Murtagh | Australia | Green Mermaid |
| Second Prize | Melinda Graham | New Zealand | Pod of Dolphin |
| Third Prize | Jamari Yoneda | U.S. | Hearst Castle |
| Fourth Prize | John Peters | Brazil | Pirate Ship |
| Fifth Prize | Jimar Guimond | Canada | Sea Creatures |

## What's new in Halifax?

### By Eileen Tao

The annual Summer Sand Sculpture Contest took place last week and it was the perfect way to say farewell to the summer season. Thanks to the especially beautiful weather, the number of visitors was double that of the previous year.

The contest drew sculptures for both the solo and team categories. Shells, seaweeds, driftwood, and other natural materials were incorporated in some of the larger-than-life sculptures that depicted everything from sea life to free-form designs.

Rachel Murtagh from Australia beat two-time champion Melinda Graham from New Zealand with her Green Mermaid sculpture which was richly ornamented with sea glasses. All the sculptures were great but my personal favorite was Pirate Ship. The use of driftwood for a base for the sculpture was something I have never seen before.

Spectators could join the fun, too. Sculpting experts who were not competing led a free class in which everyone could participate. This, as well as entertainment and foods, provided the perfect way to enjoy the end of the summer.

186 What is indicated about contestants?

(A) They are all amateurs.
(B) They are asked to sign up in advance.
(C) They personally know Mr. Chan.
(D) They are from a variety of countries.

187 In the article, the word "drew" in the paragraph 2, line 1, is closest in meaning to

(A) withdrew
(B) attracted
(C) transferred
(D) pictured

188 What is indicated about this year's event?

(A) It had more than 20,000 visitors.
(B) It cost $10 per person to attend.
(C) It was longer than last year's event.
(D) It was held in Marquise Beach for the first time.

189 What is stated about Ms. Graham?

(A) She used seashells in her sculpture.
(B) She has given sand sculpting classes.
(C) She has won the competition previously.
(D) She recently moved to New Zealand.

190 Whose sculpture did Ms. Tao like the most?

(A) Ms. Murtagh's
(B) Mr. Yoneda's
(C) Mr. Peters'
(D) Ms. Guimond's

GO ON TO THE NEXT PAGE

## Refer acquaintances to PineTop Financial, and everyone benefits!*

We appreciate the trust that you place in PineTop Financial. As a Loyal Member, you have access to our complete line of financial products and get our best rates.

To express our sincere thanks, we would like to give you $20 for each friend or family member you refer to us who opens an account. We will also give them $20 immediately after making an initial deposit of over $200 into a PineTop Online Savings Account or PineTop Investment Brokerage Account. All they need to do is register at www.PineTop.com and use special code PP880.

*This offer is only available to Loyal Members in good standing. Referrals must be new customers. Existing and former PineTop Financial employees are ineligible to participate.

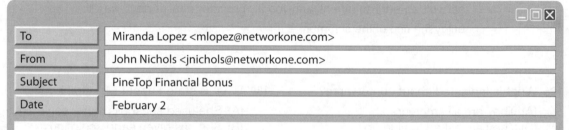

| To | Miranda Lopez <mlopez@networkone.com> |
| --- | --- |
| From | John Nichols <jnichols@networkone.com> |
| Subject | PineTop Financial Bonus |
| Date | February 2 |

Hi, Miranda,

I remember that you were worried about getting started with your retirement savings. Well, here is something that might help you. PineTop Financial will give you $20 just to open an account there! I have been using their services for almost six years now and have had only satisfactory experiences. Their online checking and savings accounts are secure and easy to use.

I enclosed a flyer that explains how to sign up.

Best,

John

Miranda Lopez
201 Newport Road
Salem, MA 50084

April 25

Dear Ms. Lopez:

Welcome to PineTop Financial. We opened a PineTop Online Savings Account in your name on April 15. Please check the attached Terms & Conditions and Fee Schedule.

To thank you for your new membership, we will deposit $20 into your account. The deposit should be made within 30 days of your opening date.

You can access your account by visiting www.PineTop.com. Please enter your account number and the temporary password below. Once you log in, you should reset your username and password.

Account Number: 78082210
Temporary Password: jj99-0dff-8822-ss

Should you have any inquiries, don't hesitate to call us at 1-600-555-6690.

Sincerely,

Lynn Cardona
New Accounts Representative

191 For whom is the announcement intended?

(A) PineTop Financial employees
(B) Potential investors
(C) Stockholders
(D) Existing account holders

192 Why did Mr. Nichols write to Ms. Lopez?

(A) To give some tips on investment
(B) To extend a special offer to her
(C) To confirm a recent account deposit
(D) To introduce a financial consultant

193 What is most likely true about Mr. Nichols?

(A) He is a PineTop Financial Loyal Member.
(B) He barely knows Ms. Lopez.
(C) He is employed by PineTop Financial.
(D) He recently opened a new account.

194 In the e-mail, the word "flyer" in paragraph 2, line 1, is closest in meaning to

(A) application
(B) newspaper
(C) handout
(D) receipt

195 What is suggested about Ms. Lopez?

(A) She is an existing PineTop Financial customer.
(B) She works at the same place as Lynn Cardona.
(C) She deposited more than $200 in her account.
(D) She is planning to retire in the near future.

GO ON TO THE NEXT PAGE

# Management Training Seminars

### New Seminar This Spring!
### Basic Supervision

Congratulations on your promotion to a supervisory position. You are now the one who is in charge.

Learn the skills necessary for success in this new and challenging job. Our Basic Supervision Seminar will teach you what you need to get started. You will learn how to . . .

- delegate tasks effectively
- motivate employees
- deliver criticism
- plan and meet deadlines
- train new employees

This one-day seminar introduces you to many of the skills you will need to be an effective supervisor. The skills you learn will not only benefit you but will also enhance your effectiveness within your organization. To download a brochure, visit www.abc.com.

## Management Training Seminars
### Dover, DE     April 7-10

| | |
|---|---|
| **Basic Supervision** | Tuesday, April 7   9:00 A.M. – 5:00 P.M. |
| | Learn the skills needed to become an effective supervisor. |
| **Leadership and Team Building** | Wednesday, April 8   8:30 A.M. – 4:30 P.M. |
| | Develop a set of strategies for building and leading a winning team. |
| **Constructive Criticism** | Thursday, April 9   9:00 A.M. – 5:00 P.M. |
| | Learn ways to bring about positive change in employees. This seminar covers effective techniques for delivering constructive criticism without making enemies. |
| **Mastering Management** | Friday, April 10   8:30 A.M. – 4:30 P.M. |
| | Become the best manager you can be. Learn how to implement proven techniques in today's professional workplace. Prerequisite: Advanced Management Course. |

Seminars include instructional materials. In addition, participants will receive access to our online resource library.

**From:** vincent.baca@valenza.com
**To:** mpoplar@abc.com
**Subject:** Dover Management Seminars
**Date:** April 15

Dear Mr. Poplar:

I want to thank you again for the generous discount you provided to Valenza Designs that enabled nine of our employees to attend your seminars in our city last week. All of the participants, including me, have been talking about how much we learned in last week's training sessions. As in past seminars, I learned a lot from Reginald Carter. Not only is he a knowledgeable instructor, but he also models the leadership skills he teaches. I thought I had learned everything I could in his advanced management course. But I was wrong!

Sincerely,
Vincent Baca

---

**196** In the announcement, the word "enhance" in paragraph 4, line 2, is closest in meaning to

(A) complement
(B) desire
(C) improve
(D) lead

**197** What is indicated about the Dover seminars?

(A) They will be repeated at a later date.
(B) They are being offered at a discount.
(C) They require advanced registration.
(D) They give learning materials to participants.

**198** What skills will probably NOT be taught at the April 7 seminar?

(A) How to instruct new staff members
(B) How to ask for promotions
(C) How to manage one's time
(D) How to correct others

**199** What seminar did Mr. Carter most likely lead in Dover?

(A) Basic Supervision
(B) Leadership and Team Building
(C) Constructive Criticism
(D) Mastering Management

**200** What is suggested about Mr. Baca?

(A) He supervises other employees.
(B) He attended a seminar for no charge.
(C) He is the owner of Valenza Designs.
(D) He used to work with Mr. Carter.

**Stop! This is the end of the test. If you finish before time is called, you may go back to Parts 5, 6, and 7 and check your work.**

- 請當作實際考試般，將書桌收拾乾淨，做好心理準備。
- 請將手機關機，並善用時鐘或手錶計時。
- 規定作答時間為 120 分鐘，請務必遵守規定時間。
- 請盡可能按照題目順序作答，碰到難題時，切勿直接跳過。

# Actual Test

# 03

 開始時間　：
完成時間　：

# LISTENING TEST

In the Listening test, you will be asked to demonstrate how well you understand spoken English. The entire Listening test will last approximately 45 minutes. There are four parts, and directions are given for each part. You must mark your answers on the separate answer sheet. Do not write your answers in your test book.

# PART 1

**Directions:** For each question in this part, you will hear four statements about a picture in your test book. When you hear the statements, you must select the one statement that best describes what you see in the picture. Then find the number of the question on your answer sheet and mark your answer. The statements will not be printed in your test book and will be spoken only one time.

**Example**

**Sample Answer**

(A) ● (C) (D)

Statement (B), "The man is working at a desk," is the best description of the picture, so you should select answer (B) and mark it on your answer sheet.

**1**

**2**

**3**

**4**

**5**

**6**

**GO ON TO THE NEXT PAGE**

# PART 2 🎧⟨10⟩

**7** Mark your answer on your answer sheet.

**8** Mark your answer on your answer sheet.

**9** Mark your answer on your answer sheet.

**10** Mark your answer on your answer sheet.

**11** Mark your answer on your answer sheet.

**12** Mark your answer on your answer sheet.

**13** Mark your answer on your answer sheet.

**14** Mark your answer on your answer sheet.

**15** Mark your answer on your answer sheet.

**16** Mark your answer on your answer sheet.

**17** Mark your answer on your answer sheet.

**18** Mark your answer on your answer sheet.

**19** Mark your answer on your answer sheet.

**20** Mark your answer on your answer sheet.

**21** Mark your answer on your answer sheet.

**22** Mark your answer on your answer sheet.

**23** Mark your answer on your answer sheet.

**24** Mark your answer on your answer sheet.

**25** Mark your answer on your answer sheet.

**26** Mark your answer on your answer sheet.

**27** Mark your answer on your answer sheet.

**28** Mark your answer on your answer sheet.

**29** Mark your answer on your answer sheet.

**30** Mark your answer on your answer sheet.

**31** Mark your answer on your answer sheet.

# PART 3 🎧

**Directions:** You will hear some conversations between two or more people. You will be asked to answer three questions about what the speakers say in each conversation. Select the best response to each question and mark the letter (A), (B), (C), or (D) on your answer sheet. The conversations will not be printed in your test book and will be spoken only one time.

**32** What is the man's complaint?
(A) His heating system does not work.
(B) His booking was cancelled.
(C) His taxi was late.
(D) His luggage is missing.

**33** What does the woman offer the man?
(A) A free lift to the concert
(B) A complimentary meal
(C) An upgraded accommodation
(D) Early check-in options

**34** What does the man request?
(A) An apology
(B) A partial refund
(C) Free taxi rides
(D) Assistance with his bags

**35** What does the woman want to do?
(A) Volunteer at a gallery
(B) Register for health care
(C) Get some legal advice
(D) Undergo surgery

**36** What does the man say the woman has to do?
(A) Provide her date of birth
(B) Make a contribution
(C) Attend a medical test
(D) Present her health card

**37** What does the man give the woman?
(A) A list of staff
(B) A policy document
(C) A disclaimer
(D) A replacement card

**38** What are the speakers discussing?
(A) Ordering supplies
(B) Installing software
(C) Scheduling an event
(D) Buying devices

**39** What does the woman say she will do next?
(A) Meet with a superior
(B) Finish her work
(C) Speak with a coworker
(D) Check her schedule

**40** What does the man mean when he says, "I'd say that's not anytime soon"?
(A) They are too busy to meet with the manager.
(B) They have other projects to focus on now.
(C) They are unable to purchase keyboards now.
(D) They have not received the keyboards yet.

GO ON TO THE NEXT PAGE

41 Where is the conversation taking place?

   (A) At a warehouse
   (B) At a delivery office
   (C) At a florist shop
   (D) At a hospital

42 According to the woman, why is the room number wrong?

   (A) The room is occupied by a male.
   (B) The patients are not allowed packages.
   (C) The building only has a small number of rooms.
   (D) The street name is incorrect.

43 What does the woman say she will do next?

   (A) Arrange for a delivery
   (B) Order some food
   (C) Call for a porter
   (D) Contact Ms. Callard

---

44 Why is the woman calling?

   (A) To report to a customer
   (B) To propose a project
   (C) To request some changes
   (D) To ask for information

45 What does the woman ask the man to do?

   (A) Go over her work
   (B) Add color to visual aids
   (C) Contact a client
   (D) Remove some colors on the graphs

46 Why does the man say, "That's not an issue"?

   (A) He currently has been assigned a lot of projects.
   (B) He is worried about a deadline being affected.
   (C) He is almost finished writing a report.
   (D) He has no problem meeting the woman's request.

47 What does the woman ask the man to do?

   (A) Bring an item from stock
   (B) Contact some students
   (C) Turn out the lights
   (D) Rearrange a cupboard

48 Why is the man unable to help?

   (A) A delivery has been delayed.
   (B) Some equipment has been damaged.
   (C) A student requires his assistance.
   (D) A lab has been closed down.

49 What will happen at 12:00?

   (A) A replacement tutor will be sent.
   (B) The man will buy some light bulbs.
   (C) The woman's students will arrive.
   (D) Different equipment will be used.

---

50 What does Carstairs Inc. want to advertise?

   (A) A job opportunity
   (B) A product
   (C) An event
   (D) A warehouse

51 What does the woman suggest?

   (A) Offering online discounts
   (B) Hiring a marketing expert
   (C) Advertising in specialist media
   (D) Advertising on the radio

52 What does the man say about the woman's suggestion?

   (A) It was unsuccessful in the past.
   (B) It will take too long.
   (C) It was not possible for the company.
   (D) It was too expensive to run.

**53** According to the woman, what is the problem with the dress?

(A) The dress didn't fit.
(B) The fastener was faulty.
(C) The size is too small.
(D) The price is too high.

**54** What will the man send to the woman?

(A) A document
(B) A new dress
(C) A discount voucher
(D) A full refund

**55** What does the woman say she would prefer?

(A) To change the color of the dress
(B) To choose a different item
(C) To receive a refund
(D) To wait for a replacement

---

**56** What problem has the woman identified?

(A) A training session has not been finished.
(B) Some documents are out of date.
(C) Some registration forms have not been collected.
(D) Some employees have given false information.

**57** What does the woman say about workers who were certified more than a year ago?

(A) They need to resubmit their details.
(B) They need to undergo a written test.
(C) They have to pay for extra tuition.
(D) They must contact their supervisors.

**58** What does the man ask the woman to do?

(A) Archive some documents
(B) Send some warnings
(C) Organize a workshop
(D) Provide names of workers

**59** What are the speakers discussing?

(A) A growing population in certain areas
(B) An industry's hiring trend
(C) Business expansion
(D) A popular city for sales people

**60** What is implied about professionals in their 30s?

(A) They are willing to relocate for work.
(B) They want to live in cities.
(C) They are a new market.
(D) They are paid well.

**61** What does the woman offer to do?

(A) Collect market data
(B) Speak with building designers
(C) Put together a report
(D) Tour some buildings

**62** Where do the speakers work?

    (A) At a fitness club
    (B) At a doctor's surgery
    (C) At a theater
    (D) At a police station

**63** Why will the man miss work today?

    (A) He is not feeling well.
    (B) He has lost his voice.
    (C) He does not have a car.
    (D) He has a crisis at home.

**64** What do the speakers say about Miguel?

    (A) He needs to be fitted for a costume.
    (B) He is always reliable.
    (C) He needs some additional training.
    (D) He is not happy about the role.

| Room | Day of reservation |
|------|--------------------|
| 4A | Monday |
| 7B | Tuesday |
| 4C | Wednesday |
| 2D | Thursday |

**65** What most likely will the man do tomorrow?

    (A) Pick up some materials
    (B) Meet a client
    (C) Test some devices
    (D) Finish a presentation

**66** What problem does the man mention?

    (A) A screen is malfunctioning.
    (B) An event needs to be put off.
    (C) A room is not available.
    (D) Some equipment is not working.

**67** Look at the graphic. What room did the man reserve?

    (A) Room 4A
    (B) Room 7B
    (C) Room 4C
    (D) Room 2D

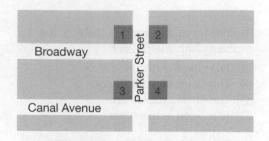

**68** What does the man want to do?

    (A) Visit an exhibit
    (B) Book a room
    (C) Park his car
    (D) Take a bus

**69** Look at the graphic. Where is the National Museum?

    (A) 1
    (B) 2
    (C) 3
    (D) 4

**70** What does the woman offer to do?

    (A) Write down directions
    (B) Walk the man to his destination
    (C) Give the man a map
    (D) Call a taxi

# PART 4 🎧12🎧

**Directions:** You will hear some talks given by a single speaker. You will be asked to answer three questions about what the speaker says in each talk. Select the best response to each question and mark the letter (A), (B), (C), or (D) on your answer sheet. The talks will not be printed in your test book and will be spoken only one time.

**71** Where does the announcement most likely take place?

(A) On a train
(B) On a boat
(C) On a plane
(D) On a bus

**72** What does the speaker point out as unusual?

(A) An animal at the castle
(B) A ruined tower structure
(C) A treat for the local community
(D) An unusual weather pattern

**73** What does the speaker recommend the listeners do?

(A) Book a meal
(B) Watch the birds
(C) Listen to music
(D) Take pictures

**74** What type of product is being discussed?

(A) Electronic devices
(B) Clothing
(C) Athletic equipment
(D) Office supplies

**75** What does the speaker say she will give the listeners?

(A) A product sample
(B) Completed questionnaires
(C) Sales updates
(D) A revised budget

**76** What are listeners asked to think about?

(A) Ideas for cutting costs
(B) Strategies for attracting customers
(C) Locations for a new shopping center
(D) Names for new products

**77** What is the speaker planning to do next weekend?

(A) Go on a sporting trip
(B) Purchase some ice skates
(C) Visit a sporting event
(D) Attend a convention

**78** According to the speaker, what must people do to receive a discount?

(A) Arrive by bus
(B) Show a membership card
(C) Present a discount voucher
(D) Make a group booking

**79** What does the speaker say he wants to do on Monday morning?

(A) Make a booking
(B) Reserve a hotel room
(C) Deliver some items
(D) Go on a trip

**80** According to the speaker, what is taking place tomorrow?

(A) A major delivery
(B) A factory tour
(C) A management meeting
(D) A safety audit

**81** Who will visit the plant?

(A) Suppliers
(B) Paramedics
(C) Inspectors
(D) Management

**82** What are listeners asked to do later today?

(A) Check compulsory instructions
(B) Upload guidelines
(C) Submit a purchase order
(D) Evacuate the building

GO ON TO THE NEXT PAGE

83 What is being discussed?

(A) A press conference
(B) A client seminar
(C) A product launch
(D) A company anniversary

84 According to the speaker, what is surprising?

(A) Rapid decrease of competitors
(B) The growth of the business
(C) The success of the advertising
(D) A change in a work schedule

85 Why are listeners asked to email Mel Cushing?

(A) To take part in a survey
(B) To assist with preparations
(C) To distribute leaflets
(D) To book a conference room

86 What topic will the woman talk about?

(A) Hiring team leaders
(B) Raising productivity
(C) Improving sales
(D) Transferring employees

87 Why does the woman say, "Now, here's my understanding"?

(A) She recently presented some findings.
(B) She wants to write a summary.
(C) She trained her staff.
(D) She is going to tell her opinion.

88 What are listeners asked to do?

(A) Write down some thoughts
(B) Talk with their coworkers
(C) Read some information
(D) Change their work station

89 Where does the speaker most likely work?

(A) At a cleaning product manufacturer
(B) At a commercial airline
(C) At a car dealership
(D) At a food market

90 When can listeners get the information packets?

(A) Today
(B) Tomorrow
(C) Next week
(D) In two weeks

91 What does the man mean when he says, "So this is it then"?

(A) He will demonstrate how the product works.
(B) He is ready to end the meeting.
(C) He will go over the packets next time.
(D) He wants listeners to design some ideas.

| Train | From | Arriving At |
|-------|------|-------------|
| 121 | JFK | Platform 2 |
| 141 | Newark | Platform 7 |
| 161 | Union | Platform 1 |
| 171 | Jay | Platform 10 |

92 What are the listeners asked to do?

(A) Store their belongings properly
(B) Not get off the train before an announcement
(C) Check their belongings before disembarking
(D) Move to a different platform

93 Look at the graphic. Where did the train leave from?

(A) JFK        (B) Newark
(C) Union      (D) Jay

94 Why can't passengers use the main entrance?

(A) Improvement work is being done.
(B) The place is too crowded at the moment.
(C) It has been shut down for a routine inspection.
(D) Cleaning work is taking place.

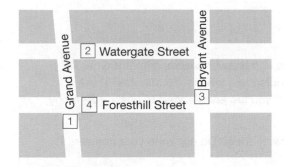

| New Work Schedule | |
|---|---|
| Area | Day |
| Cafeteria | Monday |
| Breakroom | Tuesday Thursday |
| Storage space | Wednesday Friday |
| Lobby | Saturday |

**95** What is the broadcast about?

(A) Building maintenance
(B) Traffic congestion
(C) A road closure
(D) A new bus schedule

**96** What are commuters advised to do?

(A) Leave earlier
(B) Take a detour
(C) Avoid using public transportation in the area
(D) Drive slowly

**97** Look at the graphic. What number shows where the construction will take place?

(A) 1
(B) 2
(C) 3
(D) 4

**98** What is the purpose of the announcement?

(A) To get feedback
(B) To assign a task
(C) To promote a product
(D) To change a plan

**99** What is mentioned about the new material?

(A) It takes longer to settle in.
(B) It is less expensive.
(C) It is more durable.
(D) It is easier to use.

**100** Look at the graphic. What day was the lobby originally scheduled to be worked on?

(A) Monday
(B) Tuesday
(C) Wednesday
(D) Saturday

This is the end of the Listening test. Turn to Part 5 in your test book.

GO ON TO THE NEXT PAGE

# READING TEST

In the Reading test, you will read a variety of texts and answer several different types of reading comprehension questions. The entire Reading test will last 75 minutes. There are three parts, and directions are given for each part. You are encouraged to answer as many questions as possible within the time allowed.

You must mark your answers on the separate answer sheet. Do not write your answers in your test book.

# PART 5

**Directions:** A word or phrase is missing in each of the sentences below. Four answer choices are given below each sentence. Select the best answer to complete the sentence. Then mark the letter (A), (B), (C), or (D) on your answer sheet.

101 Mr. Kim ------- his thesis on the financial state of the automobile industry next Wednesday.

(A) finished
(B) finishing
(C) to finish
(D) will finish

102 Sales representatives should be as ------- as possible when negotiating prices with customers.

(A) flexible
(B) flexed
(C) flexing
(D) flexibility

103 Please allow at least two to three weeks for ------- of your order.

(A) method
(B) quantity
(C) delivery
(D) model

104 Clarks offers the region's widest ------- of winter footwear for both adults and young people.

(A) selection
(B) selected
(C) selects
(D) selecting

105 All guests to the Solnova Solar Power Plant must report to the reception desk ------- upon arrival.

(A) partially
(B) timely
(C) closely
(D) immediately

106 When taking a holiday, leave your coworkers ------- instructions regarding how to deal with client requests in your absence.

(A) whole
(B) blank
(C) repetitive
(D) clear

107 The deadline for ------- of business proposals is Wednesday, June 6th, at 5:00 P.M.

(A) submit
(B) submission
(C) submits
(D) submitted

108 The American Equestrian Association's Web site provides members ------- easy access to the latest news about horses.

(A) with
(B) into
(C) beside
(D) up

109 Yamaha ------- requires groups of five or above to sign up in advance for factory tours.
(A) normal
(B) normality
(C) norm
(D) normally

110 Zrinka Milioti ------- assumed the role of chief information officer at Hansard Electricals on October 9th.
(A) namely
(B) collectively
(C) officially
(D) densely

111 Before activating the projector, firmly connect ------- cable to your device.
(A) there
(B) which
(C) its
(D) those

112 All part-time and full-time employees of Mantello's Snacks and Drinks are ------- to attend the president's annual information gatherings.
(A) contributed
(B) expected
(C) noticed
(D) conducted

113 The recording of the public hearing will be available on the city council Web site ------- the meeting.
(A) since
(B) between
(C) within
(D) throughout

114 While the building is being repaired, some staff members may be temporarily relocated ------- different workspaces.
(A) at
(B) on
(C) to
(D) as

115 Visit the Jarrah Placement Project Web site and ------- today for the computer programming seminar.
(A) registering
(B) registered
(C) registration
(D) register

116 Congressman Robert Smith is going to ------- his bid for reelection during a broadcast news conference at 7:00 P.M. tomorrow.
(A) announce
(B) notify
(C) interfere
(D) level

117 *The Devizes Weekly* has been ------- ranked among the most popular publications in Woodland Hills.
(A) consistency
(B) consistencies
(C) consistently
(D) consistent

118 Please confirm that all packages are packed properly ------- they are shipped to the warehouse.
(A) as much as
(B) such as
(C) whether
(D) before

119 Renovations to the lobby are not ------- to be finished before the beginning of next month.
(A) typical
(B) probably
(C) likely
(D) usual

120 *Operating System Magazine* forecasts that the ------- for iron and steel used in electronic parts will peak during the next ten years.
(A) materials
(B) demand
(C) appliances
(D) resource

121 Neo Country Club may require customers to show identification for ------- their personal belongings.

(A) retrieve
(B) retrieved
(C) retrieval
(D) retrieving

122 ------- wishes to visit this year's marketing seminar must contact Mr. Qureshi by August 1.

(A) Nobody
(B) Whoever
(C) Whatever
(D) Somebody

123 CFO Rowan Winsvold expressed her ------- to everyone who posted ideas for reducing operating costs.

(A) imitation
(B) exposure
(C) gratitude
(D) abundance

124 The air-conditioning machine will not operate without a valve ------- the flow of liquid.

(A) regulated
(B) will regulate
(C) regulates
(D) to regulate

125 The training representative sent a memo to all employees ------- the upcoming training seminar.

(A) resulting
(B) following
(C) usually
(D) concerning

126 Resch Community Airport displays artworks painted by Matthew Benton, a local aviation -------.

(A) enthusiast
(B) enthused
(C) enthusiastically
(D) enthusiasm

127 The recent trend ------- investing in precious stones is expected to continue.

(A) near
(B) toward
(C) though
(D) along

128 With Blueocean Financial Services, new clients must install antivirus software ------- they can access their account information online.

(A) unless
(B) so that
(C) as though
(D) whereas

129 Because of higher-than-predicted profits in the last nine months, Giampanidou Designs is understandably ------- about its expansion.

(A) devoted
(B) optimistic
(C) impressive
(D) ample

130 Had Starship Entertainment not given the actor a chance, another company --------- so.

(A) should do
(B) has done
(C) would have done
(D) was done

# PART 6

**Directions:** Read the texts that follow. A word, phrase, or sentence is missing in parts of each text. Four answer choices for each question are given below the text. Select the best answer to complete the text. Then mark the letter (A), (B), (C), or (D) on your answer sheet.

**Questions 131-134** refer to the following article.

Nature Park Coming Soon

The opening ------- for the city's new Nature Park will be held on Sunday, April 2.
      **131.**
The mayor, city council members, reporters, and several local celebrities will be in

attendance. The official ribbon cutting is scheduled for 10:30 A.M., ------- by the
                  **132.**
mayor's welcoming speech. Light snacks and beverages will be served by a local

restaurant. There will also be entertainment events, including a dance performance

and magic show. ------- admission is free and open to the public, registration should
      **133.**
be made online in advance. Interested individuals can view the details at www.

natureparkopening.com. -------. So arrive early.
          **134.**

131 (A) remark
    (B) ceremony
    (C) demonstration
    (D) presentation

132 (A) following
    (B) follows
    (C) will follow
    (D) followed

133 (A) Now that
    (B) Although
    (C) Besides
    (D) As though

134 (A) It is important to preserve nature.
    (B) There will be food available for purchase.
    (C) The number of seats is limited.
    (D) The event has been postponed due to inclement weather.

Questions 135-138 refer to the following brochure.

Explore the village of Bourton via one of our regularly arranged bicycle tours. Sponsored by the Bourton Tourism Academy, ------- tour is headed by an expert cyclist
**135.**
and features a different perspective of the village.

The most popular route encompasses Downvale Valley, the village's industrial -------. In
**136.**
addition to three working mills and one factory, Downvale Valley is home to a working

tin mine and several craft shops that represent the history of the region. -------. It -------
**137.** **138.**
with a refreshing meal at the Green Man pub, one of Bourton's oldest public houses.

To register for the Downvale Valley tour or to find out more about the other tours, call the Bourton Tourism Academy at 050-555-6939.

135 (A) each
(B) whose
(C) either
(D) this

136 (A) factories
(B) programs
(C) district
(D) revolution

137 (A) Visitors should wear safety gear.
(B) The tour lasts approximately three hours.
(C) Riding a bike is good for health.
(D) This guide will explain the history of the town.

138 (A) concludes
(B) exits
(C) orders
(D) reserves

116

**To:** muamba@nigermail.com
**From:** subscriptions@befitmagazine.com
**Subject:** Subscription renewal
**Date:** September 20

Dear Mr. Muamba:

Your subscription to *Be Fit Magazine* ------- on September 30. To ensure you don't
**139.**
miss any of our award-winning articles on general health and fitness, don't forget to

renew your subscription for another twelve months at the specially low rate of $30.00.

-------, renewing your subscription before the end of the month entitles you to receive
**140.**
other publications from George Dent Publishing at a discounted rate. -------.
**141.**

Just complete the online renewal form at www.befitmagazine.com/subscription -------
**142.**
September 23.

Regards,

Subscription Services

139 (A) having expired
   (B) will expire
   (C) expired
   (D) expiring

140 (A) Consequently
   (B) However
   (C) Instead
   (D) Additionally

141 (A) This offer is valid only for first-time
     subscribers.
   (B) We received your submission for our
     November issue.
   (C) This includes *Exercise Routine* and
     *Dress to Impress*.
   (D) You are cordially invited to the award
     ceremony.

142 (A) into
   (B) by
   (C) at
   (D) until

NOTICE

TO: Museum Staff

As of March 5, the east wing of the main museum building will be closed owing to

-------.  The elevators and light switches in the building are old and need to be
  **143.**
replaced.

Signs will be posted alerting patrons that the area is off-limits. Staff members needing

to enter that part of the building can do so on a limited basis. -------.
                                                                    **144.**

Finally, shipments normally delivered to the east wing's loading dock will ------- be
                                                                              **145.**
rerouted to the north wing mailroom. We will return to normal delivery protocols -------
                                                                                  **146.**
work is completed.

Thank you for your patience in advance.

Ail Yasof

Director of the Goldsun Museum

143 (A) construct
    (B) constructor
    (C) construction
    (D) constructively

144 (A) Employees are advised to take time
        off during construction.
    (B) Permission must be obtained from a
        supervisor.
    (C) Some events will still be held in the
        east wing.
    (D) Confidential documents will be
        stored in protective boxes.

145 (A) hardly
    (B) temporarily
    (C) formally
    (D) permanently

146 (A) following
    (B) promptly
    (C) later
    (D) once

# PART 7

**Directions:** In this part you will read a selection of texts, such as magazine and newspaper articles, e-mails, and instant messages. Each text or set of texts is followed by several questions. Select the best answer for each question and mark the letter (A), (B), (C), or (D) on your answer sheet.

**Questions 147-148** refer to the following text message.

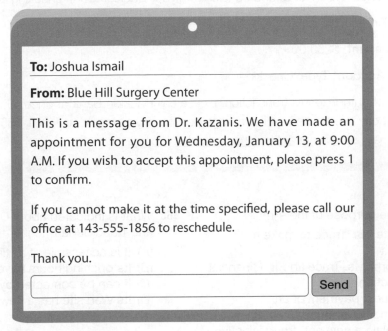

**To:** Joshua Ismail

**From:** Blue Hill Surgery Center

This is a message from Dr. Kazanis. We have made an appointment for you for Wednesday, January 13, at 9:00 A.M. If you wish to accept this appointment, please press 1 to confirm.

If you cannot make it at the time specified, please call our office at 143-555-1856 to reschedule.

Thank you.

[          ]  Send

**147** Why was the message sent?
- (A) To ask about a procedure
- (B) To announce a cancellation
- (C) To change an appointment
- (D) To ask for confirmation

**148** What is Mr. Ismail instructed to do to change an appointment?
- (A) Call the office
- (B) Visit the office
- (C) Send a text message
- (D) Send a fax

GO ON TO THE NEXT PAGE

Questions 149-150 refer to the following e-mail.

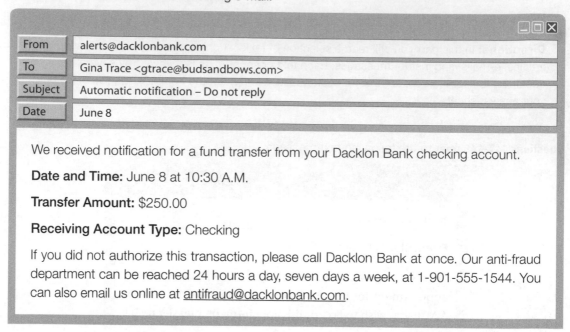

| From | alerts@dacklonbank.com |
|------|------------------------|
| To | Gina Trace <gtrace@budsandbows.com> |
| Subject | Automatic notification – Do not reply |
| Date | June 8 |

We received notification for a fund transfer from your Dacklon Bank checking account.

**Date and Time:** June 8 at 10:30 A.M.

**Transfer Amount:** $250.00

**Receiving Account Type:** Checking

If you did not authorize this transaction, please call Dacklon Bank at once. Our anti-fraud department can be reached 24 hours a day, seven days a week, at 1-901-555-1544. You can also email us online at antifraud@dacklonbank.com.

**149** What is the purpose of the e-mail?
- (A) To invite Ms. Trace to make a deposit
- (B) To inform Ms. Trace about a financial transaction
- (C) To request payment of an outstanding amount
- (D) To explain a new anti-fraud initiative

**150** What is indicated about Dacklon Bank's anti-fraud department?
- (A) It is accessible at all times.
- (B) Its opening hours have altered.
- (C) It can be contacted by post.
- (D) Its Web site has a new address.

Questions 151-152 refer to the following text message chain.

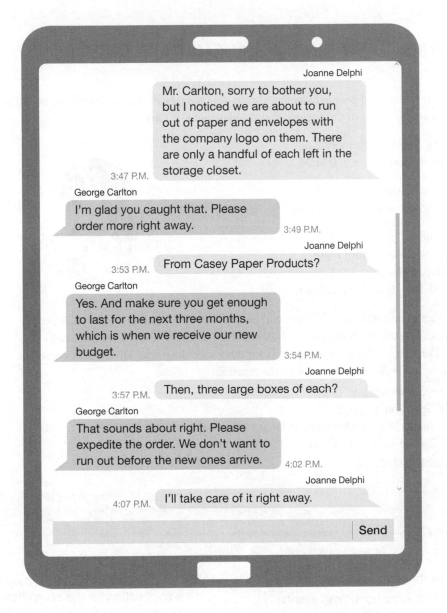

Joanne Delphi

Mr. Carlton, sorry to bother you, but I noticed we are about to run out of paper and envelopes with the company logo on them. There are only a handful of each left in the storage closet.
3:47 P.M.

George Carlton

I'm glad you caught that. Please order more right away.
3:49 P.M.

Joanne Delphi

3:53 P.M. From Casey Paper Products?

George Carlton

Yes. And make sure you get enough to last for the next three months, which is when we receive our new budget.
3:54 P.M.

Joanne Delphi

3:57 P.M. Then, three large boxes of each?

George Carlton

That sounds about right. Please expedite the order. We don't want to run out before the new ones arrive.
4:02 P.M.

Joanne Delphi

4:07 P.M. I'll take care of it right away.

Send

**151** At 4:02 P.M., what does Mr. Carlton most likely mean when he writes, "That sounds about right"?

(A) He appreciates Ms. Delphi's reporting the problem to him.
(B) He thinks Ms. Delphi estimated the correct amount.
(C) He is about to tell Ms. Delphi some additional information.
(D) He wants Ms. Delphi to pay attention to the instructions.

**152** What will Ms. Delphi most likely do next?

(A) Reschedule a shipment
(B) Mail some letters
(C) Place an order for stationery
(D) Prepare a budget

GO ON TO THE NEXT PAGE

## NOTICE OF WEIGHT MANAGEMENT MEETINGS

October 3

Local residents and people from the surrounding neighborhoods are invited to attend the following meetings of the Chamis Weight Management Group:

- Date: Saturday, October 22
  Dietary committee, 6:00 P.M.

- Date: Saturday, October 29
  Exercise committee, 6:30 P.M.

- Venue
  The Sea View, Third Floor
  Seeman Hall
  2018 Rue de la Grande, Chamis

Timetables and training schedules will be available on Tuesday, October 4 at public libraries and the foyer of Seeman Hall and the Chamis Public Swimming Pool.
Local residents who have suggestions for the weight loss program should contact the organizer at least three days before the meeting.

Send requests to:
Janis Grousson, Organizer
The Chamis Weight Management Group
2018 Rue de la Grande, Chamis
jgrousson@chamis.fr

---

**153** What is the purpose of the notice?

(A) To publicize upcoming events
(B) To inaugurate a weight gain regimen
(C) To advertise a new venue
(D) To announce a recruitment drive

**154** When will a discussion about exercise take place?

(A) On October 3
(B) On October 4
(C) On October 22
(D) On October 29

**155** What should people do if they have a suggestion for the committee?

(A) Email Ms. Grousson
(B) Call the committee
(C) Attend the first meeting
(D) Sign up at Seeman Hall

Test 03

JB Sports
El Marina
Spain 1139

## YOUR ONLINE VENDOR OF SPORT AND LEISURE GEAR

Customer: *Samira Lahon*
Shipping Address: *301 Lumago Street, Seville, SP 1295*
Order Number: *99842 (placed on November 11, 10:32 A.M.)*

| Quantity | Item | Amount |
|---|---|---|
| 1 | Blue Designer Sneakers (Manufacturer: Corrilo) | Subtotal: 58.00 |
| | | Tax: 5.80 |
| 1 | Green Slingback Sandals (Manufacturer: Grandissimo) | Expedited Shipping: 11.00 Order Total: 74.80 Amount paid via Credit Card: 74.80 Balance Due: 0.00 |

Order Shipped on November 11, 3:05 P.M.

*Thank you for your purchase. If you are not happy with the items, please return them within 14 days unworn or accompanied with the original packaging. For more details on returning or exchanging a purchase, see www.jbsports/sp/returns.

156 What kind of product does JB Sports sell?

(A) Literary material
(B) Footwear
(C) Musical instruments
(D) DVDs

157 What is indicated about Ms. Lahon?

(A) She received a parcel on November 11.
(B) She regularly buys from JB Sports.
(C) She plans to buy more shoes.
(D) She paid for quick delivery.

GO ON TO THE NEXT PAGE

http://www.raphaelcomputers.com

# Raphael Computer Repairs

| HOME | SERVICES | TESTIMONIALS | REQUEST APPOINTMENT | CONTACT US |

What our customers are saying...

**Rating:** ★★★★★

**Date of service:** August 7

**Type of service:** Installation of RZ 33 Home Automation System

Last week, I realized the computer terminal for my home automation system was faulty. –[1]–. I recalled a leaflet for Raphael Computer Repairs was posted on my front door, so I called the number. –[2]–. Even though it was late afternoon and the business was about to close, the owner, Ziggy Raphael, agreed to come round to my house straight after he closed the shop. He took a look at the computer terminal and told me I could either upgrade it or have it repaired. Since it was a few years old, I choose to have it upgraded. Mr. Raphael demonstrated a number of different models and I decided upon one with a much larger memory capacity.

I thought it would take a while for it to be ordered and delivered, but Mr. Raphael had one in his van and installed it that same day. –[3]–. His secretary called the following day to ensure that the system was working correctly. The entire experience demonstrates the excellent customer service presented by Raphael Computer Repairs and I will definitely recommend his services again. –[4]–.

Carla Lamos

**158** Why has the information most likely been included on the Web site?

(A) To explain a company policy
(B) To describe an installation process
(C) To attract potential customers
(D) To advertise a new product

**159** What is indicated about Mr. Raphael?

(A) He shares a mailbox with Ms. Lamos.
(B) He completed work for Ms. Lamos on the same day she requested it.
(C) He charges an extra fee for installing larger computer terminals.
(D) His secretary contacted Ms. Lamos on August 7.

**160** In which of the positions marked [1], [2], [3], and [4] does the following sentence best belong?

"He didn't even charge me extra for working during off hours."

(A) [1]
(B) [2]
(C) [3]
(D) [4]

GO ON TO THE NEXT PAGE

## CO Janssen's DVD is moving!

Janssen's DVD, recognized as the town's biggest collection of videos and DVDs for sale, is expanding. We began at our location on Farrier Street six years ago, and it is now time to move to 331 Sadlers Row, former home of the Flickson Bakery. We will continue to sell DVDs, videos and CDs as well as comic books, but the extra space will enable us to grow into the electronic games market.

Our Farrier Street store will close on Friday, May 18, and Janssen's DVD will host a grand opening party for the new store on Saturday, May 19, from 9 A.M. to 5 P.M. We are inviting all of our customers to join us at the event, which will be catered by Cuisine Café, our new neighbor.

Come and see our new merchandise and taste Cuisine Café's delicious sandwiches and beverages. Also present will be Randy Cloche, star of the new indie film, *Tracing James*, and he will be around to sign autographs and meet people.

To prepare for our relocation, we will be getting rid of some of our old stock. During April, the price of some DVDs and videos will be reduced by up to 50 percent, so seize the opportunity to pick up some of your favorite films at a bargain.

161 What is indicated about Janssen's DVD?

(A) It is increasing its staffing levels.
(B) It will be moving next to Flickson Bakery.
(C) It is amalgamating with Cuisine Café.
(D) It has been in business for six years.

162 What does Janssen's DVD currently NOT offer?

(A) Video games
(B) Comic books
(C) CDs
(D) DVDs

163 Who is Mr. Cloche?

(A) An actor
(B) A manager of a café
(C) A store owner
(D) A photographer

164 According to the flyer, what will happen in April?

(A) A grand opening will be held.
(B) A discount will be offered.
(C) Free DVDs will be given out.
(D) A new inventory will be delivered.

# Benzema Motor Care — Internal Job Posting

This position is open to internal candidates until the end of the month. Subsequently, the position will be advertised to external candidates.

**Title:** Chief Mechanic

**Description:**
- Support Benzema Motor Care by servicing more vehicles in the company's three main areas of maintenance, repair and servicing.
- Perform MOTs, body work repair and vehicle analytics on all vehicle models.
- Maintain customer service with key clientele.

**Principal Duties:**
- Check cars and other vehicles and diagnose problem areas
- Perform computer analytics on selected company cars
- Prepare detailed servicing using multiple repair systems
- Serve as a liaison between car manufacturers and garage staff

**Requirements:**
- A minimum of three years' experience in our Vehicle Maintenance Department
- A detailed understanding of car maintenance

To apply for this position, please submit your résumé, cover letter and contact information of two references by February 11 to Kemar Nahn, Garage Manager, at knahn@benzema.org.

**Test 03**

---

**165** What is mentioned as a requirement of the position?

(A) A business degree
(B) In-depth knowledge of car maintenance
(C) Experience working with customers
(D) A valid driving license

**166** What should a candidate do to apply?

(A) Send the requested documents to Ms. Nahn
(B) Have a supervisor refer a candidate
(C) Fill out an application form
(D) Schedule an interview by February 11

**167** Where would the notice most likely appear?

(A) In a public database of automobile jobs
(B) In a memo to staff at Benzema Motor Care
(C) In the recruitment section of a newspaper
(D) In a letter to chief mechanics

**168** What is NOT included in the responsibilities of the chief mechanic?

(A) Liaise with car manufacturers
(B) Diagnose vehicular faults
(C) Undertake car servicing
(D) Update the company's client list

GO ON TO THE NEXT PAGE

| **Pilar Ortega** | — X |
| --- | --- |

**Pilar Ortega** [8:48 A.M.] Good morning, team. I want to check in with you to see how the new e-mail program is working out. Any issues so far?

**Vincent Williams** [8:50 A.M.] I love it. Now that I get notifications directly on my phone as soon as a message arrives in my inbox, I can respond to customers faster.

**Nancy Dortmunder** [8:51 A.M.] My phone doesn't do that!

**Vincent Williams** [8:52 A.M.] It's not the phone. It's part of the actual program. You have to set it up that way.

**Nancy Dortmunder** [8:53 A.M.] How do I do that?

**Vincent Williams** [8:54 A.M.] Go to the Options tab. There is a section where you can set alerts. There, you can check the box for new messages.

**Nancy Dortmunder** [8:55 A.M.] Thanks! Overall, I think this program is way easier to use than GoBox. I'll have to thank David for recommending it.

**Adam Polar** [8:59 A.M.] I am having a problem uploading attachments. Can somebody help me?

**Pilar Ortega** [9:01 A.M.] Sure. I had the same issue, so I called Popmail's technical support team. Someone explained everything to me. It's not too difficult, but the steps are different from GoBox. I can show you how to do it at the departmental lunch meeting tomorrow. Will you be able to make it?

**Adam Polar** [9:02 A.M.] Yes. I'll try to arrive early, so we can have time to go over everything.

| | Send |
| --- | --- |

**169** At 8:51 A.M., why does Ms. Dortmunder write, "My phone doesn't do that"?

(A) She wants to adjust her phone's settings.
(B) She is unable to check e-mail on her phone.
(C) She is surprised that Mr. Williams gets alerts.
(D) She wants to respond to customer e-mails faster.

**170** Why did Ms. Ortega contact technical support?

(A) To set up alerts on her phone
(B) To install a new e-mail program
(C) To learn how to attach files
(D) To upgrade GoBox software

**171** What is suggested about Mr. Polar?

(A) He recommended Popmail to the team.
(B) He will give a presentation at the meeting.
(C) He has a lunch appointment today.
(D) He will get assistance from Ms. Ortega tomorrow.

March 30

Duncan Kamal, CEO
Erin Call Center
1000 Sprint Road
Birmingham, Alabama USA

Dear Mr. Kamal,

I'm writing to tell you that Temps Today has been taken over by WRE Employment, one of the biggest names in the supply of temporary staff. Temps Today will continue to operate under the same name, but some of our prices will be affected. −[1]−. As one of our most valued customers,
I would like to personally inform you of the changes so you can make appropriate decisions.

While the cost of supplying temporary agency staff largely remains the same, the hourly rate for our call center operatives has been revised. −[2]−. Our new hourly rates are as follows:

Up to 4 operatives, $15 per person per hour
5-9 operatives, $11 per person per hour
10-24 operatives, $10 per person per hour
25-49 operatives, $9 per person per hour
50 or more operatives, $8 per person per hour

Under the new pricing system, we calculate the charges for supplying call center staff based on the number of people you require per month. −[3]−. Therefore, if on your next request you ask for the same number of operatives as you did in February, you will be charged the lowest monthly fee ($8 per person per hour), only fifty cents more than under the old system.

As a WRE Employment company, we will also supply additional skilled temporary staff. −[4]−. In addition, our Web site now offers numerous convenient extra features, including account history and personnel skills requirements.

If you have any questions regarding the changes, please do not hesitate to contact us. We will continue to provide you with the same excellent and upmarket service that you have been enjoying for a number of years. Thank you for your continued business.

Sincerely,

*Alexis Chan*
Alexis Chan
Temps Today
Vice President, Customer Service

**172** What is a purpose of the letter?

(A) To report a staffing shortage
(B) To announce a new training scheme
(C) To advertise the opening of a new Web site
(D) To explain a change in the fee structure

**173** According to the letter, what did WRE Employment recently do?

(A) Acquire another company
(B) Change its location
(C) Hire a new vice president
(D) Relocate to Alabama

**174** Who is Mr. Kamal?

(A) A temporary call center worker
(B) An owner of WRE Employment
(C) A personal financial advisor
(D) A customer of Temps Today

**175** In which of the positions marked [1], [2], [3], and [4] does the following sentence best belong?

"For example, we can supply caterers for any event at a moment's notice."

(A) [1]
(B) [2]
(C) [3]
(D) [4]

# Spanish Vacation Home

| | |
|---|---|
| ⌂ Property: 2619 Madrid | ⌂ Property: 9110 Aragon |
| Exclusive 3-bedroom town-house<br>Minimum stay: 4 nights | Stay three consecutive nights<br>and enjoy 4th night free.<br>Suitable for those wanting to escape from<br>the busy pace of life to a peaceful haven.<br>Sea view. |
| For more information, click *here*. | For more information, click *here*. |
| ⌂ Property: 4716 Castilla | ⌂ Property: 6130 Andalusia |
| 2-bedroom apartments<br>Close to the city and excellent base for<br>modern city life<br>Vibrant environment | With private jetty<br>$1400 per week |
| For more information, click *here*. | For more information, click *here*. |

---

**E-Mail Message**

**To:** Alberto Uemura <auemura@spholidayrentals.co.esp>
**From:** Gayle Ince <gince@ckalltd.co.esp>
**Date:** September 21
**Re:** Property 4716

Hello, Mr. Uemura:

I dealt with you last summer when I went on holiday with my fiancé to Andalusia and I was very happy with both our accommodations and the level of service you provided. However, the destination was not to my taste. It was too quiet and remote. This year, I would prefer something in the city, preferably with more than two bedrooms and access to the nightlife. I am also reluctant to spend more than $900–1,000 for a week. I'm interested in property 4716. Could you provide me with availability and details for this? It seems to meet my needs.

I look forward to your reply.

Regards,

Gayle Ince

176 What property offers a free night's stay?

(A) Property 2619
(B) Property 9110
(C) Property 4716
(D) Property 6130

177 Why did Ms. Ince send the e-mail?

(A) To cancel a deposit
(B) To pay for a booking
(C) To request information
(D) To ask for travel advice

178 What aspect of her previous vacation did Ms. Ince find unsatisfactory?

(A) Cleanliness in the rented apartment
(B) Service provided by the booking agent
(C) Slow pace of life in the region nearby
(D) Distance to her rented property

179 Why is the property 6130 probably unsuitable for Ms. Ince?

(A) She wants accommodation with more than two bedrooms.
(B) She is looking for something cheaper.
(C) She wants to stay in a town house.
(D) She doesn't want to travel to the coast.

180 What location is Ms. Ince interested in?

(A) Madrid
(B) Aragon
(C) Castilla
(D) Andalusia

GO ON TO THE NEXT PAGE

**To:** All employees
**From:** Angharad Reece, Director of HR
**Subject:** Survey Feedback
**Date:** December 30

In November, our human resources department carried out a comprehensive customer questionnaire that covered several areas of our business. The results showed that the majority of our customers are generally pleased with our services, particularly when compared to other loan approval firms. However, some areas for improvement were identified.

A general complaint was that it takes an unacceptably long time to process new accounts. Currently, when we are approached by a customer, the initial loan procedure requires three signatures from our loans department and financial checking office. Thus, it often takes as long as three weeks for money to be transferred into bank accounts.

Therefore, beginning next month, new loan approvals of less than $1,000 require only one signature from the senior loan officer. This policy will reduce the processing time and help us better serve our customers.

If you have any questions, please don't hesitate to contact me.

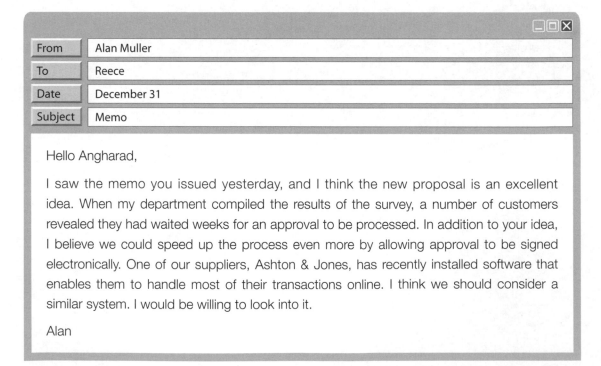

| From | Alan Muller |
|---|---|
| To | Reece |
| Date | December 31 |
| Subject | Memo |

Hello Angharad,

I saw the memo you issued yesterday, and I think the new proposal is an excellent idea. When my department compiled the results of the survey, a number of customers revealed they had waited weeks for an approval to be processed. In addition to your idea, I believe we could speed up the process even more by allowing approval to be signed electronically. One of our suppliers, Ashton & Jones, has recently installed software that enables them to handle most of their transactions online. I think we should consider a similar system. I would be willing to look into it.

Alan

**181** What does Ms. Reece announce in the memo?

(A) A merger with another firm
(B) More surveys for senior sales staff
(C) Hiring of extra financial staff
(D) A new procedure for approving contracts

**182** According to the memo, what is the purpose of the change?

(A) To reduce loan officers' workload
(B) To eliminate unnecessary delays
(C) To improve communication within the organization
(D) To expand the size of the workforce

**183** When will the change go into effect?

(A) In January
(B) In February
(C) In November
(D) In December

**184** What department does Mr. Muller work?

(A) Financial
(B) Sales
(C) Human Resources
(D) Client Relations

**185** What does Mr. Muller recommend?

(A) Participating in a survey
(B) Trying a computer software program
(C) Reducing client fees
(D) Increasing the loan approval limit

Test 03

**Questions 186-190** refer to the following schedule, e-mail, and notice.

Key Building
Schedule for Janitors
Weeks of September 1 – October 4

| Employee | Days (Hours) |
|---|---|
| Tom Jackson | Monday-Friday (9:30 A.M. – 1:30 P.M.) |
| Alan Chin | Monday-Friday (6:30 P.M. – 10:30 P.M.) |
| James Kumar | Monday, Wednesday, Friday (2:30 P.M. – 8:30 P.M) |
| Rodney Reinhardt | Tuesday, Thursday (2:30 P.M. – 8:30 P.M.)<br>Saturday (8:00 A.M. – 2:00 P.M.) |

If you are unable to work an assigned shift, please contact your supervisor as soon as possible.

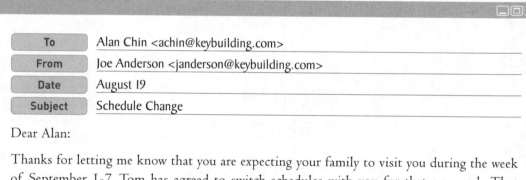

| To | Alan Chin <achin@keybuilding.com> |
|---|---|
| From | Joe Anderson <janderson@keybuilding.com> |
| Date | August 19 |
| Subject | Schedule Change |

Dear Alan:

Thanks for letting me know that you are expecting your family to visit you during the week of September 1-7. Tom has agreed to switch schedules with you for that one week. That week after that, both you and Tom will return to your assigned shifts for the remainder of the month.

Since the requested shift is not your regular one, please talk with Tom about what specific tasks need to be completed. You might also need to contact Security so that they can let you in to clean locked rooms.

Let me know if you have any questions.

Thanks,

Joe

## NEW TIME ENTRY SYSTEM

All Key Building employees will be required to use a new Web-based time entry system, called Synergy, starting the week of September 29 – October 4. Because Synergy can be accessed from any mobile device, employees will no longer have to come in to the Personnel Office to submit paper timesheets. Instead, they need to log on with a username and password and enter their hours worked.

To show employees how to use Synergy, David Harrison will be offering training sessions on the following dates:

| | |
|---|---|
| Security | Monday, September 22 (10:00 A.M. – 11:30 A.M.) |
| Accounting | Tuesday, September 23 (3:00 P.M. – 4:30 P.M.) |
| Maintenance | Wednesday, September 24 (2:00 P.M. – 3:30 P.M.) |
| Administration | Thursday, September 25 (8:30 A.M. – 10:00 A.M.) |

Employees should attend the training session on the date their department is scheduled. If that is not possible, please contact Mr. Harrison at extension 1212 to arrange to attend another session.

**186** What is indicated about Mr. Jackson?

(A) He normally works on Saturdays.
(B) His family lives in the Key Building.
(C) He will change his schedule for one month.
(D) He will work five evenings in September.

**187** What is suggested about Mr. Anderson?

(A) He will lead the Synergy training sessions.
(B) He is Mr. Chin's manager.
(C) He will take one week off.
(D) He owns the Key Building.

**188** In the e-mail, the word "regular" in paragraph 2, line 1, is closest in meaning to

(A) assigned
(B) lengthy
(C) trained
(D) usual

**189** Why are employees asked to attend a training session?

(A) To obtain their usernames and passwords
(B) To learn a new program
(C) To meet their personnel officer
(D) To update their timesheets

**190** On what day will Mr. Reinhardt most likely be trained to use Synergy?

(A) September 22
(B) September 23
(C) September 24
(D) September 25

## People Mover Is Expanding

People Mover, the nation's fastest growing city-to-city bus service, is planning to begin offering services to nineteen new destinations, including Bolton, Newport, Westville, Allentown, and Grover City. People Mover will start serving Bolton and Newport on April 15. Service to smaller cities will be rolled out in May and June.

To celebrate the expansion, we are giving away 100 round-trip tickets to/from any of the new destinations. No purchase is necessary to enter. Simply fill out the form on our Web site at www.peoplemover.com. Entries must be received by March 31.

*Charlestown (June 3)*

Charlestown residents have waited nearly three years for the restoration of direct intercity bus service. That all changed on Saturday when the first People Mover bus picked up 28 passengers in front of the now shuttered Union Street Terminal.

"I'm looking forward to seeing my relatives in Richmond," said Danica Baker, who eagerly boarded the bus. Since National Bus Lines shut down, Ms. Baker has taken local buses and taxies all the way to the city. "I'm so happy that People Mover is here now," she added.

Representatives from the mayor's office say they plan to renovate and reopen the city's only intercity bus terminal later this year. In the meantime, People Mover will stop on Eldritch Street directly in front of the building. Current schedules can be found at www.peoplemover.com or by calling 1-888-555-8399.

Elizabeth Lewis
873 Harper Road
Charlestown
June 28

Dear Ms. Lewis:

Congratulations! You have been selected to receive a trip on People Mover to any destination of your choice. You can claim your ticket by bringing this letter to any bus terminal served by People Mover or by calling 1-888-555-8789. The ticket will remain valid for up to twelve months from the date it is issued.

We look forward to serving you.

Karen Coleman
Vice President of Client Services
People Mover

Test 03

**191** What is suggested about Charlestown?

(A) It is less populous than Newport.
(B) It received new bus service before Bolton.
(C) It used to be served by People Mover.
(D) It no longer has public transportation.

**192** What is indicated about National Bus Lines?

(A) It used to offer service to Bolton.
(B) It was recently acquired by People Mover.
(C) It currently operates out of Richmond.
(D) It went out of business three years ago.

**193** What is suggested about Charlestown's local government?

(A) It currently employs Ms. Lewis.
(B) It plans to fix up Union Street Terminal.
(C) It operates a taxi service.
(D) It signed a contract with People Mover.

**194** What is most likely true about Ms. Lewis?

(A) She entered the People Mover contest online.
(B) She received her ticket in the mail.
(C) She occasionally travels to Richmond.
(D) She will travel before the end of the year.

**195** In the letter, the word "claim" in paragraph 1, line 2, is closest in meaning to

(A) assert
(B) obtain
(C) purchase
(D) reserve

GO ON TO THE NEXT PAGE

**Questions 196-200** refer to the following e-mail, Web page, and article.

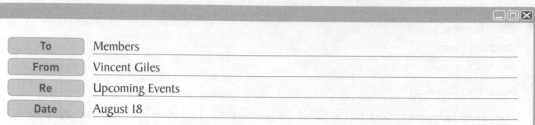

To: Members
From: Vincent Giles
Re: Upcoming Events
Date: August 18

Thanks to all of you who came out to the opening of "Wild at Heart" earlier this month. For those who were unable to attend, this traveling exhibit features over one hundred photographs by Alejandro Saragossa. His work will remain on display at the Newberry Museum until February of next year. "Wild at Heart" features stunning black and white portraits and landscapes from Brazil.

In addition to a special lecture by Mr. Saragossa, the Newberry Museum has some exciting events planned for the month of September. Visit our Web site for an up-to-date schedule. Members do not have to pay admission for Third Thursday events.

http://www.newberrymuseum.org

| Exhibits | Planning a Visit | Events | Membership |

**September 3 Family Day: 10:00 A.M. – 5:00 P.M.**
Free admission for parents and their children. Arts and crafts activities for the kids in the atrium.

**September 10 Book Signing: Noon – 2:00 P.M.**
Local historian Daniel Colton will be signing copies of his newest work, *Chase Ford: Past and Present*, available for sale in the museum's gift shop. (Members get 10% off.)

**September 22 Third Thursday: 6:00 P.M. – 9:00 P.M.**
Socialize, stroll through the galleries, and enjoy live jazz by Earth Sounds. Food and beverages available for purchase from the museum café.

**September 25 Special Event: 2:00 P.M. – 4:00 P.M.**
Join Alejandro Saragossa for a lecture. Mr. Saragossa will talk about his life and work, currently on display at the museum.

# Soulful Photos Come to the Newberry

*by Richard Dean*

Painter Manuel Solares once said that great art can touch the soul. Perhaps he was thinking of the photography of Alejandro Saragossa. His photographs are remarkably beautiful. When I visited the Newberry Museum last weekend, Mr. Saragossa talked about the inspiration for his art, his love of travel, and the challenges faced by artistic photographers in today's media-saturated world. Even if you missed the talk, you still have time to view an exhibit of his favorite photos of the past decade, many in his native country. Details available at www.newberrymuseum.com.

**196** What is NOT indicated about "Wild at Heart"?

(A) It features pictures of people.
(B) It includes a lecture by the artist.
(C) It opened in August.
(D) It will stay at the Newberry Museum permanently.

**197** What is suggested about Newberry Museum members?

(A) They receive special invitations.
(B) They can see Earth Sounds for free.
(C) They get discounts on all gift shop purchases.
(D) They pay a monthly membership fee.

**198** When did Mr. Dean most likely visit the Newberry Museum?

(A) On September 3
(B) On September 10
(C) On September 22
(D) On September 25

**199** What is indicated about Mr. Saragossa?

(A) He is traveling for five months.
(B) His career started ten years ago.
(C) He was born in Brazil.
(D) His work is displayed online.

**200** In the article, the word "missed" in paragraph 1, line 8, is closest in meaning to

(A) arrived late to
(B) avoided seeing
(C) failed to attend
(D) felt sad about

**Stop! This is the end of the test. If you finish before time is called, you may go back to Parts 5, 6, and 7 and check your work.**

# Actual Test

# 04

開始時間 ：

完成時間 ：

# LISTENING TEST

In the Listening test, you will be asked to demonstrate how well you understand spoken English. The entire Listening test will last approximately 45 minutes. There are four parts, and directions are given for each part. You must mark your answers on the separate answer sheet. Do not write your answers in your test book.

# PART 1 🎧13

**Directions:** For each question in this part, you will hear four statements about a picture in your test book. When you hear the statements, you must select the one statement that best describes what you see in the picture. Then find the number of the question on your answer sheet and mark your answer. The statements will not be printed in your test book and will be spoken only one time.

**Example**

**Sample Answer**

Statement (B), "The man is working at a desk," is the best description of the picture, so you should select answer (B) and mark it on your answer sheet.

1

2

GO ON TO THE NEXT PAGE

**3**

**4**

**5**

**6**

**GO ON TO THE NEXT PAGE**

## PART 2 🎧 14

**7** Mark your answer on your answer sheet.

**8** Mark your answer on your answer sheet.

**9** Mark your answer on your answer sheet.

**10** Mark your answer on your answer sheet.

**11** Mark your answer on your answer sheet.

**12** Mark your answer on your answer sheet.

**13** Mark your answer on your answer sheet.

**14** Mark your answer on your answer sheet.

**15** Mark your answer on your answer sheet.

**16** Mark your answer on your answer sheet.

**17** Mark your answer on your answer sheet.

**18** Mark your answer on your answer sheet.

**19** Mark your answer on your answer sheet.

**20** Mark your answer on your answer sheet.

**21** Mark your answer on your answer sheet.

**22** Mark your answer on your answer sheet.

**23** Mark your answer on your answer sheet.

**24** Mark your answer on your answer sheet.

**25** Mark your answer on your answer sheet.

**26** Mark your answer on your answer sheet.

**27** Mark your answer on your answer sheet.

**28** Mark your answer on your answer sheet.

**29** Mark your answer on your answer sheet.

**30** Mark your answer on your answer sheet.

**31** Mark your answer on your answer sheet.

# PART 3 🔊15

**Directions:** You will hear some conversations between two or more people. You will be asked to answer three questions about what the speakers say in each conversation. Select the best response to each question and mark the letter (A), (B), (C), or (D) on your answer sheet. The conversations will not be printed in your test book and will be spoken only one time.

32 Where is the conversation most likely taking place?

(A) At an outdoor concert
(B) At a tourist information office
(C) At a riverside
(D) At a general store

33 What does the woman recommend?

(A) Walking along the hillside
(B) Swimming in the local pool
(C) Exploring the environment
(D) Experiencing water sport activities

34 What does the woman give the man?

(A) An invoice
(B) A map
(C) A booklet
(D) A ticket

35 What did the man write about?

(A) His unique tours
(B) Working with Alaskans
(C) His favorite TV film
(D) Writing for television

36 Why is the man pleased?

(A) He was offered a job in Alaska.
(B) His idea will be published.
(C) His television will be replaced.
(D) His script has been accepted.

37 Why does the woman want to meet with the man?

(A) To talk about some programs
(B) To perform an audition
(C) To take part in a documentary
(D) To discuss film rights

38 What does the man offer to do?

(A) Replace an old machine
(B) Call a coworker
(C) Email an acquaintance
(D) Look up the schedule

39 Why is Jorge needed?

(A) To install a program
(B) To make photocopies
(C) To call technical support
(D) To make some repairs

40 Why does the man say, "Haley in our office is pretty good at office equipment"?

(A) To revise some schedule
(B) To recommend Haley for a promotion
(C) To suggest that Haley help with some machines
(D) To propose using another piece of equipment

41 What event has the woman recently attended?

(A) A computer seminar
(B) A fund-raising lunch
(C) A presentation
(D) A writing conference

42 What alternative does the woman suggest?

(A) Hiring an external consultant
(B) Producing an updated memo
(C) Adjusting the layout of a brochure
(D) Getting someone else to prepare a presentation

43 What do the speakers agree to do?

(A) Meet today
(B) Talk with a manager
(C) Arrange a date
(D) Present a paper

GO ON TO THE NEXT PAGE

44 Who most likely is the woman contacting?

(A) A paint supplier
(B) A clothing designer
(C) A garden expert
(D) A furniture manufacturer

45 What does the woman want to do?

(A) Select a decorator
(B) See a product sample
(C) Speak to a designer
(D) Receive an estimate

46 According to the man, how can the woman place a future order?

(A) By completing an online form
(B) By calling directly
(C) By sending an e-mail
(D) By mailing a request

47 What did the man do recently?

(A) He set up a new establishment.
(B) He developed new software.
(C) He signed up for a course.
(D) He demonstrated a new product.

48 What does the man mean when he says, "It's now progressing quite fast"?

(A) He has become busy recently.
(B) The class is picking up speed.
(C) He thinks the course is easy.
(D) The class is very difficult to follow.

49 What is the man going to participate in?

(A) An upcoming lecture
(B) His favorite show
(C) A project
(D) A professional workshop

50 Who are the speakers expecting?

(A) Business customers
(B) Job applicants
(C) Health enthusiasts
(D) Luncheon guests

51 What will the man do later this evening?

(A) Present some merchandise
(B) Give a tour of the hotel
(C) Organize a party
(D) Change a schedule

52 What does the woman say she needs to do?

(A) Contact a supplier
(B) Meet the guests
(C) Prepare a menu
(D) Call a colleague

53 What are the speakers discussing?

(A) A commercial property sale
(B) A building program
(C) Travel schedules
(D) Financial matters

54 What does the woman mention about Mr. Graston?

(A) He is reluctant to sell.
(B) His debts are mounting.
(C) His lease has expired.
(D) He is moving abroad.

55 What does the man say he will suggest to Mr. Graston?

(A) Performing an inspection
(B) Reducing the price
(C) Purchasing an automobile
(D) Taking out a loan

**56** According to the man, what has changed?

(A) A travel plan
(B) The availability of a client
(C) The terms of a contract
(D) A meeting time

**57** What problem does the woman mention?

(A) She has booked the wrong flight.
(B) She is going on a vacation.
(C) Her computer keeps breaking down.
(D) She has an appointment in the morning.

**58** What does the man say the woman will have time to do?

(A) Send over a document
(B) Drive around
(C) Reserve a lunch
(D) Return to the office

---

**59** What does the woman want to know?

(A) The period of the promotion
(B) The price of a product
(C) Information about a specific item
(D) Directions to the store

**60** What does the man say about the promotion?

(A) It will last until the end of the week.
(B) It is only available online.
(C) It is only for a specific product.
(D) It hasn't started yet.

**61** Why does the man say, "Let me walk you through our Web site now"?

(A) To make an online order
(B) To negotiate a price
(C) To show some information
(D) To explain some download methods

**62** What does the woman say she needs?

(A) A booking form
(B) An entertainment room
(C) A price breakdown
(D) Rented accommodation

**63** What does the man ask the woman about?

(A) Her date of birth
(B) Her passport number
(C) The size of her party
(D) The location of her venue

**64** What will the man most likely do next?

(A) Check prior bookings
(B) Speak to a colleague
(C) Provide an estimate
(D) Source alternative arrangements

GO ON TO THE NEXT PAGE

| Discount code (Available only from 10/3 to 10/13) | |
|---|---|
| **Items** | **Discount Rates** |
| Table | 50% |
| Chair | 40% |
| Sofa | 30% |
| Bed frame (Cherrywood) | 25% |
| Bed mattress (Memory form) | 20% |
| Bed frame (Cherrywood) & Bed mattress (Memory form) as a set | 30% |

| Product Number | Descriptions | Price |
|---|---|---|
| CM1350 | High speed with 13-inch monitor | $125 |
| CM1550 | High speed with 15-inch monitor | $150 |
| CM1750 | High speed with 17-inch monitor | $185 |
| CM1950 | High speed with 19-inch monitor | $230 |

**65** What is the man planning to do?

(A) Use a discount coupon
(B) Move out of a current apartment
(C) Purchase some furniture
(D) Find more information about the promotion

**66** What does the man indicate about the business?

(A) It offers only a few kinds of products.
(B) It is popular.
(C) This is his first time to purchase from the business.
(D) All kinds of items are on sale.

**67** Look at the graphic. Which discount will the man receive?

(A) 40%
(B) 30%
(C) 25%
(D) 20%

**68** What are the speakers mainly discussing?

(A) Preparing for a new staff member
(B) Replacing computers
(C) Transferring important files
(D) Furnishing a lobby

**69** What does the woman say she did?

(A) Rescheduled a date
(B) Contacted another department
(C) Replaced some furniture
(D) Located missing files

**70** Look at the graphic. What product will the woman most likely purchase?

(A) CM1350
(B) CM1550
(C) CM1750
(D) CM1950

# PART 4  🎧16

**Directions:** You will hear some talks given by a single speaker. You will be asked to answer three questions about what the speaker says in each talk. Select the best response to each question and mark the letter (A), (B), (C), or (D) on your answer sheet. The talks will not be printed in your test book and will be spoken only one time.

**71** Why is the speaker calling?

(A) To approve a design
(B) To arrange a meeting
(C) To extend a deadline
(D) To place an order

**72** What event is the speaker planning?

(A) A global gathering
(B) An advertising presentation
(C) A construction project
(D) A store renovation

**73** What information does the speaker request?

(A) Expected time
(B) A printing deadline
(C) A cost estimate
(D) A meeting agenda

---

**74** What type of business is Hannaford's?

(A) A travel agency
(B) A beauty shop
(C) A dental clinic
(D) A café

**75** What day is the business open late?

(A) On Tuesday
(B) On Wednesday
(C) On Thursday
(D) On Saturday

**76** What does the speaker recommend?

(A) Asking for a discount
(B) Visiting another salon
(C) Changing an appointment
(D) Leaving a message

**77** Where most likely is the announcement being heard?

(A) In a train station
(B) At the airport
(C) In a plane
(D) In a bus

**78** What should people traveling to Switzerland do?

(A) Take transport to the customs hall
(B) Go to another terminal
(C) Wait for luggage removal
(D) Exit via the main hall

**79** According to the announcement, what is offered to some passengers?

(A) Car park payment
(B) Ticket machines
(C) Refreshment stands
(D) Transportation

---

**80** What event is ending?

(A) A company picnic
(B) A computer demonstration
(C) A sporting event
(D) A nature tour

**81** What must participants in the competition do?

(A) Translate names correctly
(B) Identify wild flowers
(C) Map out a route
(D) Draw a diagram

**82** What are the listeners cautioned about?

(A) Feeding the animals
(B) Getting out of the designated paths
(C) Leaving trash
(D) Walking through the enclosures

**GO ON TO THE NEXT PAGE**

**83** Where is the announcement being made?

(A) At a harbor
(B) At a theme park
(C) At a lake
(D) At a museum

**84** Why are listeners told they will need to wait?

(A) A tour guide is delayed.
(B) A dinner has not been delivered.
(C) The transport has not arrived.
(D) The weather is inclement.

**85** What are listeners asked to do?

(A) Form two separate groups
(B) Return at another time
(C) Find a viewpoint as quickly as possible
(D) Board the boat in an orderly manner

---

**86** Where does the listener most likely work?

(A) At a gallery
(B) At a stationery store
(C) At a paint manufacturer
(D) At a graphic design firm

**87** What does the man imply when he says, "it's not what we were expecting"?

(A) He was surprised with a quick response.
(B) He wants a better result.
(C) He doesn't like the color scheme.
(D) He wants to cancel the order.

**88** What does the speaker want to do?

(A) Reschedule the appointment
(B) Order more products
(C) Arrange a meeting
(D) Change the colors

**89** What is available in the reception hall?

(A) Brochures
(B) Maps
(C) Food and drinks
(D) A gift shop

**90** What does the speaker imply when she says, "Please remember the Modern Precious collection is not expected to last very long"?

(A) The product sale has ended recently.
(B) Many people are waiting to buy items.
(C) People need to purchase the items quickly.
(D) There is only a small selection of artwork.

**91** What will the listeners do next?

(A) Buy some souvenirs
(B) Look over a special collection
(C) Introduce themselves to each other
(D) Leave the building

---

| Agenda | |
| --- | --- |
| Welcoming speech | Paul Baker |
| Financial report | Yohey Ogawa |
| New product | Beda Hari |
| Team restructuring | Lisa Whang |

**92** Where does the speaker most likely work?

(A) At a stock trading company
(B) At a computer manufacturer
(C) At an Internet service provider
(D) At an electronics retailer

**93** Look at the graphic. Who is most likely speaking?

(A) Paul Baker
(B) Yohey Ogawa
(C) Beda Hari
(D) Lisa Whang

**94** According to the speaker, what will the business do in two weeks?

(A) Sign an exclusive deal
(B) Open a new branch
(C) Release new software
(D) Begin selling new items online

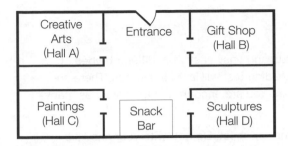

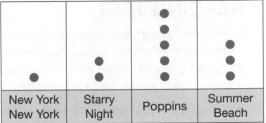

**95** Look at the graphic. Which area is unavailable to the public?

(A) Hall A
(B) Hall B
(C) Hall C
(D) Hall D

**96** What does the speaker recommend the listeners do?

(A) Visit another museum
(B) Meet a painter
(C) See a live demonstration
(D) Purchase some gifts

**97** Who is John Grisham?

(A) A collector
(B) A local potter
(C) A museum curator
(D) The tour guide

**98** Look at the graphic. Which production will be selected?

(A) New York New York
(B) Starry Night
(C) Poppins
(D) Summer Beach

**99** Why does the speaker praise Sophia?

(A) She wrote scripts well.
(B) She performed her role well.
(C) She made social media updates.
(D) She sold lots of tickets.

**100** What does the speaker remind the listeners to do?

(A) Cast actors for roles
(B) Call Sophia
(C) Inform people of updates
(D) Buy many tickets

This is the end of the Listening test. Turn to Part 5 in your test book.

GO ON TO THE NEXT PAGE

# READING TEST

In the Reading test, you will read a variety of texts and answer several different types of reading comprehension questions. The entire Reading test will last 75 minutes. There are three parts, and directions are given for each part. You are encouraged to answer as many questions as possible within the time allowed.

You must mark your answers on the separate answer sheet. Do not write your answers in your test book.

# PART 5

**Directions:** A word or phrase is missing in each of the sentences below. Four answer choices are given below each sentence. Select the best answer to complete the sentence. Then mark the letter (A), (B), (C), or (D) on your answer sheet.

101 Jonas Pet Supplies will soon open factories in ------- Holland and Spain.
(A) yet
(B) but
(C) either
(D) both

102 Please donate money to the Moonlight Gallery and show ------- support for the visual arts.
(A) your
(B) yourselves
(C) yours
(D) yourself

103 New Age Eye customers will be delighted to find out about our new ------- rates on plastic lenses.
(A) easier
(B) lower
(C) thicker
(D) louder

104 Bachman Machinery professionals can ------- design custom-tailored solutions to suit your production needs.
(A) skillful
(B) skills
(C) skill
(D) skillfully

105 ------- the workshop is over, all participants are welcome to enjoy free refreshments next door.
(A) When
(B) Still
(C) Though
(D) Soon

106 Ms. Rosy ------- her business associates that the merger should be completed by August 30.
(A) stated
(B) informed
(C) confirmed
(D) agreed

107 Professor Franco is planning a general meeting to obtain feedback ------- senior tax professionals.
(A) from
(B) as
(C) past
(D) at

108 Mr. Han ------- offered to help his co-workers learn to use the network software.
(A) variably
(B) accurately
(C) generously
(D) entirely

**109** Our computer store has secured a 30 percent discount on the ------- cost of new software.

(A) totaling
(B) totals
(C) total
(D) totally

**110** Merrick Financial Consultants can help retailers ------- their newly launched businesses into more lucrative enterprises.

(A) develops
(B) developed
(C) develop
(D) development

**111** The Urban Committee confirmed the sale of the historic Winchester House ------- concerns raised by the Barton Legacy Committee.

(A) except
(B) within
(C) onto
(D) despite

**112** With more than 5 million copies sold, *June Daily's Financial Guide* offers ------- information to business marketers.

(A) valuable
(B) eager
(C) aware
(D) numerous

**113** At Fabulous Drapes, all weekly salaries are deposited ------- into workers' bank accounts.

(A) directed
(B) directly
(C) direction
(D) directs

**114** In her farewell speech, Ms. Juno described her ------- path to becoming a well-known journalist.

(A) challenging
(B) challenges
(C) challenger
(D) challenge

**115** James Computers will be closed tomorrow in ------- of the public holiday.

(A) observance
(B) observant
(C) observe
(D) observer

**116** The City of Reedville owns and maintains 20 public parks, six of ------- have swimming facilities.

(A) all
(B) them
(C) which
(D) that

**117** Ms. Reynolds told her staff that overtime hours ------- to guarantee that the wind turbines can be completed in time for tomorrow's shipment.

(A) have approved
(B) approved
(C) having been approved
(D) have been approved

**118** Despite an overwhelmingly positive public ------- to the idea, raising funds to build a new park was difficult.

(A) approval
(B) response
(C) display
(D) creation

**119** Insoft Technologies has aggressively recruited ------- of the best software developers in the region.

(A) some
(B) every
(C) other
(D) much

**120** Sevenstar Shoe, which began as a small local shop, is now an internationally ------- brand.

(A) recognize
(B) recognized
(C) recognizer
(D) recognizing

GO ON TO THE NEXT PAGE

121 All employees are ------- to sign out at the end of the day so that the cleaning staff knows when the office is empty.

(A) inquired
(B) reminded
(C) denied
(D) committed

122 Renovations in the Gallery showrooms will be completed gradually ------- a six-week time period.

(A) above
(B) down
(C) over
(D) into

123 According to the long-term weather forecast report, heavy rain is expected to last for the ------- of the month.

(A) exception
(B) remainder
(C) boundary
(D) anticipation

124 In his address, Vice Chancellor Dale Clark compared the recent performance of Collins & Tuft ------- HG Consulting Group.

(A) rather
(B) indeed
(C) to that of
(D) what is more

125 It is ------- that Murray Almon will be reelected as chairman of the Civil Defense League.

(A) probable
(B) qualified
(C) constant
(D) endless

126 ------- completing the entrance test for the accounting course, please ensure you fill in your current employer and a contact number.

(A) While
(B) During
(C) In addition
(D) Assuming that

127 Following a meticulous inspection of the building, we found out that the storm damage was more ------- than first estimated.

(A) effective
(B) accurate
(C) apparent
(D) severe

128 By the time the acquisition was announced, Alpha Carriers -------- developing new business strategies.

(A) begins
(B) will begin
(C) had begun
(D) having begun

129 Shine Media will promote its new online music service, Jelly Music, ------- an extensive social media marketing campaign.

(A) under
(B) among
(C) below
(D) through

130 Animal Welfare's promotional campaign has resulted in a ------- 50 percent rise in donations over the last 3 months.

(A) receptive
(B) remarkable
(C) tedious
(D) perpetual

# PART 6

**Directions:** Read the texts that follow. A word, phrase, or sentence is missing in parts of each text. Four answer choices for each question are given below the text. Select the best answer to complete the text. Then mark the letter (A), (B), (C), or (D) on your answer sheet.

**Questions 131-134** refer to the following notice.

Increasing expenses have made us review the contracts with our suppliers. -------, we
**131.**
have decided to change ink suppliers.

As of August 1, all future purchases of ink will come from Dory Ink. The existing stock of ink should still be used until it runs out. However, workers must familiarize themselves with any instructions and procedures before using the new ink. It is essential that the ------- procedures be used with their respective product lines.
**132.**

-------. These will be distributed to all workers as soon as the first shipment of new ink
**133.**
arrives. Please review the instructions thoroughly. Any inquiries about use of the new products can be directed to me (555-2250) or our Dory Ink sales -------, Mary Henry
**134.**
(1-200-555-0444).

---

131 (A) Otherwise
   (B) Nevertheless
   (C) Namely
   (D) Consequently

132 (A) obsolete
   (B) appropriate
   (C) manual
   (D) obvious

133 (A) Dory Ink is among the bestselling brands of ink for industrial applications.
   (B) Employees should undergo special training on how to properly use a printer.
   (C) Dory Ink has instructional brochures explaining how to use their products.
   (D) We can reduce costs by using less ink and making two-sided copies.

134 (A) representative
   (B) represented
   (C) representation
   (D) represent

GO ON TO THE NEXT PAGE

Mickey Orden, Director
Clear Water Fishing Supplies
89 Hennz Road
Dayton, Ohio 45377

Dear Mr. Orden:

My supervisor, Judy Petrie, recently spoke to me about a job opportunity for a production designer in our Los Angeles office. She thought that I would be an excellent person for the job. -------.
                                                    **135.**

This transfer ------- me the chance to associate again with Jessica Antz, the interior
                    **136.**
design manager in Los Angeles. Ms. Antz and I collaborated on the National Fly Fishing project when she was working here in Dayton.

Ms. Petrie has ------- full support for the move and she has offered to put her approval
                **137.**
in writing for you. I have included my résumé and thank you in advance for your -------.
                                                                                **138.**

Sincerely,

Jason Tate
Production Design Specialist
Enclosures

135 (A) In addition, she has already completed the internship in a design firm.
    (B) Therefore, I would like you to consider my application for a transfer to the Los Angeles office.
    (C) However, my experience working overseas makes me a perfect fit for the job.
    (D) Otherwise, I will decide to relocate to another country.

136 (A) did allow
    (B) would allow
    (C) has allowed
    (D) was allowing

137 (A) relied
    (B) questioned
    (C) expressed
    (D) wanted

138 (A) ideas
    (B) progress
    (C) consideration
    (D) patience

Questions 139-142 refer to the following memo.

---

**From:** Cody Allen
**To:** All KPN employees

As you are aware, KPN has undergone some major renovations over the past six months. During that time, our Human Resources Department has made many adjustments ------- still trying to provide outstanding service. Since our employees
**139.**
are our most valuable assets, we would like to hear about your experiences with the changes.

------- is a single-page survey. This confidential survey is being conducted by Superb
**140.**
Research, a company that has provided KPN with marketing research and analysis for almost a decade. Your straightforward and timely feedback will help determine goals for the department. All responses will be kept -------. Please submit the completed
**141.**
form to HR by Monday, June 10.

-------. We always appreciate your dedication to KPN.
**142.**

---

139 (A) after
(B) without
(C) unlike
(D) while

140 (A) Enclosure
(B) To enclose
(C) Enclosed
(D) Enclosing

141 (A) anonymous
(B) unattended
(C) sustainable
(D) dependent

142 (A) We have made a considerable effort to improve employee satisfaction.
(B) It has been an honor to serve all employees at KPN.
(C) Thank you in advance for your time and opinions.
(D) Please upload your suggestions to our Web site.

Questions 143-146 refer to the following e-mail.

**To:** Catering Department Staff
**From:** Novek Ivanovic
**Date:** April 22
**Subject:** New Coffee Machine

Dear Colleagues:

Today, a new coffee machine was installed in the common room as a replacement for the old one that constantly broke down. We hope that this model will be more -------.

**143.**

It is a large-capacity reputable coffee maker. -------. To ensure effective maintenance

**144.**

for the coffee machine, only use the accessories that are supplied ------- paper cups

**145.**

and milk sachets rather than using any others.

You may experience problems initially when using the machine. If so, you can -------

**146.**

the instructions that we will put on the notice board next to the machine.

Regards,

Novek

143 (A) reliable
(B) achievable
(C) portable
(D) detectable

144 (A) We need to buy the newest line of machinery.
(B) The following is how to make a decent cup of coffee.
(C) All employees are required to attend the cooking class.
(D) We also have a warranty that it will last for at least ten years.

145 (A) of these
(B) as well
(C) such as
(D) sort of

146 (A) revise
(B) discard
(C) approve
(D) consult

# PART 7

**Directions:** In this part you will read a selection of texts, such as magazine and newspaper articles, e-mails, and instant messages. Each text or set of texts is followed by several questions. Select the best answer for each question and mark the letter (A), (B), (C), or (D) on your answer sheet.

**Questions 147-48** refer to the following schedule.

## Reservations for Room 8, November 5-9

|  | MONDAY Nov. 5 | TUESDAY Nov. 6 | WEDNESDAY Nov. 7 | THURSDAY Nov. 8 | FRIDAY Nov. 9 |
|---|---|---|---|---|---|
| 10:00 A.M. | Stories for Children |  | Stories for Children |  | Youth Writing Society |
| 11:00 A.M. |  | Lecture by Author Darryl Doolage |  | Science Fiction Reading |  |
| Noon |  |  | Summer Book Program Party |  | Friends of Literature Meeting |
| 1:00 P.M. | Stories for Children |  |  | Poetry Club Meeting |  |
| 2:00 P.M. |  |  | Board Meeting |  |  |
| 3:00 P.M. |  | Job Application and Interviewing Skills Lesson |  |  |  |

**147** Where is Room 8 most likely located?
(A) In a department store
(B) In a public library
(C) In an art gallery
(D) In an employment agency

**148** What event is scheduled on the same day as the Youth Writing Society?
(A) Stories for Children
(B) Friends of Literature Meeting
(C) Science Fiction Reading
(D) Poetry Club Meeting

GO ON TO THE NEXT PAGE

**Questions 149-151** refer to the following text message chain.

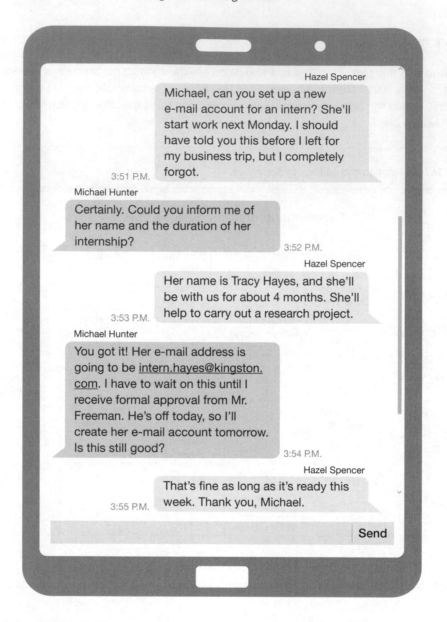

**Hazel Spencer**

Michael, can you set up a new e-mail account for an intern? She'll start work next Monday. I should have told you this before I left for my business trip, but I completely forgot.

3:51 P.M.

**Michael Hunter**

Certainly. Could you inform me of her name and the duration of her internship?

3:52 P.M.

**Hazel Spencer**

Her name is Tracy Hayes, and she'll be with us for about 4 months. She'll help to carry out a research project.

3:53 P.M.

**Michael Hunter**

You got it! Her e-mail address is going to be intern.hayes@kingston.com. I have to wait on this until I receive formal approval from Mr. Freeman. He's off today, so I'll create her e-mail account tomorrow. Is this still good?

3:54 P.M.

**Hazel Spencer**

That's fine as long as it's ready this week. Thank you, Michael.

3:55 P.M.

Send

**149** What is implied about Tracy Hayes?

(A) She is on a business trip.
(B) She needs to send an e-mail now.
(C) She will start her internship soon.
(D) She will work full-time after her internship.

**150** At 3:54 P.M., what does Mr. Hunter mean when he writes, "You got it"?

(A) He will make a new e-mail account.
(B) He will forward an e-mail to someone.
(C) He will lead a research project.
(D) He will give an orientation to interns.

**151** What does Mr. Hunter have to wait for?

(A) A network engineer
(B) A person's approval
(C) A formal document
(D) A job interview

**Questions 152-154** refer to the following e-mail.

| To | Katilda Densch <katilda_densch@smail.com> |
| From | Bruce Kaplan <kaplanb@smail.com> |
| Date | Monday, January 9 |
| Subject | News |

Dear Katilda,

Thank you again for arranging my visit to the Memphis offices last month. It was very fruitful and enjoyable, and I look forward to visiting again soon. While I was there, you noted that you would be interested in relocating to France to be near your mother. I wanted to let you know that our Paris office currently has a position available in the accounting department. We are looking for a tax expert, a job for which I think you would be highly qualified. The job responsibilities are much like those of your management accountant position in Memphis. The opening will be publicly advertised at the end of next month, but we will begin soliciting applications from within the organization this week. If you are interested in submitting an application, please let me know, and I'll email the job details and application right away.

Best regards,
Bruce Kaplan

**152** What is the purpose of the e-mail?

(A) To discuss travel arrangements
(B) To encourage Ms. Densch to apply for a job
(C) To inform Ms. Densch of an upcoming business meeting
(D) To explain the company's recent restructuring

**153** According to the e-mail, why is Ms. Densch interested in moving to Paris?

(A) To tour the area with Mr. Kaplan
(B) To work in a position with more responsibility
(C) To live closer to a family member
(D) To collaborate with Mr. Kaplan on a project

**154** What does Mr. Kaplan offer to do for Ms. Densch?

(A) Arrange for her to meet the project manager
(B) Find a place for her to stay
(C) Send her additional information
(D) Answer her questions

# Jones & Vargoes Inc.

Positions are for the night shift (5:00 P.M. – 10:00 P.M.), unless otherwise indicated.

**Warehouse Manager**
Must have a high school diploma, strong awareness of stock control procedures, and experience in a busy production environment. Must also have a basic knowledge of technology and finance. Previous management work is desirable but not essential.

**Factory Technician**
Must have relevant qualifications, at least two years of experience working in a factory environment. Must also be capable of operating heavy equipment. Night work is a necessity.

**Personal Assistant**
Must have a high school diploma, excellent typing skills and experience in a retail establishment. Some night work is necessary.

**Distribution Manager and Stock Assistants**
Must be diligent and reliable. Some night work is required in the case of the stock assistant positions.

Please send résumés to:     Human resources
                            Jones & Vargoes Inc.
                            Distribution center
                            1415 Cambridge Rd.
                            Boston, MA, 02109

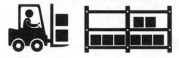

No phone calls or e-mails, please.

---

**155** What is a requirement for the warehouse manager position?

(A) A degree in marketing
(B) Some knowledge of finance
(C) Previous management experience
(D) A willingness to work the night shift

**156** What position does NOT involve night shifts?

(A) Distribution manager
(B) Personal assistant
(C) Factory technician
(D) Stock assistant

**157** How will candidates apply for the positions?

(A) Online
(B) In person
(C) By mail
(D) By telephone

# James Institute for Marketing

Are you looking for a marketing-degree program? –[1]–.

This is a twelve-month program — with entry dates in February, June, and October and a wide variety of courses in cross-cultural marketing and international advertising. Classes are led by distinguished personnel, most of whom hold senior positions in reputable advertising and trading companies and bring real-work information to the classroom. –[2]–. This, plus overseas internship options in leading international businesses, has led to the National Association of Marketers to consistently rate our program among the top three in the country.

The application fee is $100 for residents and $120 for overseas applicants. –[3]–. Mention this advertisement and you will not have to pay the application fee, provided the documents are submitted on or before October 30. The regular application deadline is November 30. Applicants are encouraged to seek scholarships and sponsorship. –[4]–. If you have questions and need more information, visit our Web site at www.jamesmarketing.edu.

**158** What is suggested about the marketing program?

(A) It takes two years to finish.
(B) It has an excellent reputation.
(C) It has two enrollment times.
(D) It recently added faculty employees.

**159** According to the advertisement, what is NOT available to students?

(A) Access to professors with professional expertise
(B) An opportunity to gain experience abroad
(C) The chance to take courses online
(D) The opportunity of getting financial assistance

**160** In which of the positions marked [1], [2], [3], and [4] does the following sentence best belong?

"Then look no further than the Excellence Marketing Program at the James Institute for Marketing."

(A) [1]
(B) [2]
(C) [3]
(D) [4]

Judy Jones
20 Hessa Street
Jefferson, Maine 04348

September 20

Paul Duveshnie, Manager
All Fashions Magazine
Dennis Road
Jefferson, Maine 04348

Dear. Mr. Duveshnie,

I'm writing to inform you that I intend to resign as photographer at *All Fashions Magazine*, to take effect on October 30. I am notifying you one month in advance, as outlined in our contract.

For some time, I have been thinking about starting my own full-time photography venture. One month ago, I won a prize from the Organization of Master Photographers as an individual photographer. The winnings included a financial prize that will allow me to start my own venture.

During my time at the magazine, I learned so much about this field. My colleagues at the photography department helped me develop not only as an artist, but also as a business professional. Even though I will build my new career as a professional photographer, I will genuinely miss my time here and all of you. It is my hope that we will stay in touch as I begin this new adventure in my life. I wish you and the company future success.

Sincerely,

*Judy Jones*
Judy Jones

**161** Why did Ms. Jones write to Mr. Duveshnie?

(A) To ask for a transfer
(B) To ask for a promotion
(C) To apply for a funding program
(D) To advise him of a decision

**162** What did Ms. Jones recently receive?

(A) Opportunity to be trained by a well-known visual artist
(B) Recognition for her outstanding work
(C) A letter of appreciation from an independent photographer for special assistance
(D) A three-year contract as supervisor for the photography department

**163** What did the Organization of Master Photographers help Ms. Jones to do?

(A) Make the decision to work part-time instead of full-time
(B) Leave her position as head of the photography department
(C) Choose to focus on a personal goal
(D) Apply for a small-business loan

---

**Rosa Patterson**                                                                                    — X

---

**Rosa Patterson** [10:03 A.M.]   Wanda, I'm interviewing now for an accounting manager position and expect to bring the right person on board by the end of this month. Could you prepare a computer for the new hire?

**Wanda Ross** [10:04 A.M.]   I think we have a desktop available from the Sales Department. A contractor finished his project last week. Let me invite Howard.

<<Howard Foster joined the chat room.>>

**Wanda Ross** [10:05 A.M.]   Howard, is Jesse Walter's machine still available?

**Howard Foster** [10:06 A.M.]   No, it was assigned to one of our research interns.

**Wanda Ross** [10:08 A.M.]   Are there any other computers available around the office?

**Howard Foster** [10:08 A.M.]   We don't have any desktops, but we have two laptops that were retrieved from the Wilson branch.

**Rosa Patterson** [10:09 A.M.]   Are they good enough to handle e-mails, spreadsheets, and presentation files?

**Howard Foster** [10:11 A.M.]   Yes, they'll be fine for normal office work. They're almost new.

**Rosa Patterson** [10:13 A.M.]   That's great. Could you set one up for my new staff member, Howard? I want this person to be productive from day one.

**Howard Foster** [10:14 A.M.]   Don't worry. I'll take care of it.

|                                                                               | Send |

**164** Why did Ms. Ross invite Mr. Foster?

(A) To explain what she wanted to order
(B) To ask questions about a new hire
(C) To request that he retrieve some computers
(D) To ask about the availability of office equipment

**165** What is suggested about Ms. Patterson?

(A) She plans to hire some interns.
(B) She wants to upgrade some computers for her staff.
(C) She wants her new staff member to work without delay.
(D) She used to work at the Wilson branch.

**166** At 10:14 A.M., what does Mr. Foster mean when he writes, "I'll take care of it"?

(A) He will review a financial report.
(B) He will reserve a conference room.
(C) He will order a computer online.
(D) He will set up a computer.

GO ON TO THE NEXT PAGE

Questions 167-168 refer to the following announcement.

Dear Local Residents,

Beginning next week, La Marler will be known as Evonia Road Bistro. The restaurant will also undergo several modifications, including an enlargement of its outside patio area and refurbishing of the main dining room to provide more space. Please be assured that under its new manager, Paul Gant, the restaurant will offer the same delicious French food at the low prices you have come to expect. Please enjoy our continued service.

167 According to the advertisement, what is being changed about the restaurant?
(A) The type of food served
(B) The pricing of the food
(C) Its location
(D) Its name

168 What is suggested about Mr. Gant?
(A) He owns other businesses in the neighborhood.
(B) He plans to develop the restaurant's seating capacity.
(C) He has lived on Evonia Road for several years.
(D) He used to work at La Marler.

# Corporate Library Cards

The state university library system extends borrowing privileges to the business community. Employees of any company with offices in our city are eligible for the privilege of a corporate card.

The yearly fee for each card issued to a worker at an organization is $40. Government and nonprofit entities are exempt from these payments.

Corporate library cards are meant for employees who conduct research for their organizations. These individuals must take responsibility for all the materials they borrow. Fines imposed by the library for overdue or missing materials are the liability of the card-holder.

To obtain a corporate card, employees must apply in person at the university library. Applicants are required to provide photo identification and a letter from their employer as proof of their employment. The fee is due with the application. A receipt can be provided for reimbursement purposes.

If you have any queries about the corporate card, please contact the circulation desk at 855-555-3001.

**169** What is the purpose of the notice?

(A) To correct a mistake
(B) To explain a service
(C) To put forward an idea
(D) To announce an event

**170** What is stated about annual fees?

(A) They can be paid by credit card.
(B) They are unlikely to increase.
(C) They are not applicable to some types of organizations.
(D) They are higher for non-local businesses.

**171** What is NOT required at the time of application?

(A) A signed contract
(B) Proof of identity
(C) A payment
(D) Employment details

June 5 – Botanist Reeva Dubchec announced yesterday that she is donating one million dollars over a period of two years to Tunney Natural Heritage project. The contribution comes at a crucial time, as the project's funding has been strained for the past three years. –[1]–.

"We're thrilled to receive Ms. Dubchec's generous gift." said Tunney Natural Heritage president James McNulty. "It will go a long way toward conserving the natural cornerstone of our community."

Natural Heritage was launched a decade ago by the Nature Reserve Society (NRS) to restore and preserve natural resorts from the town's early years. It was originally funded by tax revenue; however, three years ago the town council decided to move much of that income away from the NRS and into a new land development project. –[2]–.

Five months ago, NRS began soliciting private gifts from larger businesses in the community. "Along with a letter asking for donations, we sent photographs of several natural sites in need of maintenance," Mr. McNulty recalled. One such site was the Orchid Heritage Site where former resident Reeva Dubchec was a frequent visitor. "I didn't know about Reeva's personal connection to the site until she called me and asked how she could help." Mr. McNulty said.

Tunney residents and leadership have responded with great delight to the news of the donation. Mayor Jim Connor and members of the town council have considered putting honorary plaques in several natural landmarks to make the town appealing to new residents, visitors, and businesses. –[3]–.

"When I was a child, I was inspired by the natural sites in Tunney. They were instrumental in helping me choose my career studying plant life. This donation is not just about preserving the town's resources. –[4]–. It's about investing in its future," Ms. Dubchec said.

Richard Dobbs
Local Contributor

172 According to the article, why was the project losing funding?

(A) Because building costs increased
(B) Because the local government decreased its financial support
(C) Because the renovation work was complete
(D) Because Tunney's population had decreased

173 Who is currently NOT a resident of Tunney?

(A) James McNulty
(B) Reeva Dubchek
(C) Jim Connor
(D) Richard Dobbs

174 What does Ms. Dubchec say about the nature reserves in Tunney?

(A) They made her decide to become a botanist.
(B) They are too costly to maintain.
(C) Each one should bear a plaque indicating the year it was built.
(D) Local organizations should pay to restore them.

175 In which of the positions marked [1], [2], [3], and [4] does the following sentence best belong?

"Since then, financial support for natural resource maintenance has remained limited."

(A) [1]
(B) [2]
(C) [3]
(D) [4]

E-Mail Message

From:     Jenny Li <jli@edumail.com>
To:       Fenton Lewis <flewis@springlink.net>
Re:       Estimate
Date:     October 8

Dear Mr. Lewis,

I was referred to you by Lee-Anne Fuentes, a neighbor in the town of Ithaca. I would like to obtain an estimate for removing four Leyland cypresses from my garden, which have become a safety issue.

They are about 13 meters high: two are approximately 45 centimeters in diameter while the others have a diameter of about 75 centimeters. They are standing within 4 meters of my house and two meters of the hedge.

Would a team be available around 11 o'clock in the morning on Friday, 15 October? October, November and December are the busiest times for people like us who work in the tourist industry. The only day that I can afford is next Friday.

I look forward to hearing from you soon.

Sincerely,
Jenny Li

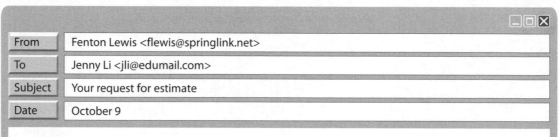

| From | Fenton Lewis <flewis@springlink.net> |
| To | Jenny Li <jli@edumail.com> |
| Subject | Your request for estimate |
| Date | October 9 |

Dear Ms. Li,

Thank you for considering Lewis Tree Service. We have the most up-to-date equipment for the service, so you can rest assured your premises will not sustain any damage when the work is completed. To learn what our clients say about the quality of our services, please visit www.fentontreeservice/customerreports.com.

We can definitely accommodate you on the day and time you have requested. An 11:00 A.M. slot is presently open. Based on the information you have submitted, I can give you an initial quote for the cost of the service. We charge $400 for trees between 20cm and 55cm in diameter and $600 for those measuring more than 55cm in diameter. Also please be informed that a $70 travel charge is applicable for work done at locations more than 40km from our company's Dune office. Consequently, the total cost will be about $2,070. To calculate the exact cost, one of my associates can stop by your property soon to measure the trees you want to remove.

Confirm at your earliest convenience if this arrangement is acceptable.

Fenton Lewis

**176** What information does Ms. Li NOT provide in the e-mail to Mr. Lewis?

(A) The height of some plants in her garden
(B) The type of employment she has
(C) The street she lives on
(D) The day she can take off from work

**177** What is suggested about Ms. Li?

(A) She previously had work done in her garden by Lewis Tree Service.
(B) She plans to go on vacation in March.
(C) She lives more than 40km from Lewis Tree Service's office.
(D) She will receive a discount from Lewis Tree Service.

**178** In the second e-mail, the word "sustain" in paragraph 1, line 2, is closest in meaning to

(A) assess
(B) suffer
(C) support
(D) cause

**179** What does Mr. Lewis recommend that Ms. Li do?

(A) Buy new equipment for her garden
(B) Telephone him at 11 A.M.
(C) Visit his office to provide him with exact measurement of the trees
(D) Read on-line customer reviews about his service

**180** When does Mr. Lewis agree to do the work?

(A) On November 10
(B) On October 15
(C) On October 3
(D) On October 2

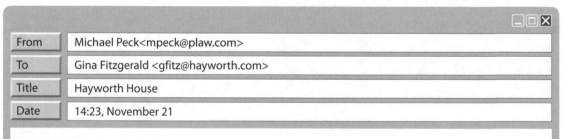

**Questions 181-185** refer to the following advertisement and e-mail.

---

### Hayworth House
in the heart of Downtown Lanshow

New Mixed-Use Property Opening February 1
Residential, Business, and Commercial Spaces for Rent

Modern, state-of-the-art construction flanked by shops and cafés. Close to bus stop. Across the street from Hayworth Lake and Hiking. Spring-fed lake and hiking trails nearby.

**Apartments (Floor 4-8)**: one-, two-, and three-bedroom apartments, each with kitchen, full bathroom, living/ dining room, and spacious closets. Storage facilities in basement available for a minor monthly fee. Free underground parking for tenants and visitors. Shared laundry facilities on floor 6 and 8. Roof garden to be added.

**Offices (Floor 2-3)**: Flexible office spaces can be divided as needed while space is available. Suitable for single offices and complete company office suites. Several layout options to choose from.

**Retail Stores (Street level)**: Two storefronts offered. Both 500 square meters. Retail use only.

**Prices and leasing information provided on request**:
Please direct residential inquiries to Leonora Dean (080) 555-6705 or ldean@hayworth.com. Direct commercial inquiries to Gina Fitzgerald (080) 555-6707 or gfitz@hayworth.com.

---

| From | Michael Peck<mpeck@plaw.com> |
|------|------------------------------|
| To | Gina Fitzgerald <gfitz@hayworth.com> |
| Title | Hayworth House |
| Date | 14:23, November 21 |

Dear Ms. Fitzgerald,

If it would be possible to organize the office space at Hayworth House to accommodate a total of 50 employees, both lawyers and support workers, I would be interested in visiting the property at your earliest convenience.

Our current premises, just a few blocks from Hayworth House, is too small to accommodate any additional people. My firm's business has been growing rapidly, and we will be employing several new staff members in the near future to handle our growing caseload.

Sincerely,
Peck

181 What is indicated about Hayworth House?

(A) It's on a bus route.
(B) It was designed by a local professional.
(C) Its opening has been delayed.
(D) It's on the edge of the city.

182 According to the advertisement, what is available to residential tenants for an additional cost?

(A) Underground parking
(B) Basement storage
(C) Use of a shared garden
(D) Shared laundry facilities

183 What type of tenant is NOT allowed to occupy the building?

(A) A wholesaler
(B) A clothing store
(C) An advertising agency
(D) A family of three people

184 What is suggested about Mr. Peck's firm?

(A) It recently increased its fees.
(B) It is relocating to Lanshow.
(C) It has enjoyed increasing success.
(D) It buys and renovates commercial properties.

185 What part of Hayworth House would most likely interest Mr. Peck?

(A) Floors 4-8
(B) Floors 2-3
(C) Street level spaces
(D) The basement

Test 04

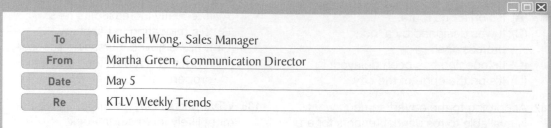

| To | Michael Wong, Sales Manager |
| From | Martha Green, Communication Director |
| Date | May 5 |
| Re | KTLV Weekly Trends |

Dear Michael:

Thank you for informing me that you have been contacted by a TV broadcasting station. I have reviewed the program summary you submitted, and it looks like they want you because of your professional expertise. I discussed this issue with Vice President Lauren Parker, and she gave permission for you to appear on the show. Jeremy Diaz from the General Administration Department will help you to prepare for the show. Please give him a list of products that you need for the show.

Before the show, please keep in mind the following rules that you should follow when communicating with the media.

• Do not talk about personnel issues at the company.
• Do not discuss any future business plans that have not been mentioned in press releases.
• Do not disclose sensitive information that is related to the company's clients and customers.
• Please avoid discussing any emergencies or crises at the company.

I hope you can positively portray our brand and products. Good luck.

Best Wishes,
Martha Green

# Our Employee on KTLV Weekly Trends

On Saturday, May 24, Michael Wong from the Marketing Department will be a guest on the TV show Weekly Trends. The senior sales manager will talk about recent trends in the camping market. On the show, he will talk about our tents, sleeping bags, and cookware as he gives some tips on camping. Weekly Trends is one of the top-rated shows and has a 12.3 rating with adults ages 18-49. We hope his appearance on the show helps promote our brand and products. The show will air from 8 to 9 P.M. on Channel 15. It will also be streamed at www.KTLV.com. If you don't make it on time or want to watch the show again, please visit the KTLV Web site.

May 28

Michael Wong
Orleans Sports, Inc.
1610 Wisconsin Ave,
Milwaukee, WI 53233

Dear Mr. Wong:

We are so happy that we had you as a guest on our show. The show on May 24 was quite successful, and the ratings were higher than we had expected. We have received a lot of positive feedback from our viewers. They said your tips on outdoor camping were very useful and informative. Thank you for your efforts and contributions.

In spite of your request, we didn't edit out what you said about the new product launch in a few months. Despite your concerns, the new camping equipment was officially mentioned in a press release by your company. We double-checked with Martha Green at your company.

I would like to ask if you could appear on our show one more time in July. We are planning to air a summer special show about outdoor activities on July 19. The show will start airing at 8 P.M. and will last for 2 hours. We really hope we can have you back on our show then. We look forward to hearing from you as soon as possible.

Sincerely,
Brian Duff
Senior Producer, KTLV

186 According to the e-mail, who will assist Mr. Wong with his TV appearance?

(A) Martha Green
(B) Lauren Parker
(C) Jeremy Diaz
(D) Brian Duff

187 In the e-mail, the word "expertise" in paragraph 1, line 3, is closest in meaning to

(A) knowledge
(B) impression
(C) look
(D) opinion

188 What is the purpose of the announcement?

(A) To promote new camping equipment
(B) To provide camping tips for people
(C) To tell the ratings of a TV show
(D) To encourage people to watch a TV program

189 Why did Mr. Wong ask that what he said on the show be edited?

(A) He disclosed sensitive information about his client.
(B) He talked about a personnel issue regarding a coworker.
(C) He mentioned a future business plan of his company.
(D) He indicated that his company was having financial difficulties.

190 How will the special show differ from the regular show?

(A) It will start at 9 P.M.
(B) It will air one hour longer.
(C) It will be broadcast on Sunday.
(D) It will be on Channel 16.

GO ON TO THE NEXT PAGE

# Ottawa Online Business Conference

October is the biggest month for the staff members at the Ottawa Online Business Conference because our annual conference takes place then. However, the biggest month for attendees is June. That is the early-bird registration month for the upcoming 27th OOBC. It means that rates go up on July 1. Now is the best time to save on registration fees, especially for companies sending a group of people. If you register this month, you can save $100 per person. In addition to giving you an early-bird discount, we will present you with a $50 gift card which can be used at the Royal Hotel, Ace Hotel, or Next Hotel. The best news for all registrants in June is that one lucky participant will receive a free 3-night hotel stay during the conference. You must be registered by June 30 to have a chance to be the winner.

We can't wait to see you at the Ottawa Online Business Conference. The best chance to learn about sustainable online business practices is waiting for you. Register today for the best rates.

---

### E-Mail Message

| | |
|---|---|
| To: | reservations@royalhotel.com |
| From: | richard.morris@estrada.com |
| Date: | June 28 |
| Re: | Reservation |

Hello. My name is Richard Morris, and I work at Estrada, Inc. My company plans to dispatch some employees to attend the 27th Ottawa Online Business Conference in October. We talked with some OOBC people, and they recommended your hotel because of the location and service provided by your hotel staff. I would like to know if you have any rooms available for them. I tried to make a reservation at your Web site but could not find an option for a group reservation.

Eleven of them will stay from October 12 to 14, and they need three single rooms and four double rooms. If it is possible, they would prefer to stay on the same floor. I want to make sure that they can use their OOBC gift cards, too.

If the rooms are available, please contact me and tell me what to do to reserve the rooms at your hotel.

Sincerely,
Richard Morris
General Department
Estrada, Inc.

| To | olga.carter@estrada.com |
|---|---|
| From | james.stanley@royalhotel.com |
| Date | October 22 |
| Re | Reservation |

Dear Ms. Carter,

Thank you for contacting the Royal Hotel, Ottawa. I am writing to respond to your e-mail on October 20. As you requested, we checked your account immediately and discovered that we overcharged you. A staff member didn't apply the OOBC gift card you presented. We recently hired a new payment service company, and some of our staff members have not gotten accustomed to using the new system. We sincerely apologize for the mistake. Since you stayed in a single room at a rate of $100 for three nights, we were supposed to charge you $250 after applying the gift card.

We want to reassure you that we are doing our best to correct this error. The overcharged amount will be refunded to your credit card account in two business days. As a token of our apology, we would also like to give you a free night pass, which you can use to stay for one night for free at any Royal Hotel around the world.

Once again, we apologize for any inconvenience this may have caused you. We look forward to serving you again.

James Stanley
General Manager
Royal Hotel, Ottawa

191 What is implied about the Ottawa Online Business Conference?

(A) The staff members are busiest in June.
(B) It will last for five days in June.
(C) The registration fee is the lowest in June.
(D) All attendees will have a chance to win a lottery.

192 In the advertisement, the word "sustainable" in paragraph 2, line 2, is closest in meaning to

(A) likely to occur
(B) existing in reality
(C) able to be moved easily
(D) capable of being continued

193 What is NOT mentioned about employees at Estrada, Inc.?

(A) Eleven of them will attend a conference.
(B) They need seven rooms at a hotel.
(C) They would like to stay on the same floor.
(D) They want to have rooms with a good view.

194 What did Mr. Stanley say about the cause of the problem?

(A) The payment system was temporarily broken.
(B) An employee was unfamiliar with a new system.
(C) The gift card expired in October.
(D) The guest's name was changed at the last minute.

195 How much did the hotel charge Ms. Carter?

(A) $300      (B) $350
(C) $400      (D) $500

Questions 196-200 refer to the following notice, article, and Web page.

# NOTICE OF PUBLIC HEARING

This notice is to inform you of a public hearing. After the hearing, the Richmond Department of City Planning will decide whether to adopt the proposed plan. All interested people are invited to attend. You may listen and will have a chance to speak regarding the proposed project.

**TOPIC OF HEARING**: Pamela Boulevard Project
Proposal for roadway improvements including restoring the sewage system, pavement construction, and traffic signal upgrades on Pamela Boulevard.

**PLACE**: Richmond City Hall
523 West 8th Street
Richmond City, GA 30003

**HEARING DATE**: Thursday, September 9
**TIME**: 6:00 P.M. – 8:00 P.M.
**FOR ADDITIONAL INFORMATION CONTACT**: Richmond Department of City Planning at 555-3217

## *Pamela Boulevard Project Approved*

Richmond City, Georgia - Richmond City has approved a $1.2 million restoration of Pamela Boulevard, which is a critical roadway for residents. City officials say construction is scheduled to start early next year. The construction comes after the roadway was severely flooded and shut down during heavy rainfall last summer. The sewage system was also damaged as Richmond City's aging sewers were not designed for heavy rain. The project also includes pavement reconstruction and traffic signal upgrades.

"When the roadway becomes impassable due to heavy rain, those living in the southern part of the city cannot gain access to the major roads," Mayor James Norris said. "The road upgrade project will enhance access to the main highway entrance during the rainy season."

The city held a public hearing on September 9, and more than 200 citizens participated by raising their voices. They said that the money should be put directly into replacing the old sewage system.

"We listened to the citizens, and their biggest concern was the reconstruction of Pamela Boulevard. It was a big deal, so that's where we put most of the city's budget," the mayor said.

www.RichmondCity.gov/notice

During the weeks from February 1 to October 31, the following road repairs may cause a reduction in lanes or lane closures. The Department of City Planning will make every effort to complete the necessary work as quickly as possible. We hope the citizens of Richmond City will enjoy the improvements once they are complete.

**Pamela Boulevard Project**
  • When: February – June
  • Description: Sewage system improvements and upgrading of traffic signals on Pamela Boulevard

**Hayman Road Project**
  • When: March – September
  • Description: Addition of a bike trail and updating of the pedestrian crossings on Hayman Road

**Westfield Bridge Project**
  • When: May – October
  • Description: Repairs on the bridge and bridge railing

**Annapolis Street Project**
  • When: June – October
  • Description: Reconstruction of the intersection

Information on expected traffic disruptions and detours will be posted on the city's Web page. To receive automatic alerts of all the updates, please sign up for our e-mail and text alerts HERE.

**196** What is NOT proposed for the Pamela Boulevard Project?

(A) Roadway pavement
(B) Traffic light installation
(C) Sewage pipe replacement
(D) Repairs of sidewalks

**197** What is true about the hearing?

(A) It was about a bridge repair project.
(B) The mayor didn't attend it because of heavy rain.
(C) It was held at City Hall with a few hundred people present.
(D) Citizens disapproved of the project.

**198** According to the article, what problem was mentioned about Pamela Boulevard?

(A) It was too dark to drive on.
(B) It was flooded in the summer.
(C) It was too narrow for traffic to pass through.
(D) It was slippery in winter.

**199** In the article, the word "impassable" in paragraph 2, line 1, is closest in meaning to

(A) renovated
(B) blocked
(C) dirty
(D) lifted

**200** What is the purpose of the Web page?

(A) To announce community events
(B) To give alerts of upcoming storms
(C) To provide information on traffic disruptions
(D) To hire construction companies

**Stop! This is the end of the test. If you finish before time is called, you may go back to Parts 5, 6, and 7 and check your work.**

**慢著**！作答前請務必**確認**！

- 請當作實際考試般，將書桌收拾乾淨，做好心理準備。
- 請將手機關機，並善用時鐘或手錶計時。
- 規定作答時間為 120 分鐘，請務必遵守規定時間。
- 請盡可能按照題目順序作答，碰到難題時，切勿直接跳過。

# Actual Test

## 05

開始時間　　：
完成時間　　：

# LISTENING TEST

In the Listening test, you will be asked to demonstrate how well you understand spoken English. The entire Listening test will last approximately 45 minutes. There are four parts, and directions are given for each part. You must mark your answers on the separate answer sheet. Do not write your answers in your test book.

# PART 1

**Directions:** For each question in this part, you will hear four statements about a picture in your test book. When you hear the statements, you must select the one statement that best describes what you see in the picture. Then find the number of the question on your answer sheet and mark your answer. The statements will not be printed in your test book and will be spoken only one time.

**Example**

**Sample Answer**

Ⓐ ● Ⓒ Ⓓ

Statement (B), "The man is working at a desk," is the best description of the picture, so you should select answer (B) and mark it on your answer sheet.

1

2

GO ON TO THE NEXT PAGE

3

4

5

6

GO ON TO THE NEXT PAGE

## PART 2 🎧 18

**Directions:** You will hear a question or statement and three responses spoken in English. They will not be printed in your test book and will be spoken only one time. Select the best response to the question or statement and mark the letter (A), (B), or (C) on your answer sheet.

**7** Mark your answer on your answer sheet.

**8** Mark your answer on your answer sheet.

**9** Mark your answer on your answer sheet.

**10** Mark your answer on your answer sheet.

**11** Mark your answer on your answer sheet.

**12** Mark your answer on your answer sheet.

**13** Mark your answer on your answer sheet.

**14** Mark your answer on your answer sheet.

**15** Mark your answer on your answer sheet.

**16** Mark your answer on your answer sheet.

**17** Mark your answer on your answer sheet.

**18** Mark your answer on your answer sheet.

**19** Mark your answer on your answer sheet.

**20** Mark your answer on your answer sheet.

**21** Mark your answer on your answer sheet.

**22** Mark your answer on your answer sheet.

**23** Mark your answer on your answer sheet.

**24** Mark your answer on your answer sheet.

**25** Mark your answer on your answer sheet.

**26** Mark your answer on your answer sheet.

**27** Mark your answer on your answer sheet.

**28** Mark your answer on your answer sheet.

**29** Mark your answer on your answer sheet.

**30** Mark your answer on your answer sheet.

**31** Mark your answer on your answer sheet.

# PART 3 🎧19

**Directions:** You will hear some conversations between two or more people. You will be asked to answer three questions about what the speakers say in each conversation. Select the best response to each question and mark the letter (A), (B), (C), or (D) on your answer sheet. The conversations will not be printed in your test book and will be spoken only one time.

32 Who most likely is the woman?
(A) A supplier
(B) A restaurant worker
(C) A chef
(D) An office employee

33 Why does the woman apologize?
(A) She provided the wrong meal.
(B) There is a mistake in the order.
(C) A business is closing late.
(D) An order was not completed on time.

34 What will the man do next?
(A) Go to a neighbor
(B) Pay for an order
(C) Send an e-mail
(D) Do some shopping

35 What did the woman have to do this week?
(A) Go on a vacation
(B) Cancel her account
(C) Join a different department
(D) Work extra hours

36 Where will the woman go on Monday?
(A) To a mountainous area
(B) To a station
(C) To a park
(D) To a concert

37 What does the man suggest the woman do?
(A) Work from home
(B) Negotiate a pay raise
(C) Ride in a cable car
(D) Go to watch a sports event

38 What are the speakers mainly discussing?
(A) A computer system
(B) A delivery charge
(C) A work agenda
(D) A piece of item

39 What does the man plan to do?
(A) Talk to a customer
(B) Write up an order
(C) Make an appointment
(D) Send an invoice

40 According to the woman, what will happen in two weeks?
(A) An order will be cancelled.
(B) A catalog will be released.
(C) Some products will be back in stock.
(D) A computer brand will become obsolete.

41 What type of position has been advertised?
(A) Architect
(B) Designer
(C) Legal clerk
(D) Lab Technician

42 Where did the woman work most recently?
(A) In Ireland
(B) In Scotland
(C) In England
(D) In Wales

43 What does the man ask the woman to do?
(A) Send in further information
(B) Fill out an online form
(C) Check for more details
(D) Submit a portfolio

GO ON TO THE NEXT PAGE

44 What does the man ask about the office?

(A) Where it is located
(B) When it is available
(C) How many other businesses are there
(D) How much is the rent

45 What is unique about the unit?

(A) Its scenic view
(B) Its storage space
(C) Its historic site
(D) Its reduced price

46 When will the woman meet the man?

(A) At 10:00 A.M.
(B) At 11:00 A.M.
(C) At 1:00 P.M.
(D) At 11:00 P.M.

47 What will the man probably do this afternoon?

(A) Have a meeting with coworkers
(B) Attend an appointment with a client
(C) Pick up a friend
(D) Go to a show downtown

48 What was the man supposed to do at 3:00 P.M.?

(A) Attend a workshop
(B) Visit a branch office
(C) Meet with new employees
(D) Discuss issues with the marketing team

49 What does the man mean when he says, "Come to think of it, I'd better do it myself"?

(A) He will cancel a reservation.
(B) He will contact a coworker.
(C) He will attend a meeting.
(D) He will email some reports.

50 What does the woman ask the man to help her with?

(A) Serving drinks
(B) Moving some tables
(C) Preparing meals
(D) Changing his shifts

51 Why is the man concerned?

(A) They might be short staffed.
(B) The party might get out of hand.
(C) The kitchen will not be open.
(D) The ingredients may not be available.

52 What did some customers request?

(A) More floor space
(B) A vegetarian menu
(C) A beachfront view
(D) An event calendar

53 What is the conversation mainly about?

(A) A sales result
(B) A retiring employee
(C) Candidates for a position
(D) A company's anniversary

54 What does the woman mean when she says, "I couldn't agree more"?

(A) Now is the time for recruiting.
(B) 10 years' working experience is a requirement.
(C) An internal promotion is a fast way to fill a position.
(D) The company needs to contact a staffing agency.

55 According to the woman, what do the board members want?

(A) Increased sales
(B) Relocation of one of their branches
(C) Adding new delivery locations
(D) Restructuring of the sales team

56 According to the woman, why did Mr. Bloomberg call her?

(A) To inquire about the status of the project
(B) To discuss costs
(C) To reschedule a deadline
(D) To change a flooring material

57 What does the man mention about Mr. Bloomberg?

(A) He doesn't like changing plans.
(B) He asked for an additional discount.
(C) He is unpredictable.
(D) He is a frequent client.

58 What does the woman mean when she says, "That is what I was going to propose, actually"?

(A) A new floor plan is needed for the client.
(B) Mr. Bloomberg is a demanding client.
(C) Hiring workers will help meet the deadline.
(D) Mr. Ferrell is a popular contractor.

59 Why is the man calling?

(A) To ask about a special deal
(B) To reply to a consumer survey
(C) To track a delivery
(D) To inquire about his savings

60 What products are the speakers discussing?

(A) Electronic products
(B) Gardening equipment
(C) Cooking appliances
(D) Vehicle accessories

61 What information is the man told to submit on the Web site?

(A) A delivery schedule
(B) A shipping number
(C) A promotional code
(D) A credit card billing address

62 Who is the woman?

(A) A florist
(B) A shop owner
(C) A customer
(D) A sales representative

63 What concern does the man mention about the display?

(A) The cost involved in the process
(B) The time consumption for his employees
(C) The amount of space required
(D) The timespan of delivery

64 What information does the brochure contain?

(A) A timetable
(B) Cost information
(C) A list of other stores
(D) A flower sample

GO ON TO THE NEXT PAGE

| Hubert Research Center - 3rd Floor | |
|---|---|
| Laboratory | Room 301 |
| Incubation Room | Room 302 |
| Low-Pressure Chamber | Room 303 |
| High-Pressure Chamber | Room 304 |

| Mr. Brooks' schedule | |
|---|---|
| Tuesday | Urban Kitchen |
| Wednesday | Polly's Restaurant |
| Thursday | Top Cloud (in Hotel Dublin) |
| Friday | New York Diner |

**65** Look at the graphic. Where did the man stay last night?

(A) Room 301
(B) Room 302
(C) Room 303
(D) Room 304

**66** What happened to the man?

(A) He lost a garage key.
(B) He left his house door open.
(C) He was locked inside a space.
(D) He was under pressure with his task.

**67** According to the man, why didn't he sleep well?

(A) The space was cold.
(B) The space was scary.
(C) The space was stuffy.
(D) The space was too noisy.

**68** What are the speakers preparing for?

(A) An appreciation event
(B) A retirement party
(C) A grand opening
(D) An employee workshop

**69** What does the woman say she did last night?

(A) Searched for a location
(B) Sampled some food
(C) Paid a deposit
(D) Picked up supplies

**70** Look at the graphic. What is the name of the catering service that the woman contacted?

(A) Urban Kitchen
(B) Polly's Restaurant
(C) Top Cloud
(D) New York Diner

# PART 4 🎧20

**Directions:** You will hear some talks given by a single speaker. You will be asked to answer three questions about what the speaker says in each talk. Select the best response to each question and mark the letter (A), (B), (C), or (D) on your answer sheet. The talks will not be printed in your test book and will be spoken only one time.

**71** What is being advertised?

(A) A beverage
(B) A store
(C) A food bar
(D) A dessert

**72** According to the speaker, what can be found at the Plusto Web site?

(A) Details of ingredients
(B) A list of vegetable growers
(C) A map of store locations
(D) Discount coupons

**73** What will happen next month?

(A) A new flavor will be launched.
(B) Different-colored packaging will be offered.
(C) Prices will be reduced.
(D) A company name will change.

**74** What type of business created the message?

(A) A delivery service
(B) A bus company
(C) A telephone exchange
(D) A travel agency

**75** What new service does the business offer?

(A) A web-based payment option
(B) Mobile message alerts
(C) Priority delivery options
(D) An online tracking system

**76** Why would a listener press star?

(A) To speak to an operator
(B) To return to the main menu
(C) To have this message repeated
(D) To hear the message again

**77** Who most likely is the speaker?

(A) A fitness trainer
(B) An army doctor
(C) A sports journalist
(D) A medical expert

**78** What are the listeners preparing to do in two months?

(A) Run a race
(B) Take part in an endurance test
(C) Travel overseas
(D) Participate in a fitness program

**79** What does the speaker encourage the listeners to do?

(A) Take weekly breaks
(B) Purchase appropriate weapons
(C) Consult a medical professional daily
(D) Keep a personal log

**80** Where does the talk most likely take place?

(A) At a factory
(B) At a restaurant
(C) At a photographic studio
(D) At a museum

**81** What does the speaker say listeners will receive?

(A) Food samples
(B) A choice of desserts
(C) A photograph
(D) A cookery opportunity

**82** What does the speaker ask the listeners to do in the reception?

(A) Check out a picture
(B) Leave their possessions
(C) Form a line
(D) Listen to an audio message

GO ON TO THE NEXT PAGE

83 What is the main topic of the report?

(A) A concert opening
(B) A community
(C) A sports competition
(D) A municipal fair

84 What problem does the speaker mention?

(A) Bad weather is forecast.
(B) Traffic is expected to be heavy.
(C) Parking is limited.
(D) Some events have been cancelled.

85 What does the speaker suggest listeners do?

(A) Bring a packed lunch
(B) Use public transport
(C) Run in the park
(D) Wear suitable clothing

86 Who most likely are the listeners?

(A) Library users
(B) Librarians
(C) Shoppers
(D) Seminar participants

87 What is being announced?

(A) An art exhibition
(B) A community fair
(C) An art class
(D) A painting action

88 What does the speaker imply when she says, "This is to avoid interruptions"?

(A) The listeners should register for the event.
(B) The listeners should be punctual for the event.
(C) The listeners should wait in a line.
(D) The listeners should hold their questions for a while.

89 What is the purpose of the advertisement?

(A) To publicize a grand opening
(B) To advertise job openings
(C) To inform the customers of the origin of the produce
(D) To promote a sale

90 What is Fresh Groceries mainly selling?

(A) Meat
(B) Dairy products
(C) Bakery
(D) Fruits and vegetables

91 What does the speaker mean when he says, "That's our trick of the trade"?

(A) Their products are cheap.
(B) Their products are grown locally.
(C) They import products.
(D) The products are all organic.

| Received | Vendor | Item | Quantity |
|----------|--------|------|----------|
| 12/14 | Ralph | Blazer | 25 |
| 12/15 | Dash | Sweater | 30 |
| 12/16 | Custom | Trousers | 40 |
| 12/17 | Hiller | Accessory | 120 |

92 What most likely is the speaker's job?

(A) Clothing designer
(B) Store manager
(C) Delivery person
(D) Inspector

93 Look at the graphic. What quantity will the speaker add to the inventory?

(A) 25
(B) 30
(C) 40
(D) 120

94 What does the speaker say he will do when he returns?

(A) Change the price tags
(B) Send back arrivals
(C) Inspect the displays
(D) Alter some pants

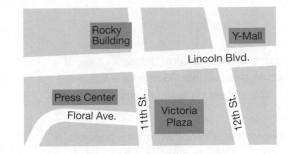

| Winner | Trumpet Shell Weight (Pound) |
|--------|:---:|
| Brian | 5 |
| Jim | 4.5 |
| John | 3 |
| Jason | 4 |

**95** What will visitors receive?

(A) A complimentary gift
(B) A voucher for a meal
(C) A discount coupon
(D) A gift certificate

**96** What does the speaker mention about Tom & Stephany's products?

(A) They are shipped at no charge.
(B) They are custom made.
(C) They are popular.
(D) They are made by top designers.

**97** Look at the graphic. Where is Tom & Stephany most likely located?

(A) At the Press Center
(B) At Y-Mall
(C) At Victoria Plaza
(D) At the Rocky Building

**98** According to the speaker, what is the purpose of the event?

(A) To raise trumpet shells
(B) To revitalize local business
(C) To honor a person
(D) To celebrate the opening of a season

**99** Look at the graphic. Who won the special prize?

(A) Brian
(B) Jim
(C) John
(D) Jason

**100** What will listeners probably hear next?

(A) Music
(B) Local news
(C) Advertisements
(D) A traffic report

This is the end of the Listening test. Turn to Part 5 in your test book.

Test 05

# READING TEST

In the Reading test, you will read a variety of texts and answer several different types of reading comprehension questions. The entire Reading test will last 75 minutes. There are three parts, and directions are given for each part. You are encouraged to answer as many questions as possible within the time allowed.

You must mark your answers on the separate answer sheet. Do not write your answers in your test book.

# PART 5

**Directions:** A word or phrase is missing in each of the sentences below. Four answer choices are given below each sentence. Select the best answer to complete the sentence. Then mark the letter (A), (B), (C), or (D) on your answer sheet.

**101** The members of the committee will ------- in Heart Lane Hall for the shareholder meeting.

(A) convene
(B) implement
(C) nominate
(D) initiate

**102** Employees have been requested to update ------- working hours.

(A) theirs
(B) their
(C) them
(D) they

**103** The company's bi-monthly budget report was ------- explained by Mr. Pam Isley.

(A) brief
(B) briefly
(C) briefness
(D) briefing

**104** All personal items ------- behind in the lounge are kept for 30 days before being discarded.

(A) left
(B) leave
(C) leaving
(D) leaves

**105** Joyce Appliances has recalled this year's line of microwave ovens in ------- to reports of defective components.

(A) response
(B) responsibility
(C) responsible
(D) responsive

**106** All workers who ------- electrical equipment must wear hard hats.

(A) are operated
(B) operates
(C) to operate
(D) operate

**107** At Shalting Management Consultants, we ------- our ideas to clients as concisely as possible.

(A) believe
(B) insert
(C) decide
(D) explain

**108** The structure of the building -------, but the interior has been completely remodeled.

(A) preserving
(B) preserved
(C) had been preserving
(D) has been preserved

109 A ------- the information seemed to be missing from the report at first, but it was quickly identified.

(A) little
(B) few of
(C) few
(D) little of

110 Harleque Industries is currently exploring methods to more ------- manufacture its air conditioning units.

(A) produce
(B) production
(C) productive
(D) productively

111 An increasing ------- of homeowners are refinancing their mortgages to make use of lower interest rates.

(A) number
(B) amount
(C) type
(D) supply

112 Kortra Software has unveiled a music player that can ------- any type of sound file.

(A) dispose
(B) contain
(C) reconcile
(D) accommodate

113 ------- the board comes to a conclusion today, the vote will have to be postponed until next month's meeting.

(A) Whereas
(B) If
(C) Unless
(D) Even

114 Forecasters anticipate an increase in public spending in Lancetown ------- the next three years.

(A) between
(B) upon
(C) against
(D) over

115 Directors of the zoo are predicting an ------- in visitors following the birth of a rare white tiger cub.

(A) insert
(B) effort
(C) increase
(D) array

116 Not many of the consumers questioned were familiar with the product line manufactured by Grantham Cosmetics, ------- advertisement appears in glossy magazines.

(A) whose
(B) what
(C) which
(D) who

117 Mr. Lao from Price Financial Services will be using the main boardroom while he ------- the company's annual reports.

(A) compiles
(B) responds
(C) proceeds
(D) realizes

118 The Fitness for Life promotion DVD will feature a number of exercises for a healthy body, with an ------- on upper body strength.

(A) emphasize
(B) emphasized
(C) emphasis
(D) emphasizes

119 Harris Supermarkets' ------- is to encourage more people to shop at the stores by insisting on better customer service.

(A) inquiry
(B) structure
(C) objective
(D) transfer

120 The town of Santos has been evacuated ------- a bush fire heading towards Netherman Falls.

(A) provided that
(B) owing to
(C) instead of
(D) even if

GO ON TO THE NEXT PAGE

121 ------- a minor decline in kitchen appliance sales, Boldwon Electrical has experienced a surge across all of its industries.

(A) Aside from
(B) Compared to
(C) Although
(D) For instance

122 After discussion with the labor union started, Foxtune Industries ------- to raise wages and reduce working hours for all employees.

(A) permitted
(B) included
(C) consented
(D) complied

123 Customers who purchased the third edition of the Gloria coffee maker are ------- to complete the customer survey card and return it.

(A) circulated
(B) encouraged
(C) conducted
(D) considered

124 Weather forecasters predict five ------- days of sunshine, which should provide a welcome reprieve from recent unprecedented rainfall.

(A) refreshed
(B) atmospheric
(C) deliberate
(D) consecutive

125 With just 2 weeks to go before the start of the annual Glastonbury Festival, the organizers have ------- to decide which act is headlining.

(A) yet
(B) not
(C) finally
(D) already

126 A local oil corporation, Petro Co., plans to start ------- of its new line of oil products.

(A) production
(B) producing
(C) product
(D) productivity

127 The appointment of Russ Heiskell as CEO will ------- Marbeck's position as one of the leading pharmaceutical institutions in Egypt.

(A) incline
(B) accomplish
(C) administer
(D) solidify

128 ------- adopting the Kiving production method, Qantros Corporation has experienced a reduction in product defects.

(A) That
(B) Because
(C) For
(D) Since

129 Although the revised return policy will go into ------- on June 1, customers who made a purchase before May 15 will be exempt from it.

(A) effect
(B) effective
(C) effectively
(D) effectiveness

130 Ucham Construction builds energy-efficient residential structures worldwide and ------- requires skilled and experienced workers.

(A) because
(B) therefore
(C) however
(D) rather

# PART 6

**Directions:** Read the texts that follow. A word, phrase, or sentence is missing in parts of each text. Four answer choices for each question are given below the text. Select the best answer to complete the text. Then mark the letter (A), (B), (C), or (D) on your answer sheet.

**Questions 131-134** refer to the following article.

May 1 — Interling Credit Union and Royalwin Credit Union yesterday unveiled

------- plans to merge. The new entity will be named Victory Credit Union. It will
**131.**
become the largest locally headquartered ------- corporation with a total of 120,000
**132.**
members, holding over $5 billion in assets.

The boards of both credit unions convened several months ago to consider merging.

This past week, they voted unanimously for the merger. -------.
**133.**

The ------- of the new joint entity is supposed to take several weeks. During that time,
**134.**
members are advised to continue using the services of their respective institutions.

However, they will also be able to access the services of their new partner institution.

131 (A) its
(B) our
(C) their
(D) his

132 (A) finance
(B) financed
(C) financial
(D) financially

133 (A) Specifics were first released to the public yesterday.
(B) The official records show the entity is compliant with all federal regulations.
(C) Banking is one of the fastest emerging industries.
(D) Membership is available to certain groups of people.

134 (A) distinction
(B) assessment
(C) estimate
(D) formation

**To:** sanrao@kignet.com

**From:** accounts@osn.com

**Date:** November 15

**Subject:** Your Phone Bill


Dear Ms. Rao:

Your OSN phone bill for the account ending in 5110 is now available online. The total

amount ------- is $25.80
       **135.**

No action is required at this time. You have registered for our autopay option. -------,
                                            **136.**
your credit card will be charged in the amount of the current balance on November 25.


------- your bill, log in to your account at www.osntelecom.net. You will also be able to
**137.**
download or print any current or previous bills.


-------. For that reason, we encourage you to review it thoroughly every month.
**138.**


Sincerely,

Account Services

135 (A) obtained
    (B) due
    (C) kept
    (D) returned

136 (A) In fact
    (B) Otherwise
    (C) Hence
    (D) However

137 (A) Check
    (B) To check
    (C) Checking
    (D) Having checked

138 (A) Enclosed in this e-mail is a special coupon for loyal customers.
    (B) Thank you for doing business with OSN Telecom.
    (C) Important changes about your account may be included on your bill.
    (D) You will be charged an extra fee due to a late payment.

**Questions 139-142** refer to the following e-mail.

---

**To:** harvey@koln.com
**From:** kyra@koln.com
**Subject:** Interviews
**Date:** September 2
**Attachment:** contact_list.doc

Dear Harvey:

You may remember that the hiring committee I work for is planning to interview some

job candidates in the following weeks. I would like to ask you to contact each of the

------- and schedule their individual interviews. Included is a document containing their
   **139.**
names and contact information. It also ------- their preferred dates and times for the
          **140.**
interviews. Once you have scheduled the interviews, please immediately report to me.

-------. Should you have any further inquiries, just let me know. I will be out of town until
**141.**
tomorrow, ------- I will be checking my e-mail and text messages.
      **142.**

Best,

Kyra

---

139 (A) employees
(B) acquaintances
(C) applicants
(D) residents

140 (A) lists
(B) would have listed
(C) will list
(D) listed

141 (A) We can meet tomorrow to discuss the details.
(B) I appreciate your patronage as a regular customer.
(C) All you need to do is train new employees.
(D) Thanks for handling this important issue.

142 (A) whereas
(B) although
(C) but
(D) unless

Questions 143-146 refer to the following memo.

**FROM:** Jan Grady

**TO:** Packaging Department

**DATE:** December 2

One of the objectives for our department's planning team has been to ------- expenses
**143.**
over the following year. We have identified three areas for potential cost-cutting: labor,

materials, and processes. -------. Therefore, we have decided to focus on the other two
**144.**
areas. As for the second area, the department will begin using new, cheaper boxes.

Details ------- these and other new packing materials will be determined soon. As for
**145.**
the third area, we are still evaluating our current packaging process to identify potential

ineffectiveness. As soon as those have been found, ------- will be made. We should
**146.**
familiarize employees with the new processes. If you have any questions about these

changes, please forward them to your supervisor.

143 (A) evaluate
   (B) promote
   (C) curtail
   (D) calculate

144 (A) New workers are encouraged to
       attend the training session.
   (B) We already allocate employee work
       hours efficiently.
   (C) Cutting-edge equipment will be
       installed in the coming weeks.
   (D) Our success is attributed to your
       contributions.

145 (A) regards
   (B) regarded
   (C) regarding
   (D) to regard

146 (A) promotions
   (B) transactions
   (C) installments
   (D) adjustments

# PART 7

**Directions:** In this part you will read a selection of texts, such as magazine and newspaper articles, e-mails, and instant messages. Each text or set of texts is followed by several questions. Select the best answer for each question and mark the letter (A), (B), (C), or (D) on your answer sheet.

**Questions 147-148** refer to the following advertisement.

## Callan's Seafood

**235 Ocean Drive**
**Monday – Saturday: 8 A.M. – 7 P.M.**
**Sunday: 10 A.M. – 5 P.M.**
**339-555-4481**

The region's best wholesaler for fresh seafood, including:
squid, fresh fish, and shellfish
cod and haddock
halibut and eel

Weekly special! Save 25 percent on oysters, mussels, crabs and lobsters.
Offer ends on February 2.

**147** What is stated about Callan's Seafood?

(A) It sells frozen food.
(B) It is open every day of the week.
(C) It takes orders from overseas.
(D) It specializes in exotic fish.

**148** According to the advertisement, what has been discounted?

(A) White fish
(B) Boating equipment
(C) Deep sea fish
(D) Shellfish

GO ON TO THE NEXT PAGE

# Welcome to Luigi's Vehicle Service and Repair

Open Monday through Saturday
8:30 A.M. to 5:00 P.M.

**Customer:** Alex Jang
**Order #:** 20201187
Wednesday, October 8, 8:37 A.M.

| Item | Service | Pick-Up Date/ Time | Cost |
|------|---------|--------------------|------|
| Van | Wheel Alignment | Wed. October 8/ 4 P.M. | $8.00 |
| Hatchback | Interior Cleaning | Fri. October 10/ 6 P.M. | $20.00 |
| Motorcycle | Service | Mon. October 13/ 10 A.M. | $30.00 |
| Scooter | Service | Mon. October 13/ 10 A.M. | $30.00 |

Total cost: $88.00
Amount paid: $88.00
Balance due: $ 0.00

Thank you for choosing Luigi's
Ask about our Monday Interior Cleaning

149 For what vehicle did Ms. Jang receive same-day service?

(A) Motorcycle
(B) Hatchback
(C) Scooter
(D) Van

150 What is indicated in the receipt about Ms. Jang's service?

(A) It will be invoiced
(B) It was billed on October 10.
(C) It was paid for in full.
(D) It contained a number of vans.

Questions 151-153 refer to the following chart.

http://www.appliancereviewer.com

## Microwave Appliances Under $200

| MODEL | DETAILS | REVIEWER COMMENTS |
|---|---|---|
| Access T-L | Weight: 3kg<br>Baking Function: Yes<br>Suggested retail price: $199 | Available in stainless steel only<br>Very fast defrost |
| Vista 4 | Weight: 3kg<br>Baking Function: No<br>Suggested retail price: $49 | Simple, easy-to-use controls<br>Replacement parts very expensive |
| Caterham Special | Weight: 5kg<br>Baking Function : No<br>Suggested retail price: $99 | Ten-year guarantee on motor<br>Powerful roast facility |
| Plasma 700 | Weight: 6kg<br>Baking Function: Yes<br>Suggested retail price: $99 | Very cumbersome<br>High energy-efficiency rating |

151 Why would someone refer to the chart?

(A) To learn about microwaves in a certain price range
(B) To find the components of each microwave
(C) To determine how many microwaves a store sells each week
(D) To compare the energy efficiency of microwaves

152 What is a stated advantage of Access T-L?

(A) It is available in several colors.
(B) It defrosts food quickly.
(C) It has a ten-year warranty.
(D) It uses energy efficiently.

153 How are Caterham Special and Plasma 700 similar?

(A) They cost the same amount.
(B) They both have baking capacity.
(C) They are the same weight.
(D) They both received negative reviews.

Test 05

GO ON TO THE NEXT PAGE

Questions 154-155 refer to the following text message chain.

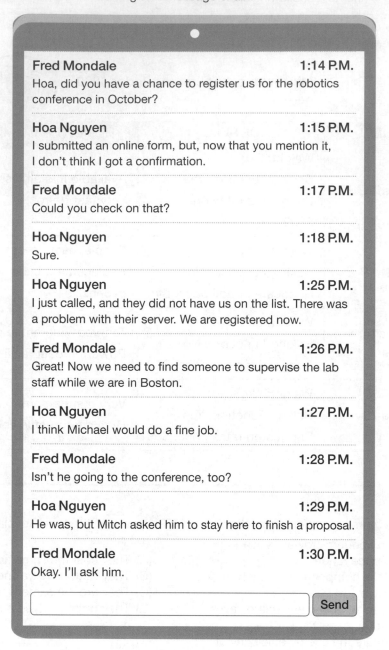

**Fred Mondale**           1:14 P.M.
Hoa, did you have a chance to register us for the robotics conference in October?

**Hoa Nguyen**           1:15 P.M.
I submitted an online form, but, now that you mention it, I don't think I got a confirmation.

**Fred Mondale**           1:17 P.M.
Could you check on that?

**Hoa Nguyen**           1:18 P.M.
Sure.

**Hoa Nguyen**           1:25 P.M.
I just called, and they did not have us on the list. There was a problem with their server. We are registered now.

**Fred Mondale**           1:26 P.M.
Great! Now we need to find someone to supervise the lab staff while we are in Boston.

**Hoa Nguyen**           1:27 P.M.
I think Michael would do a fine job.

**Fred Mondale**           1:28 P.M.
Isn't he going to the conference, too?

**Hoa Nguyen**           1:29 P.M.
He was, but Mitch asked him to stay here to finish a proposal.

**Fred Mondale**           1:30 P.M.
Okay. I'll ask him.

Send

**154** What is suggested about Michael?

(A) He cannot supervise the lab.
(B) He is a new employee.
(C) He is presenting at a conference.
(D) He will not go to Boston.

**155** At 1:15 P.M., what does Ms. Nguyen mean when she writes, "Now that you mention it"?

(A) She is embarrassed that she forgot to check on the registration.
(B) She realizes that she needs to be less forgetful about details.
(C) She just realized something because of what Mr. Mondale said.
(D) She thought Mr. Mondale was going to submit the registration.

# Emiron Losing Market Share

By Junaid Kasim

Hong Kong, April 11 — Following recent market research into customer satisfaction, Emiron Energy was ranked the tenth most customer-friendly energy supplier, with 60% of users claiming to be satisfied. -[1]-. The survey was conducted by Aston Research in the previous month and revealed that although Emiron is rated higher than its main rival, Tivol Power, its position has dropped dramatically from last year's survey, which placed Emiron in fourth position. -[2]-.

"Despite the fact that we have fallen behind other competitors, our aim is to concentrate on our customers' needs," comments Adam Rawling, spokesperson for Emiron. -[3]-. "As for next year, we are putting certain changes in place to improve our customer service. For example, we are consolidating all technical service staff in one building for better training and quality-control monitoring. This will be completed by March of next year." -[4]-.

**156** What did the customers most likely say about Emiron?

(A) Its energy supply is too slow.
(B) Its prices are too high.
(C) Its call center is short-staffed.
(D) Its technical service is inconsistent.

**157** What will Emiron do next year?

(A) It will use new technology.
(B) It will merge with other competitors.
(C) It will place all technical staff in one location.
(D) It will carry out more market research.

**158** In which of the positions marked [1], [2], [3], and [4] does the following sentence best belong?

"It is hoped these changes will increase the popularity of Emiron in the customers' opinions."

(A) [1]
(B) [2]
(C) [3]
(D) [4]

Test 05

```
                        E-Mail Message
```

| | |
|---|---|
| **To:** | cbowden@washngo.com |
| **From:** | rmansell@plumbbase.com |
| **Date:** | June 30 |
| **Re:** | Elite Washer Dryer |

Dear Mr. Bowden,

I'm contacting you regarding one of the washer-dryers your organization manufactures, the Elite Washer Drier. A significant number of customers who bought this item have complained that the internal liquid holder is loose due to a missing screw. Luckily, we have that size of screw available in stock and were able to supply it for customers.

I would be grateful if you would replace the screws that we have had to give to customers so we do not lose any of our stock profits.

Due to the concerns about this fault in the machine, we have decided to delay ordering any additional washer-dryers from you until the matter has been rectified. When we receive assurance that this is resolved, we will be more than happy to resume our orders.

Thank you for assisting me in this matter.

Sincerely,

Raine Mansell
Manager
Plumbbase

**159** Why did Ms. Mansell write the e-mail?

(A) To question an invoice
(B) To recommend an appliance
(C) To address a problem
(D) To reply to a customer

**160** What does Ms. Mansell ask Mr. Bowden to do?

(A) Explain how to use a machine
(B) Help promote the washer-dryer
(C) Replace some items
(D) Speed up an order

**161** What decision has Plumbbase made?

(A) It will postpone placing orders for a particular product.
(B) It will sell a variety of washing machines.
(C) It will charge customers for screws.
(D) It will return some unsatisfactory merchandise.

# Weekly Catering News

On Friday, Saloma's nightclub agreed on the terms to purchase three Galant casinos. One of the casinos is located in Antrim and the other two in Belfast. -[1]-.

For the foreseeable future, the venues will continue under the Galant brand name, with nothing announced as yet for a change in name. -[2]-. In a press release, the CEO of Saloma, Ansar Quidar announced: "I am delighted to incorporate these venues under the Saloma brand. We are aiming to become the leading name in entertainment in Antrim and Belfast. Our long-term strategy is to provide these communities with affordable and exciting leisure entertainment." Mr. Quidar also stressed that no jobs were under threat. -[3]-.

Saloma's nightclub was the brainchild of Mr. Quidar's great-grandfather, who opened the first bar in Omaghe over a century ago. Mr. Quidar took over ownership after the death of his father 7 years ago. There are now Saloma bars in many towns and cities in Ireland. -[4]-.

**162** What is the purpose of the article?

(A) To announce an acquisition
(B) To report on the gaming market
(C) To recruit new bar staff
(D) To comment on the relocation of a company

**163** What does Mr. Quidar say about employment at the Antrim and Belfast branches?

(A) He wants to experiment with new hiring practices.
(B) He expects support within the community.
(C) He intends to retain current employees.
(D) He plans to offer performance-based bonuses.

**164** What is indicated about Saloma's Nightclub?

(A) It is a family-owned business.
(B) It has international clubs.
(C) It will soon expand into Scotland.
(D) It offers free gaming.

**165** In which of the positions marked [1], [2], [3], and [4] does the following sentence best belong?

"The sale price has not yet been announced."

(A) [1]
(B) [2]
(C) [3]
(D) [4]

Questions 166-168 refer to the following online chat discussion.

**Irma Vega**                                                  — X

| | |
|---|---|
| **Irma Vega** [10:08 A.M.] | Good morning. I just prepared a sales report on our last quarter. Sales are down 20% compared to the same time last year. We need to reverse that. |
| **Ron Couloir** [10:09 A.M.] | Why don't we have a big promotional offer to get people into the store? Maybe a buy-one-get-one-free sale. |
| **Irma Vega** [10:10 A.M.] | Let's hold off on that. I want to see what other options we can come up with first. |
| **Katherine Baker** [10:11 A.M.] | Why don't we increase advertising? Maybe people have forgotten about us since the new mall opened. |
| **Ron Couloir** [10:12 A.M.] | That's true, but advertisements are expensive. |
| **Katherine Baker** [10:13 A.M.] | Not radio advertisements. We can do it without spending any extra money. |
| **Irma Vega** [10:14 A.M.] | Okay, go on. |
| **Katherine Baker** [10:15 A.M.] | Look, right now we are paying $1,500 a month to run advertisements in the local newspaper. For the same price, we can get advertisements on 3-4 stations every day. |
| **Irma Vega** [10:16 A.M.] | That's a lot of advertisements. |
| **Ron Couloir** [10:17 A.M.] | I like it. It also makes it easier to target young people. They are the ones who like the trendy shoes. |
| **Irma Vega** [10:18 A.M.] | Let's try it. Kat, can you call a few stations and get estimates for what this will cost? |
| **Katherine Baker** [10:19 A.M.] | Sure thing. |
| **Irma Vega** [10:20 A.M.] | Ron, I'd like you to jot down some ideas for scripts for the advertisements. We sell the same shoes that they have in the mall. We need to make sure consumers know our prices are lower. |
| **Ron Couloir** [10:20 A.M.] | Got it. |

| Send |

**166** Where do the writers most likely work?

    (A) At a radio station

    (B) At a clothing store

    (C) At a shopping mall

    (D) At a shoe store

**167** What does Mr. Couloir agree to do?

    (A) Generate advertising ideas

    (B) Check the prices at some competitors

    (C) Design a promotional offer

    (D) Talk with mall shoppers

**168** At 10:14 A.M., what does Ms. Vega mean when she says, "Okay, go on"?

    (A) She wants to finish the discussion so she can get going.

    (B) She is reconsidering the idea proposed by Mr. Couloir.

    (C) She wants Ms. Baker to explain the details of her idea.

    (D) She is skeptical that radio advertisements will work.

GO ON TO THE NEXT PAGE

Questions 169-171 refer to the following e-mail.

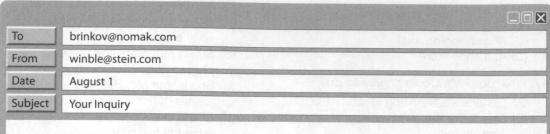

To: brinkov@nomak.com
From: winble@stein.com
Date: August 1
Subject: Your Inquiry

Dear Mr. Brinkov,

Thank you for your e-mail inquiry, which I reviewed today. I can now tell you a bit about how we can help Nomak Print increase traffic through the redesign of your Web site.

Stein Design was established five years ago. We have been appointed as an Internet consultant for a number of large companies, many of which are also overseas. Some of our biggest clients include KKS Clothing of Mombasa, Signet Designs of New York, and Falas Inc. of Hong Kong. As a result of our consulting work, these companies have seen a dramatic increase in visitors to their Web site, many of whom have become interested customers.

If you would like to work with us, I can assure you of the highest possible standards of work. Stein Design has an impressive record of completing projects on time and within budget. I am positive your company will see increased profitability.

Please feel free to call me directly at 901-555-1232 to arrange a meeting during which we will analyze your requirements further. I look forward to hearing from you.

Sincerely,

Lena Wimble
Senior Sales Manager
Stein Design

**169** Why does Ms. Wimble send the e-mail?

(A) To confirm an upcoming meeting at Nomak Print
(B) To encourage a company to pursue a business relationship
(C) To give information about a design forum
(D) To describe how to set up a new Web page

**170** What is mentioned about Stein Design?

(A) It does business overseas.
(B) Its fees are lower than those of other consultants.
(C) It has recently hired several designers.
(D) Its headquarters are in Mombasa.

**171** The word "assure" in paragraph 3, line 1, is closest in meaning to

(A) promise
(B) inform
(C) convince
(D) promote

**Questions 172-175** refer to the following article.

SEATTLE(March 3) — Seattle-based Mallins Cosmetics has recently revealed plans to construct another research and development facility. At the moment, the organization's only such facility is situated in Maine, a distance of more than 200 kilometers from its Seattle main headquarters. The cost of the new facility has been announced as $4 million and this move is at the forefront of a new initiative to expand into the European market.

Management executives are hoping this bold move to Berlin, Germany will boost the company's reputation as a major player in the European cosmetics industry. Once the project is completed, the two R&D facilities will easily accommodate the requirements of the American and the European markets. "An important advantage is that we will now have access to European products and ingredients, which previously we had to source and import. This took time and added to our cost margins," said company president Steve Baker.

Mr. Baker's father, David Baker, founded Mallins Cosmetics in 1981 after graduating from a university in California. When he returned to Seattle, he began a part-time job selling imported cosmetics to students in the region. Within six months, his part-time business had managed to bring in large profits, which increased when he went full time the next year. Today, Mallins Cosmetics is recognized internationally as a quality producer with outlets in more than 20 countries worldwide. Recently, however, sales have fallen off with the new R&D team under Mr. Baker aggressively attempting to find new angles.

The full range of Mallins Cosmetic's existing products should be available in the majority of European countries by the end of the year, according to R&D director Anna Bottram. Ms. Bottram has a long-term vision to introduce a line of anti-ageing creams aimed at the older generation to complement the company's current product line. "Our aim is to grow and develop new items our customers will appreciate," she said.

**172** Why is Mallins Cosmetics building a new facility?

(A) Because the production department is too far away from its headquarters

(B) Because operation costs at the current location have increased

(C) Because it needs to introduce modernized equipment

(D) Because its leaders want to sell their products in a new location

**173** Where will the new facility be located?

(A) Seattle

(B) Maine

(C) Berlin

(D) California

**174** What is mentioned about Mallins Cosmetics?

(A) Sales of its products have stopped growing recently.

(B) It sells more products overseas.

(C) Customers can currently buy its products only in Seattle.

(D) It is planning to fire several executives.

**175** What new type of product is Mallins Cosmetics planning to develop?

(A) Lipsticks

(B) Lotions

(C) Creams

(D) Powder

Questions **176-180** refer to the following e-mail and online article.

| To | Andrea Golding <agolding@coverart.com> |
|---|---|
| From | Toyah Labon <tlabon@sequencepress.com> |
| Subject | Ingleton |
| Date | June 14, 2:44 P.M. |
| Attachment | Tennis illustration.zip |

Hi Andrea,

Earlier today, I received a call from Larss Ingleton about the cover for *Tennis Players through the Ages*, his latest book in what is to be a three-volume series on sports heroes in the modern era. He does not approve of the neutral tone images we were intending to use and wants this cover to be similar in design to his previous book, *Soccer in the Americas*. So as soon as possible, can I rely on you to come up with some initial designs so we can send them for approval to Mr. Ingleton? I've also attached some illustrations of tennis for your reference.

As this is not the only design-related issue that Mr. Ingleton has raised when I spoke to him, I think it would be highly beneficial for everyone in the design department involved in the project to hear what he has to say. So I've arranged a conference call with him on Tuesday at midday from his home in the Austrian Alps. I'll email over the list of recipients for the call. Please let me know if you have any questions.

Toyah

# The Art of Covers
www.theaustrianreview.com/book-review

### Tuesday August 11

The Austrian Review annually asks prominent artists to vote for their favorite book cover designs. Iliana Drobvik, who is director of art design at the University of Altrecht in Belgium, reveals his favorites this week.

Iliana Drobvik: I love to see book covers that show a myriad of images about the content itself and are interesting enough for me to recognize some of the people mentioned in the book. So when I came across the cover of <Tennis Players through the Ages> designed by Andrea Golding, I was quite taken. The book was written by Mr. Larss Ingleton, an Austrian writer, and it was published by Sequence Press. The cover bears illustrations of tennis stars past and present, with no title or author on the cover itself. Instead, the cover makes use only of black and white drawings with a red background. This cover is remarkably similar in design to the first book in the trilogy planned by Mr. Larss Ingleton; that first book's cover also makes use of black and white drawing but with a blue background. Golding is obviously an expert in line drawing and I applaud her design work.

**176** What is one purpose of the e-mail?

(A) To request that a coworker return some books she borrowed
(B) To inform a staff member that adjustments need to be made
(C) To set a deadline for additional work to be done on a project
(D) To announce the publication date of an author's latest book

**177** What is implied about Toyah Labon?

(A) She invited Mr. Larss Ingleton to participate in a meeting.
(B) She is an expert on structural engineering.
(C) She will visit the Austrian Alps next week.
(D) She is the author of five books.

**178** What is indicated about the cover of *Soccer in the Americas*?

(A) It features only three colors.
(B) Iliana Drobvik designed it.
(C) Larss Ingleton was dissatisfied with it.
(D) It is covered in photographs.

**179** In the online article, the word "bears" in paragraph 2, line 5, is closest in meaning to

(A) accepts
(B) requires
(C) displays
(D) fits

**180** What is NOT suggested about Andrea Golding?

(A) Her work is on a book published by Sequence Press.
(B) She designed one of the books in the trilogy.
(C) Her work makes extensive use of color.
(D) An art critic named her work as his favorite book cover.

13 September

# Press Release

Luizi Corporation is delighted to announce the unveiling of its new factories in Pampa and Corboba on Saturday, September 13. In addition, we can also reveal the merger with Rassoul Manufacturing, a centrally located organization in Tucuman, has finally been approved this week. According to Luizi's President, Amande Resok, these transactions consolidate the corporation's determination to increase its presence in Argentina.

Luizi was established by Joachim Fillen after he was made redundant at Bolero Industries, five years ago. Having been employed there for a decade, he was ready to return back to his home in Parana, where, in partnership with his family and friends, he began his fruit wholesale business there. Mr. Fillen's plan was to concentrate on domestic produce using only a local supply network. The strategy was massively lucrative and Fillen's idea was soon adopted by similar wholesalers throughout the country. This led to the company becoming one of the most revered and esteemed firms of its kind.

Even with its unprecedented growth in the market, the company's original office, purpose-built five years ago, is still used as the company's main base, and the business has continued its quest for innovation. The IT team has recently introduced a picking system that can relay orders almost twice as fast as earlier models.

---

**From :** Amande Resok [AmandeResok@Luizi.com]
**To :** Tim Janke [TimJanke@Luizi.com]
**Date :** September 21
**Subject :** Good News

Dear Mr. Janke,

I'm delighted to inform you that the Human Resources Department has decided to honor you as a recipient of this year's long service awards. The award was based on your commitment and contribution to the company since you joined Luizi. Since then, you have been consistent in helping Luizi's transition from a local business to one of the leading companies in South American wholesaling. In addition, the work ethic you have displayed as a team leader, particularly as a manager of the shipping division, is exemplary.

In celebration of this year's awards, a gourmet dinner will be held at the company's headquarters on Tuesday, 25 September, 5 P.M., after which, I will present the awards. Thank you again for your hard work and dedication and I'm looking forward to seeing you there.

Amande Resok
Chief Executive Officer

181 According to the press release, why has Luizi Corporation been successful?

(A) It rapidly expanded into the overseas market.
(B) It offered lower prices than its competitors.
(C) It installed a wholesaler system that is widely used.
(D) It formed a partnership with Bolero.

182 What is NOT mentioned as an activity Luizi Corporation is involved in?

(A) Merging with a company
(B) Opening new offices
(C) Introducing an upgraded system
(D) Offering training opportunities

183 How long did Mr. Fillen work at Bolero Industries?

(A) For 2 years
(B) For 5 years
(C) For 10 years
(D) For 15 years

184 Why will Luizi Corporation host a reception?

(A) To celebrate the conclusion of a business deal
(B) To attract more business opportunities in Argentina
(C) To honor the service of several workers
(D) To mark the anniversary of the company's founding

185 Where will Mr. Janke most likely be on September 25?

(A) In Tucuman
(B) In Pampa
(C) In Parana
(D) In Cordoba

GO ON TO THE NEXT PAGE

# OFFICE EXPRESS

Store # 840 - San Pedro
555-8203

WEEKLY SPECIALS (March 2 – March 9)

Tax preparation software $25
All laptops 10% off – Starting at just $300 (regular: $330)
All Dextra brand printers 20% off – Starting at just $100 (regular: $120)
Office supplies from 5% – 50% off
SPEND $75 or more and get a complimentary USB drive ($5 value).

Sign up for our rewards card and earn points with both in-store purchases and those made at www.officeexpress.com. For every dollar spent, you get a point. Bonus points can be earned on select purchases. Points cannot be earned on sale items.

---

Thank you for purchasing a Dextra T950 printer. Included with your printer are one three-color cartridges and one black ink cartridge. Please follow the instructions on the other side of the card when inserting the cartridges into your printer. It is advised that you print a test page before using the printer for the first time. This helps ensure that the print heads are lined up correctly.

Replacement cartridges can be purchased from many retailers. In addition, they are available at our online store at www.dextra.com. Cartridges ordered from our Web site will be shipped within 48 hours at no extra charge. You can use coupon code DT2000 to take an additional 10% off your first order. This discount is only available for purchases made on our Web site.

Feel free to contact us 24 hours a day, 7 days a week if you have any questions about your new printer.

Customer support: 1-800-555-1818 / customersupport@dextra.com

Technical support: 1-800-555-0909 / techsupport@dextra.com

| From | Dan Farmer <dfarm@jetmail.net> |
| To | Dextra, Inc. <customersupport@dextra.com> |
| Subject | Order #8945 |
| Date | March 25 |

To Whom It May Concern:

On March 2, I purchased a T950 printer at an Office Express store while I was visiting a friend in San Pedro. The printer is awesome. It is exactly what I needed to print high-quality flyers for my business. I have been using it so much that I have almost run out of ink. There is no Office Express in my area, so I ordered four replacement cartridges (Order #8945) from your Web site with code DT2000. Unfortunately, the ones that were sent to me are the wrong size. I would like to exchange these for correct ones. Please advise me what to do.

Sincerely,

Dan Farmer

**186** According to the advertisement, what is true about rewards card points?

(A) They can be earned for online purchases.
(B) They can be redeemed for discounts.
(C) They can be earned on discounted items.
(D) They are only available to loyal customers.

**187** What is suggested about Mr. Farmer?

(A) He regularly shops at Store #840.
(B) He received a free USB drive.
(C) He signed up for a rewards card.
(D) He paid less than $100 for his printer.

**188** What is most likely true about order #8945?

(A) It took four days to arrive.
(B) There was a fee for shipping.
(C) It included a 10% discount.
(D) There was an incorrect address.

**189** In the information, the word "ensure" in paragraph 1, line 5, is closest in meaning to

(A) adjust
(B) transmit
(C) measure
(D) confirm

**190** What is indicated about Dextra's customer support?

(A) It can be reached by phone on weekends.
(B) It processes orders placed on Dextra's Web site.
(C) Its members prefer being contacted by e-mail.
(D) It can assist with installation issues.

GO ON TO THE NEXT PAGE

Test 05

# From the Office of Dr. Sharron Wilson
## 27 Mustang Road • Billings, MT 61520
### (894) 555-0128
### office@doctorwilson.com

Dear Ms. Sainsbury:

Your health is important to us. That's why we would like to remind you that you have scheduled an appointment with us on

Tuesday, October 5, at 8:30 A.M.

If you are a new patient, please arrive ten minutes prior to your scheduled appointment to fill out a patient information form and a payment authorization form.

If, for any reason, you need to cancel or change your appointment, please contact us at least 24 hours in advance to preclude a cancelation fee.

We look forward to seeing you!

---

| From | ms2002@netmail.com |
|------|--------------------|
| To | office@doctorwilson.com |
| Date | October 3, 3:45 P.M. |

Thank you for sending me the reminder. I had almost forgotten about my appointment. The past few weeks have been very hectic at work. Still, I know how important it is to get my annual physical. Is there any way I could change my appointment to Friday, October 8? Any time will work for me. I will make sure I arrive ten minutes early to fill out the paperwork.

In addition, people at work keep saying it would be a good idea for me to get a flu shot. I'm not sure they are really effective. I would like to discuss this with Dr. Wilson before agreeing to get a shot.

Thanks,
Marsha Sainsbury

## PATIENT BILLING STATEMENT

Marsha Sainsbury
1898 Jasper Canyon Ln.
Billings, MT 61520

Dr. Sharron Wilson
27 Mustang Road
Billings, MT 61520

**Summary of Services**

Physical Examination          $125.00
Vaccination, Influenza        $ 25.00

**Account Summary**

Account #: 8093-034
Service Date: October 8
Billed Charges: $150.00
Payment Method: Insurance
Provider Name: Health One

**NOTE**: All charges billed to an insurance provider must be approved by the provider. If the provider rejects the charge, the patient will be responsible for the payment in full. Please check with your insurance provider before authorizing services.

**191** What is NOT mentioned in the notice?

(A) The time of the appointment
(B) The location of the appointment
(C) The reason for the appointment
(D) The deadline to cancel an appointment

**192** What is suggested about Ms. Sainsbury?

(A) She has had recent health problems.
(B) She is a new patient of Dr. Wilson's.
(C) She frequently gets sick at work.
(D) She had to pay a cancelation fee.

**193** Why did Ms. Sainsbury write the e-mail?

(A) To request additional information
(B) To make an appointment
(C) To submit paperwork
(D) To change an appointment

**194** What is most likely true about Ms. Sainsbury's visit?

(A) It took place in the morning.
(B) She arrived later than scheduled.
(C) It was on her preferred date.
(D) She decided not to get a flu shot.

**195** In the bill, the word "authorizing" in paragraph 4, line 3, is closest in meaning to

(A) allowing
(B) considering
(C) refusing
(D) paying

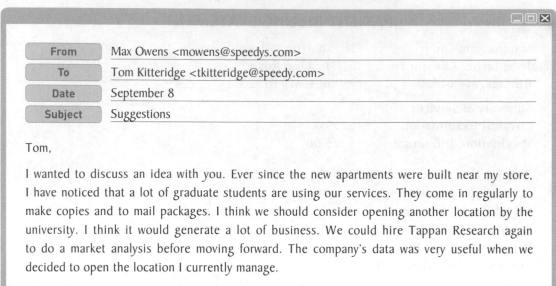

**From** Max Owens <mowens@speedys.com>

**To** Tom Kitteridge <tkitteridge@speedy.com>

**Date** September 8

**Subject** Suggestions

Tom,

I wanted to discuss an idea with you. Ever since the new apartments were built near my store, I have noticed that a lot of graduate students are using our services. They come in regularly to make copies and to mail packages. I think we should consider opening another location by the university. I think it would generate a lot of business. We could hire Tappan Research again to do a market analysis before moving forward. The company's data was very useful when we decided to open the location I currently manage.

What do you think?

Max

BURLINGTON — (May 8) Speedy's, the nationwide chain of copying and printing centers, announced that it will be opening a new location in the neighborhood just south of the university campus next month.

The company, which also offers mail services, says it wants to provide students with a faster, more affordable alternative to making photocopies in the library.

"Our market data showed there was tremendous demand for our services in this part of the city," explained regional manager Tom Kitteridge.

The new location on Wheeler Street, next to Java Max coffee shop, will be open 24 hours a day.

Unlike its other Burlington locations, this Speedy's will allow students to open prepaid accounts. Students pay in advance and receive a student PIN. This system avoids the hassle of having to carry cash or a credit card. Students can easily check and add to their account balances in the store.

# SELF-SERVICE PRINTERS/ COPIERS

**Instruction**

**1.** Insert your credit/debit card OR enter your student PIN.

**2.** Select the type of service: printing/copying.
  a. If printing, insert your USB drive and follow the prompts on the display to print files on this storage device.
  b. If copying, select the type of copy and size.

**3.** Indicate the number of pages needed.

**4.** Press start.

**5.** When the job is complete, you will be asked if you would like to receive a paper or electronic receipt. If using a credit/debit card, an e-mail address must be provided for e-receipts.

Need help? Ask a friendly associate at the front desk.

**196** What is the purpose of the e-mail?
  (A) To report on sales
  (B) To file a complaint
  (C) To make a suggestion
  (D) To request data

**197** What is most likely true about Mr. Kitteridge?
  (A) He will manage the new Speedy's location.
  (B) He is one of Mr. Owens's employees.
  (C) He is a resident of Burlington.
  (D) He hired a marketing research firm again.

**198** In the article, the word "hassle" in paragraph 5, line 5, is closest in meaning to
  (A) inconvenience
  (B) interaction
  (C) expense
  (D) contradiction

**199** What is NOT mentioned in the instructions?
  (A) Payments can be made with a credit card.
  (B) Printing can be done from a USB drive.
  (C) Assistance is available if needed.
  (D) Students can print in full color.

**200** What is suggested about the self-service copiers?
  (A) They are only available at the university location.
  (B) Students can send files to them from their phones.
  (C) Students with prepaid accounts can use them.
  (D) They are identical to the type used in the library.

**Stop! This is the end of the test. If you finish before time is called, you may go back to Parts 5, 6, and 7 and check your work.**

**慢著！作答前請務必確認！**

- 請當作實際考試般，將書桌收拾乾淨，做好心理準備。
- 請將手機關機，並善用時鐘或手錶計時。
- 規定作答時間為 120 分鐘，請務必遵守規定時間。
- 請盡可能按照題目順序作答，碰到難題時，切勿直接跳過。

# Actual Test

# 06

開始時間 ：
完成時間 ：

# LISTENING TEST

In the Listening test, you will be asked to demonstrate how well you understand spoken English. The entire Listening test will last approximately 45 minutes. There are four parts, and directions are given for each part. You must mark your answers on the separate answer sheet. Do not write your answers in your test book.

# PART 1 🎧 21

**Directions:** For each question in this part, you will hear four statements about a picture in your test book. When you hear the statements, you must select the one statement that best describes what you see in the picture. Then find the number of the question on your answer sheet and mark your answer. The statements will not be printed in your test book and will be spoken only one time.

**Example**

**Sample Answer**

Statement (B), "The man is working at a desk," is the best description of the picture, so you should select answer (B) and mark it on your answer sheet.

1

2

**GO ON TO THE NEXT PAGE**

3

4

5

6

# PART 2 🎧22

7   Mark your answer on your answer sheet.

8   Mark your answer on your answer sheet.

9   Mark your answer on your answer sheet.

10   Mark your answer on your answer sheet.

11   Mark your answer on your answer sheet.

12   Mark your answer on your answer sheet.

13   Mark your answer on your answer sheet.

14   Mark your answer on your answer sheet.

15   Mark your answer on your answer sheet.

16   Mark your answer on your answer sheet.

17   Mark your answer on your answer sheet.

18   Mark your answer on your answer sheet.

19   Mark your answer on your answer sheet.

20   Mark your answer on your answer sheet.

21   Mark your answer on your answer sheet.

22   Mark your answer on your answer sheet.

23   Mark your answer on your answer sheet.

24   Mark your answer on your answer sheet.

25   Mark your answer on your answer sheet.

26   Mark your answer on your answer sheet.

27   Mark your answer on your answer sheet.

28   Mark your answer on your answer sheet.

29   Mark your answer on your answer sheet.

30   Mark your answer on your answer sheet.

31   Mark your answer on your answer sheet.

## PART 3 🎧23

**Directions:** You will hear some conversations between two or more people. You will be asked to answer three questions about what the speakers say in each conversation. Select the best response to each question and mark the letter (A), (B), (C), or (D) on your answer sheet. The conversations will not be printed in your test book and will be spoken only one time.

32 Where does the man work?

(A) At a café
(B) At an appliance store
(C) At a repair shop
(D) At a distribution center

33 Why is the woman's order delayed?

(A) A fault has occurred in the factory.
(B) A delivery van has broken down.
(C) A payment was refused.
(D) Her appliance is out of stock.

34 What does the woman say she will do?

(A) Select an alternative appliance
(B) Cancel the order
(C) Use a different credit card
(D) Collect her own order

35 Why is the woman calling?

(A) To ask about a theater schedule
(B) To find out the cost for children
(C) To sign up for membership
(D) To arrange a show

36 What is the theater going to offer during the winter?

(A) Membership packages
(B) Discounted tickets
(C) Free admission
(D) Special shows

37 What does the man recommend?

(A) Purchasing from the Web site
(B) Checking the times of the shows
(C) Arriving early for tickets
(D) Signing up for discounts

38 What does the woman request?

(A) A lab coat
(B) A temporary security pass
(C) An alternative entrance
(D) Directions to a department

39 What does the man ask to see?

(A) A registration form
(B) A driver's license
(C) A safety certificate
(D) A form of identification

40 What does the man suggest?

(A) Contacting a different department
(B) Paying with cash
(C) Changing her ID details
(D) Searching for her wallet

41 What is the man's problem?

(A) He left his confirmation at home.
(B) He cannot attend the exhibition.
(C) He forgot to register.
(D) His name is missing from a list.

42 What does the woman ask to see?

(A) A letter of confirmation
(B) A payment receipt
(C) A form of identification
(D) A coordinators badge

43 What is being offered to some conference participants?

(A) Free entry to an exhibition
(B) A voucher for a meal
(C) Access to a conference
(D) A gift shop coupon

**GO ON TO THE NEXT PAGE**

Actual Test 06  235

**44** Where most likely do the speakers work?

(A) At an office
(B) At a jewelry shop
(C) At a supermarket
(D) At a catering business

**45** What problem does the man mention?

(A) A delivery did not arrive.
(B) A colleague was late.
(C) A dinner was postponed.
(D) A freezer was faulty.

**46** Why will the man make a telephone call?

(A) To find an alternative supplier
(B) To ask for more time
(C) To confirm the status of an order
(D) To check on a client's booking

**47** Where do the speakers most likely work?

(A) At a printing company
(B) At a financial institute
(C) At a construction firm
(D) At an office furniture design firm

**48** What does the man mean when he says, "You know I really want to be a part of it"?

(A) He needs some part for repairs.
(B) His supervisor didn't give him permission.
(C) He is interested in joining the team.
(D) He will go on a business trip soon.

**49** What does the woman suggest?

(A) Talking to a supervisor
(B) Checking schedules
(C) Postponing a deadline
(D) Borrowing some equipment

**50** What did the woman do last week?

(A) She spoke at a seminar.
(B) She inspected a college.
(C) She went on a vacation.
(D) She visited a headquarters.

**51** What does the man ask the woman to do?

(A) Talk to a superior
(B) Go on a vacation
(C) Attend a workshop
(D) Repeat a seminar

**52** What problem does the woman mention?

(A) She cannot travel to the office.
(B) She has forgotten her notes.
(C) She has not received her fee.
(D) She is away for a fortnight.

**53** What are the speakers mainly discussing?

(A) A new contract
(B) A marketing report
(C) An employee evaluation
(D) A travel itinerary

**54** Why does the man say, "we don't have any specific procedure for this"?

(A) To put off an announcement
(B) To give the woman an approval
(C) To clarify an issue
(D) To suggest a policy change

**55** Why is the supervisor unavailable?

(A) She is meeting some clients.
(B) She is training new employees.
(C) She is finalizing a contract.
(D) She is speaking at a convention.

**56** Why is the woman calling?

(A) To discuss travel arrangements
(B) To complain about a service
(C) To request a taxi
(D) To inquire about a missing item

**57** Where will the woman most likely go in an hour?

(A) To a client's office
(B) To a restaurant
(C) To a taxi firm
(D) To a department store

**58** What does the man tell the woman to bring?

(A) A form of identification
(B) An application form
(C) A description of the item
(D) Her car

---

**59** What is mentioned about the products?

(A) They are all the same design.
(B) They can be ordered for a limited time.
(C) They are only available online.
(D) They will not be delivered on time.

**60** What does the woman imply when she says, "I'm actually short of cash now"?

(A) She only has credit cards.
(B) She left some money in her car.
(C) She does not have enough money.
(D) She can lend some cash to the man.

**61** What will the man probably do next?

(A) Place an order
(B) Borrow some money from the woman
(C) Give the woman a lift
(D) Show the woman around the facility

**62** What item are the speakers discussing?

(A) A mobile phone
(B) A child seat
(C) A television
(D) A watch

**63** What does the woman suggest?

(A) Reviewing an advertising strategy
(B) Canceling production
(C) Delaying a consumer survey
(D) Altering a product design

**64** What topic does the man say he will bring up at the meeting?

(A) A request for funding
(B) More time for research
(C) A changed schedule
(D) An alternative product

| Vacation Packages | Price (per person) |
|---|---|
| Single ticket | $700 |
| Couple ticket | $500 |
| Family member | $450 |
| Group of 6 or more | $400 |

| Conference Room A | |
|---|---|
| Accounting | 11:00 A.M. |
| Marketing | 2:00 P.M. |
| Sales | 3:00 P.M. |
| Advertising | 4:00 P.M. |

**65** What are the speakers talking about?

(A) A vacation
(B) An overseas business trip
(C) A package delivery
(D) An accounting staff

**66** Look at the graphic. What ticket price will the speakers most likely pay?

(A) $700
(B) $500
(C) $450
(D) $400

**67** What does the man suggest the woman do?

(A) Go to an accounting office
(B) Buy tickets as soon as possible
(C) Work overtime
(D) Call a colleague

**68** Where do the speakers most likely work?

(A) At a shipping company
(B) At a pharmaceutical company
(C) At a real estate agency
(D) At a software manufacturer

**69** Look at the graphic. In which department does Ron most likely work?

(A) Accounting
(B) Marketing
(C) Sales
(D) Advertising

**70** What will the woman probably do next?

(A) Bring some presentation materials
(B) Conduct an online survey
(C) Ask a coworker to change rooms
(D) Reschedule a meeting

## PART 4 🎧(24)

**Directions:** You will hear some talks given by a single speaker. You will be asked to answer three questions about what the speaker says in each talk. Select the best response to each question and mark the letter (A), (B), (C), or (D) on your answer sheet. The talks will not be printed in your test book and will be spoken only one time.

**71** What kind of business is Ziggy's?
(A) A gaming store
(B) A bookstore
(C) A video store
(D) A music store

**72** What does Ziggy's offer for families with children?
(A) Free drinks in the evenings
(B) A parental list of safe games
(C) A supervised gaming area
(D) A monthly free workshop

**73** What does the advertisement say about online orders?
(A) They are shipped at a small cost.
(B) They are delivered overnight.
(C) They will come with special discounts.
(D) They can be gift wrapped.

**74** Where most likely is the announcement being made?
(A) On a tour bus
(B) On an airplane
(C) In a hotel
(D) In a bank

**75** What does the speaker apologize for?
(A) Early closure
(B) A cancelled service
(C) Delayed payments
(D) A bomb alert

**76** What are customers paying bills assured of?
(A) Their payments will not be accepted.
(B) Their bills will be paid at once.
(C) Another option will be offered.
(D) Refunds will be issued.

**77** What is the speaker discussing?
(A) A television program
(B) A theater production
(C) An advertising campaign
(D) A performance competition

**78** What does the speaker say happened two years ago?
(A) The company won an award.
(B) A new director was appointed.
(C) The company changed its dance routine.
(D) An alternative schedule was introduced.

**79** What are listeners asked to do?
(A) Appoint a trustee
(B) Contact an audience
(C) Make recommendations
(D) Plan a new routine

**80** Where most likely does the speaker work?
(A) At a photographic store
(B) At a supermarket
(C) At an art gallery
(D) At a travel agency

**81** Why does the speaker ask the listener to come to the business?
(A) To refund a holiday
(B) To enter a competition
(C) To pick up a prize
(D) To retrieve a lost item

**82** What does the speaker ask the listener to bring?
(A) An invoice
(B) Holiday brochures
(C) Passport identification
(D) Account details

83 What is the purpose of the message?

(A) To provide a referral
(B) To change a date
(C) To provide a driving test
(D) To confirm an appointment

84 What does the speaker remind Mr. Landau to do on Friday morning?

(A) Submit an insurance claim
(B) Bring eye glasses if necessary
(C) Call back for examination results
(D) Arrive half an hour early

85 What information does the speaker need from Mr. Laundau?

(A) The address of his workplace
(B) An alternative contact number
(C) An identification number
(D) A date for a repeat visit

86 Where is the speaker most likely calling from?

(A) An airport
(B) A taxi stand
(C) A bus stop
(D) A pet shop

87 What does the speaker imply when she says, "but it isn't easy thus far"?

(A) She cannot get a taxi.
(B) She is stuck in traffic.
(C) She doesn't know where the taxi stand is.
(D) She thinks the destination is too far away.

88 What does the speaker ask the listener to do?

(A) Call back
(B) Walk the pet
(C) Feed her pet
(D) Close the bedroom door

89 Who most likely are the listeners?

(A) Competition participants
(B) Festival goers
(C) Security guards
(D) Conference attendees

90 What does the speaker imply when she says, "I'm going to need you for a little more time"?

(A) The listeners are in a hurry to leave.
(B) The event will go longer than expected.
(C) The speaker is busy with other projects.
(D) The audience wants the event to end soon.

91 What is the speaker distributing to the listeners?

(A) Brochures
(B) Greeting cards
(C) Survey forms
(D) Vouchers

| Types of services | Fastshipping | BSS |
|---|---|---|
| Additional charge for an international shipping | O | O |
| Arrival notification service | O | O |
| Package pickup | O | O |
| Breakage insurance | | O |

92 Who most likely is the speaker?

(A) A business owner
(B) A retiring employee
(C) A technician
(D) A professor in a college

93 What is the main purpose of the meeting?

(A) To recruit more employees
(B) To open a new branch
(C) To improve the service
(D) To analyze a rival company

94 Look at the graphic. What will the speaker most likely discuss next?

(A) Additional charge for international shipping
(B) Arrival notification service
(C) Package pickup
(D) Breakage insurance

| Survey Results | |
| --- | --- |
| Waste treatment system | 35% |
| Enlarging Parking Lot | 30% |
| Fitness Facility | 25% |
| Repainting work | 10% |

| Departing Flight | Destination | Departure Time |
| --- | --- | --- |
| 742 | London | 2:00 P.M. |
| 707 | Seattle | 3:15 P.M. |
| 747 | Los Angeles | 3:30 P.M. |
| 778 | Hawaii | 5:30 P.M. |

**95** What is the focus on the meeting?

(A) Improving the community center
(B) Meeting residents' requests
(C) Raising money
(D) Remodeling commercial facilities

**96** Look at the graphic. What does the speaker want to focus on?

(A) Waste treatment system
(B) Enlarging parking lot
(C) Fitness facility
(D) Repainting work

**97** What does the speaker want from the listeners?

(A) A decision on whether to increase rent
(B) A suggestion for a new parking lot
(C) A tentative contract
(D) A new floor plan

**98** What is the cause of the delay?

(A) Inclement weather
(B) A mechanical flaw
(C) A human error
(D) A routine maintenance

**99** Look at the graphic. What is the updated time for the flight?

(A) 2:00 P.M.
(B) 3:15 P.M.
(C) 3:30 P.M.
(D) 5:30 P.M.

**100** What are the listeners asked to do?

(A) Board the airplane in advance
(B) Wait for the announcement
(C) Follow the staff members
(D) Buy some food

This is the end of the Listening test. Turn to Part 5 in your test book.

GO ON TO THE NEXT PAGE

# READING TEST

In the Reading test, you will read a variety of texts and answer several different types of reading comprehension questions. The entire Reading test will last 75 minutes. There are three parts, and directions are given for each part. You are encouraged to answer as many questions as possible within the time allowed.

You must mark your answers on the separate answer sheet. Do not write your answers in your test book.

## PART 5

**Directions:** A word or phrase is missing in each of the sentences below. Four answer choices are given below each sentence. Select the best answer to complete the sentence. Then mark the letter (A), (B), (C), or (D) on your answer sheet.

**101** Sanmark has ------- introduced a new kitchen appliance to the market.

(A) successes
(B) successfully
(C) successful
(D) success

**102** Broadband access may be cut off by ------- Manote Communications or the service provider.

(A) either
(B) both
(C) however
(D) plus

**103** Carmen Sanchez, a well-known -------, received praise for her campaign to save the polar bear.

(A) environmental
(B) environmentalist
(C) environmentally
(D) environments

**104** With such a positive response to the Alansi organic food promotion, the marketing team plans ------- production by 40 percent in the next six months.

(A) increase
(B) increasing
(C) increases
(D) to increase

**105** Our partnership on the publicity drive is an example of how efficient teamwork can lead to ------- results.

(A) excellently
(B) excellent
(C) excel
(D) excellence

**106** The Reventure software is ------- specifically for organizations that want to monitor workers when they are away from the office.

(A) designed
(B) appointed
(C) accomplished
(D) informed

**107** Two days ago, Ms. Hayes told people that the piles of paperwork in the corner were -------.

(A) she
(B) hers
(C) her
(D) herself

**108** Reconstruction of the pipeline was ------- planned to be completed by February 11.

(A) originally
(B) extremely
(C) strongly
(D) highly

109 As a response to employee -------, our offices will be opened earlier in the morning.
(A) suggestions
(B) suggest
(C) suggests
(D) suggested

110 As well as soft drinks, a selection of canapés will be provided ------- the employee orientation course.
(A) during
(B) along
(C) onto
(D) about

111 Mr. McBride applauded the workers for ------- dedication during the recent production run.
(A) their
(B) them
(C) theirs
(D) they

112 Laymon's DVD store received positive ------- for its customer service from members of the public.
(A) impact
(B) access
(C) feedback
(D) experience

113 Before ------- the winners of the awards, please make sure that they are all in attendance in the main dining hall.
(A) announcing
(B) announced
(C) announcement
(D) announcer

114 Several efforts were made to ease traffic congestion on the main highway, ------- of which addressed any problems.
(A) none
(B) nothing
(C) nobody
(D) neither

115 The Dunlop County History Museum ------- by the local historical research society.
(A) maintained
(B) is maintained
(C) is maintaining
(D) can maintain

116 Amaize County has attracted a large number of new businesses ------- its low taxes and bountiful workforce.
(A) as a result
(B) owing to
(C) now that
(D) because

117 We will notify you ------- our employment decision on or after November 1st.
(A) to
(B) of
(C) for
(D) from

118 Acquisition of the newest equipment can have a significant impact on a company's overall -------.
(A) profitable
(B) profitability
(C) profitably
(D) profited

119 Our staffing assignments are adjusted ------- to make sure that all employees have an opportunity to work directly with our customers.
(A) previously
(B) accordingly
(C) periodically
(D) extremely

120 ------- the hotel's reception desk is open around the clock, the free shuttle service to and from the airport is only available from 6 A.M. to 10 P.M.
(A) Despite
(B) However
(C) Although
(D) Nevertheless

GO ON TO THE NEXT PAGE

121 ------- that the recent inclement weather will reduce tourism to Sunnyside Island, several local hotel operators have announced special offers.

(A) Concerning
(B) Concerned
(C) Been concerned
(D) To have been concerning

122 ------- company policy, sales associates must obtain a permit from a supervisor before using company equipment personally.

(A) Instead of
(B) As well as
(C) On behalf of
(D) In accordance with

123 At Bergen National Park, you can enjoy a trek up the mountainside and a ------- walk by a lake.

(A) persistent
(B) conclusive
(C) leisurely
(D) tolerant

124 The financial district is located in downtown Starnberg and is easily ------- by public transport.

(A) accessible
(B) active
(C) necessary
(D) transportable

125 ------- Wesler employee revealing confidential company information to others will be terminated.

(A) All
(B) Several
(C) Few
(D) Any

126 Starkland officials and Thronin Construction Engineers are currently engaged in ------- over the proposals to construct a new ring road.

(A) negotiations
(B) receipts
(C) construction
(D) increase

127 The initiative that Mayor Tomlinson ------- to improve the highways, involved sectioning off a part of Route 22 for use by public transport only.

(A) implementing
(B) implement
(C) implemented
(D) implements

128 Employees must have been employed for a minimum of a year to be ------- for the company's pension scheme.

(A) compatible
(B) eligible
(C) responsive
(D) flexible

129 Mr. Khalid has indicated that he is willing to travel abroad ------- it would be of benefit to his organization's future prospects.

(A) somewhere
(B) whenever
(C) himself
(D) whether

130 A reduction in operating costs is one ------- for investing in new technology in the workplace.

(A) justification
(B) condolence
(C) translation
(D) diagnosis

# PART 6

**Directions:** Read the texts that follow. A word, phrase, or sentence is missing in parts of each text. Four answer choices for each question are given below the text. Select the best answer to complete the text. Then mark the letter (A), (B), (C), or (D) on your answer sheet.

**Questions 131-134** refer to the following flyer.

---

### Attention Performing Artists!

Are you interested in an exclusive opportunity to perform on stage at our theater?

-------, you are invited to sign up for a chance to display your talent at the York Open
 **131.**
Festival on June 23.

Entry forms are available online at www.yorkopen.org and your performance will be

judged by several performers from events staged at our local theater. Together with

your completed entry form, please upload ------- of your specialist area. -------.
                                        **132.**                              **133.**

The application deadline is May 1, and the judges' decisions will be made on that day.

------- applicants will have use of the stage facilities and will be expected to stay for the
 **134.**
duration of the event.

---

131 (A) Instead
 (B) Even so
 (C) If so
 (D) After that

132 (A) developments
 (B) instructions
 (C) details
 (D) requirements

133 (A) We have already finished reviewing all of the entry forms.
 (B) This will help the judges to put you into the correct category.
 (C) You need to obtain necessary forms at the reception desk.
 (D) Performing on stage requires courage and the ability to react instantly.

134 (A) Invited
 (B) Invites
 (C) Invitation
 (D) Inviting

GO ON TO THE NEXT PAGE

Montana (March 15) — Max-Gas, a popular national chain of gas stations, will be opening its first two stations in Montana soon. The company's stations feature large 24-hour convenience stores with a wide array of snacks, beverages, and other daily necessities. -------, Max-Gas stations are well known for being efficiently managed and **135.**
having friendly staff. -------.
**136.**
Montana's first Max-Gas will be constructed at the corner of Lloyd Street and 10th Avenue. The ------- one, to be situated at Kisco Street and 20th Avenue, will be a **137.**
special Max-Gas station, equipped with a small kitchen facility. Like other special stations, this one will have tables and chairs ------- patrons can sit down and eat.
**138.**

135 (A) Nonetheless
(B) After all
(C) Besides
(D) Namely

136 (A) Improvements of highways are attributed to government's effort.
(B) They also pride themselves on their safe and clean amenities.
(C) Commuters are driving their cars less and less as the price of gasoline rises.
(D) The availability of consumer goods will increase in the near future.

137 (A) similar
(B) former
(C) rival
(D) second

138 (A) there
(B) whose
(C) which
(D) where

**To:** dcarlton@jetmail.net

**From:** jdelphi@houndban.com

**Date:** April 5

**Subject:** Your Interview

Dear Mr. Carlton:

I am writing on behalf of the hiring team at Houndban, Inc. The team was very impressed with your interview on Thursday. -------, you were one of the most promising candidates.
**139.**
-------. Instead we would like to invite you to send your résumé to our Fineville office.
**140.**
It is currently looking for a senior accountant. ------- your experience and knowledge,
**141.**
you would be an asset to Houndban, Inc. If you are willing to consider relocating to Fineville, we would be happy to recommend you for the ------- there.
**142.**

Sincerely,

Joanne Delphi

---

**139** (A) Otherwise
(B) Meanwhile
(C) In fact
(D) As always

**140** (A) We never received a copy of your reference letter.
(B) We think you don't have enough experience.
(C) We would like you to intern with our company.
(D) Unfortunately, we are unable to offer you a position at this time.

**141** (A) Now that
(B) Given
(C) Unlike
(D) Also

**142** (A) program
(B) lodging
(C) vacancy
(D) training

**GO ON TO THE NEXT PAGE**

Test 06

---

### New Library Opens

September 10 — The city's new library branch at Victory Center began serving patrons two days ago. The mayor was ------- for the opening ceremony. Moreover, members of
**143.**
several local community groups and schoolchildren ------- in the event.
**144.**

The new 1,200-square-meter library was designed with environmental considerations in mind. -------. In addition, 60% of the building's electricity comes from solar panels
**145.**
on its roof.

One of the library's objectives is to connect users to cutting-edge -------. While there
**146.**
are plenty of reference materials, there are also lots of computer terminals. Patrons can also bring their own devices to use the library's free ultra-high-speed Internet.

---

**143** (A) presented
(B) presenting
(C) present
(D) presently

**144** (A) participated
(B) participating
(C) will participate
(D) would have participated

**145** (A) It has five large air-conditioning units.
(B) A famous architect designed it.
(C) It is heated entirely by the sun.
(D) It is close to a subway station.

**146** (A) technology
(B) vehicles
(C) education
(D) appliance

# PART 7

**Directions:** In this part you will read a selection of texts, such as magazine and newspaper articles, e-mails, and instant messages. Each text or set of texts is followed by several questions. Select the best answer for each question and mark the letter (A), (B), (C), or (D) on your answer sheet.

**Questions 147-148** refer to the following advertisement.

## *Newhaven Retirement Village*

Newhaven Retirement Village is now leasing!

- One-and two-bedroom apartments

- Located in the center of downtown Newhaven, this new 48-unit residential village caters to retired people.

- On-site amenities include two communal lounges, a swimming pool and fitness center, and ample parking, all included in the monthly rental charge.

- This village is in a perfect location, overlooking Waterdown Bridge and close to shops and public amenities.

- Visit our showroom apartments and see what we have available. Our leasing agents are on hand to take prospective tenants around the village.

Newhaven Retirement Village
32 Treetop Road
Newhaven
857-555-4125
www.newhavenretirementvillage.com

**147** What does the advertisement describe?

(A) Retirement homes for rent
(B) Corporate relocation service
(C) Local visitors' attractions
(D) Vacation homes for sale

**148** What are the readers invited to do?

(A) Purchase a membership
(B) Take a tour
(C) Sign an agreement
(D) Send a deposit payment

GO ON TO THE NEXT PAGE

Questions 149-150 refer to the following e-mail.

---

**E-Mail Message**

**To:** Kelmer Manufacturing Employees
**From:** Sally Arnold <arsally@kelmer.com>
**Date:** February 12
**Subject:** Company Information

---

Recently, we sent all staff members a copy of our new employee manual, together with
a separate acknowledgement form.

The manual contains complete information regarding the policies and procedures of Kelmer Manufacturing. Additionally, it contains details about job descriptions and employee benefits. Please read the manual carefully and sign the acknowledgement form enclosed, confirming that you have read and understood the rules and procedures as described in the manual, and that you undertake to follow company rules.

Please send your signed forms to John Feathers in Human Resources.
Thank you for your cooperation in this matter.

Sally Arnold
Managing Director, Human Resources

---

**149** What does Ms. Arnold discuss in the e-mail?

(A) A training course
(B) An employment opportunity
(C) A company publication
(D) A change in employment procedures

**150** What does Ms. Arnold ask employees to do?

(A) Sign and send a form
(B) Review their job benefits
(C) Attend a meeting
(D) Return a book

Thank you for purchasing a Mission B-452 laptop computer. Our free anti-virus software is included in your laptop purchase. As this is our introductory version, it is recommended that you purchase the complete edition soon. You can order the full version directly from Mission at our online store, www.missioncomputers.com. We guarantee that you will receive an immediate download and the software package will be delivered to you within five working days. If you do not receive it by that time, we will provide a full refund. As a valued customer, you will receive a 15 percent discount off your first software purchase. Just type in code 41230 when placing your order. If you would prefer to purchase software through a retail outlet, our packages are stocked by all leading computer equipment stores. However, please be aware that most retailers do not allow customers our corporate discount.

Call 800-555-3412, 24 hours a day for technical support or 800-555-3412 Monday through Friday 8 A.M. to 9 P.M. with any questions or feedback about your purchase.

**Test 06**

**151** For whom was the notice written?
(A) Owners of new laptop computers
(B) Sales advisors
(C) Technical support professionals
(D) Software developers

**152** What promise is made about placing orders for software?
(A) The introductory software continues for three months.
(B) The buyer receives the software for free if delivery is late.
(C) The technical department will respond to queries promptly.
(D) Customer service is provided 24/7.

**153** How can shoppers receive a discount?
(A) By purchasing items from a computer store
(B) By mailing a voucher
(C) By calling customer support
(D) By entering numbers when ordering online

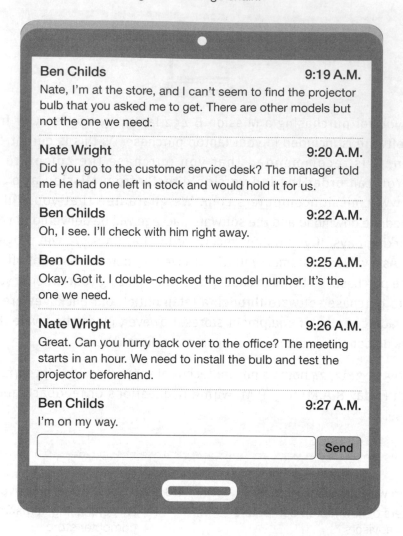

**Ben Childs**        9:19 A.M.

Nate, I'm at the store, and I can't seem to find the projector bulb that you asked me to get. There are other models but not the one we need.

**Nate Wright**        9:20 A.M.

Did you go to the customer service desk? The manager told me he had one left in stock and would hold it for us.

**Ben Childs**        9:22 A.M.

Oh, I see. I'll check with him right away.

**Ben Childs**        9:25 A.M.

Okay. Got it. I double-checked the model number. It's the one we need.

**Nate Wright**        9:26 A.M.

Great. Can you hurry back over to the office? The meeting starts in an hour. We need to install the bulb and test the projector beforehand.

**Ben Childs**        9:27 A.M.

I'm on my way.

Send

**154** What is most likely true about Mr. Wright?

(A) He gave Mr. Childs the wrong model number.

(B) He contacted the store about a projector bulb.

(C) He plans to return to the office right away.

(D) He is going to give a presentation.

**155** At 9:22 A.M., what does Mr. Childs mean when he writes, "Oh, I see"?

(A) He found the last projector bulb.

(B) He is still looking around the store.

(C) He understands the situation now.

(D) He can see the customer service desk.

# A Note from the Editor

This September issue of *Thailand Cuisine* coincides with the magazine's second anniversary. It has been two years since we published our first issue, and since then we have become one of the area's most popular magazines on ethnic cooking. Our circulation recently reached 22,000, and the number continues to rise.

Local food lovers have praised our publication, and we were awarded the accolade of Best New Food Magazine at last month's World Food Festival. As Senior Editor, I would like to express my appreciation for our dedicated staff, our writers, our advertisers, and our growing community of readers, all of whom have contributed greatly to our success.

Stella Morgan

**156** What is the purpose of Ms. Morgan's note?

(A) To make an offer available
(B) To ask for contributions
(C) To express appreciation
(D) To introduce a writer

**157** What is indicated about *Thailand Cuisine*?

(A) It is becoming increasingly popular.
(B) It has increased its advertising charges.
(C) It will soon be distributed worldwide.
(D) It is seeking additional contributors.

**158** Why does Ms. Morgan mention the World Food Festival?

(A) Because the magazine received an award at the event
(B) Because the publishers sponsored the event
(C) Because she recruited extra volunteers there
(D) Because she held a cooking demonstration

**From:** Geraldine Compton
**To:** Bickford Marketing employees
**Subject:** Stanley Haynes

We are pleased to announce that Mr. Stanley Haynes, Managing Director of our Singapore branch office, is due to visit our office in Washington, D.C., in two weeks' time. Mr. Haynes has worked with Bickford Marketing for five years as a research analyst and Web site designer before transferring to Asia.

Mr. Haynes has successfully worked for the last two years setting up the online division of our Singapore branch. As a result, sales figures have continued to rise significantly, and Bickford has now become an established name in Asia.

Mr. Haynes will be leading a discussion focusing on social media marketing. The presentation, which will be very detailed, will be followed by a question-and-answer session. We encourage participants to take notes during the meeting.

All staff are required to attend, but in the case of a scheduling conflict, please contact Ms. Walker or your office manager.

We look forward to seeing you soon.

Sincerely,
Bickford Marketing

159 What does the memo announce?

(A) An upcoming business presentation
(B) The celebration of a company's five-year anniversary
(C) Employment opportunities in the Singapore office
(D) The appointment of a new company director

160 What is indicated about Mr. Haynes?

(A) He was recently hired by Mr. Bickford.
(B) He referred a client to Bickford Marketing.
(C) He will be managing the Washington office.
(D) He has experience in online marketing development.

161 According to the memo, what should participants bring with them to the meeting?

(A) A sheet of prepared questions
(B) A list of marketing topics
(C) Copies of their résumés
(D) Note-taking materials

Sharm Ra Hotels

50 Merino Street

Cairo, Egypt

August 7

To all interested applicants:

Thank you for your inquiry concerning training opportunities at Sharma Ra Hotels. We offer a small number of paid summer traineeships to qualified applicants who wish to make a career in the holiday and hotel industries. Applicants selected to participate in our training scheme gain hands-on experience in a true life working environment and work with tutors on specific projects related to their individual aspirations.

Please find enclosed an application packet and job descriptions for each department. After reading these thoroughly, please apply directly to the section in which you are interested. Completed applications should be received by the end of this month. Interviews will be held with selected applicants during the first week of September. The trainee programs begin February 1 and end on March 10. We look forward to receiving your applications shortly.

Sincerely,

Selma Banks

Selma Banks

Traineeships organizer

Enclosures

Test 06

162 What is suggested about the recipients of the letter?

(A) They have already contacted Sharm Ra Hotels.
(B) They will be interviewed by Selma Banks.
(C) They are planning their vacations.
(D) They work at tourist offices.

163 What are the recipients of the letter asked to review?

(A) A brochure describing the hotels
(B) The company's financial procedures
(C) A list of changes to a program
(D) Information about training projects

164 When are applications due?

(A) On August 31
(B) On September 4
(C) On February 1
(D) On March 10

GO ON TO THE NEXT PAGE

**Sam Jenkins**    − X

**Sam Jenkins** [10:15 A.M.]    Since we are preparing our budget for the next fiscal year, we should discuss replacing the laptops our sales team have been using. They have been complaining about them for some time now.

**Louise Parker** [10:17 A.M.]    What's the problem? I thought we gave them new laptops.

**Eddie Swanson** [10:22 A.M.]    It's been five years already. They are getting slow, but the bigger issue is that they are not going to handle our next software upgrades. They just don't have the power.

**Jeff Long** [10:25 A.M.]    We are scheduled to install the new inventory database in a few months. So we don't have a lot of time to make a decision.

**Eddie Swanson** [10:28 A.M.]    Right. I would also suggest getting something that can better withstand wear and tear this time.

**Jeff Long** [10:29 A.M.]    Then I would suggest a Kingston. The company just came out with a new model in the XM line that has gotten great reviews.

**Louise Parker** [10:30 A.M.]    What are we talking about in terms of price?

**Jeff Long** [10:31 A.M.]    They start at $1,000 each. Equipping 22 employees is not going to be cheap.

**Louise Parker** [10:32 A.M.]    No, but if it saves us money in the long run, then it's worth it.

**Sam Jenkins** [10:33 A.M.]    Okay, well, before we decide, I think we should compare at least three or four options.

**Jeff Long** [10:36 A.M.]    I'll look into that.

Send

**165** What is indicated about the sales team?

(A) They recently updated their inventory software.
(B) They have used the same equipment for several years.
(C) They recently submitted a budget request for laptops.
(D) They are having problems processing sales orders.

**166** What is suggested about the current laptops?

(A) They cost more than $1,000.
(B) Their power supplies failed.
(C) They will soon be obsolete.
(D) They were bought at a discount.

**167** What is implied about Kingston?

(A) Its laptops are durable.
(B) The company cannot afford them.
(C) It makes one model.
(D) It is the top-rated brand.

**168** At 10:36 A.M., what does Mr. Long mean when he writes, "I'll look into that"?

(A) He will determine how money can be saved.
(B) He will gather information on different models.
(C) He will ask employees what laptop they prefer.
(D) He will confirm the price of the Kingston.

GO ON TO THE NEXT PAGE

**Integrated Irrigation and Vegetable Production in Brazil (IIVPB)**

54 Rua 3
Gravata, Brazil
www.vpb.br

# POSITION VACANT

For 10 years, IIVPB has been educating smallholders in the use of organic growing methods. -(1)-. The aim is to increase production while using the latest research in irrigation methods and maintaining the high quality of organic growing methods. -(2)-. We are an independently-funded organization based in São Paolo, with additional locations in the Brazilian states of Paraiba, Bahia, Pernambuco, and Rio Grande do Norte.

-(3)-. The successful candidate will lead the research and act as a liaison between the research team and owners of smallholdings. The successful applicant must have a solid scientific research background, preferably agricultural, and have a minimum of four years of professional managerial experience.

Please submit applications, accompanied by a cover letter and résumé, in person, by e-mail, by regular mail or on our Web site, www.iivpb.br/careers, by November 10. The successful applicant is expected to begin his or her duties on December 10. –(4)–.

**169** What is indicated about IIVPB?

(A) It is committed to using modern irrigation procedures.
(B) It is revising its corporate mission.
(C) It sells irrigation equipment.
(D) It receives financial assistance from the government.

**170** What is NOT suggested about the position?

(A) It will be filled before the end of the year.
(B) It involves liaison between parties.
(C) It requires experience in project management.
(D) It is restricted to Brazilian nationals.

**171** In which of the positions marked [1], [2], [3], and [4] does the following sentence best belong?

"We are looking to fill the position of Project Manager at our Paraiba location."

(A) [1]
(B) [2]
(C) [3]
(D) [4]

## Employee Focus: Stacey May

Stacey May, who plans to step down as senior underwriter in March, has served Trafford Insurance in many roles for 25 years. Insurance company president Geoffrey Marks said, "It's seldom that one finds the range of experience at Trafford that Stacey has." –[1]–.

Ms. May began her career in insurance as a temporary administrative assistant at Simpson Insurance Brokers in Harlowe. She found the work to be very satisfying, and at the end of her contract, started to seek a permanent position in the industry. –[2]–. After eighteen months of answering telephones and routine administrative duties, Ms. May was hired as a trainee underwriter at Trafford Insurance's Eggington branch, and in less than just six months, was promoted to junior underwriter. –[3]–.

However, Ms. May continued her climb upwards in the ranks. She explained, "I enjoyed learning about insurance policies and wanted to become a senior underwriter. My manager at the Eggington branch, Craig Ling, gave me advice on how to proceed. On Craig's recommendation, I decided to apply for the insurance studies program at Butterick College in Anderton, just as Craig had done five years before. I financed my course by applying for a student loan and continued to work as a junior underwriter part-time. It took me six years to complete the insurance degree." –[4]–.

Once she had graduated from Butterick College, Ms. May joined the insurance department at Trafford Insurance's headquarters. Two years later, she was appointed assistant to Senior Underwriter Hope Bennett, and when Ms. Bennett transferred to the large claims division, Ms. May was chosen to take her place. "Just think about that," Ms. May said, "I started out doing the filing, and I ended up as senior underwriter at the company's headquarters."

Test 06

**172** What is the purpose of the article?

(A) To introduce an employee who is retiring after long years of service
(B) To give information regarding applications for training courses
(C) To describe all the job openings at the insurance company
(D) To report on the varied duties of an employee

**173** What is indicated about Mr. Ling?

(A) He was interviewed for the article.
(B) He studied insurance.
(C) He has teaching experience.
(D) He is a part-time underwriter at an insurance company.

**174** What is suggested about Trafford Insurance?

(A) It offers its employees discounts on college fees.
(B) It recently merged with Simpson Insurance Brokers.
(C) Its headquarters are in Eggington.
(D) It has a large claims department.

**175** In which of the positions marked [1], [2], [3], and [4] does the following sentence best belong?

"She found employment as a permanent administrative officer at Trafford's Anderton branch."

(A) [1]
(B) [2]
(C) [3]
(D) [4]

GO ON TO THE NEXT PAGE

# The 10th Mansfield Art and Drama Festival

## October 10-12

The Mansfield Art and Drama Festival, sponsored by Mansfield Cultural Association, has something for everyone. The events, lasting three days, will feature exhibits by prominent artists and entertainment by local musicians and actors. Refreshments and crafts will be available for purchase and a variety of children's activities are scheduled.

Here are some of the events:

### Friday, October 10, 4 PM, Art Gallery Picasso
The opening of Elena Martin's Portraits of My Family. Exhibition runs through 17 November. Open Monday to Friday, 10.30 A.M. to 8 P.M., Saturday and Sunday, noon to 6 P.M. Admission is free.

### Saturday & Sunday, October 11-12, 11 AM to 7 PM, St. Mary's RC Church
Children's arts and crafts and play activities. Admission is free.

### Saturday, October 11, 3 PM, Risedale Open Air Theater
(Rain relocation: Welbury Theater) Concert by the Peruvian Youth Choir (as requested by popular demand). Tickets available at the door.

### Saturday & Sunday, October 11-12, 1 PM to 7 PM, McLean Memorial
Ethnic Food and Crafts Fair

### Sunday, October 12, 6 PM to 8 PM, Fennymore Theater
The Stowbridge Theater Company presents Summer at the Farm by the playwright Stel Gosse. Tickets available at the door.

Pre-booking available beginning October 1. For further details and a complete list of events, please visit us at www.madf.org.

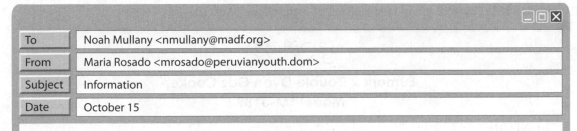

| To | Noah Mullany <nmullany@madf.org> |
| From | Maria Rosado <mrosado@peruvianyouth.dom> |
| Subject | Information |
| Date | October 15 |

Dear Mr. Mullany,

This is to thank you once again for inviting us to perform our Peruvian music at the Mansfield Arts and Drama Festival. It was such bad luck that it rained so heavily that we had to perform indoors, since that meant a much smaller audience could enjoy our performance. However, we were delighted with the ovation we received from the audience. Many people purchased our CDs or asked us whether our music could be downloaded from popular music Web sites.

We hope we will have the privilege of participating in future festivals.

Sincerely,
Maria Rosado
Events manager
Peruvian Youth Choir

**176** What event is NOT scheduled to take place at 6 P.M. on Sunday?

(A) A craft-making program
(B) An art showing
(C) An ethnic food market
(D) A ballet performance

**177** What is indicated about the Festival?

(A) It is being advertised online.
(B) It starts at 11 A.M. each morning.
(C) It takes place three times a year.
(D) It has the duration of one week.

**178** When is a play to be performed?

(A) October 1
(B) October 9
(C) October 10
(D) October 12

**179** Why did Ms. Rosado send Mr. Mullany an e-mail?

(A) To express her thanks
(B) To request tickets for a performance
(C) To cancel her reservation
(D) To cancel a performance

**180** What is suggested about the Peruvian Youth Choir?

(A) It has more people accessing its Web site.
(B) It is currently on tour in South America.
(C) It performed at Welbury Theater.
(D) It participated in the Festival for the first time.

## Eumark 2 Double Oven Gas Cooker
## Model EM-3189

FEATURES:

- Extra-large double oven accommodates more cooking than standard cookers.
- Heat-treated steel exterior offers excellent protection from rust and easier cleaning.
- Integral automatic timer lets you know when your food is cooked. Control panel lights indicate the optimum cooking temperature.
- New SaveEnergy technology provides a varied temperature control that uses less gas than most other models.
- A variety of burners for small, medium and large cooking pans
- Three-shelf design enables the cooker to bake, roast and warm food at the same time so your meals are totally coordinated.

---

WWW.EUMARK.COM

| **Review** | **Products** | **Terms and Conditions** | **Locations** |

**"Great value for money"**

Posted by: Abigail Davies
Posted on: September 14
Located in: Berkshire, UK

My previous cooker was manufactured by another company and only lasted three years. I was delighted when Eumark designed this very advanced but inexpensive model. I didn't think it would be as economical as my previous appliance, but I was pleasantly surprised. This appliance cooks all types of food perfectly. The oven has three tiers internally (bake, roast and warm) and four different burners (small, medium and two large) to suit a variety of pot sizes. I am also particularly impressed with the fact that the oven turns itself off when cooking is complete, so that I can leave it and go out. It is also available in a wide range of bright colors. Best of all, Eumark has designed the cooker to be long lasting. My only complaint is that it has so many functions that it took me a long time to figure them out. I had to study the manual very carefully to follow all the instructions.

181 What is indicated in the list of features?

(A) A set of instructions for cooking recipes
(B) The positive characteristics of a product
(C) Information about the various types of oven gas cooker
(D) All types of food which can be made by Eumark 2 Double Oven Gas Cooker

182 According to the list of features, what is an advantage of SaveEnergy technology?

(A) It uses less energy.
(B) It saves the customer time.
(C) It extends the durability of the appliance.
(D) It makes the item easier to clean.

183 In the Web site, the word "suit" in paragraph 1, line 6, is closest in meaning to

(A) accommodate
(B) dress up
(C) qualify
(D) appeal to

184 What criticism does Ms. Davies make about the product?

(A) It is complicated.
(B) It is too heavy.
(C) It is too noisy.
(D) It is expensive.

185 What feature does Ms. Davies like that is NOT mentioned in the product description?

(A) Its number of hobs
(B) Its large oven size
(C) Its variety of appearance
(D) Its cooking settings

GO ON TO THE NEXT PAGE

## Upgrade your computer skills with
### New Technology Campus
### Fall Course Offerings (Term 1)

Working with Databases (Basic-level Course)                      $975
  8 sessions (9:30 A.M. – 11:45 A.M.)
  Starting: September 3

Word Processing Boot Camp (Intermediate-level Course)    $825
  6 sessions (8:30 A.M. – 11:30 A.M.)
  Starting: September 10

Perfecting Presentation Software (Advanced-level Course)   $775
  5 sessions (1:00 P.M. – 5:30 P.M.)
  Starting: September 17

Spreadsheet Secrets (Intermediate-level Course)          $450
  4 sessions (9:00 A.M. – 12:15 P.M.)
  Starting: September 24

All classes are held on Saturdays at

Lowman Continuing Education Building
8904 Lightfoot Avenue, Vernon
(818) 555-9303

Register at www.newtechnologycampus.com.
A nonrefundable deposit (10% of tuition)
is due at the time of registration.

---

| | |
|---|---|
| From | Tom Barton <tbarton@nevis.com> |
| To | Brenda Lane <blane@newtechnologycampus.com> |
| Date | August 20 |
| Subject | Fall Courses |

Dear Ms. Lane:

I am writing because I am having trouble submitting my online registration. I would like to join the class for beginners you are offering next month. Please let me know how to arrange the payment. I am prepared to pay the full tuition up front, but will request reimbursement from my company.

Therefore, I need a receipt.

Sincerely,
Tom Barton

Dear Mr. Barton,

Your course will start next week. Please note that a room has not yet been assigned. Therefore, we ask that you come at least fifteen minutes prior to your class' scheduled starting time. Upon arrival, please check in at the security desk located at the building's east entrance. You will receive a temporary parking permit and ID badge. In addition, you will be directed to your classroom at that time.

If you have not paid the balance of your tuition, you will need to do so on your starting date. A representative from the admissions office will be present in the lobby.

If you have any questions, please feel free to call us at (818) 555-8787.

**186** What is indicated about the New Technology Campus courses?

(A) They allow for in-person registration.
(B) They require advanced payment.
(C) They are only offered in the morning.
(D) They limit the number of participants.

**187** What is true about the course Mr. Barton wants to take?

(A) It will meet a total of six times.
(B) It will be held in the afternoon.
(C) It will cost his company $450.
(D) It will meet for fewer than three hours.

**188** In the e-mail, the word "full" in paragraph 1, line 3, is closest in meaning to

(A) entire
(B) extra
(C) important
(D) overdue

**189** According to the postcard, what should Mr. Barton do?

(A) Arrive early for his first class
(B) Bring a form of identification
(C) Park in a special area
(D) Issue a parking permit

**190** What is suggested about the postcard?

(A) It was mailed to Mr. Barton's workplace.
(B) It was written by Ms. Lane.
(C) It requires a response from Mr. Barton.
(D) It was sent before September 3.

GO ON TO THE NEXT PAGE

**Questions 191-195** refer to the following Web site, article, and e-mail message.

www.fabulousfoods.com

| About Us | Products | Branches | Online Sales | Contact Us |

Our Story

Fabulous Foods started in 1920 as Fabulous Bakery in a small town in western New York. Owner and founder David Hecht baked breads and sweets by using his family's secret recipes. The company started making potato chips and other snack foods in the 1950s. Hecht decided to sell the company in 1958 to a group of investors who renamed it Fabulous Foods. The new owners sold the bakery operation and focused exclusively on the development and production of potato chips, corn chips, popcorn, and other tasty snacks, including a popular low-fat line for health-conscious consumers. Today, Fabulous Foods distributes its products to retail stores in all 50 U.S. states, Canada, and Mexico.

BUFFALO (July 16) — On Sunday, July 21, a series of foot races will be held at the city's Burlington Park to raise money for health education. The Race for Your Health features 15 km, 10 km, and 5 km races, with the earliest starting at 7:30 A.M. Participants can compete in six different categories based on age and gender. Prizes will be awarded to the top three finishers in each category. There will also be a noncompetitive 2 km fun walk for people of all ages. Several local businesses, including Burlington Sports Drinks and Fabulous Foods, as well as St. James Hospital are sponsoring the event. To register, visit www.racehealth. org. There is a $25 fee for the fun walk and a $45 fee for the races. Participants will receive a T-shirt, complimentary beverages and promotional items from the sponsors.

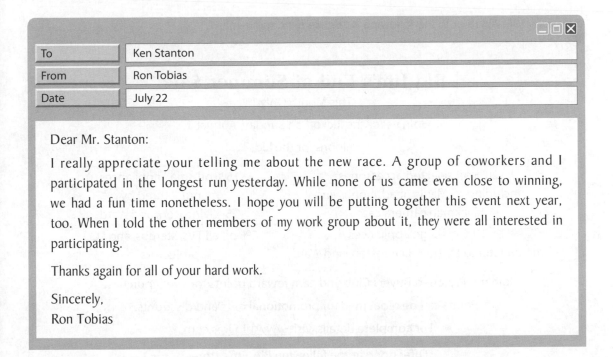

To          Ken Stanton

From        Ron Tobias

Date        July 22

Dear Mr. Stanton:

I really appreciate your telling me about the new race. A group of coworkers and I participated in the longest run yesterday. While none of us came even close to winning, we had a fun time nonetheless. I hope you will be putting together this event next year, too. When I told the other members of my work group about it, they were all interested in participating.

Thanks again for all of your hard work.

Sincerely,

Ron Tobias

**191** On the Web site, the word "operation" in paragraph 1, line 5, is closest in meaning to

(A) business
(B) equipment
(C) procedure
(D) surgery

**192** What is indicated about Fabulous Foods?

(A) It regularly sponsors events.
(B) It donates money to schools.
(C) It has a factory in Canada.
(D) It is located in Buffalo.

**193** In the article, what is NOT mentioned about the event?

(A) Children are eligible to participate.
(B) A payment is required to register.
(C) Eighteen prizes will be awarded.
(D) All races will be finished by noon.

**194** Who most likely is Mr. Stanton?

(A) The winner of the 15 km race
(B) The organizer of the Race for Your Health
(C) A public health worker at St. James Hospital
(D) A colleague at Mr. Tobias's company

**195** What is suggested about Mr. Tobias?

(A) He ran in the 10 km event.
(B) He paid $25 to participate.
(C) He received free food.
(D) He was given a prize.

GO ON TO THE NEXT PAGE

# Big Jim's End of Summer Sale

This Month Only

Join us for the kickoff on Sunday, August 1

Balloons for the kids

| | |
|---|---|
| 20% off selected accessories, including all Magic headphones and Blackman camera cases | 15% off small appliances manufactured by G5, Livingston, and Ward |
| 10% off large appliances manufactured by Titus, Livingston, and Ward | 5% off all TVs, stereos, and LCD projectors |

Join our Preferred Buyers Club and earn reward points for every purchase.

Points can be redeemed for promotional gifts and discounts.

For complete details, visit www.bigjims.com.

Offer good at the following Big Jim's stores

88 Reese Road in Marston 555-0340

7816 Eagle Road in Lincoln 555-2149

908 Jasper Ave in Winston 555-3873

Some products are eligible for free delivery. Check with a store manager.

---

**E-Mail Message**

To:       Sam Long <slong@bigjims.com>
From:     Donna Kingsley <dkingsley@netnet.com>
Subject:  Delivery
Date:     September 2, 8:29 A.M.

Dear Mr. Long:

When I bought my Ward brand dishwasher at your store last week, I originally asked you to deliver it on the third. However, something has come up, and that plan now conflicts with my schedule. Could you deliver it on the sixth at 4:00 P.M. or the seventh at 10:00 A.M.? Please let me know if any of these dates and times work for you. Since your Jasper Avenue store is not that far from my home, I hope that you can do this for me. I'm sorry I was not able to contact you about this matter sooner.

Thanks,

Donna Kingsley

To: Donna Kingsley <dkingsley@netnet.com>
From: Sam Long <slong@bigjims.com>
Subject: RE: Delivery
Date: September 2, 9:09 A.M.

Dear Ms. Kingsley:

We would be happy to accommodate your request for the morning delivery you suggested. One of our drivers will contact you to confirm your address and delivery time. In the meantime, if you have any questions or concerns, feel free to contact us.

Thank you for choosing to do business with us.

Sincerely,
Sam Long

**196** What is NOT indicated about Big Jim's?

(A) It has multiple locations.
(B) It carries electronic equipment.
(C) It gives incentives to loyal shoppers.
(D) It sells products online.

**197** Why did Ms. Kingsley contact Mr. Long?

(A) To confirm a recent order
(B) To inquire about a discount
(C) To change an appointment
(D) To provide a delivery address

**198** What is most likely true about Ms. Kingsley?

(A) She paid for the delivery.
(B) She received a 10% discount.
(C) She lives in Lincoln.
(D) She earned reward points.

**199** In the second e-mail, the word "accommodate" in paragraph 1, line 1, is closest in meaning to

(A) accept
(B) adjust
(C) review
(D) shelter

**200** When will Ms. Kingsley receive her purchase?

(A) On September 2
(B) On September 3
(C) On September 6
(D) On September 7

**Stop! This is the end of the test. If you finish before time is called, you may go back to Parts 5, 6, and 7 and check your work.**

# 新制多益計分換算參考對照表

| 答對題數 | 聽力分數 | 答對題數 | 閱讀分數 |
|---|---|---|---|
| 96-100 | 480-495 | 96-100 | 460-495 |
| 91-95 | 435-490 | 91-95 | 410-475 |
| 86-90 | 395-450 | 86-90 | 380-430 |
| 81-85 | 355-415 | 81-85 | 355-400 |
| 76-80 | 325-375 | 76-80 | 325-375 |
| 71-75 | 295-340 | 71-75 | 295-345 |
| 66-70 | 265-315 | 66-70 | 265-315 |
| 61-65 | 240-285 | 61-65 | 235-285 |
| 56-60 | 215-260 | 56-60 | 205-255 |
| 51-55 | 190-235 | 51-55 | 175-225 |
| 46-50 | 160-210 | 46-50 | 150-195 |
| 41-45 | 135-180 | 41-45 | 120-170 |
| 36-40 | 110-155 | 36-40 | 100-140 |
| 31-35 | 85-130 | 31-35 | 75-120 |
| 26-30 | 70-105 | 26-30 | 55-100 |
| 21-25 | 50-90 | 21-25 | 40-80 |
| 16-20 | 35-75 | 16-20 | 30-65 |
| 11-15 | 20-55 | 11-15 | 20-50 |
| 6-10 | 15-40 | 6-10 | 15-35 |
| 1-5 | 5-20 | 1-5 | 5-20 |
| 0 | 5 | 0 | 5 |

註：上述表格僅供參考，實際計分以官方分數為準。

# Answer Sheet

## READING SECTION

| | A | B | C | D |
|---|---|---|---|---|
| 101 | Ⓐ | Ⓑ | Ⓒ | Ⓓ |
| 102 | Ⓐ | Ⓑ | Ⓒ | Ⓓ |
| 103 | Ⓐ | Ⓑ | Ⓒ | Ⓓ |
| 104 | Ⓐ | Ⓑ | Ⓒ | Ⓓ |
| 105 | Ⓐ | Ⓑ | Ⓒ | Ⓓ |
| 106 | Ⓐ | Ⓑ | Ⓒ | Ⓓ |
| 107 | Ⓐ | Ⓑ | Ⓒ | Ⓓ |
| 108 | Ⓐ | Ⓑ | Ⓒ | Ⓓ |
| 109 | Ⓐ | Ⓑ | Ⓒ | Ⓓ |
| 110 | Ⓐ | Ⓑ | Ⓒ | Ⓓ |
| 111 | Ⓐ | Ⓑ | Ⓒ | Ⓓ |
| 112 | Ⓐ | Ⓑ | Ⓒ | Ⓓ |
| 113 | Ⓐ | Ⓑ | Ⓒ | Ⓓ |
| 114 | Ⓐ | Ⓑ | Ⓒ | Ⓓ |
| 115 | Ⓐ | Ⓑ | Ⓒ | Ⓓ |
| 116 | Ⓐ | Ⓑ | Ⓒ | Ⓓ |
| 117 | Ⓐ | Ⓑ | Ⓒ | Ⓓ |
| 118 | Ⓐ | Ⓑ | Ⓒ | Ⓓ |
| 119 | Ⓐ | Ⓑ | Ⓒ | Ⓓ |
| 120 | Ⓐ | Ⓑ | Ⓒ | Ⓓ |
| 121 | Ⓐ | Ⓑ | Ⓒ | Ⓓ |
| 122 | Ⓐ | Ⓑ | Ⓒ | Ⓓ |
| 123 | Ⓐ | Ⓑ | Ⓒ | Ⓓ |
| 124 | Ⓐ | Ⓑ | Ⓒ | Ⓓ |
| 125 | Ⓐ | Ⓑ | Ⓒ | Ⓓ |
| 126 | Ⓐ | Ⓑ | Ⓒ | Ⓓ |
| 127 | Ⓐ | Ⓑ | Ⓒ | Ⓓ |
| 128 | Ⓐ | Ⓑ | Ⓒ | Ⓓ |
| 129 | Ⓐ | Ⓑ | Ⓒ | Ⓓ |
| 130 | Ⓐ | Ⓑ | Ⓒ | Ⓓ |
| 131 | Ⓐ | Ⓑ | Ⓒ | Ⓓ |
| 132 | Ⓐ | Ⓑ | Ⓒ | Ⓓ |
| 133 | Ⓐ | Ⓑ | Ⓒ | Ⓓ |
| 134 | Ⓐ | Ⓑ | Ⓒ | Ⓓ |
| 135 | Ⓐ | Ⓑ | Ⓒ | Ⓓ |
| 136 | Ⓐ | Ⓑ | Ⓒ | Ⓓ |
| 137 | Ⓐ | Ⓑ | Ⓒ | Ⓓ |
| 138 | Ⓐ | Ⓑ | Ⓒ | Ⓓ |
| 139 | Ⓐ | Ⓑ | Ⓒ | Ⓓ |
| 140 | Ⓐ | Ⓑ | Ⓒ | Ⓓ |
| 141 | Ⓐ | Ⓑ | Ⓒ | Ⓓ |
| 142 | Ⓐ | Ⓑ | Ⓒ | Ⓓ |
| 143 | Ⓐ | Ⓑ | Ⓒ | Ⓓ |
| 144 | Ⓐ | Ⓑ | Ⓒ | Ⓓ |
| 145 | Ⓐ | Ⓑ | Ⓒ | Ⓓ |
| 146 | Ⓐ | Ⓑ | Ⓒ | Ⓓ |
| 147 | Ⓐ | Ⓑ | Ⓒ | Ⓓ |
| 148 | Ⓐ | Ⓑ | Ⓒ | Ⓓ |
| 149 | Ⓐ | Ⓑ | Ⓒ | Ⓓ |
| 150 | Ⓐ | Ⓑ | Ⓒ | Ⓓ |
| 151 | Ⓐ | Ⓑ | Ⓒ | Ⓓ |
| 152 | Ⓐ | Ⓑ | Ⓒ | Ⓓ |
| 153 | Ⓐ | Ⓑ | Ⓒ | Ⓓ |
| 154 | Ⓐ | Ⓑ | Ⓒ | Ⓓ |
| 155 | Ⓐ | Ⓑ | Ⓒ | Ⓓ |
| 156 | Ⓐ | Ⓑ | Ⓒ | Ⓓ |
| 157 | Ⓐ | Ⓑ | Ⓒ | Ⓓ |
| 158 | Ⓐ | Ⓑ | Ⓒ | Ⓓ |
| 159 | Ⓐ | Ⓑ | Ⓒ | Ⓓ |
| 160 | Ⓐ | Ⓑ | Ⓒ | Ⓓ |
| 161 | Ⓐ | Ⓑ | Ⓒ | Ⓓ |
| 162 | Ⓐ | Ⓑ | Ⓒ | Ⓓ |
| 163 | Ⓐ | Ⓑ | Ⓒ | Ⓓ |
| 164 | Ⓐ | Ⓑ | Ⓒ | Ⓓ |
| 165 | Ⓐ | Ⓑ | Ⓒ | Ⓓ |
| 166 | Ⓐ | Ⓑ | Ⓒ | Ⓓ |
| 167 | Ⓐ | Ⓑ | Ⓒ | Ⓓ |
| 168 | Ⓐ | Ⓑ | Ⓒ | Ⓓ |
| 169 | Ⓐ | Ⓑ | Ⓒ | Ⓓ |
| 170 | Ⓐ | Ⓑ | Ⓒ | Ⓓ |
| 171 | Ⓐ | Ⓑ | Ⓒ | Ⓓ |
| 172 | Ⓐ | Ⓑ | Ⓒ | Ⓓ |
| 173 | Ⓐ | Ⓑ | Ⓒ | Ⓓ |
| 174 | Ⓐ | Ⓑ | Ⓒ | Ⓓ |
| 175 | Ⓐ | Ⓑ | Ⓒ | Ⓓ |
| 176 | Ⓐ | Ⓑ | Ⓒ | Ⓓ |
| 177 | Ⓐ | Ⓑ | Ⓒ | Ⓓ |
| 178 | Ⓐ | Ⓑ | Ⓒ | Ⓓ |
| 179 | Ⓐ | Ⓑ | Ⓒ | Ⓓ |
| 180 | Ⓐ | Ⓑ | Ⓒ | Ⓓ |
| 181 | Ⓐ | Ⓑ | Ⓒ | Ⓓ |
| 182 | Ⓐ | Ⓑ | Ⓒ | Ⓓ |
| 183 | Ⓐ | Ⓑ | Ⓒ | Ⓓ |
| 184 | Ⓐ | Ⓑ | Ⓒ | Ⓓ |
| 185 | Ⓐ | Ⓑ | Ⓒ | Ⓓ |
| 186 | Ⓐ | Ⓑ | Ⓒ | Ⓓ |
| 187 | Ⓐ | Ⓑ | Ⓒ | Ⓓ |
| 188 | Ⓐ | Ⓑ | Ⓒ | Ⓓ |
| 189 | Ⓐ | Ⓑ | Ⓒ | Ⓓ |
| 190 | Ⓐ | Ⓑ | Ⓒ | Ⓓ |
| 191 | Ⓐ | Ⓑ | Ⓒ | Ⓓ |
| 192 | Ⓐ | Ⓑ | Ⓒ | Ⓓ |
| 193 | Ⓐ | Ⓑ | Ⓒ | Ⓓ |
| 194 | Ⓐ | Ⓑ | Ⓒ | Ⓓ |
| 195 | Ⓐ | Ⓑ | Ⓒ | Ⓓ |
| 196 | Ⓐ | Ⓑ | Ⓒ | Ⓓ |
| 197 | Ⓐ | Ⓑ | Ⓒ | Ⓓ |
| 198 | Ⓐ | Ⓑ | Ⓒ | Ⓓ |
| 199 | Ⓐ | Ⓑ | Ⓒ | Ⓓ |
| 200 | Ⓐ | Ⓑ | Ⓒ | Ⓓ |

## LISTENING SECTION

| | A | B | C | D |
|---|---|---|---|---|
| 1 | Ⓐ | Ⓑ | Ⓒ | Ⓓ |
| 2 | Ⓐ | Ⓑ | Ⓒ | Ⓓ |
| 3 | Ⓐ | Ⓑ | Ⓒ | Ⓓ |
| 4 | Ⓐ | Ⓑ | Ⓒ | Ⓓ |
| 5 | Ⓐ | Ⓑ | Ⓒ | Ⓓ |
| 6 | Ⓐ | Ⓑ | Ⓒ | Ⓓ |
| 7 | Ⓐ | Ⓑ | Ⓒ | Ⓓ |
| 8 | Ⓐ | Ⓑ | Ⓒ | Ⓓ |
| 9 | Ⓐ | Ⓑ | Ⓒ | Ⓓ |
| 10 | Ⓐ | Ⓑ | Ⓒ | Ⓓ |
| 11 | Ⓐ | Ⓑ | Ⓒ | Ⓓ |
| 12 | Ⓐ | Ⓑ | Ⓒ | Ⓓ |
| 13 | Ⓐ | Ⓑ | Ⓒ | Ⓓ |
| 14 | Ⓐ | Ⓑ | Ⓒ | Ⓓ |
| 15 | Ⓐ | Ⓑ | Ⓒ | Ⓓ |
| 16 | Ⓐ | Ⓑ | Ⓒ | Ⓓ |
| 17 | Ⓐ | Ⓑ | Ⓒ | Ⓓ |
| 18 | Ⓐ | Ⓑ | Ⓒ | Ⓓ |
| 19 | Ⓐ | Ⓑ | Ⓒ | Ⓓ |
| 20 | Ⓐ | Ⓑ | Ⓒ | Ⓓ |
| 21 | Ⓐ | Ⓑ | Ⓒ | Ⓓ |
| 22 | Ⓐ | Ⓑ | Ⓒ | Ⓓ |
| 23 | Ⓐ | Ⓑ | Ⓒ | Ⓓ |
| 24 | Ⓐ | Ⓑ | Ⓒ | Ⓓ |
| 25 | Ⓐ | Ⓑ | Ⓒ | Ⓓ |
| 26 | Ⓐ | Ⓑ | Ⓒ | Ⓓ |
| 27 | Ⓐ | Ⓑ | Ⓒ | Ⓓ |
| 28 | Ⓐ | Ⓑ | Ⓒ | Ⓓ |
| 29 | Ⓐ | Ⓑ | Ⓒ | Ⓓ |
| 30 | Ⓐ | Ⓑ | Ⓒ | Ⓓ |
| 31 | Ⓐ | Ⓑ | Ⓒ | Ⓓ |
| 32 | Ⓐ | Ⓑ | Ⓒ | Ⓓ |
| 33 | Ⓐ | Ⓑ | Ⓒ | Ⓓ |
| 34 | Ⓐ | Ⓑ | Ⓒ | Ⓓ |
| 35 | Ⓐ | Ⓑ | Ⓒ | Ⓓ |
| 36 | Ⓐ | Ⓑ | Ⓒ | Ⓓ |
| 37 | Ⓐ | Ⓑ | Ⓒ | Ⓓ |
| 38 | Ⓐ | Ⓑ | Ⓒ | Ⓓ |
| 39 | Ⓐ | Ⓑ | Ⓒ | Ⓓ |
| 40 | Ⓐ | Ⓑ | Ⓒ | Ⓓ |
| 41 | Ⓐ | Ⓑ | Ⓒ | Ⓓ |
| 42 | Ⓐ | Ⓑ | Ⓒ | Ⓓ |
| 43 | Ⓐ | Ⓑ | Ⓒ | Ⓓ |
| 44 | Ⓐ | Ⓑ | Ⓒ | Ⓓ |
| 45 | Ⓐ | Ⓑ | Ⓒ | Ⓓ |
| 46 | Ⓐ | Ⓑ | Ⓒ | Ⓓ |
| 47 | Ⓐ | Ⓑ | Ⓒ | Ⓓ |
| 48 | Ⓐ | Ⓑ | Ⓒ | Ⓓ |
| 49 | Ⓐ | Ⓑ | Ⓒ | Ⓓ |
| 50 | Ⓐ | Ⓑ | Ⓒ | Ⓓ |
| 51 | Ⓐ | Ⓑ | Ⓒ | Ⓓ |
| 52 | Ⓐ | Ⓑ | Ⓒ | Ⓓ |
| 53 | Ⓐ | Ⓑ | Ⓒ | Ⓓ |
| 54 | Ⓐ | Ⓑ | Ⓒ | Ⓓ |
| 55 | Ⓐ | Ⓑ | Ⓒ | Ⓓ |
| 56 | Ⓐ | Ⓑ | Ⓒ | Ⓓ |
| 57 | Ⓐ | Ⓑ | Ⓒ | Ⓓ |
| 58 | Ⓐ | Ⓑ | Ⓒ | Ⓓ |
| 59 | Ⓐ | Ⓑ | Ⓒ | Ⓓ |
| 60 | Ⓐ | Ⓑ | Ⓒ | Ⓓ |
| 61 | Ⓐ | Ⓑ | Ⓒ | Ⓓ |
| 62 | Ⓐ | Ⓑ | Ⓒ | Ⓓ |
| 63 | Ⓐ | Ⓑ | Ⓒ | Ⓓ |
| 64 | Ⓐ | Ⓑ | Ⓒ | Ⓓ |
| 65 | Ⓐ | Ⓑ | Ⓒ | Ⓓ |
| 66 | Ⓐ | Ⓑ | Ⓒ | Ⓓ |
| 67 | Ⓐ | Ⓑ | Ⓒ | Ⓓ |
| 68 | Ⓐ | Ⓑ | Ⓒ | Ⓓ |
| 69 | Ⓐ | Ⓑ | Ⓒ | Ⓓ |
| 70 | Ⓐ | Ⓑ | Ⓒ | Ⓓ |
| 71 | Ⓐ | Ⓑ | Ⓒ | Ⓓ |
| 72 | Ⓐ | Ⓑ | Ⓒ | Ⓓ |
| 73 | Ⓐ | Ⓑ | Ⓒ | Ⓓ |
| 74 | Ⓐ | Ⓑ | Ⓒ | Ⓓ |
| 75 | Ⓐ | Ⓑ | Ⓒ | Ⓓ |
| 76 | Ⓐ | Ⓑ | Ⓒ | Ⓓ |
| 77 | Ⓐ | Ⓑ | Ⓒ | Ⓓ |
| 78 | Ⓐ | Ⓑ | Ⓒ | Ⓓ |
| 79 | Ⓐ | Ⓑ | Ⓒ | Ⓓ |
| 80 | Ⓐ | Ⓑ | Ⓒ | Ⓓ |
| 81 | Ⓐ | Ⓑ | Ⓒ | Ⓓ |
| 82 | Ⓐ | Ⓑ | Ⓒ | Ⓓ |
| 83 | Ⓐ | Ⓑ | Ⓒ | Ⓓ |
| 84 | Ⓐ | Ⓑ | Ⓒ | Ⓓ |
| 85 | Ⓐ | Ⓑ | Ⓒ | Ⓓ |
| 86 | Ⓐ | Ⓑ | Ⓒ | Ⓓ |
| 87 | Ⓐ | Ⓑ | Ⓒ | Ⓓ |
| 88 | Ⓐ | Ⓑ | Ⓒ | Ⓓ |
| 89 | Ⓐ | Ⓑ | Ⓒ | Ⓓ |
| 90 | Ⓐ | Ⓑ | Ⓒ | Ⓓ |
| 91 | Ⓐ | Ⓑ | Ⓒ | Ⓓ |
| 92 | Ⓐ | Ⓑ | Ⓒ | Ⓓ |
| 93 | Ⓐ | Ⓑ | Ⓒ | Ⓓ |
| 94 | Ⓐ | Ⓑ | Ⓒ | Ⓓ |
| 95 | Ⓐ | Ⓑ | Ⓒ | Ⓓ |
| 96 | Ⓐ | Ⓑ | Ⓒ | Ⓓ |
| 97 | Ⓐ | Ⓑ | Ⓒ | Ⓓ |
| 98 | Ⓐ | Ⓑ | Ⓒ | Ⓓ |
| 99 | Ⓐ | Ⓑ | Ⓒ | Ⓓ |
| 100 | Ⓐ | Ⓑ | Ⓒ | Ⓓ |

**Actual Test 1**

# Answer Sheet

**Actual Test 2**

## READING SECTION

| 101 | 102 | 103 | 104 | 105 | 106 | 107 | 108 | 109 | 110 |
|-----|-----|-----|-----|-----|-----|-----|-----|-----|-----|
| Ⓐ Ⓑ Ⓒ Ⓓ | Ⓐ Ⓑ Ⓒ Ⓓ | Ⓐ Ⓑ Ⓒ Ⓓ | Ⓐ Ⓑ Ⓒ Ⓓ | Ⓐ Ⓑ Ⓒ Ⓓ | Ⓐ Ⓑ Ⓒ Ⓓ | Ⓐ Ⓑ Ⓒ Ⓓ | Ⓐ Ⓑ Ⓒ Ⓓ | Ⓐ Ⓑ Ⓒ Ⓓ | Ⓐ Ⓑ Ⓒ Ⓓ |

| 111 | 112 | 113 | 114 | 115 | 116 | 117 | 118 | 119 | 120 |
|-----|-----|-----|-----|-----|-----|-----|-----|-----|-----|
| Ⓐ Ⓑ Ⓒ Ⓓ | Ⓐ Ⓑ Ⓒ Ⓓ | Ⓐ Ⓑ Ⓒ Ⓓ | Ⓐ Ⓑ Ⓒ Ⓓ | Ⓐ Ⓑ Ⓒ Ⓓ | Ⓐ Ⓑ Ⓒ Ⓓ | Ⓐ Ⓑ Ⓒ Ⓓ | Ⓐ Ⓑ Ⓒ Ⓓ | Ⓐ Ⓑ Ⓒ Ⓓ | Ⓐ Ⓑ Ⓒ Ⓓ |

| 121 | 122 | 123 | 124 | 125 | 126 | 127 | 128 | 129 | 130 |
|-----|-----|-----|-----|-----|-----|-----|-----|-----|-----|
| Ⓐ Ⓑ Ⓒ Ⓓ | Ⓐ Ⓑ Ⓒ Ⓓ | Ⓐ Ⓑ Ⓒ Ⓓ | Ⓐ Ⓑ Ⓒ Ⓓ | Ⓐ Ⓑ Ⓒ Ⓓ | Ⓐ Ⓑ Ⓒ Ⓓ | Ⓐ Ⓑ Ⓒ Ⓓ | Ⓐ Ⓑ Ⓒ Ⓓ | Ⓐ Ⓑ Ⓒ Ⓓ | Ⓐ Ⓑ Ⓒ Ⓓ |

| 131 | 132 | 133 | 134 | 135 | 136 | 137 | 138 | 139 | 140 |
|-----|-----|-----|-----|-----|-----|-----|-----|-----|-----|
| Ⓐ Ⓑ Ⓒ Ⓓ | Ⓐ Ⓑ Ⓒ Ⓓ | Ⓐ Ⓑ Ⓒ Ⓓ | Ⓐ Ⓑ Ⓒ Ⓓ | Ⓐ Ⓑ Ⓒ Ⓓ | Ⓐ Ⓑ Ⓒ Ⓓ | Ⓐ Ⓑ Ⓒ Ⓓ | Ⓐ Ⓑ Ⓒ Ⓓ | Ⓐ Ⓑ Ⓒ Ⓓ | Ⓐ Ⓑ Ⓒ Ⓓ |

| 141 | 142 | 143 | 144 | 145 | 146 | 147 | 148 | 149 | 150 |
|-----|-----|-----|-----|-----|-----|-----|-----|-----|-----|
| Ⓐ Ⓑ Ⓒ Ⓓ | Ⓐ Ⓑ Ⓒ Ⓓ | Ⓐ Ⓑ Ⓒ Ⓓ | Ⓐ Ⓑ Ⓒ Ⓓ | Ⓐ Ⓑ Ⓒ Ⓓ | Ⓐ Ⓑ Ⓒ Ⓓ | Ⓐ Ⓑ Ⓒ Ⓓ | Ⓐ Ⓑ Ⓒ Ⓓ | Ⓐ Ⓑ Ⓒ Ⓓ | Ⓐ Ⓑ Ⓒ Ⓓ |

| 151 | 152 | 153 | 154 | 155 | 156 | 157 | 158 | 159 | 160 |
|-----|-----|-----|-----|-----|-----|-----|-----|-----|-----|
| Ⓐ Ⓑ Ⓒ Ⓓ | Ⓐ Ⓑ Ⓒ Ⓓ | Ⓐ Ⓑ Ⓒ Ⓓ | Ⓐ Ⓑ Ⓒ Ⓓ | Ⓐ Ⓑ Ⓒ Ⓓ | Ⓐ Ⓑ Ⓒ Ⓓ | Ⓐ Ⓑ Ⓒ Ⓓ | Ⓐ Ⓑ Ⓒ Ⓓ | Ⓐ Ⓑ Ⓒ Ⓓ | Ⓐ Ⓑ Ⓒ Ⓓ |

| 161 | 162 | 163 | 164 | 165 | 166 | 167 | 168 | 169 | 170 |
|-----|-----|-----|-----|-----|-----|-----|-----|-----|-----|
| Ⓐ Ⓑ Ⓒ Ⓓ | Ⓐ Ⓑ Ⓒ Ⓓ | Ⓐ Ⓑ Ⓒ Ⓓ | Ⓐ Ⓑ Ⓒ Ⓓ | Ⓐ Ⓑ Ⓒ Ⓓ | Ⓐ Ⓑ Ⓒ Ⓓ | Ⓐ Ⓑ Ⓒ Ⓓ | Ⓐ Ⓑ Ⓒ Ⓓ | Ⓐ Ⓑ Ⓒ Ⓓ | Ⓐ Ⓑ Ⓒ Ⓓ |

| 171 | 172 | 173 | 174 | 175 | 176 | 177 | 178 | 179 | 180 |
|-----|-----|-----|-----|-----|-----|-----|-----|-----|-----|
| Ⓐ Ⓑ Ⓒ Ⓓ | Ⓐ Ⓑ Ⓒ Ⓓ | Ⓐ Ⓑ Ⓒ Ⓓ | Ⓐ Ⓑ Ⓒ Ⓓ | Ⓐ Ⓑ Ⓒ Ⓓ | Ⓐ Ⓑ Ⓒ Ⓓ | Ⓐ Ⓑ Ⓒ Ⓓ | Ⓐ Ⓑ Ⓒ Ⓓ | Ⓐ Ⓑ Ⓒ Ⓓ | Ⓐ Ⓑ Ⓒ Ⓓ |

| 181 | 182 | 183 | 184 | 185 | 186 | 187 | 188 | 189 | 190 |
|-----|-----|-----|-----|-----|-----|-----|-----|-----|-----|
| Ⓐ Ⓑ Ⓒ Ⓓ | Ⓐ Ⓑ Ⓒ Ⓓ | Ⓐ Ⓑ Ⓒ Ⓓ | Ⓐ Ⓑ Ⓒ Ⓓ | Ⓐ Ⓑ Ⓒ Ⓓ | Ⓐ Ⓑ Ⓒ Ⓓ | Ⓐ Ⓑ Ⓒ Ⓓ | Ⓐ Ⓑ Ⓒ Ⓓ | Ⓐ Ⓑ Ⓒ Ⓓ | Ⓐ Ⓑ Ⓒ Ⓓ |

| 191 | 192 | 193 | 194 | 195 | 196 | 197 | 198 | 199 | 200 |
|-----|-----|-----|-----|-----|-----|-----|-----|-----|-----|
| Ⓐ Ⓑ Ⓒ Ⓓ | Ⓐ Ⓑ Ⓒ Ⓓ | Ⓐ Ⓑ Ⓒ Ⓓ | Ⓐ Ⓑ Ⓒ Ⓓ | Ⓐ Ⓑ Ⓒ Ⓓ | Ⓐ Ⓑ Ⓒ Ⓓ | Ⓐ Ⓑ Ⓒ Ⓓ | Ⓐ Ⓑ Ⓒ Ⓓ | Ⓐ Ⓑ Ⓒ Ⓓ | Ⓐ Ⓑ Ⓒ Ⓓ |

## LISTENING SECTION

| 1 | 2 | 3 | 4 | 5 | 6 | 7 | 8 | 9 | 10 |
|---|---|---|---|---|---|---|---|---|----|
| Ⓐ Ⓑ Ⓒ Ⓓ | Ⓐ Ⓑ Ⓒ Ⓓ | Ⓐ Ⓑ Ⓒ Ⓓ | Ⓐ Ⓑ Ⓒ Ⓓ | Ⓐ Ⓑ Ⓒ Ⓓ | Ⓐ Ⓑ Ⓒ Ⓓ | Ⓐ Ⓑ Ⓒ Ⓓ | Ⓐ Ⓑ Ⓒ Ⓓ | Ⓐ Ⓑ Ⓒ Ⓓ | Ⓐ Ⓑ Ⓒ Ⓓ |

| 11 | 12 | 13 | 14 | 15 | 16 | 17 | 18 | 19 | 20 |
|----|----|----|----|----|----|----|----|----|----|
| Ⓐ Ⓑ Ⓒ Ⓓ | Ⓐ Ⓑ Ⓒ Ⓓ | Ⓐ Ⓑ Ⓒ Ⓓ | Ⓐ Ⓑ Ⓒ Ⓓ | Ⓐ Ⓑ Ⓒ Ⓓ | Ⓐ Ⓑ Ⓒ Ⓓ | Ⓐ Ⓑ Ⓒ Ⓓ | Ⓐ Ⓑ Ⓒ Ⓓ | Ⓐ Ⓑ Ⓒ Ⓓ | Ⓐ Ⓑ Ⓒ Ⓓ |

| 21 | 22 | 23 | 24 | 25 | 26 | 27 | 28 | 29 | 30 |
|----|----|----|----|----|----|----|----|----|----|
| Ⓐ Ⓑ Ⓒ Ⓓ | Ⓐ Ⓑ Ⓒ Ⓓ | Ⓐ Ⓑ Ⓒ Ⓓ | Ⓐ Ⓑ Ⓒ Ⓓ | Ⓐ Ⓑ Ⓒ Ⓓ | Ⓐ Ⓑ Ⓒ Ⓓ | Ⓐ Ⓑ Ⓒ Ⓓ | Ⓐ Ⓑ Ⓒ Ⓓ | Ⓐ Ⓑ Ⓒ Ⓓ | Ⓐ Ⓑ Ⓒ Ⓓ |

| 31 | 32 | 33 | 34 | 35 | 36 | 37 | 38 | 39 | 40 |
|----|----|----|----|----|----|----|----|----|----|
| Ⓐ Ⓑ Ⓒ Ⓓ | Ⓐ Ⓑ Ⓒ Ⓓ | Ⓐ Ⓑ Ⓒ Ⓓ | Ⓐ Ⓑ Ⓒ Ⓓ | Ⓐ Ⓑ Ⓒ Ⓓ | Ⓐ Ⓑ Ⓒ Ⓓ | Ⓐ Ⓑ Ⓒ Ⓓ | Ⓐ Ⓑ Ⓒ Ⓓ | Ⓐ Ⓑ Ⓒ Ⓓ | Ⓐ Ⓑ Ⓒ Ⓓ |

| 41 | 42 | 43 | 44 | 45 | 46 | 47 | 48 | 49 | 50 |
|----|----|----|----|----|----|----|----|----|----|
| Ⓐ Ⓑ Ⓒ Ⓓ | Ⓐ Ⓑ Ⓒ Ⓓ | Ⓐ Ⓑ Ⓒ Ⓓ | Ⓐ Ⓑ Ⓒ Ⓓ | Ⓐ Ⓑ Ⓒ Ⓓ | Ⓐ Ⓑ Ⓒ Ⓓ | Ⓐ Ⓑ Ⓒ Ⓓ | Ⓐ Ⓑ Ⓒ Ⓓ | Ⓐ Ⓑ Ⓒ Ⓓ | Ⓐ Ⓑ Ⓒ Ⓓ |

| 51 | 52 | 53 | 54 | 55 | 56 | 57 | 58 | 59 | 60 |
|----|----|----|----|----|----|----|----|----|----|
| Ⓐ Ⓑ Ⓒ Ⓓ | Ⓐ Ⓑ Ⓒ Ⓓ | Ⓐ Ⓑ Ⓒ Ⓓ | Ⓐ Ⓑ Ⓒ Ⓓ | Ⓐ Ⓑ Ⓒ Ⓓ | Ⓐ Ⓑ Ⓒ Ⓓ | Ⓐ Ⓑ Ⓒ Ⓓ | Ⓐ Ⓑ Ⓒ Ⓓ | Ⓐ Ⓑ Ⓒ Ⓓ | Ⓐ Ⓑ Ⓒ Ⓓ |

| 61 | 62 | 63 | 64 | 65 | 66 | 67 | 68 | 69 | 70 |
|----|----|----|----|----|----|----|----|----|----|
| Ⓐ Ⓑ Ⓒ Ⓓ | Ⓐ Ⓑ Ⓒ Ⓓ | Ⓐ Ⓑ Ⓒ Ⓓ | Ⓐ Ⓑ Ⓒ Ⓓ | Ⓐ Ⓑ Ⓒ Ⓓ | Ⓐ Ⓑ Ⓒ Ⓓ | Ⓐ Ⓑ Ⓒ Ⓓ | Ⓐ Ⓑ Ⓒ Ⓓ | Ⓐ Ⓑ Ⓒ Ⓓ | Ⓐ Ⓑ Ⓒ Ⓓ |

| 71 | 72 | 73 | 74 | 75 | 76 | 77 | 78 | 79 | 80 |
|----|----|----|----|----|----|----|----|----|----|
| Ⓐ Ⓑ Ⓒ Ⓓ | Ⓐ Ⓑ Ⓒ Ⓓ | Ⓐ Ⓑ Ⓒ Ⓓ | Ⓐ Ⓑ Ⓒ Ⓓ | Ⓐ Ⓑ Ⓒ Ⓓ | Ⓐ Ⓑ Ⓒ Ⓓ | Ⓐ Ⓑ Ⓒ Ⓓ | Ⓐ Ⓑ Ⓒ Ⓓ | Ⓐ Ⓑ Ⓒ Ⓓ | Ⓐ Ⓑ Ⓒ Ⓓ |

| 81 | 82 | 83 | 84 | 85 | 86 | 87 | 88 | 89 | 90 |
|----|----|----|----|----|----|----|----|----|----|
| Ⓐ Ⓑ Ⓒ Ⓓ | Ⓐ Ⓑ Ⓒ Ⓓ | Ⓐ Ⓑ Ⓒ Ⓓ | Ⓐ Ⓑ Ⓒ Ⓓ | Ⓐ Ⓑ Ⓒ Ⓓ | Ⓐ Ⓑ Ⓒ Ⓓ | Ⓐ Ⓑ Ⓒ Ⓓ | Ⓐ Ⓑ Ⓒ Ⓓ | Ⓐ Ⓑ Ⓒ Ⓓ | Ⓐ Ⓑ Ⓒ Ⓓ |

| 91 | 92 | 93 | 94 | 95 | 96 | 97 | 98 | 99 | 100 |
|----|----|----|----|----|----|----|----|----|-----|
| Ⓐ Ⓑ Ⓒ Ⓓ | Ⓐ Ⓑ Ⓒ Ⓓ | Ⓐ Ⓑ Ⓒ Ⓓ | Ⓐ Ⓑ Ⓒ Ⓓ | Ⓐ Ⓑ Ⓒ Ⓓ | Ⓐ Ⓑ Ⓒ Ⓓ | Ⓐ Ⓑ Ⓒ Ⓓ | Ⓐ Ⓑ Ⓒ Ⓓ | Ⓐ Ⓑ Ⓒ Ⓓ | Ⓐ Ⓑ Ⓒ Ⓓ |

# Answer Sheet

## READING SECTION

| 101 | 102 | 103 | 104 | 105 | 106 | 107 | 108 | 109 | 110 |
| --- | --- | --- | --- | --- | --- | --- | --- | --- | --- |
| Ⓐ Ⓑ Ⓒ Ⓓ | Ⓐ Ⓑ Ⓒ Ⓓ | Ⓐ Ⓑ Ⓒ Ⓓ | Ⓐ Ⓑ Ⓒ Ⓓ | Ⓐ Ⓑ Ⓒ Ⓓ | Ⓐ Ⓑ Ⓒ Ⓓ | Ⓐ Ⓑ Ⓒ Ⓓ | Ⓐ Ⓑ Ⓒ Ⓓ | Ⓐ Ⓑ Ⓒ Ⓓ | Ⓐ Ⓑ Ⓒ Ⓓ |

| 111 | 112 | 113 | 114 | 115 | 116 | 117 | 118 | 119 | 120 |
| --- | --- | --- | --- | --- | --- | --- | --- | --- | --- |
| Ⓐ Ⓑ Ⓒ Ⓓ | Ⓐ Ⓑ Ⓒ Ⓓ | Ⓐ Ⓑ Ⓒ Ⓓ | Ⓐ Ⓑ Ⓒ Ⓓ | Ⓐ Ⓑ Ⓒ Ⓓ | Ⓐ Ⓑ Ⓒ Ⓓ | Ⓐ Ⓑ Ⓒ Ⓓ | Ⓐ Ⓑ Ⓒ Ⓓ | Ⓐ Ⓑ Ⓒ Ⓓ | Ⓐ Ⓑ Ⓒ Ⓓ |

| 121 | 122 | 123 | 124 | 125 | 126 | 127 | 128 | 129 | 130 |
| --- | --- | --- | --- | --- | --- | --- | --- | --- | --- |
| Ⓐ Ⓑ Ⓒ Ⓓ | Ⓐ Ⓑ Ⓒ Ⓓ | Ⓐ Ⓑ Ⓒ Ⓓ | Ⓐ Ⓑ Ⓒ Ⓓ | Ⓐ Ⓑ Ⓒ Ⓓ | Ⓐ Ⓑ Ⓒ Ⓓ | Ⓐ Ⓑ Ⓒ Ⓓ | Ⓐ Ⓑ Ⓒ Ⓓ | Ⓐ Ⓑ Ⓒ Ⓓ | Ⓐ Ⓑ Ⓒ Ⓓ |

| 131 | 132 | 133 | 134 | 135 | 136 | 137 | 138 | 139 | 140 |
| --- | --- | --- | --- | --- | --- | --- | --- | --- | --- |
| Ⓐ Ⓑ Ⓒ Ⓓ | Ⓐ Ⓑ Ⓒ Ⓓ | Ⓐ Ⓑ Ⓒ Ⓓ | Ⓐ Ⓑ Ⓒ Ⓓ | Ⓐ Ⓑ Ⓒ Ⓓ | Ⓐ Ⓑ Ⓒ Ⓓ | Ⓐ Ⓑ Ⓒ Ⓓ | Ⓐ Ⓑ Ⓒ Ⓓ | Ⓐ Ⓑ Ⓒ Ⓓ | Ⓐ Ⓑ Ⓒ Ⓓ |

| 141 | 142 | 143 | 144 | 145 | 146 | 147 | 148 | 149 | 150 |
| --- | --- | --- | --- | --- | --- | --- | --- | --- | --- |
| Ⓐ Ⓑ Ⓒ Ⓓ | Ⓐ Ⓑ Ⓒ Ⓓ | Ⓐ Ⓑ Ⓒ Ⓓ | Ⓐ Ⓑ Ⓒ Ⓓ | Ⓐ Ⓑ Ⓒ Ⓓ | Ⓐ Ⓑ Ⓒ Ⓓ | Ⓐ Ⓑ Ⓒ Ⓓ | Ⓐ Ⓑ Ⓒ Ⓓ | Ⓐ Ⓑ Ⓒ Ⓓ | Ⓐ Ⓑ Ⓒ Ⓓ |

| 151 | 152 | 153 | 154 | 155 | 156 | 157 | 158 | 159 | 160 |
| --- | --- | --- | --- | --- | --- | --- | --- | --- | --- |
| Ⓐ Ⓑ Ⓒ Ⓓ | Ⓐ Ⓑ Ⓒ Ⓓ | Ⓐ Ⓑ Ⓒ Ⓓ | Ⓐ Ⓑ Ⓒ Ⓓ | Ⓐ Ⓑ Ⓒ Ⓓ | Ⓐ Ⓑ Ⓒ Ⓓ | Ⓐ Ⓑ Ⓒ Ⓓ | Ⓐ Ⓑ Ⓒ Ⓓ | Ⓐ Ⓑ Ⓒ Ⓓ | Ⓐ Ⓑ Ⓒ Ⓓ |

| 161 | 162 | 163 | 164 | 165 | 166 | 167 | 168 | 169 | 170 |
| --- | --- | --- | --- | --- | --- | --- | --- | --- | --- |
| Ⓐ Ⓑ Ⓒ Ⓓ | Ⓐ Ⓑ Ⓒ Ⓓ | Ⓐ Ⓑ Ⓒ Ⓓ | Ⓐ Ⓑ Ⓒ Ⓓ | Ⓐ Ⓑ Ⓒ Ⓓ | Ⓐ Ⓑ Ⓒ Ⓓ | Ⓐ Ⓑ Ⓒ Ⓓ | Ⓐ Ⓑ Ⓒ Ⓓ | Ⓐ Ⓑ Ⓒ Ⓓ | Ⓐ Ⓑ Ⓒ Ⓓ |

| 171 | 172 | 173 | 174 | 175 | 176 | 177 | 178 | 179 | 180 |
| --- | --- | --- | --- | --- | --- | --- | --- | --- | --- |
| Ⓐ Ⓑ Ⓒ Ⓓ | Ⓐ Ⓑ Ⓒ Ⓓ | Ⓐ Ⓑ Ⓒ Ⓓ | Ⓐ Ⓑ Ⓒ Ⓓ | Ⓐ Ⓑ Ⓒ Ⓓ | Ⓐ Ⓑ Ⓒ Ⓓ | Ⓐ Ⓑ Ⓒ Ⓓ | Ⓐ Ⓑ Ⓒ Ⓓ | Ⓐ Ⓑ Ⓒ Ⓓ | Ⓐ Ⓑ Ⓒ Ⓓ |

| 181 | 182 | 183 | 184 | 185 | 186 | 187 | 188 | 189 | 190 |
| --- | --- | --- | --- | --- | --- | --- | --- | --- | --- |
| Ⓐ Ⓑ Ⓒ Ⓓ | Ⓐ Ⓑ Ⓒ Ⓓ | Ⓐ Ⓑ Ⓒ Ⓓ | Ⓐ Ⓑ Ⓒ Ⓓ | Ⓐ Ⓑ Ⓒ Ⓓ | Ⓐ Ⓑ Ⓒ Ⓓ | Ⓐ Ⓑ Ⓒ Ⓓ | Ⓐ Ⓑ Ⓒ Ⓓ | Ⓐ Ⓑ Ⓒ Ⓓ | Ⓐ Ⓑ Ⓒ Ⓓ |

| 191 | 192 | 193 | 194 | 195 | 196 | 197 | 198 | 199 | 200 |
| --- | --- | --- | --- | --- | --- | --- | --- | --- | --- |
| Ⓐ Ⓑ Ⓒ Ⓓ | Ⓐ Ⓑ Ⓒ Ⓓ | Ⓐ Ⓑ Ⓒ Ⓓ | Ⓐ Ⓑ Ⓒ Ⓓ | Ⓐ Ⓑ Ⓒ Ⓓ | Ⓐ Ⓑ Ⓒ Ⓓ | Ⓐ Ⓑ Ⓒ Ⓓ | Ⓐ Ⓑ Ⓒ Ⓓ | Ⓐ Ⓑ Ⓒ Ⓓ | Ⓐ Ⓑ Ⓒ Ⓓ |

## LISTENING SECTION

| 1 | 2 | 3 | 4 | 5 | 6 | 7 | 8 | 9 | 10 |
| --- | --- | --- | --- | --- | --- | --- | --- | --- | --- |
| Ⓐ Ⓑ Ⓒ Ⓓ | Ⓐ Ⓑ Ⓒ Ⓓ | Ⓐ Ⓑ Ⓒ Ⓓ | Ⓐ Ⓑ Ⓒ Ⓓ | Ⓐ Ⓑ Ⓒ Ⓓ | Ⓐ Ⓑ Ⓒ Ⓓ | Ⓐ Ⓑ Ⓒ Ⓓ | Ⓐ Ⓑ Ⓒ Ⓓ | Ⓐ Ⓑ Ⓒ Ⓓ | Ⓐ Ⓑ Ⓒ Ⓓ |

| 11 | 12 | 13 | 14 | 15 | 16 | 17 | 18 | 19 | 20 |
| --- | --- | --- | --- | --- | --- | --- | --- | --- | --- |
| Ⓐ Ⓑ Ⓒ Ⓓ | Ⓐ Ⓑ Ⓒ Ⓓ | Ⓐ Ⓑ Ⓒ Ⓓ | Ⓐ Ⓑ Ⓒ Ⓓ | Ⓐ Ⓑ Ⓒ Ⓓ | Ⓐ Ⓑ Ⓒ Ⓓ | Ⓐ Ⓑ Ⓒ Ⓓ | Ⓐ Ⓑ Ⓒ Ⓓ | Ⓐ Ⓑ Ⓒ Ⓓ | Ⓐ Ⓑ Ⓒ Ⓓ |

| 21 | 22 | 23 | 24 | 25 | 26 | 27 | 28 | 29 | 30 |
| --- | --- | --- | --- | --- | --- | --- | --- | --- | --- |
| Ⓐ Ⓑ Ⓒ Ⓓ | Ⓐ Ⓑ Ⓒ Ⓓ | Ⓐ Ⓑ Ⓒ Ⓓ | Ⓐ Ⓑ Ⓒ Ⓓ | Ⓐ Ⓑ Ⓒ Ⓓ | Ⓐ Ⓑ Ⓒ Ⓓ | Ⓐ Ⓑ Ⓒ Ⓓ | Ⓐ Ⓑ Ⓒ Ⓓ | Ⓐ Ⓑ Ⓒ Ⓓ | Ⓐ Ⓑ Ⓒ Ⓓ |

| 31 | 32 | 33 | 34 | 35 | 36 | 37 | 38 | 39 | 40 |
| --- | --- | --- | --- | --- | --- | --- | --- | --- | --- |
| Ⓐ Ⓑ Ⓒ Ⓓ | Ⓐ Ⓑ Ⓒ Ⓓ | Ⓐ Ⓑ Ⓒ Ⓓ | Ⓐ Ⓑ Ⓒ Ⓓ | Ⓐ Ⓑ Ⓒ Ⓓ | Ⓐ Ⓑ Ⓒ Ⓓ | Ⓐ Ⓑ Ⓒ Ⓓ | Ⓐ Ⓑ Ⓒ Ⓓ | Ⓐ Ⓑ Ⓒ Ⓓ | Ⓐ Ⓑ Ⓒ Ⓓ |

| 41 | 42 | 43 | 44 | 45 | 46 | 47 | 48 | 49 | 50 |
| --- | --- | --- | --- | --- | --- | --- | --- | --- | --- |
| Ⓐ Ⓑ Ⓒ Ⓓ | Ⓐ Ⓑ Ⓒ Ⓓ | Ⓐ Ⓑ Ⓒ Ⓓ | Ⓐ Ⓑ Ⓒ Ⓓ | Ⓐ Ⓑ Ⓒ Ⓓ | Ⓐ Ⓑ Ⓒ Ⓓ | Ⓐ Ⓑ Ⓒ Ⓓ | Ⓐ Ⓑ Ⓒ Ⓓ | Ⓐ Ⓑ Ⓒ Ⓓ | Ⓐ Ⓑ Ⓒ Ⓓ |

| 51 | 52 | 53 | 54 | 55 | 56 | 57 | 58 | 59 | 60 |
| --- | --- | --- | --- | --- | --- | --- | --- | --- | --- |
| Ⓐ Ⓑ Ⓒ Ⓓ | Ⓐ Ⓑ Ⓒ Ⓓ | Ⓐ Ⓑ Ⓒ Ⓓ | Ⓐ Ⓑ Ⓒ Ⓓ | Ⓐ Ⓑ Ⓒ Ⓓ | Ⓐ Ⓑ Ⓒ Ⓓ | Ⓐ Ⓑ Ⓒ Ⓓ | Ⓐ Ⓑ Ⓒ Ⓓ | Ⓐ Ⓑ Ⓒ Ⓓ | Ⓐ Ⓑ Ⓒ Ⓓ |

| 61 | 62 | 63 | 64 | 65 | 66 | 67 | 68 | 69 | 70 |
| --- | --- | --- | --- | --- | --- | --- | --- | --- | --- |
| Ⓐ Ⓑ Ⓒ Ⓓ | Ⓐ Ⓑ Ⓒ Ⓓ | Ⓐ Ⓑ Ⓒ Ⓓ | Ⓐ Ⓑ Ⓒ Ⓓ | Ⓐ Ⓑ Ⓒ Ⓓ | Ⓐ Ⓑ Ⓒ Ⓓ | Ⓐ Ⓑ Ⓒ Ⓓ | Ⓐ Ⓑ Ⓒ Ⓓ | Ⓐ Ⓑ Ⓒ Ⓓ | Ⓐ Ⓑ Ⓒ Ⓓ |

| 71 | 72 | 73 | 74 | 75 | 76 | 77 | 78 | 79 | 80 |
| --- | --- | --- | --- | --- | --- | --- | --- | --- | --- |
| Ⓐ Ⓑ Ⓒ Ⓓ | Ⓐ Ⓑ Ⓒ Ⓓ | Ⓐ Ⓑ Ⓒ Ⓓ | Ⓐ Ⓑ Ⓒ Ⓓ | Ⓐ Ⓑ Ⓒ Ⓓ | Ⓐ Ⓑ Ⓒ Ⓓ | Ⓐ Ⓑ Ⓒ Ⓓ | Ⓐ Ⓑ Ⓒ Ⓓ | Ⓐ Ⓑ Ⓒ Ⓓ | Ⓐ Ⓑ Ⓒ Ⓓ |

| 81 | 82 | 83 | 84 | 85 | 86 | 87 | 88 | 89 | 90 |
| --- | --- | --- | --- | --- | --- | --- | --- | --- | --- |
| Ⓐ Ⓑ Ⓒ Ⓓ | Ⓐ Ⓑ Ⓒ Ⓓ | Ⓐ Ⓑ Ⓒ Ⓓ | Ⓐ Ⓑ Ⓒ Ⓓ | Ⓐ Ⓑ Ⓒ Ⓓ | Ⓐ Ⓑ Ⓒ Ⓓ | Ⓐ Ⓑ Ⓒ Ⓓ | Ⓐ Ⓑ Ⓒ Ⓓ | Ⓐ Ⓑ Ⓒ Ⓓ | Ⓐ Ⓑ Ⓒ Ⓓ |

| 91 | 92 | 93 | 94 | 95 | 96 | 97 | 98 | 99 | 100 |
| --- | --- | --- | --- | --- | --- | --- | --- | --- | --- |
| Ⓐ Ⓑ Ⓒ Ⓓ | Ⓐ Ⓑ Ⓒ Ⓓ | Ⓐ Ⓑ Ⓒ Ⓓ | Ⓐ Ⓑ Ⓒ Ⓓ | Ⓐ Ⓑ Ⓒ Ⓓ | Ⓐ Ⓑ Ⓒ Ⓓ | Ⓐ Ⓑ Ⓒ Ⓓ | Ⓐ Ⓑ Ⓒ Ⓓ | Ⓐ Ⓑ Ⓒ Ⓓ | Ⓐ Ⓑ Ⓒ Ⓓ |

**Actual Test 3**

# Answer Sheet

## READING SECTION

| | A | B | C | D |
|---|---|---|---|---|
| 101 | Ⓐ | Ⓑ | Ⓒ | Ⓓ |
| 102 | Ⓐ | Ⓑ | Ⓒ | Ⓓ |
| 103 | Ⓐ | Ⓑ | Ⓒ | Ⓓ |
| 104 | Ⓐ | Ⓑ | Ⓒ | Ⓓ |
| 105 | Ⓐ | Ⓑ | Ⓒ | Ⓓ |
| 106 | Ⓐ | Ⓑ | Ⓒ | Ⓓ |
| 107 | Ⓐ | Ⓑ | Ⓒ | Ⓓ |
| 108 | Ⓐ | Ⓑ | Ⓒ | Ⓓ |
| 109 | Ⓐ | Ⓑ | Ⓒ | Ⓓ |
| 110 | Ⓐ | Ⓑ | Ⓒ | Ⓓ |
| 111 | Ⓐ | Ⓑ | Ⓒ | Ⓓ |
| 112 | Ⓐ | Ⓑ | Ⓒ | Ⓓ |
| 113 | Ⓐ | Ⓑ | Ⓒ | Ⓓ |
| 114 | Ⓐ | Ⓑ | Ⓒ | Ⓓ |
| 115 | Ⓐ | Ⓑ | Ⓒ | Ⓓ |
| 116 | Ⓐ | Ⓑ | Ⓒ | Ⓓ |
| 117 | Ⓐ | Ⓑ | Ⓒ | Ⓓ |
| 118 | Ⓐ | Ⓑ | Ⓒ | Ⓓ |
| 119 | Ⓐ | Ⓑ | Ⓒ | Ⓓ |
| 120 | Ⓐ | Ⓑ | Ⓒ | Ⓓ |
| 121 | Ⓐ | Ⓑ | Ⓒ | Ⓓ |
| 122 | Ⓐ | Ⓑ | Ⓒ | Ⓓ |
| 123 | Ⓐ | Ⓑ | Ⓒ | Ⓓ |
| 124 | Ⓐ | Ⓑ | Ⓒ | Ⓓ |
| 125 | Ⓐ | Ⓑ | Ⓒ | Ⓓ |
| 126 | Ⓐ | Ⓑ | Ⓒ | Ⓓ |
| 127 | Ⓐ | Ⓑ | Ⓒ | Ⓓ |
| 128 | Ⓐ | Ⓑ | Ⓒ | Ⓓ |
| 129 | Ⓐ | Ⓑ | Ⓒ | Ⓓ |
| 130 | Ⓐ | Ⓑ | Ⓒ | Ⓓ |
| 131 | Ⓐ | Ⓑ | Ⓒ | Ⓓ |
| 132 | Ⓐ | Ⓑ | Ⓒ | Ⓓ |
| 133 | Ⓐ | Ⓑ | Ⓒ | Ⓓ |
| 134 | Ⓐ | Ⓑ | Ⓒ | Ⓓ |
| 135 | Ⓐ | Ⓑ | Ⓒ | Ⓓ |
| 136 | Ⓐ | Ⓑ | Ⓒ | Ⓓ |
| 137 | Ⓐ | Ⓑ | Ⓒ | Ⓓ |
| 138 | Ⓐ | Ⓑ | Ⓒ | Ⓓ |
| 139 | Ⓐ | Ⓑ | Ⓒ | Ⓓ |
| 140 | Ⓐ | Ⓑ | Ⓒ | Ⓓ |
| 141 | Ⓐ | Ⓑ | Ⓒ | Ⓓ |
| 142 | Ⓐ | Ⓑ | Ⓒ | Ⓓ |
| 143 | Ⓐ | Ⓑ | Ⓒ | Ⓓ |
| 144 | Ⓐ | Ⓑ | Ⓒ | Ⓓ |
| 145 | Ⓐ | Ⓑ | Ⓒ | Ⓓ |
| 146 | Ⓐ | Ⓑ | Ⓒ | Ⓓ |
| 147 | Ⓐ | Ⓑ | Ⓒ | Ⓓ |
| 148 | Ⓐ | Ⓑ | Ⓒ | Ⓓ |
| 149 | Ⓐ | Ⓑ | Ⓒ | Ⓓ |
| 150 | Ⓐ | Ⓑ | Ⓒ | Ⓓ |
| 151 | Ⓐ | Ⓑ | Ⓒ | Ⓓ |
| 152 | Ⓐ | Ⓑ | Ⓒ | Ⓓ |
| 153 | Ⓐ | Ⓑ | Ⓒ | Ⓓ |
| 154 | Ⓐ | Ⓑ | Ⓒ | Ⓓ |
| 155 | Ⓐ | Ⓑ | Ⓒ | Ⓓ |
| 156 | Ⓐ | Ⓑ | Ⓒ | Ⓓ |
| 157 | Ⓐ | Ⓑ | Ⓒ | Ⓓ |
| 158 | Ⓐ | Ⓑ | Ⓒ | Ⓓ |
| 159 | Ⓐ | Ⓑ | Ⓒ | Ⓓ |
| 160 | Ⓐ | Ⓑ | Ⓒ | Ⓓ |
| 161 | Ⓐ | Ⓑ | Ⓒ | Ⓓ |
| 162 | Ⓐ | Ⓑ | Ⓒ | Ⓓ |
| 163 | Ⓐ | Ⓑ | Ⓒ | Ⓓ |
| 164 | Ⓐ | Ⓑ | Ⓒ | Ⓓ |
| 165 | Ⓐ | Ⓑ | Ⓒ | Ⓓ |
| 166 | Ⓐ | Ⓑ | Ⓒ | Ⓓ |
| 167 | Ⓐ | Ⓑ | Ⓒ | Ⓓ |
| 168 | Ⓐ | Ⓑ | Ⓒ | Ⓓ |
| 169 | Ⓐ | Ⓑ | Ⓒ | Ⓓ |
| 170 | Ⓐ | Ⓑ | Ⓒ | Ⓓ |
| 171 | Ⓐ | Ⓑ | Ⓒ | Ⓓ |
| 172 | Ⓐ | Ⓑ | Ⓒ | Ⓓ |
| 173 | Ⓐ | Ⓑ | Ⓒ | Ⓓ |
| 174 | Ⓐ | Ⓑ | Ⓒ | Ⓓ |
| 175 | Ⓐ | Ⓑ | Ⓒ | Ⓓ |
| 176 | Ⓐ | Ⓑ | Ⓒ | Ⓓ |
| 177 | Ⓐ | Ⓑ | Ⓒ | Ⓓ |
| 178 | Ⓐ | Ⓑ | Ⓒ | Ⓓ |
| 179 | Ⓐ | Ⓑ | Ⓒ | Ⓓ |
| 180 | Ⓐ | Ⓑ | Ⓒ | Ⓓ |
| 181 | Ⓐ | Ⓑ | Ⓒ | Ⓓ |
| 182 | Ⓐ | Ⓑ | Ⓒ | Ⓓ |
| 183 | Ⓐ | Ⓑ | Ⓒ | Ⓓ |
| 184 | Ⓐ | Ⓑ | Ⓒ | Ⓓ |
| 185 | Ⓐ | Ⓑ | Ⓒ | Ⓓ |
| 186 | Ⓐ | Ⓑ | Ⓒ | Ⓓ |
| 187 | Ⓐ | Ⓑ | Ⓒ | Ⓓ |
| 188 | Ⓐ | Ⓑ | Ⓒ | Ⓓ |
| 189 | Ⓐ | Ⓑ | Ⓒ | Ⓓ |
| 190 | Ⓐ | Ⓑ | Ⓒ | Ⓓ |
| 191 | Ⓐ | Ⓑ | Ⓒ | Ⓓ |
| 192 | Ⓐ | Ⓑ | Ⓒ | Ⓓ |
| 193 | Ⓐ | Ⓑ | Ⓒ | Ⓓ |
| 194 | Ⓐ | Ⓑ | Ⓒ | Ⓓ |
| 195 | Ⓐ | Ⓑ | Ⓒ | Ⓓ |
| 196 | Ⓐ | Ⓑ | Ⓒ | Ⓓ |
| 197 | Ⓐ | Ⓑ | Ⓒ | Ⓓ |
| 198 | Ⓐ | Ⓑ | Ⓒ | Ⓓ |
| 199 | Ⓐ | Ⓑ | Ⓒ | Ⓓ |
| 200 | Ⓐ | Ⓑ | Ⓒ | Ⓓ |

## LISTENING SECTION

| | A | B | C | D |
|---|---|---|---|---|
| 1 | Ⓐ | Ⓑ | Ⓒ | Ⓓ |
| 2 | Ⓐ | Ⓑ | Ⓒ | Ⓓ |
| 3 | Ⓐ | Ⓑ | Ⓒ | Ⓓ |
| 4 | Ⓐ | Ⓑ | Ⓒ | Ⓓ |
| 5 | Ⓐ | Ⓑ | Ⓒ | Ⓓ |
| 6 | Ⓐ | Ⓑ | Ⓒ | Ⓓ |
| 7 | Ⓐ | Ⓑ | Ⓒ | Ⓓ |
| 8 | Ⓐ | Ⓑ | Ⓒ | Ⓓ |
| 9 | Ⓐ | Ⓑ | Ⓒ | Ⓓ |
| 10 | Ⓐ | Ⓑ | Ⓒ | Ⓓ |
| 11 | Ⓐ | Ⓑ | Ⓒ | Ⓓ |
| 12 | Ⓐ | Ⓑ | Ⓒ | Ⓓ |
| 13 | Ⓐ | Ⓑ | Ⓒ | Ⓓ |
| 14 | Ⓐ | Ⓑ | Ⓒ | Ⓓ |
| 15 | Ⓐ | Ⓑ | Ⓒ | Ⓓ |
| 16 | Ⓐ | Ⓑ | Ⓒ | Ⓓ |
| 17 | Ⓐ | Ⓑ | Ⓒ | Ⓓ |
| 18 | Ⓐ | Ⓑ | Ⓒ | Ⓓ |
| 19 | Ⓐ | Ⓑ | Ⓒ | Ⓓ |
| 20 | Ⓐ | Ⓑ | Ⓒ | Ⓓ |
| 21 | Ⓐ | Ⓑ | Ⓒ | Ⓓ |
| 22 | Ⓐ | Ⓑ | Ⓒ | Ⓓ |
| 23 | Ⓐ | Ⓑ | Ⓒ | Ⓓ |
| 24 | Ⓐ | Ⓑ | Ⓒ | Ⓓ |
| 25 | Ⓐ | Ⓑ | Ⓒ | Ⓓ |
| 26 | Ⓐ | Ⓑ | Ⓒ | Ⓓ |
| 27 | Ⓐ | Ⓑ | Ⓒ | Ⓓ |
| 28 | Ⓐ | Ⓑ | Ⓒ | Ⓓ |
| 29 | Ⓐ | Ⓑ | Ⓒ | Ⓓ |
| 30 | Ⓐ | Ⓑ | Ⓒ | Ⓓ |
| 31 | Ⓐ | Ⓑ | Ⓒ | Ⓓ |
| 32 | Ⓐ | Ⓑ | Ⓒ | Ⓓ |
| 33 | Ⓐ | Ⓑ | Ⓒ | Ⓓ |
| 34 | Ⓐ | Ⓑ | Ⓒ | Ⓓ |
| 35 | Ⓐ | Ⓑ | Ⓒ | Ⓓ |
| 36 | Ⓐ | Ⓑ | Ⓒ | Ⓓ |
| 37 | Ⓐ | Ⓑ | Ⓒ | Ⓓ |
| 38 | Ⓐ | Ⓑ | Ⓒ | Ⓓ |
| 39 | Ⓐ | Ⓑ | Ⓒ | Ⓓ |
| 40 | Ⓐ | Ⓑ | Ⓒ | Ⓓ |
| 41 | Ⓐ | Ⓑ | Ⓒ | Ⓓ |
| 42 | Ⓐ | Ⓑ | Ⓒ | Ⓓ |
| 43 | Ⓐ | Ⓑ | Ⓒ | Ⓓ |
| 44 | Ⓐ | Ⓑ | Ⓒ | Ⓓ |
| 45 | Ⓐ | Ⓑ | Ⓒ | Ⓓ |
| 46 | Ⓐ | Ⓑ | Ⓒ | Ⓓ |
| 47 | Ⓐ | Ⓑ | Ⓒ | Ⓓ |
| 48 | Ⓐ | Ⓑ | Ⓒ | Ⓓ |
| 49 | Ⓐ | Ⓑ | Ⓒ | Ⓓ |
| 50 | Ⓐ | Ⓑ | Ⓒ | Ⓓ |
| 51 | Ⓐ | Ⓑ | Ⓒ | Ⓓ |
| 52 | Ⓐ | Ⓑ | Ⓒ | Ⓓ |
| 53 | Ⓐ | Ⓑ | Ⓒ | Ⓓ |
| 54 | Ⓐ | Ⓑ | Ⓒ | Ⓓ |
| 55 | Ⓐ | Ⓑ | Ⓒ | Ⓓ |
| 56 | Ⓐ | Ⓑ | Ⓒ | Ⓓ |
| 57 | Ⓐ | Ⓑ | Ⓒ | Ⓓ |
| 58 | Ⓐ | Ⓑ | Ⓒ | Ⓓ |
| 59 | Ⓐ | Ⓑ | Ⓒ | Ⓓ |
| 60 | Ⓐ | Ⓑ | Ⓒ | Ⓓ |
| 61 | Ⓐ | Ⓑ | Ⓒ | Ⓓ |
| 62 | Ⓐ | Ⓑ | Ⓒ | Ⓓ |
| 63 | Ⓐ | Ⓑ | Ⓒ | Ⓓ |
| 64 | Ⓐ | Ⓑ | Ⓒ | Ⓓ |
| 65 | Ⓐ | Ⓑ | Ⓒ | Ⓓ |
| 66 | Ⓐ | Ⓑ | Ⓒ | Ⓓ |
| 67 | Ⓐ | Ⓑ | Ⓒ | Ⓓ |
| 68 | Ⓐ | Ⓑ | Ⓒ | Ⓓ |
| 69 | Ⓐ | Ⓑ | Ⓒ | Ⓓ |
| 70 | Ⓐ | Ⓑ | Ⓒ | Ⓓ |
| 71 | Ⓐ | Ⓑ | Ⓒ | Ⓓ |
| 72 | Ⓐ | Ⓑ | Ⓒ | Ⓓ |
| 73 | Ⓐ | Ⓑ | Ⓒ | Ⓓ |
| 74 | Ⓐ | Ⓑ | Ⓒ | Ⓓ |
| 75 | Ⓐ | Ⓑ | Ⓒ | Ⓓ |
| 76 | Ⓐ | Ⓑ | Ⓒ | Ⓓ |
| 77 | Ⓐ | Ⓑ | Ⓒ | Ⓓ |
| 78 | Ⓐ | Ⓑ | Ⓒ | Ⓓ |
| 79 | Ⓐ | Ⓑ | Ⓒ | Ⓓ |
| 80 | Ⓐ | Ⓑ | Ⓒ | Ⓓ |
| 81 | Ⓐ | Ⓑ | Ⓒ | Ⓓ |
| 82 | Ⓐ | Ⓑ | Ⓒ | Ⓓ |
| 83 | Ⓐ | Ⓑ | Ⓒ | Ⓓ |
| 84 | Ⓐ | Ⓑ | Ⓒ | Ⓓ |
| 85 | Ⓐ | Ⓑ | Ⓒ | Ⓓ |
| 86 | Ⓐ | Ⓑ | Ⓒ | Ⓓ |
| 87 | Ⓐ | Ⓑ | Ⓒ | Ⓓ |
| 88 | Ⓐ | Ⓑ | Ⓒ | Ⓓ |
| 89 | Ⓐ | Ⓑ | Ⓒ | Ⓓ |
| 90 | Ⓐ | Ⓑ | Ⓒ | Ⓓ |
| 91 | Ⓐ | Ⓑ | Ⓒ | Ⓓ |
| 92 | Ⓐ | Ⓑ | Ⓒ | Ⓓ |
| 93 | Ⓐ | Ⓑ | Ⓒ | Ⓓ |
| 94 | Ⓐ | Ⓑ | Ⓒ | Ⓓ |
| 95 | Ⓐ | Ⓑ | Ⓒ | Ⓓ |
| 96 | Ⓐ | Ⓑ | Ⓒ | Ⓓ |
| 97 | Ⓐ | Ⓑ | Ⓒ | Ⓓ |
| 98 | Ⓐ | Ⓑ | Ⓒ | Ⓓ |
| 99 | Ⓐ | Ⓑ | Ⓒ | Ⓓ |
| 100 | Ⓐ | Ⓑ | Ⓒ | Ⓓ |

## Actual Test 4

# Answer Sheet

## READING SECTION

| # | A | B | C | D |
|---|---|---|---|---|
| 101 | Ⓐ | Ⓑ | Ⓒ | Ⓓ |
| 102 | Ⓐ | Ⓑ | Ⓒ | Ⓓ |
| 103 | Ⓐ | Ⓑ | Ⓒ | Ⓓ |
| 104 | Ⓐ | Ⓑ | Ⓒ | Ⓓ |
| 105 | Ⓐ | Ⓑ | Ⓒ | Ⓓ |
| 106 | Ⓐ | Ⓑ | Ⓒ | Ⓓ |
| 107 | Ⓐ | Ⓑ | Ⓒ | Ⓓ |
| 108 | Ⓐ | Ⓑ | Ⓒ | Ⓓ |
| 109 | Ⓐ | Ⓑ | Ⓒ | Ⓓ |
| 110 | Ⓐ | Ⓑ | Ⓒ | Ⓓ |
| 111 | Ⓐ | Ⓑ | Ⓒ | Ⓓ |
| 112 | Ⓐ | Ⓑ | Ⓒ | Ⓓ |
| 113 | Ⓐ | Ⓑ | Ⓒ | Ⓓ |
| 114 | Ⓐ | Ⓑ | Ⓒ | Ⓓ |
| 115 | Ⓐ | Ⓑ | Ⓒ | Ⓓ |
| 116 | Ⓐ | Ⓑ | Ⓒ | Ⓓ |
| 117 | Ⓐ | Ⓑ | Ⓒ | Ⓓ |
| 118 | Ⓐ | Ⓑ | Ⓒ | Ⓓ |
| 119 | Ⓐ | Ⓑ | Ⓒ | Ⓓ |
| 120 | Ⓐ | Ⓑ | Ⓒ | Ⓓ |
| 121 | Ⓐ | Ⓑ | Ⓒ | Ⓓ |
| 122 | Ⓐ | Ⓑ | Ⓒ | Ⓓ |
| 123 | Ⓐ | Ⓑ | Ⓒ | Ⓓ |
| 124 | Ⓐ | Ⓑ | Ⓒ | Ⓓ |
| 125 | Ⓐ | Ⓑ | Ⓒ | Ⓓ |
| 126 | Ⓐ | Ⓑ | Ⓒ | Ⓓ |
| 127 | Ⓐ | Ⓑ | Ⓒ | Ⓓ |
| 128 | Ⓐ | Ⓑ | Ⓒ | Ⓓ |
| 129 | Ⓐ | Ⓑ | Ⓒ | Ⓓ |
| 130 | Ⓐ | Ⓑ | Ⓒ | Ⓓ |
| 131 | Ⓐ | Ⓑ | Ⓒ | Ⓓ |
| 132 | Ⓐ | Ⓑ | Ⓒ | Ⓓ |
| 133 | Ⓐ | Ⓑ | Ⓒ | Ⓓ |
| 134 | Ⓐ | Ⓑ | Ⓒ | Ⓓ |
| 135 | Ⓐ | Ⓑ | Ⓒ | Ⓓ |
| 136 | Ⓐ | Ⓑ | Ⓒ | Ⓓ |
| 137 | Ⓐ | Ⓑ | Ⓒ | Ⓓ |
| 138 | Ⓐ | Ⓑ | Ⓒ | Ⓓ |
| 139 | Ⓐ | Ⓑ | Ⓒ | Ⓓ |
| 140 | Ⓐ | Ⓑ | Ⓒ | Ⓓ |
| 141 | Ⓐ | Ⓑ | Ⓒ | Ⓓ |
| 142 | Ⓐ | Ⓑ | Ⓒ | Ⓓ |
| 143 | Ⓐ | Ⓑ | Ⓒ | Ⓓ |
| 144 | Ⓐ | Ⓑ | Ⓒ | Ⓓ |
| 145 | Ⓐ | Ⓑ | Ⓒ | Ⓓ |
| 146 | Ⓐ | Ⓑ | Ⓒ | Ⓓ |
| 147 | Ⓐ | Ⓑ | Ⓒ | Ⓓ |
| 148 | Ⓐ | Ⓑ | Ⓒ | Ⓓ |
| 149 | Ⓐ | Ⓑ | Ⓒ | Ⓓ |
| 150 | Ⓐ | Ⓑ | Ⓒ | Ⓓ |
| 151 | Ⓐ | Ⓑ | Ⓒ | Ⓓ |
| 152 | Ⓐ | Ⓑ | Ⓒ | Ⓓ |
| 153 | Ⓐ | Ⓑ | Ⓒ | Ⓓ |
| 154 | Ⓐ | Ⓑ | Ⓒ | Ⓓ |
| 155 | Ⓐ | Ⓑ | Ⓒ | Ⓓ |
| 156 | Ⓐ | Ⓑ | Ⓒ | Ⓓ |
| 157 | Ⓐ | Ⓑ | Ⓒ | Ⓓ |
| 158 | Ⓐ | Ⓑ | Ⓒ | Ⓓ |
| 159 | Ⓐ | Ⓑ | Ⓒ | Ⓓ |
| 160 | Ⓐ | Ⓑ | Ⓒ | Ⓓ |
| 161 | Ⓐ | Ⓑ | Ⓒ | Ⓓ |
| 162 | Ⓐ | Ⓑ | Ⓒ | Ⓓ |
| 163 | Ⓐ | Ⓑ | Ⓒ | Ⓓ |
| 164 | Ⓐ | Ⓑ | Ⓒ | Ⓓ |
| 165 | Ⓐ | Ⓑ | Ⓒ | Ⓓ |
| 166 | Ⓐ | Ⓑ | Ⓒ | Ⓓ |
| 167 | Ⓐ | Ⓑ | Ⓒ | Ⓓ |
| 168 | Ⓐ | Ⓑ | Ⓒ | Ⓓ |
| 169 | Ⓐ | Ⓑ | Ⓒ | Ⓓ |
| 170 | Ⓐ | Ⓑ | Ⓒ | Ⓓ |
| 171 | Ⓐ | Ⓑ | Ⓒ | Ⓓ |
| 172 | Ⓐ | Ⓑ | Ⓒ | Ⓓ |
| 173 | Ⓐ | Ⓑ | Ⓒ | Ⓓ |
| 174 | Ⓐ | Ⓑ | Ⓒ | Ⓓ |
| 175 | Ⓐ | Ⓑ | Ⓒ | Ⓓ |
| 176 | Ⓐ | Ⓑ | Ⓒ | Ⓓ |
| 177 | Ⓐ | Ⓑ | Ⓒ | Ⓓ |
| 178 | Ⓐ | Ⓑ | Ⓒ | Ⓓ |
| 179 | Ⓐ | Ⓑ | Ⓒ | Ⓓ |
| 180 | Ⓐ | Ⓑ | Ⓒ | Ⓓ |
| 181 | Ⓐ | Ⓑ | Ⓒ | Ⓓ |
| 182 | Ⓐ | Ⓑ | Ⓒ | Ⓓ |
| 183 | Ⓐ | Ⓑ | Ⓒ | Ⓓ |
| 184 | Ⓐ | Ⓑ | Ⓒ | Ⓓ |
| 185 | Ⓐ | Ⓑ | Ⓒ | Ⓓ |
| 186 | Ⓐ | Ⓑ | Ⓒ | Ⓓ |
| 187 | Ⓐ | Ⓑ | Ⓒ | Ⓓ |
| 188 | Ⓐ | Ⓑ | Ⓒ | Ⓓ |
| 189 | Ⓐ | Ⓑ | Ⓒ | Ⓓ |
| 190 | Ⓐ | Ⓑ | Ⓒ | Ⓓ |
| 191 | Ⓐ | Ⓑ | Ⓒ | Ⓓ |
| 192 | Ⓐ | Ⓑ | Ⓒ | Ⓓ |
| 193 | Ⓐ | Ⓑ | Ⓒ | Ⓓ |
| 194 | Ⓐ | Ⓑ | Ⓒ | Ⓓ |
| 195 | Ⓐ | Ⓑ | Ⓒ | Ⓓ |
| 196 | Ⓐ | Ⓑ | Ⓒ | Ⓓ |
| 197 | Ⓐ | Ⓑ | Ⓒ | Ⓓ |
| 198 | Ⓐ | Ⓑ | Ⓒ | Ⓓ |
| 199 | Ⓐ | Ⓑ | Ⓒ | Ⓓ |
| 200 | Ⓐ | Ⓑ | Ⓒ | Ⓓ |

## LISTENING SECTION

| # | A | B | C | D |
|---|---|---|---|---|
| 1 | Ⓐ | Ⓑ | Ⓒ | Ⓓ |
| 2 | Ⓐ | Ⓑ | Ⓒ | Ⓓ |
| 3 | Ⓐ | Ⓑ | Ⓒ | Ⓓ |
| 4 | Ⓐ | Ⓑ | Ⓒ | Ⓓ |
| 5 | Ⓐ | Ⓑ | Ⓒ | Ⓓ |
| 6 | Ⓐ | Ⓑ | Ⓒ | Ⓓ |
| 7 | Ⓐ | Ⓑ | Ⓒ | Ⓓ |
| 8 | Ⓐ | Ⓑ | Ⓒ | Ⓓ |
| 9 | Ⓐ | Ⓑ | Ⓒ | Ⓓ |
| 10 | Ⓐ | Ⓑ | Ⓒ | Ⓓ |
| 11 | Ⓐ | Ⓑ | Ⓒ | Ⓓ |
| 12 | Ⓐ | Ⓑ | Ⓒ | Ⓓ |
| 13 | Ⓐ | Ⓑ | Ⓒ | Ⓓ |
| 14 | Ⓐ | Ⓑ | Ⓒ | Ⓓ |
| 15 | Ⓐ | Ⓑ | Ⓒ | Ⓓ |
| 16 | Ⓐ | Ⓑ | Ⓒ | Ⓓ |
| 17 | Ⓐ | Ⓑ | Ⓒ | Ⓓ |
| 18 | Ⓐ | Ⓑ | Ⓒ | Ⓓ |
| 19 | Ⓐ | Ⓑ | Ⓒ | Ⓓ |
| 20 | Ⓐ | Ⓑ | Ⓒ | Ⓓ |
| 21 | Ⓐ | Ⓑ | Ⓒ | Ⓓ |
| 22 | Ⓐ | Ⓑ | Ⓒ | Ⓓ |
| 23 | Ⓐ | Ⓑ | Ⓒ | Ⓓ |
| 24 | Ⓐ | Ⓑ | Ⓒ | Ⓓ |
| 25 | Ⓐ | Ⓑ | Ⓒ | Ⓓ |
| 26 | Ⓐ | Ⓑ | Ⓒ | Ⓓ |
| 27 | Ⓐ | Ⓑ | Ⓒ | Ⓓ |
| 28 | Ⓐ | Ⓑ | Ⓒ | Ⓓ |
| 29 | Ⓐ | Ⓑ | Ⓒ | Ⓓ |
| 30 | Ⓐ | Ⓑ | Ⓒ | Ⓓ |
| 31 | Ⓐ | Ⓑ | Ⓒ | Ⓓ |
| 32 | Ⓐ | Ⓑ | Ⓒ | Ⓓ |
| 33 | Ⓐ | Ⓑ | Ⓒ | Ⓓ |
| 34 | Ⓐ | Ⓑ | Ⓒ | Ⓓ |
| 35 | Ⓐ | Ⓑ | Ⓒ | Ⓓ |
| 36 | Ⓐ | Ⓑ | Ⓒ | Ⓓ |
| 37 | Ⓐ | Ⓑ | Ⓒ | Ⓓ |
| 38 | Ⓐ | Ⓑ | Ⓒ | Ⓓ |
| 39 | Ⓐ | Ⓑ | Ⓒ | Ⓓ |
| 40 | Ⓐ | Ⓑ | Ⓒ | Ⓓ |
| 41 | Ⓐ | Ⓑ | Ⓒ | Ⓓ |
| 42 | Ⓐ | Ⓑ | Ⓒ | Ⓓ |
| 43 | Ⓐ | Ⓑ | Ⓒ | Ⓓ |
| 44 | Ⓐ | Ⓑ | Ⓒ | Ⓓ |
| 45 | Ⓐ | Ⓑ | Ⓒ | Ⓓ |
| 46 | Ⓐ | Ⓑ | Ⓒ | Ⓓ |
| 47 | Ⓐ | Ⓑ | Ⓒ | Ⓓ |
| 48 | Ⓐ | Ⓑ | Ⓒ | Ⓓ |
| 49 | Ⓐ | Ⓑ | Ⓒ | Ⓓ |
| 50 | Ⓐ | Ⓑ | Ⓒ | Ⓓ |
| 51 | Ⓐ | Ⓑ | Ⓒ | Ⓓ |
| 52 | Ⓐ | Ⓑ | Ⓒ | Ⓓ |
| 53 | Ⓐ | Ⓑ | Ⓒ | Ⓓ |
| 54 | Ⓐ | Ⓑ | Ⓒ | Ⓓ |
| 55 | Ⓐ | Ⓑ | Ⓒ | Ⓓ |
| 56 | Ⓐ | Ⓑ | Ⓒ | Ⓓ |
| 57 | Ⓐ | Ⓑ | Ⓒ | Ⓓ |
| 58 | Ⓐ | Ⓑ | Ⓒ | Ⓓ |
| 59 | Ⓐ | Ⓑ | Ⓒ | Ⓓ |
| 60 | Ⓐ | Ⓑ | Ⓒ | Ⓓ |
| 61 | Ⓐ | Ⓑ | Ⓒ | Ⓓ |
| 62 | Ⓐ | Ⓑ | Ⓒ | Ⓓ |
| 63 | Ⓐ | Ⓑ | Ⓒ | Ⓓ |
| 64 | Ⓐ | Ⓑ | Ⓒ | Ⓓ |
| 65 | Ⓐ | Ⓑ | Ⓒ | Ⓓ |
| 66 | Ⓐ | Ⓑ | Ⓒ | Ⓓ |
| 67 | Ⓐ | Ⓑ | Ⓒ | Ⓓ |
| 68 | Ⓐ | Ⓑ | Ⓒ | Ⓓ |
| 69 | Ⓐ | Ⓑ | Ⓒ | Ⓓ |
| 70 | Ⓐ | Ⓑ | Ⓒ | Ⓓ |
| 71 | Ⓐ | Ⓑ | Ⓒ | Ⓓ |
| 72 | Ⓐ | Ⓑ | Ⓒ | Ⓓ |
| 73 | Ⓐ | Ⓑ | Ⓒ | Ⓓ |
| 74 | Ⓐ | Ⓑ | Ⓒ | Ⓓ |
| 75 | Ⓐ | Ⓑ | Ⓒ | Ⓓ |
| 76 | Ⓐ | Ⓑ | Ⓒ | Ⓓ |
| 77 | Ⓐ | Ⓑ | Ⓒ | Ⓓ |
| 78 | Ⓐ | Ⓑ | Ⓒ | Ⓓ |
| 79 | Ⓐ | Ⓑ | Ⓒ | Ⓓ |
| 80 | Ⓐ | Ⓑ | Ⓒ | Ⓓ |
| 81 | Ⓐ | Ⓑ | Ⓒ | Ⓓ |
| 82 | Ⓐ | Ⓑ | Ⓒ | Ⓓ |
| 83 | Ⓐ | Ⓑ | Ⓒ | Ⓓ |
| 84 | Ⓐ | Ⓑ | Ⓒ | Ⓓ |
| 85 | Ⓐ | Ⓑ | Ⓒ | Ⓓ |
| 86 | Ⓐ | Ⓑ | Ⓒ | Ⓓ |
| 87 | Ⓐ | Ⓑ | Ⓒ | Ⓓ |
| 88 | Ⓐ | Ⓑ | Ⓒ | Ⓓ |
| 89 | Ⓐ | Ⓑ | Ⓒ | Ⓓ |
| 90 | Ⓐ | Ⓑ | Ⓒ | Ⓓ |
| 91 | Ⓐ | Ⓑ | Ⓒ | Ⓓ |
| 92 | Ⓐ | Ⓑ | Ⓒ | Ⓓ |
| 93 | Ⓐ | Ⓑ | Ⓒ | Ⓓ |
| 94 | Ⓐ | Ⓑ | Ⓒ | Ⓓ |
| 95 | Ⓐ | Ⓑ | Ⓒ | Ⓓ |
| 96 | Ⓐ | Ⓑ | Ⓒ | Ⓓ |
| 97 | Ⓐ | Ⓑ | Ⓒ | Ⓓ |
| 98 | Ⓐ | Ⓑ | Ⓒ | Ⓓ |
| 99 | Ⓐ | Ⓑ | Ⓒ | Ⓓ |
| 100 | Ⓐ | Ⓑ | Ⓒ | Ⓓ |

Actual Test 5

# Answer Sheet

## READING SECTION

| | 101 | 102 | 103 | 104 | 105 | 106 | 107 | 108 | 109 | 110 |
|---|---|---|---|---|---|---|---|---|---|---|
| | Ⓐ | Ⓐ | Ⓐ | Ⓐ | Ⓐ | Ⓐ | Ⓐ | Ⓐ | Ⓐ | Ⓐ |
| | Ⓑ | Ⓑ | Ⓑ | Ⓑ | Ⓑ | Ⓑ | Ⓑ | Ⓑ | Ⓑ | Ⓑ |
| | Ⓒ | Ⓒ | Ⓒ | Ⓒ | Ⓒ | Ⓒ | Ⓒ | Ⓒ | Ⓒ | Ⓒ |
| | Ⓓ | Ⓓ | Ⓓ | Ⓓ | Ⓓ | Ⓓ | Ⓓ | Ⓓ | Ⓓ | Ⓓ |

| | 111 | 112 | 113 | 114 | 115 | 116 | 117 | 118 | 119 | 120 |
|---|---|---|---|---|---|---|---|---|---|---|
| | Ⓐ | Ⓐ | Ⓐ | Ⓐ | Ⓐ | Ⓐ | Ⓐ | Ⓐ | Ⓐ | Ⓐ |
| | Ⓑ | Ⓑ | Ⓑ | Ⓑ | Ⓑ | Ⓑ | Ⓑ | Ⓑ | Ⓑ | Ⓑ |
| | Ⓒ | Ⓒ | Ⓒ | Ⓒ | Ⓒ | Ⓒ | Ⓒ | Ⓒ | Ⓒ | Ⓒ |
| | Ⓓ | Ⓓ | Ⓓ | Ⓓ | Ⓓ | Ⓓ | Ⓓ | Ⓓ | Ⓓ | Ⓓ |

| | 121 | 122 | 123 | 124 | 125 | 126 | 127 | 128 | 129 | 130 |
|---|---|---|---|---|---|---|---|---|---|---|
| | Ⓐ | Ⓐ | Ⓐ | Ⓐ | Ⓐ | Ⓐ | Ⓐ | Ⓐ | Ⓐ | Ⓐ |
| | Ⓑ | Ⓑ | Ⓑ | Ⓑ | Ⓑ | Ⓑ | Ⓑ | Ⓑ | Ⓑ | Ⓑ |
| | Ⓒ | Ⓒ | Ⓒ | Ⓒ | Ⓒ | Ⓒ | Ⓒ | Ⓒ | Ⓒ | Ⓒ |
| | Ⓓ | Ⓓ | Ⓓ | Ⓓ | Ⓓ | Ⓓ | Ⓓ | Ⓓ | Ⓓ | Ⓓ |

| | 131 | 132 | 133 | 134 | 135 | 136 | 137 | 138 | 139 | 140 |
|---|---|---|---|---|---|---|---|---|---|---|
| | Ⓐ | Ⓐ | Ⓐ | Ⓐ | Ⓐ | Ⓐ | Ⓐ | Ⓐ | Ⓐ | Ⓐ |
| | Ⓑ | Ⓑ | Ⓑ | Ⓑ | Ⓑ | Ⓑ | Ⓑ | Ⓑ | Ⓑ | Ⓑ |
| | Ⓒ | Ⓒ | Ⓒ | Ⓒ | Ⓒ | Ⓒ | Ⓒ | Ⓒ | Ⓒ | Ⓒ |
| | Ⓓ | Ⓓ | Ⓓ | Ⓓ | Ⓓ | Ⓓ | Ⓓ | Ⓓ | Ⓓ | Ⓓ |

| | 141 | 142 | 143 | 144 | 145 | 146 | 147 | 148 | 149 | 150 |
|---|---|---|---|---|---|---|---|---|---|---|
| | Ⓐ | Ⓐ | Ⓐ | Ⓐ | Ⓐ | Ⓐ | Ⓐ | Ⓐ | Ⓐ | Ⓐ |
| | Ⓑ | Ⓑ | Ⓑ | Ⓑ | Ⓑ | Ⓑ | Ⓑ | Ⓑ | Ⓑ | Ⓑ |
| | Ⓒ | Ⓒ | Ⓒ | Ⓒ | Ⓒ | Ⓒ | Ⓒ | Ⓒ | Ⓒ | Ⓒ |
| | Ⓓ | Ⓓ | Ⓓ | Ⓓ | Ⓓ | Ⓓ | Ⓓ | Ⓓ | Ⓓ | Ⓓ |

| | 151 | 152 | 153 | 154 | 155 | 156 | 157 | 158 | 159 | 160 |
|---|---|---|---|---|---|---|---|---|---|---|
| | Ⓐ | Ⓐ | Ⓐ | Ⓐ | Ⓐ | Ⓐ | Ⓐ | Ⓐ | Ⓐ | Ⓐ |
| | Ⓑ | Ⓑ | Ⓑ | Ⓑ | Ⓑ | Ⓑ | Ⓑ | Ⓑ | Ⓑ | Ⓑ |
| | Ⓒ | Ⓒ | Ⓒ | Ⓒ | Ⓒ | Ⓒ | Ⓒ | Ⓒ | Ⓒ | Ⓒ |
| | Ⓓ | Ⓓ | Ⓓ | Ⓓ | Ⓓ | Ⓓ | Ⓓ | Ⓓ | Ⓓ | Ⓓ |

| | 161 | 162 | 163 | 164 | 165 | 166 | 167 | 168 | 169 | 170 |
|---|---|---|---|---|---|---|---|---|---|---|
| | Ⓐ | Ⓐ | Ⓐ | Ⓐ | Ⓐ | Ⓐ | Ⓐ | Ⓐ | Ⓐ | Ⓐ |
| | Ⓑ | Ⓑ | Ⓑ | Ⓑ | Ⓑ | Ⓑ | Ⓑ | Ⓑ | Ⓑ | Ⓑ |
| | Ⓒ | Ⓒ | Ⓒ | Ⓒ | Ⓒ | Ⓒ | Ⓒ | Ⓒ | Ⓒ | Ⓒ |
| | Ⓓ | Ⓓ | Ⓓ | Ⓓ | Ⓓ | Ⓓ | Ⓓ | Ⓓ | Ⓓ | Ⓓ |

| | 171 | 172 | 173 | 174 | 175 | 176 | 177 | 178 | 179 | 180 |
|---|---|---|---|---|---|---|---|---|---|---|
| | Ⓐ | Ⓐ | Ⓐ | Ⓐ | Ⓐ | Ⓐ | Ⓐ | Ⓐ | Ⓐ | Ⓐ |
| | Ⓑ | Ⓑ | Ⓑ | Ⓑ | Ⓑ | Ⓑ | Ⓑ | Ⓑ | Ⓑ | Ⓑ |
| | Ⓒ | Ⓒ | Ⓒ | Ⓒ | Ⓒ | Ⓒ | Ⓒ | Ⓒ | Ⓒ | Ⓒ |
| | Ⓓ | Ⓓ | Ⓓ | Ⓓ | Ⓓ | Ⓓ | Ⓓ | Ⓓ | Ⓓ | Ⓓ |

| | 181 | 182 | 183 | 184 | 185 | 186 | 187 | 188 | 189 | 190 |
|---|---|---|---|---|---|---|---|---|---|---|
| | Ⓐ | Ⓐ | Ⓐ | Ⓐ | Ⓐ | Ⓐ | Ⓐ | Ⓐ | Ⓐ | Ⓐ |
| | Ⓑ | Ⓑ | Ⓑ | Ⓑ | Ⓑ | Ⓑ | Ⓑ | Ⓑ | Ⓑ | Ⓑ |
| | Ⓒ | Ⓒ | Ⓒ | Ⓒ | Ⓒ | Ⓒ | Ⓒ | Ⓒ | Ⓒ | Ⓒ |
| | Ⓓ | Ⓓ | Ⓓ | Ⓓ | Ⓓ | Ⓓ | Ⓓ | Ⓓ | Ⓓ | Ⓓ |

| | 191 | 192 | 193 | 194 | 195 | 196 | 197 | 198 | 199 | 200 |
|---|---|---|---|---|---|---|---|---|---|---|
| | Ⓐ | Ⓐ | Ⓐ | Ⓐ | Ⓐ | Ⓐ | Ⓐ | Ⓐ | Ⓐ | Ⓐ |
| | Ⓑ | Ⓑ | Ⓑ | Ⓑ | Ⓑ | Ⓑ | Ⓑ | Ⓑ | Ⓑ | Ⓑ |
| | Ⓒ | Ⓒ | Ⓒ | Ⓒ | Ⓒ | Ⓒ | Ⓒ | Ⓒ | Ⓒ | Ⓒ |
| | Ⓓ | Ⓓ | Ⓓ | Ⓓ | Ⓓ | Ⓓ | Ⓓ | Ⓓ | Ⓓ | Ⓓ |

## LISTENING SECTION

| | 1 | 2 | 3 | 4 | 5 | 6 | 7 | 8 | 9 | 10 |
|---|---|---|---|---|---|---|---|---|---|---|
| | Ⓐ | Ⓐ | Ⓐ | Ⓐ | Ⓐ | Ⓐ | Ⓐ | Ⓐ | Ⓐ | Ⓐ |
| | Ⓑ | Ⓑ | Ⓑ | Ⓑ | Ⓑ | Ⓑ | Ⓑ | Ⓑ | Ⓑ | Ⓑ |
| | Ⓒ | Ⓒ | Ⓒ | Ⓒ | Ⓒ | Ⓒ | Ⓒ | Ⓒ | Ⓒ | Ⓒ |
| | Ⓓ | Ⓓ | Ⓓ | Ⓓ | Ⓓ | Ⓓ | Ⓓ | Ⓓ | Ⓓ | Ⓓ |

| | 11 | 12 | 13 | 14 | 15 | 16 | 17 | 18 | 19 | 20 |
|---|---|---|---|---|---|---|---|---|---|---|
| | Ⓐ | Ⓐ | Ⓐ | Ⓐ | Ⓐ | Ⓐ | Ⓐ | Ⓐ | Ⓐ | Ⓐ |
| | Ⓑ | Ⓑ | Ⓑ | Ⓑ | Ⓑ | Ⓑ | Ⓑ | Ⓑ | Ⓑ | Ⓑ |
| | Ⓒ | Ⓒ | Ⓒ | Ⓒ | Ⓒ | Ⓒ | Ⓒ | Ⓒ | Ⓒ | Ⓒ |
| | Ⓓ | Ⓓ | Ⓓ | Ⓓ | Ⓓ | Ⓓ | Ⓓ | Ⓓ | Ⓓ | Ⓓ |

| | 21 | 22 | 23 | 24 | 25 | 26 | 27 | 28 | 29 | 30 |
|---|---|---|---|---|---|---|---|---|---|---|
| | Ⓐ | Ⓐ | Ⓐ | Ⓐ | Ⓐ | Ⓐ | Ⓐ | Ⓐ | Ⓐ | Ⓐ |
| | Ⓑ | Ⓑ | Ⓑ | Ⓑ | Ⓑ | Ⓑ | Ⓑ | Ⓑ | Ⓑ | Ⓑ |
| | Ⓒ | Ⓒ | Ⓒ | Ⓒ | Ⓒ | Ⓒ | Ⓒ | Ⓒ | Ⓒ | Ⓒ |
| | Ⓓ | Ⓓ | Ⓓ | Ⓓ | Ⓓ | Ⓓ | Ⓓ | Ⓓ | Ⓓ | Ⓓ |

| | 31 | 32 | 33 | 34 | 35 | 36 | 37 | 38 | 39 | 40 |
|---|---|---|---|---|---|---|---|---|---|---|
| | Ⓐ | Ⓐ | Ⓐ | Ⓐ | Ⓐ | Ⓐ | Ⓐ | Ⓐ | Ⓐ | Ⓐ |
| | Ⓑ | Ⓑ | Ⓑ | Ⓑ | Ⓑ | Ⓑ | Ⓑ | Ⓑ | Ⓑ | Ⓑ |
| | Ⓒ | Ⓒ | Ⓒ | Ⓒ | Ⓒ | Ⓒ | Ⓒ | Ⓒ | Ⓒ | Ⓒ |
| | Ⓓ | Ⓓ | Ⓓ | Ⓓ | Ⓓ | Ⓓ | Ⓓ | Ⓓ | Ⓓ | Ⓓ |

| | 41 | 42 | 43 | 44 | 45 | 46 | 47 | 48 | 49 | 50 |
|---|---|---|---|---|---|---|---|---|---|---|
| | Ⓐ | Ⓐ | Ⓐ | Ⓐ | Ⓐ | Ⓐ | Ⓐ | Ⓐ | Ⓐ | Ⓐ |
| | Ⓑ | Ⓑ | Ⓑ | Ⓑ | Ⓑ | Ⓑ | Ⓑ | Ⓑ | Ⓑ | Ⓑ |
| | Ⓒ | Ⓒ | Ⓒ | Ⓒ | Ⓒ | Ⓒ | Ⓒ | Ⓒ | Ⓒ | Ⓒ |
| | Ⓓ | Ⓓ | Ⓓ | Ⓓ | Ⓓ | Ⓓ | Ⓓ | Ⓓ | Ⓓ | Ⓓ |

| | 51 | 52 | 53 | 54 | 55 | 56 | 57 | 58 | 59 | 60 |
|---|---|---|---|---|---|---|---|---|---|---|
| | Ⓐ | Ⓐ | Ⓐ | Ⓐ | Ⓐ | Ⓐ | Ⓐ | Ⓐ | Ⓐ | Ⓐ |
| | Ⓑ | Ⓑ | Ⓑ | Ⓑ | Ⓑ | Ⓑ | Ⓑ | Ⓑ | Ⓑ | Ⓑ |
| | Ⓒ | Ⓒ | Ⓒ | Ⓒ | Ⓒ | Ⓒ | Ⓒ | Ⓒ | Ⓒ | Ⓒ |
| | Ⓓ | Ⓓ | Ⓓ | Ⓓ | Ⓓ | Ⓓ | Ⓓ | Ⓓ | Ⓓ | Ⓓ |

| | 61 | 62 | 63 | 64 | 65 | 66 | 67 | 68 | 69 | 70 |
|---|---|---|---|---|---|---|---|---|---|---|
| | Ⓐ | Ⓐ | Ⓐ | Ⓐ | Ⓐ | Ⓐ | Ⓐ | Ⓐ | Ⓐ | Ⓐ |
| | Ⓑ | Ⓑ | Ⓑ | Ⓑ | Ⓑ | Ⓑ | Ⓑ | Ⓑ | Ⓑ | Ⓑ |
| | Ⓒ | Ⓒ | Ⓒ | Ⓒ | Ⓒ | Ⓒ | Ⓒ | Ⓒ | Ⓒ | Ⓒ |
| | Ⓓ | Ⓓ | Ⓓ | Ⓓ | Ⓓ | Ⓓ | Ⓓ | Ⓓ | Ⓓ | Ⓓ |

| | 71 | 72 | 73 | 74 | 75 | 76 | 77 | 78 | 79 | 80 |
|---|---|---|---|---|---|---|---|---|---|---|
| | Ⓐ | Ⓐ | Ⓐ | Ⓐ | Ⓐ | Ⓐ | Ⓐ | Ⓐ | Ⓐ | Ⓐ |
| | Ⓑ | Ⓑ | Ⓑ | Ⓑ | Ⓑ | Ⓑ | Ⓑ | Ⓑ | Ⓑ | Ⓑ |
| | Ⓒ | Ⓒ | Ⓒ | Ⓒ | Ⓒ | Ⓒ | Ⓒ | Ⓒ | Ⓒ | Ⓒ |
| | Ⓓ | Ⓓ | Ⓓ | Ⓓ | Ⓓ | Ⓓ | Ⓓ | Ⓓ | Ⓓ | Ⓓ |

| | 81 | 82 | 83 | 84 | 85 | 86 | 87 | 88 | 89 | 90 |
|---|---|---|---|---|---|---|---|---|---|---|
| | Ⓐ | Ⓐ | Ⓐ | Ⓐ | Ⓐ | Ⓐ | Ⓐ | Ⓐ | Ⓐ | Ⓐ |
| | Ⓑ | Ⓑ | Ⓑ | Ⓑ | Ⓑ | Ⓑ | Ⓑ | Ⓑ | Ⓑ | Ⓑ |
| | Ⓒ | Ⓒ | Ⓒ | Ⓒ | Ⓒ | Ⓒ | Ⓒ | Ⓒ | Ⓒ | Ⓒ |
| | Ⓓ | Ⓓ | Ⓓ | Ⓓ | Ⓓ | Ⓓ | Ⓓ | Ⓓ | Ⓓ | Ⓓ |

| | 91 | 92 | 93 | 94 | 95 | 96 | 97 | 98 | 99 | 100 |
|---|---|---|---|---|---|---|---|---|---|---|
| | Ⓐ | Ⓐ | Ⓐ | Ⓐ | Ⓐ | Ⓐ | Ⓐ | Ⓐ | Ⓐ | Ⓐ |
| | Ⓑ | Ⓑ | Ⓑ | Ⓑ | Ⓑ | Ⓑ | Ⓑ | Ⓑ | Ⓑ | Ⓑ |
| | Ⓒ | Ⓒ | Ⓒ | Ⓒ | Ⓒ | Ⓒ | Ⓒ | Ⓒ | Ⓒ | Ⓒ |
| | Ⓓ | Ⓓ | Ⓓ | Ⓓ | Ⓓ | Ⓓ | Ⓓ | Ⓓ | Ⓓ | Ⓓ |

**Actual Test 6**

直指新制多益命題趨勢，
# New TOEIC完整六回實戰演練，
## 高效提升多益成績！

**多益權威針對新制多益最新命題趨勢，精心撰寫六回實戰模擬測驗，**
**輕鬆戰勝 NEW TOEIC 新制多益！**

## 本書特色

本書針對新制多益最新命題趨勢方向，編寫六回聽力閱讀模擬實戰考題，並針對
各大題型標示解題線索，有效幫助考生短時間達成目標分數。同時提供不同分數
目標讀者自我學習計畫，考生可針對自己的程度來分配研讀進度，有效掌握學習
成效並強化弱點，培養扎實的應試實力！

### 多益權威精闢出題，命中新制多益出題方針

**1** 本書係多益權威在多年授課鑽研後，針對新制多益命題趨勢，精闢編寫出符合實際
多益考題難度，且題型相似的百分百仿真模擬試題。完整六回聽力閱讀實戰訓練，
讓考生迅速掌握新制多益命題方向，培養實際應考臨場感。

### 詳盡中譯解析，秒懂出題重點與命題邏輯

**2** 每回模擬測驗皆附詳盡中譯解答，作者以多年授課及研究的獨門解題技巧，
針對 Part 5 及 Part 6 詳加分析解題過程，說明選項正確理由，釐清選項錯誤原因。
在聽力對話／獨白與閱讀測驗中，並貼心標示出每題解答線索所在位置，
一眼找出破題關鍵，完美突破解題障礙。

### 提供自我學習計畫表，依據個人程度擬訂作戰計畫

**3** 提供自我學習計畫表，為目標分數設定為 700、800 及 900 以上的不同程度讀者，
擬訂專屬的研讀日程規畫，考生可依據自我的程度分級，掌握自己的學習成效，
有效提升學習效率。

### 由專業外師錄製 MP3，輕鬆克服口音障礙

**4** 附有由專業外師所錄製的 MP3 音檔，含英美加澳四國口音，讓考生快速熟悉各國
口音特色，戰勝新制多益聽力測驗。

寂天 文化事業股份有限公司
Cosmos Culture Ltd.
www.icosmos.com.tw

C1373-1614

# 戰勝
# 新制多益
## 高分演練

NEW
TOEIC

解答&中譯解析本

# 戰勝
# 新制多益
# 高分演練

NEW
TOEIC

# 目錄

# 1 解答

| | | | | | | | | | |
|---|---|---|---|---|---|---|---|---|---|
| 1. (A) | 2. (C) | 3. (B) | 4. (A) | 5. (D) | 6. (C) | 7. (A) | 8. (B) | 9. (C) | 10. (C) |
| 11. (A) | 12. (B) | 13. (B) | 14. (C) | 15. (B) | 16. (A) | 17. (B) | 18. (B) | 19. (A) | 20. (C) |
| 21. (A) | 22. (A) | 23. (B) | 24. (B) | 25. (B) | 26. (C) | 27. (C) | 28. (B) | 29. (C) | 30. (C) |
| 31. (A) | 32. (A) | 33. (D) | 34. (C) | 35. (A) | 36. (C) | 37. (A) | 38. (B) | 39. (A) | 40. (D) |
| 41. (A) | 42. (C) | 43. (C) | 44. (A) | 45. (B) | 46. (A) | 47. (C) | 48. (D) | 49. (A) | 50. (B) |
| 51. (B) | 52. (D) | 53. (C) | 54. (D) | 55. (A) | 56. (C) | 57. (A) | 58. (C) | 59. (D) | 60. (D) |
| 61. (A) | 62. (B) | 63. (D) | 64. (A) | 65. (C) | 66. (A) | 67. (B) | 68. (B) | 69. (C) | 70. (A) |
| 71. (B) | 72. (A) | 73. (A) | 74. (A) | 75. (D) | 76. (D) | 77. (B) | 78. (A) | 79. (A) | 80. (D) |
| 81. (A) | 82. (C) | 83. (D) | 84. (C) | 85. (C) | 86. (B) | 87. (C) | 88. (D) | 89. (A) | 90. (D) |
| 91. (B) | 92. (B) | 93. (C) | 94. (A) | 95. (D) | 96. (C) | 97. (A) | 98. (A) | 99. (C) | 100. (D) |
| 101. (B) | 102. (C) | 103. (B) | 104. (B) | 105. (B) | 106. (A) | 107. (D) | 108. (C) | 109. (A) | 110. (C) |
| 111. (C) | 112. (B) | 113. (D) | 114. (A) | 115. (A) | 116. (A) | 117. (B) | 118. (B) | 119. (D) | 120. (B) |
| 121. (C) | 122. (C) | 123. (A) | 124. (D) | 125. (D) | 126. (A) | 127. (A) | 128. (A) | 129. (C) | 130. (C) |
| 131. (B) | 132. (D) | 133. (B) | 134. (B) | 135. (C) | 136. (C) | 137. (B) | 138. (A) | 139. (C) | 140. (B) |
| 141. (A) | 142. (D) | 143. (D) | 144. (B) | 145. (A) | 146. (B) | 147. (B) | 148. (A) | 149. (C) | 150. (C) |
| 151. (B) | 152. (D) | 153. (A) | 154. (A) | 155. (D) | 156. (A) | 157. (D) | 158. (C) | 159. (A) | 160. (D) |
| 161. (D) | 162. (B) | 163. (A) | 164. (B) | 165. (B) | 166. (C) | 167. (A) | 168. (B) | 169. (A) | 170. (B) |
| 171. (D) | 172. (A) | 173. (D) | 174. (C) | 175. (B) | 176. (A) | 177. (D) | 178. (C) | 179. (A) | 180. (A) |
| 181. (A) | 182. (B) | 183. (A) | 184. (D) | 185. (C) | 186. (B) | 187. (D) | 188. (A) | 189. (D) | 190. (C) |
| 191. (A) | 192. (A) | 193. (B) | 194. (D) | 195. (D) | 196. (C) | 197. (D) | 198. (A) | 199. (B) | 200. (A) |

# PART 1
P. 014

**1** (A) He is taking notes.
美M (B) He is signing a paper.
(C) He is typing on a keyboard.
(D) He is cleaning the computer monitor.

(A) 他正在記筆記。
(B) 他正在簽文件。
(C) 他正在鍵盤上打字。
(D) 他正在擦拭電腦螢幕。

字彙 **take a note** 記下 **type** 打字

**2** (A) A woman is putting on some boots.
英M (B) A woman is sweeping the driveway.
(C) A woman is grasping a broomstick.
(D) A woman is standing under the tree.

(A) 一名女子正穿上靴子。
(B) 一名女子正在掃車道。
(C) 一名女子正抓著長柄掃帚。
(D) 一名女子正站在樹下。

字彙 **put on** 穿、戴　**sweep** 清掃
**driveway** 住宅的車道　**grasp** 抓牢、握緊
**broomstick** 長柄掃帚、掃帚柄

**3** (A) Leaves are being cleared on a path.
美W (B) Some cars are parked at the side of the street.
(C) Snow is being piled along a walkway.
(D) The vehicles are facing opposite directions.

(A) 正在清掃小徑上的樹葉。
(B) 有些車停在路邊。
(C) 雪沿著人行道堆積。
(D) 車輛們彼此面向相反的方向。

字彙 **path** 小徑、小路　**pile** 堆積、累積
**walkway** 人行道　**face** 面向、朝
**opposite** 相反的、對面的　**direction** 方向

**4** (A) Some bicycles have been left on the street.
澳M (B) A vehicle is approaching an archway.
(C) The roof of a building is being fixed.
(D) The pavement is decorated with potted plants.

(A) 有些腳踏車被留在街道上。
(B) 有輛車正接近拱門。
(C) 有棟建築物的屋頂正在整修。
(D) 人行道上有盆栽裝飾。

字彙 **leave** 留下
**approach** 接近、即將到達
**archway** 拱門、拱廊
**pavement** （英）人行道、鋪過的路面
**potted plant** 盆栽

**5** (A) The seats are being arranged in a semi-circle.
美M (B) Folding chairs have been set up on the stage.
(C) A concert is being given inside an auditorium.
(D) A man has his back to a group of people.

(A) 座位排成半圓形。
(B) 舞台上排著摺疊椅。
(C) 禮堂裡正在舉行音樂會。
(D) 一名男子背對著一群人。

字彙 **semi-circle** 半圓形
**folding chairs** 摺疊椅
**set up** 擺放或豎起某物
**auditorium** 禮堂、會堂

**6** (A) A vehicle is stopped at a stop sign.
美W (B) Shipping containers are being lifted by a crane.
(C) Rows of containers have been stacked up.
(D) Workers are smoothing the road surface.

(A) 一輛車停在停止標誌前。
(B) 起重機正吊起船運貨櫃。
(C) 貨櫃成排堆放。
(D) 工人正把道路鋪平。

字彙 **stop sign** 停止標誌
**shipping container** 船運貨櫃
**crane** 起重機　**row** 一排、一列
**stack up** 堆起、把……放成堆
**smooth** 鋪平（道路）

🎧02

## PART 2

P. 018

**7** Where can I find the financial report?
(美M) (A) I saw it on your desk.
(美W) (B) There was a sale at the store.
(C) I'm going to Beijing.

我要去哪裡找財務報表？
(A) 我看到在你桌上。
(B) 店裡正在特價促銷。
(C) 我要去北京。

字彙 **financial report** 財務報表

**8** Who's in charge of the meeting today?
(美M) (A) I'll stand over there.
(美W) (B) It's Ms. Cortez.
(C) Our aim for the next quarter.

今天的會議由誰負責？
(A) 我會站在那邊。
(B) 是柯蒂茲女士。
(C) 我們下一季的目標。

字彙 **in charge of** 負責管理、負責掌管
**aim** 目標、目的 **quarter** 季度；四分之一

**9** Which train are you catching?
(美W) (A) Sure, I'll catch it.
(美M) (B) Yes, aren't you?
(C) The one at noon.

你要搭哪一班火車？
(A) 當然，我會趕上的。
(B) 是的，你不是嗎？
(C) 中午那一班。

字彙 **catch** 搭乘（飛機、火車、公車等）；趕上

**10** Where can I get my laptop repaired?
(美M) (A) I didn't know you were moving.
(美W) (B) It's the newest product.
(C) I gave mine to Andy's shop.

我的筆記型電腦要送去哪裡修理？
(A) 我不知道你在搬家。
(B) 這是最新產品。
(C) 我的是送去安迪的店。

字彙 **laptop** 筆記型電腦

**11** Did Mr. Yang talk through our pension benefits
(美M) with you?
(美W) (A) Very meticulously.
(B) Yes, she was.
(C) Thanks, I feel great.

楊先生和你詳細談過我們的退休金津貼了嗎？
(A) 非常詳細。
(B) 是的，她是。
(C) 謝謝，我很好。

字彙 **talk through** 討論……的細節
**pension benefit** 退休金津貼
**meticulously** 非常仔細地；一絲不苟地

**12** How many people have registered for the
(美M) team game?
(英W) (A) It's a new concept.
(B) About half a dozen.
(C) There are three different lines.

有多少人登記參加團隊運動比賽？
(A) 那是個新的概念。
(B) 大約 6 個。
(C) 有不同的 3 排。

字彙 **half a dozen** 6 個、半打 **line** 排、列

**13** Let's finish at lunch today.
(美M) (A) Stop it at the end.
(美W) (B) That's a good idea.
(C) I already ate.

我們在今天午餐前完成吧。
(A) 停在結尾的地方。
(B) 好主意。
(C) 我已經吃過了。

字彙 **at the end** （時間、地點的）盡頭

**14** Dinner yesterday was delightful, wasn't it?
(美W) (A) Sorry, I wasn't available then.
(美M) (B) No, she's the new creative director.
(C) Yes, the fish was delicious.

昨天的晚餐很愉快，不是嗎？
(A) 抱歉，我當時沒空。
(B) 不是，她是新來的創意總監。
(C) 是的，魚很鮮美。

字彙 **delightful** 令人愉快的
**creative director** 創意總監

🎧01
🎧02

**15** Would you rather travel on the highway or the scenic route?
(A) It's easier like that.
(B) The quickest route is best.
(C) I've been here twice.

你比較喜歡走公路還是走風景優美的那條路？
(A) 像那樣比較容易。
(B) 最快到的路最好。
(C) 我來過這裡二次。

字彙 highway 公路；幹道
scenic route 風景優美的道路

**16** Why is the light on the photocopier red?
(A) Maybe it's out of ink.
(B) Thank you, but I've decided not to.
(C) It is too light in here.

影印機為什麼亮紅燈？
(A) 可能沒有墨水了。
(B) 謝謝你，但我決定不要。
(C) 這裡太亮了。

字彙 be out of 沒有……；用完……

**17** Isn't Kelvin having an operation soon?
(A) Sure, I'd love to try some.
(B) In March, I believe.
(C) No, it's not too difficult.

凱爾文不是快要動手術了嗎？
(A) 當然，我很樂意試試。
(B) 我想是三月時。
(C) 不，不太困難。

字彙 operation 手術

**18** When will the debate on human rights be aired?
(A) At the accounting office.
(B) On Wednesday in the daytime.
(C) Yes, it was thought-provoking.

關於人權的辯論什麼時候會播出？
(A) 在會計部。
(B) 星期三白天。
(C) 是的，很令人深思。

字彙 debate 辯論　human rights 人權
air 廣播、播送
accounting office 會計部門
thought-provoking 引人深思；發人深省地

**19** I'm having difficulty locating Mr. Rozenberg's dinner suit.
(A) Maybe I can be of assistance.
(B) I have twelve in total.
(C) Where did you find it?

我找不到羅森伯格先生的晚宴服。
(A) 也許，我可以幫忙。
(B) 我總共有 12 個。
(C) 你在哪裡找到的？

字彙 have difficulty V-ing 做某事有困難
locate 找出
dinner suit 晚宴服；無尾禮服
be of assistance 有幫助　in total 總共

**20** Would you like me to add up your expenses before you hand them in?
(A) Oh, I paid with credit card.
(B) I'd like a little extra, please.
(C) Thanks, but Ms. Washington already helped.

在你交出去之前，你想要我把你的費用加起來嗎？
(A) 噢，我用信用卡支付了。
(B) 我想再多一點，謝謝。
(C) 謝謝，但華盛頓女士已經幫我算過了。

字彙 add up 合計；把……加起來
expense 費用；支出　hand in 遞交；上交

**21** Which pair of shoes did you finally buy?
(A) Actually, I couldn't choose any yet.
(B) Just a small measure, please.
(C) Thanks for your help.

你最後買了哪一雙鞋？
(A) 其實，我還無法決定。
(B) 只要少量，謝謝。
(C) 謝謝你的幫忙。

字彙 measure 分量；尺寸

**22** You'll be arriving in Dunkirk on Thursday,
[英M] won't you?
[美W] (A) No, my ferry was cancelled.
    (B) Could I use those next week?
    (C) Yes, he emailed to say he'd arrived.

你會在星期四抵達敦克爾克，不是嗎？
(A) 不，我的渡輪取消了。
(B) 我下星期可以用那些嗎？
(C) 是的，他寄了電子郵件說他已經到了。

字彙 ferry 渡輪

**23** Isn't the assessor meant to come to lunch
[美W] today?
[英M] (A) Two new assessments.
    (B) Yes, he's held up in traffic.
    (C) Most days of the year.

估價員不是打算今天來吃午餐嗎？
(A) 兩份新的估價。
(B) 是要來，他遇到了塞車。
(C) 一年中大部分的時間。

字彙 assessor 估價員；估稅員
    mean to 打算做某事
    assessment 估價；評估
    be held up in traffic 塞車

**24** I think I left my umbrella in the taxi.
[美M] (A) We left after midnight.
[美W] (B) You should call them immediately.
    (C) We have one just round the corner.

我想，我把傘忘在計程車上了。
(A) 我們午夜之後離開。
(B) 你應該立刻打電話給他們。
(C) 附近就有一個。

字彙 midnight 半夜；午夜
    just round the corner 就在附近

**25** Why has the transport system been
[美W] disrupted?
[英M] (A) A train and a bus.
    (B) There was an accident.
    (C) I've read the comments.

交通系統為什麼中斷？
(A) 一輛火車和一輛公車。
(B) 有車禍。
(C) 我看過評論了。

字彙 disrupt 中斷　comment 評論；意見

**26** Could you swap Janghir's shift this Tuesday?
[美M] (A) I didn't realize that.
[美W] (B) Yes, it shifted perfectly.
    (C) Let me check who's working.

你這個星期二可以和賈合爾換班嗎？
(A) 我沒意識到。
(B) 是的，換擋很順暢。
(C) 讓我查一下誰有上班。

字彙 swap 與……交換
    shift 輪班；輪班工作時間

**27** Were you involved in the Milicent fund
[美W] investigation?
[英M] (A) That's not her workload.
    (B) A vital clue.
    (C) Yes, together with Rachel and Chloe.

你有參與米利森基金的調查嗎？
(A) 那不是她的工作。
(B) 一個很重要的線索。
(C) 有，和瑞秋及克蘿伊一起。

字彙 involved in 使參與……　fund 基金
    investigation 調查；偵查
    workload 工作量　vital 極其重要的
    clue 線索

**28** Have you put the tablecloths in the wash yet?
[美M] (A) I'll take twenty, thanks.
[美W] (B) Actually, I've just dried them.
    (C) Not as often as I would like.

你把桌布拿去洗了嗎？
(A) 我要 20 個，謝謝。
(B) 事實上，我剛把它們烘乾。
(C) 沒有我想要的次數多。

字彙 tablecloth 桌布
    wash 待洗、在洗或洗好的衣服　dry 弄乾

02

**29** Would you prefer to book this hotel or the one in the next town?
(A) I've worked as a receptionist for 20 years.
(B) I bought them from a street vendor.
(C) Either will be fine.

你比較想訂這家飯店還是鄰鎮的那家？
(A) 我當接待人員當了 20 年。
(B) 我跟一個街頭小販買的。
(C) 兩家都好。

字彙 book 預訂　receptionist 接待人員
street vendor 街頭小販

**30** Why don't you ask Larry about the rodent issue?
(A) Yes, I brought some poison.
(B) I think you're making a mistake.
(C) It's already been taken care of.

老鼠的問題，你為什麼不問問賴瑞？
(A) 是的，我買了一些毒餌。
(B) 我想，你犯了錯。
(C) 問題已經處理好了。

字彙 rodent 齧齒動物　take care of 處理、照顧

**31** Who will replace Mr. Landrake as financial officer?
(A) It hasn't been confirmed.
(B) That sounds like an excellent start.
(C) Lisa provided the catering.

誰會接替藍卓克先生當財務長？
(A) 還沒確定。
(B) 那聽起來是很棒的開始。
(C) 麗莎供應外燴。

字彙 replace 替換；取代
financial office 財務長
catering 承辦酒席；準備或提供食物的工作

---

🎧 03

P. 019

# PART 3

**Questions 32-34 refer to the following conversation.**
美M 美W

M Ms. Kitayama, I have an inquiry. ㉜ I have a position for a beautician and I know you recently recruited for a similar job last week. Where did you place the job advertisement?

W ㉝ I emailed the beauty department at Westland College and they put forward a number of graduates for the job.

M That's an excellent idea. Although by now the majority of graduates have probably got jobs, I am going to require an extra person within the next two weeks.

W Then, ㉞ you should post the position on the Health and Beauty Web site. A number of people use the site, amateurs and professionals. You are bound to get a large amount of interest.

---

對話
男：北山女士，我有件事想問妳。我有個美容師的缺，我知道妳上星期才為一個類似的職缺招人。妳的徵人廣告登在哪裡？
女：我寄了電子郵件給衛斯蘭大學的美容系，他們推薦了一些畢業生。
男：真是個很棒的主意。雖然大部分畢業生現在很可能都有工作了，但我打算在未來兩星期內再招一個人。
女：那麼，你應該把徵人廣告貼在「健康與美麗」網站上。不少人會上那個網站，業餘和專業人士都有。一定很多人有興趣。

字彙 inquiry 詢問　beautician 美容師
recruit 招募新成員
place an advertisement 刊登廣告
put forward 推薦；提出
graduate 大學畢業生
majority of 大多數　post 貼出（布告等）
professional 專門人員
be bound to 一定會
navigate 瀏覽、訪問（網站）

**32** What does the man want to do?
(A) Recruit an assistant
(B) Get a degree
(C) Have a facial
(D) Visit a Web site

男子想做什麼？
(A) 僱一位助手
(B) 拿到學位
(C) 做臉
(D) 造訪一個網站

**33** Why did the woman contact the college?
(A) To locate a suitable salon
(B) To sign up for a college course
(C) To rent some equipment
(D) To find trained job applicants

女子為什麼和大學聯絡？
(A) 為了設置一個合適的沙龍
(B) 為了註冊一門大學課程
(C) 為了租用一些設備
(D) 為了找到受過訓練的應徵者

**34** Why does the woman recommend the Health and Beauty Web site?
(A) It features useful advice.
(B) It is only for professionals.
(C) It has a lot of users.
(D) It is simple to navigate.

女子為什麼推薦「健康與美麗」網站？
(A) 它以提供實用建議為特色。
(B) 它只供專業人士使用。
(C) 它有很多用戶。
(D) 它很容易瀏覽。

**Questions 35-37 refer to the following conversation.**
英M 美W

**M** Hi, Claire. ㉟ **Could you let me know when you are available this week**? I'd like to arrange a time for a meeting with you. We have to ensure we're organized for the annual tax return.
**W** Hmm, I can't really arrange anything for the next three days as ㊱ **I'm attending a wedding in Las Vegas.** Isn't the tax return due next week?
**M** No, I'm afraid all the revenue forms have to be submitted by Friday at 5 P.M. ㊲ **Why don't we arrange an afternoon for a video conference call** about the annual submissions when you return from your trip?

---

對話
**男**：嗨，克萊兒。妳可以告訴我，這星期妳何時有空嗎？我想排個時間和妳開會。我們必須確認已經安排好年度報稅的事情。
**女**：嗯，接下來三天，我真的沒辦法排任何事情，因為我要去拉斯維加斯參加婚禮。報稅不是下星期才截止嗎？
**男**：不是，恐怕所有的收入表都得在星期五下午5點前交出。等妳旅行回來後，我們何不找個下午開視訊會議，討論繳交年度表格的事？

字彙 **tax return** 納稅申報表
**due** 到期的；預計的
**revenue** 收入；稅收
**video conference call** 視訊會議
**tax office** 稅務局
**documentation** （總稱）文件

**35** What does the man ask about?
(A) The woman's availability
(B) The amount of tax to be returned
(C) The return from a vacation
(D) The call to a client

男子詢問什麼事？
(A) 女子有空的時間
(B) 將要退回的稅金金額
(C) 何時休完假回來
(D) 打給客戶的電話

**36** What does the woman plan to do this week?
(A) Finalize a seminar
(B) Visit the tax office
(C) Attend a ceremony
(D) Provide some paperwork

女子計劃這星期要做什麼？
(A) 敲定研討會
(B) 造訪稅務局
(C) 參加一場典禮
(D) 提供一些文件

**37** What does the man suggest doing?
(A) Setting up a conference call
(B) Filling out a registration form
(C) Submitting the required documentation
(D) Making a phone call

03

男子建議做什麼？

(A) 安排一場視訊會議

(B) 填寫一份註冊表格

(C) 交出需要的文件

(D) 打一通電話

**Questions 38-40 refer to the following conversation.**

美W 英M

> **W** Hi, ㊳ **I am keen on seeing the game at the baseball center** on Saturday. I tried to buy four tickets over the phone but my calls weren't being answered.
>
> **M** I apologize. ㊴ **We are having some technical issues with the phone company today.** Would you like to book the tickets with me?
>
> **W** Yes, thank you. I'd like four sixth row seats for the Saturday morning match at the Pedusa Stadium. Are there any available?
>
> **M** Certainly. If you ㊵ **let me have your credit card information,** I can reserve these straight away.

對話

女： 嗨，我很想去看星期六在棒球中心的比賽。我試著用電話訂 4 張票，但沒人接電話。

男： 抱歉，電話公司今天有些技術性的問題，您要跟我訂票嗎？

女： 好的，謝謝你。我想要 4 張星期六早上派都沙體育場第 6 排的票，還有嗎？

男： 當然有。如果您給我信用卡資料，我可以馬上預訂票券。

字彙 **keen on** 喜愛某事／某人
**row** 一排；一排座位　　**match** 比賽
**stadium** 體育場；球場
**straight away** 馬上；即刻
**premiere** 首映
**representative** 代表；代理人
**reference number** 代碼

**38** What event does the woman want to attend?

(A) A movie premiere

(B) A sporting event

(C) A book launch

(D) A theater performance

女子想要參加什麼活動？

(A) 電影首映會

(B) 體育活動

(C) 新書發表會

(D) 戲劇演出

**39** What is the problem?

(A) A phone system is not working.

(B) A representative reserved the wrong tickets.

(C) A credit card was stolen.

(D) A game is sold out.

有什麼問題？

(A) 電話系統故障。

(B) 有個專員訂錯票了。

(C) 有張信用卡被偷了。

(D) 有場比賽票賣完了。

**40** What information does the man request?

(A) A reference number

(B) A business address

(C) The name of an event

(D) Credit card details

男子要求什麼資訊？

(A) 訂位代號

(B) 公司地址

(C) 活動名稱

(D) 信用卡詳細資料

**Questions 41-43 refer to the following conversation.**

美M 美W

> **M** Hello, Ms. Mayall. This is Mark Tolley. I am calling to introduce myself. I did some freelance design work for your company a year ago and ㊶ **I believe you are the new head of the technical department.** ㊷ **I was inquiring whether you have any design work I can assist with.** I'd appreciate working with you.
>
> **W** Well, thank you for the call. To be honest, though, Mark, we're keeping the majority of our designing in house for now. That's not to say it won't change in the future though. I'd be happy to file your details in case we need help.
>
> **M** OK. That would be good. If it's acceptable to you then, ㊸ **I'd like to email you my updated portfolio.** And I hope you bear me in mind if anything turns up.

**對話**

男：哈囉，梅耶爾女士，我是馬克・托利。我打電話來是要自我介紹。我是自由職業者，一年前接了你們公司的設計工作。我想您是技術部門的新任主管，我想詢問，您是否有任何我可以協助的設計工作。若能和您合作，我會很感謝。

女：嗯，謝謝你打電話來。不過說實話，馬克，我們現在把大部分的設計工作都留給我們的內部人員，但這不代表未來不會有變動。我很樂意把你的詳細資料歸檔，以備我們需要協助時使用。

男：好的，太好了。如果您可以接受的話，我想把更新的作品集用電子郵件寄給您。我希望如果出現任何機會的話，您會想到我。

**字彙** freelance（不受僱於人的）自由職業者
head 負責人　inquire 詢問
in house 內部的；存在於機構內的
that's not to say 不代表；不表示
file 把……歸檔　in case 以防萬一
updated 更新的；最新的
portfolio 代表作選輯
bear in mind 把……記在心裡
turn up（機會）出現、到來
reference 推薦（信）
forthcoming 即將到來的

**41** Who most likely is the woman?
(A) A technical director
(B) A human resources manager
(C) A temporary worker
(D) A factory worker
女子最可能是什麼人？
(A) 一位技術主管
(B) 一位人事經理
(C) 一名臨時員工
(D) 一名工廠工人

**42** Why is the man calling?
(A) To request a reference
(B) To submit his portfolio
(C) To ask about employment
(D) To explain a forthcoming training session
男子為什麼打電話？
(A) 為了要求推薦信
(B) 為了交出他的作品集
(C) 為了詢問工作
(D) 為了解釋即將開始的訓練課程

**43** What does the man offer to send?
(A) An extended contract
(B) A draft design
(C) An upgraded portfolio
(D) An updated résumé
男子提議寄送什麼？
(A) 一份延長的合約
(B) 一份設計草稿
(C) 一份最新的作品集
(D) 一份更新的履歷表

**Questions 44-46 refer to the following conversation.**
美W 美M

**W** Good morning. My name is Marsha Juncker. ㊹ I have made a booking to rent a room.

**M** Yes, Ms. Juncker. I have your details here. You booked a single room for three days, right?

**W** Yes, but I'm thinking about staying an extra night. ㊺ I saw your promotion that promised an extra night's stay free if I book three nights.

**M** I'm sorry but ㊻ that promotion only applies to stays that include the weekend and the cost for an extra weekday stay is our normal rate. Would you like to extend your stay?

**對話**

女：早安，我是瑪莎・江克。我預訂了一個房間。

男：是的，江克女士。您的資料在這裡。您預訂了三晚的單人房，對嗎？

女：是的，但我在考慮要多住一晚。我看到你們的促銷宣傳上保證，如果我預訂三個晚上的話，可以免費多住一晚。

男：很抱歉，但那個促銷只適用於住宿期間包含週末在內，而另外住的週間日費用是我們的一般房價。您想要延長您的住宿嗎？

**字彙** booking 預訂；預約
single room 單人房
promotion 促銷；宣傳
normal rate 一般價；正常價
retreat 靜居處；僻靜處

解答&中譯解析　Actual Test 1　PART **3**

13

**44** Where does the conversation most likely take place?
(A) At a hotel
(B) At a rental agency
(C) At a weekend retreat
(D) At a conference hall

這段對話最可能發生在什麼地方？
(A) 飯店
(B) 租賃公司
(C) 幽靜度週末的居所
(D) 會議中心

**45** What does the woman mention about the promotion?
(A) A free bus service
(B) Details of a special offer
(C) The date of a new hotel opening
(D) Discounts at the restaurant

關於促銷，女子提到什麼？
(A) 免費巴士服務
(B) 特別優惠的細節
(C) 一家新飯店的開幕日期
(D) 餐廳的折扣

**46** What does the man explain to the woman?
(A) The discount applies only on certain days.
(B) There will be a two-hour delay.
(C) The hotel is closed to the public.
(D) The promotion has false information.

男子跟女子解釋什麼？
(A) 折扣只適用於特定的日子。
(B) 會延遲 2 小時。
(C) 飯店不對外開放。
(D) 促銷資訊有錯。

**Questions 47-49 refer to the following conversation with three speakers.** 美M 美W 英M

**M1** 47 Two of our team members called in sick, but we have a big banquet tonight and need to come up with a plan.
**W** The guests are going to arrive in two hours.
**M2** The good news is that we have most of the food prepared. So maybe I can ask someone on the kitchen staff to help set up the tables.

**M1** Good idea. 48 What about serving the food?
**W** 48 Since we are going to need one more person for that, I can help. That means I need to have everything organized perfectly before dinner is served.
**M1** 49 If you need someone to help coordinate with the kitchen, I might be able to do it.
**W** I don't think you have to worry about that.

---

三人對話

男1：我們有兩名員工打電話請病假，但我們今天晚上有個大型宴會，必須想出應變計畫。

女：客人 2 小時後就會抵達。

男2：好消息是，我們大部分的菜都準備好了。所以，我也許可以請一位廚房的人員幫忙擺桌。

男1：好主意。那上菜怎麼辦？

女：既然我們需要一個額外的人手上菜，我可以幫忙妳表示，我需要在晚餐上菜前，把每件事都安排妥當。

男1：如果妳需要有人幫忙和廚房協調，我或許可以做。

女：我想你不需要擔心這件事。

字彙 **call in sick** 打電話請病假
**come up with** （針對問題等）想出
**coordinate** 協調；調節

**47** What problem are the speakers discussing?
(A) Changing a menu
(B) Rescheduling an event
(C) Being understaffed
(D) Hiring employees

說話者在討論什麼問題？
(A) 換菜單
(B) 重新安排活動的時間
(C) 人手不足
(D) 僱用員工

**48** What does the woman offer to do?
(A) Wash dishes
(B) Meet a client
(C) Move tables
(D) Serve food

女子提議做什麼？
(A) 洗碗盤
(B) 迎接一位客人
(C) 搬桌子
(D) 上菜

**49** What does the woman mean when she says, "I don't think you have to worry about that"?
(A) She believes she can handle the task.
(B) She is able to help cooking.
(C) She is having some trouble with the customer.
(D) She thinks the men can't solve the problem.

當女子說：「我想你不需要擔心這件事」時，她的意思是什麼？
(A) 她相信她可以應付這個工作。
(B) 她可以幫忙做菜。
(C) 她和客戶有些問題。
(D) 她認為那些男子無法解決問題。

**Questions 50-52 refer to the following conversation.**
英M 美W

**M** Good morning, Ms. Jamison. This is Bill Lowell from *Modern Life Magazine*. **50** I'm calling to let you know that we would like you to write the article on weekend farms near cities that you proposed.

**W** That's great news! I'm so glad that you liked my idea. I think your readers will find it as fascinating a topic as I do.

**M** **51** We believe they will be as impressed as we are by your passion for your topics in the writing samples you sent us. How soon do you think you can have a draft ready?

**W** Hmm . . . in about a month I believe.

**M** Great. **52** How about if we set March 15 as the deadline? If you have any questions regarding this, just give me a call.

**W** Absolutely.

對話
男：潔米森女士，早安，我是《現代生活雜誌》的比爾·洛威。我打來是要告訴妳，我們希望由妳來寫那篇妳所提案的城市近郊週末農場的文章。

女：真是好消息！我很高興你們喜歡我的提案。我想你們的讀者會和我一樣覺得這是個很迷人的主題。

男：我們相信，他們會和我們一樣，對妳寄給我們的試寫稿中就妳主題所展現的熱情印象深刻。妳覺得妳多快可以寫好草稿？

女：嗯……我想，大約一個月。

男：太好了。如果，我們把截稿日定在 3 月 15 日，妳覺得如何？如果妳有任何關於交稿日期的問題，就打個電話給我。

女：當然。

字彙 fascinating 迷人的；極好的
draft 草稿；草圖　landscaping 景觀美化

**50** What does the woman plan to write about?
(A) Professional landscaping
(B) Farming
(C) Public transportation
(D) Fashion trends

女子打算寫什麼主題？
(A) 專業景觀美化
(B) 農業
(C) 大眾運輸
(D) 流行趨勢

**51** What did the man receive from the woman?
(A) A billing statement
(B) Samples of her work
(C) A rental contract
(D) References

男子收到女子的什麼東西？
(A) 帳單明細
(B) 她的寫作範本
(C) 租賃合約
(D) 推薦信

**52** What does the woman mean when she says, "Absolutely"?
(A) She will answer some questions.
(B) She can't call at the moment.
(C) She will not be able to complete the draft by the deadline.
(D) She agrees to the man's suggestion.

03

當女子說：「當然」時，她的意思是什麼？
(A) 她會回答一些問題。
(B) 她目前無法打電話。
(C) 她無法在截稿日前完成草稿。
(D) 她同意男子的提議。

**Questions 53-55 refer to the following conversation.**
美M 美W

**M** Kaya, Amanda called. She's not going to be able to make it onsite **53** because there's a major traffic accident on the highway. **54** She asked me to find the keys to Jamid's site office but I can't find them on her desk.

**W** Oh, I'm sorry. I have them here. I took them off her desk meaning to get another duplicate set of keys cut. Should we wait until she gets here before we head over to the site?

**M** No, Amanda said carry on with the plans. We don't want to delay work anymore. **55** I'll just get my hard hat from the office.

-----------------

對話

男：卡雅，亞曼達打電話來。她無法趕到現場，因為公路上發生了重大車禍。她要我找出傑米德的工地辦公室鑰匙，但我在她桌上找不到。

女：噢，真抱歉，鑰匙在我這裡。我從她的桌上拿走鑰匙，想要再打一副。我們應該等她來，再過去工地嗎？

男：不用，亞曼達說照計畫進行。我們不想再耽擱任何工作了。我去辦公室拿我的安全帽。

字彙 **make it** 做或完成某事
**onsite** 在工地、在現場
**major** 重大的；較大範圍的
**site office** 工地辦公室
**mean to** 打算做某事、有意做某事
**duplicate** 複製的
**head** （向特定方向）出發　**site** 工地
**carry on with** 繼續　**fetch** （去）拿來
**hard hat** （建築工人等戴的）安全帽

**53** Why will Amanda be late for the meeting?
(A) She is still on site.
(B) She has to make a phone call.
(C) She is caught in traffic congestion.
(D) She has lost the keys to the office.

為什麼亞曼達參加會議遲到？
(A) 她還在工地現場。
(B) 她必須打個電話。
(C) 她遇到塞車。
(D) 她掉了辦公室的鑰匙。

**54** What did Amanda ask the man to do?
(A) Fetch a hard hat
(B) Drive straight to the office
(C) Take notes at a meeting
(D) Get some keys from her desk

亞曼達要求男子做什麼？
(A) 拿一頂安全帽來
(B) 直接開車到辦公室
(C) 在開會時記筆記
(D) 從她的桌上拿鑰匙

**55** What does the man say he will do next?
(A) Pick up some work supplies
(B) Contact a supervisor
(C) Link up his computer
(D) Call the site manager

男子說他接下來要做什麼？
(A) 拿一些工作用品
(B) 聯絡主管
(C) 連上他的電腦
(D) 打電話給工地主任

**Questions 56-58 refer to the following conversation.**
美W 英M

**W** That's all the interview questions that I have, Robert. Do you have any questions for me?

**M** Actually, yes. You asked me about my availability. **57** However, I am still not clear what you had in mind for the starting date.

**W** Well, we need someone right away. **56** So, ideally, we would like to hire a new assistant for my stationery store no later than next week. We could be a little flexible with the starting date though. Are you still interested?

**M** Yes, I am. I was afraid you needed someone this week. I already committed to help my cousin's shop this week.

**W** Great. Then I would like to offer you the job. **58** Can you start on Monday next week?

**M** Not a problem.

- - - - - - - - - - - - - - - - - - - - - - - - - - - - - - - - - -

對話

女：我要問的面試問題就這些了，羅伯特。你有什麼問題要問我的嗎？

男：其實有。您問我何時能上班，然而，我還不知道您設想的開始上班日是什麼時候。

女：嗯，我們馬上需要人手。因此，理想上，我們想要在下星期之前為我的文具店僱用一位新助理。不過，對於開始上班日，我們可以有點彈性。你還有興趣嗎？

男：是的，有。恐怕您這星期得找別人。我已經答應我表親這星期去店裡幫忙。

女：很好。那麼你被錄取了。你下星期一可以開始上班嗎？

男：沒問題。

字彙 availability 能出席；(人或物)可得性
**ideally** 理想地
**flexible** 有彈性的；可變通的
**commit** 承諾；保證　**stationery** 文具

**56** Where does the woman work?
(A) At an educational institute
(B) At a convention center
(C) At a stationery store
(D) At a staffing agency

女子在哪裡工作？
(A) 教育機構
(B) 會議中心
(C) 文具店
(D) 職業介紹所

**57** What does the man ask about the job?
(A) The starting date
(B) The salary
(C) The duration
(D) The location

關於這份工作，男子問了什麼問題？
(A) 開始上班的日期
(B) 薪水
(C) 持續時間
(D) 地點

**58** Why does the man say, "Not a problem"?
(A) He doesn't have any questions at the moment.
(B) He wants to start on a different date.
(C) He can start working on Monday.
(D) He can take the job right away.

男子為什麼說：「沒問題」？
(A) 他目前沒有任何問題。
(B) 他想要改天開始上班。
(C) 他可以從星期一開始上班。
(D) 他可以立刻接下工作。

**Questions 59-61 refer to the following conversation.**
美W 英M

**W** Hello, I'm contacting you because **59** I'd like to have a studio specially designed for dance club activities. You don't build custom constructions, do you?

**M** No, we don't. But we occasionally subcontract them from a building firm. If you can tell me what you want, **60** I can get a quote for you.

**W** Thanks, but I would rather do it myself. **61** If you'd care to give me the contact details and Web site, I'll be happy to contact them directly.

- - - - - - - - - - - - - - - - - - - - - - - - - - - - - - - - - -

對話

女：哈囉，我打來是因為，我想要打造一間特別為舞蹈社活動而設計的練習室。你們不接客製化工程，對嗎？

男：沒有，我們沒有做。但是，我們偶爾會向一家營造公司接這類的外包工程。如果，您可以告訴我您的需求，我可以報價給您。

女：謝謝，但我想自己來。如果，你願意給我聯絡資訊和網站，我很樂意和他們直接聯絡。

字彙 **studio** (舞蹈)練習室；(藝術家的)工作室；(電視或廣播節目的)攝影棚；錄音室
**custom** 訂做的；訂製的
**occasionally** 偶爾
**subcontract** 外包；分包　**quote** 報價
**approximate** 大約的；近似的

**59** What does the woman want to do?
(A) Request a collection service
(B) Hold a new dance class
(C) Alter a previous order
(D) Have an area specially designed

03

女子想要做什麼？
(A) 要求收貨服務
(B) 開一個新的舞蹈班
(C) 更改先前的訂單
(D) 特別設計一個區域

**60** What does the man say he can do?
(A) Comment on her work
(B) Design a dance stage
(C) Check a building guarantee
(D) Obtain an approximate estimate

男子說他能做什麼？
(A) 評論她的工作
(B) 設計一個舞蹈舞台
(C) 查看建築保證
(D) 取得大約的估價

**61** What does the woman request?
(A) Contact information
(B) Design samples
(C) Blueprint drawings
(D) A stock catalog

女子要求什麼？
(A) 聯絡資料
(B) 設計樣本
(C) 圖紙藍圖
(D) 存貨目錄

**Questions 62-64 refer to the following conversation.**
美W 美M

**W** Hi, Titan. I'm hoping you would give me some suggestions. 62 **I want to buy some security cameras** for my factory. I know you install a lot of security equipment, and I was wondering what you'd suggest.

**M** Well, I just read a review in a magazine about the new ultra sensitive sensors from Jeynes Office Security Company. Apparently, they've been receiving positive customer feedback.

**W** Oh, really? I've seen that brand advertised. 63 **Could you tell me which issue of the magazine the feature is in** so I can read more about them?

**M** Sure, I'd be happy to. But while you're here, 64 **why don't I give you my copy instead**?

----

對話

女：嗨，泰坦。我希望你可以給我點建議。我想幫我的工廠買些監視器。我知道你裝了不少監視器，不知道你會建議什麼。

男：嗯，我才在雜誌上看到一篇，關於傑尼斯辦公室安全公司出的新型超敏銳感應器的評論。顯然，他們一直得到顧客的正面回饋意見。

女：噢，真的嗎？我看過那個牌子的廣告。你可以告訴我，那個專題報導是在雜誌的哪一期，好讓我看看更多內容嗎？

男：當然，我很樂意。不過，既然妳在這裡，何不把我的這本給妳就好？

字彙 security camera 監視器
ultra sensitive 超靈敏的；極為敏感的
sensor 感應器　apparently 顯然地
issue （報刊）期號
feature （報紙或雜誌的）特寫；專題
copy （書報等印刷品的）一冊、一本

**62** What are the speakers mainly discussing?
(A) Factory installations
(B) Security systems
(C) A new brand launch
(D) A fashion magazine

說話者主要在討論什麼？
(A) 工廠的裝置
(B) 保全系統
(C) 一個新品牌上市
(D) 一本時尚雜誌

**63** What does the woman ask for?
(A) A list of security cameras
(B) An Internet address
(C) A purchase order number
(D) Details of a magazine

女子要求什麼？
(A) 一份監視器的清單
(B) 一個網址
(C) 一份採購訂單的號碼
(D) 一本雜誌的詳細資料

**64** What does the man offer to do?
(A) Give the woman his magazine
(B) Install a security device
(C) Review a feature
(D) Purchase products online

男子提議做什麼？
(A) 把他的雜誌給女子
(B) 裝設保全設備
(C) 看一篇專題報導
(D) 上網購買產品

**Questions 65-67 refer to the following conversation and floor plan.** 英M 美W

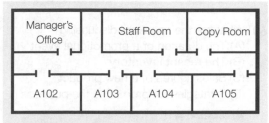

| Manager's Office | Staff Room | Copy Room |
|---|---|---|
| A102 | A103 | A104 | A105 |

**M** 65 Hi. I'm calling to let you know that the **LCD computer monitor and color printer that you ordered just arrived. Where do you want them delivered?**

**W** 66 Well, the LCD computer monitor is for Mr. Wilcox. His office is immediately across from the manager's office. As for the color printer, it goes in the copy room.

**M** Okay. I should be able to drop by this afternoon. Will you be there to let me into the office?

**W** I'm going out for lunch meeting with a client and should be back by 2:30 P.M. So as long as you come after that time and before 6:00 P.M., then yes.

**M** 67 Let's tentatively say 3:00 P.M. then. If I come any later, I might not have enough time to help you set everything up.

**W** That works for me. Thanks.

對話與樓層平面圖

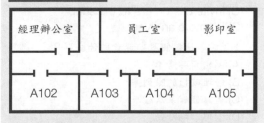

| 經理辦公室 | 員工室 | 影印室 |
|---|---|---|
| A102 | A103 | A104 | A105 |

男：嗨，我打電話來是要告訴妳，妳訂購的電腦液晶螢幕和彩色印表機剛剛到貨。要送到哪裡？

女：嗯，電腦液晶螢幕是威爾考克斯先生要用的，他的辦公室就在經理辦公室的正對面。至於彩色印表機，要放在影印室裡。

男：好的，我應該今天下午可以送過去。妳會在那裡開門讓我進辦公室嗎？

女：我中午會出去和客戶開午餐會報，應該下午2點半前會回來。所以，只要你在那個時間之後，並在6點以前來，那我就會在。

男：那麼，我們先暫定3點。如果我過了3點才到，可能就沒有足夠時間幫妳把機器都裝好。

女：那個時間可以，謝謝。

字彙 immediately 直接地；緊接地
tentatively 暫時地；臨時地

**65** Why is the man calling?
(A) To cancel an appointment
(B) To place an order
(C) To arrange a delivery
(D) To obtain contact information

男子為什麼打這通電話？
(A) 為了取消一個約會
(B) 為了下訂單
(C) 為了安排送貨
(D) 為了取得聯絡資訊。

**66** Look at the graphic. Where is the LCD computer monitor supposed to go?
(A) A102
(B) A103
(C) A104
(D) A105

請見圖表，電腦液晶螢幕應該要放在哪裡？
(A) A102
(B) A103
(C) A104
(D) A105

**67** When will the speakers most likely meet?
(A) At 2:00 P.M.
(B) At 3:00 P.M.
(C) At 4:00 P.M.
(D) At 5:30 P.M.

說話者最可能在何時碰面？
(A) 下午 2:00
(B) 下午 3:00
(C) 下午 4:00
(D) 下午 5:30

03

Questions 68-70 refer to the following conversation and inventory. 美W 美M

| Inventory | |
|---|---|
| Item | Quantity |
| Dining table | 6 |
| Stool | 5 |
| Table cloth | 2 |
| Small-sized rug | 7 |

**W** Wow! The sale was a huge success. **68 It looks like we sold out of several items.** There are no more dining tables, stools, table cloths or small-sized rugs in the store displays.

**M** **68 According to the inventory, we still have some extras in the storeroom.**

**W** That's good news. Can you restock the displays then? Put 5 of each of the missing items out. We'll need them just in case new customers come in next week.

**M** Okay. **69 But what if we don't have 5?**

**W** **69 Then put out what we have and order more of those items right away.** I just want to make sure we have the minimum that we need for now. **70 I will take complete inventory in a few weeks anyway.**

**M** You've got it.

---

對話與存貨清單

| 存貨清單 | |
|---|---|
| 商品 | 數量 |
| 餐桌 | 6 |
| 凳子 | 5 |
| 桌布 | 2 |
| 小地毯 | 7 |

女：哇，特賣會大成功。看來我們有好幾樣產品都已售完，店裡的陳列架上已經沒有餐桌、凳子、桌布或小地毯了。

男：從存貨清單來看，我們倉庫裡還有一些庫存。

女：真是好消息。那麼，你可以補一下貨架嗎？每一項賣完的貨品補 5 個。我們需要這些商品，以防下星期有新顧客來。

男：好的。但是，如果沒有 5 個怎麼辦？

女：那麼，把我們有的放上去，然後立刻再訂一些。我只想要確定，我們目前有沒有所需的最少量。反正，我幾個星期後會全面盤點。

男：沒問題。

字彙 inventory 存貨清單；存貨
storeroom 儲藏室；庫房

**68** What are the speakers discussing?
(A) The duration of a promotional event
(B) The recent inventory
(C) Sales figures of a new product
(D) Strategies for promoting the business

說話者在討論什麼？
(A) 促銷活動的持續時間
(B) 近期的存貨
(C) 一項新產品的銷售數字
(D) 宣傳生意的策略

**69** Look at the graphic. Which item will the man order right away?
(A) Dining table
(B) Stool
(C) Table cloth
(D) Small-sized rug

請見圖表，男子會立刻訂購哪一項商品？
(A) 餐桌
(B) 凳子
(C) 桌布
(D) 小地毯

**70** What does the woman say she will do in a few weeks?
(A) Make a list of items
(B) Repair a broken display
(C) Invite customers to the shop
(D) Promote an event

女子說，她幾個星期後會做什麼事？
(A) 列出商品清單
(B) 修理破損的陳列架
(C) 邀請顧客來店裡
(D) 宣傳一場活動

# PART 4

P. 023

**Questions 71-73 refer to the following telephone message.** 美M

Hello, **❼ this is Cal Khan calling from Poco Building Supplies.** We processed the order you placed through our Web site yesterday, but **❼ I have a question about one of the items you asked for.** You stated that you required 200 PVC window panels. Before we approve the delivery, I wanted to check the amount and confirm that you actually want 200 items and not 2 or 20. **❼ Please email me** to verify the quantity of items in your order. You can reach me on ckahn@pbsupplies.com. I'll be on the shop floor until the store closes tonight at 8 P.M. Thank you.

----

**電話留言**

　　哈囉，我是波可建材公司的卡爾・汗。我們處理了您昨天在我們的網站下的訂單，但我對您要的一個商品有個問題。您說需要 200 個 PVC 塑膠窗板。在我們核准出貨前，我想要核對一下數量，確認您真的要 200 個、而不是 2 個或 20 個。請寄電子郵件給我，確認您訂單上的數量。您可以寄到 ckahn@pbsupplies.com。我今天會在店裡待到晚上 8 點打烊，謝謝您。

----

**字彙** building supplies 建材　state 陳述；說明
**panel** 嵌板；壁板　**verify** 核實；核對
**quantity** 數量　shop floor 工作場所；店面

**71** Where does the speaker work?
(A) At an accounting firm
**(B) At a construction materials supplier**
(C) At an office supply store
(D) At a window replacement company
說話者在哪裡工作？
(A) 會計師事務所
(B) 建材供應商
(C) 辦公用品店
(D) 更換窗戶的公司

**72** Why is the speaker calling?
**(A) To query an order**
(B) To offer a discount
(C) To explain shipment costs
(D) To cancel a delivery

說話者為什麼打這通電話？
(A) 為了詢問一張訂單
(B) 為了提供折扣
(C) 為了解釋運費
(D) 為了取消送貨

**73** What is the listener asked to do?
(A) Email a reply
(B) Return a phone call
(C) Check an estimate
(D) Provide a credit card
聽話者被要求做什麼？
(A) 以電子郵件回覆
(B) 回電話
(C) 核對估價單
(D) 提供信用卡

04

**Questions 74-76 refer to the following tour information.** 英M

Hi! **❼ I'm Hugh Dancy from Last Minute Cruises. Welcome to our cruise ship,** The Age of the Ocean. This evening, we will be hosting a talent show as well as karaoke, which commences at 8 P.M. Before that, **❼ we have a gala barbecue on the Main Deck** and **❼ a special event, an after-dinner solo by international singer,** Caitlin Marriel, who is a special guest on the ship for the summer season. Now if you follow me, we will settle you in.

----

**旅遊資訊**

　　嗨！我是「最後一刻遊輪」的休・丹西。歡迎登上我們的郵輪「海洋年代號」。今天晚上，我們會舉辦才藝比賽以及卡拉 OK，將於晚上 8 點開始。在那之前，我們在主甲板上會有大型 BBQ 烤肉活動，晚餐後還有一項特別活動，是國際級歌手凱特琳・瑪瑞兒的獨唱會，她是我們夏季的船上貴賓。現在，請你們跟著我，我們將帶大家到房間安頓。

----

**字彙** cruise ship 郵輪　host 主辦、主持
**talent show** 才藝比賽；選秀比賽
**A as well as B** 除 A 之外還有 B
**karaoke** 卡拉 OK　**commence** 開始
**gala** 慶典；盛會　**main deck** 主甲板
**settle in** 安頓下來；適應新環境
**park attendant** 停車管理員
**welcome speech** 致歡迎辭

**74** Who most likely is the speaker?
(A) A ship employee
(B) A local singer
(C) A park attendant
(D) An entertainer

說話者最可能是什麼人？
(A) 一艘船上的員工
(B) 一位當地的歌手
(C) 一名停車管理員
(D) 一位藝人

**75** According to the speaker, where will dinner be served?
(A) On the beach
(B) In the lobby
(C) In the cafeteria
(D) On the deck

根據說話者所述，晚餐會在哪裡供應？
(A) 在海灘上
(B) 在大廳
(C) 在自助餐廳
(D) 在甲板上

**76** What will the listeners attend after dinner?
(A) A play
(B) A welcome speech
(C) A film
(D) A concert

聽者在晚餐後會參加什麼活動？
(A) 戲劇演出
(B) 歡迎致詞
(C) 電影欣賞
(D) 演唱會

**Questions 77-79 refer to the following talk.** 美W

I hope you all benefit from our first **77 IT training session** at Barrats. Remember that you can perform all of these tasks at your own workstations, so don't forget to practice during your breaks. Before you leave the classroom, **78 please fill out the questionnaire that is given to each of you.** We would like to know what you learned in the training and any further areas that you would like us to cover in future training sessions. If you would like to be contacted about advanced classes, please **79 state your e-mail address on the test form and we will get back to you with a proposed timetable.**

----

**談話**

　　我希望巴瑞特的第一期資訊科技訓練課程對你們都有所獲益。記得，你們都可以在你們自己的工作站裡運用所有這些技巧，所以，別忘了在休息時練習。在你們離開教室前，請填寫發給你們每個人的問卷。我們想要知道你們在訓練課程學到什麼，還有任何想要我們在未來的訓練課程裡涵蓋的領域。如果，你們想要接到進階課程的通知，請在測試表上寫明你們的電子郵件信箱，我們就會把規畫的課程表寄給你們。

**字彙** benefit 得益；受惠
workstation 工作站；個人工作區
questionnaire 問卷；意見調查表
further 進一步地；深一層地
advanced 高等的；先進的
state 陳述；說明
get back to 給（某人）回話或回信
proposed 計畫的；提議地　　first aid 急救
consent form 同意書

**77** What have listeners been learning?
(A) New employee orientation
(B) Technology training
(C) First aid in the office
(D) Improving production techniques

聽者在學習什麼？
(A) 新進員工訓練
(B) 科技訓練
(C) 辦公室急救
(D) 改進生產技術

**78** What does the speaker ask listeners to complete?
(A) A questionnaire
(B) A timetable
(C) A consent form
(D) A test

說話者要求聽者完成什麼？
(A) 一份問卷
(B) 一份課程表
(C) 一份同意書
(D) 一項測驗

**79** Why would listeners provide an e-mail address?
(A) To receive a list of advanced classes
(B) To apply for employment opportunities
(C) To cancel a reservation
(D) To get details of trainer's notes

聽者為什麼要提供電子郵件信箱地址？
(A) 為了接到進階課程表
(B) 為了應徵工作機會
(C) 為了取消預約
(D) 為了收到訓練講師的詳細筆記

**Questions 80-82 refer to the following advertisement.**
美M

Do you have a corporate sales business in the Sao Paulo region? ⑧⓪ **Do you often require training and consultancy services?** Sales Training is here to assist. We provide expert consultation packages by the day, week or month. You will have a dedicated expert individual consultant for your organization, skilled with the latest corporate knowledge. Book one of our trainers today to take advantage of this new service. We provide training for staff in sales techniques, customer service and ⑧① **we have recently added online selling.** Also, if you are in the sales business in the Rio area, visit our Web site now to see ⑧② **our new facility to open next month.** Find us on the web at www.salestraining.com.

廣告

　　您在聖保羅地區有企業銷售業務嗎？您是否常需要訓練與諮詢服務？銷售訓練公司在此協助您。我們提供按日、按週或按月計算的專家諮詢套裝服務。您的組織會單獨有一位盡心盡力的專家級顧問，且嫻熟最新的企業知識。今日就簽訂一位我們的訓練師，以利用這項新服務。我們提供員工業務技巧、客戶服務的訓練，同時，我們最近還增加了網路銷售訓練。此外，如果您在里約地區有業務，現在就造訪我們的網站，看看我們下個月要啟用的新分處。您可以在這個網站找到我們：www.salestraining.com。

字彙 **corporate** 公司的；企業的
**consultancy service** 諮詢服務
**expert** 專家　**consultation** 諮詢；磋商
**dedicated** 盡心盡力的；專用的
**individual** 單個的；個人的
**consultant** 顧問；諮詢師
**skilled with** 熟悉運用；擅長

04

**80** What is being advertised?
(A) Retail opportunities
(B) Offices for hire
(C) Sports training
(D) Sales consulting

這是在廣告什麼？
(A) 零售機會
(B) 辦公室租賃
(C) 運動訓練
(D) 銷售諮詢

**81** What new service did the company recently add?
(A) Internet selling
(B) Web page design
(C) Facility management
(D) Mail handling

這家公司最近增加了什麼新服務？
(A) 網路銷售
(B) 網頁設計
(C) 設施管理
(D) 郵件處理

**82** What will happen next month?
(A) Prices will increase.
(B) More staff will be recruited.
(C) A new location will open.
(D) An online seminar will be offered.

下個月會發生什麼事？
(A) 價格會上升。
(B) 會招募更多員工。
(C) 新場所會啟用。
(D) 會提供線上研討會。

**Questions 83-85 refer to the following excerpt from a talk.** 英W

Next, I've got some thrilling news. ㊳ **Our digital illustration company** is going to begin work in a brand-new field of industry. We will be entering the fitness and sports business. In fact, ㊴ **we've just signed the deal this morning** to create cartoon characters for Health Comes First, a fitness company based in Hamburg. This means that ㊵ **we'll be spending the next few weeks creating animated characters to show our new customers.**

- - - - - - - - - - - - - - - - - - - - - - - - - -

談話摘錄

接下來，我有個令人興奮的消息。我們的數位繪圖公司將在一個全新的產業展開工作，我們要進軍健身與運動產業。事實上，我們今天早上剛與健康第一公司簽下合約，要為這家總部在漢堡的健身公司創造卡通人物角色。這意謂著，我們接下來幾星期要創造動畫角色，展示給我們的新客戶看

字彙 **thrilling** 令人興奮的；令人激動的
**illustration** 插圖；圖示
**brand new** 全新的；嶄新的　**field** 領域；界
**enter** 進入；開始從事　**sign a deal** 簽約
**cartoon** 卡通片；（以政治、時事為題材的）諷刺畫
**based in** 總部設在……
**animated** 動畫的；卡通片的
**launch** 啟動；推出

**83** What kind of company does the speaker work for?
(A) A retail store
(B) A packaging company
(C) A fitness corporation
(D) An illustration company
說話者在什麼樣的公司工作？
(A) 零售商店
(B) 包裝公司
(C) 健身企業
(D) 繪圖公司

**84** What has the company recently done?
(A) Moved to Germany
(B) Opened a new branch
(C) Signed a contract
(D) Launched a new product range
這家公司最近做了什麼？
(A) 搬到德國
(B) 開了新的分公司
(C) 簽下一份合約
(D) 推出新系列產品

**85** According to the speaker, what will listeners do over the next few weeks?
(A) Recruit new employees
(B) Design a building
(C) Prepare work samples
(D) Join a health club
根據說話者所言，聽者在接下來幾星期會做什麼？
(A) 招募新員工
(B) 設計一棟大樓
(C) 準備作品範本
(D) 加入健康俱樂部

**Questions 86-88 refer to the following advertisement.**
澳M

Energy costs are on the rise. That's why smart consumers are shifting to Ultimate Solar Heating Systems. ㊱ **Our systems utilize the power of the sun to heat your home and provide you with hot water constantly.** ㊲ **You might be surprised to know that after paying for the installation, you will need to pay almost nothing to use and maintain an Ultimate Solar Heating System.** That's right. You will see your heating and hot water utility bills disappear. Plus, if you order a system with us, we will provide you with a free energy inspection of your home, a service that our competitors charge at least $300 to do. So give us a call today and find out how we can help you save money. This is as good as it gets. Call us at 555-7828.

- - - - - - - - - - - - - - - - - - - - - - - - - -

能源成本持續上漲。所以，聰明的消費者才會改用終極太陽能暖氣系統。我們的系統運用太陽能讓您的家變溫暖，並不斷為您提供熱水。您可能會很吃驚地發現，在付錢安裝設備後，您幾乎不用再付錢使用及維護終極太陽能暖氣系統。沒錯。您會看到您的暖氣及熱水費帳單消失了。此外，如果您向我們訂購設備，我們會免費提供居家能源檢測，我們的競爭對手對於這項服務收費至少要 300 元。所以，今天就打電話給我們，了解我們如何幫您省錢。這是筆再划算不過的交易了。請撥打 555-7828。

字彙 **shift** 更換；移動　**utilize** 利用
**constantly** 不斷地；時常地
**utility bill** 公用事業費用帳單(如水、電、瓦斯費)
**inspection** 檢查
**insulation** 隔熱；隔音；絕緣

**86** What products are being discussed?
(A) Solar cells
(B) Heating systems
(C) Computer programs
(D) Home insulation

文中在討論的是什麼產品？
(A) 太陽能電池
(B) 暖氣系統
(C) 電腦程式
(D) 居家隔熱設備

**87** According to the speaker, what might surprise listeners about these products?
(A) They are cheap to install.
(B) They are selling very well.
(C) They cost little to maintain.
(D) They teach directions to use.

根據說話者，這些產品的什麼部分可能會讓聽者很吃驚？
(A) 它們的安裝費很便宜。
(B) 它們賣得很好。
(C) 它們的維護費微乎其微。
(D) 他們教授使用指南。

**88** What does the speaker mean when he says, "This is as good as it gets"?
(A) The system is in good condition.
(B) He can't make the system better.
(C) His staff is very knowledgeable.
(D) He thinks he is offering a good deal.

當說話者說：「這是筆再划算不過的交易了」，他的意思是什麼？
(A) 這套系統狀況很好。
(B) 他無法讓系統更好了。
(C) 他的員工非常博學。
(D) 他認為，他給了一個好價錢。

**Questions 89-91 refer to the following telephone message.** 英W

Hi, Kevin. **89 This is Mary from City Residence. We met last week when you signed the rental contract for a two-bedroom apartment in the building I manage.** Well, I know that I said you could move in before the end of this month. But I have to say that's not an option anymore. While performing an inspection of the unit you will be renting, it was determined that the flooring and the refrigerator need to be replaced. **90 So it will take us a bit longer to make those upgrades.** I promise that the unit will be ready by the first of next month. **91 If we are able to have it ready a day or two early, I will certainly let you know.** I'm sorry things didn't work out as I had promised.

電話留言

嗨，凱文，我是城市住宅的瑪莉。我們上星期見過，你簽下我管理的一棟大樓裡的二房公寓租約。嗯，我知道我說過你可以在這個月底前搬進去。但我得說，這件事現在不可能了。在對你要承租的公寓進行檢查後，判定地板和冰箱需要更換。因此，我們需要再花更長時間進行更新工程。我保證，最晚下個月 1 號公寓就會一切就緒。如果，我們能提早一或兩天完工，我一定會讓你知道。很抱歉，事情無法像我答應過的那樣順利進行。

字彙 **rental contract** 租賃合約
**inspection** 檢查；檢驗
**contractor** 承包商；承包人　**lease** 租約
**terminate** 使停止；使結束

**89** Who is the speaker?
(A) A building manager
(B) A contractor
(C) A mover
(D) An inspector

說話者是什麼人？
(A) 一位大樓經理
(B) 一位承包商
(C) 一位搬家工人
(D) 一位檢查員

90 What does the woman mean when she says, "that's not an option anymore"?
(A) A service is no longer available.
(B) A lease has been terminated.
(C) A building failed to pass inspection.
(D) A date needs to be changed.

當女子說：「這件事現在不可能了」，她的意思是什麼？
(A) 有項服務不再提供了。
(B) 有份租約已經終止了。
(C) 有棟大樓未能通過檢查。
(D) 有個日期必須更改。

91 What does the woman offer to do?
(A) Arrange a moving service
(B) Contact the listener under certain conditions
(C) Supervise an installation
(D) Give a discount

女子提議做什麼？
(A) 安排搬家服務
(B) 在某些狀況下，與聽話者聯絡
(C) 監督一項設備的安裝
(D) 提供優惠折扣

**Questions 92-94 refer to the following telephone message and receipt.** 澳M

| Receipt | |
|---|---|
| Doughnut | $1.75 |
| Chocolate cake | $2.50 |
| Apple pie | $3.00 |
| Pastry | $4.25 |
| Total | $11.50 |

Hi. This is Paulo. I bought some bread from your bakery about half an hour ago. ❸❸ Well, when I got home, I realized that one of the items that I bought —an apple pie, — ❾❷ was not in my shopping bag, but there is a charge for it on my receipt. The cashier probably forgot to put it in my shopping bag. Could you kindly see if it is still there? If not,

could I stop by and get a replacement? I need it to prepare a small dinner party. ❾❹ Please let me know as soon as possible. My name, again, is Paulo. My number is 555-3457. I look forward to hearing from you.

電話留言與收據

| 收據 | |
|---|---|
| 甜甜圈 | $1.75 |
| 巧克力蛋糕 | $2.50 |
| 蘋果派 | $3.00 |
| 糕點 | $4.25 |
| 總計 | $11.50 |

嗨，我是保羅。我大約半小時前在你們麵包店買了一些麵包。嗯，等我回到家，我發現我買的其中一項商品，一個蘋果派並沒有在購物袋裡，但收據上有列出費用。收銀員可能忘記把派放進我的購物袋裡。可以麻煩你看一下東西是否還在那裡嗎？如果沒有，我可以過去拿一個新的嗎？我準備的一場小型晚餐派對會需要用到。請盡快通知我，我再說一次，我的名字是保羅，電話是555-3457。期待接到你的回電。

字彙 replacement 更換；取代

92 Why is the speaker calling?
(A) To cancel an order
(B) To report a missing item
(C) To arrange a delivery
(D) To request a refund

說話者為什麼打這通電話？
(A) 為了取消一份訂單
(B) 為了告知不見的商品
(C) 為了安排送貨
(D) 為了要求退回貨款

93 Look at the graphic. What is the price of the item the speaker refers to?
(A) $1.75
(B) $2.50
(C) $3.00
(D) $4.25

請見圖表，說話者提到的商品價格是多少？
(A) $1.75
(B) $2.50
(C) $3.00
(D) $4.25

**94** What does the speaker want the listener to do?
(A) Get in touch with him
(B) Give him a refund
(C) Email the list
(D) Upgrade the shipping method

說話者想要聽者做什麼？
(A) 和他聯絡
(B) 把錢退給他
(C) 以電子郵件把清單寄給他
(D) 更新送貨方式

**Questions 95-97 refer to the following excerpt from a meeting and chart.** 英W

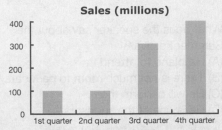

**Sales (millions)**

I want to move on to some good news. **95** I know all of you worked very hard to improve the design of our company's line of water purifiers. Well, it appears that your hard work paid off. If you look at the chart by the sales division, you can see that the month after the new designs were released onto the market, sales started to rise. **96** For the first six months of the year, they had been flat at around $100 million. Then, they jumped by $200 million during the month of the release and have continued to increase since then. You've done a great job, everyone! To celebrate, I would like to invite all of you out to Marilyn Hotel this Friday evening. **97** Dinner is on me!

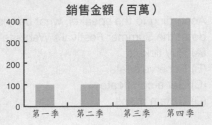

**銷售金額（百萬）**

---

接下來，我想要說些好消息。我知道，你們全都很努力改進我們公司淨水器的設計。嗯，看起來你們的努力有了收穫。如果你們看看這張銷售部門做的圖，可以看到在新設計上市後的一個月，銷售金額開始上升。今年前6個月，銷售金額一直維持在大約一億元左右。然後，在產品上市的那個月，銷售金額飆升，增加了兩億元，而且在那之後持續上升。各位，你們表現得很棒！為了慶祝，我邀請大家這個星期五晚上到瑪麗蓮飯店去，我請大家吃晚餐！

字彙 purifier 淨化器
pay off 取得成功；得到好結果
flat （利潤、銷售等）無增長的
incentive 激勵；刺激

🎧04

**95** Where most likely does the speaker work?
(A) At a phone company
(B) At an accounting firm
(C) At a lighting maker
(D) At an appliance manufacturer

說話者最可能在哪裡工作？
(A) 電話公司
(B) 會計師事務所
(C) 燈具製造商
(D) 家用電器廠商

**96** Look at the graphic. When did the company release the new products?
(A) 1st quarter
(B) 2nd quarter
(C) 3rd quarter
(D) 4th quarter

請見圖表，這家公司在何時讓新產品上市？
(A) 第一季
(B) 第二季
(C) 第三季
(D) 第四季

**97** What does the speaker say she will do for the listeners?
(A) Treat them to dinner
(B) Give them a financial incentive
(C) Present an award
(D) Let them take a vacation

說話者說，她會為聽者做什麼？
(A) 請他們吃晚餐
(B) 給他們獎金獎勵
(C) 頒獎
(D) 讓他們去度假

**Questions 98-100 refer to the following radio broadcast and map.** 澳M

Summer Festival Map

| Visual Arts | | Info |
| Booth #111 | Lake | Booth #113 |
| Food Stands | | Market |
| Booth #112 | | Booth #114 |

Before we get back to listening to the music, I want to remind you that this weekend is the 10th annual Summer Festival. It will take place on Saturday from 9 A.M. to 10 P.M. in Bryant Park. It's a great place to see the work of artists, both local and those from out of town. You can also sample food from a variety of restaurants. Plus, there will be great musical performances. That's what I am looking forward to most of all. Be sure to stop by to meet your favorite Rock musicians broadcasting live during the fair. **98 99 Our booth will be next to the information tent on the eastern side of the lake. 100 For more information, visit the festival's Web site at www.summerfestival.org. There, you can download maps and a schedule of performances.**

電台廣播與地圖

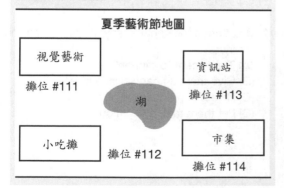

夏季藝術節地圖

| 視覺藝術 | | 資訊站 |
| 攤位 #111 | 湖 | 攤位 #113 |
| 小吃攤 | | 市集 |
| | 攤位 #112 | 攤位 #114 |

在我們繼續播放音樂之前，我要提醒你們，這個週末是第十屆年度夏季藝術節。活動將於星期六上午9點到晚上10點在布萊恩公園舉行。那是個很棒的地方，可以看到來自本地和外地的藝術家的作品。你們也可以吃到各家餐廳的佳餚。此外，還有很讚的音樂表演，那是我最期待的部分。務必要前往你們最喜歡的搖滾音樂家在活動期間的現場演出。我們的攤位在湖東邊的資訊站帳蓬旁邊。更多資訊請上藝術節官網：www.summerfestival.org。你可以從網站上下載地圖和表演節目的時間表。

字彙 broadcast 播送；廣播　challenging 挑戰 certificate 證書

**98** What does the speaker say about the Summer Festival?
(A) He plans to attend it.
(B) There is not much room to park cars.
(C) He will perform there.
(D) He is one of the sponsors.

關於夏季藝術節，說話者說了什麼？
(A) 他打算參加。
(B) 沒有太多地方可以停車。
(C) 他會在那裡表演。
(D) 他是贊助者之一。

**99** Look at the graphic. Where will the radio station be broadcasting from?
(A) Booth #111
(B) Booth #112
(C) Booth #113
(D) Booth #114

請見圖表，廣播電台會從哪裡播送節目？
(A) 攤位 #111
(B) 攤位 #112
(C) 攤位 #113
(D) 攤位 #114

**100** According to the speaker, what can listeners do at the Summer Festival's Web site?
(A) Buy tickets
(B) Reserve seats
(C) Get a certificate
(D) Obtain maps

根據說話者所言，聽者在夏季藝術節的官網上可以做什麼？
(A) 買票
(B) 預訂座位
(C) 拿到證書
(D) 拿到地圖

## PART 5
P. 026

**101**

阿摩提管理公司的行政主管決定支持研究團隊的資金決策。
(A) deciding 決定性的
(B) decisions 決定
(C) decide 決定
(D) decides 決定

解析 空格要與冠詞（the）以及後方的 funding 組合成「融資決策」，因此答案為 (B)。deciding 可以當作分詞或動名詞；decide 為動詞，無法與前方名詞組合成複合名詞。

字彙 executive 行政部門的；經營管理的
uphold 贊成；維持 funding 資金
research 研究；調查

**102**

為了節省能源，請在離開工作場所前，關閉電器設備。
(A) to leave 將離開
(B) leaves 離開
(C) leaving 離開
(D) left 離開

解析 空格位在 before 後方，又連接受詞（the workplace），因此要填入動名詞 (C)。before 可以當作介系詞、或是從屬連接詞使用，兩者後方都可以連接 -ing 的形態。

字彙 conserve 節省；保存
switch off 關上
electrical appliance 電器；電氣設備
workplace 工作場所

**103**

全國油漆與裝潢展的特色是，有機會聽到經驗豐富工匠的具體建議。
(A) case 案例
(B) advice 建議
(C) songs 歌曲
(D) house 房屋

解析 本題為名詞詞彙題。根據題意，表達「有機會聽取具體的建議」最為適當，因此答案為 (B)。

字彙 decorate 粉刷裝潢；裝飾
feature 以……為特色；
（電影）由……主演
specific 具體的；特殊的
craftsman 工匠；工藝師

**104**

KKL 集團有一個有經驗管理會計師的職缺。
(A) across 穿過
(B) for 在……方面
(C) through 通過
(D) off 離開

解析 本題要選出適當的介系詞。根據題意，表達「開出一個有經驗的管理會計師職缺」最為適當，因此答案為 (B)。

請熟記 vacancy for 的用法，表示「開出……職缺」。其餘選項 across（橫越）、through（穿過）、off（離開、脫落）皆為經常出現在考題中的介系詞。

字彙 have a vacancy 有……的職缺
experienced 有經驗的；熟練的
management accountant 管理會計師

**105**

由於國內消費量的驟降，本季的薪資很可能維持不變。
(A) liked 喜歡
(B) likely 很可能
(C) likened 比喻
(D) likeable 討人喜歡的

解析 若有背過常見用法 be likely to 不定詞（有可能……），便能輕鬆選出答案 (B)。雖然 likely 為 ly 結尾，卻屬於形容詞，請務必熟記。

字彙 plunge 驟降；猛跌
consumption 消費；消費量

**106**

盧卡斯女士預測，整個再生計畫應該在月底前完成。

(A) by 在……之前
(B) until 直到
(C) of 屬於
(D) on 在……的時候

解析 本題考的是介系詞。根據題意，表達「月底之前」最為適當，因此要從 by 和 until 當中選出答案。請務必熟記：by 用於表示動作在某個時間點完成，適合搭配 complete、register、pay、submit 使用；until 用於表示動作持續到某個時間點，適合搭配 wait、stay、continue 使用，因此答案要選 (A) by。

字彙 forecast 預測；預言
entire 全部的；整個的
regeneration 重建；（使）再生

**107**

一份近期問卷調查顯示，超過 50% 的線上顧客打算和同一家公司的寬頻連線續約。

(A) them 他們
(B) theirs 他們的東西
(C) they 他們
(D) their 他們的

解析 空格後方為名詞 broadband connection，扮演受詞的角色，因此空格要填入所有格，放在名詞前方使用。them 要放在受詞的位置；theirs 為所有格代名詞，要放在主詞、受詞或補語的位置；they 要放在主詞的位置，不能放在名詞前方，因此答案要選 (D)。

字彙 questionnaire 問卷調查
reveal 顯露出；展現
renew 更新；延長……的期限；給……展期
broadband connection 寬頻連線

**108**

要和客服專員通話，請撥打列在本表格最下面的號碼。

(A) tell 告訴
(B) mention 提及
(C) speak 說話
(D) inform 通知

解析 空格後方沒有連接受詞，因此要填入不及物動詞。tell 為及物動詞，適用兩種句型「主詞＋動詞＋受詞」和「主詞＋動詞＋受詞 1 ＋受詞 2」；mention 也是及物動詞，適用句型「主詞＋動詞＋受詞」。

inform（告知）的後方要直接加上告知的對象作為受詞，同樣適用兩種句型「主詞＋動詞＋受詞」和「主詞＋動詞＋受詞 1 ＋受詞 2」。綜合前述，答案要選不及物動詞 (C) speak。

字彙 representative 代表；代理人

**109**

即使歐納西斯女士無法出席本週的研討會，她和所有的部門主管也會參加下週的研討會。

(A) she 她
(B) her 她
(C) hers 她的東西
(D) herself 她自己

解析 空格前方為由 Even though 引導的子句，而空格位在主要子句裡，要填入主詞。人稱代名詞當中，主格（she）和所有格代名詞（hers）都可以填入主詞的位置，但根據題意，表示「她」比起「她的」更為適當，因此答案要選主格 (A) she。

字彙 along with 和……一起

**110**

收購泰坦工業應該有助太平洋控股的商業策略多樣化。

(A) diversity 多樣性
(B) diverse 多樣的
(C) diversify 使多樣化
(D) diversely 多樣地

解析 空格要填入 help 的受詞補語。原形動詞和 to 不定詞皆可作為 help 的受詞補語使用，因此答案要選動詞 (C) diversify。

字彙 acquisition 收購物（房屋、土地、公司等）；收購

**111**

沒有最新的安全軟體，電腦系統容易受到許多病毒攻擊。

(A) superior 優越的
(B) exemplary 值得仿效的
(C) vulnerable 易受攻擊的
(D) cautious 小心謹慎的

**解析** 本題的四個選項皆為形容詞，因此要透過單字的意思來解題。superior（優秀的）、exemplary（模範的）、cautious（小心謹慎的）皆不符合題意，因此答案為 (C) vulnerable（脆弱的；易受攻擊的）。請一併熟記常見用法 be vulnerable to（易受……；易於……）。

**112**

伊萊亞斯百貨的保全部門對員工擔心的可疑包裹迅速作出回應。

(A) prompt 迅速的
(B) promptly 迅速地
(C) prompting 促使
(D) promptness 迅速

**解析** 空格前方為不及物動詞 react，因此填入副詞 (B) 最為適當。prompt 可以當作名詞、形容詞或動詞使用；prompting 可以當作動名詞或分詞使用；promptness 為名詞，無法用來修飾動詞。另外，除了 react 之外，還有其他意思相近的不及物動詞，例如 respond、reply 等等，其後方皆會搭配介系詞 to 一起使用，請務必熟記。

**字彙** security department 保全部門
react 反應；作出反應
suspicious 可疑的
prompt 迅速的；及時的
promptly 迅速地；及時地

**113**

旅客在登上任何國內班機時，必須出示適當的身分證件。

(A) in addition 此外
(B) such as 例如
(C) although 雖然
(D) when 當……時

**解析** 本題考的是具修飾作用的連接詞。「Travelers . . . identification」的部分為結構完整的句子，因此空格至 flights 要扮演修飾的角色。空格後方連接 -ing，可以填入介系詞或從屬連接詞作修飾，因此應從 although 和 when 當中選出答案。

根據題意，表達「搭乘國內線的時候」最為適當，因此答案要選 (D)。若填入 although，不符合題意；in addition 為副詞片語；such as 用於列出前方名詞的具體事例時，並不符合題意。

**字彙** appropriate 適當的
identification 身分證明；識別
board 上（船、車、飛機等）
domestic flight 國內班機

**114**

由於道路過於狹窄，長途貨車駕駛禁止進入帕克大道。

(A) narrow 狹窄的
(B) narrowly 狹窄地
(C) narrows 使狹窄
(D) narrower 較窄的

**解析** be 動詞後方可以連接名詞或形容詞，副詞 too 後方可以連接形容詞 narrow 或比較級 narrower。根據題意，表達「因為道路太窄」較為適當，因此答案要選 (A)。narrowly 為副詞；narrows 為動詞，不能扮演補語的角色。

**字彙** long-distance 長途的；長距離的
lorry 貨車；卡車　forbidden 禁止的
narrowly 狹窄地

**115**

艾科霍國際的總公司座落於史普林希爾的郵局附近。

(A) near 在……附近
(B) besides 除……之外
(C) close 緊密的
(D) next 緊接在後的

**解析** 空格用來引導名詞片語，要填入介系詞。close 和 next 僅能當作形容詞或副詞使用，因此並非答案。near（接近）和 besides（除……之外）皆為介系詞，根據題意，選擇 (A) 較為適當。另外補充一點，besides 當作副詞使用時，意思為「還有；此外」。

**字彙** headquarters（公司、機關等的）總部；總公司

**116**

由於還沒決定出優勝者，評審必須進一步評估參賽者。
(A) decided 決定出
(B) decisive 果斷的
(C) deciding 決定
(D) decision 決定

**解析** 後方句子提到還需要針對參賽者進行評價，表示尚未決定出優勝者，因此答案為 (A) decided。

**字彙** judge 裁判；評審
assess 評估；評估
entry 參賽者；參賽作品

**117**

如果你申請的大學額滿了，你的名字會自動列入備取名單，以備如果有人退出不念。
(A) intermittently 間歇地
(B) automatically 自動地
(C) progressively 逐漸地
(D) considerably 相當多地

**解析** 本題為副詞詞彙題。根據題意，表達「你的名字將自動被排進備取名單」最為適當，因此答案為 (B)。

**字彙** waiting list 候補名單；備取名單
in case 以防萬一；假使
drop out 退出；退學
intermittently 間歇地；斷斷續續地
progressively 逐漸地；日漸增加地
considerably 非常；相當多的

**118**

藉由把老舊巴士換成更省油的新款車輛，肯尼威克得以省下保養與維修的費用。
(A) replacement 更換
(B) replacing 更換
(C) replace 更換
(D) replaced 更換

**解析** 介系詞後方要連接名詞，因此應從 replacement 和 replacing 當中選出答案。而當中只有動名詞 (B) 的後方可以連接受詞 old buses。雖然 replaced（替換、取代的）當作形容詞使用時，可以修飾後方的名詞，但是填入空格後並不符合題意。replace A with B 的意思為「把 A 換成 B」，請特別熟記。

**字彙** fuel-efficient 省油的；油耗低的
maintenance 維修；保養
replacement 更換

**119**

評審委員會必須在星期一下午 3 點前收到年度藝術家獎的提名人選。
(A) Authorities 當局
(B) Performances 表演
(C) Occurrences 事件
(D) Nominations 提名

**解析** 本題為名詞詞彙題。根據題意，應為將從審查委員會收到今年的藝術家「提名」，因此答案選 (D) 最為適當。

**字彙** judging committee 評審委員會
authority 當局；權力
occurrence 事件；發生
nomination 提名；任命

**120**

多虧我們的優異業績，我們的業務主管全都可以期待這個月的分紅。
(A) which 哪個
(B) all 所有的
(C) another 另一個
(D) any 任何一個

**解析** 空格位在助動詞（can）和原形動詞（look forward to）之間，要填入副詞。another 和 any 可以當作形容詞或代名詞使用；which 可以當作關係代名詞或名詞子句連接詞使用，不能放在副詞的位置。all 可以當作形容詞、代名詞、或副詞使用。當作副詞使用時，意思為「完全、全部都」，因此答案為 (B)。

**字彙** record 紀錄
sales executive 業務主管；業務主任

**121**

理察‧K‧諾斯的推理小說《霧中之屋》被吹捧為十年來最棒的小說。

(A) totaled 總計
(B) alleviated 減輕
(C) billed 透過廣告宣傳
(D) consisted 組成

**解析** 本題的四個選項皆為 p.p.，因此要透過單字的意思來解題。total 的意思為「總計」；alleviate 的意思為「減輕、緩和」；consist 要搭配介系詞 of 一起使用，意思為「組成」，填入後皆不符合題意。

bill 當作名詞使用時，意思為「帳單；海報」。但是當作動詞使用時，可以表示「開立帳單；把……宣傳為」的意思，請特別熟記，因此答案為 (C) billed。

**字彙** total 總計；合計　alleviate 減輕；緩和
bill 透過廣告宣傳；做廣告（常與 as 連用）

**122**

大部分的消費者，在面對要選擇廉價或高品質電器設備時，會優先考慮產品的品質。

(A) who ……的人
(B) which ……的那些
(C) when 當……時
(D) what 凡是……的事物

**解析** 空格所引導的句子（. . . appliance）中缺少動詞，因此並非子句，而是要視為分詞構句（given）省略後的句型結構。因此答案要選從屬連接詞 (C) when。

**123**

霍華德金融公司樂於為忠實客戶提供該地區最佳的諮詢服務。

(A) provide 提供
(B) providing 提供
(C) provided 提供
(D) provider 提供者

**解析** 請熟記 be pleased to（對……感到高興）的用法。此處的「to 不定詞」扮演副詞的角色，用來表示產生情緒的原因。另外，請一併熟記相似用法 be delighted to。因此答案要選 (A)。

**字彙** loyal customer 忠實顧客

**124**

如果沃克斯科技公司同意簽合約，所需的資金早就到位了。

(A) send 傳遞
(B) would have sent 當時就會傳了
(C) were sent 被傳遞了
(D) would have been sent 當時就被傳送了

**解析** 假設語氣 if 子句的時態為過去完成式（had agreed），因此主要子句中的助動詞也要使用過去完成式。空格後方並未連接受詞，因此要從 (B) 和 (D) 當中，選出被動語態 (D) would have been sent 作為答案。

**125**

等到有人通報柏德西巷的火災時，火勢已蔓延到鄰近地區。

(A) spreading 蔓延
(B) spreads 蔓延
(C) were spread 被蔓延
(D) had spread 已蔓延

**解析** When 或 By the time 開頭的子句使用過去式時，主要子句要使用相同的時態，或是過去完成式。雖然 (C) were spread 的時態正確，但是與主詞的單複數不一致，不能作為答案，因此答案要選 (D) had spread。

另外補充一點，When 或 By the time 開頭的子句使用現在式時，實際上要表達的是未來，因此主要子句要使用未來式或未來完成式才行。

**126**

八月時，康諾斯藝廊將展出著名藝術家詹姆斯‧麥克尼爾的一些作品。

(A) distinguished 著名的
(B) founded 有基礎的
(C) estimated 估計的
(D) allocated 分配的

**解析** 本題為形容詞詞彙題。根據題意，表達「著名的藝術家 James McNeil」最為適當，因此答案為 (A)。distinguished 除了可以解釋為「著名的」之外，還有「區分的、卓越的」意思，請特別熟記。

**字彙** distinguished 著名的；傑出的；卓越的
founded 有基礎的；創立的
estimated 估計的；估價的
allocated 分配的；分派的

**127**

預定於 6 月 20 日開始的訓練延後了三個星期。

(A) which ⋯⋯的那個
(B) this 這個
(C) what 所有⋯⋯的事物
(D) that ⋯⋯那個

**解析** 句中有兩個動詞（was scheduled 和 was put off），因此空格要填入連接詞。選項中，(B) this 不能當作連接詞使用，因此並非答案。其餘選項皆為連接詞，但是 (D) that 不能置於逗點後方，因此不能作為答案；(C) what 為名詞子句連接詞，不能放在名詞（The training）的後方；空格引導的子句為形容詞子句，置於名詞後方作修飾，(A) which 可以當作形容詞子句連接詞使用，故為正確答案。

**字彙** put off 延後

**128**

即使今天晚上天氣轉好，明天將在珍金斯公園舉行音樂祭的主辦單位仍考慮延後活動。

(A) even if 即使
(B) nevertheless 仍然
(C) regardless of 不管
(D) so that 以便

**解析** 空格後方連接子句，因此要填入連接詞。(B) nevertheless 為副詞、(C) regardless of 為介系詞，都不是答案。從 (A) 和 (D) 當中選擇時，根據題意，答案要選 (A)，意思為「即使」。

**129**

雖然適清淨水器今年夏天賣得很好，它仍被品質指南協會視為不可靠。

(A) inspected 檢查
(B) conducted 實施
(C) deemed 視為
(D) allowed 允許

**解析** 被動語態（be p.p.）的動詞後方連接形容詞（unreliable），表示該形容詞為受詞補語，空格要填入不完全及物動詞。因此答案要選 (C) deemed（視為）。

**字彙** unreliable 不可靠的；無法信賴的

**130**

好幾個桑德林大樓的住戶都報告，他們經常得面對大量噪音。

(A) participate in 參加
(B) put forth 提出
(C) contend with 面對
(D) aspire to 渴求

**解析** 本題為動詞詞彙題。根據題意，表達「得應付噪音問題」最為適當，因此答案為 (C)。

**字彙** tenant 住戶；房客　report 報告；描述
put forth 提出；發表
contend with 必須面對、處理（困境或不愉快的事）
aspire to 渴求

# PART 6

P. 029

## 131-134 電子郵件

收件者：service@blueoceanair.com
寄件者：james.gimbel@cmail.com
關於：訂位錯誤

　　你好，我是詹姆斯‧金貝爾。我訂了 7 月 12 日星期二從雪梨到華盛頓的機票。我計劃回華盛頓和太太慶祝結婚十週年。我的訂位號碼是 5774001。在我要出發的那一天——7 月 15 日，我提早一個小時到機場。我立刻走到藍海航空的其中一台自助報到機。當我在機器上輸入我的訂位資訊後，機器顯示我的報到狀態無效。我衝去找你們的一位客服代表，出示列印出來的確認電子郵件，讓她知道我所遭遇的事。然後，她把我排進候補名單。她說，我必須等到有空位。我在櫃檯旁邊緊張不安地站了兩個小時，才在最後一刻登上飛機。

　　我非常不高興，而且對你們的系統真的很失望。我希望你們針對這個問題解釋，請盡快撥打我的手機回電給我。

謝謝你，
詹姆斯‧金貝爾

**字彙** status 狀態；身分
invalid 無效的；作廢的
representative 代表；代理人
embarrassed 使人尷尬的；令人為難的

### 131

(A) book 預訂
(B) booking 預訂
(C) booked 預訂
(D) bookable 可預訂的

**解析** 請熟記複合名詞「預訂號碼」（booking number）。比起動名詞和分詞，booking 更常作為名詞使用，因此答案要選 (B)。

### 132

(A) gradually 逐漸地
(B) substantially 實質上
(C) comprehensively 廣泛地
(D) immediately 立即

**解析** 根據前後文意，表達的是抵達機場後，「立即」前往自助報到機，因此答案要選 (D)。

### 133

(A) 因此，我必須額外付費。
(B) 然後，她把我排進候補名單。
(C) 不巧，印表機故障了。
(D) 之後，她要求我打開行李。

**解析** 空格後方提到必須等到有空的機位出來為止，因此答案要選 (B)，表示已加入候補名單。

### 134

(A) beyond 超出
(B) concerning 關於
(C) along 沿著
(D) up to 至多

**解析** 空格後方連接 this issue，表達「『關於』這項問題」較為適當，因此答案為 (B)。

## 135-138 信件

安娜・魯本
80-5 溫斯頓公寓
加州 89723 河濱市伍迪大道 2917 號

親愛的魯本女士：

　　謝謝您詢問關於您銀行帳戶的資料。您的最新一期帳單中會包含 20 元的費用，是因為我們晚收到您八月份的帳款。然而，我們了解您是一位信用良好的長期客戶。因為這樣，我們將取消這筆通常會收的費用，您的帳戶也就此更正。

　　為了確保您的每月帳款都能準時入帳，我們建議您申請我們的自動扣款功能。有了這項服務，您可以定期支付應付款項的最低繳款金額。詳細資料請上 www.chvasbankingservice.com/payments 查詢。

　　如果您有任何問題或疑慮，可以透過電子郵件聯絡我 d.adelaide@chvasbankingservice.com。

　　謝謝您的惠顧。

丹娜・阿德雷德
會計專員

**字彙** bank account 銀行帳戶
　　　 fee 服務費；費用（如學費、入場費等）
　　　 statement （銀行的）對帳單；報告單
　　　 payment 支付的金額；付款
　　　 revise 修改；修正
　　　 accordingly 相對應地；因此
　　　 guarantee 保證
　　　 sign up for 註冊；登記；申請
　　　 automatic debit 自動扣款
　　　 amount due 應付金額
　　　 on a regular basis 定期地
　　　 of good standing 信用良好
　　　 reimburse 償還；退款　waive 取消；放棄

### 135
(A) 您可以以電子方式或臨櫃支付這筆滯納金。
(B) 我們鼓勵您開一個新的儲蓄帳戶。
(C) 然而，我們了解您是一位信用良好的長期客戶。
(D) 您應該填完月底前退款所需的表格。

**解析** 空格前方提到要繳交滯納金，後方則提到撤回這件事，因此答案要選 (C)，表示其原因為對方是信用良好的長期客戶。

### 136
(A) expecting 預期
(B) imposing 徵（稅）
(C) waiving 取消
(D) honoring 致敬

**解析** 開頭提到由於錢延遲入帳，未準時付款，必須支付 20 美元的滯納金。因此此處表達「信用良好的客戶，免除此筆費用」較為適當，答案要選 (C)。

### 137
(A) already 已經
(B) always 總是
(C) evenly 均勻地
(D) shortly 不久

**解析** 根據前後文意，表達「為了確保『一直』能準時付款，建議申請自動扣款功能」較為適當，因此答案要選 (B)。

### 138
(A) specified 特定的
(B) specifying 特定的
(C) specifically 特別地
(D) specification 規格

**解析** 冠詞與名詞之間要填入形容詞，因此請優先刪除 (C) 與 (D)。根據前後文意，表達「特定的金額」最為適當，因此答案為過去分詞 (A)。

## 139-142 通知

### 健身中心休館

由於進行大規模整修，大部分的一流體態健身中心將從 8 月 14 日星期一起休館。主要改進工程包括最新的運動健身器材、室內新上一層漆，以及新的地板與燈具。在考量過我們中心老顧客的意見後，我們會增加更多團體運動教室和桑拿設施。由於二樓將有更多團體運動教室，有些設備如臥推和跑步機將移到一樓。

休館時間可能持續數個月。我們預計在 12 月 1 日重新開館。

您仍可以到下列分館健身：

—威勒分館（緬因大道 25 號）
—樂園分館（布雷亞路 8 號）
—水生分館（東街 110 號）

想找到離你最近的分館，請上 www.acebodyfit.com，並透過線上聊天服務和健身房工作人員通話。

**字彙** renovation 更新；整修
coat （油漆等的）塗層
flooring （總稱）室內地板
fixtures 固定裝置；燈具
GX (Group Exercising) 團體運動
bench presses 臥推；重量訓練機；胸部訓練機　treadmills 跑步機

### 139
(A) extend 延長
(B) extensively 大規模地
(C) extensive 大規模的
(D) extending 延伸的

**解析** 冠詞與名詞之間要填入形容詞，用來修飾名詞。選項中只有 (C) extensive（大範圍的）和 (D) extending（延伸的）可以扮演形容詞的角色，而根據文意，表達「大範圍的整修」較為適當，因此答案為 (C)。

### 140
(A) candidates 候選人
(B) patrons 老顧客
(C) pedestrians 行人
(D) passengers 乘客

**解析** 向健身中心提供意見的人應為顧客（patrons），因此答案要選 (B)。

### 141
(A) 我們預計在 12 月 1 日重新開館。
(B) 您可以上 www.acebodyfit.com 報名舞蹈課。
(C) 規律運動被視為健康所需。
(D) 健身房預定在明天早上十時開門。

**解析** 空格前方提到可能會閉館數個月，因此答案要選 (A)，表示預計於 12 月 1 日重新開放。

### 142
(A) Find 找到
(B) Having found 已找到
(C) To be found 要被找到
(D) To find 要找到

**解析** 根據文意，表達「『如欲尋找』鄰近的分館」較為適當，因此答案為 to 不定詞 (D)。

## 143-146 備忘錄

發文人：所有員工
受文人：人事部總監
關於：人事異動

在董事會於二月十日通過一項決議後，梅爾羅斯系統很高興宣布下列的人事異動。我們相信，梅爾羅斯系統在新的管理階層領導下，會繼續穩定成長。

資深會計總監安琪拉·藍斯博瑞被任命為財務長，她主要負責監督所有的預算管理和投資策略。

既然我們正在擴展我們的國際業務，公司因此設置了一個新職位：國際業務總監。國內業務經理安迪·萬里芬斯已被任命擔任此一職務，他將監管公司的所有全球營運。

資深行銷經理約翰·華頓晉升為國內業務經理，他將接手安迪·萬里芬斯的職務，負責發展用來讓我們在國內市場的業務達到短期與長期成長的銷售策略。

**143**

(A) resolves 解決
(B) resolved 解決
(C) resolving 解決
(D) resolution 決議

解析 空格位在 After 子句中主詞的位置，一定要填入名詞，因此答案為 (D) resolution（決議）。

**144**

(A) regularly 規律地
(B) primarily 主要地
(C) relatively 相對地
(D) positively 明確地

解析 該句話列出財務長「主要」負責的業務內容，因此答案要選 (B) primarily。

**145**

(A) Now that 既然
(B) Rather than 寧願
(C) During 在……期間
(D) Whether 是否

解析 空格要填入從屬連接詞。選項中只有 Now that（既然；由於）為從屬連接詞，因此答案要選 (A)。另外補充一點，Whether 可以用來引導名詞子句或副詞子句，但是當作從屬連接詞使用時，後方一定要加上 or 或 or not 才行。

**146**

(A) 從下個月起，他將到海外工作。
(B) 他將接手安迪‧葛里芬斯的職務。
(C) 這將是他作為財務長的另一項職責。
(D) 他將處理公司的所有預算評估。

解析 空格前一段提到原任國內業務經理的 Andy Griffith 先生接下新的職務，而空格前方提到 John Walton 已升為國內業務經理，這表示他將接手 Andy Griffith 先生的工作，因此答案為 (B)。

## PART 7

P. 033

### 147-148 簡訊

收件者：漢彌爾頓・哈珊　下午 2 時 46 分
寄件者：內馬爾航空旅客服務
警訊通知：請見內馬爾航空 4492 班機時刻表變動的簡訊

**4492 班機**
布理斯托地區機場到艾克希特聖大衛機場

誤點
原定起飛：下午 4 時 20 分
實際起飛：下午 4 時 50 分
原定到達：下午 7 時 30 分
預估到達：下午 7 時 40 分
登機門：31
行李提領：4 號轉盤

如果您預訂要轉機，請查看航空公司的轉機資訊。

〔發送〕

**字彙** alert 警報；警戒
flight （飛機的）班次
regional 地區的
departure 出發；啟程；離開
estimated 估計的
baggage claim 行李提領處
carousel 行李輸送帶；行李轉盤
connecting flight 轉機航班；轉接班機
transfer 轉機
status 狀態

**147** 為什麼發送這則簡訊？
(A) 為了確認預訂的航班
(B) 為了宣布航班狀態的變動
(C) 為了通知一位旅客登機門資料
(D) 為了提供轉機航班的更新資料

**148** 關於哈珊先生，可由文中得知什麼？
(A) 他會從布理斯托起飛。
(B) 他在艾克希特付機票錢。
(C) 他托運了二件行李上飛機。
(D) 他遺失了他的機票資料。

### 149-151 傳單

和我們一起歡慶傑克森 4 月 18 日的盛大開幕！

為了慶祝我們新店開幕，傑克森在營業第一週推出「買一件，第二件半價」活動。所以，來看我們的手提袋和鞋子。從 20 多個品牌中挑選，其中包括：

- 楊朵
- 西爾格德
- 拉蒙謝
- 印弟歌
- 桃子媽媽

傑克森位於切里希谷購物中心裡，海爾頓服飾和全民料理中間。我們的營業時間是每週七天的正常購物時間。

請看 3 月 30 日的《切里希谷先驅報》，內有傑克森新任店經理艾莉・朱諾的人物專訪。

每位顧客限購 5 件商品。

**字彙** grand opening 盛大開幕
trading 營業；買賣
be located 位於……
take a look at 看一看
issue （報刊）期號
be situated 位於……

**149** 傑克森販賣什麼？
(A) 食物
(B) 服裝
(C) 時尚配件
(D) 運動設備

**150** 根據傳單，顧客在 4 月 18 日到 24 日間可以做什麼？
(A) 免費得到一份《切里希谷先驅報》
(B) 參加新分店開幕的記者招待會
(C) 買一件，第二件半價
(D) 出示傳單獲得更多折扣優惠

**151** 關於傑克森，文中提及什麼？
(A) 它登廣告徵聘員工。
(B) 它位於購物商場內。
(C) 艾莉・朱諾將訪問商店老闆。
(D) 它的開幕日是 3 月 30 日。

納瑪斯基

納瑪斯基集團致力於保護環境，及確保盡一切努力不讓我們的廢棄物被送去掩埋場。我們有項政策鼓勵我們的消費者，在產品的生命週期結束時，要有責任地處理我們的產品。如果，您在我們的任何一家納瑪斯基商店購買產品，我們很樂意送貨給您。同時，我們也很高興回收您的舊電器，將它送到我們的處理場。或者，您可以安排把您的舊電器送到我們的處理廠。您所在地的納瑪斯基商店也可以給您一張離您較近的處理場清單，他們提供類似的環保方式處理任何尺寸的電器。

**字彙** be dedicated to 專心致志於做某事
attempt 嘗試；企圖
prevent 防止；阻止　waste 廢棄物；廢料
landfill 垃圾掩埋；垃圾掩埋場
dispose of 處理；處置
lifecycle 生命週期
appliance 器具；設備　collect 收集；接走
disposal facility 處理設施
alternatively 或者；要不
environmentally friendly 環保的；對生態環境無害的
method 方法　depot 倉庫；儲藏處

**152** 這則告示的目的是什麼？
(A) 為了宣傳新系列的電器產品
(B) 為了指出送貨延遲了
(C) 為了提醒消費者有折扣
(D) 為了敘述可用的服務

**153** 根據告示，納瑪斯基提供什麼資訊？
(A) 附近處理中心的名稱
(B) 顧客對產品評價的印刷品
(C) 環保處理方式的近期研究
(D) 公司產品儲藏庫的說明

明視電影公司
英國薩里郡惠爾大道 686 號
三月三十日

伊摩珍·克倫福特女士
英國薩里郡泰晤士街 34 號 克萊倫頓公寓 121 室

親愛的克倫福特女士：

感謝您對明視電影公司的關注。我們的客戶伊恩·布連曾提過你是餐飲部經理一職的合適人選，而我們現在收到您的應徵函。

我想要安排四月十七日下午一時和您面談。請盡快和我的助理席瑪拉·夏姆聯絡，確認這個時間可以接受。您可以撥打 010-555-9234 和她聯絡。

此外，如果您可以用電子郵件重新傳送您的履歷表給我，我會很感激。您透過我們的網站線上傳送的履歷表有問題，我們無法瀏覽文件的最後一頁。

最後，請查看看隨信付上的數個您必須完成的表格，並在面談時帶過來。我們期待收到您的回音。

誠摯地，

愛德華·特倫
人事經理

附件

**字彙** suitable 合適的
candidate 應徵者；候選人
catering 外燴；準備或提供食物的工作
assistant 助理
acceptable 可以接受的；值得接受的
reach 與……取得聯繫
corrupted （電腦上的資訊）被破壞的；有錯誤的
enclosed 隨函附上的
mandatory 強制的；必須履行的
enclosure 附件　alteration 變更；修改
glitch （設備、機器等的）小故障
vacancy 空缺　reference 推薦人；推薦函

**154** 特倫先生為什麼寫信給克倫福特女士？
(A) 為了安排會面
(B) 為了要求推薦
(C) 為了詢問一個職缺
(D) 為了要求修改一份線上表格

**155** 文中要求克倫福特女士和誰聯絡？
(A) 布連先生
(B) 產品經理
(C) 公司的行政主管
(D) 夏姆女士

**156** 特倫先生提及什麼問題？
(A) 他無法查看一份電子文件的某個部分。
(B) 克倫福特女士應徵的職缺已經找到人。
(C) 無法聯絡到克倫福特女士提及的推薦者。
(D) 過了截止日期才收到克倫福特女士寄的應徵信。

**157-158 訊息串**

| 貝絲・錢德勒 | 14 時 21 分 |
|---|---|

吉姆，你可以去中央車站接林先生嗎？

**吉姆・羅傑斯**　14 時 24 分
我以為妳要去接他。

**貝絲・錢德勒**　14 時 25 分
我本來要去，但他剛發簡訊給我，說他的火車會晚點到，我那個時間有約。

**吉姆・羅傑斯**　14 時 27 分
了解，我何時要到那裡？

**貝絲・錢德勒**　14 時 28 分
波士頓來的火車預計 5 點 30 分到，但你過去之前，也許要再查一下。

**吉姆・羅傑斯**　14 時 29 分
我可以開公司的車去嗎？

**貝絲・錢德勒**　14 時 30 分
當然，只是務必要開一輛好車去，我們想要留下好印象。他的公司是我們最重要的買主之一。

**字彙** head over 前往、朝……方向前進
get in touch with 與……聯繫

**157** 關於林先生，下列何者最可能為真？
(A) 他重新安排了會議時間。
(B) 他上火車的時間晚了。
(C) 他是錢德勒女士的老闆。
(D) 他從波士頓來。

**158** 在 14 時 27 分處，當羅傑斯先生寫道：「了解」，他的意思最可能是什麼？
(A) 他知道中央車站在哪裡。
(B) 他將要聯絡林先生。
(C) 他了解提出這個要求的原因。
(D) 他了解火車有時會誤點。

**159-161 電子郵件**

寄件者：佐藤由紀 <ysatou@tabe.org>
收件者：山本伊茲 <iyamamoto@antifren.org>
日期：八月三日
主旨：您的報名請求

親愛的山本先生：

謝謝您對我們計劃於九月十五日召開的營建業升級大會感興趣。很遺憾，因為活動門票已售罄，我們不再接受報名參加。請告知您是否想要排進我們的候補名單。萬一，任何已經註冊的人無法出席，我們會提供那些在名單上的人位置。如果我們無法提供您這次活動的座位，請留意，營建業升級大會每季都會舉辦，我們的下次活動預計安排在一月。

我能否也利用這個機會邀請您成為東京建築工程師協會（TABE）的會員？會員年費 300 元，您會得到許多好處，包括被列入業界名錄、一張當地營建供應商的折扣卡，以及參加我們每季雞尾酒派對的機會。要申請會員，請打給我們的會員處：(440) 555-9943 或上我們的網站：www.tabe.org 看相關網頁。

我希望，在我們即將舉行的大會中會有您的位置，還有您會考慮成為 TABE 的會員。

祝安好
佐藤由紀
東京營建工程師協會
www.tabe.org
電話：(440) 555-9943
傳真：(440) 555-4631

**字彙** registration 登記；註冊
convention 大會；會議
regrettably 遺憾地；抱歉地
attendance 出席；出席人數
sold out 銷售一空的；(門票等)全部預售完的
cancellation 取消
note 注意；留意
quarter 四分之一；季度；一刻鐘
association 協會；聯盟
building engineer 營建工程師
inclusion 包括；把……包括在內
directory 姓名住址簿；工商名錄
relevant 有關的
chair 任(會議的)主席；主持(會議)
venue (事件、活動等的)發生地
advance registration 提早報名

**159** 關於營建業升級大會，可由文中得知什麼？
(A) 一年舉行四次。
(B) 由佐藤女士主持。
(C) 這是個新作法。
(D) 大會換到一個更大的場地。

**160** 佐藤女士建議山本先生做什麼？
(A) 要求退費
(B) 傳送他的聯絡資料給她
(C) 和她約見面
(D) 加入一個組織

**161** 文中提及會提供給 TABE 會員什麼樣的好處？
(A) 一份推薦律師的名單
(B) 提前報名研討會
(C) 研討會的預留席
(D) 社交活動的邀請函

### 162-164 備忘錄

收件者：S&L 製造集團
寄件者：財務預測委員會
日期：四月十四日
關於：分析報告

---

　　S&L 一直是以生產高品質的包裝食品而聲譽卓著，從事大型外燴業已多年。然而，我們現在面臨危機。也許正如你所知，包裝成本在過去三年已大幅上漲了 12%。我們討論過許多讓我們得以支付這些成本的辦法。一致的共識是，我們提高各系列產品的價格，但漲價意味有流失顧客的風險。

　　請記得，我們有極為有效的商業策略。我們的社群媒體宣傳促銷有很多人看，而我們也得到顧客的良好回應。我們建議，我們應該維持同樣的廣告費用。然而，我們必需嘗試找到更新、更符合成本效益的包裝設計。這樣的話，我們可以維持我們的定價策略，不會讓潛在顧客卻步，同時這也有助我們彌補任何損失。

珍‧考克斯

字彙 **forecast** 預測　**analysis** 分析
**well-established** 信譽卓著的
**reputation** 名聲；名譽
**mass** 大規模的；大型的
**crisis** 危機　**significantly** 顯著地
**consensus** 共識　**bear in mind** 記住

**advocate** 擁護；提倡
**discourage** 使沮喪；打消
**potential** 潛在的；可能的
**recoup** 彌補；補償
**universally** 普遍地；全體地
**economical** 經濟的；節約的
**shut down** 關閉；停止

**162** 關於 S&L 製造集團，文中陳述了什麼？
(A) 他們製造外燴業的包裝材料。
(B) 他們在業界很受敬重。
(C) 他們是家全球企業。
(D) 他們投資新產品的研發。

**163** S&L 製造集團為什麼有問題？
(A) 生產變得更昂貴。
(B) 他們的商業策略幾乎沒有一個奏效。
(C) 他們的產品品質下降。
(D) 他們的廣告不受歡迎。

**164** 委員會建議 S&L 製造集團做什麼？
(A) 全面漲價
(B) 投資更省錢的包裝
(C) 停止生產
(D) 加強開發新產品

### 165-168 文章報導

**聚焦亞力山卓雅的商家**

　　主廣場商業協會和支持亞力山卓雅組織攜手主辦第一屆亞力山卓雅商業平台。時間安排在八月二十四日星期六上午 11 點 30 分到晚上 8 點 30 分，活動將在主廣場舉行，提供本地商家展示各自商品與服務的機會。對任何想要提高知名度的商家來說，這會是理想的展示場地。

　　活動的目的在提供亞力山卓雅地區的各種不同商家和表演者一個平台，以突顯他們的能力。本地商家與精品店會展示他們的商品，而本地餐廳與咖啡館則會提供試吃，有些店家甚至會在戶外烹煮。此外，業餘表演者與藝術家會在整個活動期間演出。

　　活動免費開放給大眾參加。有興趣者，攤位一天的租金是 100 歐元。由於攤位數量有限，我們鼓勵攤販盡快預訂攤位。申請者應填寫活動報名表，並將表格與 50 歐元不退還的訂金在七月三日前寄到 henani@alex.org 給胡薩馬‧艾爾‧厄奈尼。

**165** 這篇文章最可能寫給誰看？
(A) 胡薩馬·艾爾·厄奈尼
(B) 本地商家的老闆
(C) 烹飪專業人士
(D) 主廣場商業協會的員工

**166** 對有意設攤的小販應採取的行動，文中並未提
及下列何者？
(A) 預先支付一筆錢
(B) 填寫一份表格
(C) 提供產品樣本
(D) 以電子郵件傳送細節

**167** 關於展示活動，可由文中得知什麼？
(A) 兩個組織贊助這個活動。
(B) 要求訪客付費參加。
(C) 會有多餘的攤位供租用。
(D) 之前活動的出席率很高。

**168** 在標示 [1]、[2]、[3] 和 [4] 的地方，下列句子
最適合放在何處？
「此外，業餘表演者與藝術家會在整個活動期
間演出。」
(A) [1]
(B) [2]
(C) [3]
(D) [4]

### 169-171 線上聊天

| 蘿拉·艾貝兒 | 上午 8 時 45 分 |
| --- | --- |

我兩年前畢業，拿到生物學士學位，之後一直
在餐廳當服務生。工作很辛苦，而且薪水很低。
我曾在我大學的健康中心工作，主要做檢驗的
工作，但我不想再拿針刺病人。有人告訴我，
應該試著在製藥業找工作，我該從哪裡找起？

| 肯·洛克威爾 | 上午 9 時 01 分 |
| --- | --- |

查看妳所在地的工作布告欄，了解誰在徵才。
查看妳有興趣的公司。然後，試著和在那裡工
作的人建立關係。

| 保羅·史密斯 | 上午 10 時 10 分 |
| --- | --- |

我以前在克來倫斯當化學師，那家公司生產數
種受歡迎的止痛藥。妳需要有紮實的實驗研究
經驗，才好應徵他們或任何其他的大公司的工
作。既然妳有醫療檢驗的經驗，我建議先找醫
院檢驗室的工作，先增加妳的資歷。

| 甘蒂斯·派克 | 上午 10 時 20 分 |
| --- | --- |

我附議肯，開始認識妳有興趣行業的人是第一
步。

| 肯·洛克威爾 | 上午 11 時 01 分 |
| --- | --- |

如果妳在妳的所在地找不到任何公司，妳也許
得搬家，以展開妳的新職業生涯。

| 甘蒂斯·派克 | 下午 12 時 20 分 |
| --- | --- |

妳要不要考慮搬到紐澤西？好幾家主要製藥公
司的總部都在那裡。

| 蘿拉·艾貝克 | 下午 4 時 45 分 |
| --- | --- |

謝謝大家的指點！我和大學的指導老師聯絡上
了，她指引我一個在聖詹姆斯醫學中心的空缺。
我明天要去面試，祝我好運吧！

（發送）

**169** 關於史密斯先生，可由文中得知什麼？
(A) 他以前在製藥業工作。
(B) 他以前管理一個實驗室。
(C) 他目前住在紐澤西。
(D) 他的公司正在找人。

**170** 上午 10 時 20 分處，當派克女士寫道：
「我附議肯」，她的意思最可能是什麼？
(A) 她以前遵照過洛克威爾先生的建議。
(B) 她認為建立關係很重要。
(C) 她目前在藥廠工作。
(D) 她想要認識新朋友。

**171** 關於艾貝兒女士，下列何者最可能為真？
(A) 她會回去找前一個雇主。
(B) 她最近修改了她的履歷表。
(C) 她計劃回學校讀書。
(D) 她應徵了一個醫院的工作。

## 172-175 電子郵件

寄件者：hamish@dunfair.com
收件者：lmckenzie@hotline.com
主旨：丹費爾島美食祭
日期：六月二日

親愛的麥肯琪女士：

謝謝妳詢問有關丹費爾島美食祭的事情。五年多來，我們一直主辦這個完全由丹費爾島居民獨家舉辦的慶典。蛋糕、鹹點、糖果、特殊盛會的菜單和主菜，是其中一些供應的料理，全出自本地大廚之手。我們只允許使用本地食材在慶典當天新鮮烹調的食品，而且，我們會派督察員檢查這些食品，我們不允許任何事先準備的包裝食品。價格從 1 英鎊的餅乾到 100 英鎊以上的結婚蛋糕都有。小販所販售的食品必須支付 10% 的佣金。

每月的第一個星期六，我們也舉辦丹費爾手工藝之夜，以本地居民與商家製作的商品為特色，我們並在下午 4 到 6 點提供免費餐點。這項活動總是有很多人參加，通常會吸引超過 50 位遊客和居民。買賣往往很熱絡，尤其是在整個夏季，那是旅遊的旺季。

如果妳想要加入丹費爾島美食祭家族，請以電子郵件傳送妳拿手菜的圖像，並附上所用的食材清單。此外，請說明妳的餐飲資歷。我們會在七天內和妳聯絡，提供進一步說明。

祝安好
哈米許‧葛林
丹費爾島美食祭行政管理主管

**172** 這封電子郵件的目的是什麼？
(A) 要解釋一項活動如何執行
(B) 要宣傳丹費爾手工藝之夜
(C) 要訂購一些手作用的商品
(D) 要宣傳烹飪比賽

**173** 麥肯琪女士最有可能是誰？
(A) 一名工藝師
(B) 一名觀光客
(C) 一名餐廳員工
(D) 一名大廚

**174** 關於在丹費爾美食祭販售的商品，可由文中得知什麼？
(A) 商品的定價都未高於 100 英鎊。
(B) 六月、七月和八月的商品價格打七折。
(C) 商品是由丹費爾島的居民所製作。
(D) 商品使用來自世界各地的材料。

**175** 在標示 [1]、[2]、[3] 和 [4] 的地方，下列句子最適合放在何處？
「小販所販售的食品必須支付 10% 的佣金。」
(A) [1]
(B) [2]
(C) [3]
(D) [4]

## 176-180 廣告與文章報導

### 窩添吧不動產公司

在布里斯班、凱恩斯和黃金海岸服務超過十年

**精選房源**

**萊恩斯廣場 395 號：**170 平方公尺。位於專門建造的綜合大樓內，屋況絕佳的辦公空間。主要接待區，數個辦公室和三個中型會議室。與大樓其餘住戶共用停車區。黃金海岸的絕佳位置。

**貝蘭觀 229 號：**280 平方公尺。位於布里斯班喬治亞建築的一樓整層。全套外燴設備。屋況良好，含電器。

**瓦塔瑪大道 12 號：**320 平方公尺。位於布里斯班觀光區中心的高級雙層商業大樓。全新固定裝置與配件，包含 20 公尺長內嵌象牙的大理石地板。

**阿德雷得街 7 號：**320 平方公尺。適合餐廳或外燴用途，但也可用來做零售生意。位於緬因街的繁忙地點。近凱恩斯。

我們還有更多待售或待租的辦公和零售空間！

完整房源清單請上我們的網站：www.wotambarealty.com 或透過電話 (330) 555-3593，或電子郵件 properties@wotambarealty.com 聯絡我們。

### 餐廳宣布搬新家

十二月一日——受歡迎的泰式餐廳茉莉宮，昨天在位於麥汀大道 211 號的新址重新開幕。當地民間團體「跳躍節拍」帶來音樂表演，老闆楊齊和楊藍則以豪華盛宴招待賓客，其中的特色菜餚在他們的家鄉曼谷通常只有特殊場合才吃得到。有數百賓客到場，忠實顧客排在來賓名單的最前面。楊齊發表簡短演說，感謝當地社群的慷慨與支持。「謝謝布里斯班的居民，在我們從泰國來此地時接納我們，從那之後也一直支持我們餐廳。」

茉莉宮 7 年前開幕，從那之後，餐廳變得非常受歡迎，因此現有的場地簡直無法容納顧客的數量。「我們的前一家餐廳樓面地板面積不到 300 平方公尺，而且，停車是個問題，因此顧客必須停在相鄰的停車場，」楊先生說：「窩添吧不動產的業務代表把我們的舊餐廳列入他公司的精選房源之一，並提供無價協助幫我們找到這個地方，有很棒的餐飲和外燴設備，還有它位於布里斯本市中心的位置。」

最熱情支持餐廳的顧客之一是詹姆斯·泰勒議員，他和這一家人建立了緊密關係。他對賓客簡短致詞。泰勒議員對關於重新開幕問題的回答是：「茉莉宮已牢牢立足於布里斯班當地社區。我確信，這個新地點只會更增它的人氣。」

**字彙**　real estate 不動產
square meter 平方公尺
purpose-built 為特定目的建造的
complex 綜合大樓；建築群
ground floor 一樓〔英〕(=first floor〔美〕)
upmarket 高級的；高檔的
double tiered 雙層的
fixture （房屋等的）固定裝置
fitting 可拆除裝置；配件　ivory 象牙
inset 嵌入；插入　marble 大理石
sumptuous 奢華的；昂貴的
generosity 慷慨；慷慨的行為
adjacent 相鄰的；鄰近的
invaluable 無價的；無法估價的
fervent 熱情的；熱誠的
councilor （州、市、鎮等）議會議員
strike up a relationship 建立關係
secure 把……弄牢；獲得
enhance 增加（價值、品質、吸引力等）
profile 簡要介紹

**176** 關於窩添吧不動產公司，可由文中得知什麼？
(A) 它銷售數個城市的房地產。
(B) 它的主力在租賃市場。
(C) 它目前只有四件房地產在出售。
(D) 它偏好和賣方面對面打交道。

**177** 這篇文章的主要目的是什麼？
(A) 教授傳統泰式料理
(B) 宣布出售一家當地餐廳
(C) 簡要介紹一位布里斯班的市政官員
(D) 報導一個商業活動

**178** 根據文章報導，茉莉宮為什麼搬家？
(A) 新租約被拒。
(B) 老闆決定搬到布里斯班。
(C) 前一個地點太小。
(D) 新址有較多現代化設備。

**179** 茉莉宮之前最可能位於哪裡？
(A) 貝蘭觀
(B) 阿德雷得街
(C) 瓦塔馬大道
(D) 萊恩斯廣場

**180** 關於楊家，可由文中得知什麼？
(A) 他們是泰勒議員的朋友。
(B) 他們是音樂家。
(C) 他們是茉莉宮的常客。
(D) 他們原本來自黃金海岸。

## 181-185 電子郵件與發貨單

收件者：吉塔・莉托維克
　　　　<glitovic@voicedesign.com>
寄件者：莎夏・提摩維斯
　　　　<stimovis@manatidesign.com>
主旨：快樂設計
日期：十二月十二日

親愛的吉塔・莉托維克女士：

　　身為馬納提設計的熟客，您會對我們最近推出的快樂設計更新版有興趣。市面上最先進、最有效的設計解決方案套裝軟體，現在甚至有了更多選項！

　　快樂設計仍然有之前版本的所有標準功能，例如用來創作工程圖、形狀、標誌和動畫的繪圖工具。然而，最新版包含複雜精細向量濾鏡效果、顏色和 3D 效果的進階選項。此外，您也能更新快樂設計並附加新功能進去，因為這套軟體不斷在更新。

　　我們邀請您參加線上免費訓練課程，老師會提供專家建議，並示範如何使用軟體。而且，只要參加這個工作坊，您就會得到九折優惠，以及免費安裝日後任何馬納提設計的產品。要報名，您必須上我們的網站跟著連結進行線上註冊，您也可以看到我們所有的系列產品清單。

誠摯地
莎夏・提摩維斯
技術服務部經理

---

### 發貨單

賣方：馬納提設計　　買方：吉塔・莉托維克
保加利亞杜伯尼克　　聲音設計工作室
34963　　　　　　　英國倫敦 W11
亞薩路 11 號　　　　梅菲爾街 992 號

訂單日期：1 月 6 日
出貨日期：1 月 7 日
預定到貨日：1 月 11 日

| 品名 | 數量 | 內容 | 價格 |
| --- | --- | --- | --- |
| AC41 | 1 | 快樂設計（商業版） | $525.00 |
| | 1 | 九折 | $-52.50 |
| | 1 | 運費 | $0.00 |

貨物售出，概不退換。
技術支援請上本公司網站：www.manatidesign.com/support。

字彙 launch 推出 package 一（整）套
drawing tool 繪圖工具
standard feature 標準功能
intricate 複雜精細的 add-on 附加
constantly 不斷地；時常地
demonstration 實地示範；實物宣傳
register 登記；註冊
description 描述；形容
accounting 會計；會計學
release 發行；發表
residential 居住的；住宅的

**181** 提摩維斯女士為什麼寫電子郵件給莉托維克女士？
(A) 為了推薦一個新產品
(B) 為了提供安裝建議
(C) 為了要求關於工作坊的意見回饋
(D) 為了提醒她參加一場會議

**182** 關於快樂設計，下列何者為真？
(A) 它能建立會計資料庫。
(B) 它是先前發行產品的更新版。
(C) 它只能在線上購買。
(D) 它的效能是競爭者類似產品的二倍。

**183** 莉托維克女士何時購買產品？
(A) 1 月 6 日
(B) 1 月 7 日
(C) 1 月 11 日
(D) 1 月 14 日

**184** 關於莉托維克女士，可由文中得知什麼？
(A) 她付了隔日送達的費用。
(B) 她買這套軟體是要在家使用。
(C) 同一套軟體，她訂購了一份以上。
(D) 她參加過訓練課程。

**185** 關於馬納提設計，文中提及什麼？
(A) 它提供一對一的訓練課程。
(B) 它提供軟體退換貨。
(C) 它提供線上顧客支援。
(D) 它接受郵寄註冊。

## 186-190 廣告、電子郵件與表單

### 齊洛影像
#### 首屈一指的婚禮攝影公司

　　無論是傳統式、現代式還是介於二者之間，你的婚禮都是非常特別的。齊洛影像會和你合作，確保婚禮是以你自己的特殊角度記錄下來。過去十年來，我們和數百對新人一起創造了令人難忘的照片和影片。我們的總部位於羅哈頓，距此 200 公里內的地方，我們才華洋溢的專業團隊都能到。除了婚禮的儀式與宴會外，我們也辦新娘婚前送禮派對、新郎／新娘告別單身派對，和婚禮後的早午餐。請上 info@cieloimages.com 與我們聯絡。

收件者：mjones@jmail.com
寄件者：info@cieloimages.com
日期：1 月 28 日
關於：空檔
附件：預約表

親愛的瓊斯女士：

　　謝謝您表示對齊洛影像有興趣。您婚禮那天我們有空。我們可以到達您提到的地點。如果您想要預約，請填寫附件中的表格，並以電子郵件寄回給我們，以便暫時保留那一天，然後我們會和您聯絡，安排一個初步會議。會議上，我們會討論您的需求和預算。為了保留預約資格，我們要求您同時支付 200 元不可退還的訂金。大約在您實際結婚日之前兩星期，我們會安排和您的最後一次會面，以再次檢視您的計畫。如果有任何問題，歡迎隨時以這個電子郵件和我聯絡，或撥打 555-9090。

誠摯地
蘿娜·泰勒
齊洛影像

## 齊洛影像　　　　　　　預約表

姓名：瑪麗恩·瓊斯
電話號碼：(412) 555-6736
需求日：5 月 1 日星期六
需求時間：下午 2 時到 7 時
地點：畢克福公園薩伯里庭園宴會中心
描述您的需求：我未婚夫和我想要請你們拍攝我們的婚禮和婚宴。我們還在討論同時錄影的可能性，但我們想要先和你們討論價格。如果可以，能否給我們看一些你們作品的範本？

---

**字彙**
premier 首要的；最重要的
reception 宴會；歡迎會
bridal shower 新娘婚前送禮派對
tentatively 暫時地
nonrefundable 無法退還的
deposit 訂金；押金
staff （為機構）提供人員

---

**186** 關於齊洛影像，可由文中得知什麼？
(A) 它會收取初步的諮詢費。
(B) 5 月 1 日的活動，它可以提供人員。
(C) 它可以派十名員工。
(D) 它會為瓊斯女士拍一支影片。

**187** 關於瓊斯女士，下列何者最可能為真？
(A) 她計劃在室內結婚。
(B) 她要辦一場大型婚宴。
(C) 她先打電話給泰勒女士。
(D) 她會在四月和齊洛影像的人見面。

**188** 根據電子郵件，瓊斯女士必須做什麼以確保齊洛會幫她的活動拍照？
(A) 先付初期費用
(B) 出示適當的身分證件
(C) 聯絡婚禮顧問
(D) 造訪泰勒女士的辦公室

**189** 關於畢克福公園，可由文中得知什麼？
(A) 那是個租金不貴的場地。
(B) 那裡一年舉辦很多場婚禮。
(C) 那裡能招待很多賓客。
(D) 它距離羅哈頓 200 公里內。

**190** 表單中，第 6 行的「shoot」，意義最接近下列何者？
(A) 出席
(B) 紀錄
(C) 照像
(D) 服務

---

## 191-195 布告、表單與電子郵件

受文者：所有住戶
主旨：托兒所即將開幕

　　珍貴願望公司已簽約，將在波頓大樓開一間托兒中心。該中心會設在三樓。有執照的合格幼兒照顧專業人員將為三個月到五歲的兒童，提供基本的日間托兒服務和優質的教育性內容。

**時間**：星期一到星期五，上午 7 時到下午 6 時 30 分

　　現在開始接受員工或本大樓住戶的孩子申請。名額有限，申請截止日為 1 月 31 日。

　　月費、用餐時間、申請表等更多資訊，請上 www.preciouswishes.com

---

### 珍貴願望
**申請表**
姓名：蘿莉·華特斯
雇主：傑克森顧問公司
電話（公司）：(505)555-0334
電話（個人）：(505)555-2217
電子郵件：lwaters@jacksonconsulting.com
報名兒童人數：2
報名兒童年齡：14 個月，4 歲
需要的天數：[√]星期一　[√]星期二
　　　　　　[√]星期三　[√]星期四　[√]星期五
需要的時間：[ ]半天（5 小時或以下）
　　　　　　[√]全天（5 小時以上）
其他資訊：我女兒對花生過敏。

---

收件者：lwaters@jacksonconsulting.com
寄件者：poliver@preciouswishes.com
主旨：您的申請
日期：2 月 8 日

親愛的華特斯女士：

　　謝謝您申請我們最新地點的名額。對這個地方感興趣的人遠超過我們的容納人數，因此，我們將孩童按照所收到的申請順序排列。

　　雖然我們這一次無法提供名額給您，但您已排入候補名單。您目前在 42 人中排在第七個。當有名額空出時，您會收到通知。然後，您會有 48 小時決定要接受還是拒絕這個名額。

如果您在任何時候想要退出名單，麻煩告訴我們。不過，我們無法退還在你申請時所附上的每位兒童 50 元的申請費。

誠摯地
派翠西亞·奧利佛

字彙 **component** 組成部分　**allergic** 過敏的
**exceed** 超過　**capacity** 容量；容積
**status** 地位；狀態

**191** 關於珍貴願望公司，沒有提到什麼？
(A) 它會擴大它的新場所。
(B) 它有好幾個點。
(C) 它僱用訓練有素的工作人員。
(D) 它提供嬰兒的照護。

**192** 在布告中，第三段、第一行的「rates」，意義最接近下列何者？
(A) 費用
(B) 數字
(C) 等級
(D) 速度

**193** 關於傑克森顧問公司，可由文中得知什麼？
(A) 它位於三樓。
(B) 它租用波頓大樓的空間。
(C) 它的許多員工有小孩。
(D) 它是珍貴願望公司的房東。

**194** 奧利佛女士為什麼寫信給華特斯女士？
(A) 為了提供她新地點的名額
(B) 為了要求支付兒童的費用
(C) 為了把她在名單上往前排
(D) 為了通知她，她的申請狀況

**195** 關於華特斯女士，下列何者最可能為真？
(A) 她會找到另一個托兒所。
(B) 她一星期工作四天。
(C) 她會取消申請。
(D) 她付給珍貴願望公司 100 元。

## 196-200 文章報導、電子郵件與公告

丹頓（七月一日）——上週末，數千名林伍德的居民出門慶祝陽光超市盛大開幕。佔地 5000 平方公尺的新雜貨超市，位於新近整修完成的六層樓藍新大樓一樓，供應各種新鮮農產品、肉品、麵包還有很多商品。

雖然，林伍德地區在過去十年來顯著成長，但它所缺的一樣東西就是一家雜貨店。事實上，居民為了買食品，至少必需跑五公里。這家位於林伍德市中心地帶的新商店，附近一公里內住了一萬五千人。

市政府去年買下藍新大樓，這是賈斯汀·班迪克斯市長的市中心與鄰近地區計畫的一部分。自從二年前就任以來，市長一直以市中心及週邊地區的經濟發展作為他的首要任務。

收件者：凱蕾·柴斯
　　　　<kchase@sunshinemarket.com>
寄件者：賈斯汀·班迪克斯
　　　　<jbendix@cityofdanton.org>
主旨：停車問題
日期：8 月 28 日

親愛的柴斯女士：

謝謝您聯絡我，提出您對緬因街上停車的憂慮。我了解您和您的顧客想必都遭受到的沮喪。請放心，市政府正致力於補救這個狀況。我們目前正進行到我們開發計畫的第二階段。它包含在第十大道與緬因街交叉口建造一座新的停車場，大約離您的店 500 公尺。您的顧客可以免費停車。

祝安好，

賈斯汀·班迪克斯

## 公告

受文者：所有顧客

　　我們接到許多關於在店前面停車狀況的客訴。請不要停在那裡，請改停在店後面的柯曼街或附近任何一條街道。如果您無法把你的食品雜貨搬上車，我們的員工會非常樂意協助您。

　　市政府已經跟我們保證，他們正努力找出這個迫切問題的解決之道。在此期間，我們十分感謝您的耐心與合作。

誠摯地
陽光超市管理部

> **字彙** ground floor 一樓　significant 顯著的
> rest assured that （用於安慰某人）請放心；
> 別擔心
> pressing 緊迫的；迫切的

**196** 關於林伍德，可由文中得知什麼？
(A) 市公車不開到這一區。
(B) 很多居民在市中心工作。
(C) 在陽光超市之前，沒有合適的雜貨店。
(D) 那裡的經濟發展受限。

**197** 關於市中心與鄰近地區計畫，下列何者最可能為真？
(A) 它提議增加更多住宅。
(B) 它會在兩年內完成。
(C) 它是由前任市長啟動的。
(D) 它會擴大可用的停車空間。

**198** 這則公告的目的是什麼？
(A) 解釋一個狀況
(B) 提出抱怨
(C) 批評顧客
(D) 建議一項新服務

**199** 在公告中，第二段、第一行的「hard」，意義最接近下列何者？
(A) 強烈地
(B) 勤奮地
(C) 堅定地
(D) 主要地

**200** 關於陽光超市，可由文中得知什麼？
(A) 它座落於緬因街。
(B) 它有大約五千名顧客。
(C) 很少顧客有自己的車。
(D) 它將要蓋一座新的停車場。

| 1. (B) | 2. (A) | 3. (C) | 4. (D) | 5. (C) | 6. (C) | 07. (B) | 08. (A) | 09. (B) | 10. (B) |
|---|---|---|---|---|---|---|---|---|---|
| 11. (C) | 12. (C) | 13. (C) | 14. (A) | 15. (A) | 16. (A) | 17. (C) | 18. (C) | 19. (C) | 20. (C) |
| 21. (B) | 22. (B) | 23. (A) | 24. (B) | 25. (B) | 26. (A) | 27. (A) | 28. (C) | 29. (B) | 30. (A) |
| 31. (C) | 32. (A) | 33. (A) | 34. (C) | 35. (D) | 36. (B) | 37. (D) | 38. (A) | 39. (C) | 40. (C) |
| 41. (A) | 42. (C) | 43. (B) | 44. (C) | 45. (D) | 46. (C) | 47. (D) | 48. (B) | 49. (C) | 50. (C) |
| 51. (A) | 52. (D) | 53. (B) | 54. (B) | 55. (A) | 56. (C) | 57. (B) | 58. (A) | 59. (C) | 60. (A) |
| 61. (C) | 62. (A) | 63. (C) | 64. (D) | 65. (C) | 66. (D) | 67. (C) | 68. (A) | 69. (D) | 70. (B) |
| 71. (A) | 72. (C) | 73. (A) | 74. (D) | 75. (A) | 76. (B) | 77. (A) | 78. (B) | 79. (C) | 80. (B) |
| 81. (A) | 82. (D) | 83. (A) | 84. (D) | 85. (C) | 86. (A) | 87. (D) | 88. (C) | 89. (D) | 90. (B) |
| 91. (D) | 92. (C) | 93. (A) | 94. (B) | 95. (C) | 96. (A) | 97. (B) | 98. (B) | 99. (A) | 100. (B) |
| 101. (A) | 102. (A) | 103. (B) | 104. (A) | 105. (B) | 106. (B) | 107. (B) | 108. (C) | 109. (C) | 110. (C) |
| 111. (D) | 112. (B) | 113. (A) | 114. (C) | 115. (D) | 116. (D) | 117. (D) | 118. (A) | 119. (B) | 120. (B) |
| 121. (A) | 122. (D) | 123. (A) | 124. (C) | 125. (D) | 126. (D) | 127. (D) | 128. (A) | 129. (C) | 130. (B) |
| 131. (D) | 132. (B) | 133. (C) | 134. (B) | 135. (C) | 136. (B) | 137. (A) | 138. (C) | 139. (D) | 140. (A) |
| 141. (B) | 142. (A) | 143. (A) | 144. (B) | 145. (B) | 146. (B) | 147. (A) | 148. (D) | 149. (B) | 150. (D) |
| 151. (B) | 152. (C) | 153. (C) | 154. (A) | 155. (B) | 156. (C) | 157. (B) | 158. (C) | 159. (C) | 160. (A) |
| 161. (D) | 162. (D) | 163. (B) | 164. (C) | 165. (A) | 166. (C) | 167. (A) | 168. (D) | 169. (A) | 170. (D) |
| 171. (A) | 172. (A) | 173. (A) | 174. (B) | 175. (C) | 176. (D) | 177. (A) | 178. (D) | 179. (D) | 180. (B) |
| 181. (A) | 182. (D) | 183. (A) | 184. (A) | 185. (A) | 186. (D) | 187. (B) | 188. (A) | 189. (C) | 190. (C) |
| 191. (D) | 192. (B) | 193. (A) | 194. (C) | 195. (C) | 196. (C) | 197. (D) | 198. (B) | 199. (D) | 200. (A) |

# PART 1
P. 058

**1**
(A) He is moving some furniture.
(美M) (B) He is handling some boxes.
(C) He is opening a cabinet.
(D) He is setting up a sign.

(A) 他正在移動一些家具。
(B) 他正在搬一些箱子。
(C) 他正打開櫥櫃。
(D) 他正在豎立一個標誌。

字彙 handle 搬動;拿　cabinet 櫥櫃;陳列櫃
set up 擺放或豎起某物　sign 標誌;招牌

**2**
(A) They are working on the floor.
(美W) (B) They are measuring a wall.
(C) They are rolling up their sleeves.
(D) They are sweeping the sidewalk.

(A) 他們正在地板上工作。
(B) 他們正在測量一面牆。
(C) 他們正捲起袖子。
(D) 他們正在清掃人行道。

字彙 measure 測量;計算
roll up one's sleeves
捲起袖子(準備行動)
sweep 打掃;清掃　sidewalk 人行道

**3**
(A) The fruits are being placed in bags.
(英M) (B) Plants are growing in pots.
(C) Apples have been piled in the baskets.
(D) Crates of fruit are being delivered.

(A) 正在把水果放進袋子裡。
(B) 植物在花盆裡生長。
(C) 蘋果被堆放在籃子裡。
(D) 正在運送一箱箱的水果。

字彙 place 放置;安置
pot 花盆;罐;壺　pile 堆;疊
crate 板條箱;貨箱

**4**
(A) A mirror is being adjusted on a shelf.
(美W) (B) Some items are being removed from a case.
(C) A woman is polishing some glass cabinets.
(D) A woman is examining a pair of sunglasses.

(A) 正在調整架子上的一面鏡子。
(B) 正從盒子裡拿出一些商品。
(C) 女子正在擦亮一些玻璃櫃。
(D) 女子正在仔細查看一副太陽眼鏡。

字彙 adjust 調整;調節
shelf (通常指固定在牆上或櫥櫃中的)架子
polish 擦亮;磨光　examine 細查;檢查

**5**
(A) Shoppers are lining up to buy some products.
(澳M) (B) A customer is winding a watch.
(C) Some merchandise is displayed for sale.
(D) Some vendors are standing inside the shop.

(A) 顧客們正在排隊要買一些商品。
(B) 一位顧客正在給手錶上發條。
(C) 一些貨物陳列待售。
(D) 一些小販站在商店裡。

字彙 line up 排成隊　wind 給(鐘錶)上發條
merchandise 商品;貨物
vendor 小販

**6**
(A) A row of plants have been placed on a shelf.
(美W) (B) Potted plants are hanging from the ceiling.
(C) She is holding a watering can with both hands.
(D) She is pouring the soil into a container.

(A) 一排植物放在架子上。
(B) 盆栽從天花板上吊掛下來。
(C) 她正用雙手拿著灑水壺。
(D) 她正把土倒進容器裡。

字彙 a row of 一排;一行　potted plant 盆栽
hang 懸掛;吊著　ceiling 天花板
watering can (用於澆灌園藝植物的)長嘴噴水壺;灑水壺
pour 倒;灌　soil 土壤;泥土
container 容器

# PART 2

P. 062

**7** Who will I need to speak to?
(A) Kathleen Moore was.
(B) You should contact Janine.
(C) It was signed last week.

我需要和誰談談？
(A) 凱薩琳‧摩爾曾是。
(B) 你應該聯絡珍寧。
(C) 上星期簽約。

字彙 sign 簽名；簽署

**8** The album got a good review, didn't it?
(A) Yes, and it deserved it.
(B) The apartment has a great view.
(C) She went too late.

這張唱片得到好評，不是嗎？
(A) 是的，而且它實至名歸。
(B) 這間公寓視野良好。
(C) 她太晚去了。

字彙 review 評論　deserve 值得；應得

**9** Why did Damson Inc. relocate their offices?
(A) She never offered.
(B) They needed more room.
(C) Not too long.

丹森公司為什麼搬遷？
(A) 她從來沒提議過。
(B) 他們需要更大的空間。
(C) 不用太久。

字彙 relocate 搬遷；重新安置
　　 offer 提議；主動給予

**10** Do you know if Mr. Chilt is arriving this afternoon?
(A) Not every one of them.
(B) I believe so.
(C) Sorry, it's faulty.

你知不知道，奇爾特先生是否今天下午會到？
(A) 不是他們每個人都是。
(B) 我想是的。
(C) 抱歉，這個有問題。

字彙 faulty 有缺陷的；故障的

**11** The session has been changed to a new location.
(A) They're leaving on Monday.
(B) I saw that film.
(C) Yes, it's in the main convention hall.

會議改到新的地點了。
(A) 他們星期一離開。
(B) 我看過那部電影。
(C) 是的，在大會議中心。

字彙 session 會議；集會　location 位置；場所
　　 convention hall 會議中心

**12** When can we expect the documents?
(A) The shipping merchandise.
(B) In dreadful condition.
(C) Within 48 hours.

我們何時會收到文件？
(A) 運送的貨物。
(B) 狀況很糟。
(C) 48 小時內。

字彙 shipping 運輸、(尤指)船運
　　 dreadful 可怕的；糟透的

**13** How many people will be attending the seminar?
(A) It went well, thank you.
(B) Because it's undersubscribed.
(C) Most of our team.

有多少人要參加研討會？
(A) 進行得很順利，謝謝你。
(B) 因為很少人訂購。
(C) 我們團隊的人大部分都會去。

字彙 go well 進展順利
　　 undersubscribed 訂購人數不足

**14** What is the precise time now in Tokyo?
(A) A quarter to four.
(B) Another 25 kilometers or so.
(C) Yes, many times.

東京現在確切時間是幾點？
(A) 3 點 45 分。
(B) 大約再 25 公里。
(C) 是的，很多次。

字彙 precise 精確的；確切的
　　 a quarter to 差 15 分鐘……點　or so 大約

05
06

**15** Would you like to buy two jars of sauce as they're reduced?

(A) I think I'll just buy one for now.

(B) No, I didn't get that.

(C) A ticket for one, please.

既然降價，你要不要買兩罐醬汁？

(A) 我想，我現在只要買一罐就好。

(B) 沒有，我沒有收到。

(C) 一張單人票，謝謝。

字彙 jar 罐子　reduced 降低的
　　　for now 現在；暫時

**16** Do you want the first contract or can I send you the amended one?

(A) The latter will do.

(B) A manager's signature.

(C) It's out of control.

你要第一版的合約，還是我可以把修訂版寄給你？

(A) 後者就可以。

(B) 經理的簽名。

(C) 失控了。

字彙 amend 修訂；修改
　　　latter （二者中的）後者　manager 經理
　　　signature 簽名
　　　out of control 失去控制；不受控制

**17** When did you return to Singapore?

(A) No, it's in Malaysia.

(B) Please put it there.

(C) Four years ago.

你何時回新加坡的？

(A) 不是，那在馬來西亞。

(B) 請放在那裡。

(C) 4 年前。

字彙 return 返回；回復

**18** Where can I find a list of our past customers?

(A) That's not good for me.

(B) I'll have one, thanks.

(C) It's in our internal archives.

哪裡可以找到我們過去的客戶名單？

(A) 那對我沒好處。

(B) 我要一個，謝謝。

(C) 在我們的內部資料庫裡。

字彙 internal 內部的；內在的
　　　archive 資料庫；檔案

**19** Who is in charge of choosing the product color?

(A) A new blender.

(B) It was commissioned three years ago.

(C) The team leader is.

誰負責選擇產品的顏色？

(A) 一台新的攪拌器。

(B) 三年前任命的。

(C) 小組領導人。

字彙 in charge of 負責
　　　blender （做菜用的）攪拌器
　　　commission 任命

**20** I heard you've been put forward for promotion.

(A) He didn't tell us his details.

(B) Why don't you book it now?

(C) Yes, it was unexpected.

我聽說你受到推薦升職。

(A) 他沒有告訴我們他的詳細資料。

(B) 你何不現在預訂？

(C) 是的，出乎意料之外。

字彙 put forward 推薦；提出
　　　unexpected 想不到的；意外的

**21** Should we label the last bottles in the morning?

(A) Look in the closet on the left.

(B) I'd rather do it this evening.

(C) We can always check again.

我們應該早上再把最後一批瓶子貼上標籤嗎？

(A) 看看左邊的櫃子。

(B) 我寧可今天晚上做。

(C) 我們可以隨時再檢查一次。

字彙 label 貼標籤　rather 寧可；偏好

**22** How did you learn about this recruitment fair?
(美W) (A) We close at 9.
(英M) (B) From the newspaper advertisement.
　　 (C) Yes, it was very tidy.

你是如何得知這次就業博覽會的？
(A) 我們 9 點打烊。
(B) 從報紙的廣告欄。
(C) 是的，非常整齊。

字彙 recruitment fair 就業博覽會
　　 tidy 整齊的；有條理的

**23** Aren't you supposed to be in the meeting
(美W) upstairs?
(美M) (A) No, Alexis went in my place.
　　 (B) It's my phone number.
　　 (C) I think I missed her.

你不是應該參加樓上的會議嗎？
(A) 沒有，亞歷克斯代替我去參加。
(B) 這是我的電話號碼。
(C) 我想，我錯過她了。

字彙 go in one's place 代替某人去　 miss 錯過

**24** Where do you place the completed samples
(英M) when we're done?
(美W) (A) Sit anywhere you like.
　　 (B) There's a container on the floor.
　　 (C) No, I'm not finished yet.

等我們完成後，你要把做好的樣品放在哪裡？
(A) 隨便坐。
(B) 地板上有個容器。
(C) 沒有，我還沒做完。

字彙 place 放置；安置　 container 容器

**25** The train I take to get home is cancelled for
(美M) the foreseeable future.
(美W) (A) By next week.
　　 (B) What transport are you taking then?
　　 (C) It's not that close.

我回家要搭的火車，在可預見的未來都取消了。
(A) 下個星期前。
(B) 那麼，你要搭什麼交通工具？
(C) 沒那麼近。

字彙 cancel 取消
　　 foreseeable future 可預見的未來
　　 transport 交通工具；運輸

**26** Why don't you find out if Mr. Eyres can
(美M) approve the students' request?
(英M) (A) He is busy, regrettably.
　　 (B) A student loan.
　　 (C) No, I couldn't find it.

你何不查查，艾爾斯先生能否同意學生們的
請求？
(A) 很遺憾，他很忙。
(B) 學生貸款。
(C) 不，我找不到。

字彙 regrettably 遺憾地；抱歉地
　　 student loan 學生貸款

**27** Was this order placed online or over the
(美W) phone?
(美M) (A) It was an online order.
　　 (B) A new project.
　　 (C) Please order more boxes.

這份訂單是從網路還是電話下單的？
(A) 那是網路訂單。
(B) 一個新的專案。
(C) 請多訂些箱子。

字彙 over the phone 透過電話

**28** Why was the delivery early this week?
(美M) (A) In June, I believe.
(美W) (B) I'll have time to do it.
　　 (C) The order was completed.

為什麼這星期這麼早就送貨？
(A) 我想是在 6 月。
(B) 我會有時間做的。
(C) 訂單完成了。

**29** Isn't anyone working late in the laboratory?
(美M) (A) I don't have much left.
(美W) (B) Maybe they're at dinner.
　　 (C) The experiment procedures.

不是有人要在實驗室待到很晚嗎？
(A) 我剩下的不多。
(B) 也許他們去吃晚餐了。
(C) 實驗步驟。

字彙 laboratory 實驗室
　　 procedure 步驟；程序

06

**30** I might have left my phone in your taxi.
英M (A) Okay, I'll hunt for it.
美W (B) There's a problem with the car.
(C) No, I'll be here all evening.

我的手機可能掉在你的計程車上。
(A) 好的，我會找找看。
(B) 車子有問題。
(C) 不，我整個晚上都會待在這裡。

字彙 hunt for 尋找；搜尋

**31** Should we give the manager our resignation
美W letters now?
美M (A) Until the middle of the week.
(B) The residential building on Kings Street.
(C) Let's wait for the meeting in the morning.

我們應該現在把我們的辭呈交給經理嗎？
(A) 直到這星期中。
(B) 京士街的住宅大樓。
(C) 讓我們等到早上的會議再說吧。

字彙 resignation letter 辭呈
residential building 住宅大樓

 07

# PART 3

P. 063

**Questions 32-34 refer to the following conversation.**
美M 美W

**M** Excuse me, ㉜ **do you know where I can find the Porter History Exhibition?** I've been looking all over, but the information I was given at the coach station seems to be incorrect.

**W** Actually, I'm going there now. I help out at the place where the exhibition is being held. We can go over there together.

**M** Would it be better to take public transport? ㉝ **I'm meeting a colleague there in 20 minutes** and I don't want to miss him.

**W** Don't worry. ㉞ **The exhibition is just around the corner.** It would take us longer to find public transport than it would to walk as it's less than ten minutes away.

-------------------------

對話

男：不好意思，請問你知道波特歷史展的地點在哪裡嗎？我四處都看過了，但我在長途汽車站拿到的資訊似乎是錯的。

女：其實，我現在正要去那裡。我在展覽舉行的地方幫忙，我們可以一起過去。

男：搭大眾運輸工具會不會比較快？我 20 分鐘後要和一位同事在那裡碰面，我不想和他錯過。

女：別擔心，展覽就在附近。去找大眾運輸工具花的時間會比走過去更久，因為離這裡走路不到 10 分鐘。

字彙 exhibition 展覽；展覽品
look all over 到處看
coach station 長途汽車站
help out 幫助；幫忙做    colleague 同事
just around the corner 就在附近
venue （事件、行動等的）發生地

**32** Where are the speakers going?
(A) To an exhibition
(B) To a museum
(C) To a taxi stand
(D) To a friend's house

說話者正要去哪裡？
(A) 展覽
(B) 博物館
(C) 計程車招呼站
(D) 朋友家

**33** What will happen in 20 minutes?
(A) A meeting
(B) A bus ride
(C) A talk
(D) A display

20 分鐘後會發生什麼事？
(A) 一次會面
(B) 搭一趟公車
(C) 一次談話
(D) 一次展覽

**34** Why does the woman suggest that she and the man walk?
(A) There are no available taxis.
(B) The walk would do them good.
(C) They are close to the venue.
(D) Buses are expensive.

女子為什麼建議她和男子走路？
(A) 沒有空計程車可搭。
(B) 走路對他們有益。
(C) 他們離展覽場地很近。
(D) 公車很貴。

**Questions 35-37 refer to the following conversation.**
美W 英M

**W** Mr. Foucault, here is the confirmation for your new table. Now, **㉟ when would you prefer us to deliver it**? We do local deliveries from Sunday to Monday.

**M** Well, **㊱ the only time I'll be able to take off work is Thursday**. It will have to be on that day. Is there anything extra to pay?

**W** No, delivery is free of charge. But **㊲ if you want us to remove your old table, you'll have to pay a minimal amount**.

**M** I'll have to get back to you on that. My coworker might want it, as it's still in excellent condition.

- - - - - - - - - - - - - - - - - - - - - - - - - - - -

**對話**
女：佛寇先生，我打來確認您新訂購的桌子。您比較想要我們什麼時候送貨？我們從星期日到星期一可以送本地的貨物。

男：嗯，我唯一可以休假的時間是星期四，必須在這一天送貨。要付額外的費用嗎？

女：不用，免運費。但如果，您想要我們回收您的舊桌子，您必須付一點點費用。

男：關於這一點，我再回電話給你。我同事可能想要，因為桌子狀況還很好。

**字彙** confirmation 確認；證實
local delivery 本地送貨
take off work 休假
minimal 最小的；極微的
get back to 之後再回覆某人
co-worker 同事
extended 延長的；延伸的
overnight shipping 夜間送貨
bespoke 訂做的；訂製的
removal 移動；除去

**35** What are the speakers mainly discussing?
(A) Returning an item
(B) Repairing an item of clothing
(C) Hiring a furniture maker
(D) Arranging a delivery

說話者主要在討論什麼？
(A) 退回一個物品
(B) 修補一件衣服
(C) 僱用一位家具師傅
(D) 安排送貨

**36** What day will the man be available?
(A) Monday
(B) Thursday
(C) Friday
(D) Sunday

男子哪一天有空？
(A) 星期一
(B) 星期四
(C) 星期五
(D) 星期日

**37** According to the woman, what requires an extra fee?
(A) An extended guarantee
(B) Overnight shipping
(C) A bespoke design
(D) Removal of the existing item

根據女子所述，什麼需要額外費用？
(A) 延長保固
(B) 隔日送達
(C) 客製化設計
(D) 移走現有的物品

**Questions 38-40 refer to the following conversation.**
美M 美W

**M** Hey, Ruth. Some of us from the sports center are booking tickets for **㊳ the Slingbacks game next week**. Are you available to come with us?

**W** Oh, the Slingbacks are one of my favorite teams. **㊴ I'm amazed tickets are still on sale**, though. I imagined they were sold out.

07

**M** Yes, they had to change the venue to accommodate demand. I'm going to book seats online for everyone tomorrow, so we can all sit together. I can reserve one for you as well, but ⓐ **please tell me by later this evening if you'd like to go to see them or not.**

---

對話

男：嘿，露絲。我們運動中心有些人正要訂史林貝克隊下星期比賽的票。妳有空和我們一起去看嗎？

女：噢，史林貝克是我最喜歡的隊伍之一。不過，我很驚訝還有票在賣。我以為全都賣完了。

男：是的，他們必須換場地以容納所需的人數。我明天要幫大家上網訂票，這樣我們就都可以坐在一起。我也可以幫妳訂一張票，但請在今晚晚點告訴我，妳是否要去看比賽。

字彙 **be amazed** 吃驚的
**sold out** 銷售一空
**venue** （事件、行動等的）發生地
**accommodate** 容納　**seat** 座位
**as well** 也、同樣地　**mid** 中央的；中間的
**relocate** 重新安置　**charge** 收費；索價
**intention** 意向；打算；目的

**38** What event does the man plan to attend?
(A) A sports event
(B) A concert
(C) A theater performance
(D) A school play

男子計劃參加什麼活動？
(A) 運動賽事
(B) 音樂會
(C) 戲劇表演
(D) 校園劇場

**39** Why is the woman surprised?
(A) A performance has been relocated.
(B) An event has been cancelled.
(C) Space is available.
(D) Parking is charged.

女子為什麼很驚訝？
(A) 有一場表演換了地點。
(B) 有個活動取消了。
(C) 還有空位。
(D) 停車要收費。

**40** What should the woman do by the end of the day?
(A) Contact the booking desk
(B) Change a schedule
(C) Confirm her intention to attend
(D) Issue an invitation

今天結束前，女子應該要做什麼？
(A) 聯絡訂票處
(B) 更改行程表
(C) 確認她參加的意向
(D) 發出邀請

**Questions 41-43 refer to the following conversation.**
美W 美M

**W** Kolen, this is Ann. I am the owner of the storage unit you are leasing. I just wanted to tell you that ⓐ **I've made a decision to sell the unit.**

**M** Oh, really? My rental agreement doesn't end until March. Will I be able to use it until then?

**W** Of course, that's not an issue. But ⓐ **on Saturday, some of my friends will be repairing the exterior and repairing some small damage on the roof.** Just a few repairs to prepare it for sale.

**M** ⓐ **Is there any possibility this can be done at the end of next week?** I'll be clearing my current stock out before then. So they could do the work when the unit is empty.

---

對話

女：庫倫，我是安，是你所承租倉庫的屋主。我只是要告訴你，我已經決定把倉庫賣掉了。

男：噢，真的嗎？我的租約要到三月才到期，我可以使用到那個時候嗎？

女：當然可以，沒有問題。但星期六，我的幾個朋友要整修外觀，還有修理屋頂的幾處略微破損問題。只是一些修理工作，好準備出售。

男：有沒有可能下個星期底再進行？我會在那之前把我目前的庫存品清空。這樣的話，他們就可以在倉庫空著的情況下進行工程。

**41** What has the woman decided to do?
(A) Sell a building
(B) Extend the lease
(C) Increase the rent
(D) Renovate a house

女子決定要做什麼？
(A) 賣掉一棟建物
(B) 延長租約
(C) 調高租金
(D) 翻修一間房子

**42** According to the woman, who will come to the unit on Saturday?
(A) A contracting team
(B) A vendor
(C) A few friends
(D) A work crew

根據女子所述，誰會在星期六到倉庫去？
(A) 一組承包團隊
(B) 一個小販
(C) 一些朋友
(D) 一組工作人員

**43** What request does the man make?
(A) That a contract be renewed
(B) That the dates be rearranged
(C) That the rent be reduced
(D) That the exterior be painted

男子提出什麼要求？
(A) 續租約
(B) 重新安排日期
(C) 降低租金
(D) 粉刷外觀

W Well, this has been a beneficial meeting, Andrew, and ④④ ④⑤ **I'd like to offer you the opportunity of a franchise with the Chinese Chicken.** Now, as you are aware, there's a probation period for six months but after that, there'll be the opportunity for you to take over the franchise permanently.

M Thank you, Ms. Jackson. I'm pleased you agreed to give me a chance even though I am new to the fast food industry.

W Well, ④⑥ **I was particularly impressed with the portfolio** of successful businesses you have managed in the past. We're looking forward to working with you.

對話

女：嗯，這次會議真有助益，安德魯，我想提供你加盟中華雞的機會。如你所知，會有 6 個月的試用期，但過了之後，你就有機會永久接手加盟店。

男：謝謝您，傑克森女士。我很高興您同意給我機會，即使我在速食業來說是個新人。

女：嗯，我對你過去經營成功的企業表現尤其印象深刻，我們期待與你合作。

**44** Where does the woman work?
(A) At a travel agency
(B) At an employment agency
(C) At a fast food chain
(D) At a clothing store

女子在哪裡工作？
(A) 旅行社
(B) 職業介紹所
(C) 速食連鎖店
(D) 服飾店

🎧07

**45** What does the woman offer the man?
(A) An apprenticeship
(B) Some food samples
(C) Travel opportunities
(D) A franchise

女子要給男子什麼？
(A) 見習期
(B) 一些試吃品
(C) 旅行的機會
(D) 一家加盟店

**46** What was the woman particularly interested in?
(A) A résumé
(B) A reference letter
(C) A portfolio
(D) A travel schedule

女子對什麼特別感興趣？
(A) 履歷表
(B) 推薦信
(C) 代表作
(D) 旅程行程表

**Questions 47-49 refer to the following conversation with three speakers.** 英M 美W 英W

**M** ㊼ I'm expecting another patient in a few minutes. Could one of you please prepare examining room three?
**W1** That would be Mr. Todd Atkinson. I'll get it ready for him.
**M** Thanks. ㊽ I also need to review his medical file before I see him.
**W2** I have been looking for it, but it isn't in the cabinet where it is supposed to be.
**W1** Sorry, I got busy and forgot to tell you that I already took it out. I put it in room three.
**W2** Please tell me next time. I was worried it had gotten lost under all these billing statements.
**M** No harm done. Please take Mr. Atkinson to room three as soon as it is ready.
**W1** Sure.

---

**三人對話**

男：幾分鐘後會有另一個病人來，可以請你們其中一個人準備好 3 號檢查室嗎？

女1：那是陶德‧艾金森先生，我會準備好給他用。

男：謝謝。在我見他前，我還需要看看他的病歷檔案。

女2：我一直在找他的病歷表，但檔案不在它應該在的櫃子裡。

女1：抱歉，我忙到忘了告訴妳，我已經把檔案拿出來了，我放在 3 號室裡。

女2：下次請告訴我，我擔心檔案消失在這堆繳費單下面了。

男：沒出錯就好，等 3 號室準備好就帶艾金森先生過去。

女1：當然。

**字彙** examining room 檢查室；抽檢室
billing statement 繳費單；帳單

**47** Where do the speakers most likely work?
(A) At a pharmacy
(B) At a fitness center
(C) At a copy center
(D) At a doctor's office

說話者最可能在哪裡工作？
(A) 藥局
(B) 健身中心
(C) 影印中心
(D) 診所

**48** What does the man say he needs to see?
(A) A bill
(B) Medical information
(C) A billing statement
(D) A label

男子說他需要看什麼？
(A) 帳單
(B) 醫療資料
(C) 繳費單
(D) 標籤

**49** Why does the man say, "No harm done"?
(A) He is glad the bills are found.
(B) He has an idea to organize files.
(C) He is not concerned about the issue.
(D) He is satisfied with the women's performance.

男子為什麼說：「沒出錯就好」？

(A) 他很高興繳費單找到了。

(B) 他有個整理檔案的構想。

(C) 他不擔心這個問題。

(D) 他很滿意女子的表現。

**Questions 50-52 refer to the following conversation.**

美W 英M

**W** Hi. This is Beth Rivers calling. I rented one of your pensions in Miami last month. (50) **I just received an e-mail from one of your staff saying that I owe $200. I thought I paid the bill.**

**M** Let me check our computer system. It says here that you were charged a damage fee.

**W** I don't get it.

**M** According to the employee who inspected the property after you left, (51) **the door to the terrace was cracked.**

**W** I don't know what you are talking about. I never even went into the terrace during my stay. If there was a problem, I would have reported it when I checked out.

**M** Let me get my supervisor. Only he can process this type of issue. Hold on, please.

**對話**

女：嗨，我是貝絲·瑞佛斯。我上個月租了你們在邁阿密的一間公寓。我剛剛接到你們一位員工寄來的電子郵件，說我還欠 200 元。我以為我已經付了帳單。

男：讓我查看一下電腦系統。這上面說要跟您收取賠償金。

女：我不明白。

男：根據在您離開後檢查房子的員工表示，通往陽台的門裂開了。

女：我不知道你在說什麼。在我居住期間，我連陽台都沒去過。如果有問題，我結帳時就會呈報了。

男：請讓我問一下主管，只有他能處理這種問題，請稍等。

**字彙** **pension** (歐洲大陸國家的)膳宿公寓
**terrace** 陽台；露台 **crack** 裂開；爆裂
**dispute** (對……)有異議、爭執、糾紛

**50** Why is the woman calling?

(A) To return a key

(B) To change a reservation

(C) To dispute a charge

(D) To inform the man of the payday

女子為什麼打這通電話？

(A) 為了歸還鑰匙

(B) 為了更改預約

(C) 為了對一筆費用提出異議

(D) 為了通知男子付款日

**51** What does the man say happened?

(A) A door was damaged.

(B) A reservation was cancelled.

(C) A key was lost.

(D) All pensions were already rented out.

男子說發生了什麼事？

(A) 有扇門損壞了。

(B) 預訂取消了。

(C) 鑰匙遺失了。

(D) 所有的公寓都租出去了。

**52** What does the woman mean when she says, "I don't get it"?

(A) She was lost in the area.

(B) She never received an inspection report.

(C) She thinks the door is too expensive.

(D) She doesn't understand the reason for the fee.

當女子說：「我不明白」時，她的意思是什麼？

(A) 她在那一區迷路了。

(B) 她從來沒有收到檢查報告。

(C) 她認為那扇門太貴了。

(D) 她不明白收那筆費用的原因。

07

**Questions 53-55 refer to the following conversation.**

美M 美W

**M** Hi, Shelley. (53) **Have you heard any news about the bid you submitted to Patriot Corporation for the construction contract?**

**W** We didn't get it.

**M** Oh, that's a shame. I know you put a lot of effort into it, but I hope you don't see it as wasted effort.

**W** It certainly feels like I wasted a lot of time since we didn't get the contract.

**M** Remember that this was your first time preparing a bid. There will be many more contracts to try. ⑤⑤ **Now you have some solid experience that will help you next time.**

**W** Thanks, Donald. That's a better way to look at the situation. I'll keep that in mind.

------

對話

男：嗨，雪莉。關於妳投標愛國者企業的營建工程合約，妳有收到任何消息了嗎？

女：我們沒有得標。

男：噢，真是遺憾。我知道妳投入了很多心力，但我希望妳不要認為那是白費力氣。

女：因我們沒有拿到合約，的確會感覺我浪費了很多時間。

男：別忘了，這是妳第一次準備標案，以後還會有更多的合約要努力爭取。現在妳有了一些紮實完整的經驗，下次這些經驗就能幫上忙了。

女：謝謝，唐納德。那是個看事情的好角度，我會記在心裡。

字彙 bid 投標

**53** What are the speakers mainly discussing?
(A) A construction material
(B) A bid for a contract
(C) An affected deadline
(D) A completed task

說話者主要在討論什麼？
(A) 建材
(B) 投標一份合約
(C) 受到影響的截止日期
(D) 一項完成的任務

**54** Why does the man say, "that's a shame"?
(A) He is not proud of what the woman did.
(B) He is expressing sympathy.
(C) He expected the result.
(D) He is excited to hear the news.

男子為什麼說：「真是遺憾」？
(A) 他對女子的作為並不感到光彩。
(B) 他在表達同情。
(C) 他預期會有這個結果。
(D) 他很興奮聽到這個消息。

**55** What does the man remind the woman about?
(A) She has gained experience.
(B) She will need his help soon.
(C) She has to put in a higher bid.
(D) She was recently hired.

男子提醒女子什麼事？
(A) 她得到了經驗。
(B) 她很快會需要他的幫助。
(C) 她必須要以更高的價格投標。
(D) 她最近才被僱用。

**Questions 56-58 refer to the following conversation.**
美W 美M

**W** So, Miguel! ⑤⑥ **Thanks for applying for Colonel in chief.** I see from your credentials that you served abroad before. Why don't we begin by discussing your most recent army position?

**M** Sure, my last posting was at the Mozambique Barracks. ⑤⑦ **I was in charge of training a number of military divisions,** and we protected a number of important military installations.

**W** That's impressive. But it appears you only served there for three months. Why did you have to leave?

**M** Well, ⑤⑧ **it was only a temporary posting.** I was covering the absence of the chief lieutenant who was on sick leave. So he returned and I had to go back to my unit.

------

對話

女：啊，米蓋爾！謝謝你應徵名譽上校一職。我從你的資歷中看到，你之前曾在海外服役。我們何不先來討論你最近的軍隊職務？

男：當然，我的上一個駐紮地是在莫三比克營區。我負責訓練幾個師團，我們保護不少重要的軍事設施。

女：令人欽佩。但是，看起來你只在那裡服役3個月，你為何必須離開？

男：嗯，那只是個臨時職務。我是去代理休病假的中尉的缺。所以，他回來了，我就得回我的單位。

字彙 colonel in chief 名譽上校
credentials 資格；證書
serve 服役；服務  abroad 在國外；海外
posting 派駐  barrack 營房；兵營
be in charge of 負責；主管
division （軍隊的）師
military installation 軍事設施
impressive 令人印象深刻；令人欽佩
temporary 暫時的；臨時的
cover 代替；頂替  absence 缺席
lieutenant 中尉  sick leave 病假
second in command 副手；副司令
diversify 多樣化

**56** What position is the man applying for?
(A) Second in command
(B) Company engineer
(C) Colonel in chief
(D) Chief lieutenant

男子應徵的是什麼職位？
(A) 副司令
(B) 連隊工兵
(C) 名譽上校
(D) 中尉

**57** What does the man say he was in charge of?
(A) Planning a campaign
(B) Training army personnel
(C) Teaching at a school
(D) Constructing a building

男子說他負責什麼事？
(A) 策劃活動
(B) 訓練軍事人員
(C) 在學校教書
(D) 建造房屋

**58** Why did the man leave his last post?
(A) He was employed on a temporary basis.
(B) He was offered a better position.
(C) He wanted to diversify.
(D) He moved to a different city.

男子為什麼離開上一個駐地？
(A) 他的工作是暫時性的。
(B) 他得到更好的職務。
(C) 他想多些變化。
(D) 他搬到另一個城市。

Questions 59-61 refer to the following conversation.
英M 美W

**M** Leanne, ⑥⓪ do you know where Simon Jack's application form is? He is the third interviewee this afternoon.
**W** Yes, I took out all the files for the applicants invited to come in today. ⑤⑨ They should be on your desk next to the pile of employer files.
**M** Oh, okay. You're one step ahead of me, thanks.
**W** No problem. ⑥① Today is the date of decorating the administration department office. Remember? The filing system is in a bit of disarray. So when I arrived, I took out all the application forms we need today from the office.

對話
男：黎安，妳知道賽門‧傑克的應徵表格在哪裡嗎？今天下午的面試，他排在第三位。
女：是的，我把今天要面試的應徵者檔案都拿出來了。應該在你桌上，僱主檔案的旁邊。
男：噢，好。妳的動作比我快一步，謝謝。
女：沒問題。今天是行政部門辦公室裝潢的日子，記得嗎？檔案系統有點亂，所以，我來的時候，就把我們今天需要的所有應徵表格從辦公室拿出來了。

字彙 application form 應徵表；申請表
take out 取出
ahead of 在……之前
decorate 裝飾；布置
administration department 行政部門
in a disarray 凌亂；混亂
refurbish 整修；把……翻新

**59** Where do the speakers most likely work?
(A) In a doctor's office
(B) In a decorating shop
(C) In an employment agency
(D) At a music store

說話者最可能在哪裡工作？
(A) 診所
(B) 裝潢公司
(C) 職業介紹所
(D) 樂器行

解答&中譯解析 Actual Test 2 PART 3

63

**60** What does the man ask the woman about?
(A) The location of some information
(B) The time of an interview
(C) The contact details of a painter
(D) The cost of an item

男子問女子什麼事？
(A) 某些資料的位置
(B) 面試的時間
(C) 一位油漆師傅的聯絡方式
(D) 某個物品的價格

**61** What does the woman say is happening today?
(A) A business is relocating.
(B) New equipment is being installed.
(C) An office is being refurbished.
(D) A filing system is being updated.

女子說今天有什麼事將發生？
(A) 有間公司要搬家。
(B) 要裝設新的設備。
(C) 有間辦公室要裝修。
(D) 檔案系統要升級。

**Questions 62-64 refer to the following conversation.**
美W 美M

**W** Zack, how is the design of ❻❸ **the new suction cleaner** progressing? I noticed your department has been working hard these past few months.
**M** Well, ❻❷ **we devised a powerful wireless cleaner that can be operated without a cable.** People will be able to clean easily to reach places, even outdoors.
**W** I'm a gardener, and I'd certainly want to try a product like that. When do you anticipate it'll be ready for launch?
**M** Later this week, ❻❹ **we're going to ask some volunteers to try out a prototype as members of a research group** so that we can make any required changes. With luck, we'll start manufacturing within the next six months.

----

**對話**

女：查克，新型吸塵器的設計進度如何？我注意到，你們部門過去這幾個月來一直很努力工作。

男：嗯，我們設計了一款強力無線吸塵器，不用電線就能操作。人們可以輕鬆清潔各個地方，甚至是戶外。

女：我喜歡園藝，肯定想要試試那樣的產品。你預料何時能準備好上市？

男：這個星期稍後，我們會要一些志願者，以研發人員的身分試用一台原型機，這樣我們就能進行任何所需的修改。運氣好的話，我們在未來 6 個月內會開始生產。

**字彙** suction cleaner 吸塵器
progress 進展；前進　department 部門
devise 設計；發明　wireless 無線的
cable 電線；電纜　anticipate 預料；預期
launch 推出；啟動
volunteer 志願者　try out 試用
prototype 原型
research group 研究團隊
with luck 幸運的話；運氣好的話
manufacture （大量）製造；大量生產
coordinate 協調　landscape 風景

**62** What type of work does the man most likely do?
(A) He designs products.
(B) He coordinates training sessions.
(C) He provides landscape services.
(D) He heads advertising campaigns.

男子最可能做什麼樣的工作？
(A) 他設計產品。
(B) 他協調訓練課程。
(C) 他提供景觀美化服務。
(D) 他率領廣告宣傳活動。

**63** What are the speakers mainly discussing?
(A) Sports equipment
(B) Gardening clothing
(C) A cleaning product
(D) A wireless computer

說話者主要在討論什麼？
(A) 運動裝備
(B) 園藝服飾
(C) 清潔產品
(D) 無線電腦

**64** According to the man, what will happen this week?
(A) A marketing campaign will be launched.
(B) A manufacturing process will start.
(C) A product will be ready for sale.
(D) A research study will take place.

根據男子所述，這個星期將會發生什麼事？
(A) 將會展開行銷活動。
(B) 將會啟動製造程序。
(C) 將準備販售產品。
(D) 將會進行研究調查。

**Questions 65-67 refer to the following conversation and phone directory.** 英M 美W

| Staff | Extension |
|---|---|
| Paul Smith | 234 |
| Ronny Hanks | 235 |
| Ginger Harrison | 236 |
| Kelly Shaffer | 237 |

**M** Kelly, now that I am a full-time employee, am I eligible for the company's health insurance plan?
**W** Of course. **65 You have 45 days from the date of your promotion to decide if you want to enroll.** The same goes for the other benefits available only to full-time employees. Any benefits you received as a part-time employee, you can keep.
**M** 45 days? I'd better make a decision soon. **66 Do you know how I can get more information about the insurance plan?**
**W** You need to contact Human Resources. **67 The benefits specialist for our department is Ginger Harrison.** I suggest you call his extension. You can find his number in the employee phone directory.
**M** Thanks, I'll do that.

對話與電話分機表

| 員工 | 分機 |
|---|---|
| 保羅・史密斯 | 234 |
| 羅尼・漢克斯 | 235 |
| 金傑・哈里森 | 236 |
| 凱莉・薛佛 | 237 |

男：凱莉，既然我現在是全職員工了，我有資格加入公司的健康保險方案嗎？女：
當然，從你升職後，你有 45 天可以決定是否要加入，其他只有全職員工享有的福利也是如此。你在當兼職員工時享有的福利，可以保留。
男：45 天？我最好快點做決定。妳知道我要如何才能得到更多關於保險方案的資訊嗎？
女：你需要聯絡人事部門，專門負責我們部門福利的是金傑・哈里森。我建議你打他的分機，你可以在員工電話簿裡找到他的號碼。
男：謝謝，我會打的。

字彙 now that 既然　eligible for 有資格做……
enroll （使）加入、註冊
benefit （雇主提供給員工的）福利
extension 電話分機
directory 姓名住址簿；電話簿

**65** According to the woman, what does the man have 45 days to do?
(A) Apply for a promotion
(B) Register his driving license
(C) Enroll in an insurance plan
(D) Hire a full-time employee

根據女子所述，男子有 45 天可以做什麼？
(A) 申請升職
(B) 登記他的駕駛執照
(C) 加入保險方案
(D) 僱用一名全職員工

**66** What does the man want to obtain?
(A) An insurance card
(B) A list of entire staff
(C) A new phone number
(D) Information about specific benefits

男子想要獲得什麼？
(A) 一張保險卡
(B) 一份所有員工的名單
(C) 一個新的電話號碼
(D) 特定福利的資訊

**67** Look at the graphic. What number will the man call?
(A) 234
(B) 235
(C) 236
(D) 237

07

請見圖表，男子會打哪個號碼？
(A) 234
(B) 235
(C) 236
(D) 237

**Questions 68-70 refer to the following conversation and menu.** (美W)(美M)

| Lunch Menu | |
|---|---|
| Fresh Salad | $8 |
| Hearty Soup | $9 |
| Personal Pizza | $12 |
| Salmon Sandwich | $7 |

**W** Hello. My name is Linzie, and I will be your server today. Could I get you something to drink to get you started?

**M** Yes, please. I'd like a glass of wine.

**W** Okay. Do you need some time to look at the menu?

**M** No, I'm actually kind of in a hurry. 68 I have to meet with a client at 12:00. 69 So could you please bring me a grilled salmon sandwich?

**W** Would you like it on white or wheat bread? And would you like anything on it?

**M** I'd like wheat bread, and please add honey-mustard, mayonnaise, lettuce, tomatoes, and onions.

**W** Got it. 70 I'll be back with your drink in a moment.

----

**對話與菜單**

| 午餐菜單 | |
|---|---|
| 新鮮沙拉 | $8 |
| 暖心湯 | $9 |
| 個人獨享披薩 | $12 |
| 鮭魚三明治 | $7 |

女：您好，我是琳茲，今天由我為您服務。您要先喝點什麼再開始點餐嗎？

男：好，謝謝。我要一杯葡萄酒。

女：好的，您需要點時間看菜單嗎？

男：不用，我其實有點趕時間，我得在 12 點去見一位客戶。所以，妳可以給我一份烤鮭魚三明治嗎？

女：您要白麵包還是小麥麵包？還有，上面要加什麼嗎？

男：我要小麥麵包，還有，請加蜂蜜芥茉醬、美乃滋、生菜、番茄和洋蔥。

女：知道了，我馬上送飲料來。

**字彙** in a hurry 匆忙；倉促　grilled 燒烤的　salmon 鮭魚

**68** What does the man say he needs to do at noon?
(A) Have a business meeting
(B) Take a bus
(C) See a friend
(D) Return to the office

男子說他中午必須做什麼事？
(A) 有個商務會議
(B) 搭公車
(C) 見個朋友
(D) 回辦公室

**69** Look at the graphic. How much will the man pay for his food?
(A) $8
(B) $9
(C) $12
(D) $7

請見圖表，男子要付多少餐費？
(A) $8
(B) $9
(C) $12
(D) $7

**70** What does the woman say she will do next?
(A) Set the man's table with dishes
(B) Return with a part of the man's order
(C) Bring the check
(D) Buy a bottle of wine

女子說她接下來將會做什麼？
(A) 為男子擺放餐具
(B) 送一部分男子點的餐過來
(C) 拿帳單來
(D) 買一瓶葡萄酒

# PART 4

P. 067

**Questions 71-73 refer to the following announcement.**
美M

In regional news, **71 today the municipal library opened its newly built media center.** The first visitors to the new space is a group of school children from St. Monarch School, whose fundraising helped to build the extension to the building. **72 Library curator, Richard Blaine,** says that he is pleased to welcome the pupils of St. Monarch. To commemorate the opening, **73 the library is providing free refreshments** to the general public this Sunday from 10 A.M. to 4 P.M.

宣告

　　在地方新聞部分，市立圖書館今天啟用了新建的媒體中心。新空間的首批訪客是來自聖莫納克小學的一群學童，該校的捐款幫助圖書館得以擴建。圖書館館長理察·布連說，他很高興歡迎聖莫納克的學生來。為慶祝媒體中心開幕，圖書館將在這個星期日上午 10 點到下午 4 點，免費供應大眾飲料和點心。

字彙　regional 地區的；局部的
　　　municipal library 市立圖書館
　　　newly 新近；最近
　　　fundraising 募款；募捐
　　　extension 增建部分
　　　curator 館長；管理人　pupil 小學生
　　　commemorate 慶祝；紀念
　　　refreshments 茶點、點心和飲料
　　　general public 公眾；大眾
　　　instructional 教學的；教育的

**71** What happened today at the municipal library?
(A) An extension was opened.
(B) A new curator was appointed.
(C) An exhibit space closed.
(D) Some media were invited.

市立圖書館今天發生什麼事？
(A) 增建部分啟用
(B) 任命新館長
(C) 有個展覽場地關閉
(D) 有些媒體獲邀前來

**72** Who is Richard Blaine?
(A) A teacher
(B) A librarian
(C) A curator
(D) An architect

理察·布連是誰？
(A) 一位教師
(B) 一位圖書館員
(C) 一位館長
(D) 一位建築師

**73** According to the speaker, what will the library offer on Sunday?
(A) Free food and drink
(B) Free computer access
(C) Instructional videos
(D) Library vouchers

根據說話者所述，圖書館會在星期日提供什麼？
(A) 免費的食物和飲料
(B) 免費使用電腦
(C) 教學影片
(D) 圖書館優惠卡

**Questions 74-76 refer to the following recorded message.** 美W

Hello, **74 you've reached the Government Customs Department. 75 We are currently unavailable due to the Queen's Birthday holiday.** If this is an emergency and you wish to speak to someone urgently, please call Sir Andre Wilson at 20-555-2121. Otherwise, if you'd like to speak personally to an advisor or make an inquiry, **76 call back tomorrow during our working hours of 08:00 A.M. to 7:00 P.M.**

留言錄音

　　哈囉，這裡是政府海關部門。由於女王誕辰假期，我們今天不上班。如果是緊急狀況，您急著想要和某人通話，請撥打 20-555-2121，找安德烈·威爾森爵士。除此之外，若您想要親自和顧問洽談或詢問事情，請在明天上班時間上午 8 點至下午 7 點再來電。

**74** What kind of business did the caller reach?
(A) A department store
(B) A solicitor's firm
(C) A royal residence
(D) A governmental department

打電話的人打到什麼機構？
(A) 一家百貨公司
(B) 一家律師事務所
(C) 一處皇室宅邸
(D) 一個政府部門

**75** Why is the business closed?
(A) A national holiday is observed.
(B) Some departments have merged.
(C) A ceremony is taking place.
(D) The office has shut down.

這個機構為什麼沒上班？
(A) 慶祝國定假日。
(B) 有些部門合併了。
(C) 正在舉行某個儀式。
(D) 辦公室關閉了。

**76** When will the business reopen?
(A) After a few hours
(B) Tomorrow
(C) In two days
(D) Next week

這個機構何時會再開放？
(A) 幾個小時之後
(B) 明天
(C) 兩天後
(D) 下星期

**Questions 77-79 refer to the following advertisement.**
美M

Every year, home owners throw away hundreds of pounds by not maintaining their oven appliances. Why not make sure that your oven is working to its full capacity? Call Acoven Services at 070-555-9464 and arrange a free call-out, by ⑦ ⑱ one of our repair experts who will check your appliance and explain exactly how our maintenance programs work. And ⑲ from the beginning of this month, there's a 15 percent discount on any service agreement that you take out with us. So call today!

廣告

　　自用住宅的屋主每年都因沒有維修他們的爐具，而白白浪費掉數百鎊。為什麼不確認一下，您的爐具是否有發揮到最大功效？請打070-555-9464，找艾可文服務公司安排免費到府服務，我們的維修專家會檢查您的設備，並確實解說我們的維修方案會如何進行。而且，從這個月開始，您同意選用我們的任何一項服務都享有85折優惠。所以，今天就拿起電話吧！

**77** What is being advertised?
(A) Appliance maintenance
(B) Residential repairs
(C) Technician training
(D) Cooking classes

這是在廣告什麼？
(A) 器具維修
(B) 住宅整修
(C) 技術人員訓練
(D) 烹飪課

**78** Why are listeners asked to call?
   (A) To reach an agreement
   (B) To arrange an inspection
   (C) To receive a new oven
   (D) To sign up for discounts

為什麼聽者被要求打電話？
   (A) 為了達成協議
   (B) 為了安排檢查
   (C) 為了得到新爐子
   (D) 為了報名享受折扣

**79** What will happen at the beginning of the month?
   (A) Payments will be collected.
   (B) A program will start.
   (C) A discount scheme comes into force.
   (D) A report will be issued.

從這個月開始會發生什麼事？
   (A) 將會收款。
   (B) 將開始一個方案。
   (C) 一項優專方案將生效。
   (D) 將會發出一份報告。

**Questions 80-82 refer to the following talk.** 英W

⓼⓪ **Welcome to the 20th annual award ceremony for creative writing.** We were overwhelmed to see applications from so many talented writers. People whose creativity challenges a conservative way of writing. After hours of reflection, ⓼① **we unanimously awarded Ms. Femke Jukkin the Newcomer of the Year.** Her latest, *the Life Choices to be Made*, shows incredible imagination and skill. Before we invite Ms. Jukkin to the podium, ⓼② **I would like you to open the brochure that you received when you arrived.** We have included in it a short excerpt from Ms. Jukkin's novel.

----

談話

　　歡迎參加第 20 屆創意寫作頒獎典禮。看到有這麼多才華洋溢的作家報名，讓我們滿心激動。人們的創意挑戰了傳統的寫作方式。經過數小時的審慎思考，我們一致決定頒給芬克・朱金女士年度新人獎。她的最新作品《必須做出的人生抉擇》展現了不可思議的想像力與技巧。在我們邀請朱金女士上台之前，我希望你們打開抵達會場時拿到的小冊子，我們在裡面摘錄了一小段朱金女士的小說內容。

字彙 award ceremony 頒獎典禮
creative writing 創意寫作
overwhelm （強烈的情感）充溢；使難以承受
talented 有天賦的；技藝高超的
creativity 創意
conservative 傳統的；保守的
reflection 審慎思考；深思熟慮
unanimously 一致通過的；意見一致的
newcomer 新來者；新手
incredible 不可思議的；驚人的
podium 演講台；領獎台

**80** What type of event is being held?
   (A) An art gallery opening
   (B) An awards ceremony
   (C) A conservative meeting
   (D) A play preview

正在舉行什麼樣的活動？
   (A) 藝廊開幕
   (B) 頒獎典禮
   (C) 保守黨大會
   (D) 戲劇預演

**81** What field does Ms. Jukkin work in?
   (A) Writing
   (B) Teaching
   (C) Catering
   (D) Publishing

朱金女士在哪個領域工作？
   (A) 寫作
   (B) 教學
   (C) 外燴
   (D) 出版

**82** What will listeners most likely do next?
   (A) Watch a video
   (B) Hear a speech
   (C) Eat a meal
   (D) Pick up a brochure

聽者接下來最可能做什麼事？
   (A) 看一段影片
   (B) 聽一場演講
   (C) 吃一餐飯
   (D) 拿起一本小冊子

**Questions 83-85 refer to the following telephone message.** 澳M

Hi, Mr. Ubamo. ⑧ **This is Mtama from MJ's Vehicle Exchange.** ⑧ **I'm calling about the second hand truck you wanted us to look at.** Well, I have an offer for you as we'd like to take it off your hands. Because of the damage to the paintwork, we can't offer you your asking price. In the past, we purchased similar models for about 300 euros. However, ⑧ **we are willing to negotiate if you find a better offer.** Give me a call so we can discuss this. This is Mtama and you can reach me at 44-555-6687.

---

電話留言

嗨，尤巴摩先生。我是 MJ 舊換新汽車的莫塔瑪。我打來是關於您要我們檢查的那輛二手卡車。嗯，我要給您報個價，因為我們想要接手這輛車。由於烤漆受損，所以，我們無法提供您所要求的價格。以前，我們曾用大約 300 歐元買過類似的車款。不過，如果您可以找到有人出更好的價格，我們願意協商。請回我電話討論這件事。我是莫塔瑪，您可以撥 44-555-6687。

---

字彙  vehicle 車輛
　　 second hand 二手的；中古的
　　 take . . . off a person's hands 接手
　　 paintwork 油漆部分；漆面
　　 asking price 要價　negotiate 協商；談判
　　 lot 場地；一塊地
　　 outlet 廉價商品經銷點；專賣店
　　 estimate 估價；估算

**83** Where most likely does the speaker work?
(A) At a used car lot
(B) At a gas station
(C) At a supermarket
(D) At a vehicle repair outlet

說話者最可能在哪裡工作？
(A) 中古車行
(B) 加油站
(C) 超級市場
(D) 修車場

**84** What does Mr. Ubamo want to do?
(A) Ask for a job
(B) Repair his truck
(C) Advertise a business
(D) Sell a vehicle

尤巴摩先生想要做什麼？
(A) 要求一份工作
(B) 修理他的卡車
(C) 宣傳一個生意
(D) 賣掉一輛車

**85** What should Mr. Ubamo do when he returns the call?
(A) Speak to a manager
(B) Ask for an estimate
(C) Negotiate the price
(D) Provide credit card details

當尤巴摩先生回電時，他應該做什麼？
(A) 和經理談話
(B) 要求估價
(C) 協商價格
(D) 提供信用卡資料

**Questions 86-88 refer to the following talk.** 英M

Good morning, and welcome to Yellow Stone State Park. My name is Mark Williams. ⑧ **I'll be leading today's hike.** Right now, we are standing in front of the information center. In a moment, we'll stroll along the pond, cross over a bridge, and climb a small hill. The park is a habitat for hundreds of types of native plants. We also have dozens of species of birds, small mammals, and other wildlife that make their home here. If we are quiet, we might get to see them. No one can guarantee anything, though. ⑧ **We recommend that all of you bring a water bottle.** Although this is just a one-hour walk, it can get quite warm this time of the year.

---

談話

早安，歡迎來到黃石州立公園。我是馬克·威廉斯，由我帶領今天的健行活動。我們現在站在服務中心前面。等一下，我們會沿著池塘漫步，走過一座橋，然後爬上一座小山丘。這座公園是數百種原生植物的棲息地，我們也有許多種鳥類、小型哺乳動物和其他野生動物以此為家。如果我們很安靜，我們可能看得到牠們。不過，沒有人可以保證什麼。我們建議你們大家都帶一瓶水。雖然，這只是一小時的健行，但這個時節，天氣可能會變得相當暖和。

**86** Who most likely is the speaker?
(A) A guide
(B) An animal activist
(C) A fitness trainer
(D) A logger

說話者最可能是什麼人？
(A) 一名嚮導
(B) 一名動保人士
(C) 一位健身教練
(D) 一名伐木工人

**87** What does the man mean when he says, "No one can guarantee anything, though"?
(A) He is uncertain if they are going in the right direction.
(B) He is uncertain if the weather will be good.
(C) He cannot be sure this hike is not hard.
(D) He cannot be sure they will see any animals.

當男子說：「不過，沒有人可以保證什麼」時，他的意思是什麼？
(A) 他不確定他們是否走對方向。
(B) 他不確定天氣是否會很好。
(C) 他不確定這趟健行不會很難走。
(D) 他不確定他們可以看到任何動物。

**88** What does the speaker suggest the listeners do?
(A) Wear warm clothes
(B) Bring a map
(C) Carry water
(D) Stay with a group

說話者建議聽者做什麼？
(A) 穿保暖衣物
(B) 帶著地圖
(C) 帶水
(D) 不脫隊

**Questions 89-91 refer to the following excerpt from a seminar.** 英W

Well, that's all we have for today. ❽❾ I hope that this seminar on prioritizing tasks has been useful to you. We discussed several techniques for helping you and your employees to plan strategically. It has been my experience that if you practice these strategies, you will get work done more efficiently. ❾⓿ The handouts I just gave you summarize the key points we went over today. They also include a list of Web sites with additional resources. Make sure to go over all of these. I think you will find them useful. Before you leave, please take a moment to complete the comment card on your table. Your feedback will help us improve this and other seminars. Thanks again for taking part in the seminar.

研討會摘錄

好了，今天就到這裡結束。我希望這次關於排定工作優先順序的研討會，對你們都有幫助。我們討論了好幾項技能，幫助你和你的員工進行策略規畫的技巧。我的經驗是，如果你練習這些策略，會更有效完成工作。我剛剛發給你們的講義，總結了我們今天仔細討論的重點，裡面也包含一份提供額外資源的網站名單。務必要仔細看過這些資料。我想，你們會發現它們很有用。在你們離開之前，請花點時間填寫桌上的意見卡。你們的回饋意見，可以幫助我們改進這次以及其他的研討會。再次感謝各位參加這次的研討會。

**89** What most likely was the topic of the seminar?
(A) Organizing a task force
(B) Cooperating with colleagues
(C) Coordinating a hiring process
(D) Arranging assignments effectively

研討會的主題最可能是什麼？
(A) 組織專門小組
(B) 和同事合作
(C) 協調僱用程序
(D) 有效安排工作

**90** What did the speaker pass out to the listeners?
(A) A recent article
(B) A list of resources
(C) An enrollment form
(D) A list of attendees

說話者分發了什麼給聽者？
(A) 一篇最近的文章
(B) 一份資源清單
(C) 一份報名表
(D) 一份出席名單

**91** Why does the speaker say, "Make sure to go over all of these"?
(A) To celebrate a product launch
(B) To give an assignment
(C) To promote other seminars
(D) To recommend Web sites

說話者為什麼說：「務必要仔細看過這些資料」？
(A) 為了慶祝產品上市
(B) 為了分派工作
(C) 為了宣傳其他研討會
(D) 為了推薦網站

**Questions 92-94 refer to the following news report and map.** 澳M

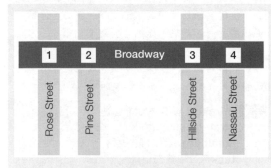

It's time for our 7 A.M. traffic update. Commuters planning to take the highway into the city today might want to consider avoiding exit number 4. **92 Work crews are filling up a huge sink hole near the exit ramp.** As a result, you will experience delays if you have to use this exit. If you can use another exit to get where you need to go, **93 then the Transportation Department recommends taking exits 6 or 9 instead.** If you are going to be downtown today, **94 please use extra caution at the intersection of Pine Street and Broadway.** The traffic lights there are not

working due to a temporary power outage. Police are stationed to help direct traffic until an electrical utility crew can get power restored.

---

新聞報導與地圖

　　現在播報早上 7 點的最新路況。今天打算走公路進城的通勤族，可能要考慮避開 4 號匝道。工作人員正在填補出口坡道附近的一個大坑洞。因此，如果你必須走這個出口，將會受到延誤。如果，你可以走另一個出口去你需要去的地方，那麼交通局建議改走 6 號或 9 號出口。如果你今天要去市中心，在派恩街與百老匯大道的交叉路口，請格外注意。那裡的交通號誌燈由於暫時停電而不亮。在電力公司工作人員恢復電力之前，警察已被派去幫忙指揮交通。

| 字彙 | commuter 通勤者　fill up 填補；裝滿 |
| ramp 坡道；斜坡　caution 小心；謹慎 |
| temporary 暫時的 |
| power outage 停電；斷電 |
| station 派駐；部署 |
| utility 公用事業；公共設施 |
| slippery 濕滑的；容易打滑的　detour 繞道 |

**92** What is causing traffic delays at exit number 4?
(A) A car accident
(B) A slippery road
(C) Road repair work
(D) A scheduled town event

是什麼原因造成 4 號出口的交通延誤？
(A) 車禍
(B) 路面濕滑
(C) 道路修補工程
(D) 安排好的市內活動

**93** What does the Transportation Department recommend?
(A) Using detours
(B) Commuting by public transportation
(C) Not passing through downtown
(D) Avoiding a certain bridge

交通局建議什麼？

(A) 繞道而行

(B) 搭乘大眾運輸工具通勤

(C) 不要經過市中心

(D) 避開某座橋樑

**94** Look at the graphic. What traffic light is not working?

(A) 1

(B) 2

(C) 3

(D) 4

請見圖表，哪個交通號誌燈不亮？

(A) 1

(B) 2

(C) 3

(D) 4

**Questions 95-97 refer to the following excerpt from a meeting and chart.** 英W

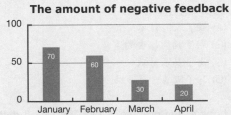

The next topic on today's meeting is customer service. Overall, I want to point out that our customer service team is exceptional. ⑨⑤ **They are extremely efficient, and the additional associates who were hired to join the team earlier this year have done a great job.** Nevertheless, we saw an increase in negative feedback a few months ago. ⑨⑥ **We determined that the cause was an unclear return and exchange policy.** To address this problem, we simplified the policy and retrained all the customer service representatives. ⑨⑦ **Well, if you take a look at the chart on the screen, you can see that the amount of negative feedback decreased from 60 to 30 in the month after the training session.** And it is continuing to fall.

會議摘錄與圖表

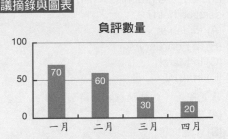

今天會議的下個主題是客戶服務。整體而言，我要指出，我們的客戶服務團隊非常優秀。他們極有效率，而且今年初受僱加入團隊的其他同事表現非常傑出。然而，幾個月前，我們看到負評數量增加。我們判斷原因為退換貨政策不明。為了處理這個問題，我們簡化了規定，並重新訓練所有的客服專員。嗯，如果你們看一下螢幕上的圖表，你們會看到在訓練課程後那個月的負評數量從 60 減到 30。而且，還在持續減少。

字彙 overall 全面地　point out 指出；提出
exceptional 優秀的；卓越的
associate 夥伴；同事
nevertheless 然而；不過　fall 減少；下降
workforce 人力；勞動力
ambiguous 含糊不清的；不明確的

**95** What does the speaker say about the customer service team?

(A) It was recently transferred.

(B) It received a pay increase.

(C) Its workforce has been expanded.

(D) It still needs to improve.

關於客服團隊，說話者說了什麼？

(A) 團隊最近有調動。

(B) 團隊得到加薪。

(C) 團隊的人力擴編。

(D) 團隊仍然需要改進。

**96** What was the cause of negative comments?

(A) An ambiguous policy

(B) An expensive service price

(C) Untrained staff

(D) A defective product

造成負評的原因是什麼？

(A) 不明的政策

(B) 昂貴的服務費

(C) 未經訓練的員工

(D) 產品有瑕疵

**97** Look at the graphic. When was the training session held?
(A) In January
(B) In February
(C) In March
(D) In April

請見圖表，訓練課程在何時舉行？
(A) 一月
(B) 二月
(C) 三月
(D) 四月

Questions 98-100 refer to the following telephone message and invoice. 澳M

| INVOICE | |
| --- | --- |
| **Product Number** | **Description** |
| P365 | Soccer ball (# 3) |
| P345 | Basketball (# 2) |
| P443 | Running shoes (# 2 pairs) |
| P334 | Track Jacket (# 1) |

Hello, Ms. Williams. This is Paul Grey at East Athletics. You placed an order on our Web site yesterday. ㊙ **I am just calling to let you know that one of the items on your order, the soccer ball, is currently out of stock.** We expect to receive a new shipment and to fully restock the item at our warehouse within 5-6 days. If you would like, we can send you the other items first and send the soccer ball to you later. ⑩ **There will be no additional shipping costs for you.** Otherwise, we can wait until we have all the items and ship them to you together. ㊙ **Please let me know which option you prefer.** The number is 555-5783. Thanks and have a great day!

電話留言與發貨單

| 發貨單 | |
| --- | --- |
| **產品編號** | **說明** |
| P365 | 足球（＃3） |
| P345 | 籃球（＃2） |
| P443 | 跑步鞋（＃2雙） |
| P334 | 運動外套（＃1） |

哈囉，威廉斯女士，我是東方運動公司的保羅·萬瑞。您昨天在我們的網站上下了訂單。我打來只是要告訴您，您訂單中的一個商品——足球，目前缺貨。我們預計會在 5 到 6 天內會收到新的一批貨，並重新補齊我們倉庫裡的這項商品。如果您願意，我們可以先把其他商品送去給您，足球稍後再送，不會向您收額外的運費。或者，我們可以等到所有的商品都來了，再一起送去給您。請告訴我，您比較喜歡哪種做法，我的電話是 555-5783。謝謝您，並祝您有個愉快的一天！

字彙 otherwise 除此之外；用別的方法
waive 免除　out of stock 缺貨；無庫存

**98** Why is the speaker calling?
(A) To cancel an order
(B) To ask a preference
(C) To ask for a payment
(D) To sell a product

說話者為什麼打這通電話？
(A) 為了取消訂單
(B) 為了詢問偏愛的選擇
(C) 為了要求付款
(D) 為了販售一項產品

**99** Look at the graphic. Which item is currently out of stock?
(A) P365
(B) P345
(C) P443
(D) P334

請見圖表，哪一項商品目前缺貨？
(A) P365
(B) P345
(C) P443
(D) P334

**100** What does the speaker offer to do?
(A) Refund some money
(B) Waive a shipping fee
(C) Upgrade a shipping method
(D) Cancel an order

說話者提議做什麼？
(A) 退回一些費用
(B) 免除運費
(C) 升級運送方式
(D) 取消訂單

## PART 5

P. 070

**101**

林先生已經提交費用核銷單，但安克女士還沒提出她的。
(A) hers 她的東西
(B) her 她的
(C) herself 她自己
(D) she 她

**解析** 空格要填入動詞（has not yet finished）的受詞。除了 she 為主格之外，其他皆能扮演受詞的角色。而根據題意，表達的是 Anker 小姐尚未完成她的費用報銷單，因此要選所有格代名詞，代替前方的費用報銷單，答案為 (A)。

**字彙** hand in 提出；繳交
expense claim 費用核銷

**102**

HTR 公司以實惠的年費提供可靠無線服務。
(A) reliable 可靠的
(B) reliant 依賴的
(C) reliably 可靠地
(D) reliability 可靠

**解析** 空格用來修飾名詞（wireless service），因此要填入形容詞。選項中的形容詞有 (A) reliable（可靠的；可信賴的）和 (B) reliant（依賴的），根據題意，選擇 (A) 較為適當。

**字彙** wireless 無線的
affordable 負擔的起的

**103**

「樂翻頁」出版一份電子報，以電子郵件傳給顧客。
(A) publisher 出版商
(B) publishes 出版
(C) publish 出版
(D) publishable 可出版的

**解析** 主詞為 Fun & Turn，空格位在該句子的動詞位置，因此答案為 (B)。主詞為單數，所以答案不能選 (C)。

**字彙** online newsletter（機構定期發送給成員的）線上通訊；簡報；電子報
publisher 出版商；出版社
publish 出版　publishable 可出版的

**104**

因為網路是個交換想法的絕佳地方，因此現在很多人加入網路論壇。
(A) Because 因為
(B) So 所以
(C) Owning to 由於
(D) After 在……之後

**解析** 本題考的是從屬連接詞。主要子句 many people now join online forums 為一個結構完整的句子，因此 the Internet . . . ideas 的作用為修飾。答案要選從屬連接詞，連接空格後方的子句，扮演修飾的角色，因此應從 Because 和 After 當中選出答案。根據題意，表達「因為……」較為適當，因此答案為 (A)。So 為對等連接詞，僅能放在句子與句子之間做連接，不能放在句首使用。

**字彙** exchange 交換
forum（尤指討論與公共利益相關問題的）論壇

**105**

在選擇搬家公司時，你應該要求確實報價。
(A) choice 選擇
(B) choosing 正選擇
(C) chosen 被選
(D) choose 選擇

**解析** 該句話為副詞子句（When you choose a moving company）改寫成分詞構句。省略主詞（you）後，要將動詞（choose）改為分詞，而主詞和動詞的關係為主動，因此答案要選 (B)。

**字彙** moving company 搬家公司

**106**

由於擁有豐富的專業知識，杜爾森先生被視為是財經團隊中受歡迎的新成員。
(A) output 產量
(B) addition 增加的人或物
(C) response 回應
(D) reception 接待

**解析** 請熟記慣用語 a welcome addition（新加的東西／新增的設施／新加入的人大家都開心接受），答案要選 (B)。

**字彙** extensive 廣大的；大量的

**107**

有了「找工作」程式的幫助，要為你自己創作一份令人印象深刻的履歷表會很容易且簡單。
(A) you 你
(B) your own 你自己的
(C) your 你的
(D) yourself 你自己

**解析** of 表示所屬的意思時，後方會加上所有格代名詞（yours）使用。〈所有格＋own〉可以用來代替所有格代名詞，因此答案為 (B)。

**字彙** impressive 令人印象深刻的

**108**

筆記型電腦不用的時候就關機，可以延長電池的壽命。
(A) extends 延長
(B) have extended 已延長
(C) be extended 被延長
(D) extending 延長

**解析** 助動詞（can）後方要連接原形動詞。選項中僅有 (B) have extended 和 (C) be extended 為原形動詞，兩者的差異為語態。(B) 為主動語態，後方必須連接受詞；(C) 為被動語態，後方不能連接受詞。而空格後方僅連接修飾語（by . . .），並未連接受詞，因此答案為 (C)。

**字彙** extend 延長；擴展

**109**

想要在假期中使用辦公室的員工，必須事先獲得許可。
(A) since 自從
(B) among 在……之中
(C) during 在……期間
(D) next 下一個

**解析** 空格位在修飾語的位置，置於名詞後方作修飾，因此要填入介系詞。(D) next 可以當作形容詞或副詞使用，並非答案。其餘選項中，表達「在……期間」最符合題意，因此答案為 (C) during。

**110**

為了努力確保遵守規定，稽查員必須檢查工廠所有的區域。
(A) ensures 確保
(B) to be ensured 為了被確保
(C) to ensure 為了確保
(D) were ensured 被確保

**解析** 空格置於介系詞（in）和名詞（effort）後方作修飾。to 不定詞可以用來修飾名詞 effort，因此答案為 (C)。〈in an effort to 不定詞〉的意思為「為了……而努力」；〈make an effort to 不定詞〉的意思為「努力做……」，兩者皆為常見用法，請特別熟記。另外，可以用 to 不定詞修飾的名詞還有 chance、opportunity、right、ability、way、plan、time，建議一併熟記。

**字彙** ensure 保證；擔保
compliance 遵守；服從
auditor 稽核員；查帳員

**111**

在修習線上課程之前，你應該徹底熟悉這套軟體。
(A) familiarization 熟悉
(B) familiarize 使……熟悉
(C) familiarity 親近
(D) familiar 熟悉的

**解析** 動詞 become 為連綴動詞，屬於不完全不及物動詞，因此空格要填入主詞補語。名詞或形容詞皆可置於主詞補語的位置，但是副詞（thoroughly）無法用來修飾名詞，表示空格僅能填入形容詞，因此答案為 (D)。

**字彙** thoroughly 徹底地；極其

**112**

不管你目前的財務狀況如何，JPR 貸款公司都讓獲得住宅貸款變得容易。
(A) depending 依……而定
(B) regardless of 不管
(C) even if 即使
(D) as long as 只要

**解析** 空格後方連接的是名詞片語，並非子句（S＋V），因此空格不能填入連接詞，而是要填入介系詞。選項中只有 (B) regardless of（不管……）可以當作介系詞使用。

**字彙** housing loan 住宅貸款
　　　 status 狀況；身分

**113**

在漫長的討論之後，更新大廳陳設的提案終於獲得同意。
(A) finally 終於
(B) rarely 很少
(C) exactly 精確地
(D) immensely 廣大地

**解析** 本題的四個選項皆為副詞，因此要選出最符合題意的單字。(A) finally（最後）與介系詞 Following（在……以後）的意思最為貼近，故為正確答案。

**字彙** proposal 提案
　　　 furnishing 家具；室內陳設

**114**

透過飯店網站的訂房，必須在登記入住前 12 小時確認。
(A) make 做
(B) are made 被做
(C) made 做了
(D) will make 將要做

**解析** 空格用來修飾名詞（Reservations）因此要填入形容詞。選項中僅有 made（過去分詞）可以用來扮演形容詞的角色，因此答案為 (C)。其餘選項皆屬於主要動詞。

**115**

今年初，巴席爾‧汗訪問了幾位出現在《舞台明星》雜誌封面的名人。
(A) since 自從
(B) recently 最近
(C) where 在那裡
(D) who ……的人。

**解析** Bashir . . . celebrities 的部分為結構完整的句子，因此從空格開始用來修飾前方內容。關係代名詞可以連接動詞，同時用來修飾前方名詞，因此答案為 (D)。

　since 可以當作介系詞或從屬連接詞使用，當作介系詞使用時，後方要連接過去的時間點、或是表示過去事件的名詞；當作從屬連接詞使用時，則要連接完整的句子。

　recently 為副詞；where 可以當作關係副詞或名詞子句連接詞，其後方皆要連接完整的句子。

**字彙** earlier 稍早　celebrity 名人；名流

**116**

儘管這個地區的經濟不振，好幾家本地商家的代表都報告今年的銷售額亮眼。
(A) even though 就算
(B) in case 萬一
(C) provided that 假如
(D) notwithstanding 儘管

**解析** 空格加上後方的名詞片語為修飾語，故要填入介系詞。(A)、(B)、(C) 皆為連接詞，因此並非答案。(D) notwithstanding（儘管……）為選項中唯一的介系詞，故為正確答案。

**字彙** remarkable 非凡的；卓越的

**117**

馬斯頓釀酒廠額外招募了員工，以應付整個假期間的空前需求。
(A) estimate 估計
(B) advertise 廣告
(C) propose 提議
(D) accommodate 應付

**解析** 本題為動詞詞彙題。根據題意，表達「因應史無前例的需求」較為適當，因此答案為 (D)。

**字彙** brewery 釀酒廠　recruit 招聘；吸收
unprecedented 空前的；史無前例的
throughout 從頭到尾；遍及
estimate 估計；估價

**118**

您的問題會得到立即的關注，而且您將會在三個工作天內接到電話。
(A) prompt 及時的
(B) promptly 及時地
(C) promptness 及時性
(D) more promptly 更迅速地

**解析** 空格用來修飾名詞（attention），要填入形容詞，因此答案為 (A)。

**字彙** business day 工作天

**119**

克萊夫與唐健身中心五年多來專營拳擊與武術。
(A) offered 提供
(B) specialized 專攻
(C) maintained 維持
(D) consisted 組成

**解析** 本題的四個選項皆為動詞，因此要選出最符合題意的單字。但是當中僅有不及物動詞 specialize 可以搭配介系詞 in 一起使用，因此答案為 (B)。

**字彙** fitness center 健身中心
martial arts 武術
specialize 專攻；專營
document 文件

**120**

在大廳遭受的損害修復之前，所有為三角飯店規劃的活動都將延期。
(A) are postponing 正在延期
(B) will be postponed 將被延期
(C) should postpone 應該延期
(D) postponing 延期

**解析** 主詞為 All events，planned . . . Hotel 的部分為修飾主詞的子句，因此空格要填入動詞。postponing 可以當作分詞或動名詞使用，不適合填入；are postponing 和 should postpone 皆為主動語態；will be postponed 則為被動語態。空格後方沒有連接受詞，因此答案為 (B)。

**字彙** main hall 大廳；主廳

**121**

辛克托有限公司在過去 12 個月來，更加侷限在社群媒體廣告上。
(A) narrowly 嚴格地
(B) narrowing 減小
(C) narrower 更小
(D) narrows 減少

**解析** 本題的四個選項為同個單字不同的形態變化，因此要選出適合填入空格的形態。become 和 focused 之間要填入副詞，用來修飾分詞，因此答案為 (A)。narrowing 可以當作分詞或動名詞使用；narrower 為比較級；narrows 為動詞，不能填入副詞的位置。

**字彙** social media 社群媒體
narrowly 嚴格地；狹窄地；勉強地

**122**

這個活動場地夠寬敞，足以容納超過一千名來自全市各地的人。
(A) included 包含的
(B) overall 全部的
(C) insufficient 不足的
(D) spacious 寬敞的

**解析** 本題的四個選項皆為形容詞，因此要透過單字的意思來解題。根據題意，表達「活動場地『寬敞』到足以容納所有人」較為適當，因此答案為 (D)。(A) 的意思為「包含的」、(B) 的意思為「全部的」、(C) 的意思為「不充分的」，皆不符合題意。

**字彙** venue （事件、活動等的）場地
accommodate 容納

**123**

英太汽車公司是否要展開日本的業務，要依它的財政顧問正在進行的可行性報告而定。
(A) Whether 是否
(B) Although 雖然
(C) While 當⋯⋯的時候
(D) Despite 儘管

**解析** 句中有兩個動詞 begins 和 is，因此空格要填入連接詞。空格到 in Japan 的部分扮演句子的主詞角色，因此答案為引導名詞子句的從屬連接詞 (A)。although 和 while 為從屬連接詞；despite 為介系詞。

字彙　trading 生意；貿易；買賣
feasibility 可行性
undertake 從事（尤指耗時或困難的事）
financial consultant 財務顧問；金融顧問

**124**

最佳老饕餐廳正在找一名有強烈學習廚藝意願的學徒。
(A) to learn 為了學習
(B) will learn 將要學習
(C) learning 學習
(D) learns 學習

解析 空格前方為介系詞 in，因此答案為動名詞 (C)。

字彙　apprentice 學徒
culinary art 廚藝；烹調藝術

**125**

市場研究報告指出，一家飯店的乾淨程度會直接影響顧客的滿意度。
(A) clean 乾淨的
(B) cleanly 乾淨地
(C) cleanlier 較乾淨地
(D) cleanliness 乾淨

解析 空格為介系詞的受詞，要填入名詞，因此答案為 (D)。

字彙　customer satisfaction 顧客滿意度

**126**

普瑞克頓有限公司生產的咳嗽藥，是專為成人配製的，不應給兒童服用。
(A) alternatively 或者
(B) partially 部分地
(C) mutually 互相地
(D) exclusively 專門地

解析 本題考的是副詞詞彙，必須透過單字的意思選出最符合題意的副詞。根據題意填入 (D) 最為適當。formulate、manufacture 等表示「生產或製造」的單字，經常搭配 exclusively 一起使用，請特別熟記。

字彙　cough 咳嗽
medication 藥物；藥物治療
manufacture （大量）製造
formulate 配製；制定……的配方
alternatively 或；二者擇一
partially 部分地

mutually 互相；彼此
exclusively 專門地；獨佔地；排外地

**127**

研發特定尺寸與形狀的貨櫃，有助促進整個運輸業的標準化。
(A) standardize 標準化
(B) standardized 標準化的
(C) more standardized 更標準化的
(D) standardization 標準化

解析 準動詞 boost 後方需要連接受詞，空格應填入名詞，因此答案為 (D)。另外補充一點，該句話的主要動詞為 helped，而動詞 help 後方可以省略受詞，直接連接受詞補語，因此其後方可以連接原形動詞 boost。help 可以連接原形動詞或 to 不定詞作為受詞補語。

字彙　standardization 標準化；規格化；統一

**128**

在使用我們的線上繳費系統前，您必須先填寫註冊表。
(A) Before 在……之前
(B) So that 以便
(C) In order 為了
(D) According to 根據

解析 該句話為副詞子句（Before you use our online bill payment system）改寫為分詞構句，因此答案要選 (A)。(B) So that 雖然是從屬連接詞，但是後方一定要連接子句，因此不適合填入；(C) In order 後方要連接 to 不定詞，因此也不正確；(D) According to 為介系詞，按照文法規則，雖然可以連接動名詞形態（using），但是它的意思為「根據……」，並不符合題意。

字彙　fill in 填寫；填好

**129**

要分辨古董家具和仿製品愈來愈困難了。

(A) integrate 使結合
(B) suppose 認為應該
(C) distinguish 分辨
(D) modify 修改

**解析** distinguish A from B（將 A 和 B 區分開來）為慣用片語，建議熟記此用法。因此答案要選 (C)。(A) integrate 的用法為 integrate A into B（將 A 合併為 B）；(B) suppose 的意思為「假定、猜想」；(D) modify 的意思為「修改」，不符合題意。

**字彙** increasingly 逐漸地；越來越多地
authentic 真實的；可信的
imitation 仿製品；模仿

**130**

德里公司打算舉辦公司野餐會，以促進所有員工間的合作與團隊精神。

(A) proceed 繼續進行
(B) facilitate 促進
(C) retrieve 重新得到
(D) convince 說服

**解析** (A) proceed（進行、開展）為不及物動詞，後方要連接介系詞 to 或 with。而空格後方連接受詞，因此並不適合填入；(C) retrieve（重新得到）和 (D) convince（說服）雖然都屬於及物動詞，但是不符合題意。根據題意，表達「為了『促進』合作和團隊精神」較為適當，因此答案為 (B)。

**字彙** cooperation 合作

---

**131-134 備忘錄**

**備忘錄**

收件者：技術支援部全體員工
發件者：菲歐娜・諾頓
主旨：訓練課程

接下來兩個星期，我們將提供數個可選的教育訓練課程，給我們部門的員工。這些課程的目的，是要提供技術支援人員加強他們的專業技術和知識的機會。六小時的工作坊將討論很多主題，包括處理常見的技術問題、滿足特殊的顧客需求，以及改善生產力。儘管這些課程並沒有強制性，但強烈建議員工參加。所有訓練的相關費用都由公司支付。

這些課程是由喬伊斯訓練公司（www.joicetraining.com）所規劃，有興趣的人可以上該公司網站看課程表。

**字彙** objective 目的；目標
enhance 增加（價值、品質、吸引力等）
expertise 專門技術；專門知識
an array of 一系列；大量
address 處理；應付
productivity 生產力；生產率
mandatory 強制的；義務的

**131**

(A) compulsory 強制的
(B) constant 固定的
(C) lengthy 冗長的
(D) optional 非強制的

**解析** 本題要從 (A)「強制的」、(B)「持續的」、(C)「冗長的」、(D)「可供選擇的、非強制的」中選出最符合文意的單字。第四句話提到「該課程並未強制參加」，因此答案要選 (D)。

**132**

(A) Due to 由於
(B) Even though 儘管
(C) So that 以便
(D) While 當……的時候

**解析** 空格後方連接子句（S + V），因此要填入連接詞。(A) Due to 為介系詞，因此並非答案；副詞子句表達「該課程並非強制性」，而主要子句表達「強烈建議參加」，兩句話相互對比，因此適合填入的從屬連接詞為 (B) Even though（儘管；雖然）；So that 的意思為「以便⋯⋯；為了⋯⋯」；While 的意思為「當⋯⋯的時候、然而」。

**133**

(A) were covered 被支付
(B) will have covered 將已支付
(C) will be covered 將被支付
(D) have covered 已支付

**解析** 本題考的是動詞的時態和語態。空格後方並未連接受詞，因此要填入動詞的被動語態，應從 (A) 和 (C) 當中選出答案。開頭提到「往後兩週」將提供教育訓練課程，表示相關費用「將會由公司負擔」，因此答案為未來式 (C)。

**134**

(A) 我們為此事可能造成的不便致歉。
(B) 有興趣的人可以上該公司網站看課程表。
(C) 只有那些已上完一門課的主管可以得到證書。
(D) 謝謝你幫忙解決了這個非常有挑戰性的狀況。

**解析** 空格前方提到公司名稱「Joice Training」，因此答案要選 (B)，表示「可以在該公司的網站上查看課程表」。

**135-138 新聞稿**

洛杉磯——托康金融公司宣布將在本月底前，推出一項給散戶的新投資諮詢服務。這項新服務將結合專業顧問的專業知識與便利的行動應用程式。

它是這樣運作的。用戶應該先下載一個應用程式到他們的智慧型手機裡。在回答了一串問題，並輸入個人金融資料後，金融顧問會和用戶聯絡，為每一個獨特狀況提供客製化的指導。如果用戶有進一步的問題，可以不分日夜隨時和指派給他們的顧問聊聊。

這項服務的費用預期大約是每年管理資產的 0.5%。用戶的資產必須留在托康金融的帳戶內，那裡有數百種投資方案可供選擇。

**字彙** advisory 諮詢的；顧問的
retail client 散客；散戶
combine 結合
expertise 專門知識；專門技術
convenience 方便；便利的設施
a series of 一系列；一連串
customized 客製化的；訂做的
assigned 分配的；分派的
around the clock 全天候；日以繼夜地

**135**

(A) waive 放棄
(B) imitate 模仿
(C) unveil 推出
(D) cancel 取消

**解析** 本題要從 (A)「放棄」、(B)「模仿」、(C)「公開」、(D)「取消」中選出最符合文意的單字。本文內容為業者介紹新的服務，因此答案為 (C) unveil（公開）。

**136**

(A) profession 職業
(B) professional 專業的
(C) professionally 專業地
(D) professionalism 專業性

**解析** 冠詞（a）和名詞（advisor）之間要填入形容詞，用來修飾名詞，因此答案為 (B) professional（專業的）。

**137**

(A) 用戶應該先下載一個應用程式到他們的智慧型手機裡。
(B) 顧客擔心個人資料外洩。
(C) 請瀏覽我們的網站，查看更多產品。
(D) 電腦軟體近來大幅發展。

**解析** 空格前方提到要開始說明步驟，且後方也是步驟的相關說明，因此答案要選 (A)。

**138**

(A) expects 預期
(B) expected 預期了
(C) is expected 被預期
(D) has expected 已預期

解析 本題考的是動詞的變化。費用（The cost）為被預估的對象，因此空格應填入動詞的被動語態，答案為 (C) is expected。

### 139-142 電子郵件

收件者：坎培拉財政局
寄件者：布瑞特‧凌
日期：8 月 12 日
主旨：合法歸檔

各位：

　　我寫信來是關於政府財政局的一則新聞與最新消息。顯然，有一條新法要求所有稅金發票和公司文件要以電子檔傳送。

　　我知道我們有些人已經熟悉 www.canberracorp/govfiling 的線上系統，而且已經發現該系統相當複雜。首先，你需要找到要輸入資料的正確網頁。然後輸入密碼，確定你輸入正確的查詢代碼，如此你個人的詳細資料才能鍵入正確的位置。

　　如有任何關於這個步驟的問題，請以電子郵件和我聯絡。

誠摯地，
布瑞特‧凌

字彙 Finance Department 財政局；財政部
　　legal 法律的；合法的
　　filing 歸檔；存檔　tax invoice 稅金發票
　　corporation 大公司；集團公司
　　electronically 透過電子手段；以電子方式
　　familiar with 熟悉的；熟知的
　　complex 複雜的　access 使用；接近
　　reference 參考；查閱　via 經由；透過
　　relevant 有關的；正確的
　　impose 強制實行；強行收取

**139**

(A) Additionally 此外
(B) Initially 起初地
(C) Conversely 相反地
(D) Apparently 顯然地

解析 空格前方表示將告知最新消息，後方應提出消息為何，因此答案要選 (D)，表示「事實上顯然為……」。

**140**

(A) 首先，你需要找到要輸入資料的正確網頁。
(B) 你應該印出報名表。
(C) 你可以修習線上課程以漸漸習慣。
(D) 除非你遵守稅務法規，否則可能會被處以罰款。

解析 空格後方的句子以 Then 開頭，表示要輸入密碼，因此前方填入表示「輸入資訊前先找出相關頁面」的內容較為適當，答案要選 (A)。

**141**

(A) their 他們的
(B) your 你的
(C) his 他的
(D) my 我的

解析 本題考的是輸入個人資訊的人。空格所在句子的前一句話為「你要先找出相關頁面」，這句話的主詞為 you，因此空格填入 (B) your 較為適當。

**142**

(A) procedure 步驟
(B) research 研究
(C) report 報告
(D) problem 問題

解析 最後一句話之前都在說明在電腦上輸入個人資訊的「步驟」，因此選 (A) 最為適當。

## 143-146 電子郵件

收件者：西西莉亞・費利狄諾
　　　　<cferidino@hmail.net>
寄件者：達西・柯爾 <dkerr@homedecor.com>
主旨：您的來稿
日期：6 月 10 日

親愛的費利狄諾女士：

　　謝謝您投稿到我們的刊物。您的文章〈如何讓你家看起來更好〉將會刊登在七月號的《家居裝潢》，只有小小的修改一下。您寄給我們的兩張照片會搭配文章刊出。正如您的合約所載，您的作品將收到 300 元稿費。我記得您說過想要讓稿費直接存入您的支票帳戶。如果是這樣，請和我們的付款部核對您的帳戶資料。

　　和您合作總是很愉快。如果您對未來的刊物有其他的構想，請告訴我。

誠摯地，
達西・柯爾
總編輯
家居裝潢

**字彙** submission 投稿；提出
issue （報刊）期號　accompany 伴隨
as indicated 如……所示
deposit 存放（銀行等）
checking account 支票戶頭
renegotiate 重新談判　verify 核對；證實

### 143

(A) publication 刊物
(B) photographer 攝影師
(C) council 議會
(D) exhibition 展覽

**解析** 本題要選出符合文意的單字。空格後方句子提到「預計將你的文章刊登在七月號」，表示與「出版、出刊」有關，因此答案為 (A)。

### 144

(A) appeared 發表
(B) will appear 將發表
(C) to appear 為了發表
(D) has appeared 已發表

**解析** 本題考的是動詞的時態。本文撰寫的日期為 6 月 10 日，這個時間七月號尚未出刊，因此答案要選未來式 (B)。

### 145

(A) 合約的條款可以在兩年後重新談。
(B) 如果是這樣，請和我們的付款部核對您的帳戶資料。
(C) 這是個調薪的大好機會。
(D) 因此，我們目前無法處理您的帳款。

**解析** 空格前方提到對方說過想要直接匯到他的帳戶，因此空格應詢問對方的帳戶資訊，答案為 (B)。

### 146

(A) adding 增加
(B) additional 額外的
(C) addition 附加
(D) additionally 額外地

**解析** 空格位在動詞（have）和受詞（ideas）之間，應填入形容詞，用來修飾名詞。因此答案可能為分詞形的形容詞 adding（添加的）、或是一般形容詞 additional（額外的）。根據文意，表示「額外的想法」較為適當，因此答案為 (B)。

## PART 7
P. 077

## 147-148 資訊

　　以下幾頁說明如何操作您的新坦維克印表機，以及如何將它連接到您家裡的電子裝置。如果這些說明有任何部分讓您看不懂，請在上班時間打電話給坦維克客服人員。客服中心及所有的聯絡資料按字母順序列在第四頁。

**字彙** illustrate （用圖、實例等）說明
work 操作；開動
electronic device 電子裝置
instructions 用法說明、操作指南
contact detail 聯絡資料；聯絡方式
list 把……編列成表、列舉
alphabetically 照字母順序排列地
return policy 退貨規定　clarify 澄清；闡明

**147** 這個資訊最可能出現在哪裡？
(A) 在使用手冊上
(B) 在產品型錄上
(C) 在電話簿上
(D) 在員工手冊上

**148** 根據資訊，坦維克的專員能如何協助？
(A) 透過解釋退貨規定
(B) 透過處理發票
(C) 透過安排撥打服務電話
(D) 透過說明讓操作指南變得清楚

### 147-148 小冊子摘錄

**拉瑪斯遺產中心**

　　拉瑪斯遺產中心保有超過一百萬件與本地文化歷史相關的書籍、照片和手工藝品。中心提供歷史上著名且有特殊意義事件的資料與資源，這些事件塑造了我們的傳統。除了包羅萬象的歷史書籍與信件收藏外，中心還擁有來自其他社區和國家的精選照片與影像，它們影響了我們的遺產。我們收藏的大量出版品與檔案，本地居民，以及觀光客和遊客也可以查看。中心的歷史區包含一些古代文物，還有一個包含數千張照片的攝影展，其中有些是本地人所拍攝。我們可以提供任何照片的影本，只收取少許費用。想要取用我們檔案的人，提出要求即可安排時間與查閱協助。

字彙 heritage 遺產　artifact 手工藝品
historic 歷史上著名的；歷史上有重大意義的
significant 有意義的；意義深長的
shape 塑造
comprehensive 包羅萬象的；詳盡的
archive 檔案
access 使用某物的權利或機會
display 陳列；展覽
charge （尤指對某一服務或活動）收費
replica 複製品；摹本
reprint 翻印；重印；再版

**149** 這些資訊與什麼有關？
(A) 一個社區活動
(B) 一間研究圖書館
(C) 一個本地攝影課程
(D) 一個遊客服務中心

**150** 可以購買什麼東西？
(A) 傳統禮品
(B) 複製的文件
(C) 雜誌文章的影本
(D) 翻印的照片

### 151-152 訊息串

**山姆・菲克西茲**　上午 9 時 29 分
嗨，蕾妮，新進員工歡迎會的案子進行得如何？

**蕾妮・卡莫**　上午 9 時 30 分
我找到一家可以做你要求的餐點的外燴業者。而且，業者可以在我們的預算之內做。

**山姆・菲克西茲**　上午 9 時 32 分
聽起來很棒。妳找到演講嘉賓了嗎？

**蕾妮・卡莫**　上午 9 時 33 分
本地的一位企業家和我們一位董事很熟，已經同意演講。

**山姆・菲克西茲**　上午 9 時 34 分
所以，看起來妳差不多都處理好了。

**蕾妮・卡莫**　上午 9 時 35 分
並沒有，我們還需要準備視聽設備。也許，我現在該打給零售商。

**山姆・菲克西茲**　上午 9 時 37 分
我想妳應該要。

發送

字彙 entrepreneur 企業家
acquaintance 熟人；相識的人
audiovisual 視聽的

**151** 關於歡迎會，可由文中得知什麼？
(A) 一位董事會成員將是演講者。
(B) 食物的花費不會超過預期。
(C) 設備已設置好。
(D) 卡莫女士是新員工。

**152** 上午 9 時 37 分時，菲克西茲先生寫道：「我想妳應該要」，他的意思是什麼？
(A) 他想要卡莫女士去拿設備。
(B) 他認同歡迎會是個好主意。
(C) 他想要卡莫女士聯絡商家。
(D) 他必需立刻結束對話。

## 153-155 雜誌目錄表

> **字彙** weight loss 減重　effectively 有效地
> raw （食物）生的、未經烹煮的
> editor 編輯　essential 必要的；重要的
> routine 慣例；一套固定動作
> home grown 自家種植的
> cosmetic surgery 整型手術
> low fat 低脂
> preview 預覽；（電視節目或電影的）預告

**153** 這本雜誌關注的是什麼？
(A) 鍛鍊與運動
(B) 園藝與農事
(C) 健康與美麗
(D) 食物與烹飪

**154** 根據目錄表，誰最近出國旅行？
(A) 葛瑞格女士
(B) 斯托娃女士
(C) 瑪薩女士
(D) 蕭女士

**155** 最可能在雜誌的哪裡找到食譜？
(A) 第 15 頁
(B) 第 20 頁
(C) 第 25 頁
(D) 第 45 頁

## 156-158 布告

### 布蘭瑞莎才藝競賽

　　你有別人想看到的才藝嗎？那就來報名布蘭瑞莎才藝競賽。

**布蘭瑞莎才藝競賽是什麼？**

　　這項競賽是由亞歷克斯·波登所創辦，他是布蘭瑞莎的居民，也是高街上紅獅酒吧的老闆。他當時正在尋找演員在他的酒吧表演。競賽的優勝者會獲得100鎊獎金，以展開他們的演藝生涯。例如，去年的冠軍在英國各地場場爆滿的地方演出。冠軍將由當地居民以及來自聖安德魯音樂劇學院的代表，在 8 月 21 日於布蘭瑞莎社區活動中心選出。

**我有資格嗎？**

　　競賽開放給每一位蘇格蘭人參加，無論年齡、地位或能力。歡迎業餘和半職業性的藝術家參加。也歡迎那些往年曾參加過比賽的人報名。

**我要如何報名？**

　　報名表必需以實體郵件或電子郵件在七月二日前送出。報名表和參賽細節可以上我們的網站：www.blenratha/sc/entry_form 查看。如果你有任何問題，哈米許·羅斯科是你的主要聯絡人，電話 (050) 555-0258。如果你想推薦自己成為評審團的一員，請聯絡我們的評估專員布蘭達·萊斯，電話 (050) 555-0259。

> **字彙** talent contest 才藝競賽
> public house 酒吧；酒館
> venue （事件、活動等的）發生地
> competition 比賽　reward 獎賞、獎勵
> eligible 有資格的；具備條件的
> regardless of 不管、不顧
> semi-professional 半職業性的
> entry 參賽；參賽作品
> put forward 提出；推薦
> judging panel 評審團；評審委員
> evaluation 評估；估價
> coordinator 協調者　solicit 請求
> inquire about 詢問；打聽

**156** 關於紅獅，文中說了什麼？
(A) 它每週主辦才藝秀。
(B) 它位於布蘭瑞莎城外。
(C) 它的老闆是亞歷克斯‧波登。
(D) 它位在聖安德魯音樂劇學院隔壁。

**157** 根據布告，為什麼有人要聯絡萊斯女士？
(A) 為了要求延後截止日期
(B) 為了志願協助判定比賽的冠軍人選
(C) 為了確認出席
(D) 為了詢問正式的規定

**158** 在標示 [1]、[2]、[3] 和 [4] 的地方，下列句子最適合放在何處？
「也歡迎那些往年曾參加過比賽的人報名。」
(A) [1]
(B) [2]
(C) [3]
(D) [4]

### 159-162 文章報導

#### 市內不要再有反社會行為

葛瑞絲‧嘉蘭托 撰

為了努力減少安特比街頭的反社會行為，市議會打算改變合法飲酒的時間。「我們的城市在夜裡最吵鬧、最混亂，」安特比市議會發言人亞魯巴‧查莉斯說，「那是因為本地人和觀光客都前往鬧區享受那裡的娛樂設施，包括酒吧、夜總會和賭場。當旅客進城時，他們通常搭乘免費公車，這樣他們就不用擔心會酒駕。這就導致街頭的亂象日益加劇。

目前，某些酒吧從晚上 6 到 8 時半價供應酒類，而有些酒吧整個晚上都供應廉價酒類。「這狀況必需改變，」查莉斯女士說，「我們想要像其他城市的作法一樣，引進公定價格體系，讓每個地方的價格都一樣。」

如果提案的變動生效，將是最近採用的眾多改變之一。五月時，一項新的卡片系統限制每人在晚間 6 點至 8 點間購買的酒品數量。卡片在門口發放，每次買酒就會蓋個章。

**字彙** anti-social 反社會的；擾亂社會的
ease 減少；減輕　rowdy 混亂的；粗暴的
spokesperson 發言人
alike 相同的、相像的
head to 朝特定方向行進
participate in 參與；參加
entertainment 娛樂、娛樂表演
lead to 導致、引起　disruption 擾亂；中斷
go into effect 開始生效、開始實施
stamp 蓋章於　surcharge 額外費用
disorderly 混亂的；無秩序的
measure 措施；手段

**159** 關於安特比，可由文中得知什麼？
(A) 它有太多娛樂場所。
(B) 它的酒類必須額外付費。
(C) 它遇到脫序行為的麻煩。
(D) 它有酒駕的問題。

**160** 市議會正在考慮什麼事？
(A) 提高酒類價格
(B) 打造新的停車區
(C) 減少酒吧的容許人數
(D) 引進保全人員

**161** 安特比最近發生什麼事？
(A) 有些鬧區的商店被破壞。
(B) 要取得酒吧的營業執照愈來愈困難。
(C) 開了更多間酒吧和俱樂部。
(D) 採用監督酒客的新措施。

**162** 在標示 [1]、[2]、[3] 和 [4] 的地方，下列句子最適合放在何處？
「卡片在門口發放，每次買酒就會蓋個章。」
(A) [1]
(B) [2]
(C) [3]
(D) [4]

## 163-165 線上聊天

**保羅・卡本特**      上午 11 時 35 分
紐馬克公司要舉辦員工感謝活動，想要我們供應開胃菜、主菜、飲料和甜點。問題是，時間是這個星期五晚上，但我們那天下午已經接了兩場活動，晚上還有另一場。

**肯・德比**      上午 11 時 37 分
我們會忙死！你要我打電話給工作人員，看誰有空嗎？

**保羅・卡本特**      上午 11 時 38 分
請打。

**米亞・秦**      上午 11 時 39 分
食物呢？沒有太多時間可以準備所有的東西。

**肯・德比**      上午 11 時 40 分
我們可以在星期三和星期四先準備一些東西。

**保羅・卡本特**      上午 11 時 41 分
我想沒辦法。食物必需新鮮。紐馬克是我們最好的客戶之一，而且該公司要求很高。

**米亞・秦**      上午 11 時 42 分
讓廚房人員提早上班並加班怎麼樣？

**肯・德比**      上午 11 時 43 分
我會和丹談談，看看我們能否說服他們這麼做。

**保羅・卡本特**      上午 11 時 45 分
他們必須這麼做。

**米亞・秦**      上午 11 時 46 分
菜單敲定了嗎？

**保羅・卡本特**      上午 11 時 47 分
我已處理了。我會以電子郵件傳一份紐馬克的合約，裡面有你所需要的一切活動資訊。

發送

**字彙** appetizer 開胃菜　entrée 主菜
demanding 要求高的、苛求的
convince 使信服；說服

**163** 訊息撰寫人最可能在哪種公司工作？
(A) 餐廳
(B) 外燴公司
(C) 雜貨店
(D) 飯店

**164** 訊息撰寫人為什麼需要更多工作人員？
(A) 一位客戶要求額外的服務。
(B) 有份訂單未及時完成。
(C) 他們的工作時程表中加了一場活動。
(D) 時程安排上出了差錯。

**165** 在 11 時 45 分時，當卡本時先生寫下：「他們必須這麼做」，他的意思是什麼？
(A) 他要求廚房人員加班。
(B) 他想要他們更細心服務客戶。
(C) 他沒有時間跟丹解釋狀況。
(D) 他需要服務人員提早上班。

## 166-167 電子郵件

**收件者：** 馬克・藍儂
**寄件者：** 瑪格莉特・金
**日期：** 9 月 10 日星期六
**主旨：** 小問題

親愛的馬克：

　　我知道，你要求我幫你看看星期一下午會議要用的筆記，並給你一些建議強化你的簡報。但當我今天晚上查看我的電子郵件時，我發現我給你的是我辦公室的郵件信箱，而不是我私人的信箱。今天晚上已經太晚了，我現在來不及看，但因為我們早餐時會在自助餐廳碰到，而我知道你在早餐前會查看你公司的電子郵件，所以，你可以就在那裡把筆記給我，我應該有足夠的時間，在你開會前看。好好享受夜晚時光。

祝你安好
瑪格莉特・金

**166** 金女士遇到什麼問題？
(A) 她遺失了藍儂先生的筆記。
(B) 她沒時間和藍儂先生見面。
(C) 她給了錯誤的聯絡資料。
(D) 她忘了查看她的電子郵件信箱。

**167** 金女士要求藍儂先生做什麼？
(A) 親自把資料交給她
(B) 請另一個員工幫忙
(C) 把文件傳真過去
(D) 早上去她的辦公室

## 168-171 傳單

你是否最近剛搬到邁阿密？
來參加我們的環境介紹：在邁阿密趴趴走

### 簡報時間表

| 上午 10 時 | 抵達城市——大眾運輸工具的選擇（212 室） |
|---|---|

| 上午 11 時<br>在邁阿密租一間公寓或平房（212 室） | 上午 11 時<br>和財務及銀行打交道（206 室） |
|---|---|
| 中午 12 時<br>認識你的鄰居（208 室） | 中午 12 時<br>在邁阿密找工作（206 室） |

| 下午 1 時　走逛邁阿密——概述本地的活動與景點（204 室） |
|---|

請注意，有些簡報的時間相衝，因此你必須決定參加哪一個會對你最有利。關於大眾運輸工具與找到合適住處的演講非常受歡迎，所以為了確保你的座位，請早點來。

這些演講都以英文發表，但會有法文、西班牙文和阿拉伯文的紙本翻譯。有食物和飲料可以購買。

在最後一場簡報之後，你將受邀參加主要景點的導覽。導覽將由一位邁阿密海灘市的長期住民和一位適應委員會成員帶領。更多資訊，請上 www.miamiwelcoming.com。

**字彙** orientation 適應；熟悉；（對新人的）情況介紹
presentation 簡報；提出
public transport 大眾運輸；公共交通
rent 租用；出租　condominium 公寓；大樓
finance 財政；金融　banking 銀行業
get to know 逐漸熟悉；逐漸了解
round-up 簡報；概述
attraction 吸引力；有吸引力的事物
clash 發生衝突；抵觸
time-wise 就時間而言；在時間方面
accommodation 住處；膳宿
translate 翻譯　transcript 文字紀錄；紙本
resident 居民；住戶

**168** 這份廣告傳單最可能為誰而設計？
(A) 邁阿密市的官員
(B) 去美國的觀光客
(C) 邁阿密觀光委員會成員
(D) 新近來到這個地區的居民

**169** 最受歡迎的簡報在哪裡進行？
(A) 212 室
(B) 208 室
(C) 206 室
(D) 204 室

**170** 關於邁阿密適應委員會，可由文中得知什麼？
(A) 它提供訪客免費交通工具。
(B) 它很快會提供更多服務。
(C) 它在很多地方都有辦公室。
(D) 它提供數種不同語言的資料。

**171** 根據傳單，在簡報之後，參加者可以做什麼？
(A) 繼續遊覽城市
(B) 詢問會員卡的詳情
(C) 預約公眾活動的座位
(D) 享受免費午餐

## 172-175 文章報導

七月十五日——提供逼真影像給大受讚揚的「保持活躍」電視活動的 24 軸公司，獲得國際西佛獎的提名。20 多年來，這個獎項一直在獎勵已出版的優秀攝影作品與平面插圖作品。從超過 3 千名參賽者中脫穎而出，24 軸公司是有史以來唯一一家位在喀拉蚩而獲得提名的攝影工作室。八月二十日在德國科隆舉行的典禮上，將宣布今年的西佛獎得主。

「我們對這次提名極為自豪，這是對公司高標準專業精神、專業知識和創造力的讚揚，」公司創辦人兼執行長阿斯蘭、米尼許說道。

西佛獎的評審由六位來自全世界各廣告公司的高階主管所組成。他們的講評指出，24 軸是因他們在攝影作品集中的品質與創新而獲選。

「我們從野生動植物到體育活動、人與大自然都拍，」米尼許先生繼續說：「而且，我們和客戶保持聯絡，以確保最後的作品比他們所能想像的更好。」

除了獲得提名帶來的名望外，24 軸的業務也已增加，同時也吸引更多人關注。當被提名名單宣布後，工作室被來自感興趣團體的詢問淹沒，都想委任工作給他們。「我們唯一能滿足這些增量需求的方法，就是僱用更多專業攝影師和技術人員，而這也正是我們下一步要做的事，」米尼許先生說。

更多關於 24 軸的資訊，可上 www.axis24. co.pk。關於西佛獎的詳細資料請瀏覽 www. schifferprize.org。

**字彙** acclaimed 受到讚揚的　nominate 提名
illustration 插圖；圖解
entrant 參賽者；新會員
tribute 致敬；稱頌
professionalism 專業精神；職業精神
expertise 專門技術；專門知識
creativity 創造力　founder 創辦人
judge 評審；法官
comprise 由……組成；包含
top executive 最高階主管
innovation 創新　portfolio 代表作選輯
wildlife 野生動植物　liaise 保持聯絡
end product 成品；最終結果
aside from 除……以外
prestige 聲望；威信
profile 大眾的注意；外觀；形象
nominee 被提名人
inundated 應接不暇的；淹沒的
commission 委任；委託
meet demand 滿足需求
prestigious 有名望的；聲望很高的

**172** 這篇文章的目的是什麼？
(A) 為了突顯一家公司的成就
(B) 為了描述一位知名藝術家的作品
(C) 為了邀請新人參加攝影比賽
(D) 為了提名一位行政主管參加一個獎項

**173** 關於西佛獎，可由文中得知什麼？
(A) 它是負有聲望的獎項，影響力遍及全球。
(B) 它以前曾有來自喀拉蚩的公司得獎。
(C) 它是由單獨一人所創辦。
(D) 它是首度頒給一家攝影公司。

**174** 關於 24 軸的攝影範疇，未提及下例何者？
(A) 體育活動
(B) 大型廣告牌
(C) 大自然
(D) 人

**175** 根據本文，米尼許先生打算做什麼？
(A) 增加公關預算
(B) 開另一間攝影工作室
(C) 僱用更多員工
(D) 參加在喀拉蚩的一場典禮

### 176-180 網頁與電子郵件

| 首頁 | 聯絡我們 | 下訂單 | 顧客評論 |
| --- | --- | --- | --- |

廣告選熱那亞藝術：熱那亞藝術是歷史悠久的網站，追蹤人數將近 2 萬人，他們因為本站提供可靠、詳盡的熱那亞地區娛樂與景點資訊而上我們的網站。

我們網頁上的廣告可以有下列的顯示方式：

| 格式 1 | 格式 2 |
| --- | --- |
| 垂直橫幅出現在網頁的側邊，右邊或左邊均可。無法顯示視聽效果。 | 中型廣告出現在網頁開頭的中間處。文字可以搭配一個圖像和一支影片。 |
| **格式 3** | **格式 4** |
| 橫過網頁最上方展開的水平標題橫幅。可以包含聲音。 | 我們最大的廣告，一個框起來的廣告，最多包含 10 張照片、影片、聲音和文字。 |

要購買廣告，請聯絡艾洛絲‧樂君 elejeune@artsingenoa.com。

寄件者：英格麗‧佛羅倫
　　　　[admin@florensgallery.com]
收件者：艾洛絲‧樂君
　　　　[elejeune@artsingenoa.com]
主旨：佛羅倫斯藝廊的廣告
日期：4 月 23 日

親愛的樂君女士：

　　我寫信來是要詢問我要再次在熱那亞藝術上刊登廣告的事。我想要再一次選擇框型廣告。我要你們使用我們上次用過的照片和音檔。不過，我需要修改文字。我會把我想要放進去的文字寄給你，那是關於即將舉行的展覽。可以讓你們製作部確定會把廣告中的文字特別標出來以吸引注意嗎？此外，你可以告知我最多幾個字嗎？

誠摯地
英格麗‧佛羅倫
佛羅倫斯藝廊所有人

**176** 樂君女士在哪裡工作？
　　(A) 在一家廣告公司
　　(B) 在一家市場研究公司
　　(C) 在熱那亞的一家藝廊
　　(D) 在一個藝術相關網站

**177** 關於格式 1，文中說了什麼？
　　(A) 它不允許視覺資料。
　　(B) 它是最貴的。
　　(C) 它可以含最多文字。
　　(D) 它可以很快做好。

**178** 佛羅倫斯女士對哪一種廣告格式最有興趣？
　　(A) 格式 1
　　(B) 格式 2
　　(C) 格式 3
　　(D) 格式 4

**179** 關於佛羅倫斯藝廊，可由文中得知什麼？
　　(A) 它正在整修。
　　(B) 它最近展出一場新展覽。
　　(C) 它將閉館到進一步通知為止。
　　(D) 它以前在熱那亞藝術登過廣告。

**180** 關於文字，佛羅倫女士問了什麼？
　　(A) 它的字體應該多大
　　(B) 它的長度應該有多長
　　(C) 哪一種格式最好
　　(D) 刊登文字的費用多少

**181-185 廣告與表格**

### 阿尼斯頓果農
水果與蔬菜
YL3 桑默塞特郡威斯特利亞路 87 號
(013) 90 72 65 58
www.aniston.co.uk

如果您想種自己的水果和蔬菜，就來阿尼斯頓果農。我們有大量來自全世界的農作物和種子可供選擇。來一趟橫跨我們佔地 6 英畝的營運農場之旅，再決定您想要種哪種水果和蔬菜。我們提供 4 種類型的產品：

1 區：長在地上的水果和蔬菜
2 區：長在樹上的水果
3 區：根類蔬菜
4 區：來自全世界的異國水果和蔬菜

我們的園丁會講多種語言，而且很樂意回答任何關於種植、培育和採摘水果與蔬菜的最佳做法的問題。

想找有異國情調的不同作物嗎？在入口處洽詢我們的總園丁，他會給您看我們的國際農產品。

在您選完後，阿尼斯頓果園可以把您的貨送到英國的任何地方。

### 阿尼斯頓果園訂單

| 種類 | 數量 |
| --- | --- |
| 1. 紅甜椒 | 100 |
| 2. 青辣椒 | 100 |
| 3. 果樹：蘋果 | 1 |
| 4. 覆盆子苗 | 300 |
| 5. 草莓苗 | 200 |

**顧客姓名：**安琪拉‧史達勒德
**送貨日期：**三月十二日
**地址：**桑默塞特郡約維爾市希爾萊斯路 26 號
**電話：**(01398) 319553

填完訂單後，請交到服務櫃。助理會查看您的訂單、回答問題，並確認該品項是否有存貨。顧客應會在下訂後一星期內收到貨品。種苗或種樹如有受損，必須在貨送達後一天內回報。

| 字彙 | root vegetable 根類蔬菜 |

exotic 異國情調的；外國產的
nurture 培育；培植　ship 運送；裝運
raspberry 覆盆子　hand in 交出
damaged 受損的；損害的
orchard 果園；果林
flourish （植物等）茂盛
geographical 地理的；地理學的
origin 起源；產地　plus 加上；另有

**181** 關於阿尼斯頓果園，可由文中得知什麼？
(A) 它允許顧客探索果園。
(B) 它通常把外國蔬菜運送到全球。
(C) 它大部份的產品會賣給當地農場和果園。
(D) 它會換掉任何無法長得茂盛的果樹。

**182** 根據廣告，員工可以給顧客什麼資訊？
(A) 為異國農產品選擇最佳食譜
(B) 每一種水果和蔬菜的原始產地
(C) 大量訂購的價格折扣
(D) 如何種植水果和蔬菜的建議

**183** 顧客如何詢問特別的植物？
(A) 和總園丁談
(B) 郵寄不同的申請書給公司
(C) 上果園的網站
(D) 把訂單交給園藝專家

**184** 果園的員工要去哪裡找史達勒德女士訂購的大部分商品？
(A) 1 區
(B) 2 區
(C) 3 區
(D) 4 區

**185** 根據訂單，史達勒德女士必需在 3 月 13 日前做什麼？
(A) 通知公司她所購買商品的任何問題
(B) 支付她的果樹訂單加上運費
(C) 退還任何誤送的多餘植物
(D) 種植她所購買的品項

### 186-190 網頁、表單與文章

活動名稱：夏季沙雕賽
地點：新斯科西亞馬奎斯海灘
日期：八月十五日到十八日
聯絡人：傑瑞米·陳
關於：這項如今已邁入第五年的年度活動，吸引了來自世界各地超過 80 名職業與業餘選手，包含個人與團體項目，前一年有大約一萬二千名遊客前來參加。這項比賽已成為新斯科西亞最受歡迎的海灘活動之一。馬奎斯海灘是加拿大這個區域最大的沙灘之一，距離哈利法克斯約 40 分鐘的路程。除了沙雕之外，這個四天的慶祝活動還有音樂表演、成排的小吃攤和開給遊客的沙雕課。免費入場，但停車費 10 元。

#### 第五屆年度夏季沙雕賽優勝者
*個人賽

| 名次 | 姓名 | 國家 | 作品名稱 |
| --- | --- | --- | --- |
| 第一名 | 瑞秋·莫塔夫 | 澳洲 | 綠色美人魚 |
| 第二名 | 梅琳達·葛拉漢 | 紐西蘭 | 海豚群 |
| 第三名 | 賈馬里·尤南達 | 美國 | 赫斯特城堡 |
| 第四名 | 約翰·彼德斯 | 巴西 | 海盜船 |
| 第五名 | 吉邁爾·古蒙德 | 加拿大 | 海洋生物 |

#### 哈利法克斯有什麼新鮮事？
艾琳·陶 撰

年度夏季沙雕賽於上週舉行，而這是和夏季道別的完美方式。由於天公特別作美，遊客人數比前一年倍增。

個人與團體賽項目都吸引雕塑家來參加。貝殼、海草、漂流木和其他天然材質融入某些具有傳奇色彩的雕塑中，它們描繪了從海洋生物到不拘形式的設計都有的一切事物。

來自澳洲的瑞秋·莫塔夫以她裝飾著大量海洋玻璃的綠色美人魚雕塑，打敗獲得二次冠軍的紐西蘭選手梅琳達·葛拉漢。所有的雕塑都很棒，但我個人最愛的是海盜船。使用漂流木做為雕塑的底座是我從未見過的做法。

觀眾也可以加入其中。沒有參賽的雕塑專家帶領一堂免費課程，所有人都可以參加。這課程和娛樂節目以及美食，提供了享受夏末的完美方式。

**186** 關於參賽選手,可由文中得知什麼?

　　(A) 他們全是業餘者。

　　(B) 他們要事先報名。

　　(C) 他們自己認識陳先生。

　　(D) 他們來自不同的國家。

**187** 在文章中,第二段、第一行的「drew」一字,意思最接近下列何者?

　　(A) 撤回

　　(B) 吸引

　　(C) 轉移

　　(D) 描繪

**188** 關於今年的活動,可由文中得知什麼?

　　(A) 有超過二萬名遊客。

　　(B) 參加者每人要繳 10 元。

　　(C) 比去年活動的時間要長。

　　(D) 這是第一次在馬奎斯海灘舉行。

**189** 關於萬拉漢女士,文中說了什麼?

　　(A) 她在她的沙雕作品中使用貝殼。

　　(B) 她教授沙雕課。

　　(C) 她之前贏過比賽。

　　(D) 她最近搬到紐西蘭。

**190** 陶女士最喜歡誰的雕塑品?

　　(A) 莫塔夫女士

　　(B) 尤南達先生

　　(C) 彼德斯先生

　　(D) 古蒙德女士

## 191-195 布告、電子郵件與信件

**轉介熟人到松頂金融,大家都得利!***

　　我們感謝你對松頂金融的信任。身為忠實客戶,你得以選用我們的全系列金融產品,並得到我們最好的價格。

　　為了表達我們誠摯的謝意,你每轉介一位朋友或家人來我們這裡開戶,我們就送給你 20 元。我們也會在他們於松頂線上儲蓄帳戶或松頂投資經紀帳戶首次存入 200 元以上時,立即送給他們 20 元。他們只需要上 www.PineTop.com 註冊,並使用優惠代碼 PP880。

*這項優惠只有信用良好的忠實客戶可享有。被介紹人必需是新客戶。松頂金融的現有或過去的員工不能參加。

---

收件者:米蘭達．羅佩茲
　　　　<mlopez@networkone.com>
寄件者:約翰．尼可斯
　　　　<jnichols@networkone.com>
主旨:松頂金融獎金
日期:2 月 2 日

---

嗨,米蘭達:

　　我記得,妳在擔心如何開始妳的退休儲蓄計畫。嗯,這是有可能幫助妳的產品。只要在松頂金融開戶,就會送給妳 20 元!我使用他們的服務,到現在已將近六年,只有一些令人滿意的經驗。他們的線上支票與儲蓄帳戶很安全且便於使用。

　　隨信附上一張解釋如何註冊的傳單。

祝好,
約翰

---

米蘭達．羅佩茲
麻州 50084 塞勒姆郡新港路 201 號
4 月 25 日

---

親愛的羅佩茲女士:

　　歡迎加入松頂金融。我們在四月十五日開通了您名下的松頂線上儲蓄帳戶。請查看附件的合約條款以及收費表。

　　為了感謝您的加入,我們會在您的戶頭存入 20 元,錢應該會在您開戶後的 30 天內入帳。

　　您可以上 www.PineTop.com 登入你的帳戶。請輸入您的帳號和下方的臨時密碼。一旦登入後,您應該重新設定你的使用者名稱和密碼。

帳號：78082210
臨時密碼：jj99-Odff-8822-ss

如果您有任何問題，歡迎隨時打給我們 1-600-555-6690。

誠摯地，
琳恩・卡多娜
新帳戶服務代表

字彙 **refer** 介紹
**acquaintance** 熟人；相識的人
**initial** 開始的；最初的　**deposit** 存（款）
**referral** 被推薦人　**ineligible** 無資格的

**191** 這則布告是要給誰看的？
(A) 松頂金融的員工
(B) 潛在的投資人
(C) 股東
(D) 現在帳戶持有人

**192** 尼可斯先生為什麼寫信給羅佩茲女士？
(A) 為了給一些投資的建議
(B) 為了提供她特別優惠
(C) 為了確認帳戶最近的一筆存款
(D) 為了介紹一位金融顧問

**193** 關於尼可斯先生，下最何者最可能為真？
(A) 他是松頂金融的忠實客戶。
(B) 他幾乎不認識羅佩茲女士。
(C) 他受僱於松頂金融。
(D) 他最近開了新帳戶。

**194** 在電子郵件裡，第二段、第一行的「flyer」一字，意思最接近下列何者？
(A) 申請
(B) 報紙
(C) 傳單
(D) 收據

**195** 關於羅佩茲女士，可由文中得知什麼？
(A) 她是松頂金融的現有客戶。
(B) 她和琳恩・卡多娜在同一個地方工作。
(C) 她在戶頭裡存入 200 元以上。
(D) 她打算在不久的將來退休。

## 196-200 布告、時程表與電子郵件

### 管理培訓研討會
今年春季的新研討會！
基礎管理

恭喜你晉升管理職務，你現在是負責管理的人了。

學習做好這份有挑戰性的新工作所需的技巧。我們的基礎管理研討會將教你邁出第一步所需的一切。你會學到如何……

—有效分派工作
—激勵員工
—提出批評
—規畫截止日期並按時完成
—訓練新進員工

這個一天的研討會帶你認識很多要成為成功管理人所需的技巧。你學到的技巧不但讓你獲益，也會增強你在組織內的效率。下載宣傳手冊，請上 www.abc.com。

### 管理培訓研討會
德拉瓦州多佛市
四月七日到十日

| | |
|---|---|
| **基礎管理** | 四月七日星期二<br>上午 9 時到下午 5 時<br>學習成為有效管理者所需的技巧。 |
| **領導能力與建立團隊** | 四月八日星期三<br>上午 8 時 30 分到下午 4 時 30 分<br>發展一套能建立並領導致勝團隊的策略。 |
| **建設性的批評** | 四月九日星期四<br>上午 9 時到下午 5 時<br>學習帶給員工正面改變的方法。<br>這個研討會包含提出建設性批評而不會樹敵的有效技巧。 |
| **精通管理之道** | 四月十日星期五<br>上午 8 時 30 分到下午 4 時 30 分<br>成為你能力所及的最佳管理人。學習如何將已證實的技巧運用在今天的專業職場上。<br>先修課程：高階管理課程 |

研討會包含教材。此外，參加者得以使用我們的線上資源圖書館。

寄件者：vincent.baca@valenza.com
收件者：mpoplar@abc.com
主旨：多佛管理研討會
日期：四月十五日

親愛的派普勒先生：

　　我要再次感謝你，提供給瓦倫薩設計公司的大量折扣，讓我們有九名員工得以參加上週在本市舉行的研討會。所有的參加者，包括我在內，都一直在談我們在上週的訓練課程中學到了多少。就像過去的研討會一樣，我從雷吉諾德·卡特獲益良多。他不但是位學識豐富的講師，也親身展示了他所教授的領導技巧。我以為我在他的高階管理課程裡已經學到了一切。但我錯了！

真誠地，
文森·巴卡

字彙 **supervisory** 管理的；監督的
　　 **challenging** 挑戰性的；考驗能力的
　　 **delegate** 委派（某人）做
　　 **constructive** 建設性的；有助益的
　　 **implement** 實施；執行
　　 **prerequisite** 必修的；事先需要的；先決條件的
　　 **model** 展示

**196** 在布告中，第四段、第二行的「enhance」一字，意思最接近下列何者？
(A) 補充
(B) 渴望
(C) 改善
(D) 領導

**197** 關於多佛研討會，可由文中得知什麼？
(A) 它們之後會重覆。
(B) 它們正推出優惠價格。
(C) 它們需要事先註冊。
(D) 它們會分發學習教材給參加者。

**198** 在四月七日的研討會上，很可能不會教什麼技巧？
(A) 如何指導新員工
(B) 如何要求升職
(C) 如何管理一個人的時間
(D) 如何糾正其他人

**199** 卡特先生最可能指導多佛的哪一場研討會？
(A) 基礎管理
(B) 領導能力與建立團隊
(C) 建設性的批評
(D) 精通管理之道

**200** 關於巴卡先生，可由文中得知什麼？
(A) 他管理其他員工。
(B) 他免費參加一場研討會。
(C) 他是瓦倫薩設計的老闆。
(D) 他以前和卡特先生一起工作。

| | | | | | | | | | |
|---|---|---|---|---|---|---|---|---|---|
| 1. (B) | 2. (C) | 3. (C) | 4. (D) | 5. (A) | 6. (B) | 7. (A) | 8. (A) | 9. (A) | 10. (C) |
| 11. (C) | 12. (B) | 13. (B) | 14. (C) | 15. (B) | 16. (B) | 17. (C) | 18. (A) | 19. (B) | 20. (B) |
| 21. (C) | 22. (B) | 23. (A) | 24. (C) | 25. (A) | 26. (A) | 27. (A) | 28. (C) | 29. (C) | 30. (C) |
| 31. (B) | 32. (A) | 33. (C) | 34. (D) | 35. (B) | 36. (D) | 37. (A) | 38. (B) | 39. (C) | 40. (C) |
| 41. (D) | 42. (C) | 43. (D) | 44. (C) | 45. (B) | 46. (D) | 47. (A) | 48. (A) | 49. (C) | 50. (B) |
| 51. (C) | 52. (A) | 53. (B) | 54. (A) | 55. (C) | 56. (B) | 57. (A) | 58. (D) | 59. (C) | 60. (D) |
| 61. (B) | 62. (C) | 63. (D) | 64. (A) | 65. (A) | 66. (C) | 67. (D) | 68. (D) | 69. (B) | 70. (A) |
| 71. (D) | 72. (A) | 73. (D) | 74. (B) | 75. (B) | 76. (B) | 77. (A) | 78. (D) | 79. (A) | 80. (D) |
| 81. (C) | 82. (A) | 83. (D) | 84. (B) | 85. (B) | 86. (B) | 87. (D) | 88. (A) | 89. (A) | 90. (C) |
| 91. (B) | 92. (C) | 93. (B) | 94. (A) | 95. (C) | 96. (B) | 97. (C) | 98. (D) | 99. (A) | 100. (A) |
| 101. (D) | 102. (A) | 103. (C) | 104. (A) | 105. (D) | 106. (D) | 107. (B) | 108. (A) | 109. (D) | 110. (C) |
| 111. (C) | 112. (B) | 113. (D) | 114. (C) | 115. (D) | 116. (A) | 117. (C) | 118. (D) | 119. (C) | 120. (B) |
| 121. (D) | 122. (B) | 123. (C) | 124. (D) | 125. (D) | 126. (A) | 127. (B) | 128. (B) | 129. (B) | 130. (C) |
| 131. (B) | 132. (D) | 133. (B) | 134. (C) | 135. (A) | 136. (C) | 137. (B) | 138. (A) | 139. (B) | 140. (D) |
| 141. (C) | 142. (B) | 143. (C) | 144. (B) | 145. (B) | 146. (D) | 147. (D) | 148. (A) | 149. (B) | 150. (A) |
| 151. (B) | 152. (C) | 153. (A) | 154. (D) | 155. (A) | 156. (B) | 157. (D) | 158. (C) | 159. (B) | 160. (C) |
| 161. (D) | 162. (A) | 163. (A) | 164. (B) | 165. (B) | 166. (A) | 167. (B) | 168. (D) | 169. (C) | 170. (C) |
| 171. (D) | 172. (D) | 173. (A) | 174. (D) | 175. (D) | 176. (B) | 177. (C) | 178. (C) | 179. (B) | 180. (C) |
| 181. (D) | 182. (B) | 183. (A) | 184. (C) | 185. (B) | 186. (D) | 187. (B) | 188. (D) | 189. (B) | 190. (C) |
| 191. (A) | 192. (D) | 193. (B) | 194. (A) | 195. (B) | 196. (D) | 197. (B) | 198. (D) | 199. (C) | 200. (C) |

## PART 1

P. 100

**1** (A) People are entering the train station.
(美M) (B) Passengers are waiting to board the train.
(C) Some workers are repairing railway tracks.
(D) Pedestrians are crossing a busy street.

(A) 人們正進入火車站。
(B) 乘客正等著上火車。
(C) 有些工人在修理火車鐵軌。
(D) 行人正穿越繁忙的街道。

字彙 **board** 上（船、車、飛機等）
**railway track** 鐵軌
**pedestrian** 行人、步行者
**busy street** 繁忙的街道

**2** (A) Plants are growing in pots.
(美W) (B) Some trees are growing next to a column.
(C) The worker is raking the soil.
(D) The gardener is trimming bushes.

(A) 植物在花盆裡生長。
(B) 有些樹在柱子旁邊生長。
(C) 工人正在耙土。
(D) 園丁正在修剪灌木叢。

字彙 **pot** 花盆　**column** 圓柱
**rake** （用耙）耙平、耙鬆
**trim** 修剪；修整　**bush** 灌木叢

**3** (A) Some people are walking down a hallway.
(英M) (B) Some people are glancing at a statue.
(C) A bridge leads to some buildings.
(D) Banners have been suspended from some lampposts.

(A) 有些人正沿著走廊走。
(B) 有些人瞥了一眼雕像。
(C) 一座橋通往幾棟建築物。
(D) 有些路燈柱上掛著旗幟。

字彙 **hallway** 走廊；門廳
**glance** 迅速看一眼；掃視
**statue** 雕像；雕塑　**lead to** 通向某處
**banner** 旗幟；（遊行隊伍等用的）橫布條
**suspend** 懸掛　**lamppost** 路燈柱

**4** (A) Some merchandise is being displayed for sale.
(澳M) (B) Some books are being distributed in a store.
(C) Shoppers are waiting in line to make purchases.
(D) Bookshelves have been filled with reading materials.

(A) 有些商品陳列供販售。
(B) 有家店正經銷一些書。
(C) 顧客正排隊等候購物。
(D) 書架上放滿讀物。

字彙 **merchandise** 商品；貨物
**distribute** 經銷、分發
**wait in line** 排隊等候
**make a purchase** 買東西
**bookshelf** 書架
**reading material** 讀物；閱讀材料

**5** (A) They are collaborating on a project.
(英M) (B) One of the workers is taking off his tool belt.
(C) One of the workers is plugging in some equipment.
(D) They are moving some wooden materials into a warehouse.

(A) 他們正在合作一個工程。
(B) 其中一個工人脫下他的工具帶。
(C) 其中一個工人正把某個設備插上插頭。
(D) 他們正把一些木料搬進倉庫。

字彙 **collaborate** 合作　**take off** 脫去（衣物）
**tool belt** 工具帶　**plug in** 插上……的插頭
**wooden** 木製的；木的　**warehouse** 倉庫

**6** (A) The building overlooks the mountain.
(美W) (B) Mountains can be seen from an outdoor pool.
(C) Swimmers are stepping down into a pool.
(D) A pool is surrounded by trees.

(A) 這棟建物俯瞰著山。
(B) 從戶外泳池可以看到群山。
(C) 泳客正往下走進泳池。
(D) 游泳池四周環繞著樹木。

字彙 **overlook** 俯瞰；俯視　**step down** 走下來
**be surrounded by** 被……環繞

## PART 2

P. 104

**7** How long will it take to cycle to the stadium?
(美M) (A) About half an hour.
(英M) (B) By bus, I think.
　　(C) Maybe tomorrow.

騎腳踏車到體育場要花多久的時間？
(A) 大約半小時。
(B) 搭公車，我想。
(C) 也許明天。

字彙 cycle 騎腳踏車　stadium 體育場；運動場
　　half an hour 半小時

**8** You two haven't worked together, have you?
(美W) (A) No, not yet.
(美M) (B) I have too many.
　　(C) The day before.

你們倆人還沒有合作過，對吧？
(A) 沒有，還沒有過。
(B) 我有太多了。
(C) 前一天。

字彙 the day before 前一天

**9** Didn't you want to catch a faster flight?
(英M) (A) Yes, but I missed it.
(美W) (B) The east terminal.
　　(C) I took some back.

你不是想搭快一點的航班嗎？
(A) 是的，但我錯過了。
(B) 東航廈。
(C) 我拿了一些回來。

字彙 catch a flight 搭飛機
　　take back 拿回；收回

**10** Where's a cheap place to get breakfast?
(美W) (A) Let's line up for it.
(美M) (B) I can't lend you any money.
　　(C) At the café downtown.

在哪裡可以買到平價早餐？
(A) 我們排隊買吧。
(B) 我不能再借你錢了。
(C) 在市中心的咖啡館。

字彙 downtown 市中心；鬧區

**11** When will your driving license expire?
(美M) (A) It's right along the sidewalk.
(美W) (B) Return it by secure delivery, please.
　　(C) Not until March.

你的駕照什麼時候到期？
(A) 就在人行道邊。
(B) 請以掛號郵件寄回。
(C) 到三月。

字彙 expire 到期；結束　sidewalk 人行道
　　secure delivery 掛號

**12** Shouldn't we try going in the main entrance?
(美W) (A) We don't check any more.
(美M) (B) No, it's locked as well.
　　(C) There's a trial download.

我們不是應該試著從大門進去嗎？
(A) 我們不再檢查了。
(B) 不，它也鎖著。
(C) 有個試用版可以下載。

字彙 main entrance 大門入口；主要入口
　　trial 試用

**13** Did the Cairo office call today?
(美M) (A) No, that will suffice.
(美W) (B) Yes, Ms. Jenkins left a contact number for you.
　　(C) Try this one as an alternative.

開羅辦公室今天有打電話來嗎？
(A) 沒有，那就夠了。
(B) 有的，簡金斯女士留了聯絡電話給你。
(C) 試試這個替代方案吧。

字彙 suffice 足夠
　　contact number 聯絡電話號碼
　　alternative 替代方案

**14** Let's see if another shop has these glasses at a lower price.
(美W) (A) The window exhibit.
(美M) (B) Thanks. I bought them last summer.
　　(C) Yes, it's worth looking.

讓我們看看另一家店的這副眼鏡價格是否較低。
(A) 櫥窗陳列。
(B) 謝謝，我去年夏天買了。
(C) 好的，值得看看。

**15** Who can I speak to about selling my stocks
英M and shares?
美M (A) Yes, marketing is on the second floor.
(B) Mr. Ypres can guide you.
(C) You can email it now.

我可以找誰談談要賣掉我的股票和股份的事？
(A) 是的，行銷部在二樓。
(B) 伊普瑞斯先生可以指導你。
(C) 你可以現在用電子郵件寄過來。

字彙 stocks and shares 股票和股份
guide 指導；指引

**16** Which design did the research group prefer?
美M (A) I thought that, as well.
美W (B) The one A-One Design created.
(C) Four males and six females.

研究小組比較喜歡哪一種設計？
(A) 我也覺得是那個。
(B) 「一一設計」創作的那個。
(C) 4 男 6 女。

字彙 research group 研究小組　male 男性
female 女性

**17** Have you finished the clients' details?
英M (A) No, I just rented it.
美W (B) I saw it on the morning bulletin.
(C) Not quite, but they'll be completed soon.

你完成客戶的詳細資料了嗎？
(A) 沒有，我剛剛才租下來。
(B) 我在晨間新聞快報上看到的。
(C) 還沒有全部完成，但很快就會完成了。

字彙 client 客戶
morning bulletin 晨間新聞快報
not quite 不完全地

**18** Here, you left your wallet in the café.
美W (A) Thanks for returning it.
美M (B) It's at one o'clock.
(C) Please call Sammi.

嘿，你的皮夾掉在咖啡館了。
(A) 謝謝你送回來給我。
(B) 一點鐘。
(C) 請打給山米。

字彙 leave 遺忘；丟下　wallet 皮夾、錢包

**19** Wasn't that documentary program
美W fascinating?
英M (A) Directly to your television.
(B) I haven't watched it yet.
(C) On the second page.

那個紀錄片節目不是很吸引人嗎？
(A) 直接傳到到你的電視。
(B) 我還沒有看過。
(C) 在第 2 頁。

字彙 documentary 紀錄片
fascinating 吸引人的；極有趣的

**20** How was the play you saw at the NY
美W Theater?
美W (A) I tried the new recipe.
(B) We've really enjoyed it.
(C) By the end of today.

你們在紐約劇院看的戲如何？
(A) 我試了新的食譜。
(B) 我們真的很喜歡。
(C) 在今天結束之前。

字彙 recipe 食譜

**21** Why does Mr. Planter look tanned today?
英M (A) We tried on many occasions.
美W (B) Because it's in the morning.
(C) He just came back from vacation.

普蘭特先生今天為什麼看起來曬黑了？
(A) 我們在很多不同場合都試過。
(B) 因為是在早上。
(C) 他剛度完假回來。

字彙 tan 使曬成棕褐色　occasion 場合；時刻

**22** What should we buy for a wedding gift?
美W (A) Around 8 P.M.
英M (B) Why don't you ask Katy?
(C) The food is excellent here.

我們該買什麼當結婚禮物？
(A) 大約晚上 8 點。
(B) 你何不問問凱蒂？
(C) 這裡的餐點非常美味。

字彙 wedding gift 結婚禮物

**23** We could place the item in the local shop
(美M) window.
(美W) (A) And advertise it on a Web site, too.
    (B) Several different offers as well.
    (C) She's advertised there every year.

我們可以把這個物品放在本地商店的櫥窗裡賣。
(A) 同時也在網站上廣告。
(B) 還有好幾個不同的出價。
(C) 她每年都在那裡打廣告。

字彙 **place** 放置；安置

**24** Who's going to pick up Ms. Lejeune from the
(美W) bus station?
(美M) (A) A domestic journey.
    (B) From the 6th to the 12th.
    (C) I nominated Pierre to do it.

誰要去公車站接樂君女士？
(A) 一趟國內的旅行。
(B) 從 6 日到 12 日。
(C) 我指定皮耶去接。

字彙 **pick up** 用汽車搭載某人或接某人
    **domestic journey** 國內旅行
    **nominate** 指定；提名；任命

**25** Do you think Mark will rent a larger van or
(英M) transport everything in his car?
(美W) (A) Hiring a removal van would be easier.
    (B) It's quite a few miles away.
    (C) Were you pleased with them?

你覺得馬克會租一輛較大的廂型車，還是用他
的車載所有東西？
(A) 租一輛搬家的貨車會比較方便。
(B) 有好幾英里遠。
(C) 你對他們滿意嗎？

字彙 **van** 有蓋小貨車；廂型客貨兩用車
    **removal van** 搬家貨車
    **be pleased with** 對……感到滿意

**26** The last assembly of the convention starts at
(美W) 5.
(英M) (A) I might not be on time.
    (B) Dr. Karacki will.
    (C) Could you pass me one, please?

大會的最後一場會議 5 點開始。
(A) 我可能無法準時到。
(B) 卡拉奇博士將會。
(C) 可以麻煩你遞一個給我嗎？

字彙 **assembly** 集會　**convention** 大會
    **be on time** 準時

**27** Would you like me to sort out the basement
(英M) later?
(美M) (A) Karen Lasorda said she'd do it.
    (B) It lasts twenty minutes.
    (C) He usually cycles to work.

你要我晚點整理地下室嗎？
(A) 凱倫‧拉索達說她會整理。
(B) 持續了 20 分鐘。
(C) 他通常騎腳踏車上班。

字彙 **sort out** 整理某事物　**basement** 地下室
    **last** 持續

**28** There's a discount on everything at Klein's
(美W) Hardware Store all week.
(英M) (A) I applied two days ago.
    (B) But I shipped it yesterday.
    (C) I read about it in the newspaper.

這一整個星期，克連五金行的所有東西都在
打折。
(A) 我兩天前申請的。
(B) 但我昨天寄出去了。
(C) 我在報上看到了。

字彙 **hardware store** 五金行
    **all week** 整個星期

**29** Would you rather eat Cantonese or Italian?
(美W) (A) I like this option.
(美M) (B) You should sign up for this course.
    (C) Which one would you choose?

你比較想吃廣東菜還是義大利菜？
(A) 我喜歡這個選項。
(B) 你應該報名參加這個課程。
(C) 你要選哪一個？

字彙 **Cantonese** 廣東的　**option** 選擇；選項

🎧 10

**30** Please look over this company handbook before the training starts.
(A) Yes, but there are not enough questionnaires.
(B) At the resource center.
(C) I'll make sure I do that.

在訓練開始之前，請仔細看看這本公司手冊。
(A) 好的，但問卷不夠。
(B) 在資源中心。
(C) 我一定會看。

字彙 **look over** 仔細查看　**handbook** 手冊　**resource** 資源　**make sure** 確定；確保

**31** You don't mind if I switch the lights on, do you?
(A) Change direction at the corner.
(B) Not in the least.
(C) In fair condition.

你不介意我開燈，對吧？
(A) 在街角轉彎。
(B) 一點也不。
(C) 狀況尚佳。

字彙 **mind** 介意　**not in the least** 一點也不　**fair condition** 情況尚佳；無甚損壞

## PART 3

P. 105

**Questions 32-34 refer to the following conversation.**
美M 美W

**M** Hello, this is Mr. Allison, in room 3219.
**㉜ My heating system isn't working too well.** The radiators turn on, but the air coming out of it isn't warm.

**W** I'm sorry about that, sir. Unfortunately, all our heating engineers are unavailable at present. I can offer you an alternative room. In fact, **㉝ I'll upgrade you to a family room at the same cost** as your single room.

**M** That would be ideal. **㉞ But could you send a porter to bring my cases** to the new room straight away? I don't have time to do it. A taxi is picking me up in fifteen minutes to take me to a concert.

對話
男：哈囉，我是 3219 號房的艾利森先生。我的暖氣系統運作不太順暢，暖氣機開了，但吹出來的風不熱。

女：真是抱歉發生這種事，先生。很不湊巧，我們所有的暖氣工程師現在都沒空。我可以幫您換個房間。事實上，我會幫您升級到家庭房，費用和您的單人房一樣。

男：那真是太好了。不過，妳可不可以派個行李員來，馬上把我的行李箱都拿到新的房間去？我沒時間搬行李，15 分鐘後，計程車就要來接我去音樂會了。

字彙 **heating system** 暖氣系統
**work** 運轉　**radiator** 暖氣裝置；散熱器
**engineer** 工程師
**unavailable** 抽不開身的；沒空的；忙的
**at present** 目前；現在
**alternative** 替代的
**upgrade** 使升級　**single room** 單人房
**porter** 行李員；搬運工
**straight away** 即刻；馬上
**pick up** 用汽車搭載某人或接某人
**complimentary** 贈送的
**accommodation** 住宿　**partial** 部分的
**assistance** 幫助

**32** What is the man's complaint?
(A) His heating system does not work.
(B) His booking was cancelled.
(C) His taxi was late.
(D) His luggage is missing.

男子投訴什麼事？
(A) 他的暖氣系統故障。
(B) 他的預訂被取消了。
(C) 他的計程車晚到了。
(D) 他的行李遺失了。

**33** What does the woman offer the man?
(A) A free lift to the concert
(B) A complimentary meal
(C) An upgraded accommodation
(D) Early check-in options

女子提議給男子什麼？
(A) 免費載他到音樂會
(B) 免費餐點
(C) 住宿升級
(D) 提早入住方案

**34** What does the man request?
(A) An apology
(B) A partial refund
(C) Free taxi rides
(D) Assistance with his bags

男子要求什麼？
(A) 道歉
(B) 退回部分費用
(C) 免費搭計程車
(D) 幫他拿行李箱

**Questions 35-37 refer to the following conversation.**
美W 美M

**W** 35 **I'm trying to get a doctor's appointment.** I've only recently moved into the area.
**M** OK, I can assist you with that. 36 **I just have to see your health card with your new address.** A doctor or nurse will be able to see you once you have registered here at the St. Johns Surgery.
**W** Oh, I don't remember where I put that document. I suppose I had better go and look for it.
**M** Well, just remember that you can't register without it. Meanwhile, 37 **here's a list of our regular doctors.**

- - - - - - - - - - - - - - - - - - - - - - - - - -

對話
女：我試著要跟醫師約診，我最近才剛搬到這一區來。
男：好，我可以幫妳，我只是需要看上面有妳新地址的健保卡。只要在聖約翰診所這裡完成掛號，就能看到醫師或護理師了。
女：噢，我不記得我把那張卡放在那裡了。我想，我最好回去找一找。
男：嗯，只要記得，沒有卡就沒辦法掛號。還有，這是我們固定看診醫師的名單。

字彙 doctor's appointment 醫師約診
health card 健保卡
surgery 診所；門診處；外科手術
meanwhile 與此同時；在此期間
regular 固定的；定期的
undergo surgery 接受手術
contribution 捐款 disclaimer 免責聲明

**35** What does the woman want to do?
(A) Volunteer at a gallery
(B) Register for health care
(C) Get some legal advice
(D) Undergo surgery

女子想要做什麼？
(A) 在藝廊當志工
(B) 為醫療保健掛號
(C) 聽取法律意見
(D) 接受手術

**36** What does the man say the woman has to do?
(A) Provide her date of birth
(B) Make a contribution
(C) Attend a medical test
(D) Present her health card

男子說，女子必須做什麼？
(A) 提供她的出生日期
(B) 捐款
(C) 接受醫療檢測
(D) 出示她的健保卡

**37** What does the man give the woman?
(A) A list of staff
(B) A policy document
(C) A disclaimer
(D) A replacement card

男子給女子什麼？
(A) 一份工作人員名單
(B) 一份政策文件
(C) 一份免責聲明
(D) 一張補發的卡

**Questions 38-40 refer to the following conversation.**
英M 美W

**M** Carol, were you able to check the computers in the Marketing Department?
**W** Yeah, I just got back from there. They all still have the outdated version of the data management software.
**M** Okay. 39 **In that case, we need to make time on Thursday to install the new version.** Can you do that?
**W** I'm sorry. I'm going to be at our branch office on Parker Avenue for training that day.

M Right. I forgot about that. **㊴ Can you ask Mike if he can do the work?**

W **㊴ Sure, I can ask him.** I'm heading back to the office right now. Oh, one more thing. The marketing manager asked me when they will be getting new computer keyboards.

M I'd say that's not anytime soon. We don't have money in the budget right now. Maybe in the spring.

---

對話

男：卡羅，妳檢查行銷部的電腦了嗎？

女：有的，我剛從他們辦公室回來。他們全都還在用舊版的資料管理軟體。

男：好的，那樣的話，我們必須在星期四挪出時間安裝新的版本，妳可以去嗎？

女：抱歉，我那天要去派克大道的分公司培訓。

男：對，我忘了。妳可以去問麥克看他可以嗎？

女：當然，我可以問他，我現在正要回辦公室。噢，還有一件事。行銷部經理問我，他們什麼時候會拿到新的電腦鍵盤。

男：我會說近期內還不會，我們現在沒有預算，也許春天吧。

字彙 outdated 舊式的；過時的
management 管理

**38** What are the speakers discussing?
(A) Ordering supplies
(B) Installing software
(C) Scheduling an event
(D) Buying devices

說話者們在討論什麼？
(A) 訂購用品
(B) 安裝軟體
(C) 安排活動時間
(D) 購買設備

**39** What does the woman say she will do next?
(A) Meet with a superior
(B) Finish her work
(C) Speak with a coworker
(D) Check her schedule

女子說她接下來要做什麼？
(A) 和主管碰面
(B) 完成她的工作
(C) 和同事談話
(D) 查看她的行事曆

**40** What does the man mean when he says, "I'd say that's not anytime soon"?
(A) They are too busy to meet with the manager.
(B) They have other projects to focus on now.
(C) They are unable to purchase keyboards now.
(D) They have not received the keyboards yet.

當男子說：「我會說近期內還不會」時，他的意思是什麼？
(A) 他們太忙了，沒空和經理碰面。
(B) 他們現在要專心做別的專案。
(C) 他們現在無法買鍵盤。
(D) 他們還沒收到鍵盤。

**Questions 41-43 refer to the following conversation.**
英M 美W

M Hello, I have a food basket **㊶ here for a patient in room 312.**

W That can't be the right room. **㊷ We are a two-story building with only 20 rooms.** What's the name on the delivery?

M The package is for Anita Callard. Someone ordered it last week and wanted it delivered today.

W Oh! Ms. Callard is in room 12. If you leave the basket over there, **㊸ I'll get her to come and collect it.**

---

對話

男：哈囉，我這裡有個食物籃，要送給312號房的病人。

女：不可能是那個病房。我們這裡是兩層樓的建築，只有20個病房。送貨單上的名字是什麼？

男：這一籃是要給安妮塔‧柯拉德的。有人上星期訂了，要求今天送。

女：噢，柯拉德女士住12號房。如果你把籃子放在那邊，我會請她過來拿。

字彙 two-story 兩層樓的　package 包裹
collect 領取（信件等）
porter 行李員、搬運工

**41** Where is the conversation taking place?
(A) At a warehouse
(B) At a delivery office
(C) At a florist shop
(D) At a hospital

這段對話發生在哪裡？
(A) 倉庫
(B) 貨運辦公室
(C) 花店
(D) 醫院

**42** According to the woman, why is the room number wrong?
(A) The room is occupied by a male.
(B) The patients are not allowed packages.
(C) The building only has a small number of rooms.
(D) The street name is incorrect.

根據女子所述，房間號碼為什麼是錯的？
(A) 那個房間住的是一名男子。
(B) 病人不准收包裹。
(C) 這棟建物只有少許房間。
(D) 街道名稱不對。

**43** What does the woman say she will do next?
(A) Arrange for a delivery
(B) Order some food
(C) Call for a porter
(D) Contact Ms. Callard

女子說她接下來將會做什麼？
(A) 安排送貨
(B) 點一些食物
(C) 叫行李員來
(D) 聯絡柯拉德女士

**Questions 44-46 refer to the following conversation.**
美W 美M

W Hi, Kenny. This is Sharon. How are things going this morning?
M Everything's good. I came in early so I could get ahead start on the report.
W Great. Actually that's the reason I am calling. Yesterday, I reviewed the first chapters you wrote. The writing is exactly what we have wanted. **44 However, I was wondering if you could make some revisions to the graphs.**
M Sure. What about them?
W **45 Well, the client asked for full-color graphs, but you made them in black and white. Do you think you could change them to the client's requests?**
M That's not an issue. I just need a couple of hours.
W That's fine. We are still ahead of schedule.

---

**對話**

女：嗨，肯尼，我是雪倫。今天早上好嗎？
男：一切都很好。我很早就來了，所以，我可以先開始做報告。
女：很好。其實，那正是我打電話的原因。昨天，我仔細看了你寫的前幾章，文字內容正是我們想要的。不過，我在想你是否可以修改一下圖表。
男：當然，圖表怎麼了？
女：嗯，客戶要求全彩圖表，但你做的是黑白圖表。你覺得你可以修改圖表、以符合客戶的要求嗎？
男：那不是問題，我只需要幾個小時。
女：好的，我們的進度仍超前。

**字彙** revision 修正；修訂
black and white 黑白　go over 仔細察看
visual aid 視覺輔助工具

**44** Why is the woman calling?
(A) To report to a customer
(B) To propose a project
(C) To request some changes
(D) To ask for information

女子為什麼打這通電話？
(A) 為了向客戶報告
(B) 為了提案
(C) 為了要求修改
(D) 為了要一些資料

**45** What does the woman ask the man to do?
(A) Go over her work
(B) Add color to visual aids
(C) Contact a client
(D) Remove some colors on the graphs

女子要求男子做什麼？
(A) 仔細察看她的工作
(B) 為圖表加上顏色
(C) 聯絡一位客戶
(D) 移除圖表上的一些顏色

**46** Why does the man say, "That's not an issue"?
(A) He currently has been assigned a lot of projects.
(B) He is worried about a deadline being affected.
(C) He is almost finished writing a report.
(D) He has no problem meeting the woman's request.

男子為什麼說：「那不是問題」？
(A) 目前有很多專案指派給他。
(B) 他擔心有個截止日期會受到影響。
(C) 他快要寫完一份報告了。
(D) 他可以達成女子的要求。

**Questions 47-49 refer to the following conversation.**
美W 美M

**W** Hi, Jason. It's Margot. The light on the optic laser in the laboratory has broken. ㊼ **Could you get me a new one from the stock cupboard?**
**M** Unfortunately, I can't do that at the moment. We've run out. I ordered some more bulbs two days ago but ㊽ **the delivery hasn't arrived yet.** The wholesalers promised me that the shipment with a new batch of specialist lights will arrive within an hour.
**W** Well, I sincerely hope that's the case and the delivery comes soon. ㊾ **My students are arriving at midday** to practice on the equipment.

**對話**
女：嗨，傑森，我是瑪歌。實驗室的光學雷射儀的燈壞了，你可以從儲物櫃幫我拿一個新的來嗎？
男：很不湊巧，我現在沒辦法辦到，我們沒有燈泡了。我兩天前訂了些燈泡，但貨還沒送來，批發商跟我保證，新一批專業燈泡會在一小時內送到。
女：嗯，我真心希望是這樣，貨很快就會送來。我的學生中午會來練習操作設備。

**字彙** **optic laser** 光學雷射
**laboratory** 實驗室 **cupboard** 櫥櫃
**run out** 用完；耗盡 **bulb** 電燈泡
**wholesaler** 批發商
**shipment** 運輸的貨物 **batch** 一批
**specialist** 專門的、專業的
**case** 事實；具體情況

**47** What does the woman ask the man to do?
(A) Bring an item from stock
(B) Contact some students
(C) Turn out the lights
(D) Rearrange a cupboard

女子要求男子做什麼？
(A) 從存貨裡拿個物品過來
(B) 聯絡一些學生
(C) 關掉電燈
(D) 重新整理櫥櫃

**48** Why is the man unable to help?
(A) A delivery has been delayed.
(B) Some equipment has been damaged.
(C) A student requires his assistance.
(D) A lab has been closed down.

男子為什麼無法幫上忙？
(A) 貨物延遲送來。
(B) 有些設備受損。
(C) 有個學生需要他幫忙。
(D) 有間實驗室關閉。

**49** What will happen at 12:00?
(A) A replacement tutor will be sent.
(B) The man will buy some light bulbs.
(C) The woman's students will arrive.
(D) Different equipment will be used.

12 點時會發生什麼事？
(A) 會派一位代課助教來。
(B) 男子會買一些電燈泡。
(C) 女子的學生會過來。
(D) 會使用不同的設備。

**Questions 50-52 refer to the following conversation.**
美M 美W

**M** Hi, Lisa. Do you have a minute to talk about the Carstairs Inc. account? ㊿ **They want to initiate a marketing campaign for one of their plumbing products,** Linked Rollers. It appears that it hasn't been selling much, but they believe it will be well accepted once it is publicized.
**W** Have they thought of relevant advertising? (51) **Maybe they could put out an advertisement in trade magazines to boost its familiarity with customers.**
**M** (52) **They actually trialed that two months ago and didn't have much response.** They are looking for something totally different this time.

## 對話

男：嗨，麗莎，妳有空可以談一下卡斯德爾公司這個客戶嗎？他們想要為他們的一種管道器材——連接滾軸，發起一個廣告活動。看起來，這個產品似乎沒有賣得很好，但他們相信，只要打廣告以後，就會被大眾廣為接受。

女：他們有沒有考慮過相關的廣告宣傳？也許，他們可以在貿易雜誌上登廣告，以增加消費者對這個產品的熟悉度。

男：其實，他們兩個月前已經試過這個方法，沒有引起太多迴響。這一次，他們要找完全不同的做法。

## 字彙 Do you have a minute . . . ?
你有空做……嗎？
account 客戶
initiate 開始
plumbing 水管裝置、管路系統
publicize 宣傳、廣告
relevant 有關的；相關聯的
put out an advertisement 刊登廣告
trade 貿易　boost 促進；增加
familiarity 熟悉　trial 嘗試；試驗
warehouse 倉庫

**50** What does Carstairs Inc. want to advertise?
(A) A job opportunity
(B) A product
(C) An event
(D) A warehouse
卡斯德爾公司想要廣告什麼？
(A) 一個工作機會
(B) 一個產品
(C) 一場活動
(D) 一間倉庫

**51** What does the woman suggest?
(A) Offering online discounts
(B) Hiring a marketing expert
(C) Advertising in specialist media
(D) Advertising on the radio
女子建議什麼？
(A) 提供網路折扣
(B) 僱用行銷專家
(C) 在專業媒體上打廣告
(D) 在廣播上廣告

**52** What does the man say about the woman's suggestion?
(A) It was unsuccessful in the past.
(B) It will take too long.
(C) It was not possible for the company.
(D) It was too expensive to run.
關於女子的建議，男子說了什麼？
(A) 過去並不成功。
(B) 會花很久的時間。
(C) 公司不可能做。
(D) 要執行太昂貴了。

**Questions 53-55 refer to the following conversation.**
美W 英M

W Hi, I bought a long sleeved dress from your online store last week, only when I went to fasten it up, 53 the zipper broke.

M Oh, it's not difficult to return faulty items. 54 I'll send you a returns form. What you must do is fill in the form with your reference number, and enclose it in the original packaging. If you do that, there won't be a fee to mail it back to us. Would you like us to send a replacement dress or do you want to choose a different one from the site?

W 55 I'd like to get my money back if that's possible. I had to have a new dress for a wedding yesterday, so I ended up borrowing one from a friend.

## 對話

女：嗨，我上星期在你們的網路商店買了一件長袖洋裝，就在我要把它拉上時，拉鍊壞掉了。

男：噢，退回瑕疵品並不難，我會寄一份退貨表給你。妳必須要做的就是把妳的訂單編號填在表上，然後把它放進原本的包裝裡。如果妳這麼做，寄回來給我們就不會有費用。妳要我們另外寄一件洋裝替換，還是要從網站上另外選一件？

女：如果可以的話，我想退費。我是為了昨天的婚禮才不得不買一件新洋裝，因此，我最後跟朋友借了一件。

## 字彙 long sleeved 長袖的
fasten up 扣緊；繫牢　faulty 有缺陷的
fill in 填寫；填好
reference number 編號
enclose 隨信（或包裹）附上
packaging 包裝；包裝材料
replacement 更換　end up 結果成為……

53 According to the woman, what is the problem with the dress?
(A) The dress didn't fit.
(B) The fastener was faulty.
(C) The size is too small.
(D) The price is too high.
根據女子所述，洋裝有什麼問題？
(A) 洋裝不合身。
(B) 拉鍊有問題。
(C) 尺寸太小。
(D) 價格太高。

54 What will the man send to the woman?
(A) A document
(B) A new dress
(C) A discount voucher
(D) A full refund
男子會寄什麼給女子？
(A) 一份文件
(B) 一件新洋裝
(C) 一張折價券
(D) 全額退費

55 What does the woman say she would prefer?
(A) To change the color of the dress
(B) To choose a different item
(C) To receive a refund
(D) To wait for a replacement
女子說她比較想要什麼？
(A) 更換洋裝的顏色
(B) 選不同的商品
(C) 收到退款
(D) 等候換貨

**Questions 56-58 refer to the following conversation.**
美W 美M

**W** Mr. Hawkins, I've just been looking at our employee criminal record check certificate, and I realized that 56 **some of our workers' certificates are out of date.**

**M** Really? But I thought we had notification two months ago so that all of our workers will have regular checks. Aren't the certificates valid for six months?

**W** They are, but that legislation is just for new employees. We need another check for those workers who have been here for more than a year. 57 **They just need to update their current details to get recertified.**

**M** Okay, 58 **could you give me a list of workers** who need to be recertified? Then we can send off their details.

**對話**

女：霍金斯先生，我剛剛一直在仔細檢查我們員工的犯罪紀錄查驗證明書，發現有些員工的證明已經失效了。

男：真的嗎？但我以為我們兩個月前就有通知了，如此一來，我們所有的員工都會定期查核。證書的有效期不是六個月嗎？

女：是的，但那條法規只適用於新進員工。我們需要對已經工作超過一年的員工進行另一次檢查。他們只需要更新他們現在的詳細情況，以便重新認證。

男：好，妳可以給我一份需要重新認證的員工名單嗎？然後，我們就可以寄出他們的詳細資料。

**字彙**
criminal record 犯罪紀錄；刑事紀錄
certificate 證明書
out of date 過時的；無用的；過期的
notification 通知；告示
regular checks 定期查核
valid 有效的；合法的
legislation 法規；法律
recertify 重新認證
send off 郵寄　collect 收集
resubmit 重新提出　tuition 學費
archive 把……存檔

56 What problem has the woman identified?
(A) A training session has not been finished.
(B) Some documents are out of date.
(C) Some registration forms have not been collected.
(D) Some employees have given false information.
女子發現了什麼問題？
(A) 有個訓練課程沒有完成。
(B) 有些文件過期了。
(C) 有些報名表沒有收取。
(D) 有些員工給了假的資料。

**57** What does the woman say about workers who were certified more than a year ago?
(A) They need to resubmit their details.
(B) They need to undergo a written test.
(C) They have to pay for extra tuition.
(D) They must contact their supervisors.

關於認證超過一年的員工，女子說了什麼？
(A) 他們需要重新提出他們的詳細狀況。
(B) 他們需要接受筆試。
(C) 他們必須需繳交額外的學費。
(D) 他們必須和主管聯絡。

**58** What does the man ask the woman to do?
(A) Archive some documents
(B) Send some warnings
(C) Organize a workshop
(D) Provide names of workers

男子要求女子做什麼？
(A) 把一些文件存檔
(B) 發出警告
(C) 舉辦一場工作坊
(D) 提供員工姓名

**Questions 59-61 refer to the following conversation with three speakers.** 美M 美W 英M

| | |
|---|---|
| **M1** | **㉙ So we got approved to open six new retail locations in the southern part of the United States.** |
| **W** | That's great news. So I guess that means we need to narrow down where exactly we want to open the new stores. |
| **M2** | Well, most of our sales growth has been coming from consumers in their 30s. |
| **W** | It would make sense then to target cities with the largest populations of that consumer group. |
| **M1** | **㉚ We don't just want spots that have lots of people in their 30s, but those who have decent salaries.** |
| **M2** | **㉚ So cities with lots of professionals.** |
| **M1** | That's what I am talking about. Well, we have collected lots of market data. I can analyze them and put together a list for the best locations. |
| **W** | **㉛ While you do that, I'll talk with our architectural team about building designs.** |

**三人對話**

男1：我們獲准在美國南部開 6 家新的零售店。
女：真棒的消息。那麼，我猜這表示，我們必須縮小我們想要開新店的確切地點範圍。
男2：嗯，我們大部分的銷售額成長，向來都來自 30 幾歲的顧客。
女：那麼，鎖定有最多該消費族群人口的城市就合理了。
男1：我們不只想要有很多 30 多歲人口的地方，還要有收入不錯的顧客。
男2：那就是有很多專業人士的都市。
男1：那正是我的意思。嗯，我們已經蒐集了很多市場資料。我可以加以分析，然後匯集成一份最佳地點的名單。
女：你在做那個的同時，我會和我們的建築團隊談建物設計。

**字彙** retail 零售　decent 相當不錯的；像樣的
professional 專業人員；專家
put together 匯集；組合

**59** What are the speakers discussing?
(A) A growing population in certain areas
(B) An industry's hiring trend
(C) Business expansion
(D) A popular city for sales people

說話者在討論什麼？
(A) 某些地區的人口成長
(B) 某個產業的用人趨勢
(C) 業務擴展
(D) 受業務人員歡迎的城市

**60** What is implied about professionals in their 30s?
(A) They are willing to relocate for work.
(B) They want to live in cities.
(C) They are a new market.
(D) They are paid well.

關於 30 幾歲的專業人士，文中暗示什麼？
(A) 他們願意為了工作搬家。
(B) 他們想要住在都市裡。
(C) 他們是新興市場。
(D) 他們的收入很好。

**61** What does the woman offer to do?
(A) Collect market data
(B) Speak with building designers
(C) Put together a report
(D) Tour some buildings

女子提議做什麼？
(A) 蒐集市場資料
(B) 和建築設計師談談
(C) 匯集一份報告
(D) 巡視一些建物

## Questions 62-64 refer to the following conversation.
英M 美W

**M** Hi, Bella. It's Ramon. I'm sorry to let you down at the last minute, but ㊅ **I won't be able to perform in the play** this evening. ㊆ **I've got a domestic crisis** and I don't want to leave my family.

**W** Oh, I'm sorry to hear that, Ramon. You're right to stay and sort it out though. Have you contacted your understudy to let him know he is to take your part?

**M** I just spoke to Miguel. He said he'd be delighted to do it. But he doesn't have a costume that will fit him.

**W** That's okay. I'll give him a call and ask him to come in early. ㊈ **That would give us time to find a costume for him that fits.**

對話

男：嗨，貝拉，我是拉蒙。很抱歉在最後一刻要讓妳失望了，但我無法在今天晚上的戲裡演出了。我家裡出了事，我不想丟下我的家人。

女：噢，很遺憾聽到這件事，拉蒙。但你留下來處理事情是對的。你和你的替補演員聯絡，讓他知道他要演你的角色了嗎？

男：我剛和米蓋爾談過。他說他很樂意演，但他沒有合身的戲服。

女：沒關係，我會打電話請他早點過來，那會讓我們有時間幫他找件適合的戲服。

字彙 **let someone down** 令某人失望
**at the last minute** 在最後一刻　**play** 戲劇
**domestic** 家庭的；家事的　**crisis** 危機
**sort out** 解決（問題等）
**understudy** 候補演員；替角　**part** 角色
**be delighted to** 高興做……
**costume** 戲裝；服裝　**fit** 合身；適合
**lose one's voice** 失聲
**reliable** 可靠的；可信賴的

**62** Where do the speakers work?
(A) At a fitness club
(B) At a doctor's surgery
(C) At a theater
(D) At a police station

說話者在哪裡工作？
(A) 健身俱樂部
(B) 診所
(C) 劇院
(D) 警察局

**63** Why will the man miss work today?
(A) He is not feeling well.
(B) He has lost his voice.
(C) He does not have a car.
(D) He has a crisis at home.

男子今天為什麼無法工作？
(A) 他覺得不舒服。
(B) 他失聲了。
(C) 他沒有車。
(D) 他家裡有急事。

**64** What do the speakers say about Miguel?
(A) He needs to be fitted for a costume.
(B) He is always reliable.
(C) He needs some additional training.
(D) He is not happy about the role.

關於米蓋爾，說話者說了什麼？
(A) 他需要合適的戲服。
(B) 他總是很可靠。
(C) 他需要額外訓練。
(D) 他對這個角色不滿意。

## Questions 65-67 refer to the following conversation and schedule. 美W 美M

| Room | Day of reservation |
|------|--------------------|
| 4A | Monday |
| 7B | Tuesday |
| 4C | Wednesday |
| ㊆ 2D | Thursday |

**W** The orientation for new hires is next week. How are things coming along?

**M** I have almost everything done that I had planned. ㊅ **I dropped off the information packets at the printer this morning. They should be ready by tomorrow.** I'm almost finished preparing my part of the presentation.

**W** Me, too. I just need to add a few more graphs to my part. 🌀 **Were you able to reserve the second floor conference room for next Thursday?**

**M** Unfortunately, 🌀 **it's already booked.**

**W** Really? That's not good. I like the video projector and screen in that room. They are easy to use.

**M** I was able to reserve a room on the third floor though. It's not as big as the one on the second floor, but it still has everything that we need.

**W** Then, it's going to be fine.

對話與時程表

| 室別 | 預訂日 |
|---|---|
| 4A | 星期一 |
| 7B | 星期二 |
| 4C | 星期三 |
| 2D | 星期四 |

女：下星期是新進員工訓練，事情進展得如何？

男：我規劃的一切差不多都完成了。我今天早上把資料袋送去印刷，應該明天會好。我負責的那部分簡報差不多準備完成了。

女：我也是，我只需要在我的部分再加幾張圖。你預訂了下星期四的 2 樓會議室了嗎？

男：不巧，該會議室已經有人訂了。

女：真的嗎？這可不妙。我喜歡那間的視訊投影機和螢幕，它們很容易操作。

男：但我訂到 3 樓的會議室，它沒有 2 樓那間那麼大，但還是有我們需要的所有設備。

女：那麼，一切就沒問題了。

字彙 **come along** 進展　**packet** 小包；小袋
**malfunction** 失靈、故障
**put off** 延後；拖延

**65** What most likely will the man do tomorrow?
(A) Pick up some materials
(B) Meet a client
(C) Test some devices
(D) Finish a presentation

男子明天最可能做什麼？
(A) 去取一些資料
(B) 見一位客戶
(C) 測試一些裝置
(D) 完成簡報

**66** What problem does the man mention?
(A) A screen is malfunctioning.
(B) An event needs to be put off.
(C) A room is not available.
(D) Some equipment is not working.

男子提到什麼問題？
(A) 有個螢幕故障。
(B) 有場活動必須延後。
(C) 有個房間無法使用。
(D) 有些設備故障。

**67** Look at the graphic. What room did the man reserve?
(A) Room 4A
(B) Room 7B
(C) Room 4C
(D) Room 2D

請見圖表，男子預訂了哪間會議室？
(A) 4A 室
(B) 7B 室
(C) 4C 室
(D) 2D 室

**Questions 68-70 refer to the following conversation and map.**
英M 美W

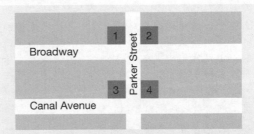

**M** Excuse me. I was wondering if you could help me. 🌀 **I'm trying to find where to catch a bus that goes to Shelton Hotel.**

**W** You mean the one on Wellington Road?

**M** Yes, that's correct. My hotel is also on that road.

**W** The number 21 bus will take you to where you want to go. The nearest bus stop is right in front of the National Museum.

**M** I'm not familiar with this area of the city. Is it close by?

**W** Well, I'm afraid you're going to have to do some walking. ⑥⑨ The museum is on the corner of Broadway and Parker Street. You are on Canal Avenue now. Walk down this street about 100 meters. Then, turn left on Parker Street. Walk along the street about 50 meters. Then you will find it on your right at the intersection.

**M** I hope I can remember all of that.

**W** ⑦⓪ How about if I write it down for you?

男：不好意思，不知道妳可不可幫我？我正在找去喜來登飯店的公車站。

女：你是指在威靈頓路的那家？

男：是的，沒錯。我的飯店也在那條路上。

女：21 路公車會載你到你想去的地方，最近的公車站就在國立博物館前面。

男：我對城市的這一區不熟，離這裡很近嗎？

女：嗯，恐怕你得走點路，博物館在派克街和百老匯大道交會口。你現在在運河大道，沿這條街走大約 100 公尺，然後在派克街左轉，沿著路走大約 50 公尺，然後你會在十字路口看到它在你的右邊。

男：我希望我能把這些都記住。

女：我把它寫下來給你如何？

**字彙** intersection 十字路口

---

**68** What does the man want to do?
(A) Visit an exhibit
(B) Book a room
(C) Park his car
(D) Take a bus
男子想要做什麼事？
(A) 看一個展覽
(B) 預訂一個房間
(C) 停車
(D) 搭公車

**69** Look at the graphic. Where is the National Museum?
(A) 1
(B) 2
(C) 3
(D) 4
請見圖表，國立博物館在哪裡？
(A) 1
(B) 2
(C) 3
(D) 4

**70** What does the woman offer to do?
(A) Write down directions
(B) Walk the man to his destination
(C) Give the man a map
(D) Call a taxi
女子提議做什麼？
(A) 寫下方向
(B) 帶男子到他的目的地
(C) 給男子一張地圖
(D) 打電話叫計程車

**PART 4**
P. 109

**Questions 71-73 refer to the following announcement.**
美M

Ladies and gentlemen, this is your tour guide. If you take a look to your right, facing southeast, you should be able to spot Blackstone Castle. This Castle is the oldest structure in the country and has become a shrine for the more superstitious in the local community who believe it is haunted. ⑦② Oh look, we can clearly see the eagles at their nest on top of the tower. This is a treat as most of the time, the eagles' nest is hidden away. ⑦① I have been a bus tour guide for many years and I've only seen the birds nesting a couple of times. If you have access to a camera, ⑦③ I recommend you take a picture as a keepsake.

## 宣告

各位女士和先生，我是你們的導遊。如果你往右邊看，面向東南方，你應該能認出黑石城堡。這座城堡是我國最古老的建築物，而且已經成為當地社區較迷信居民的聖地，他們相信那裡鬧鬼。噢，看那邊，我們可以清楚看到老鷹在塔頂的鳥巢裡。這真是難得的景象，因為大部分的時候，老鷹的巢都隱而不見。我當觀光巴士導遊很多年了，我只看過老鷹的巢幾次。如果你們有相機，我建議你們拍張照留作紀念。

**字彙** tour guide 導遊　take a look 看一看
face 朝、向　spot 認出；發現
structure 建築物；結構
shrine 聖地；神殿　superstitious 迷信的
local community 當地社區
haunted 鬧鬼的　treat 難得的樂事、招待
hide away 躲藏
have access to 可以使用……
keepsake 紀念品　ruined 毀壞的

**71** Where does the announcement most likely take place?
(A) On a train
(B) On a boat
(C) On a plane
(D) On a bus

這則宣告最有可能在哪裡發出？
(A) 在火車上
(B) 在船上
(C) 在飛機上
(D) 在巴士上

**72** What does the speaker point out as unusual?
(A) An animal at the castle
(B) A ruined tower structure
(C) A treat for the local community
(D) An unusual weather pattern

說話者指出什麼很不尋常？
(A) 城堡裡的一種動物
(B) 一座毀壞的塔狀物
(C) 當地社區的招待
(D) 奇特的天氣型態

**73** What does the speaker recommend the listeners do?
(A) Book a meal
(B) Watch the birds
(C) Listen to music
(D) Take pictures

說話者建議聽者做什麼？
(A) 預訂餐點
(B) 賞鳥
(C) 聽音樂
(D) 拍照

**Questions 74-76 refer to the following excerpt from a meeting.** 美W

Thank you all for attending this extraordinary general meeting. As you are aware, **74 our winter range of women's coats, dresses and tunics** hasn't been selling in stores as we had anticipated. We have surplus clothing in all store locations. So in an attempt to work out how to increase sales, we gave customers a questionnaire to survey what category of outfits or accessories they are most prone to purchase and under what circumstances. And **75 I'm going to distribute some of the completed questionnaires now for you** to have a look. For the remainder of the meeting, let's use this information to dream up **76 new tactics to encourage our shoppers**, especially women between the ages of 35 and 55.

## 會議摘錄

謝謝你們大家來參加這次的年度股東特別大會。如你們所知，我們的冬季系列女裝外套、洋裝和寬鬆無袖上衣，在店裡的銷售狀況並不如預期，每間店都有多的庫存。因此，為試圖想出如何增加銷量，我們發給顧客問卷，調查他們最傾向購買的服裝種類或配件，還有在什麼情況下購買。我現在要把一些完成的問卷發給你們看。在會議剩下的時間裡，讓我們運用這些資訊發想出新的策略激勵顧客，尤其是 35 到 55 歲的女性。

**字彙** extraordinary 非凡的；特別的
general meeting 股東大會
range of 一批；一系列　tunic 寬鬆無袖上衣
anticipate 預期；期望
surplus 過剩的；剩餘的
in an attempt to 試圖……
work out 想出　questionnaire 問卷
category 種類
outfit （為特定場合或活動而穿的）全套服裝
prone to 有……傾向的
under the circumstance 在某種情況下
distribute 分發、散發
have a look 看一看　remainder 剩餘部分
dream up 憑空想出　tactics 策略

**74** What type of product is being discussed?
(A) Electronic devices
(B) Clothing
(C) Athletic equipment
(D) Office supplies

正在討論何種產品？
(A) 電器設備
(B) 服裝
(C) 運動用品
(D) 辦公室用品

**75** What does the speaker say she will give the listeners?
(A) A product sample
(B) Completed questionnaires
(C) Sales updates
(D) A revised budget

說話者說，她會給聽者什麼東西？
(A) 產品的樣本
(B) 完成的問卷
(C) 最新的銷售量
(D) 修訂後的預算

**76** What are listeners asked to think about?
(A) Ideas for cutting costs
(B) Strategies for attracting customers
(C) Locations for a new shopping center
(D) Names for new products

聽者被要求思考什麼？
(A) 降低成本的方法
(B) 吸引顧客的策略
(C) 新購物中心的地點
(D) 新產品的名稱

**Questions 77-79 refer to the following telephone message.** 英M

Hi, Moritz. This is Haman. I'm organizing a group of colleagues **77** to go ice-skating at Elmer Outdoor Park next weekend. The weather is forecast to be sunny. Would you care to join us? So far, 12 people have said they'd like to come along. If we can persuade a few more people, so **78** we have twenty minimum, we qualify for a discount on boots and helmet hire. **79** I want to make the booking first thing on Monday morning, so please get back to me and let me know if you're able to come.

電話留言

　　嗨，莫里茲，我是哈曼。我正在規劃同事下週末去艾默戶外公園溜冰的事，天氣預報會是晴天，你想要加入嗎？到目前為止，有 12 個人說他們想要一起來。如果我們可以再說服多一點人，至少有 20 個人參加的話，我們就可以在租溜冰鞋和安全帽時有折扣。我想要星期一一大早預訂，所以請回電給我，告訴我你是否能來。

字彙 colleague 同事　forecast 預測；預報
Would you care to . . . ? 你想要做……嗎？
so far 到目前為止
come along 一同去；跟隨
persuade 說服；勸服
minimum 最少的；最小的
qualify for 有……的資格
booking 預訂；預約
get back to 給某人回電話
voucher 現金券；票券

**77** What is the speaker planning to do next weekend?
(A) Go on a sporting trip
(B) Purchase some ice skates
(C) Visit a sporting event
(D) Attend a convention

說話者計劃下週末做什麼？
(A) 來趟運動之旅
(B) 買溜冰鞋
(C) 參加體育活動
(D) 參加會議

**78** According to the speaker, what must people do to receive a discount?
(A) Arrive by bus
(B) Show a membership card
(C) Present a discount voucher
(D) Make a group booking

根據說話者所述，人們必須做什麼才能有折扣？
(A) 搭巴士去
(B) 出示會員卡
(C) 拿出優惠券
(D) 以團體為單位預訂

**79** What does the speaker say he wants to do on Monday morning?
(A) Make a booking
(B) Reserve a hotel room
(C) Deliver some items
(D) Go on a trip

說話者說他星期一早上想要做什麼？
(A) 預訂
(B) 預訂飯店房間
(C) 運送一些物品
(D) 去旅行

**Questions 80-82 refer to the following excerpt from a meeting.** 美W

As you all know, **80 tomorrow afternoon, we'll have a health and safety audit** for the main production plant. **81 The National Safety Inspectorate will be visiting to assess the standards of our company.** So it's crucial that everyone stores your belongings properly. **82 This afternoon, ensure you check the mandatory guidelines for safe storage** so when we get the visit tomorrow, you'll already have removed any hazardous items from the plant. Thank you for your consideration and collaboration.

會議摘錄

正如你們所知，明天下午，我們的主要生產廠房會進行衛生與安全審查，國家安全稽核局將前來評估我們公司的標準。因此，每個人把個人物品儲放在適當的地方相當重要。今天下午，務必查看安全儲存的強制規定，這樣，當我們明天接受審核時，你們就已經把所有的危險物品從工廠裡移除了。謝謝你們的體諒和配合。

字彙 audit 審核　production plant 生產工廠
safety inspectorate 安全稽核
assess 評估　crucial 關鍵的、決定性的
belongings 所有物
mandatory 強制的；義務的
guideline 準則；指導方針
hazardous 危險的
collaboration 合作
paramedic 急救護理人員
compulsory 必須做的；強制的
evacuate 撤離

**80** According to the speaker, what is taking place tomorrow?
(A) A major delivery
(B) A factory tour
(C) A management meeting
(D) A safety audit

根據說話者所述，明天會發生什麼事？
(A) 運送大量貨品
(B) 參觀工廠
(C) 管理會議
(D) 安全稽核

**81** Who will visit the plant?
(A) Suppliers
(B) Paramedics
(C) Inspectors
(D) Management

誰將要造訪工廠？
(A) 供應商
(B) 急救護理人員
(C) 檢查員
(D) 管理階層

**82** What are listeners asked to do later today?
(A) Check compulsory instructions
(B) Upload guidelines
(C) Submit a purchase order
(D) Evacuate the building

聽者今天稍晚被要求要做什麼？
(A) 查看強制規定
(B) 上傳準則
(C) 交出訂購單
(D) 撤離建物

**Questions 83-85 refer to the following excerpt from a meeting.** 美M

And last, I want to remind you that **83 the 10th anniversary of our organization** is approaching. Temp Workers Limited started with just three employees and a handful of clients and **84 it's astonishing to see how big a business we've become since then.** It's especially inspiring when you consider how much time it takes for the majority of new companies to become established. I am pleased to announce that our office coordinator, Mel Cushing, has agreed to organize the anniversary festivities but we'll require many more people to help out with the preparations. So **85 please send Mel an e-mail if you are able to help.**

12

最後，我要提醒你們，我們機構的 10 週年紀念日快到了。「派遣人員有限公司」創立時只有三名員工和少許客戶，看到我們從那時之後，發展成了如今的大企業，真是令人大為驚訝。當想到大部分的新公司，要花多少時間才能站穩腳步，就更加激勵人心。我很高興地宣布，我們的辦公室協調聯絡人，梅爾·庫辛已同意籌劃紀念日慶祝活動，但我們需要更多人幫忙籌備工作。因此，如果你們能幫忙，請寄電子郵件給梅爾。

字彙 approach 接近；即將達到
temp 臨時僱員　a handful of 少量；少數
astonishing 令人驚訝的
inspiring 激勵人心的　majority 大多數
established 已建立的；已確立的
office coordinator 辦公室協調人
festivity 慶祝活動
help out with 幫忙做某事

**83** What is being discussed?
(A) A press conference
(B) A client seminar
(C) A product launch
(D) A company anniversary

正在討論什麼？
(A) 記者會
(B) 客戶研討會
(C) 產品發表會
(D) 公司的週年紀念日

**84** According to the speaker, what is surprising?
(A) Rapid decrease of competitors
(B) The growth of the business
(C) The success of the advertising
(D) A change in a work schedule

根據說話者所述，什麼事令人驚訝？
(A) 競爭者快速減少
(B) 公司的成長
(C) 廣告的成功
(D) 工作時程表的改變

**85** Why are listeners asked to email Mel Cushing?
(A) To take part in a survey
(B) To assist with preparations
(C) To distribute leaflets
(D) To book a conference room

為什麼聽者被要求寄電子郵件給梅爾·庫辛？
(A) 為了參加調查
(B) 為了協助籌備工作
(C) 為了分發傳單
(D) 為了預訂會議室

**Questions 86-88 refer to the following talk.** 英W

**86** Today, I'm going to talk with you about some techniques team leaders can use to improve their employees' productivity. Nearly every company I have worked with has said that this is one of their top priorities. Yet, they often fail to get their workers to be more motivated or more efficient. Now, here's my understanding. The goals are good, but the implementation is often not good enough. And, as a result, they often blame the employees. But there are better ways, and that's what we are going to talk about today. **88** Before I do that, I want each of you to write down your ideas for what you think makes some employees more productive than others. There are a notepad and a pen in front of you.

談話

今天，我要和你們談談，團隊領導人可以用來改進員工生產力的一些技巧。幾乎所有我合作過的公司都說，這是他們最優先的事項之一，然而他們卻常常無法讓員工變得更有動力或更有效率。現在，我了解的狀況是這樣。目標是很好，但執行起來卻常常不夠好。因此結果是，他們通常都怪罪在員工身上。但是有更好的做法，而那正是我們今天要談的主題。在我開始之前，我要你們每個人寫下你的想法，你認為是什麼讓有些員工比其他人更有生產力。你們面前有筆記本和筆。

字彙 productivity 生產力；生產率
priority 優先考慮的事
implementation 實施；實踐；執行
summary 摘要
work station 工作站（檯）；個人工作區

**86** What topic will the woman talk about?
(A) Hiring team leaders
(B) Raising productivity
(C) Improving sales
(D) Transferring employees

女子將要談的主題是什麼？
(A) 僱用團隊領導人
(B) 提高生產力
(C) 改善業績
(D) 調動員工

**87** Why does the woman say, "Now, here's my understanding"?
(A) She recently presented some findings.
(B) She wants to write a summary.
(C) She trained her staff.
(D) She is going to tell her opinion.

為什麼女子說：「現在，我了解的狀況是這樣」？
(A) 她最近提出了一些發現。
(B) 她想要寫一篇摘要。
(C) 她訓練她的下屬。
(D) 她要說出她的意見。

**88** What are listeners asked to do?
(A) Write down some thoughts
(B) Talk with their coworkers
(C) Read some information
(D) Change their work station

聽者被要求做什麼？
(A) 寫下一些想法
(B) 和同事談談
(C) 讀一些資料
(D) 改變他們的工作站

**Questions 89-91 refer to the following excerpt from a meeting.** 澳M

There is one more item on our agenda. **89 As you may have heard, we are getting ready to launch a new line of stain remover for all types of vehicles.** They were designed to remove tough stains on cars like tar. We have tested these new products with customer focus groups, and they are well liked. I have prepared information packets to familiarize you with the products. They were supposed to be ready for me to hand out today, but we encountered a production delay. **90 So you can pick them up from my office next Tuesday.** I would have liked to go over them with you, but we are not able to do that today. **So this is it then.** The next meeting is on the twenty-fifth.

---

🔊12

**會議摘錄**

我們還有一項議程。你們可能已經聽說，我們正準備發表一款供所有車輛使用的新型去汙劑。它們設計來去除汽車上的頑強髒汙，如瀝青。我們已經給消費者焦點團體測試過這些新產品，他們都很喜歡。我準備了資料袋讓你們熟悉產品。資料原本今天應該準備好讓我可以發給你們，但製作過程遇到延誤。所以，你們可以在下星期二到我辦公室拿。我很願意和你們一起細看這些資料，但今天無法辦到。那麼，今天就到這裡。下次會議是 25 日。

**字彙** stain 污漬；污點　tar 瀝青；柏油
familiarize 使熟悉
encounter 遇到（困難、危險等）
commercial 商業的；商務的
demonstrate 展示；顯示

**89** Where does the speaker most likely work?
(A) At a cleaning product manufacturer
(B) At a commercial airline
(C) At a car dealership
(D) At a food market

說話者最可能在哪裡工作？
(A) 清潔用品廠商
(B) 商用航空公司
(C) 汽車經銷商
(D) 食品市場

**90** When can listeners get the information packets?
(A) Today
(B) Tomorrow
(C) Next week
(D) In two weeks

聽者什麼時候可以拿到資料袋？
(A) 今天
(B) 明天
(C) 下個星期
(D) 兩個星期後

**91** What does the man mean when he says, "So this is it then"?
(A) He will demonstrate how the product works.
(B) He is ready to end the meeting.
(C) He will go over the packets next time.
(D) He wants listeners to design some ideas.

115

當男子說：「那麼，今天就到這裡」時，他的意思是什麼？

(A) 他將展示產品如何作用。

(B) 他準備結束會議。

(C) 他下次會仔細看資料袋。

(D) 他想要聽者構思一些點子。

**Questions 92-94 refer to the following announcement and schedule.** 英W

| Train | From | Arriving at |
|-------|------|-------------|
| 121 | JFK | Platform 2 |
| 141 | Newark | Platform 7 |
| 161 | Union | Platform 1 |
| 171 | Jay | Platform 10 |

Attention, passengers. ❸ This train will be arriving at Platform 7 in Penn Station in about fifteen minutes. This is our final destination. All passengers must exit the train at Penn Station. ❷ Please check the overhead compartments and luggage areas for any personal items before exiting the train. Once you enter the station, you will not be able to return to the train. For passengers transferring to other trains, please check the departure board inside the station to check on your connecting train. Staff members are also available to assist you at the information desk. ❹ Please note that due to maintenance work, the station's main doors are closed. Please use the rear doors on Pine Street to exit the station. Thank you.

---

宣告與時程表

| 火車 | 起站 | 抵達 |
|------|------|------|
| 121 | 甘迺迪機場 | 第 2 月台 |
| 141 | 紐華克機場 | 第 7 月台 |
| 161 | 聯合車站 | 第 1 月台 |
| 171 | 傑伊街 | 第 10 月台 |

　　各位旅客請注意。本列車將於約 15 分鐘後抵達賓州車站第 7 月台。這是我們的終點站，所有旅客必須在賓州車站下車。請在下車前檢查上方的行李架和行李區的所有個人物品。一旦進入車站，就無法返回火車上。要轉搭其他火車的旅客，請查看車站內的離站看板，以查看您的轉乘列車資訊。車站服務台的工作人員也能協助您。請注意，由於維修作業，車站的大門關閉。請由派恩街的後門離開車站。謝謝您。

字彙 overhead compartment 座位上方的行李架或置物櫃

maintenance 維護；保養

rear 後面的；背部的

belongings 擁有物；行李

disembark 下車；登陸　　routine 例行的

**92** What are the listeners asked to do?

(A) Store their belongings properly

(B) Not get off the train before an announcement

(C) Check their belongings before disembarking

(D) Move to a different platform

聽者被要求做什麼？

(A) 把他們的東西儲放在適當的地方

(B) 在廣播之前不要下車

(C) 下車前檢查他們的隨身行李

(D) 移到另一個月台

**93** Look at the graphic. Where did the train leave from?

(A) JFK

(B) Newark

(C) Union

(D) Jay

請見圖表，這班火車是從哪裡開來的？

(A) 甘迺迪機場

(B) 紐華克機場

(C) 聯合車站

(D) 傑伊街

**94** Why can't passengers use the main entrance?

(A) Improvement work is being done.

(B) The place is too crowded at the moment.

(C) It has been shut down for a routine inspection.

(D) Cleaning work is taking place.

旅客為什麼無法使用大門？

(A) 正在進行改善工程。

(B) 這個地方現在太擁擠了。

(C) 由於例行性檢查而關閉。

(D) 正在進行清掃作業。

12

**Questions 95-97 refer to the following broadcast and map.** 澳M

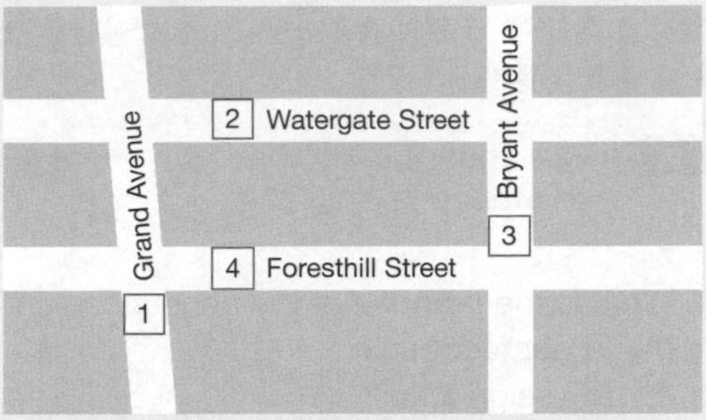


This is Sam Smith with your 6 o'clock traffic news. Everything looks good on the city's main streets and highways. That should make it easier for everyone heading back home this evening. ⑨⑦ **I have a reminder for all of you who use Bryant Avenue to get downtown.** ⑨⑤ ⑨⑦ **Starting tomorrow, that street will be closed between Watergate Street and Foresthill Street.** Work crews will be doing maintenance work on electric cables under the Avenue. They are going to use the opportunity to repave the surface of the area. Construction is expected to last for three days at the most. ⑨⑥ **During that time, commuters should follow the yellow signs to detour the site.** They will direct you to safely bypass the work area to your downtown destination.

**廣播與地圖**

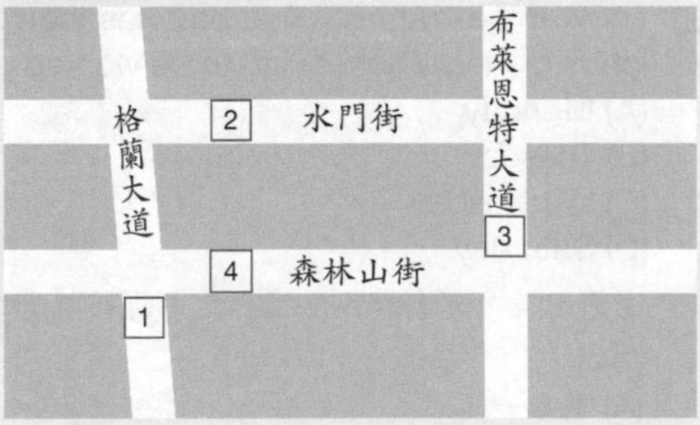


我是山姆·史密斯，為您播報6點的路況報導。本市的主要道路與公路看來都很順暢，這應該會讓大家今晚回家的路較為順利。我要提醒所有走布萊恩特大道進入市區的用路人，從明天開始，那條路在水門街和森林山街之間的路段將封閉。工作人員將進行大道地下電纜的維修工程，他們將利用這個機會重鋪該段路面。工程預計最多進行三天。在這段期間，用路人應遵照黃色標誌繞行施工地點，他們會指引你們安全地繞過施工區，前往你們的市區目的地。

字彙 **crew** 工作人員 **repave** 再鋪；重鋪 **surface** 表面；地面 **detour** 繞道 **bypass** 繞過

**95** What is the broadcast about?
(A) Building maintenance
(B) Traffic congestion
(C) A road closure
(D) A new bus schedule

這則廣播的主題是什麼？
(A) 建物維修
(B) 交通壅塞
(C) 道路封閉
(D) 新的公車時刻表

**96** What are commuters advised to do?
(A) Leave earlier
(B) Take a detour
(C) Avoid using public transportation in the area
(D) Drive slowly

用路人被建議做什麼？
(A) 提早動身
(B) 繞道而行
(C) 避免在該區搭乘大眾運輸工具
(D) 慢慢開

**97** Look at the graphic. What number shows where the construction will take place?
(A) 1
(B) 2
(C) 3
(D) 4

請見圖表，哪個號碼顯示工程將要進行之處？
(A) 1
(B) 2
(C) 3
(D) 4

| New Work Schedule | |
| --- | --- |
| Area | Day |
| Cafeteria | Monday |
| Breakroom | Tuesday<br>Thursday |
| Storage space | Wednesday<br>Friday |
| Lobby | Saturday |

Okay, before we get started working this morning, I just want to let everybody know about the new interior flooring material that we will be using. Our supplier recently let us know that they were planning to discontinue the material we normally use. They were kind enough to send us some samples of their new one to try out. Now, it's really important to understand that the new flooring material is thicker in consistency than the stuff you are familiar with. ❾❾ So it takes a little longer to apply, and it also needs more time to settle down. ❾❽ As a result, we have to adjust our schedule slightly. ❿ Initially, we had planned to start on the lobby of the building and then work on other places. But we have to change that as we need more time. So the lobby should be the last.

宣告與時程表

| 新工作時程表 | |
| --- | --- |
| 區域 | 工作日 |
| 自助餐廳 | 星期一 |
| 休息室 | 星期二<br>星期四 |
| 儲藏區 | 星期三<br>星期五 |
| 大廳 | 星期六 |

好的，在我們今天早上開始工作之前，我只是要告訴大家，我們將要採用的新室內地板建材的事。我們的供應商最近通知我們，他們打算停止供應我們以往使用的建材。他們很體貼地寄了一些新建材給我們試用。現在，特別需要熟知的是，這種新的地板建材，比你們平常熟悉的還要厚。因此，要多花一點時間鋪設與安置。所以，我們得稍微調整一下我

們的工作時程。起初，我們打算從大樓的大廳開始更換，然後施作其他地方。但是由於我們需要更多時間，所以我們必須改變計畫。因此大廳會最後進行。

字彙 discontinue 停止；中斷
consistency 堅硬度；濃度

**98** What is the purpose of the announcement?
(A) To get feedback
(B) To assign a task
(C) To promote a product
(D) To change a plan

這則宣告的目的是什麼？
(A) 為了得到回饋意見
(B) 為了分派一項任務
(C) 為了促銷一個產品
(D) 為了改變一項計畫

**99** What is mentioned about the new material?
(A) It takes longer to settle in.
(B) It is less expensive.
(C) It is more durable.
(D) It is easier to use.

關於新材料，提到了什麼？
(A) 要花較長時間適應。
(B) 較便宜。
(C) 較耐用。
(D) 較容易使用。

**100** Look at the graphic. What day was the lobby originally scheduled to be worked on?
(A) Monday
(B) Tuesday
(C) Wednesday
(D) Saturday

請見圖表，大廳原先安排要施工的日期是哪一天？
(A) 星期一
(B) 星期二
(C) 星期三
(D) 星期六

# PART 5

P. 112

**101**

金先生下週三將完成關於汽車業財務狀況的論文。

(A) finished 完成了
(B) finishing 完成
(C) to finish 完成
(D) will finish 將完成

**解析** 主詞為 Mr. Kim，空格置於句中的動詞位置，因此請先刪去 finishing 和 to finish。而句尾出現 next Wednesday，所以答案要選未來式 (D)。「next . . .」、「by/until ＋未來時間點」、「as of ＋未來時間點」、soon、shortly 皆為答題線索，表示未來。

**字彙** thesis 論文　financial 財務的
state 狀況　automobile 汽車

**102**

業務在與客戶談判價格時，應盡可能靈活。

(A) flexible 靈活的
(B) flexed 彎曲的
(C) flexing 彎曲
(D) flexibility 靈活性

**解析** 本題考的是形容詞原級。as 和 as 之間要填入形容詞或副詞的原級，因此 flexible、flexed、flexing 皆可填入空格中。但是根據題意，表達「有彈性的；靈活的」最為適當，因此答案為 (A)。

**字彙** flexible 靈活的　flex 彎曲
flexibility 靈活性

**103**

請允許您的訂單有至少兩到三週的交貨期。

(A) method 方法
(B) quantity 數量
(C) delivery 運送
(D) model 模型

**解析** 根據題意，與商品有關、最適合填入的單字為 (C)。另外補充一點，allow 適用的句型結構為〈allow ＋受詞＋ to ＋原形動詞〉和〈allowed to ＋原形動詞〉，請特別熟記。

**字彙** quantity 數量

**104**

克拉克斯公司為這區域的成人和年輕人提供最多冬季鞋款的選擇。

(A) selection 選擇
(B) selected 選擇了
(C) selects 選擇
(D) selecting 選擇

**解析** 形容詞（widest）和介系詞（of）之間只能填入名詞。選項中，selection 和 selecting 皆屬於名詞的角色。而根據題意，表達「提供最多種類的鞋類」較為適當，因此答案為 (A)。selecting 可以當作動名詞使用，但是不受形容詞修飾，而是要受副詞修飾，請特別熟記。

**字彙** region 地區　footwear 鞋類
selection 選擇

**105**

所有參觀索爾諾瓦太陽能發電廠的外賓必須在抵達時立刻向接待櫃台報告。

(A) partially 部分地
(B) timely 及時地
(C) closely 緊密地
(D) immediately 立即地

**解析** 根據題意，表達「賓客抵達就要馬上報告接待櫃檯」最為適當，因此答案為 (D)。另外補充一點，雖然 timely 為 ly 結尾，但它是形容詞，請務必記住。

**字彙** solar 太陽（能）的
power plant 發電廠

**106**

當你度假不在時，請向同事清楚指示，說明應該如何在你不在時處理客戶的要求。

(A) whole 完整的
(B) blank 空白的
(C) repetitive 重複的
(D) clear 清楚的

**解析** 本題考的是形容詞詞彙。根據題意，最適合填入的形容詞為 (D)。blank 的意思與空格後方的 absence 相近，為答題陷阱。

**字彙** take a holiday 度假
instruction 說明
regarding 有關……
absence 不在；缺席　whole 整體的
blank 空白的　repetitive 重複的

**107**

提交商業計畫書的截止日期為 6 月 6 日星期三下午 5 點。
(A) submit 提交
(B) submission 提交
(C) submits 提交
(D) submitted 提交了

解析 介系詞（for）和介系詞（of）之間要填入名詞，因此答案為 (B)。submit 為動詞、submitted 僅可當作動詞或分詞使用，無法扮演名詞的角色。

字彙 deadline 截止日期
business proposal 商業計畫書
submission 提交

**108**

美國馬術協會的網站，讓會員可以輕易獲得馬匹的最新消息。
(A) with 有……
(B) into 進入到……
(C) beside 在……旁邊
(D) up 上

解析 本題要選出適當的介系詞。provide A with B 或 provide B to A 皆可以表示「提供 B 給 A」，因此答案為 (A)。

字彙 equestrian 馬術 association 協會
access 接近；進入；通道；獲得

**109**

雅馬哈公司通常會要求五人或五人以上的團體提前報名參加工廠參觀。
(A) normal 正常的
(B) normality 正態性
(C) norm 規範
(D) normally 通常

解析 空格要填入副詞，用來修飾動詞（requires），因此答案為 (D)。normal 可以當作形容詞或名詞；normality 為名詞；norm 為名詞，三者皆不能用來修飾動詞。另外，請熟記句型〈require ＋受詞＋ to do〉，意思為「要求……做……」。

字彙 sign up 報名參加 in advance 提前
normal 正常的 normality 正態性
norm 規範 normally 通常

**110**

茲林卡・米利奧蒂於 10 月 9 日正式擔任漢薩德電氣公司」資訊科技總監一職。
(A) namely 也就是
(B) collectively 集體地
(C) officially 正式地
(D) densely 密集地

解析 本題考的是副詞詞彙。根據題意，表達「正式」就任某項職位較為適當，因此最適合填入的選項為 (C)。

字彙 assume 承擔；就任
chief information officer 首席資訊官；
資訊科技總監 namely 即；也就是
collectively 集體地 officially 正式地
densely 密集地

**111**

在啟動投影機之前，請將其電線牢牢地連接到設備上。
(A) there 那裡
(B) which 那
(C) its 它的
(D) those 那些

解析 本題考的是代名詞。空格後方連接名詞（cable），因此請優先刪去副詞（there）；those 後方要連接複數名詞，因此也請刪去該選項；which 可以當作關係代名詞、或是名詞子句連接詞使用，不適合填入本題空格中；(C) 為代名詞的所有格，故為正確答案。

字彙 activate 啟動 projector 投影機
firmly 牢固地 device 設備

**112**

曼泰洛小吃飲料公司的所有兼職和全職員工，預計都將參加總裁的年度資訊交流集會。
(A) contributed 貢獻
(B) expected 預計
(C) noticed 通知
(D) conducted 執行

解析 本題考的是動詞詞彙。根據題意，表達「預計會參加資訊交流集會」較為適當，因此答案為 (B)。(A) contributed 後方連接的是介系詞 to，因此並非答案。

字彙 gathering 聚會 conduct 進行；執行

## 113

公聽會的錄音於整場會議期間將可在市議會的網站上取得。

(A) since 自從
(B) between 在……之間
(C) within 在……之內
(D) throughout 貫穿

**解析** 本題要選出適當的介系詞。根據題意，表達「會議期間可以在市議會網站上收聽」最為適當，因此答案為 (D)。since 當作介系詞使用時，後方要連接表示過去的時間或事件的名詞，意思為「自……以來」；between 的意思為「在……之間」，不適合搭配單數名詞 meeting 使用。

**字彙** recording 錄音
public hearing 公聽會

## 114

當大樓正在整修時，一些工作人員可能暫時移到不同的工作區。

(A) at 在……
(B) on 在……上
(C) to 到……
(D) as 當……

**解析** 空格位在地點前方，根據題意，表達「可能要臨時搬移至其他工作場所」較為適當，因此答案為 (C)。as 當作介系詞使用時，意思為「作為……」，不適合填入本題的空格中。

**字彙** temporarily 暫時　relocate 搬遷
workspace 工作區

## 115

請至賈拉分班專案的網站，並且今天就報名參加電腦程式設計的研討會。

(A) registering 報名參加
(B) registered 報名參加了
(C) registration 報名參加
(D) register 報名參加

**解析** 空格前方為對等連接詞 and，前方連接的動詞為 visit，因此空格要填入原形動詞，答案為 (D)。registering 可以當作現在分詞或動名詞使用；registered 可以當作過去分詞或動詞使用；registration 為名詞，皆不能作為答案。另外，請熟記 register、sign up for、enroll in 的意思皆為「報名參加……」。

**字彙** placement 安置；分班
registration 註冊；報名；登記

## 116

國會議員羅伯特·史密斯，將在明天晚上7點的廣播新聞記者招待會上宣布競選連任。

(A) announce 宣布
(B) notify 通知
(C) interfere 干擾
(D) level 級別

**解析** 本題的四個選項皆為動詞，因此請選出最適當的動詞詞彙。根據題意，只要思考廣播節目上可以做的行為，便能輕鬆選出答案。表達「在廣播節目上宣告他的意圖」最為適當，因此答案為 (A)。

**字彙** bid 企圖；努力　reelection 連任
interfere 干擾　level 級別

## 117

《開發週刊》在伍德蘭山區始終被列為最受歡迎的出版物。

(A) consistency 一致性
(B) consistencies 一致性
(C) consistently 一貫地
(D) consistent 一致的

**解析** 空格用來修飾動詞（has been ranked），應填入副詞，因此答案為 (C)。consistency 為名詞、consistent 為形容詞，皆不適合填入。

**字彙** rank 名列　publication 出版物
consistency 一致性
consistently 一貫地；始終如一地
consistent 一致的

## 118

請確認所有包裹在送到倉庫之前都已妥善包裝好。

(A) as much as 與……一樣多
(B) such as 例如
(C) whether 是否
(D) before 在……之前

**解析** that 後方到空格前為完整的子句（all . . . properly），空格後方也是完整的子句（they . . . warehouse），因此空格要填入從屬連接詞或是對等連接詞。as much as、whether、before 皆可當作從屬連接詞使用，但是根據題意，表達「在包裹運送之前」較為適當，因此答案為 (D)。such as 的用法為〈名詞＋such as A〉，意思為「像是 A 之類的名詞」，並不適合填入。

**字彙** properly 妥善地　ship 運送
warehouse 倉庫
as much as 和……一樣多

**119** 大廳的翻修工程不可能在下個月初之前完工。
(A) typical 典型的
(B) probably 可能地
(C) likely 可能的
(D) usual 通常的

**解析** 空格應填入形容詞，因此請先刪去副詞 probably。根據題意，使用「be likely to 不定詞」，表達「有可能……」最為適當，因此答案為 (C)。句中的 likely 雖然為 ly 結尾，看似副詞，卻屬於形容詞，請特別熟記。

**字彙** renovation 翻修　typical 典型的

**120** 《作業系統雜誌》預測，用於製作電子零件的鋼鐵需求，將在未來十年達到高峰。
(A) materials 材料
(B) demand 需求
(C) appliances 器具
(D) resource 資源

**解析** 本題考的是名詞詞彙。根據題意「往後十年，用於電子零件上的鋼鐵＿＿＿將會達到高峰」，最適合填入空格的選項為 (B)。名詞 demand、request、need 後方會搭配介系詞 for 一起使用，請務必熟記。

**字彙** forecast 預測　iron and steel 鋼鐵
electronic parts 電子零件
peak 頂峰；高峰　material 材料
appliance 器具　resource 資源

**121** 新鄉村俱樂部可能會要求顧客在取回個人物品時出示證件。
(A) retrieve 取回
(B) retrieved 取回了
(C) retrieval 取回
(D) retrieving 取回

**解析** 介系詞後方可以連接名詞或動名詞，但空格後方連接了受詞，因此答案要選動名詞 (D)。

**字彙** identification 身分證件；身分證
belongings 物品；所有物
retrieve 取回

**122** 想參加今年行銷研討會的人必須在 8 月 1 日之前與古雷西先生聯繫。
(A) Nobody 沒有人
(B) Whoever 任何人
(C) Whatever 不管什麼
(D) Somebody 某人

**解析** 句中有兩個動詞 wishes 和 must contact，因此空格要填入適當的連接詞，連接這兩個動詞。Nobody 和 Somebody 皆為代名詞，不能作為答案。空格至 seminar 在句子中扮演主詞的角色，因此空格應填入名詞子句連接詞。

whoever 和 whatever 皆可當作名詞子句連接詞使用，且兩者後方皆可以連接不完整的子句，因此必須透過意思來選出正確答案。根據題意，表達「無論誰想參加今年的行銷研討會」較為適當，因此答案為 (B)。填入 Whatever 並不符合題意。

**123** 財務長羅文・溫斯沃爾德，向所有提出降低運營成本想法的人表達了她的感謝。
(A) imitation 模仿
(B) exposure 暴露
(C) gratitude 感謝
(D) abundance 豐富

**解析** 本題考的是名詞詞彙。根據題意，表達「向提供降低成本的構想的人表達感謝」最為適當，因此答案為 (C)。

**字彙** CFO (Chief Financial Officer) 財務長
post 發表　reduce 降低
imitation 模仿　exposure 曝光；暴露
abundance 豐富

**124**

空調機如果沒有控制液體流動的閥門，將無法運作。
(A) regulated 管理了
(B) will regulate 將管理
(C) regulates 管理
(D) to regulate 管理

**解析** 開頭到空格前方為一個結構完整的句子，因此空格開始應屬於修飾語。will regulate 和 regulates 皆為動詞，請優先排除；regulated 為過去分詞，但空格後方連接了受詞（the flow of liquid），因此不能填入空格中。答案要選 to 不定詞 (D)。

**字彙** operate 運作　valve 閥門
flow 流動　regulate 規範；管理；控制

**125**

培訓專員就即將舉行的培訓研討會，向全體員工發送了一份公司內部通知單。
(A) resulting 結果
(B) following 接著
(C) usually 通常
(D) concerning 關於

**解析**「The training . . . all employees」為一個結構完整的句子，因此空格至句尾是用來修飾前方的內容。空格後方連接了名詞（training meetings），因此空格應填入介系詞，搭配名詞一同作為修飾語。following 和 concerning 皆為介系詞，但是根據題意，表達「發送有關即將到來的培訓研討會的通知單」較為適當，因此答案為 (D)。

另外補充一點，介系詞 about、on、over、as to、as for、regarding、concerning 的意思皆為「關於；有關」，請務必熟記。

**字彙** representative 代表員；代理人
upcoming 即將舉行的　result 結果

**126**

雷施社區機場展示了當地航空愛好者馬修‧本頓所繪製的藝術品。
(A) enthusiast 對……熱衷之人
(B) enthused 充滿熱情的
(C) enthusiastically 熱情地
(D) enthusiasm 熱忱

**解析** 空格位在冠詞（a）和形容詞（local）的後方，因此空格應填入名詞。根據題意，該名詞用來指前方的 Matthew Benton，因此答案為人物名詞 (A)。雖然 enthusiasm 也是名詞，但是並不符合題意。

**字彙** aviation 航空
enthusiast 對……熱衷的人；熱心者
enthuse 使充滿熱情
enthusiastically 熱情地
enthusiasm 熱情；熱忱

**127**

最近投資珍貴寶石的趨勢有望延續下去。
(A) near 靠近……
(B) toward 對於……
(C) though 雖然
(D) along 沿著……

**解析** 空格後方連接動名詞（investing），因此空格應填入介系詞。雖然 (A) near（鄰近……）和 (D) along（沿著……）也是介系詞，但是其意思皆不適合填入空格中。trend 的意思為「趨勢、動向」，(B) 為表示「對於；關於」的介系詞，因此適合與其搭配使用。

**128**

使用藍海金融服務公司的新客戶必須安裝防毒軟體，才可以線上讀取帳戶資料。
(A) unless 除非
(B) so that 如此一來
(C) as though 彷彿
(D) whereas 然而

**解析** 本題的四個選項皆為從屬連接詞，因此要透過單字的意思來解題。so that 後方引導的子句通常會使用助動詞 can 或 may，表示「讓……能夠」，因此答案為 (B)。

**字彙** antivirus 防毒

**129**

由於過去 9 個月的利潤高於預期,因此可以理解為何吉安帕尼杜設計公司對於公司擴張是很樂觀的。

(A) devoted 致力的
(B) optimistic 樂觀的
(C) impressive 印象深刻的
(D) ample 充足的

**解析** 本題考的是形容詞詞彙。根據題意,表達「因為收益超乎預期的高,所以對擴張持樂觀看法」較為適當,因此答案為 (B)。

**字彙** understandably 可理解地
expansion 擴張
devoted 專心致志的;虔誠的
optimistic 樂觀的
impressive 印象深刻的
ample 充足的;大量的

**130**

當初如果星艦娛樂公司沒有給該男演員機會,另一家公司也會給。

(A) should do 應該做
(B) has done 已經做
(C) would have done 那時會做
(D) was done 被做

**解析** 本題為假設語氣倒裝句。原本的 if 子句為 If Starship Entertainment had not given the actor a chance,省略 if 之後,再將助動詞 had 移至主詞前方,形成倒裝句。if 子句的時態為過去完成式(had not given),因此主要子句的時態要用助動詞加上現在完成式,答案為 (C) would have done。

**PART 6** P. 115

**131-134 文章報導**

**「自然公園」即將開幕**

　　本市新設立的「自然公園」開幕典禮將在 4 月 2 日星期日舉行。市長、市議員、記者和幾位地方知名人士都將出席。正式的剪綵儀式將於上午 10 點 30 分舉行,緊接著是市長發表歡迎致詞。當地幾家餐廳將提供點心和飲料,此外也會有娛樂活動,包括舞蹈表演和魔術表演。雖然活動開放公眾免費入場,但必須事先在網路上報名參加。有興趣的人可以在 www.natureparkopening.com 上查看相關訊息。座位有限,所以請提早抵達。

**字彙** celebrity 知名人士
be in attendance 出席
registration 報名　in advance 事先

**131**

(A) remark 評論
(B) ceremony 典禮
(C) demonstration 示範
(D) presentation 簡報

**解析** 本題要選出符合文意的名詞詞彙。要選出適合搭配動詞 will be held(舉行)使用的主詞,又能與 opening 組合成複合名詞,因此答案為 (B)。

**132**

(A) following 接著
(B) follows 接著
(C) will follow 將接著
(D) followed 接著

**解析** 空格所在的句子已經有動詞(is scheduled),但並未出現連接詞,因此空格不能填入動詞。而空格所在的句子屬於分詞構句,後方並未連接受詞,因此空格應填入 p.p.,答案要選 (D) followed。

**133**

(A) Now that 既然
(B) Although 雖然
(C) Besides 並且
(D) As though 彷彿

解析 空格後方連接兩個子句，因此應填入連接詞。Now that（既然）、Although（雖然；儘管）、As though（好像）當中，最符合文意的是 (B) Although。

## 134

(A) 保育自然是很重要的。
(B) 將有供應食物可供購買。
(C) 座位有限。
(D) 由於天氣惡劣，活動已被延期。

解析 空格後方建議提早抵達，因此適合填入表示「座位數量有限」的句子，答案要選 (C)。

### 135-138 小冊子

來參加我們定期安排的自行車之旅，盡情探索伯頓村。由伯頓觀光學院公司贊助的遊覽活動，每一場都是由專業的自行車手帶領，並以不同的視角欣賞這個村莊。

最受歡迎的路線是圍繞著該村莊工業區下谷的路線。除了三個仍在運轉的麵粉廠和一個製造工廠外，下谷還擁有一個正在開採中的錫礦場、和幾家代表該地區歷史的手工藝品店。遊覽持續約三個小時。旅程包含在伯頓最古老的小酒吧之一的格林曼酒吧內享用爽口的餐點。

欲報名下谷的行程或了解其他旅遊行程，請致電伯頓觀光學院，電話是 050-555-6939。

字彙 sponsor 贊助　tourism 觀光業
head 帶領　expert 專門的；專家的
cyclist 自行車手
feature 以……為特色；是……的特色
perspective 視角；觀點　route 路線
encompass 圍繞；包括
industrial 工業的
in addition to 除了　mill 加工廠；磨坊
tin mine 錫礦場
crafts shop 工藝品商店
represent 代表
refreshing 清爽的；提神的
pub 酒吧　public house 小酒吧
register for 報名
find out 找出；發現

## 135

(A) each 每一個
(B) whose ……人的
(C) either 兩者之一
(D) this 這個

解析 本題的四個選項都能用來修飾名詞，具有形容詞的作用，因此屬於較難直接選出答案的題型。首先，關係代名詞 whose 屬於所有格、either 用於二選一的情況，皆不適合填入空格中。空格所在句子的後方出現 different，表示並非屬於「固定一個」行程，而是「各別的」，因此答案為 (A)。

## 136

(A) factories 工廠
(B) programs 計畫
(C) district 區域
(D) revolution 革命

解析 若能掌握 Downvale Valley 屬於什麼樣的地方，便能找出答案。空格後方的句子中出現麵粉廠、工廠、錫礦廠、工藝品店，因此填入工業「區」較為適當，答案要選 (C)。

## 137

(A) 訪客應配戴安全配備。
(B) 遊覽持續約三個小時。
(C) 騎自行車有益健康。
(D) 這趟導覽將解釋這座城鎮的歷史。

解析 空格後方提到最後一個行程，因此適合填入「參觀三個小時左右」，答案要選 (B)。

## 138

(A) concludes 以……結束
(B) exits 離去
(C) orders 訂購
(D) reserves 預訂

解析 空格後方連接 with，因此請先刪去及物動詞 (C) 和 (D)。根據文意，表達「結束」較為適當，因此答案為 (A)。

解答&中譯解析 Actual Test 3 PART 6

125

## 139-142 電子郵件

收件者：muamba@nigermail.com
寄件者：subscriptions@befitmagazine.com
主旨：續訂
日期：9 月 20 日

親愛的姆安巴先生：

您訂閱的《健康雜誌》將在 9 月 30 日到期。為了確保您不會錯過我們雜誌有關一般健康和健身的優質文章，別忘了以 30 元的超低優惠價格續訂十二個月的雜誌。此外，若是您在本月底之前續訂，您將能以折扣價購買喬治·登特出版社的其他出版品，這包括《運動常規》和《穿出好印象》這兩本書。

只需在 9 月 23 日之前，至 www.befitmagazine.com/subscription 填完線上續訂表格即可。

祝好，
訂閱服務部

**字彙** subscription renewal 續訂　ensure 確保
award-winning 獲獎的；優等的；一流的
publication 出版品　valid 有效的
cordially 熱誠地；誠摯地

**139**
(A) having expired 已到期
(B) will expire 將到期
(C) expired 到期了
(D) expiring 到期

**解析** 本文為建議讀者延長雜誌訂閱時間的電子郵件。本文撰寫的時間為 9 月 20 日，而第二句話開始持續説服對方延長訂閱時間，這表示目前的訂閱尚未到期。因此 9 月 30 日便是到期日，空格應填入未來式，答案為 (B)。

**140**
(A) Consequently 因此
(B) However 然而
(C) Instead 取而代之
(D) Additionally 此外

**解析** 空格前後的句子皆在説明相關優惠，説服對方延長訂閱時間。因此空格應填入適合連接前後句子的單字，以後面句子作為補充説明，(D) 表示「此外、還有」的意思，最適合填入空格中。

**141**
(A) 此報價僅提供給首次訂閱的用戶。
(B) 我們收到您為十一月號刊繳交的稿件。
(C) 這包括《運動常規》和《穿出好印象》這兩本書。
(D) 我們誠摯邀請您參加頒獎典禮。

**解析** 空格正前方提到 George Dent 出版社的刊物，應選擇與此相關的句子，因此答案為 (C)。

**142**
(A) into 進入到……
(B) by 在……之前
(C) at 在……
(D) until 直到……

**解析** 本題要選出適當的介系詞。該句話是要請用戶在 9 月 23 日前完成續約的表格，因此可以從 by 和 until 當中選出答案，兩者皆有「在……之前」的意思。by 用於一次性的動作、until 則用於持續進行的動作上，而 complete（完成）屬於一次性的動作，因此答案為 (B) by。

## 143-146 公告

**公告**

致：博物館工作人員

自 3 月 5 日起，由於工程進行緣故，博物館主館的東側館即將關閉。館內的電梯和電燈開關已經過於老舊，需要更換。

我們將會張貼告示，提醒來賓禁止進入該區域。需要進出該區的工作人員可以在管制之下進行，進出必須獲得主管許可。

最後要說明的是，以往規定要送到東側館裝卸碼頭的貨物，將暫時改送到北側館收發室。一旦工程完畢，我們將恢復成正常的運送模式。

在此先感謝您的耐心。

艾爾·亞索夫
金太陽博物館館長

字彙 wing （建築）側廳；廂房
owing to 由於　alert 警告；提醒
patron 主顧；贊助者；資助者
off-limits 禁止進入的；禁區的
on a limited basis 在受限的情況下
loading dock 裝卸碼頭
reroute 使改變路線；按新的特定路線運送
protocol 議定書；協議　in advance 事先

## 143

(A) construct 建造
(B) constructor 建造商
(C) construction 工程
(D) constructively 建設性地

解析 空格位在介系詞（owing to）的受詞位置，應填入名詞。選項中 constructor（建造者）和 construction（施工）皆為名詞，而因為施工導致建築物東側館關閉，因此答案為 (C) construction。

## 144

(A) 建議員工在工程期間休假。
(B) 進出必須獲得主管許可。
(C) 有些活動仍會在東側館舉行。
(D) 機密文件將儲放於保護箱內。

解析 空格前方提到僅限有需要的員工出入，因此空格填入「必須先獲得主管的同意」較為適當，答案為 (B)。

## 145

(A) hardly 幾乎不
(B) temporarily 暫時地
(C) formally 正式地
(D) permanently 永久地

解析 施工時無法送至東側館，表示「暫時」得送至北側館，因此答案為 (B) temporarily（臨時地）。

## 146

(A) following 接著
(B) promptly 迅速地
(C) later 之後
(D) once 一旦

解析 空格用來引導後方的子句，因此答案要選連接詞 (D) once（一旦……便）。(A) 為介系詞、(B) 和 (C) 為副詞。

PART 7

P. 119

147-148 簡訊

收件者：約書亞・伊斯梅爾
寄件者：藍山外科診所

這是卡贊尼斯醫生給您的簡訊。我們已為您預約 1 月 13 日（星期三）上午 9 點的約診。如果您希望接受此預約，請按 1 確認。

如果您無法在指定的時間到達，請致電 143-555-1856，和本診所重新安排時間。

謝謝。

寄送

字彙 surgery 手術
make an appointment 預約
confirm 確認
specify 具體指定；詳細指明
reschedule 重新安排……的時間
procedure 程序；手續

## 147

為什麼發送此訊息？
(A) 為了詢問一項程序
(B) 為了宣布取消預約
(C) 為了更改預約
(D) 為了要求確認預約

## 148

伊斯梅爾先生要做什麼才可以更改預約時間？
(A) 打電話到診所
(B) 去診所
(C) 發送簡訊
(D) 發送傳真

寄件者：alerts@dacklonbank.com
收件者：吉娜·崔西
　　　　<gtrace@budsandbows.com>
主旨：自動通知：請勿回覆
日期：6月8日

---

我們收到通知，得知您有筆資金從您達克倫銀行的支票存款帳戶轉出。

**日期和時間**：6月8日上午10點30分
**轉帳金額**：250元
**接收帳戶類型**：支票

如果您未授權此交易，請立即致電達克倫銀行。我們的反欺詐部門每天24小時為您服務，請撥 1-901-555-1544，與該部門聯繫。您也可以寫電子郵件至 antifraud@dacklonbank.com，與我們線上聯繫。

**字彙** automatic 自動的　notification 通知
fund transfer 資金轉帳
checking account 支票存款帳戶
authorize 授權　at once 立即
anti-fraud 反欺詐
reach 與……取得聯繫
make a deposit 存款
outstanding 未償貸款；未清帳款
accessible 可接近的；可進入的
alter 改變；修改

**149** 本篇電子郵件的目的是什麼？
(A) 為了邀請崔西女士存款
(B) 為了告知崔西女士財務狀況
(C) 為了要求支付欠款
(D) 為了解釋反欺詐的新措施

**150** 關於達克倫銀行反欺詐部門，文中提到什麼？
(A) 任何時候都可以聯絡上。
(B) 營業時間已更改。
(C) 可透過書面郵寄聯絡。
(D) 它的網站有一個新網址。

**喬安妮·德爾菲：** 　　　　下午3時47分
卡爾頓先生，很抱歉打擾您，但是我注意到我們快要用完印有公司標誌的信紙和信封，儲藏櫃中只有少量的庫存。

**喬治·卡爾頓：** 　　　　下午3時49分
很高興妳發現了，請立即多採購一下備品。

**喬安妮·德爾菲：** 　　　　下午3時53分
跟凱西紙製品公司訂購嗎？

**喬治·卡爾頓：** 　　　　下午3時54分
是的，並確保妳訂的量足以應付接下來的三個月，也就是我們收到新預算的時間。

**喬安妮·德爾菲：** 　　　　下午3時57分
那麼是每種三大箱嗎？

**喬治·卡爾頓：** 　　　　下午4時02分
聽起來差不多，請加快訂購。我們不想在貨送來之前就用光。

**喬安妮·德爾菲：** 　　　　下午4時07分
我立刻處理。

〔寄送〕

**字彙** run out of 用完　a handful of 少量
right away 立刻　expedite 加快
stationery 文具

**151** 下午4：02時，卡爾頓先生寫下：「聽起來不錯」，最有可能是什麼意思？
(A) 他感謝德爾菲女士向他報告問題。
(B) 他認為德爾菲女士估算出正確的數量。
(C) 他將告訴德爾菲女士一些其他訊息。
(D) 他希望德爾菲女士注意指示說明

**152** 德爾斐女士接下來最有可能做什麼？
(A) 重新安排出貨
(B) 寄一些信
(C) 訂購文具
(D) 編制預算

**體重管理會議通知**

10月3日

我們邀請本地住戶和附近街坊鄰居參加以下查米斯體重管理集團的會議：
● 日期：10月22日 星期六
　　　　飲食委員會，下午6點
● 日期：10月29日 星期六
　　　　運動委員會，下午6點30分

● 地點

海景飯店 三樓 西曼廳
查米斯市格蘭德街 2018 號
時間表和訓練時程表將於 10 月 4 日星期二公布
在公共圖書館、西曼廳的門廳和查米斯公共游
泳池。
有減肥計畫建議的當地居民，最晚應在會議開
始前三天聯繫活動計畫者。

**報名請寄：**
活動計畫者 賈尼斯·格魯森
查米斯體重管理集團
查米斯市格蘭德街 2018 號
jgrousson@chamis.fr

> **字彙** weight 體重　management 管理
> local resident 當地居民（住戶）
> surrounding 周圍的　dietary 飲食的
> committee 委員會　venue 場地；地點
> foyer 門廳　weight loss 減肥；減重
> organizer 組織者；（工會等的）組織幹部
> publicize 宣傳　inaugurate 開始；開展
> regimen 攝生；（病人的）食物療法；養生法
> recruitment 招募　drive 宣傳活動
> sign up 報名

**153** 本通知的目的是什麼？
(A) 為了宣傳即將發生的活動
(B) 為了開始增重療程
(C) 為了廣告新場地
(D) 為了宣布招募活動

**154** 什麼時候會進行運動相關的討論？
(A) 10 月 3 日
(B) 10 月 4 日
(C) 10 月 22 日
(D) 10 月 29 日

**155** 如果有人想對委員會提出建議，應該怎麼做？
(A) 寄電子郵件給格魯森女士
(B) 致電委員會
(C) 參加第一次會議
(D) 在西曼廳報名

**156-157 收據**

「JB 體育用品公司」
碼頭
西班牙 1139

### 您運動休閒裝備的網路商店

客戶：薩米拉·拉洪
送貨地址：1295 西班牙塞維利亞拉馬哥街
　　　　　301 號
訂單編號：99842（於 11 月 11 日上午 10 點
　　　　　32 分下單）

| 數量 | 品項 | 金額 |
|---|---|---|
| 1 | 藍色設計師運動鞋（製造商：科里洛） | 小計：58.00 元 |
| 1 | 綠色後跟綁帶涼鞋（製造商：格蘭迪西莫） | 稅額：5.80 元<br>快捷費：11.00 元<br>訂單總額：74.80 元<br>信用卡支付的金額：74.80 元<br>應付餘額：0.00 元 |

本訂單已於 11 月 11 日下午 3 點 5 分寄出

＊感謝您的購買。如果您對這些商品不滿意，請
在 14 天以內，將未使用的商品連同原始包裝
一起退還。有關退貨或換貨的更多訊息，請上
www.jbsports/sp/returns。

> **字彙** vendor 供應商；賣主　gear 裝備
> shipping address 運送地址
> manufacturer 製造商
> slingback 露鞋跟的（鞋跟部分有條細線的）
> expedited shipping 緊急運送；收據貨運
> unworn 沒穿過的
> packaging 包裝　literary 文學
> footwear 鞋類　parcel 包裹

**156** JB 體育用品公司銷售哪種產品？
(A) 文學資料
(B) 鞋類
(C) 樂器
(D) DVD 光碟

**157** 關於拉洪女士，文中提到什麼？
(A) 她在 11 月 11 日收到包裹。
(B) 她定期跟 JB 體育用品公司購買商品。
(C) 她計劃購買更多鞋子。
(D) 她付了快捷費。

## 158-160 網站資訊

http://www.raphaelcomputers.com

### 拉斐爾電腦維修公司

| 主頁 | 服務 | 感言 | 請求預約 | 聯絡我們 |
|---|---|---|---|---|

我們客戶的意見……

評分：★★★★★

服務日期：8 月 7 日

服務類型：安裝 RZ 33 家庭自動化系統

上週，我發現家庭自動化系統的電腦終端機出現故障。我回想起我的門口曾經貼了一張「拉斐爾電腦維修公司」傳單，所以我打了電話。儘管已經傍晚了，而且商店即將結束營業，但是老闆齊吉·拉斐爾同意在他商店關門後直接到我家。他看了看我的電腦終端機，然後告訴我，我可以將電腦升級或者修理它。由於電腦已經使用了幾年，所以我選擇升級。拉斐爾先生展示了許多不同型號的終端機，我決定選擇一款具有更大存儲容量的型號。

我以為訂購和交貨會花費一些時間，但是拉斐爾先生的貨車上就有一台，並在同一天的時間安裝好。他甚至沒有額外收取非營業時間的服務費。他的祕書第二天打電話來確認系統是否正常運作。整個過程「拉斐爾電腦維修公司」都提供了優質的客戶服務，我肯定會再次推薦他的服務。

卡拉·拉莫斯

> **字彙** testimonial 感謝狀；感言  rating 評分
> installation 安裝  terminal 終端機
> faulty 有缺點的；不完美的；故障的
> recall 回想  leaflet 傳單
> post 貼  come round 來訪；繞道
> straight 直接  upgrade 升級
> demonstrate 展示
> memory capacity 存儲容量
> potential 潛在的  extra fee 額外的費用

**158** 此資訊最可能被放在網站上的原因是什麼？
(A) 為了解釋公司政策
(B) 為了描述安裝過程
(C) 為了吸引潛在客戶
(D) 為了宣傳新產品

**159** 關於拉斐爾先生，文中提到什麼？
(A) 他與拉莫斯女士共用郵箱。
(B) 他在拉莫斯女士要求服務的同一天完成了工作。
(C) 他安裝較大型電腦終端機時收取了額外費用。
(D) 他的祕書在 8 月 7 日聯繫了拉莫斯女士。

**160** 下列句子最適合放在 [1]、[2、[3] 和 [4] 的哪個位置？
「他甚至沒有額外收取非營業時間的服務費。」
(A) [1]
(B) [2]
(C) [3]
(D) [4]

## 161-164 傳單

### 詹森 DVD 公司要搬家了！

詹森 DVD 公司是公認本鎮規模最大的錄影帶和 DVD 光碟銷售公司，而且還不斷在擴展當中。六年前，我們剛開始以費瑞爾街為據點，現在要搬到弗里克森麵包店的舊址：薩德勒斯街 331 號。我們將繼續銷售 DVD 光碟、錄影帶和 CD 光碟以及漫畫書，但是額外的空間將使我們公司能夠成長進入到電動遊戲市場。

我們在費瑞爾街的老店將於 5 月 18 日（星期五）結束營業，詹森 DVD 公司將在 5 月 19 日（星期六）上午 9 點至下午 5 點，為新商店舉辦盛大的開幕派對。我們邀請所有客戶加入我們的活動，活動餐點會由我們的新鄰居美食咖啡館提供。

快來看看我們的新商品和品嚐美食咖啡館的美味三明治和飲料。新上映的獨立電影《追尋詹姆斯》的主角蘭迪·克洛什也將出席，他將和大家見面並且簽名。

為了準備搬遷，我們會出清一些舊庫存。在 4 月份時，部分 DVD 光碟片和錄影帶將半價出清，因此請保握機會，以優惠價格購買一些您喜歡的電影。

> **字彙** collection 收藏；蒐集的東西；一批物品
> former 從前的；早前的  host 主辦；主持
> cater 提供飲食；承辦宴席
> present 出席的  indie film 獨立電影
> autograph 簽名  relocation 搬遷
> get rid of 處理掉；賣掉  seize 抓住
> bargain 特價商品；便宜貨
> amalgamate 合併  flyer 廣告傳單
> inventory 清單上開列的貨品；存貨

**161** 關於詹森 DVD 公司，文中提到什麼？
(A) 它正在增加人員編制。
(B) 它將搬到弗里克森麵包店旁邊。
(C) 它要與美食咖啡館合併。
(D) 它已經經營了六年。

**162** 詹森 DVD 公司目前不提供什麼？
(A) 電動遊戲
(B) 漫畫書
(C) CD 光碟
(D) DVD 光碟

**163** 克洛什先生是誰？
(A) 演員
(B) 一家咖啡館的經理
(C) 商店老闆
(D) 攝影師

**164** 根據傳單，4 月會發生什麼事？
(A) 將隆重開幕。
(B) 將提供折扣。
(C) 將免費贈送 DVD 光碟。
(D) 將有新庫存到貨。

## 165-168 公告

### 本澤馬汽車保養公司——內部職位發布

此職位開放給內部人員應徵，時間到月底。隨後，此職位將對外招募。

**職稱：首席技師**
**工作描述：**
- 技術支援本澤馬汽車保養公司，為三個主要部門（維護、維修和保養）提供更多車輛服務。
- 對所有車型進行汽車年檢、車身維修和車輛分析。
- 負責重要客戶的客戶服務。

**主要職責：**
- 檢查汽車和其他車輛，並診斷問題區域
- 在特定的公司汽車上執行電腦分析
- 使用多元維修系統來準備詳細的維修服務
- 作為汽車製造商和修車廠員工之間的溝通橋樑

**資格要求：**
- 在我們的車輛維修部門至少有三年工作經驗
- 詳細了解汽車保養維修

要申請此職位，請在 2 月 11 日之前將您的簡歷、求職信和兩個推薦人的聯絡資訊，呈交給修車廠經理凱瑪‧南，電子郵件為 knahn@benzema.org。

**字彙** internal 內部的　job posting 職位發布　subsequently 隨後；之後　external 外部的　chief mechanic 首席技師　description 描述　MOT 汽車年度性能檢驗　analytic 分析的　clientele 委託人；顧客　principal 主要的　duty 職責　diagnose 診斷　multiple 多元的　liaison 聯絡人；聯繫　minimum 最低；最少　understanding 了解　cover letter 求職信　reference 推薦人　degree 學位　in-depth 深入的　valid 有效的　supervisor 主管　liaise 聯絡；聯繫　undertake 進行

**165** 下列何者為此職位的要求之一？
(A) 商業學位
(B) 深入的汽車維修保養知識
(C) 與客戶合作的經驗
(D) 有效的駕駛執照

**166** 應徵者應如何申請？
(A) 將要求的文件寄給南女士
(B) 由主管推薦應徵者
(C) 填寫求職表
(D) 在 2 月 11 日之前安排面試

**167** 本篇公告最有可能出現在哪裡？
(A) 在汽車工作的公共資料庫當中
(B) 在給本澤馬汽車保養公司員工的備忘錄中
(C) 在報紙的求職欄
(D) 在致首席技師的信中

**168** 首席技師的職責不包括什麼？
(A) 與汽車製造商聯絡
(B) 診斷車輛故障問題
(C) 進行汽車維修服務
(D) 更新公司的客戶名單

## 169-171 線上聊天

**皮拉爾‧奧爾特加 [上午 8:48]**：團隊，早安。我想和你們確認看看新的電子郵件程式執行得如何，到目前為止有什麼問題嗎？

**文森特‧威廉姆斯 [上午 8:50]**：我太喜歡它了。現在有訊息寄到我的郵件信箱時，我的手機也可以直接收到通知，我可以更快回覆客戶。

**南希‧多特蒙德 [上午 8:51]**：我的手機無法做到這一點！

**文森特‧威廉姆斯 [上午 8:52]**：不是手機的問題，這是實際程式的一部分，妳必須這樣設定。

**南希‧多特蒙德 [上午 8:53]**：我該怎麼做？

**文森特‧威廉姆斯 [上午 8:54]**：到「選項」的標籤，有一個地方可以設置提醒功能。在那裡，妳可以勾選有新訊息的方框。

**南希‧多特蒙德 [上午 8:55]**：謝謝！總的來說，我認為這個程式比「谷箱」更容易使用，我要感謝大衛的推薦。

**亞當‧波拉 [上午 8:59]**：我現在上傳附件時出現問題，誰可以來幫我？

**皮拉爾‧奧爾特加 [上午 9:01]**：沒問題，我遇過同樣的問題，所以我打給流行郵箱公司的技術支援部，他們全都跟我解釋過了。不會太難，但是步驟與「谷箱」不同。我可以在明天的部門午餐會議上向你展示怎麼做，你會參加會議嗎？

**亞當‧波拉 [上午 9:02]**：會，我會儘早到，好讓我們有時間處理所有事。

〔寄送〕

**字彙** notification 通知　inbox 收件箱
overall 總的來說　attachment 附件
adjust 調整

**169** 上午 8:51 時，多特蒙德女士為什麼寫道：「我的手機無法做到這一點」？
(A) 她想調整手機的設定。
(B) 她無法在手機上查看電子郵件。
(C) 她很驚訝威廉姆斯先生收到提醒通知。
(D) 她想更快回覆客戶的電子郵件。

**170** 為什麼奧爾特加女士要聯絡技術支援部？
(A) 要在手機上設置提醒通知
(B) 要安裝新的電子郵件程式
(C) 要了解如何附加文件
(D) 要升級「谷箱」的軟體

**171** 關於波拉先生，文中提到什麼？
(A) 他向團隊推薦了「流行郵箱」。
(B) 他將在會議上簡報。
(C) 他今天有個午餐約會。
(D) 他明天將得到奧爾特加女士的幫助。

## 172–175 信件

3 月 30 日
執行長鄧肯‧卡瑪爾
艾琳電話中心
美國阿拉巴馬州伯明翰市
斯普林特路 1000 號

親愛的卡瑪爾先生：

　　我寫信是要通知您，今日臨時工公司已被 WRE 僱傭公司接管，WRE 僱傭公司是最知名的臨時人力派遣公司之一。今日臨時工公司將以相同的名稱繼續經營，但是我們的某些價格會有變動。您是我們最重要的客戶之一，我想親自通知您服務的變動，以便您做出適當的決定。

　　雖然提供臨時人力派遣的費用大體上保持不變，但是本公司客戶服務中心的時薪已經調整。我們新的計時費率如下：

**4 名派遣員以下**：每人每小時 15 元
**5-9 名派遣員**：每人每小時 11 元
**10-24 名派遣員**：每人每小時 10 元
**25-49 名派遣員**：每人每小時 9 元
**50 名以上派遣員**：每人每小時 8 元

　　在新的定價制度下，我們會根據您每個月需要的人數來計算客服中心的人力費用。因此，如果在下次需求中，您需求的派遣員人數與 2 月份相同，您當月費用，我們將以最低的價格收取（每人每小時 8 美元），僅比舊制多 0.5 元。

　　身為 WRE 僱傭公司旗下的一員，我們也將提供更多有技術性的派遣員。例如，我們可以隨叫隨到為任何活動提供餐飲服務。此外，我們的網站現在提供了許多方便的額外功能，包括帳戶歷史記錄和人員技能要求。

如果您對此變動有任何疑問，請隨時與我們聯繫。我們將繼續為您提供多年來您一直享受的優質服務。多謝您的長年支持。

真誠地，
亞歷克西斯・陳
今日臨時工公司
客戶服務副總

**字彙** take over 接管
temporary staff 臨時雇員；臨時工
operate 運作；營運
valued 寶貴的；重要的；有價值的
hourly rate 每小時費率
operative 技工；工人　revise 修改
calculate 計算　additional 額外的
skilled 熟練的；有技能的
at a moment's notice 隨時；一經通知就立即
account history 帳戶歷史記錄
upmarket 高品質的；高價位市場的
shortage 短缺　scheme 計畫
fee 費用　advisor 顧問

**172** 這封信的目的是什麼？
(A) 為了告知人員短缺
(B) 為了宣布一項新的培訓計畫
(C) 為了宣傳啟用新的網站
(D) 為了解釋費用結構的變化

**173** 根據這封信，WRE 僱備公司最近做了什麼？
(A) 收購另一家公司
(B) 換地址
(C) 僱用新的副總
(D) 搬到阿拉巴馬州

**174** 卡瑪爾先生是誰？
(A) 客服中心的臨時員工
(B) WRE 僱備公司的老闆
(C) 個人理財顧問
(D) 今日臨時工公司的客戶

**175** 下列句子最適合放在 [1]、[2]、[3] 和 [4] 的哪個位置？
「例如，我們可以隨叫隨到為任何活動提供餐飲服務。」
(A) [1]
(B) [2]
(C) [3]
(D) [4]

## 176–180 資訊與電子郵件

| 西班牙度假屋 | |
|---|---|
| **物件：2619 馬德里**<br>獨一無二的三房聯排別墅<br>最少住宿天數：4晚<br><br><br>想知道更多訊息，請點擊此處。 | **物件：9110 阿拉貢**<br>連續住3晚，可免費多住1晚<br>適合希望從步調繁忙的生活中逃離到寧靜避風港的人。<br>有海景。<br><br>想知道更多訊息，請點擊此處。 |
| **物件：4716 卡斯蒂利亞**<br>兩房公寓<br>近城市，是現代城市生活的絕佳基地充滿活力的環境<br><br>想知道更多訊息，請點擊此處。 | **物件：6130 安達盧西亞**<br>有私人碼頭<br>每週 1400 元<br><br><br><br>想知道更多訊息，請點擊此處。 |

收件者：阿爾貝托・魏穆拉
　　　　<auemura@spholidayrentals.co.esp>
寄件者：蓋爾・因斯 <gince@ckalltd.co.esp>
日期：9月21日
關於：4716 物件

您好，魏穆拉先生：

　　去年夏天，我與未婚夫到安達盧西亞度假時與您接觸過，我對我們的住宿和您提供的服務水準感到非常滿意。但是，住宿地點並不符合我的喜好。因為太安靜，也太偏遠了。今年，我比較想要住在城市裡的房子，最好有兩間以上的臥室，附近有夜生活的地方。我也不願意每週花費超過 900 到 1,000 元。我對物件 4716 感興趣。能否為我提供空房情況和詳細資料？它似乎能滿足我的需求。

　　期待您的回覆。

祝好，
蓋兒・因斯

**字彙** vacation home 度假屋
property 房產；地產
exclusive 唯一的；獨有的
consecutive 連續的　pace 步調
haven 避風港；避難所　base 基地；基礎
vibrant 充滿活力的　jetty 突碼頭；防波堤
fiancé 未婚夫／妻
be to one's taste 是某人喜歡的
remote 偏僻的

preferably 更可取地；更好地；可能的話
access 接近；進入　nightlife 夜生活
reluctant 不願意的
meet one's needs 合乎某人的需求
deposit 押金；訂金
cleanliness 清潔度
accommodation 住宿；住處　coast 海岸

**176** 什麼物件提供一晚免費的住宿？
(A) 物件 2619
(B) 物件 9110
(C) 物件 4716
(D) 物件 6130

**177** 因斯女士為什麼發送此封電子郵件？
(A) 要取消訂金
(B) 要支付預約訂金
(C) 要索取資料
(D) 要尋求旅行建議

**178** 因斯女士在上一次假期中，對哪方面感到不滿意？
(A) 出租公寓的清潔度
(B) 代訂仲介提供的服務
(C) 附近地區生活節奏緩慢
(D) 到她租的房屋的距離

**179** 為什麼物件 6130 不適合因斯女士？
(A) 她希望住宿房子有兩間以上的臥室。
(B) 她在尋找便宜的住宿。
(C) 她想住在聯排別墅中。
(D) 她不想去海邊。

**180** 因斯女士對哪個地點感興趣？
(A) 馬德里
(B) 阿拉貢
(C) 卡斯蒂利亞
(D) 安達盧西亞

## 181-185 備忘錄與電子郵件

收件者：所有員工
寄件者：人力資源部總監 安加拉德・里斯
主旨：問卷意見調查
日期：12 月 30 日

　　11 月時，我們的人力資源部進行了全面性的客戶問卷調查，內容涵蓋我們業務的多項領域。結果顯示，我們大多數的客戶對我們的服務普遍感到滿意，尤其是與其他貸款審核公司相比，但是有些地方確定需要改進。

　　普遍的抱怨是處理新帳戶時，花費的長時間令他們無法接受。目前，當我們與客戶聯繫時，首次貸款程序需要我們貸款部門和財務檢查辦公室的三位人士簽名核准。所以通常需要長達三個星期的時間，資金才會匯入銀行帳戶。

　　因此，從下個月開始，少於 1,000 元的新貸款只需要一位資深放款員簽名核准。這項政策將減少處理時間並幫助我們提供客戶更好的服務。

　　如有任何疑問，請隨時與我聯繫。

收件者：艾倫・穆勒
寄件者：里斯
日期：12 月 31 日
主旨：備忘錄

妳好，安加拉德：

　　我看過妳昨天寄出的備忘錄，我認為新提案是一個很好的想法。當我的部門蒐集好調查結果時，許多客戶都透露，他們在等貸款核准下來已經等了好幾週。除了妳的想法之外，我相信我們可以透過允許電子簽名來加快審批過程。我們的供應商之一阿什頓和瓊斯公司，最近安裝了軟體可使他們處理大部分的網路交易。我認為我們應該考慮類似的系統，我很願意研究一下。

艾倫

**字彙** carry out 執行
comprehensive 全面性的
questionnaire 問卷調查
loan approval 貸款核准
improvement 改進　firm 公司
identify 確認；識別
unacceptably 無法接受
process 處理；進行　signature 簽名

| transfer 轉帳 | loan officer 放款員 |
| --- | --- |
| hesitate 猶豫 | issue 發行；發布 |

compile 匯編；收集
electronically 電子地　handle 處理
look into 調查　workload 工作量
eliminate 消除

**181** 里斯女士在備忘錄中宣布了什麼事？
(A) 與另一家公司的合併
(B) 對資深銷售人員進行更多調查
(C) 僱用額外的財務人員
(D) 批准合約的新程序

**182** 根據備忘錄，更改的目的是什麼？
(A) 要減少放款員的工作量
(B) 要消除不必要的延誤
(C) 要改善組織內部的溝通
(D) 要擴大勞動力規模

**183** 異動將於何時生效？
(A) 1 月
(B) 2 月
(C) 11 月
(D) 12 月

**184** 穆勒先生在哪個部門工作？
(A) 財務部
(B) 銷售部
(C) 人力資源部
(D) 客戶關係部

**185** 穆勒先生推薦什麼事情？
(A) 參加調查
(B) 試用電腦軟體程式
(C) 降低客戶費用
(D) 增加貸款批准限額

**186-190 時程表、電子郵件與通知**

關鍵大樓
管理員班表
9 月 1 日至 10 月 4 日的平日

| 員工 | 天數（小時） |
| --- | --- |
| 湯姆·傑克遜 | 週一至週五<br>（上午 9:30 - 下午 1:30） |
| 艾倫·錢 | 週一至週五<br>（下午 6:30 - 晚上 10:30） |
| 詹姆斯·庫瑪 | 星期一、星期三、星期五<br>（下午 2:30 - 下午 8:30） |
| 羅德尼·萊因哈特 | 星期二、星期四<br>（下午 2:30 - 下午 8:30）<br>星期六（上午 8:00 - 下午 2:00） |

如果有無法值班的情況，請盡快與主管聯繫。

收件者：艾倫·錢 <achin@keybuilding.com>
寄件者：喬·安德森
　　　　<janderson@keybuilding.com>
日期：8 月 19 日
主旨：班表異動

親愛的艾倫：

　　感謝你讓我知道，你的家人預計在 9 月 1 日至 7 日那週來找你。湯姆已同意與你交換那週的排班。在那星期之後的那個月，你和湯姆將會恢復成原來安排好的班表。

　　由於你要求的排班時間不是你固定的時段，請與湯姆討論需要完成的具體任務。你可能還需要聯繫保全部，以便他們讓你打掃已經上鎖的房間。

　　如果您有任何問題，請告訴我。

謝謝，
喬

**新時間輸入系統**

　　關鍵大樓要求所有員工使用新的時間輸入網路系統，名字叫「協力」。從 9 月 29 日至 10 月 4 日這一週開始使用。因為可以透過任何手機設備使用「協力」，員工將不再需要進人事辦公室提交紙本的排班時間，而是需要使用用戶名稱和密碼登錄系統，然後輸入工作時間。

為了向員工展示如何使用「協力」，戴維·哈里森安排以下日期的訓練課程：

保全部　9月22日，星期一
　　　　（上午 10:00 – 上午 11:30）

會計部　9月23日，星期二
　　　　（下午 3:00 – 下午 4:30）

維修部　9月24日，星期三
　　　　（下午 2:00 – 下午 3:30）

行政部　9月25日，星期四
　　　　（上午 8:30 - 上午 10:00）

員工應參加自己部門的訓練課程。如果不行，請撥分機 1212，聯絡哈里森先生，請他安排另一場課程。

**字彙** janitor 管理員　assigned 分配的
remainder 剩餘物
access 存取（資料）；使用　obtain 獲取

**186** 關於傑克遜先生，文中提到什麼？
(A) 他通常在星期六工作。
(B) 他的家人住在關鍵大樓裡。
(C) 他將更改一個月的班表。
(D) 他將在 9 月工作五個晚上。

**187** 關於安德森先生，文中提到什麼？
(A) 他將領導「協力」程式的訓練課程。
(B) 他是錢先生的經理。
(C) 他將休假一週。
(D) 他擁有關鍵大樓。

**188** 在電子郵件中，第 2 段、第 1 行的「regular」，意思最接近於下列何者？
(A) 分配的
(B) 冗長的
(C) 訓練有素的
(D) 平常的

**189** 為什麼要求員工參加訓練課程？
(A) 要獲取其用戶名稱和密碼
(B) 要學習新程式
(C) 要與他們的人事經理會面
(D) 要更新時間班表

**190** 萊因哈特先生最有可能在哪一天參加「協力」的訓練課程？
(A) 9 月 22 日
(B) 9 月 23 日
(C) 9 月 24 日
(D) 9 月 25 日

### 191-195 宣告、文章與信件

**人民移動公司正在擴大經營**

全國成長最快的城市客運公司人民移動公司，計劃開始提供 19 個新地點的服務，包括博爾頓、紐波特、韋斯特維爾、阿倫敦和格羅弗城。「人民移動公司」將於 4 月 15 日開始在博爾頓和紐波特服務大家，較小城市的服務將於 5 月和 6 月推出。

為了慶祝擴大經營，我們將贈送 100 張往返於任何新目的地的來回車票。無需付費參加，只需在我們的網站 www.peoplemover.com 上填寫表格，最晚必須在 3 月 31 日之前填寫完畢送出。

查爾斯敦（6 月 3 日）

查爾斯敦居民等了近三年的時間，才等到恢復往返城市之間的客運直達車服務。這一切的改變就發生在星期六，第一輛人民移動公司客運巴士在現在關閉的聯合街總站前接載 28 名乘客。

迫不及待搭上客運的丹妮卡·貝克說道：「我很期待見到住在列治文市的親戚」。自從「國家客運線路」關閉以來，貝克女士一路都是坐當地公車和計程車到那個城市。她還說：「我真的很高興『人民移動公司』現在來了。」

市長辦公室的代表說他們計劃翻新，並重新開放這城市唯一一往返城市之間的客運直達車總站。在此同時，「人民移動公司」將會直接停在大樓前方的埃爾德里奇街。目前的規畫時程表公布在 www.peoplemover.com，或者請打 1-888-555-8399。

伊麗莎白·劉易斯
哈珀路 873 號
查爾斯敦
6 月 28 日

親愛的劉易斯女士：

恭喜你！您已獲選可以免費搭乘人民移動公司客運到任何您想要的目的地。

您可以將這封信帶到人民移動公司的任何一家巴士總站或致電 1-888-555-8789，以便索取您的車票。車票從開票日起 12 個月內有效。

我們期待為您服務。

卡倫·科爾曼
客戶服務副總裁
人民移動公司

字彙 roll out 推出　round-trip 來回的
entry 登記；輸入項目
restoration 恢復；復原
shuttered 已關閉的　claim 索取
valid 有效的　acquire 獲得

**191** 關於查爾斯敦，文中提到什麼？
(A) 它的人口比紐波特少。
(B) 它在博爾頓之前獲得了新的客運服務。
(C) 人民移動公司曾經在此地提供服務。
(D) 它不再有公共交通工具。

**192** 關於國家客運線路，文中提到什麼？
(A) 它曾經為博爾頓提供服務。
(B) 它最近被人民移動公司收購。
(C) 目前在列治文市以外地區經營。
(D) 三年前倒閉了。

**193** 關於查爾斯敦地方政府，文中提到什麼？
(A) 目前僱用劉易斯女士。
(B) 計劃修復聯合街總站。
(C) 它經營計程車服務。
(D) 它與人民移動公司簽訂了合約。

**194** 關於劉易斯女士，下列何者最可能為真？
(A) 她在線上參加了人民移動公司的比賽。
(B) 她透過郵件收到了車票。
(C) 她偶爾會去列治文市。
(D) 她將在今年年底之前旅行。

**195** 在信件中，第 1 段、第 2 行的「claim」，意思最接近於下列何者？
(A) 斷言
(B) 取得
(C) 購買
(D) 儲備

## 196-200 電子郵件、網頁與文章

收件者：會員
寄件者：文森特·吉爾斯
回覆：即將到來的活動
日期：8 月 18 日

感謝在本月初參加「狂野之心」開幕式的所有人。對於無法參加活動的人來說，這次巡迴展覽特別展出亞歷杭德羅·薩拉戈薩所拍攝的一百多張照片。他的作品將一直在紐伯里博物館展出，直到明年二月。「狂野之心」特別展出令人驚嘆的黑白人物相片和巴西的風景照。

除了薩拉戈薩先生的特別演講外，紐伯里博物館還計劃一些令人興奮的活動，活動預計在 9 月時舉行。請造訪我們的網站，以獲取最新的時程表。會員可免費參加第三個星期四的活動。

http://www.newberrymuseum.org

| 展覽 | 參觀 | 活動 | 會員 |
|------|------|------|------|

**9 月 3 日一家庭日**：上午 10:00 – 下午 5:00
父母及其子女免費入場。中庭舉辦孩子們的手工藝品活動。

**9 月 10 日一簽書會**：中午 – 下午 2:00
當地歷史學家丹尼爾·科爾頓將為最新作品《蔡斯·福特：他的過去和現在》簽名。本書在博物館的禮品店有販售。（會員可獲得 10% 的折扣。）

**9 月 22 日一第三個星期四**：晚上 6:00 – 9:00
來參加社交活動，並且漫步在畫廊中，然後欣賞「地球之聲」的現場爵士樂表演。食物和飲料可在博物館的咖啡廳購得。

**9 月 25 日一特別活動**：下午 2:00 – 4:00
聆聽亞歷杭德羅·薩拉戈薩的演講。薩拉戈薩先生將談論他的生活和目前在博物館展示的作品。

### 令人陶醉的照片來到了紐伯里

理查德・迪恩 報導

　　畫家曼努埃爾・索拉雷斯曾經說過，偉大的藝術可以觸動心靈。也許他想到了亞歷杭德羅・薩拉戈薩的攝影作品，他的照片非常漂亮。上週末我去「紐伯里博物館」參觀時，薩拉戈薩先生談到他的藝術靈感、對旅行的熱愛，與在當今媒體充斥的世界中，藝術攝影師所面臨的挑戰。即使您錯過了演講，您仍然有時間欣賞他過去十年中最喜歡的照片的展覽，當中很多照片是在他祖國所拍攝的。更多詳細訊息，請上 www.newberrymuseum.com。

---

**字彙** on display 展出　stunning 令人驚嘆的
portrait 肖像；畫像　up-to-date 最新的
remarkably 引人注目地；明顯地；非常地
inspiration　靈感
medias-saturated　媒體充斥的

---

**196** 關於「狂野之心」，沒有提到下列何者？
(A) 有人物相片。
(B) 包括藝術家的演講。
(C) 它於 8 月開始。
(D) 它將永久留在「紐伯里博物館」。

**197** 關於「紐伯里博物館」的會員，文中提到什麼？
(A) 他們收到特別邀請。
(B) 他們可以免費欣賞「地球之聲」。
(C) 他們在禮品店買任何東西都有折扣。
(D) 他們每月支付會員費。

**198** 迪恩先生最有可能在何時參觀「紐伯里博物館」？
(A) 9 月 3 日
(B) 9 月 10 日
(C) 9 月 22 日
(D) 9 月 25 日

**199** 關於薩拉戈薩先生，文中提到什麼？
(A) 他旅行了 5 個月。
(B) 他的職業生涯始於十年前。
(C) 他出生在巴西。
(D) 他的作品在網路上展出。

**200** 在文章中，第 1 段、第 8 行中的「missed」，意思最接近於下列何者？
(A) 遲到
(B) 避免看見
(C) 未能參加
(D) 感到難過

# 4 解答

| 1. (B) | 2. (A) | 3. (C) | 4. (B) | 5. (A) | 6. (D) | 7. (A) | 8. (A) | 9. (C) | 10. (C) |
|---|---|---|---|---|---|---|---|---|---|
| 11. (B) | 12. (B) | 13. (B) | 14. (A) | 15. (C) | 16. (A) | 17. (A) | 18. (C) | 19. (A) | 20. (A) |
| 21. (A) | 22. (C) | 23. (C) | 24. (A) | 25. (C) | 26. (B) | 27. (C) | 28. (B) | 29. (B) | 30. (B) |
| 31. (C) | 32. (B) | 33. (D) | 34. (C) | 35. (A) | 36. (D) | 37. (A) | 38. (B) | 39. (D) | 40. (C) |
| 41. (A) | 42. (D) | 43. (A) | 44. (A) | 45. (B) | 46. (A) | 47. (C) | 48. (B) | 49. (C) | 50. (D) |
| 51. (C) | 52. (A) | 53. (A) | 54. (B) | 55. (B) | 56. (D) | 57. (D) | 58. (A) | 59. (C) | 60. (B) |
| 61. (C) | 62. (B) | 63. (C) | 64. (A) | 65. (C) | 66. (C) | 67. (B) | 68. (A) | 69. (B) | 70. (C) |
| 71. (D) | 72. (A) | 73. (C) | 74. (B) | 75. (C) | 76. (D) | 77. (C) | 78. (B) | 79. (D) | 80. (D) |
| 81. (A) | 82. (B) | 83. (A) | 84. (C) | 85. (A) | 86. (D) | 87. (B) | 88. (C) | 89. (C) | 90. (C) |
| 91. (B) | 92. (D) | 93. (C) | 94. (D) | 95. (D) | 96. (C) | 97. (B) | 98. (C) | 99. (C) | 100. (C) |
| 101. (D) | 102. (A) | 103. (B) | 104. (D) | 105. (A) | 106. (B) | 107. (A) | 108. (C) | 109. (C) | 110. (C) |
| 111. (D) | 112. (A) | 113. (B) | 114. (A) | 115. (A) | 116. (C) | 117. (D) | 118. (B) | 119. (A) | 120. (B) |
| 121. (B) | 122. (C) | 123. (B) | 124. (C) | 125. (A) | 126. (A) | 127. (D) | 128. (C) | 129. (D) | 130. (B) |
| 131. (D) | 132. (B) | 133. (C) | 134. (A) | 135. (B) | 136. (B) | 137. (C) | 138. (C) | 139. (D) | 140. (C) |
| 141. (A) | 142. (C) | 143. (A) | 144. (D) | 145. (C) | 146. (D) | 147. (B) | 148. (B) | 149. (C) | 150. (A) |
| 151. (B) | 152. (B) | 153. (C) | 154. (C) | 155. (B) | 156. (A) | 157. (C) | 158. (B) | 159. (C) | 160. (A) |
| 161. (D) | 162. (B) | 163. (C) | 164. (D) | 165. (C) | 166. (D) | 167. (D) | 168. (B) | 169. (B) | 170. (C) |
| 171. (A) | 172. (B) | 173. (B) | 174. (A) | 175. (B) | 176. (C) | 177. (C) | 178. (B) | 179. (D) | 180. (B) |
| 181. (A) | 182. (B) | 183. (A) | 184. (C) | 185. (B) | 186. (C) | 187. (A) | 188. (D) | 189. (C) | 190. (B) |
| 191. (C) | 192. (D) | 193. (D) | 194. (B) | 195. (A) | 196. (D) | 197. (C) | 198. (B) | 199. (B) | 200. (C) |

## 13

## PART 1

P. 144

**1** (A) Some people are entering a restaurant.
(英M) (B) A waiter is serving some customers.
(C) A woman is sipping from a glass.
(D) A woman is ordering from a menu.

(A) 有些人正走進餐廳。
(B) 服務生正在服務幾位客人。
(C) 一名女性正小口喝著玻璃杯中的飲料。
(D) 一名女性正在用菜單點菜。

字彙 serve 服務  sip 啜飲；小口喝

**2** (A) An arched bridge stands over the waterway.
(美M) (B) Rowboats are lined up along the edge of the water.
(C) A staircase reaches to the doorway.
(D) Some people are sitting on a seashore.

(A) 一座拱橋轟立在水道上。
(B) 小船沿著水岸列隊停靠。
(C) 一道樓梯通往出入口。
(D) 有些人正坐在海邊。

字彙 arched bridge 拱橋
waterway 水道；水路；航道
rowboats 小船；輕舟
line up 使……整隊  edge 邊緣
staircase 樓梯  doorway 出入口
seashore 海岸

**3** (A) The man is lifting a tray.
(美W) (B) The man is holding a plate of food.
(C) Some food is being prepared on a stove.
(D) Some kitchen utensils are being washed.

(A) 這名男子正抬著托盤。
(B) 這名男子正端著一盤食物。
(C) 有些食物正在爐子上烤。
(D) 有些餐具正在洗。

字彙 lift 抬起；舉起  tray 托盤  plate 盤子
stove 烤爐；暖爐  kitchen utensil 餐具

**4** (A) A woman is arranging bags in the window display.
(澳M) (B) A woman is pointing at some merchandise.
(C) They are looking at themselves in a mirror.
(D) Some items are hanging near the bulletin board.

(A) 一名女性正在擺設櫥窗內展示的袋子。
(B) 一名女性正指著某些商品。
(C) 他們正看著鏡中的自己。
(D) 有些物品正掛在布告欄旁。

字彙 window display 櫥窗展示
point at 指著；指向……
merchandise 商品
bulletin board 布告欄

**5** (A) The woman is using a sponge to wipe off a plate.
(英M) (B) The woman is putting the dishes in the sink.
(C) Some dishes are being passed in a kitchen.
(D) Some water is being poured from the pitcher.

(A) 一名女性正在用海綿擦洗一個盤子。
(B) 一名女性正在把碗盤放進水槽。
(C) 廚房內正在傳送一些盤子。
(D) 正從罐中倒出一些水。

字彙 wipe 擦拭  sink 水槽  pitcher 罐

**6** (A) Lines are being painted on the road.
(美W) (B) There is a big house at the top of the hill.
(C) Vehicles are parked in a row on the sand.
(D) Pointed roofs are visible in the distance.

(A) 路面正在畫線。
(B) 山頂有間大房子。
(C) 車子在沙上停成一排。
(D) 從遠處就能看到尖頂。

字彙 vehicle 車  in a row 排成一行
pointed 尖角的  visible 可看見的
in the distance 在遠處

## PART 2

P. 148

**7** Do you need your oil changed?
(美M) (A) Yes, please.
(美W) (B) I'm a little bit exhausted.
(C) No, they haven't yet.

你需要換機油嗎？
(A) 是的，麻煩了。
(B) 我有點累。
(C) 不，他們還沒。

字彙 oil change 換機油
exhausted 極其疲憊的；精疲力竭的

**8** How much are two tickets to the game?
(美W) (A) About 30 dollars, I think.
(美M) (B) I just heard about that.
(C) At 5:30.

這場比賽的兩張票要多少錢？
(A) 我覺得大概三十美元。
(B) 我才剛聽說那件事。
(C) 五點半。

字彙 just 只；僅；剛才

**9** When are the guests coming?
(美M) (A) At the local airport.
(美W) (B) A very tight schedule.
(C) Tomorrow at midday.

賓客什麼時候到？
(A) 在當地機場。
(B) 行程很緊湊。
(C) 明天中午。

字彙 tight （行程）緊湊　midday 正午

**10** Who's the manager in your department?
(美M) (A) They are in a meeting right now.
(英M) (B) That's a brilliant idea.
(C) It's Mr. Omata.

你們部門經理是誰？
(A) 他們現在正在開會。
(B) 這個點子非常好。
(C) 是小俁先生。

字彙 brilliant 非常好的；聰慧的

**11** Would you rather work the weekend or the
(美W) weekday shift?
(美M) (A) We're going after training.
(B) Weekend is the best.
(C) 30 minute breaks.

你比較想上週末還是週間的班？
(A) 我們練完就過去。
(B) 週末最好。
(C) 休息三十分鐘。

字彙 weekday 週間　shift 輪班　break 休息

**12** Have you visited the new annex yet?
(美M) (A) No, it's on Birch Street.
(美W) (B) I haven't had a chance.
(C) That book was fascinating.

你逛過新分館了嗎？
(A) 不，它在樺木街上。
(B) 還沒有機會。
(C) 那本書很有趣。

字彙 annex 分館
fascinating 極有趣的；吸引人的

13
14

**13** Where is that large vessel going?
(美M) (A) They should be here soon.
(美W) (B) On a fishing trip.
(C) The coat's too large.

那艘大船要去哪？
(A) 他們應該很快就到。
(B) 出海捕魚。
(C) 這件外套太大。

字彙 vessel 大船

**14** Emma made the lunch booking, right?
(英M) (A) Yes, she called yesterday.
(美W) (B) I haven't seen his schedule.
(C) Actually, it's at the end.

艾瑪訂好午餐了，是嗎？
(A) 是的，她昨天打了電話。
(B) 我還沒看過他的日程表。
(C) 其實，它在最後。

字彙 booking 預訂

**15** Will you be on sick leave all week?
(美M) (A) A round trip tour.
(美W) (B) Medication is included.
(C) No, I'll be in the office.

你整個星期都會請病假嗎？
(A) 一趟往返旅程。
(B) 包括用藥。
(C) 不會，我會在辦公室。

字彙 **be on sick leave** 請病假
**round trip** 往返旅程 **medication** 用藥

**16** Have you considered hiring a freelance
(美W) supplier?
(英M) (A) I've been meaning to.
(B) Just a little lower.
(C) Yes, two or three business days.

你考慮過聘個個體供應商嗎？
(A) 我最近一直在想。
(B) 只要再低一點。
(C) 是的，兩、三個工作天。

字彙 **freelance** 自由職業的；獨立的
**supplier** （內容）提供者；供應商
**mean to** 有意做……
**business days** 工作天

**17** Why did the restaurant close so early?
(美M) (A) To prepare for a banquet.
(美W) (B) Because it's not far away.
(C) Well, he is normally late.

餐廳為什麼這麼早關？
(A) 為了準備餐會。
(B) 因為不遠。
(C) 嗯，他通常都遲到。

字彙 **banquet** （正式的）宴會 **far away** 遠處
**normally** 通常

**18** How was your trip to Atlanta?
(美W) (A) He arrives on Monday.
(英M) (B) I left it on the plane.
(C) The weather was fantastic.

你的亞特蘭大之旅如何？
(A) 他星期一到。
(B) 我忘在飛機上了。
(C) 天氣很棒。

字彙 **leave** 遺留 **fantastic** 極好的

**19** Why wasn't Ajmal at the training session?
(美M) (A) He had a scheduling conflict.
(美W) (B) A new staff member told us.
(C) In section 4.

阿吉馬爾為什麼沒去上培訓課？
(A) 他行程撞到。
(B) 一個新同仁告訴我們的。
(C) 在第四區。

字彙 **conflict** 衝突
**section** （事物的）部分；部門、組

**20** Who's doing the math seminar today?
(美W) (A) A guest lecturer.
(美M) (B) In the lobby.
(C) No, he is not available.

誰要帶今天的數學討論課？
(A) 一個客座講師。
(B) 在大廳裡。
(C) 不，他沒空。

字彙 **guest lecturer** 客座講師 **lobby** 大廳

**21** Which workstation is Dave's?
(美W) (A) He sits here.
(美M) (B) I saw one online.
(C) In the top drawer.

戴維的座位在哪？
(A) 他坐這邊。
(B) 我在網路有看到一個。
(C) 在最上層的抽屜裡。

字彙 **workstation** 個人工作區

**22** Shouldn't the food have been delivered by
(美W) now?
(英M) (A) The delivery man did.
(B) Actually, I'm not very hungry.
(C) Yes, it's usually here by noon.

食物現在不是應該要到了嗎？
(A) 外送員做的。
(B) 其實我沒有很餓。
(C) 是，通常中午前會到。

字彙 **deliver man** 送貨員；外送員

**23** Why don't we evaluate the formula again?
(英M) (A) No, he didn't.
(美W) (B) It probably will.
(C) That sounds like an excellent idea.

不如我們再把公式驗算一次？
(A) 不，他沒做。
(B) 可能會吧。
(C) 這個提議好像很不錯。

字彙 evaluate 計算　formula 公式

**24** These new cafeteria seats are comfortable.
(美W) (A) I prefer the old ones.
(美M) (B) A really low price.
(C) It's on Mark Turner's chair.

新餐廳的座位蠻舒服的。
(A) 我比較喜歡舊的座位。
(B) 價格真的很低。
(C) 它在馬克·特納的椅子上。

字彙 cafeteria （辦公大樓內的）自助餐廳

**25** Are you going away for the weekend or
(美W) staying at home?
(美W) (A) At the end of the week.
(B) Please rest a while.
(C) I'm travelling to Brisbane.

你週末要出門還是會待在家裡？
(A) 在這星期五。
(B) 請休息一下。
(C) 我要去布里斯本旅行。

字彙 go away for the weekend 週末出門
　　a while 一陣子

**26** Would you like me to email you a meeting
(美W) reminder?
(美M) (A) In the newspaper.
(B) No, I'll remember without one.
(C) Very upsetting.

你想要我發個信提醒你要開會嗎？
(A) 在報紙上。
(B) 不用，就算沒有我也會記得的。
(C) 非常令人不快。

字彙 reminder 提醒（的話、信）
　　upsetting 令人苦惱或憤怒的

**27** Didn't you sign the treaty?
(美M) (A) Sure, I will call him.
(英M) (B) You're welcome to join us.
(C) It hasn't been completed.

你沒簽約嗎？
(A) 當然，我會打給他。
(B) 很歡迎你加入我們。
(C) 還沒談完。

字彙 treaty 條約；條款

**28** Alan did a good job with that negotiation.
(英M) (A) The job's still open.
(美W) (B) Yes, I was impressed, too.
(C) When will that happen?

這次的協商艾倫做得不錯。
(A) 這個職缺還開著。
(B) 對，我也印象深刻。
(C) 那什麼時候會發生？

字彙 do a good job 做得不錯
　　negotiation 談判；協商
　　open （工作、職位）空缺的
　　impressed 感到印象深刻的

**29** How about getting a drink before the match?
(美W) (A) The parking is expensive.
(美M) (B) Do we have time?
(C) Their latest game.

比賽前來杯飲料如何？
(A) 停車很貴。
(B) 我們有時間嗎？
(C) 他們的最後一場賽事。

字彙 match 比賽　latest 最後的

**30** Do you think the head of department made
(英M) the wrong decision?
(美W) (A) I don't know whether he attends the
　　 meeting.
(B) It's too soon to tell.
(C) They already have.

你覺得部門主管的決策錯了嗎？
(A) 我不知道他會不會出席會議。
(B) 現在還言之過早。
(C) 他們已經做了。

字彙 head of department 部門主管
　　make a decision 做決策

14

**31** What's Martina planning to do with her
(美W) apartment when she relocates to Madrid?
(美M) (A) She's having a clearance sale here.
(B) Maybe she's going to go at once.
(C) She's trying to rent it out.

瑪蒂納要搬到馬德里去了，她打算怎麼處置她
的公寓呢？
(A) 她很快會在這裡做出清特賣。
(B) 她可能馬上就要出發。
(C) 她現在正在嘗試出租。

## PART 3
P. 149

**Questions 32-34 refer to the following conversation.**
(英M)(美W)

**M** Hello, my friends and I are camping in this area, so I'm here to check out some local attractions. I'm most interested in activities that would appeal to teenagers.

**W** Well, ㉝ the River Yeo is close and they organize numerous water sports for young adults. It also has a white water rafting course suitable for teenagers.

**M** That sounds like just what we want. Can you give me directions to the river?

**W** Yes, of course. ㉜ ㉞ Here's a brochure listing various summer activities in the surrounding region.

---

對話
男：嗨，我朋友和我正在這裡露營，想看看當
地的一些景點。以青少年為主的活動我最
感興趣。
女：這樣的話，約河很近，那邊為年輕人舉辦
很多的水上運動。也有適合青少年的泛舟
課程。
男：聽起來正是我們要的。可以告訴我河邊怎
麼去嗎？
女：當然可以。這本小冊子給你，上面有列出
鄰近地區的各種夏日活動。

**32** Where is the conversation most likely taking place?
(A) At an outdoor concert
(B) At a tourist information office
(C) At a riverside
(D) At a general store

這場對話最有可能在哪裡發生？
(A) 在戶外音樂會
(B) 在旅客服務中心辦公室
(C) 在河邊
(D) 在雜貨店內

**33** What does the woman recommend?
(A) Walking along the hillside
(B) Swimming in the local pool
(C) Exploring the environment
(D) Experiencing water sport activities

這名女子推薦了什麼？
(A) 沿著山邊走
(B) 在當地游泳池裡游泳
(C) 探索周遭環境
(D) 體驗水上運動

**34** What does the woman give the man?
(A) An invoice
(B) A map
(C) A booklet
(D) A ticket

女子給了男子什麼？
(A) 一張出貨明細
(B) 一張地圖
(C) 一本小冊子
(D) 一張票

**Questions 35-37 refer to the following conversation.**
美W 美M

**W** Mr. Hunt, this is Tanya Bouchon from Skylight TV. I'm calling to tell you that **㉟ ㊱ we'd like to accept your film script about your whale watching experiences in Alaska.**

**M** That's fantastic news. I've been a supporter of your nature programs for many years. You featured some of my favorite locations. So I was eager for you to realize my script would fit into your programming.

**W** We do think it's a relevant idea. In fact, **㊲ I'd like to arrange a meeting with you to discuss a series of programs** about whale activity in other locations. There's great interest in this topic right now.

----

**對話**

女：杭特先生，我是天光電視台的坦雅·布松。打這通電話是想告訴您，我們想採納您在阿拉斯加賞鯨體驗相關的拍攝腳本。

男：這個消息太棒了。我多年來都是貴生態節目的忠實支持者。您們的專題介紹了很多我最愛的地點。所以我很渴望我的腳本受到認可，適合貴節目的製作。

女：我們確實認為這個提案很切題。我們也想安排和您見面，討論有關其他地區鯨魚活動的系列節目。這是現在正熱門的主題。

----

**字彙** script （影視）腳本
whale watching 賞鯨
supporter 支持者
feature 以……為特色；主打
be eager for 熱切想要……
fit into 合適於  relevant 相關的；切題的
come along 到達；出現
a series of ……的系列
Alaskan 阿拉斯加人
film rights 影視版權（製播、重製或發行）

**35** What did the man write about?
(A) His unique tours
(B) Working with Alaskans
(C) His favorite TV film
(D) Writing for television

男子寫的東西與什麼有關？
(A) 他特別的旅程
(B) 和阿拉斯加人一起工作
(C) 他最愛的電視類電影
(D) 電視寫作

**36** Why is the man pleased?
(A) He was offered a job in Alaska.
(B) His idea will be published.
(C) His television will be replaced.
(D) His script has been accepted.

男子為何高興？
(A) 他得到了在阿拉斯加的工作。
(B) 他的構想將要出版。
(C) 他的電視機會被取代。
(D) 他的腳本剛被接納。

**37** Why does the woman want to meet with the man?
(A) To talk about some programs
(B) To perform an audition
(C) To take part in a documentary
(D) To discuss film rights

女子為何想與男子見面？
(A) 為了洽談一些節目
(B) 為了進行試鏡
(C) 為了加入紀錄片製作
(D) 為了討論影片版權

**Questions 38-40 refer to the following conversation with three speakers.** 美W 英M 英W

**W1** Hi, Mike and Helen. I am glad I caught you two! Do you happen to know where Jorge might be?

**M** Unfortunately, I don't. Is there anything you need from him? **㊳ I can call him on his mobile phone if you'd like.**

**W1** **㊴ Yeah, apparently there's a problem with the printers on the third floor.**

**M** You know, Haley in our office is pretty good at office equipment.

**W2** I fix all the machines on my floor. Would you like me to take a look at it right now?

----

女1：嗨，邁克和海倫。我很高興找到你們倆
　　個！你們會碰巧知道豪赫爾在哪裡嗎？

男：很遺憾我不知道。妳是不是需要他幫忙
　　呢？如果妳想的話，我可以打他手機。

女1：是的，三樓的印表機顯然出問題了。

男：妳知道嗎，我們辦公室的海莉很擅長修辦
　　公設備喔。

女2：我修得好我們這棟的所有機器。妳要我現
　　在就去看看嗎？

字彙 happen to 碰巧……　apparently 顯然

**38** What does the man offer to do?
(A) Replace an old machine
(B) Call a coworker
(C) Email an acquaintance
(D) Look up the schedule

男子提議做什麼？
(A) 換掉舊機器
(B) 打電話給一名同事
(C) 寄電子郵件給助理
(D) 查看行程

**39** Why is Jorge needed?
(A) To install a program
(B) To make photocopies
(C) To call technical support
(D) To make some repairs

為何需要豪赫爾？
(A) 要安裝程式
(B) 要影印
(C) 需要技術支援
(D) 需要修理一些東西

**40** Why does the man say, "Haley in our office is pretty good at office equipment"?
(A) To revise some schedule
(B) To recommend Haley for a promotion
(C) To suggest that Haley help with some machines
(D) To propose using another piece of equipment

為何男子說：「我們辦公室的海莉很擅長修辦公設備喔」？
(A) 以修改部分行程
(B) 以推薦海莉的升遷
(C) 以建議讓海莉協助設備狀況
(D) 以提議使用其他設備

---

**Questions 41-43 refer to the following conversation.**
英M 美W

**M** I understand ㊶ **you attended the conference for computer updates yesterday.** Can I ask you to prepare a short presentation for our new apprentices?

**W** Sorry, but I'm not much of a public speaker. How about I write up what I learnt from the conference and ㊷ **give you the information so you can get someone else to do the presentation**?

**M** Well, why don't I just ask you about the latest updates? Then I'll be able to prepare a presentation myself for tomorrow. ㊸ **When are you available today?**

**W** OK. That sounds like a good plan. ㊸ **Let's meet later over coffee.**

---

對話

男：我聽說妳昨天參加了電腦升級的會議。我
　　可以請妳為新進同仁準備個簡短的報告
　　嗎？

女：抱歉，我實在不是公開講話的料。還是我
　　把會議所見所聞詳細寫下後交份報告給
　　你，這樣你就可以找別人做簡報。

男：嗯，不如就我直接向妳討教最新狀況？然
　　後我明天就能自己準備簡報。妳今天何時
　　有空？

女：好啊，這做法感覺不錯。等等見面喝個咖
　　啡聊。

字彙 apprentice 新進員工
　　 not much of a 不是……的料
　　 public speaker 公開演講者
　　 write up 把……（詳細）寫成書面
　　 meet over coffee 喝咖啡見面
　　 external 外部的　adjust 調整
　　 layout 版面編排

**41** What event has the woman recently attended?
(A) A computer seminar
(B) A fund-raising lunch
(C) A presentation
(D) A writing conference

女子近來去過什麼活動？
(A) 電腦研討會
(B) 募款午餐會
(C) 簡報
(D) 寫作會議

**42** What alternative does the woman suggest?
(A) Hiring an external consultant
(B) Producing an updated memo
(C) Adjusting the layout of a brochure
(D) Getting someone else to prepare a presentation

女子建議換成哪個替代做法？
(A) 外聘諮詢人士
(B) 製作更新版的備忘錄
(C) 調整小冊的版面設計
(D) 找別人準備簡報

**43** What do the speakers agree to do?
(A) Meet today
(B) Talk with a manager
(C) Arrange a date
(D) Present a paper

談話的兩人同意怎麼做？
(A) 今天見面
(B) 和主管聊
(C) 擇日安排
(D) 呈交紙本資料

**Questions 44-46 refer to the following conversation.**
美W 美M

**W** Hi, ㊹ I'm calling because I'm painting my garden furniture and I've been searching for the right coating to protect the furniture from bad weather. Would you be able to give me some suggestions?

**M** Yes, we have a technical department available to advise you. Which brand of coating do you prefer?

**W** ㊺ I'd like to see a sample of the metallic color product I saw in your brochure. I think it's coating number 5.

**M** Okay, and if you like what we send you, ㊻ you can fill in an order form which is available on the Web site when you've made a decision of what you want to purchase.

--------

對話
女：嗨，我打給您是因為我正在塗裝花園裡的擺設，想找合適的塗料來保護家具不受壞天氣影響。您能給我一些建議嗎？

男：可以，我們有技術部門能給您建議。您偏好哪個牌子的塗料呢？

女：我想看看您產品冊中的一個金屬色式樣。我記得是五號塗料。

男：好的，如果您喜歡我們寄給您的樣品，而且決定好要購買的產品時，您可以在我們官網找到訂貨單下訂。

字彙 garden furniture 花園擺設
coating 塗料
technical department 技術部門
metallic 金屬的   brochure 樣冊
fill in 填寫   order form 訂貨單
manufacturer 製造商   decorator 裝修工
estimate 估價單

**44** Who most likely is the woman contacting?
(A) A paint supplier
(B) A clothing designer
(C) A garden expert
(D) A furniture manufacturer

女子最可能是和誰聯絡？
(A) 塗料業者
(B) 服裝設計師
(C) 園藝專家
(D) 家具業者

**45** What does the woman want to do?
(A) Select a decorator
(B) See a product sample
(C) Speak to a designer
(D) Receive an estimate

女子想做什麼？
(A) 找名裝修工
(B) 看樣品
(C) 和設計師談
(D) 收到估價單

**46** According to the man, how can the woman place a future order?
(A) By completing an online form
(B) By calling directly
(C) By sending an e-mail
(D) By mailing a request

根據男子說法，女子可以如何下訂單？
(A) 填完網路表格
(B) 直接打電話
(C) 寄電子郵件
(D) 寄信提出需求

15

**Questions 47-49 refer to the following conversation.**
美W 英M

**W** I'm glad I ran into you. ㊼ How is the accounting class going for you?

**M** It's now progressing quite fast ㊽ since we've learned all of the basic skills.

**W** Good luck with that! It should give you a lot of good practice.

**M** Definitely. ㊾ We're going to take part in a project where we can show off our skills. Our teacher is going to use this project as a way to evaluate us.

**W** Is accounting easy to learn?

**M** There's an open house where we'll demonstrate what we're learning if you're interested.

**W** I think I'll go to that. Thanks for the tip!

---

女：遇到你我很高興。你的會計課還順利嗎？

男：學完所有基礎以後，我們現在進度很快。

女：祝福你！你應該會有許多好的練習機會。

男：肯定是的。我們還會參加一項專案展現我們的技能。我們老師會拿這項專案當作評分方式。

女：學會計簡單嗎？

男：如果妳感興趣，會有一個公開活動，我們將在現場展示所學。

女：我想我會去看看。感謝提議！

字彙 **run into** 偶然遇到（某人）；無意碰見（某人）
**accounting** 會計　**progress** 進展
**evaluate** 評估；評價　**demonstrate** 展示
**establishment** 公司；機構

**47** What did the man do recently?
(A) He set up a new establishment.
(B) He developed new software.
(C) He signed up for a course.
(D) He demonstrated a new product.

男子最近做了什麼？
(A) 他開了新公司。
(B) 他開發新軟體。
(C) 他註冊參加了某個課程。
(D) 他展示了新產品。

**48** What does the man mean when he says, "It's now progressing quite fast"?
(A) He has become busy recently.
(B) The class is picking up speed.
(C) He thinks the course is easy.
(D) The class is very difficult to follow.

當男子說：「現在進度很快」時，他的意思是？
(A) 他最近變得很忙。
(B) 課程正在加快進度。
(C) 他認為課程很簡單。
(D) 很難追上課程進度。

**49** What is the man going to participate in?
(A) An upcoming lecture
(B) His favorite show
(C) A project
(D) A professional workshop

男子將參與什麼事？
(A) 一門即將開始的課程
(B) 他最喜歡的秀
(C) 一項計畫
(D) 專業工作坊

**Questions 50-52 refer to the following conversation.**
美M 美W

**M** Hi, Louisa. Is everything prepared for when the guests arrive?

**W** Yes, I've double checked and everything's going as planned. ㊿ The guests will arrive by 12:30 as scheduled so you can set the table at 1.

**M** Excellent! The dining hall is all prepared for me to serve the new healthy menu. Oh, 51 are this evening's drinks reception ready? I also need to prepare some food.

**W** Yes, I was able to contact a supplier that will provide the champagne you requested. 52 I just have to contact them to confirm the delivery time.

---

對話

男：嗨，路易莎。該為賓客做的準備一切妥當了嗎？

女：是的，我再三確認過了一切如預期。賓客按行程會在十二點半前抵達，所以你可以在一點擺設餐桌。

男：好極了！餐廳已全部就位，等著讓我擺上新的健康菜色。欸，今晚飲料招待那邊也準備好了嗎？我也需要準備一些食物。

女：好了，我已經聯絡好一家廠商，他們會提供你要的香檳。我只要再聯絡他們確認出貨時間就好。

**字彙** double check 再次確認；仔細檢查
as scheduled 照行程
dining hall（學校或其他建築物裡的）餐廳
reception 招待會　supplier 廠商
champagne 香檳　applicant 申請人
enthusiast 對……狂熱者
luncheon （正式的）午餐會
merchandise 商品

**50** Who are the speakers expecting?
(A) Business customers
(B) Job applicants
(C) Health enthusiasts
(D) Luncheon guests

對話的人等的是誰？
(A) 商業客戶
(B) 求職者
(C) 注重健康的人
(D) 午宴賓客

**51** What will the man do later this evening?
(A) Present some merchandise
(B) Give a tour of the hotel
(C) Organize a party
(D) Change a schedule

男子今晚稍晚將做什麼？
(A) 展示一些商品
(B) 提供飯店導覽
(C) 舉辦宴會
(D) 改變行程

**52** What does the woman say she needs to do?
(A) Contact a supplier
(B) Meet the guests
(C) Prepare a menu
(D) Call a colleague

女子說她需要做什麼？
(A) 聯絡廠商
(B) 見賓客
(C) 準備菜單
(D) 打給同事

**Questions 53-55 refer to the following conversation.**
英M 美W

**M** I met with ㊼ a possible buyer for Bill's Automobile Center yesterday. She is a business owner who manages similar garages in the town and she wants to expand her business.

**W** Well, we have had that business on sale for a long time now. Other interested parties said that the location was too remote. I know ㊾ the owner, Mr. Graston is becoming worried about his rising debts.

**M** You are right. This must be the perfect time to ㊿ suggest to Mr. Graston that he reduce the selling price of the business.

**對話**

男：我昨天和可能買下比爾汽車中心的對象見面了。她是在鎮上管理幾家類似維修場的老闆，想擴展業務。

女：嗯，我們這項業務到現在也經營蠻久了。其他感興趣的對象說地點太偏僻。我知道老闆格拉斯頓先生對於他持續增加的債務愈來愈擔心。

男：妳說的對。這正是向格拉斯頓先生提議降低售價的大好時機。

**字彙** possible buyer 可能買家
automobile 汽車
business owner 企業老闆
garage 汽車維修場
interested party 感興趣的對象
remote 偏遠的　selling price 售價
property 財產　reluctant to 不情願……
mount 增加　expire 到期
inspection 檢查
take out a loan 申請貸款

**53** What are the speakers discussing?
(A) A commercial property sale
(B) A building program
(C) Travel schedules
(D) Financial matters

對話的人在談什麼？
(A) 商業財產出售
(B) 建築計畫
(C) 旅遊行程
(D) 財經事務

15

**54** What does the woman mention about Mr. Graston?
(A) He is reluctant to sell.
(B) His debts are mounting.
(C) His lease has expired.
(D) He is moving abroad.

關於格拉斯頓先生，女子說了什麼？
(A) 他很抗拒出售。
(B) 他的債務增加。
(C) 他的租約過期了。
(D) 他正要搬出國。

**55** What does the man say he will suggest to Mr. Graston?
(A) Performing an inspection
(B) Reducing the price
(C) Purchasing an automobile
(D) Taking out a loan

男子說他要向格拉斯頓先生建議什麼？
(A) 進行檢查
(B) 降低價格
(C) 買輛汽車
(D) 申請貸款

**Questions 56-58 refer to the following conversation.**
美M 美W

**M** Hi, Naomi. I was just told that **56** my get-together with our German counterparts has been rearranged, so I have to travel there earlier than expected. Could you please give me your proposal for the campaign I'll be discussing with them in Hamburg? I need to receive it in two hours.

**W** I'm sorry, but regrettably **57** I'll be at the hospital all morning. But I can work on it when I return and email you all the information in time for the meeting.

**M** That would be good. It's a long drive, so **58** you have plenty of time to get it to me before I arrive.

------------

對話
男：嗨，娜歐蜜，我剛剛被告知，和德國對口的碰面被重新安排了，所以我必須比原定時間更早出發。可以請妳給我，妳想讓我在漢堡和他們討論的活動提案嗎？我需要在兩小時內收到。

女：我很抱歉，很遺憾我今天一整個早上都會在醫院。但我一回去就能處理，並把所有的開會資料準時寄給你。

男：這樣沒問題。路程很久，所以在我到之前，妳有充份的時間做好給我。

字彙 get-together 聚會；碰面
counterpart 往來客戶；對口
earlier than expected 比預期的早
proposal 提案　regrettably 遺憾地
terms 條款

**56** According to the man, what has changed?
(A) A travel plan
(B) The availability of a client
(C) The terms of a contract
(D) A meeting time

根據男子的說法，是什麼被改了？
(A) 旅行計畫
(B) 一位客戶有空的時間
(C) 合約的條款
(D) 會面時間

**57** What problem does the woman mention?
(A) She has booked the wrong flight.
(B) She is going on a vacation.
(C) Her computer keeps breaking down.
(D) She has an appointment in the morning.

女子提到什麼問題？
(A) 她訂錯班機。
(B) 她正在放假。
(C) 她的電腦一直當機。
(D) 她今天早上已有約。

**58** What does the man say the woman will have time to do?
(A) Send over a document
(B) Drive around
(C) Reserve a lunch
(D) Return to the office

男子說女子將有時間做什麼？
(A) 發出一份文件
(B) 開車晃晃
(C) 訂午餐
(D) 回到辦公室

**Questions 59-61 refer to the following conversation.**
美W 英M

**W** Hi. I saw the promotional poster for this laptop on your window, but I don't see it displayed anywhere.
**M** Ah, we have several promotions going on right now. Which one are you looking for?
**W** The model SP50T. (59) **I can't seem to find any information about it.**
**M** (60) **The reason is that the promotion is currently online only.** What do you want to know?
**W** I want to read more about the specifications.
**M** Let me walk you through our Web site now. Please come this way.

**對話**
女：您好，我在您店裡的櫥窗看到這台筆電的促銷海報，但到處都沒看到展示品。
男：噢，我們現在有多種促銷。您在找的是哪台呢？
女：SP50T 機型。我似乎找不到它的任何資訊。
男：是因為這個促銷目前只限網路。您想知道什麼呢？
女：我想要更詳細了解規格。
男：現在讓我帶您逛一下我們官網，請走這邊。

**字彙** laptop 筆電　promotion 升遷
specification 詳細規格；詳述

**59** What does the woman want to know?
(A) The period of the promotion
(B) The price of a product
(C) Information about a specific item
(D) Directions to the store
女子想知道什麼？
(A) 促銷為期多久
(B) 某產品的價格
(C) 特定品項的資訊
(D) 往店家的路

**60** What does the man say about the promotion?
(A) It will last until the end of the week.
(B) It is only available online.
(C) It is only for a specific product.
(D) It hasn't started yet.
關於促銷，男子說了什麼？
(A) 將持續到這週五為止。
(B) 只有網路上有。
(C) 只針對某個特定商品。
(D) 還沒開始。

**61** Why does the man say, "Let me walk you through our Web site now"?
(A) To make an online order
(B) To negotiate a price
(C) To show some information
(D) To explain some download methods
當男子說：「現在讓我帶您逛一下我們的官網」時，他的意思是？
(A) 要下網路訂單
(B) 要議價
(C) 要給出一些資訊
(D) 要解釋下載的一些方法

**Questions 62-64 refer to the following conversation.**
美W 英M

**W** Hi, (62) **I'm hosting a party next month and I'd like to book a room to accommodate all my guests.** Will you have any suitable rooms available on the 23rd?
**M** Well, (63) **how many guests will be in your party?** That will give us an idea of how much catering is required and the size of the venue you need to book.
**W** Okay. I have invited 200 people and expect between 100 and 150 will attend.
**M** In that case, you probably need one of our mid-sized rooms. I know two are reserved for events on that day, but I am sure one is available on the 23rd. Please give me a minute and (64) **I'll check the advanced bookings.**

**對話**
女：您好，我下個月要辦場聚會，想要訂一間能夠招待我所有賓客的房間。您 23 號會有合適的空房嗎？

男：好的，您的宴會會有多少賓客呢？這樣能讓我們大概知道需要多少酒水，還有您需要預約的場地大小。

女：好的。我邀請了 200 人，預計會有 100 到 150 人出席。

男：那樣的話，您可能需要我們一間中型房。就我所知，有兩間在當天已有活動預約了，但我確定 23 號還有一間空房。請再給我一點時間，我確認訂房狀況。

**62** What does the woman say she needs?
(A) A booking form
(B) An entertainment room
(C) A price breakdown
(D) Rented accommodation

女子說她需要什麼？
(A) 訂房表格
(B) 娛樂用房間
(C) 價格細目
(D) 租所

**63** What does the man ask the woman about?
(A) Her date of birth
(B) Her passport number
(C) The size of her party
(D) The location of her venue

男子向女子問了什麼？
(A) 她的出生日期
(B) 她的護照號碼
(C) 她的宴會規模
(D) 她的場地位置

**64** What will the man most likely do next?
(A) Check prior bookings
(B) Speak to a colleague
(C) Provide an estimate
(D) Source alternative arrangements

男子接著最有可能做什麼？
(A) 確認之前的預約
(B) 和同事說話
(C) 提供估價單
(D) 尋找替代方案

**Questions 65-67 refer to the following conversation and chart.** 美M 美W

| Discount code (Available only from 10/3 to 10/13) | |
|---|---|
| Items | Discount Rates |
| Table | 50% |
| Chair | 40% |
| Sofa | 30% |
| Bed frame (Cherrywood) | 25% |
| Bed mattress (Memory form) | 20% |
| **67** Bed frame (Cherrywood) & Bed mattress (Memory form) as a set | 30% |

**M** Hello. **65** I'm looking for a bed frame and mattress set, please.

**W** We have a wide selection you can choose from! Do you have a specific material and style you want?

**M** Hmm . . . Well, **66** I haven't purchased from your store before, but I'd like something in Cherrywood for the frame and a memory form for the mattress.

**W** You're in luck! **67** We are currently offering a limited-time discount on our entire Cherrywood bed frame and memory form sets. The promotional code will be automatically added to your order when you pay.

**M** That's great. Where can I see the products?

**對話與圖表**

| 折扣碼 （只限 10/3 到 10/13） | |
|---|---|
| 物品 | 折扣比例 |
| 桌子 | 50% |
| 椅子 | 40% |
| 沙發 | 30% |
| 床架（櫻桃木） | 25% |
| 床墊（記憶型） | 20% |
| 床架床墊組（櫻桃木＋記憶型） | 30% |

男：您好，我在找床架和床墊組。

女：我們有很多精選項目可供選購！您有想要的特定材質或風格嗎？

男：嗯……我從沒來過你們店內消費，但床架的話，我想要櫻桃木製的，至於床墊要記憶型的。

女：客人您很幸運！我們目前針對所有的櫻桃木床架和記憶床墊組均有限時折扣。您付款時，折扣碼即會自動代入訂單。

男：好棒。我可以在哪裡看產品呢？

**字彙** specific 特定的　automatically 自動地

**65** What is the man planning to do?
(A) Use a discount coupon
(B) Move out of a current apartment
(C) Purchase some furniture
(D) Find more information about the promotion

男子計劃做什麼？
(A) 用折扣券
(B) 搬出目前住的公寓
(C) 買些家具
(D) 找到更多促銷資訊

**66** What does the man indicate about the business?
(A) It offers only a few kinds of products.
(B) It is popular.
(C) This is his first time to purchase from the business.
(D) All kinds of items are on sale.

關於該公司，男子指出了什麼？
(A) 提供的產品種類不多。
(B) 非常受歡迎。
(C) 這是他第一次在那裡選購產品。
(D) 各種商品都在特價。

**67** Look at the graphic. Which discount will the man receive?
(A) 40%
(B) 30%
(C) 25%
(D) 20%

請看圖表，男子將得到多少折扣？
(A) 40%
(B) 30%
(C) 25%
(D) 20%

Questions 68-70 refer to the following conversation and catalog page. 英M 美W

| Product Number | Descriptions | Price |
|---|---|---|
| CM1350 | High speed with 13-inch monitor | $125 |
| CM1550 | High speed with 15-inch monitor | $150 |
| ❼⓿ CM1750 | High speed with 17-inch monitor | $185 |
| CM1950 | High speed with 19-inch monitor | $230 |

M ❻❽ **How are the preparations for our new associate coming along?**

W So far, so good. She is going to start next Monday. We have a space for her office. There is a desk already in there. I was able to find a phone and a printer, too. But I couldn't find a computer anywhere.

M ❻❾ **Did you ask the Maintenance Department?** Sometimes they have unused computers in storage.

W ❻❾ **I did, but they don't have any.**

M We'll just have to buy one. Our budget is pretty limited though. ❼⓿ **Get one with the largest monitor you can find for under $200.** Oh, and make sure it has a lock. She needs to keep her files secure.

**對話與型錄頁**

| 產品號碼 | 描述 | 價格 |
|---|---|---|
| CM1350 | 高速搭配 13 吋螢幕 | $125 |
| CM1550 | 高速搭配 15 吋螢幕 | $150 |
| CM1750 | 高速搭配 17 吋螢幕 | $185 |
| CM1950 | 高速搭配 19 吋螢幕 | $230 |

男：為我們的新同事做的準備進度還好嗎？

女：到目前為止還不錯。她下個星期一上工。我們有留她辦公室的空間。那裡已經有一張桌子了，我也找到一支電話和一台印表機，但我到處都沒找到電腦。

男：妳問過維修部門了嗎？他們的庫存裡有時會有沒用過的電腦。

女：我問了，他們那裡沒半台。

男：那我們需要買一台，雖然我們預算非常有限，就用 200 元以內買一台妳所能找到螢幕最大的。噢，要確保它有附鎖，她需要確保她的檔案安全無虞。

15

字彙 associate 同事；夥伴　storage 庫存
secure 安全的　transfer 轉移
furnish 給（房間）配置（傢俱等）
locate 探出；找出

**68** What are the speakers mainly discussing?
(A) Preparing for a new staff member
(B) Replacing computers
(C) Transferring important files
(D) Furnishing a lobby

對話的人主要在討論什麼？

(A) 為新同仁作準備
(B) 替換電腦
(C) 轉移重要檔案
(D) 為大廳裝設家具

**69** What does the woman say she did?
(A) Rescheduled a date
(B) Contacted another department
(C) Replaced some furniture
(D) Located missing files

女子說她做了什麼？

(A) 重新安排約會
(B) 聯絡其他部門
(C) 替換部分家具
(D) 找出遺失檔案

**70** Look at the graphic. What product will the woman most likely purchase?
(A) CM1350
(B) CM1550
(C) CM1750
(D) CM1950

請看圖表，女子最可能會買哪個產品？

(A) CM1350
(B) CM1550
(C) CM1750
(D) CM1950

**PART 4**

P. 153

Questions 71-73 refer to the following telephone message. 英M

Hello, this is Mario Cobiella calling from the Cretol Conference Center. ⓐ I'm scheduling an international convention and ⓐ would like to place an order of 2,000 name tags for all delegates. The convention is about three months from now but I'd like to finalize all the details by April 23. ⓐ Could you inform me of the cost for this amount? Please call me back at 555-5629, so we can discuss the details of the order. Thank you.

------

電話留言

　　嗨，我是科瑞托會議中心的瑪莉歐·科比亞。我正在安排一場國際會議，想要訂購給所有代表人士的名牌，共 2,000 個。會議至今還有大約三個月，但我想在 4 月 23 日前打點好所有細節。您能通知我總價多少嗎？回電給我請撥 555-5629，電話中我們可再討論訂單細節，謝謝。

字彙 schedule 安排　name tag 名牌
delegate 會議代表　finalize 完成；使結束
gathering 聚會　estimate 估計

**71** Why is the speaker calling?
(A) To approve a design
(B) To arrange a meeting
(C) To extend a deadline
(D) To place an order

說話的人為何打這通電話？

(A) 要接受設計
(B) 要安排會議
(C) 要延長期限
(D) 要下訂單

**72** What event is the speaker planning?
(A) A global gathering
(B) An advertising presentation
(C) A construction project
(D) A store renovation

說話的人正在籌備什麼活動？

(A) 國際級聚會
(B) 廣告用簡報
(C) 建案
(D) 店面整修

154

**73** What information does the speaker request?
(A) Expected time
(B) A printing deadline
(C) A cost estimate
(D) A meeting agenda

說話的人要求了什麼資訊？
(A) 預計時間
(B) 印刷截止日期
(C) 成本估價
(D) 會議議程

**Questions 74-76 refer to the following recorded message.** 美W

You've reached ❹ **Hannaford beauty technicians**. We are situated on the Hannaford's Main Street next to the Iris coffee shop. The store is closed at the moment but our beauticians are available Tuesday through Saturday from 8 A.M. to 5 P.M. We also have ❺ **late opening on Thursdays until 10 P.M.** Advance bookings are preferred to ensure you get full attention. To arrange an appointment, ❻ **please leave a message after the tone.**

留言錄音

　　您所撥打的電話是漢娜佛德美容院。我們位於漢娜佛德主大街上、愛瑞斯咖啡店旁。目前店面沒有營業，但可以在星期二到星期六、早上 8 點到下午 5 點找到我們的美容師。且我們週四營業得比較晚，到晚間 10 點。建議您提前預約以確保您享受到完整的服務。如欲預約，請在嗶聲後留言。

字彙 beauty technician 美容師　situate 位於
at the moment 目前　beautician 美容師
advance booking 預約
attention 關心；關切　appointment 約會
tone 提示聲

**74** What type of business is Hannaford's?
(A) A travel agency
(B) A beauty shop
(C) A dental clinic
(D) A café

漢娜佛德是什麼類型的店家？
(A) 旅行社
(B) 美容店
(C) 牙醫診所
(D) 咖啡廳

**75** What day is the business open late?
(A) On Tuesday
(B) On Wednesday
(C) On Thursday
(D) On Saturday

店家在哪天營業得較晚？
(A) 星期二
(B) 星期三
(C) 星期四
(D) 星期六

**76** What does the speaker recommend?
(A) Asking for a discount
(B) Visiting another salon
(C) Changing an appointment
(D) Leaving a message

說話的人建議了什麼？
(A) 可要求折扣
(B) 去別家沙龍
(C) 更改預約
(D) 留言

**Questions 77-79 refer to the following announcement.** 美M

Attention, ladies and gentlemen. ❼ **We'll be landing at La Manche Airport in ten minutes.** Please make sure you take all of your hand luggage with you when you exit the plane. ❽ **For passengers travelling onto Switzerland, please leave through terminal 1 exit and proceed to terminal 3 for your connecting flight.** ❾ **For those who are unable to walk, there is transport to take you to the customs hall.** Thank you for flying with us.

宣告

　　女士先生們請注意。我們即將在十分鐘後降落拉芒什機場。下飛機時請確保您攜帶您所有的隨身行李。前往瑞士的旅客，請從第一航廈出口離開，並前往第三航線轉乘接駁航班。不便行走的旅客也有運輸工具能帶您到海關大廳。感謝您搭乘我們的航班。

字彙 hand luggage 手提行李　exit 出口
travel onto 前往　proceed 繼續進行
connecting flight 接駁航班
transport 運輸工具
customs hall 海關大廳
refreshment 茶點　stand 小販賣部

**77** Where most likely is the announcement being heard?
(A) In a train station
(B) At the airport
(C) In a plane
(D) In a bus

這段廣播最有可能在哪裡聽到？
(A) 在火車站
(B) 在機場
(C) 在飛機上
(D) 在巴士裡

**78** What should people traveling to Switzerland do?
(A) Take transport to the customs hall
(B) Go to another terminal
(C) Wait for luggage removal
(D) Exit via the main hall

前往瑞士的人應該做什麼？
(A) 使用運輸系統到海關大廳
(B) 去其他航廈
(C) 等候行李移出
(D) 經由主大廳離開

**79** According to the announcement, what is offered to some passengers?
(A) Car park payment
(B) Ticket machines
(C) Refreshment stands
(D) Transportation

根據廣播內容，他們提供給部分旅客什麼東西？
(A) 停車費
(B) 售票機
(C) 點心販賣部
(D) 交通工具

**Questions 80-82 refer to the following instructions.** 英W

So ⑧⓪ this is the end of the tour of the **Kalua Zoo Nature Trail**. For those people who wish to remain, we will now have a simple test. Here's what we are going to do. I'll provide the Latin names of some animals and a map of the zoo. Whoever can ⑧① **accurately translate the names of the corresponding animal**, using the map to help you, will be awarded a free pass to the zoo's reptile house. Just ⑧② **make sure you don't stray out of the marked areas** while you're investigating. I hope you all decide to take part.

指示說明

　　到這裡就是卡魯瓦動物園自然步道之旅的尾聲了。想要留下來的人，我們現在有個簡單的測驗，也就是我們現在準備要做的。我將提供幾個動物的拉丁文名稱和一份動物園的地圖。藉由地圖，能夠精確翻譯相應動物名稱的人，將會得到一張動物園爬蟲館的免費入場券。請您務必確保調查過程中不會偏離指定區域。我希望你們全體都有意願參加。

字彙 nature trail 自然步道　Latin 拉丁文
corresponding 相應的　award 獎勵
pass 通行證；入場證　reptile 爬蟲類
stray 偏離　mark 劃定；標記
investigate 調查　take part 參加
demonstration 示範；演示
identify 辨識；識別　diagram 圖解
designate 標出；指定
enclosure 圍欄；圍地

**80** What event is ending?
(A) A company picnic
(B) A computer demonstration
(C) A sporting event
(D) A nature tour

什麼活動結束了？
(A) 公司野餐
(B) 一台電腦的使用示範
(C) 體育活動
(D) 自然之旅

**81** What must participants in the competition do?
(A) Translate names correctly
(B) Identify wild flowers
(C) Map out a route
(D) Draw a diagram

參加競賽的人必須要做什麼？
(A) 正確地翻譯名稱
(B) 辨識野花
(C) 擬定路線
(D) 畫圖表

**82** What are the listeners cautioned about?
(A) Feeding the animals
(B) Getting out of the designated paths
(C) Leaving trash
(D) Walking through the enclosures

聽話者被提醒要注意什麼？
(A) 餵食動物
(B) 偏離指定路線
(C) 留下垃圾
(D) 走過圍欄

**Questions 83-85 refer to the following announcement.**
英M

Hello, everyone, and welcome to The Whale Sanctuary. Regrettably, we'll have to line up for the next available transport. 83 84 The scheduled boat had a minor fault but as soon as the replacement arrives, we will go aboard. 85 Remember there are two different viewpoints of whale watching available, one from the top deck, and the other from below the water. Underwater viewers, please come forward as you will board first, everyone else please wait until called. Thanks and please enjoy your tour.

宣告

　　各位好，歡迎來到鯨魚保護區。很抱歉，我們需要排隊等待下一艘通行船班。原訂船隻有點小問題，不過等到替代船隻到達時就會開始登船。請記得共有兩個賞鯨地點，其一是從上層甲板，另一個則是從水下。水下的觀眾由於會先行登船，請到前方來，其他人則請等候通知。謝謝您並祝旅途愉快。

字彙 sanctuary 保護區　regrettably 遺憾地　line up 排隊　minor 小的　fault 錯誤　replacement 替代　top deck 上層甲板　below the water 在水下　underwater 水下的　viewer 觀眾　come forward 向前來　harbor 碼頭　inclement 天氣險惡的　in an orderly manner 有秩序地

**83** Where is the announcement being made?
(A) At a harbor
(B) At a theme park
(C) At a lake
(D) At a museum

這則廣播是在哪裡發出？
(A) 在碼頭
(B) 在主題樂園
(C) 在湖邊
(D) 在博物館

**84** Why are listeners told they will need to wait?
(A) A tour guide is delayed.
(B) A dinner has not been delivered.
(C) The transport has not arrived.
(D) The weather is inclement.

為何聽話者被告知需要等候？
(A) 一趟導覽受到耽擱。
(B) 晚餐還沒供應。
(C) 船班尚未抵達。
(D) 天氣惡劣。

**85** What are listeners asked to do?
(A) Form two separate groups
(B) Return at another time
(C) Find a viewpoint as quickly as possible
(D) Board the boat in an orderly manner

聽話者被要求做什麼？
(A) 分成兩群
(B) 其他時間再回來
(C) 盡快找到觀賞地點
(D) 有秩序地登船

Hi, Emily. This is Pablo from Parco, Inc. **86 I just received the file with the sample logo that one of your designers prepared for my company. I think it's a good start. But it's not what we were expecting.** When we spoke a few weeks ago, I explained that we are looking for a logo with bright colors but also simple. The logo I received is very bright. The red and yellow look great, but the text is too complicated. Can you replace it with something a little more basic? I remember you mentioning that you had catalogs with sample text. **88 Could we meet to review those?** I'm free afternoons next week. Let me know what your schedule looks like.

電話留言

嗨，愛蜜莉，我是帕爾可公司的保羅。我剛收到了檔案，是您一位設計師為我們公司準備的標識樣本。我想這是一個好的開始，但不是我們當初想要的。我們幾週前在談時，我解釋過我們的標識想要用色明亮、但也要簡約。我收到的標識很明亮，紅黃配色看起來很棒，但文字太過繁複。您能否用更基本的款式換掉呢？我記得您提過您有文字式樣的型錄，我們方便見面重新看過嗎？我下週下午都有空，請再告訴我您可能的行程安排。

字彙 **stationery store** 文具店　**scheme** 組合

**86** Where does the listener most likely work?
(A) At a gallery
(B) At a stationary store
(C) At a paint manufacturer
(D) At a graphic design firm
聽話者最可能在哪裡工作？
(A) 藝廊
(B) 文具店
(C) 油漆製造商
(D) 平面設計公司

**87** What does the man imply when he says, "it's not what we were expecting"?
(A) He was surprised with a quick response.
(B) He wants a better result.
(C) He doesn't like the color scheme.
(D) He wants to cancel the order.

當男子說：「和我們當時期望的不同」時，他的意思是？
(A) 他很驚訝獲得即時答覆。
(B) 他想要更好的成果。
(C) 他不喜歡配色。
(D) 他想取消訂單。

**88** What does the speaker want to do?
(A) Reschedule the appointment
(B) Order more products
(C) Arrange a meeting
(D) Change the colors
說話的人想要做什麼？
(A) 更改約會
(B) 訂更多產品
(C) 安排見面
(D) 換顏色

Good afternoon, and welcome to the grand opening party of Sunrise Gallery's SoHo location. **89 We hope that you enjoy the refreshments provided by Gourmet Catering, located in the reception hall right next to this room.** In conjunction with this event, we are showing our special painting selection, aptly named Modern Precious, which is also available for purchase at discounted prices; however, please remember the Modern Precious collection is not expected to last very long, so guests are encouraged to peruse them throughout the event. **91 Let's take a look at our special selection.**

指示

各位午安，歡迎來到日昇藝廊蘇活館的盛大開幕餐會。我們希望您能盡情享用由「美食家外燴」提供的點心，就在這個房間旁邊的接待大廳內。和這次活動一起，我們也會現場展示特藏畫作，它很貼切地就叫作現代珍寶，同時並特價開放購買；不過，請留意現代珍寶系列預計不會展出很久，所以鼓勵各位賓客在整場活動中細細品味。現在就一起來看看我們的特別收藏。

字彙 **refreshments** 茶點
**in conjunction with** 和⋯⋯一起
**aptly** 恰當地　**pursue** 細讀；仔細觀察
**souvenir** 紀念品

**89** What is available in the reception hall?
(A) Brochures
(B) Maps
(C) Food and drinks
(D) A gift shop

在接待大廳有什麼可供使用？
(A) 小冊子
(B) 地圖
(C) 餐飲
(D) 禮品店

**90** What does the speaker imply when she says, "Please remember the Modern Precious collection is not expected to last very long"?
(A) The product sale has ended recently.
(B) Many people are waiting to buy items.
(C) People need to purchase the items quickly.
(D) There is only a small selection of artwork.

說話的人說：「請留意現代珍寶系列預計不會展出很久」，她的意思是？
(A) 產品促銷最近結束了。
(B) 等著買東西的人很多。
(C) 想買東西的人要盡快。
(D) 只有少量的藝術收藏。

**91** What will the listeners do next?
(A) Buy some souvenirs
(B) Look over a special collection
(C) Introduce themselves to each other
(D) Leave the building

聽話者之後將會做什麼？
(A) 買些紀念品
(B) 瀏覽特藏
(C) 和他人介紹自我
(D) 離開建築物

**Questions 92-94 refer to the following excerpt from a meeting and agenda.** 澳M

| Agenda | |
|---|---|
| Welcoming speech | Paul Baker |
| Financial report | Yohey Ogawa |
| ❸ New product | Beda Hari |
| Team restructuring | Lisa Whang |

In spite of unfavorable domestic industrial circumstances, our company's profits continue to grow, which makes the shareholders happy. Today I would like to let you know about some new offerings that we expect will help boost profits. ❷ ❸ **As you may know, Top Technologies released a new line of tablet PCs.** ❷ **Well, I am pleased to report that we have signed a contract to be the exclusive online distributor of these products.** ❹ **We will begin selling them on our Web site in two weeks.** In addition, we are expanding our in-store offerings of accessories to include several new brands of headphones, data storage drives, and security software. Our marketing researchers say that customers are interested in having more options when it comes to these types of products.

🔊16

**會議摘錄與議程表**

| 議程 | |
|---|---|
| 致歡迎詞 | 保羅・貝克 |
| 財務報告 | 小川與平 |
| 新品介紹 | 貝達・哈里 |
| 團隊再造 | 麗莎・王 |

儘管國內產業局勢不利，但我們公司的收益仍持續成長，股東們都很高興。我今天還想告訴你們幾個預期能夠增加收益的產品。你們可能聽說過頂尖科技新開賣的平板電腦產品線。嗯，我很高興宣布，我們已簽約成為這些產品銷售的網路獨家通路。兩個星期後我們將在官網上開賣。此外，我們也正在實體店面擴大銷售配件商品，囊括多個新品牌耳機、硬碟和安全軟體。我們的行銷研究專家說，顧客選購這類產品時想要有更多選擇。

**字彙** in spite of 儘管…… unfavorable 不利的
domestic 國內的
circumstance 條件；形勢
offering （提供的）產品
boost 刺激；提振 profit 收益
exclusive 獨家的 distributor 銷售商
expand 擴展 in-store 在實體店面的
when it comes to 當談到……
stock 股票 retailer 零售業

**92** Where does the speaker most likely work?
(A) At a stock trading company
(B) At a computer manufacturer
(C) At an Internet service provider
(D) At an electronics retailer

說話的人最可能在哪裡工作？
(A) 在證券交易公司
(B) 在電腦製造業
(C) 在網路服務供應商
(D) 在電子零售業

**93** Look at the graphic. Who is most likely speaking?
(A) Paul Baker
(B) Yohey Ogawa
(C) Beda Hari
(D) Lisa Whang

請看圖表，誰最有可能是講者？
(A) 保羅・貝克
(B) 小川與平
(C) 貝達・哈里
(D) 麗莎・王

**94** According to the speaker, what will the business do in two weeks?
(A) Sign an exclusive deal
(B) Open a new branch
(C) Release new software
(D) Begin selling new items online

根據說話的人所述，公司在兩週內會做什麼？
(A) 簽署獨門交易
(B) 開設新分店
(C) 釋出新軟體
(D) 線上開賣新商品

**Questions 95-97 refer to the following talk and map.**
英W

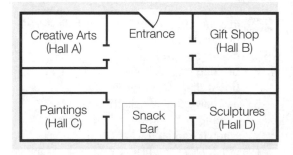

Thank you, everyone, for your interest and cooperation on our tour of the Wesley Museum. ⑨⑤ **We apologize that our wooden sculptures were made unavailable to the public as many of you expressed interest in seeing them before the tour. The room will be reopened once renovations are completed.** ⑨⑥ ⑨⑦ **However, I urge all of you to attend the live demonstration today at one o'clock for this month's pottery display, produced by John Grisham, a local artist and environmental activist.**

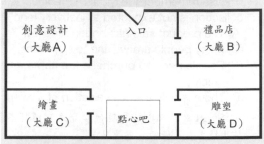

感謝各位對衛斯理美術館參訪行程的興趣和配合。很抱歉，我們的木雕沒能開放參觀，畢竟你們之中很多人行前曾表示感興趣。那個展示廳一整修完就會重新開放。我也很推薦各位去參加今天一點整的當月陶器展，將由當地藝術家兼環保運動人士約翰・葛里遜現場示範。

字彙 cooperation 合作；配合 wooden 木製的 sculpture 雕塑 urge 敦促；力薦 demonstration 示範；展示 potter 陶藝家 curator 策展人

**95** Look at the graphic. Which area is unavailable to the public?
(A) Hall A
(B) Hall B
(C) Hall C
(D) Hall D

請看圖表，哪個區域不對外開放？
(A) 大廳 A
(B) 大廳 B
(C) 大廳 C
(D) 大廳 D

**96** What does the speaker recommend the listeners do?
(A) Visit another museum
(B) Meet a painter
(C) See a live demonstration
(D) Purchase some gifts

說話的人推薦聽話者做什麼？
(A) 參觀另一間美術館
(B) 和畫家見面
(C) 欣賞現場示範
(D) 買禮品

**97** Who is John Grisham?
(A) A collector
(B) A local potter
(C) A museum curator
(D) The tour guide

約翰‧葛里遜是誰？
(A) 收藏家
(B) 當地陶藝家
(C) 美術館策展人
(D) 導遊

Questions 98-100 refer to the following excerpt from a meeting and chart. 澳M

### Survey Result

| New York New York | Starry Night | Poppins | Summer Beach |
|---|---|---|---|

I'd like to present the results of last month's survey to everyone before making a final decision. As you may remember, we asked our members to indicate which production we should perform next, and **98** it looks like there is a clear preference for what we should do. **99** Oh, and there are countless responses to Sophia for giving out teasers on social media; it's thanks to her that we had many people call and reserve tickets ahead of time. There's a lot of work ahead of us, but **100** remember to keep our fans updated!

---

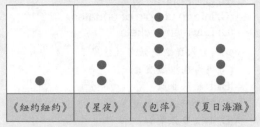

會議摘錄與圖表

### 調查結果

| 《紐約紐約》 | 《星夜》 | 《包萍》 | 《夏日海灘》 |
|---|---|---|---|

　　在做出最後決定前，我想把上個月問卷的結果給大家看。你們可能還記得，我請會員針對下次要表演哪齣戲表示看法，對於我們該怎麼做，結果出現了明顯偏好。對了，蘇菲亞也收到數不清的回應，希望在社群媒體上釋出片花；也要感謝她，才有很多人打電話來提前訂票。我們眼前還有很多工作，但也要記得讓我們的粉絲得知最新消息。

字彙 **indicate** 表明
**countless** 無數的；數不清的
**teaser** 片花（影視或表演的片段）
**ahead of time** 提前

**98** Look at the graphic. Which production will be selected?
(A) New York New York
(B) Starry Night
(C) Poppins
(D) Summer Beach

請看圖表，最有可能選擇哪齣表演？
(A) 《紐約紐約》
(B) 《星夜》
(C) 《包萍》
(D) 《夏日海灘》

**99** Why does the speaker praise Sophia?
(A) She wrote scripts well.
(B) She performed her role well.
(C) She made social media updates.
(D) She sold lots of tickets.

說話的人為何稱讚蘇菲亞？
(A) 她腳本寫得好。
(B) 她角色演得好。
(C) 她在社群媒體上更新訊息。
(D) 她賣出很多票。

16

**100** What does the speaker remind the listeners to do?
(A) Cast actors for roles
(B) Call Sophia
(C) Inform people of updates
(D) Buy many tickets

說話的人提醒聽話者做什麼？
(A) 為角色試鏡演員
(B) 打給蘇菲亞
(C) 更新給人們知道
(D) 購買多張票

## PART 5
P. 156

**101** 喬納斯寵物用品店很快會在荷蘭和西班牙兩地開設新工廠。
(A) yet 然而
(B) but 但
(C) either 兩者之一
(D) both 兩者都

**解析** 本題考的是相關連接詞。空格應搭配 and 使用，表示「A 與 B 兩個都」的意思，因此答案為 (D)。另外補充一點，either A or B 的意思為「A 或者 B」；neither A nor B 的意思為「A 與 B 兩者皆不」；not only A but also B 的意思為「不僅 A 還有 B」（= B as well as A）；not A but B 的意思為「不是 A 而是 B」。

**字彙** Holland 荷蘭
pet supply 寵物用品店

**102** 請捐款到月光藝廊表達你對視覺藝術的支持。
(A) your 你的
(B) yourselves 你們自己
(C) yours 你的（東西）
(D) yourself 你自己

**解析** 本題考的是代名詞。空格位在名詞前方，應填入代名詞的所有格，因此答案為 (A)。

**字彙** gallery 藝廊；展覽館
visual art 視覺藝術

**103** 「新時代之眼」的顧客得知我們塑膠製隱形眼鏡的最新降價幅度時將會很高興。
(A) easier 更簡單的
(B) lower 較低的
(C) thicker 更濃的
(D) louder 更吵鬧的

**解析** 本題考的是形容詞詞彙。空格後方連接 rates，根據題意，(B) 最適合與其搭配使用。另外補充一點，題目經常會考以 reasonable（合理的）、affordable（付得起的）、moderate（適度的）等形容詞來修飾價格，請特別熟記。

**字彙** delighted 高興的　find out 得知
louder 更吵鬧的　rate 幅度

**104** 巴克曼機工的專家能嫻熟地配合您的製造需求，設計客製化的解決方案。
(A) skillful 嫻熟的；熟練的
(B) skills 技巧
(C) skill 技巧
(D) skillfully 嫻熟地；熟練地

**解析** 助動詞（can）和原形動詞（design）之間應填入副詞，修飾前方動詞，因此答案為 (D)。skillful 為形容詞、skill 為名詞，都不能用來修飾動詞。

**字彙** professional 專家
custom-tailored 客製化地
solution 解決方案　suit 適合
skillfully 嫻熟地；熟練地

**105** 研討會結束後，歡迎所有與會者在隔壁房間享用免費茶點。
(A) When 當
(B) Still 仍
(C) Though 雖然
(D) Soon 很快地

**解析** all participants . . . next door 為一個結構完整的句子，因此空格至 over 扮演修飾的角色。空格應填入從屬連接詞，用來修飾後方子句。Still 和 Soon 皆為副詞，不適合填入；When 和 Though 皆為從屬連接詞，但是根據題意，表達「研討會結束的時候」較為適當，因此答案為 (A)。

**字彙** be over 結束　participant 參加者

**106**

羅茜女士告知她的事業合夥人，合併案應在 8 月 30 日前完成。

(A) stated 陳述
(B) informed 通知
(C) confirmed 確認
(D) agreed 同意

**解析** 本題考的是動詞詞彙。根據題意，表達「告知在 8 月 30 日前完成合併」最為適當，因此答案為 (B)。

**字彙** business associate 事業合夥人　merger (公司) 合併　state 陳述　inform 通知　confirm 確認

**107**

法蘭科教授正打算召開股東會，以徵詢資深稅務專家的意見。

(A) from 從……
(B) as 如同……
(C) past 經過……
(D) at 在……

**解析** 本題要選出適當的介系詞。空格後方為高階稅務專業人員，應「從他們身上」獲取意見，因此填入 (A) 最為適當。

**字彙** general meeting 股東會　obtain 取得　senior 資深的　tax professional 稅務專家

**108**

韓先生大方協助同事學習使用網路軟體。

(A) variably 多變地；反覆無常地
(B) accurately 精確地
(C) generously 大方地；慷慨地
(D) entirely 完全地

**解析** 本題考的是副詞詞彙。根據題意，最適合搭配「提供協助」使用的副詞為 (C)。

**字彙** co-worker 同事　variably 多變地；反覆無常地　accurately 精確地　generously 慷慨地；大方地　entirely 完全地

**109**

我們的電腦商場爭取到新軟體總價三成的折扣。

(A) totaling 正在合計為
(B) totals 總額
(C) total 總共的
(D) totally 完全地

**解析** 空格位在冠詞 (the) 和名詞 (cost) 之間，應填入形容詞，修飾後方名詞，因此答案為 (C)。totaling 當作現在分詞使用時，雖然能夠扮演形容詞的角色，但是其意思為「總計的、合計的」，不符合題意。

**字彙** secure 取得

**110**

梅里克財務諮詢能協助零售業者發展新業務，並成為收益更好的企業。

(A) develops 發展
(B) developed 發展了
(C) develop 發展
(D) development 發展

**解析** 動詞 help 的受詞後方要再連接原形動詞、或 to 不定詞作為受詞補語，因此空格填入 (C) 當作受詞補語最為適當。〈help ＋受詞＋ (to) 原形動詞〉該用法中可以選擇省略受詞，也就是說 help 後方可以直接連接原形動詞，請特別熟記。

**字彙** financial consultant 財務諮詢　retailer 零售業者　launch 開始　lucrative (尤指生意、職位或活動)賺錢的，盈利的　enterprise 企業

**111**

儘管巴頓遺產委員會表示關切，市政委員會仍確定出售歷史悠久的溫徹斯特故居。

(A) except 除……之外
(B) within 在……之中
(C) onto 到……之上
(D) despite 儘管

**解析** The urban . . . House 為一個結構完整的句子，因此空格至句尾扮演修飾的角色。空格後方連接名詞 (concerns)，因此空格應填入介系詞。raised 為過去分詞，用來修飾前方名詞 concerns。根據題意，表達「儘管擔憂」較為適當，因此答案為 (D)。

字彙 urban 城市的，城鎮的
committee 委員會
historic 有歷史意義的
raise 提出；發出　legacy 遺產

**112**

《六月每日財經指南》的銷量超過五百萬冊，提供商業行銷人員可貴的資訊。

(A) valuable 可貴的
(B) eager 熱切的
(C) aware 意識到的
(D) numerous 許多的；大量的

解析 本題考的是形容詞詞彙。根據題意，表達「提供有價值的資訊給商業行銷人員」較為適當，因此答案為 (A)。

字彙 financial 財經的
business marketer 商業行銷人員
valuable 可貴的；有價值的
eager 熱切的

**113**

佳美簾公司的週薪都是直接存入員工的銀行帳戶。

(A) directed 被導向
(B) directly 直接地
(C) direction 方向
(D) directs 指向；導向

解析 空格位在〈be p.p.〉後方，應填入副詞，修飾前方動詞，因此答案為 (B)。directed 可以當作動詞或分詞使用；direction 為名詞；direct 可以當作動詞或形容詞使用，皆不能用來修飾動詞。

字彙 fabulous 極好的
drape（厚布製成的）帷，幕，窗簾
deposit 存入
bank account 銀行帳戶
direct 指向；導向

**114**

朱諾女士告別演說時講述了她成為著名記者的挑戰過程。

(A) challenging 挑戰性的；考驗能力的
(B) challenges 挑戰；考驗
(C) challenger 挑戰者
(D) challenge 挑戰

解析 空格位在所有格（her）和名詞（path）之間，應填入形容詞，修飾後方名詞。因此答案為 (A)。challenge 為動詞；challenger 為名詞，皆無法扮演形容詞的角色。

字彙 farewell speech 告別演說
well-known 著名的　journalist 記者
challenging 挑戰性的；考驗能力的
challenger 挑戰者

**115**

詹姆斯電腦公司明天會因國定假日而休息一天。

(A) observance 紀念；遵守
(B) observant 善於觀察的；觀察力敏銳的
(C) observe 遵守
(D) observer 觀察員

解析 空格位在介系詞（in）和介系詞（of）之間，應填入名詞，因此要從 observance 和 observer 當中選出答案。in observance of 的意思為「慶祝、紀念……」，因此答案要選 (A)。

字彙 public holiday 國定假日
observance（節日、生日等的）紀念，慶祝；遵守，奉行
observant 善於觀察的；觀察力敏銳的
observe 遵守　observer 觀察員

**116**

里德維爾市府持有 20 個公園並負責管理，其中 6 個有游泳設施。

(A) all 所有的
(B) them 它們
(C) which（上述的、非限定關係）它們
(D) that（上述的）它們

解析 句子當中有三個動詞（owns、maintains、have），需要搭配兩個連接詞。現在句中已經有一個對等連接詞 and，因此空格需要填入另一個連接詞。(C) which 和 (D) that 可以當作連接詞，應從中選出答案。而 that 當作連接詞使用時，不能放在介系詞後方，因此答案為 (C) which。

　　值得留意的是，千萬不能只看空格前後方，就直接選 (B) them。空格填入的連接詞需同時扮演代名詞的角色，因此要填入關係代名詞才行。

字彙 public park 公園　facility 設施

**117**

雷諾女士通知員工加班獲准，以確保風機可在明天出貨前完成。
(A) have approved 已批准
(B) approved 批准
(C) having been approved 正在獲批准
(D) have been approved 已獲批准

解析 空格置於 that 子句中的動詞位置，having been approved 並非動詞，因此請先刪去該選項。have approved 和 approved 屬於主動語態、have been approved 屬於被動語態，而空格後方沒有連接受詞，因此答案為 (D)。

　　另外補充一點，本題的句型結構為「主詞＋動詞＋受詞 1 ＋受詞 2」，使用 that 子句作為第二個受詞。適用此用法的動詞有 inform、remind、tell、advise、assure、convince 等。

字彙 overtime hours 加班
guarantee 確保　wind turbine 風機
in time 及時　shipment 出貨

**118**

儘管民意一面倒支持，籌措資金蓋新公園還是很困難。
(A) approval 批准
(B) response 回應；意見
(C) display 展示
(D) creation 創作

解析 (A) approval 的意思為「批准」，用於表示市議會、或政府機關的同意，不適用於大眾上，因此不適合作為答案。(C) display（展示）和 (D) creation（創作）皆不符合題意，因此答案應選 (B)。另外，請一併熟記 response to（對……的反應）。

字彙 overwhelmingly 壓倒性的

**119**

應時軟體科技積極聘用了當地多位頂尖的軟體開發人員。
(A) some 幾位
(B) every 每一
(C) other 其他
(D) much 多

解析 空格要填入 has recruited 的受詞，(B) every 和 (C) other 皆為形容詞，因此不能作為答案。(A) some 和 (D) much 可以當作名詞或形容詞使用，因此請從中選出答案。much of 後方要連接不可數名詞，因此並不適當。(A) some 加上 of 後，後方可以連接複數可數名詞、或不可數名詞，故為正確答案。

字彙 aggressively 積極地

**120**

七星鞋業起先是地方的小店面，如今已成為國際知名品牌。
(A) recognize 認可
(B) recognized 被認可
(C) recognizer 識別器
(D) recognizing 正在認可

解析 空格用來修飾名詞（brand），因此要填入形容詞。選項中沒有一般形容詞，僅有現在分詞 (D) 和過去分詞 (B)。根據題意，並非自己認可的（recognizing）品牌，而是備受認可的（recognized）品牌，因此答案為 (B) recognized。

字彙 internationally 在國際間

**121**

全體員工務必記得下班前簽退，以便清潔人員知道辦公室已淨空。
(A) inquired 被詢問的
(B) reminded 僅記；被提醒注意
(C) denied 被拒絕
(D) committed 承諾過的

解析 請熟記 be reminded to（使想起、提醒）的用法。本題答案要選 (B)。inquire（詢問）當作不及物動詞使用時，後方要搭配 about，因此並非答案。deny（否認）不符合題意。另外，be committed（致力於）後方要連接介系詞 to，不是連接 to 不定詞，因此也不能作為答案。

字彙 sign out 簽退

**122**

藝廊展場將在六週的時間內逐步整修到好。

(A) above 在……上面
(B) down 在下面
(C) over 在……期間
(D) into 在……裡面

解析 本題考的是介系詞。空格後方連接的名詞（a six-week time period）表示一段時間，介系詞 (C) 的後方可以連接該類名詞，故為正確答案。其他相同用法的介系詞有 for、during、within、throughout、in、after 等，皆可用於時間名詞的前方，請一併熟記。

字彙 renovation 整修
showroom 陳列室；展場
gradually 逐步地　period 期間

**123**

長期天氣預報顯示，這個月接下來的日子仍會持續大雨。

(A) exception 例外
(B) remainder 其餘
(C) boundary 邊界
(D) anticipation 預期

解析 本題考的是名詞詞彙。根據題意，表達「這個月剩下的時間預計會持續暴雨」較為適當，因此答案為 (B)。

字彙 long-term 長期　last 持續
remainder 剩餘部分；其餘；剩餘物
boundary 邊界　anticipation 預期

**124**

副總理戴爾·克拉克在演說中，比較了柯林斯與塔夫茨公司和 HG 諮詢集團近期的表現。

(A) rather 相當
(B) indeed 確實
(C) to that of 和……的（近期表現）相比
(D) what is more 更有意思的是……

解析 本題考的是動詞詞彙。compare A with (to) B 表示「將 A 和 B 比較」。根據題意，表達「比較兩處的成果」較為適當。且用 that 來代替前方的名詞（performance），因此答案為 (C)。句中重複出現前方的名詞時，依照單數或複數的，可以使用代名詞 that 或 those 來代替。

字彙 address （正式場合的）演講或報告
what is more 更有意思的是……

**125**

莫瑞·阿爾蒙可望會連任民防聯隊的主席。

(A) probable 很可能發生的
(B) qualified 合格的
(C) constant 經常發生的
(D) endless 無盡的

解析 本題考的是形容詞詞彙。根據題意，表達「有可能再次當選」較為適當，因此答案為 (A)。

字彙 Civil Defence 民防
probable 很可能發生的
qualified 合格的
constant 經常發生的
endless 無盡的

**126**

寫完會計課程的入學資格考時，請確保您已填寫目前的雇主及聯絡電話。

(A) While 當
(B) During 在……期間
(C) In addition 此外
(D) Assuming that 假定

解析 本題考的是連接詞。逗點後方為原形動詞（ensure）開頭的句子，是一個結構完整的句子，因此空格開始到 course 屬於修飾語。根據題意，表達「在會計課程入學考試的時候」較為適當，因此答案為 (A)。

空格後方的 completing 並非動名詞，而是屬於分詞構句中的分詞。In addition 為副詞片語；Assuming that 為從屬連接詞，後方要連接結構完整的子句。

字彙 entrance test 入學資格考
accounting 會計　ensure 確保
fill in 填入　current 目前的　employer 雇主

**127**

我們仔細檢查建築物後，發現風暴的破壞比原先預期的更嚴重。

(A) effective 有效的
(B) accurate 精確的
(C) apparent 顯見的
(D) severe 嚴重的

**解析** 本題要選出適合用來形容「暴風雨災害」的形容詞。effective（有效率的）、accurate（準確的）、apparent（明顯的）皆不適合填入空格中。表達比預期還要「嚴重」較為適當，因此答案為 (D) severe（嚴重的）。

**字彙** meticulous 嚴謹的　accurate 精確的
apparent 顯見的

**128**

收購案宣布前，阿爾發運輸就已經開始發展新的商業策略。
(A) begins 開始
(B) will begin 將開始
(C) had begun 已經開始
(D) having begun 正在開始

**解析** When/By the time 開頭的子句使用過去式時，主要子句要使用過去式、或是過去完成式，因此答案為 (C) had begun。另外補充一點，若 When/By the time 開頭的子句使用現在式時，實際上要表達的是未來，因此主要子句要使用未來式、或未來完成式才行。

**字彙** acquisition 收購

**129**

閃耀媒體將廣泛投放社交媒體行銷活動，來推廣「果凍音樂」這項新的線上音樂服務。
(A) under 在……之下
(B) among 在……之中
(C) below 在較低處
(D) through 透過；經由

**解析** 四個選項皆為介系詞，因此要透過單字的意思來解題。social media marketing campaign 屬於宣傳方式，(D) through 的意思為「透過……」，故為正確答案。另外，among（在……之中）後方要連接複數名詞。

**字彙** extensive 廣泛的

**130**

過去三個月來的動物福利促進運動，使捐款驚人地增加了50%。
(A) receptive 樂於接受的
(B) remarkable 驚人的
(C) tedious 單調乏味的
(D) perpetual 永久的

**解析** 本題考的是形容詞詞彙。根據題意，表達「捐款有 50% 驚人的成長」較為適當，因此答案為 (B)。

**字彙** animal welfare 動物福利
promotional 促進
receptive 樂於接受的
remarkable 驚人的；出色的
tedious 單調乏味的
perpetual 永久的

## PART 6

### 131-134 告示

　　成本的增加使我們重新檢視和供應商的合約，並決定更換墨水供應商。

　　自 8 月 1 日起，所有墨水均從多莉墨水進行採購。現有的庫存會繼續用到用完為止。不過，啟用新墨水前，員工應熟悉所有指示和流程。各別產線必須使用相應且適當的程序。

　　多莉墨水提供其產品使用說明的手冊。這些小冊子在第一批新墨水到達時將一併發送給所有員工。請詳細閱讀說明。如果對於新產品的使用有任何疑問，請您聯繫我（555-2250）或多莉墨水的業務代表瑪麗・亨利（1-200-555-0444）。

**字彙** expense 成本　as of 從……起
existing 現有的；既存的　run out 用盡
familiarize 使熟悉　instruction 說明
procedure 流程；程序
respective 各別的　thoroughly 仔細地
application 應用　undergo 經歷

**131**

(A) Otherwise 否則
(B) Nevertheless 然而
(C) Namely 也就是說
(D) Consequently 因此

解析 本題要選出適合連接空格前後兩個句子的連接副詞。空格前方的句子提到要再檢查一次合約，後方的句子則提到決定要更換供應商。由此可以看出兩者為因果關係，因此答案為 (D) Consequently（因此）。

**132**

(A) obsolete 過時的
(B) appropriate 適當的
(C) manual 手工的
(D) obvious 明顯的

解析 表示「符合各生產線『適當的』程序」最符合文意，因此答案為 (B) appropriate。

**133**

(A) 多莉墨水是工業用墨水的一大暢銷品牌。
(B) 員工應受過特殊訓練以學習正確使用印表機。
(C) 多莉墨水提供其產品使用說明的手冊。
(D) 我們少用墨水並雙面列印可以減少成本。

解析 空格後方出現 These，提到會分給所有的人員，而 These 指的是 brochures，因此答案為 (C)。

**134**

(A) representative 代表；代理人
(B) represented 被呈現
(C) representation 作為……的代理人
(D) represent 代表

解析 請把 sales representative（銷售代表）當成一個複合名詞背下來，因此答案為 (A)。另外，representation 的意思為「表示、表述」。

**135-138 信件**

米奇・奧登　經理
清水釣魚用品
亨茲路 89
代頓，俄亥俄州 45377

敬愛的奧登：

　　我的主管朱迪・佩特里介紹我洛杉磯辦公室產品設計師的工作機會。她認為我是這份工作的合適人選。因此，我希望您能考慮讓我請調到洛杉磯辦公室。

　　此一調動將使我有機會再度和洛杉磯的室內設計經理潔西卡・安茲女士聯繫上。她還在代頓時，曾和我合作一項全國性的飛蠅釣企畫。

　　佩特里女士表示她全力支持此調動，並提供她的書面同意給您。我隨信附上履歷，並提前感謝您的斟酌。

傑森・泰特
產品設計專員
附件

字彙 director 經理　fishing supply 釣魚用品
supervisor 主管　transfer 調職
associate with 和……聯繫在一起
collaborate 合作　full support 全力支持
in advance 提前
enclosure （信函）附件
application 申請

**135**

(A) 此外，她已在設計公司完成實習。
(B) 因此，我希望您能考慮讓我申請調動到洛杉磯辦公室。
(C) 然而，我的海外工作經驗使我完全符合這項職務所需。
(D) 不然，我將搬到其他國家。

解析 空格前方提到他的主管告訴他適合洛杉磯分公司的工作，(B) 提出調職申請，故為正確答案。

**136**

(A) did allow 已使……能夠
(B) would allow 將使……能夠
(C) has allowed 剛使……能夠
(D) was allowing 正在使……能夠

**解析** 空格是針對想像中的事情所下的結論，適合使用 would（將⋯⋯），因此答案為 (B)。

**137**

(A) replied 答覆
(B) questioned 疑問
(C) expressed 表示
(D) wanted 想

**解析** 根據題意，使用 (C)「表達」感情或想法最符合文意，故為正確答案。

**138**

(A) ideas 想法
(B) progress 進步
(C) consideration 考慮；斟酌
(D) patience 耐心

**解析** 本文為想要申請調職的信件，因此最後以感謝對方考慮此事作結最為適當。因此答案為 (C) consideration（考慮）。

**139-142 備忘錄**

寄件者：科迪・艾倫
收件者：KPN 全體員工

眾所周知，過去六個月來 KPN 經歷了重大革新。我們人資部門這段期間一邊調整，同時戮力提供優質服務。員工是我們最寶貴的資產，我們想聽聽您對於這些變動的感想。

隨信附上問卷，僅有一頁之多。這次機密問卷由「超級調查」執行，這間公司將近十年來為 KPN 提供行銷研究和分析。您坦率且及時的意見回饋將有助於確立部門目標。答覆均會保持匿名。請在 6 月 10 日星期一前將填好的表格呈交人資部門。

提前感謝您撥冗留下意見。我們向來感謝您為 KPN 的付出。

**字彙** aware 知道的 undergo 經歷
renovation 整修；革新
adjustment 調整
outstanding 優秀的；卓越的
confidential 機密的
straightforward 坦率的 timely 及時的
determine 確定；決定 dedication 付出
considerable 相當大的

**139**

(A) after 在⋯⋯之後
(B) without 沒有
(C) unlike 不像
(D) while 與⋯⋯同時

**解析** 人力資源部提供優質的服務，「同時」進行一些調整，最符合文意，因此答案為 (D) while（和⋯⋯同時）。

**140**

(A) Enclosure （信或包裹中的）附件
(B) To enclose 為了附帶
(C) Enclosed 被附帶的
(D) Enclosing 正在附上

**解析** 由 be 動詞和空格的位置，可以得知該句話的結構為倒裝。原本的句子為「A single-page survey is enclosed」，為強調附上的東西才改成倒裝句，因此答案為 (C) Enclosed。

**141**

(A) anonymous 匿名的
(B) unattended 無人看管的
(C) sustainable 永續的
(D) dependent 依賴的

**解析** 前方提到問卷調查屬機密，因此所有的回覆採「匿名」方式最符合文意，答案要選 (A) anonymous（匿名的）。

**142**

(A) 我們付出莫大努力提升員工滿意度。
(B) 在 KPN 服務所有員工是一大榮幸。
(C) 提前感謝您撥冗留下意見。
(D) 請把您的建議上傳至官網。

**解析** 空格後方對各位的貢獻表達感謝，(C) 也是在表達感謝之意，故為正確答案。

## 143-146 電子郵件

收件者：餐飲部承辦人
寄件者：諾維克‧伊凡諾維奇
日期：4 月 22 日
標題：新咖啡機

敬愛的同仁們：

　　休息室的舊咖啡機經常故障，今天已安裝了新的咖啡機頂替。我們希望這台機器更牢靠。

　　這台大容量咖啡機的聲譽還不錯。我們收到的保固聲明也表示它可以用上至少十年。為了確保能夠保養好這台咖啡機，請務必使用原廠配件，如紙杯和牛奶粉包等，而非其他廠商所提供的材料。

　　您剛開始使用這台設備可能會遇到問題，我們很快就會把使用說明放在咖啡機旁邊的布告欄上，如有狀況即可參閱。

諾維克

**字彙** catering 餐飲　colleague 同仁
common room 休息室
replacement 代替品
constantly 經常地　break down 故障
large-capacity 大容量的
reputable 聲譽好的　maintenance 保養
accessory 配件；周邊
sachet（洗髮精、糖、奶粉等）小包裝
initially 一開始　if so 如是
instructions 使用說明
notice board 布告欄
decent 像樣的；還不錯的
warranty 保固聲明

**143**
(A) reliable 可靠的
(B) achievable 可得的
(C) portable 可攜的
(D) detectable 可發覺的

**解析** 前方提到公司休息室內的舊咖啡機換新，因此空格填入表達「期待新機為更可靠的產品」最符合文意。(A) 的意思為「值得信賴的」最適合填入。

**144**
(A) 我們需要買最新產線的機具。
(B) 下述將說明如何做出一杯好咖啡。
(C) 全體員工都需要參加烹飪課。
(D) 我們收到的保固聲明也表示它可以用上至少十年。

**解析** 空格前方針對新買的咖啡機進行說明，接著可以表示使用十年都不會有問題，因此填入 (D) 最為適當。

**145**
(A) of these 在它們之中
(B) as well 也
(C) such as 像是
(D) sort of 有幾分

**解析** 空格後方提出購買機器時附贈的東西，因此空格填入 (C) 最為適當，表達舉例的概念。

**146**
(A) revise 訂正
(B) discard 丟棄
(C) approve 通過
(D) consult 查閱

**解析** 提出發生問題時，可以尋找或參考的資訊，因此答案要選 (D)。

# PART 7

P. 163

## 147-148 日程表

**8 號室預約，11 月 5 － 9 日**

| | 星期一<br>11月5日 | 星期二<br>11月6日 | 星期三<br>11月7日 | 星期四<br>11月8日 | 星期五<br>11月9日 |
|---|---|---|---|---|---|
| 上午<br>10:00 | 兒童<br>故事 | | 兒童<br>故事 | | 青少年<br>寫作社 |
| 上午<br>11:00 | | 作家戴洛‧杜拉吉的講座 | | 科幻<br>閱讀 | |
| 正午 | | | 夏日<br>讀書會<br>派對 | | 文學<br>之友<br>聚會 |
| 下午<br>1:00 | 兒童<br>故事 | | | 詩社<br>聚會 | |
| 下午<br>2:00 | | | 董事會 | | |
| 下午<br>3:00 | | 求職與<br>面試技<br>巧課程 | | | |

字彙 youth 青少年　society 社團
lecture 講座　author 作者；作家
science fiction 科幻故事
board meeting 董事會
job application 求職
interviewing skill 面試技巧

**147** 8 號室最有可能在哪裡？
(A) 百貨公司
(B) 公立圖書館
(C) 藝廊
(D) 就業服務站

**148** 哪項活動和青少年寫作社安排在同一天？
(A) 兒童故事
(B) 文學之友聚會
(C) 科幻閱讀
(D) 詩社聚會

## 149-151 訊息串

**海澤爾‧斯賓塞 [ 下午 3:51]**：麥克，可以請你為實習生開設新的電子郵件帳號嗎？她下週一上工，我出差前應該告訴你這件事，但我完全忘了。

**麥克‧杭特 [ 下午 3:52]**：當然，妳能告訴我她的名字和實習起迄時間嗎？

**海澤爾‧斯賓塞 [ 下午 3:53]**：她叫作崔西‧海耶斯，將和我們工作大約四個月。她會協助執行研究計畫。

**麥克‧杭特 [ 下午 3:54]**：沒問題！她的電子郵件地址將會是 interm.hayes@kingston.com，我還要等弗里曼先生的正式批准，他今天休假，所以等到明天我再設置新的電子郵件帳號，這樣可以嗎？

**海澤爾‧斯賓塞 [ 下午 3:55]**：只要這星期準備好就好了，謝謝你，麥克。

字彙 duration 期間　carry out 執行；實施
formal 正式的　approval 批准

**149** 關於崔西‧海耶斯，文中提到什麼？
(A) 她正在出差。
(B) 她現在需要發電子郵件。
(C) 她快要開始實習。
(D) 她實習過後會轉全職。

**150** 下午 3:54 時，杭特先生寫道：「沒問題」，是什麼意思？
(A) 他會設立新的電子郵件帳號。
(B) 他會把信件轉寄給某人。
(C) 他將主持研究計畫。
(D) 他會給實習生新進訓練。

**151** 杭特先生需要等什麼？
(A) 網路工程師
(B) 某人的批准
(C) 正式文件
(D) 職務面試

## 152-154 電子郵件

收件者：卡蒂爾達‧丹許
寄件者：布魯斯‧卡普蘭
日期：1月9日，星期一
主旨：新聞

敬愛的卡蒂爾達：

　　再次感謝您上個月安排我到孟菲斯辦公室參訪，很有收穫也非常愉快，我期待很快能再次參訪。您上次提到，您有意為了就近陪伴母親搬到法國。我想跟您說，我們巴黎辦公室的會計部門目前有空缺。我們正在找稅務專家，而我認為您十分勝任該職位。職責和您在孟菲斯擔任管理會計師非常像。這個職缺將在下個月底前公告，但這星期將開始內部徵選。如果您有意應徵，請告訴我，我會馬上把該職位的詳細資訊和應徵方式寄給您。

祝好，
布魯斯‧卡普蘭

**字彙** fruitful 收穫豐富的　accounting 會計
highly 高度　qualified 勝任的
opening 職缺　publicly 公開地
solicit 徵求　collaborate 合作

**152** 寄此封電子郵件的目的為？
(A) 要討論旅遊安排
(B) 要鼓勵丹許女士應徵某職位
(C) 要通知丹許女士之後開會的資訊
(D) 要解釋公司近期的重整

**153** 根據電子郵件，丹許女士為何有意搬到巴黎？
(A) 想和卡普蘭先生遊覽當地
(B) 想要做責任更大的工作
(C) 想要和家人生活得更近
(D) 想和卡普蘭先生合作一項計畫

**154** 卡普蘭先生向丹許女士提議說他能做什麼？
(A) 安排她和計畫經理見面
(B) 幫她找留宿的地方
(C) 寄給她額外資訊
(D) 回答她的問題

## 155-157 廣告

### 瓊斯巴戈斯股份有限公司

職務均為晚班（下午5點至晚上10點），除非另有說明。

**倉儲經理**
需高中學歷、熟悉庫存管理流程，並有忙碌工作環境下的經驗。也須備有技術和金融的基礎知識。有管理經驗為佳，但不是必需。

**工廠技術員**
具相關檢定資格，且有至少兩年的工廠工作經驗。也須會操作重型設備。須值夜班。

**個人助理**
需高中學歷、須精通打字並有零售業的工作經驗。有時須值夜班。

**經銷經理和倉儲助理**
須勤奮可靠。倉儲助理有時須值夜班。

請把履歷寄到　人資部
瓊斯和巴戈斯物流股份有限公司
劍橋路1415號，波士頓，馬薩諸塞州02109

請勿以電話或電子郵件聯繫。

**字彙** shift 輪班
unless otherwise indicated 除非另有說明
warehouse 倉庫　diploma 學歷
awareness 對……有了解
desirable 理想的　relevant 相關的
qualification 檢定資格；證照
heavy equipment 重型設備
retail 零售業　establishment 店面；機構
distribution 經銷　diligent 勤勞的
willingness 樂意　in person 當面

**155** 應徵倉儲經理職位的需求為何？
(A) 行銷相關學位
(B) 一些金融知識
(C) 管理經驗
(D) 願意值夜班

**156** 哪項職務不需值夜班？
(A) 經銷經理
(B) 個人助理
(C) 工廠技術員
(D) 倉儲助理

**157** 求職者要怎麼應徵職位？
(A) 用網路
(B) 面對面
(C) 寄信
(D) 打電話

## 158-161 廣告

### 詹姆斯行銷學院

您正在找行銷學位學程嗎？如是，別再找了，您的首選就是詹姆斯行銷學院的卓越行銷課程。

課程為期 12 個月，在 2 月、6 月和 10 月均可入學，涵括跨文化行銷、國際廣告的各類課程。課程由傑出人士教授，多為聲譽良好的廣告或貿易公司高層，將在課程中導入實務知識。我們不只有國際領先企業的實習機會，也正是因為實務專業才會持續受到全國行銷協會肯定，並評選為國內三大頂尖學程。

國人的入學申請費用為 100 美元、外籍生為 120 美元。提及這則招生廣告並於 10 月 30 日前提出申請，則無需支付申請費。一般報名截止日期為 11 月 30 日。我們鼓勵申請人爭取獎學金和補助。如有任何疑問或需要更多資訊，請上官網 www.jamesmarketing.edu 查詢。

**字彙** institute 學院　entry 入學
cross-cultural 跨文化的
distinguished 傑出的　personnel 員工
reputable 聲譽好的　trading 貿易
real-work 實務
consistently 一貫地；始終如一地
rate 評等為　resident 居民
provided 以……為條件
scholarship 獎學金　sponsorship 補助
enrollment 註冊
faculty（高教機構）系，院

**158** 關於行銷課程，文中提到什麼？
(A) 要花兩年修完。
(B) 聲譽非常好。
(C) 有兩個註冊時間。
(D) 近來增聘系所教職員。

**159** 根據廣告，學生不能得到什麼？
(A) 認識有專業知識的教授
(B) 得到海外經驗的機會
(C) 線上修課的機會
(D) 得到財務支援的機會

**160** 在文中標記處，下列句子最適合放在哪裡？
「如是，不用再找了，首選就是詹姆斯行銷學院的卓越行銷課程。」
(A) [1]
(B) [2]
(C) [3]
(D) [4]

## 161-163 信件

茉蒂·瓊斯
黑塞街 20 號
杰斐遜，緬因州 04348

9 月 20 日
保羅·杜維希尼，經理
全時尚雜誌
丹尼斯路
杰斐遜，緬因州 04348

敬愛的杜維希尼先生：

我寫這封信是想告訴您，我想請辭《全時尚雜誌》的攝影師一職，盼能自 10 月 30 日起生效。我照合約提前一個月通知您。

我一直以來都在考慮要自己創業，轉做全職攝影師。一個月前，我以個人攝影師身分拿到攝影大師協會的獎項，也因此得到了能用來創業的資金。

我在雜誌社工作時學到了很多相關領域的知識。攝影部門的同仁不只幫助我成為一名藝術工作者，也讓我成為商務專業人士。我雖然即將開始專業攝影師的新工作，仍會真心想念在這裡以及與您共事的時光。我個人希望，在我展開人生的新冒險後，也能與您保持聯繫。祝您和公司鴻圖大展。

誠摯地，
茉蒂·瓊斯

**字彙** resign 辭職　take effect 生效
notify 通知　outline 載明
venture 商業活動；事業　field 領域
colleague 同仁　funding
advise 建議　outstanding 優秀的；出眾的
supervisor 主管　loan 借貸

**161** 瓊斯女士為何寫信給杜維希尼先生？
(A) 要求轉調
(B) 要求升遷
(C) 申請補助計畫
(D) 通知他一項決定

**162** 瓊斯女士最近得到了什麼？
- (A) 給知名視覺藝術家訓練的機會
- (B) 優秀表現的認可
- (C) 一名獨立攝影師為她特別支援所寫的感謝信
- (D) 攝影部門主管的三年期合約

**163** 攝影大師協會在什麼事情上幫了瓊斯女士？
- (A) 決定不做全職、改做兼職
- (B) 離開她攝影組長的職位
- (C) 轉而專注於個人目標
- (D) 申請小企業貸款

## 164-166 線上聊天室

**羅莎·帕特森 [上午 10:03]**：汪達，我現在正在面試會計經理的人選，預計這個月底前要找到合適對象。可以請妳為新進同仁準備電腦嗎？

**汪達·羅斯 [上午 10:04]**：我想我們業務部門有一台桌機可用。上個星期有一名約聘人員的專案結束了。我邀請浩爾進來。

<< 浩爾·佛斯特進入聊天室。>>

**汪達羅斯 [上午 10:05]**：浩爾，潔西·沃爾特的電腦還在嗎？

**浩爾·佛斯特 [上午 10:06]**：不在了，已配給我們的一名研究實習生。

**汪達·羅斯 [上午 10:08]**：辦公室內還有其他電腦可用嗎？

**浩爾·佛斯特 [上午 10:08]**：我們已經沒有桌機，但是有從威爾森分公司拿回來的兩台筆電。

**羅莎·帕特森 [上午 10:09]**：方便用來發電子郵件、做試算表和處理簡報檔嗎？

**浩爾·佛斯特 [上午 10:11]**：可以，用來做一般文書作業不是問題。近乎全新。

**羅莎·帕特森 [上午 10:13]**：太好了。浩爾，能請你為新進同仁準備一台嗎？我希望新同仁第一天上工就能多做點事。

**浩爾·佛斯特 [上午 10:14 am]**：不用擔心，我會處理好的。

**字彙** on board 到職　assign 指派
contractor 約聘人員　retrieve 取回

**164** 羅斯女士為何邀請佛斯特先生？
- (A) 要解釋她想要訂什麼
- (B) 要詢問有關新進同仁的問題
- (C) 要要求他拿回幾台電腦
- (D) 要詢問辦公室設備可否使用

**165** 關於帕特森女士，文中提到什麼？
- (A) 她計劃聘僱幾位實習生。
- (B) 她想為員工升級幾台電腦。
- (C) 她希望新進同仁的工作不受到耽擱。
- (D) 她曾在威爾森分公司工作。

**166** 上午 10:14 時，佛斯特先生寫道：「我會處理好的。」，是什麼意思？
- (A) 他會審閱財務報告。
- (B) 他會訂好會議室。
- (C) 他會在網路上訂購電腦。
- (D) 他會裝好電腦。

## 167-168 聲明

敬愛的居民好，

　　拉馬勒將從下週開始改名為艾薇妮亞路小酒館。餐廳也將進行多處改裝，包括擴大戶外露台區，並為了增加空間而重新裝潢主餐廳。敬請安心，這家餐廳在新經理保羅·甘特的帶領下，將一如往常提供美味的法國料理，也將如您所期待的平價。請您享受我們的後續服務。

**字彙** bistro 小酒館　undergo 經歷
modification 改裝　enlargement 擴建
patio 露台　refurbish 整修　assure 確保
seating capacity 座位數

**167** 根據廣告，餐廳內正在改變的是什麼？
- (A) 餐點種類
- (B) 餐點價格
- (C) 地點
- (D) 名稱

**168** 關於甘特先生，文中提到什麼？
- (A) 他在鄰近地區有其他事業。
- (B) 他打算增加餐廳的座位。
- (C) 他住在艾薇妮亞路好幾年了。
- (D) 他曾在拉馬勒工作。

## 169-171 告示

### 企業圖書證

州立大學圖書體系將特別開放商務人士借書，任何員工只要其公司在這座城市設有辦公室，即符合申辦企業卡的資格。

一般公司員工辦卡年費為 40 美元，政府和非營利組織則免收年費。

企業圖書證專為負責公司研究的員工設計。個人應對所借閱的一切資料負責，持卡人應承擔逾期或遺失所衍生的圖書罰款。

員工須當面向大學圖書館提出申請以取得企業圖書證，申請人必須出示有照片的識別證件及雇主信函茲證明其聘僱關係。申請時一併付費，可依核銷需求提供收據。

如果您對於企業證有任何疑問，請撥打 855-555-3001 聯繫借還書櫃檯。

**字彙** state university 州立大學
extend 擴展到　privilege 特權；特別待遇
issue 發行（證件）　non-profit 非營利
entity 實體；企業
be exempt from 豁免於……
fine 罰款　impose 強加於
overdue 逾期　liability（法律上對某事物的）責任，義務　employer 雇主
proof 證明　employment 聘僱關係
reimbursement 核銷　query 疑問
circulation desk 借還書櫃檯
put forward 提出　applicable 適用的
relinquish 放棄

**169** 這則公告的目的是？
(A) 訂正錯誤
(B) 說明服務
(C) 提出想法
(D) 公告活動

**170** 關於年費，文中提到什麼？
(A) 可用信用卡支付。
(B) 不太可能增加。
(C) 不適用於某些組織。
(D) 對非本地企業來說比較貴。

**171** 申請時不需要什麼？
(A) 已簽署的合約
(B) 證明身分
(C) 付款
(D) 聘僱關係的詳細資料

## 172-175 報導

6 月 5 日——植物學家里瓦・杜謝克昨天宣布，她將在兩年期間捐贈坦尼自然遺產計畫一百萬美元。該計畫過去三年資金拮据，這筆捐款來得正是關鍵時刻。

「能收到杜謝克女士的慷慨致贈，我們很激動。」坦尼自然遺產董事長詹姆斯・麥克納蒂表示：「這將對我們維護當地大自然有莫大幫助。」

自然保護協會（NRS）10 年前推動自然遺產計畫，旨在復育和保育鎮上早年留下的天然勝地。起先由稅收資助，但鎮議會三年前決定將自然保護協會的大筆資金轉挹注到新興土地開發計畫，之後，用於維護自然資源的資金便受限。

NRS 自五個月前向當地較大的企業及商家發起私人募款。麥克納蒂回憶說：「我們寫了封募款信，並附上幾張極需維護的自然景觀照片。」其一是蘭花遺址，也是前當地居民里瓦・杜謝克經常造訪的地方。麥克納蒂表示：「直到她打電話給我、詢問能如何夠協助，我才知道她和當地有這層關係。」

坦尼地區的民眾和首長團隊對捐款消息感到非常高興。市長吉姆・康納和幾名地方民代考慮在幾處自然景點設置紀念區額，以便小鎮吸引新住戶、觀光客和商家。

杜謝克表示：「我小時候受到坦尼的自然風光啟迪，它是讓我投入植物界研究的一大助力。捐贈不僅僅是為了保育小鎮的資源，也是在投資小鎮的未來。」

李察・多柏斯
地方撰稿人

**字彙** botanist 植物學家　heritage 遺產
crucial 關鍵的　strain 使緊張；使受壓
thrilled 非常高興的
go a long way toward 對……有很大的幫助
conserve 保育　cornerstone 基礎
decade 十年　restore 復育
preserve 保育　tax revenue 稅收
solicit 請求；索求　honorary 名譽的
plaque 區　landmark 地標
appealing 吸引人的
instrumental 有重大幫助的
contributor 撰稿人

**172** 根據文章報導，該計畫為何失去資金？
(A) 因為建築成本增加
(B) 因為地方政府減少資助
(C) 因為整修完成了
(D) 因為坦尼鎮的人口減少了

**173** 誰目前不是坦尼鎮的鎮民？
(A) 詹姆斯‧麥克納蒂
(B) 里瓦‧杜謝克
(C) 吉姆‧康納
(D) 李察‧多柏斯

**174** 關於坦尼的自然保護區，杜謝克女士說了什麼？
(A) 使她決定成為植物學家。
(B) 維護所費不貲。
(C) 每個人都應該有標誌建造年份的區額。
(D) 地方組織應該付錢保育它。

**175** 在文中標記處，下列句子最適合放在哪裡？
「之後，用於維護自然資源的資金便受限。」
(A) [1]
(B) [2]
(C) [3]
(D) [4]

### 176-180 兩封電子郵件

寄件者：珍妮‧李
收件者：芬頓‧路易斯
主旨：報價
日期：10 月 8 日

敬愛的路易斯先生：

我在伊薩卡鎮的鄰居李‧安妮‧福恩德斯向我推薦您。我想把我花園中四棵造成安全疑慮的雜交金柏砍掉，所以想請您報價。

它們高約 13 公尺，其中兩棵直徑約 45 公分，另外兩棵直徑約 75 公分。距離我家大約 4 公尺、籬笆 2 公尺。

不知道貴團隊在 10 月 15 日星期五上午 11 點有空嗎？對於我們這樣的旅遊業者，10 月、11 月和 12 月是大月最忙，我唯一方便的時間只有下週五。

我期待能很快收到您的答覆。

誠摯地，
珍妮李

---

寄件者：芬頓‧路易斯
收件者：珍妮‧李
主旨：答覆您的報價需求
日期：10 月 9 日

敬愛的李女士：

感謝您想到路易斯伐木服務。我們有最先進的伐木設備，您可以儘管放心，完工後您的經營場所將不會受到任何損害。如果您想參考我們顧客對服務品質的評價，請上網站 www.fentontreeservice/customerreports.com。

我們當然能配合您所要求的日期和時間動工。目前上午 11:00 的時段有空。我們從您提供的資訊可以給您伐木成本的初步報價。針對直徑 20 到 55 公分的樹木，我們的價格為 400 美元，而直徑超過 55 公分的價格為 600 美元。另外也請您注意，超過我們公司位於沙丘的辦公室 40 公里外的作業，仍須負擔 70 美元的車資。因此，總計約為 2,070 美元。為了計算確切的支出，我們的一位合夥對象能開車過去，很快到達您的地點測量您想砍伐的樹木。

請您盡快確認這項安排是否適合。

芬頓‧路易斯

**字彙** estimate 估價　refer to 推薦；介紹
cypress 柏樹　diameter 直徑
hedge 籬笆　afford 有時間做……
rest assured 放心　premises 營業場所
sustain 經歷，遭受（尤指破壞或損失）
slot （某活動安排的）時段
presently 目前　initial 最初的
quote 報價　measure 測量
applicable 適用的　consequently 因此
calculate 計算　associate 合夥對象
property 房產；地產

**176** 李女士給路易斯先生的信件中沒有提供哪項資訊？
(A) 她花園中部分植物的高度
(B) 她工作的類型
(C) 她住的街道
(D) 她可以休息不工作的日期

**177** 關於李女士，文中提到什麼？
(A) 她曾讓路易斯伐木服務在她的花園裡動工。
(B) 她計劃三月要去度假。
(C) 她住在距離路易斯服務辦公室超過40公里的地方。
(D) 她將得到路易斯伐木服務的折扣。

**178** 第二封信第一段、第二行的「secure」，意思最接近下列何者？
(A) 評估
(B) 蒙受
(C) 支持
(D) 造成

**179** 路易斯先生建議李女士做什麼？
(A) 為花園買新設備
(B) 上午11點時打電話給他
(C) 到他的辦公室來給他精確的樹木尺寸
(D) 上網看顧客對他服務的評論

**180** 路易斯先生同意在何時動工？
(A) 11月10日
(B) 10月15日
(C) 10月3日
(D) 10月2日

## 181-185 廣告與電子郵件

**海沃斯建設**
**位於蘭秀市中心**
**多用途建築2月1日開幕**
**住宅、辦公、商業空間出租**

具現代感、最新潮的建設，緊鄰多家商店和咖啡廳。近公車站。

對街是海沃斯湖及健行區。附近有湧泉湖和健行步道。

公寓（四到八樓）：一臥室、兩臥室或三臥室公寓，均設有廚房、全套衛浴，客廳／餐廳和寬敞的壁櫥。地下室的儲藏間可供使用，只需支付小額的月租費。地下停車場供房客和訪客免費停車。6樓和8樓有共用洗衣設備。附屋頂花園。

辦公室（二到三樓）：彈性的辦公空間只要空間足夠就能視需求分割。單一辦公室或整個公司的辦公空間均適用。多種平面配置可供選擇。

零售商店（地面層）：兩間店面出租，均為500平方公尺。限零售店面。

---

應要求能夠提供價格和出租資訊：
住宅諮詢請洽李歐諾拉・迪恩（080）555-6705或 ldean@hayworth.com。
商家諮詢請洽吉娜・費茲傑羅（080）555-6707或 gfitz@hayworth.com。

---

寄件者：麥克・佩克
收件者：吉娜・費茲傑羅
標題：海沃斯建設
日期：11月21日 14:23

敬愛的費茲傑羅女士，

如果海沃斯建設裡能夠打造一處辦公空間，容納律師和助理總計50名員工的話，我想盡快到場看看。

我們目前的營業地點和海沃斯建設只隔了幾條街，但規模太小了，無法容納更多人員。我們公司業務近來快速成長，為了因應持續增加的案件數，不久的將來就會招聘新員工。

誠摯地，
佩克

字彙 mixed-use 多用途；混合用途
residential 住宅用的
commercial 商業用的
state-of-the-art 最現代的；最時髦的
flank 位於……的側面
spring-fed 湧泉挹注的
hiking trail 健行步道
full bathroom 全套衛浴
spacious 寬敞的　closet 壁櫥；儲藏室
storage 倉庫；儲藏間　basement 地下室
flexible 彈性的　tenant 住戶；房客
shared 共用的
laundry facilities 洗衣設備
layout 平面配置　storefront 店面
square meter 平方公尺　lease 租賃
direct 將……寄給　caseload 案件數

**181** 關於海沃斯建設，文中提到什麼？
(A) 位於巴士路線上。
(B) 由當地專家所設計。
(C) 延後開放。
(D) 位於城市外圍。

**182** 根據廣告，住戶可額外付費使用什麼？
(A) 地下停車
(B) 地下儲藏間
(C) 使用共用的花園
(D) 共用的洗衣設備

**183** 該建築不允許哪一類用戶？
(A) 批發商
(B) 服飾店
(C) 廣告公司
(D) 一家 3 口

**184** 關於佩克先生的公司，文中提到什麼？
(A) 最近增加收費。
(B) 要搬到蘭秀。
(C) 近來愈來愈成功。
(D) 購買新的營業場所並整修。

**185** 佩克先生最可能對海沃斯建設的哪個部分感興趣？
(A) 四到八樓
(B) 二到三樓
(C) 地面層
(D) 地下室

## 186-190 電子郵件、公告與信件

收件者：麥克・王，業務經理
寄件者：瑪莎・格林，公關經理
日期：5 月 5 日
關於：KTLV 每週趨勢

---

敬愛的麥克：

感謝你告訴我電視台和你聯繫一事。我讀完你交給我的節目大綱，看起來他們是想借重你的專業知識。我和副總羅蘭・帕克討論過這件事，她已准許你上節目了。行政總部的傑瑞米・迪亞茲將協助你上電視的準備。請給他你上節目所需的產品清單。

上節目前，請你牢記以下應對媒體的規則：

- 不要談到公司人事議題
- 不要討論任何新聞稿中未提及的未來業務計畫
- 不要洩露有關公司客戶或顧客的敏感資訊
- 請避免討論任何公司的緊急狀況或危機

我希望你可以正面呈現我們的品牌和產品。祝好運。

祝好，
瑪莎・格林

---

### 我們的員工要上 KTLV 每週趨勢

行銷部的麥克・王將在 5 月 24 日星期六上電視節目《每週趨勢》作來賓。這位資深行銷經理將討論露營市場的最新趨勢。他上節目提供露營建議時會一併談到我們的帳篷、睡袋和炊具。《每週趨勢》是相當受歡迎的節目，在 18 到 49 歲的成年人當中收視率為 12.3。我們希望他在節目曝光能協助推廣我們的品牌和產品。節目將在晚上 8:00 到 9:00，於 15 頻道播出，也將在 www.KTLV.com 線上播映。如果您錯過了或想要看重播，請上 KTLV 官網。

5 月 28 日
麥克・王
奧爾良運動股份有限公司
威斯康辛街 1610
米爾瓦基，威斯康辛州 53233

敬愛的王先生：

很高興能邀請您作節目來賓。5 月 24 日播出相當成功，收視率也超乎預期。我們收到了很多觀眾的正面評價，說您對戶外露營的建議很實用、也很有教育意義。感謝您的努力和付出。

雖然您提出了要求，但我們並沒有剪掉您對未來幾個月將推出新產品的說法。儘管您有所顧慮，但貴公司的一份新聞稿中曾正式提到新的露營設備。我們也和貴公司的瑪莎・格林再次確認過了。

我也想問問您，7 月是否方便再上一次我們的節目。我們計劃在 7 月 19 日製作一集有關戶外活動的夏季特別節目。播出從晚上 8 點開始，持續兩個小時。我們真心希望到時候可以在節目上再次見到您。期待能盡快收到您的答覆。

誠摯地，
布萊恩・杜夫
KTLV 資深製作人

**字彙** expertise 專業知識
keep in mind 牢記在心
disclose 揭露 sensitive 敏感的
portray 表述；表現　cookware 炊具
rating 收視率
informative 有益的；教育性的
edit out （影片）剪掉

**186** 根據信件，誰會幫助王先生上節目？
(A) 瑪莎‧格林
(B) 羅蘭‧帕克
(C) 傑瑞米‧迪亞茲
(D) 布萊恩‧杜夫

**187** 信件中第二段、第三行的「expertise」，意思最接近下列何者？
(A) 知識
(B) 印象
(C) 長相
(D) 意見

**188** 該則公告的目的為何？
(A) 要推銷新的露營用品
(B) 要提供露營建議給民眾
(C) 要告知電視節目的收視率
(D) 要鼓勵人們去看某一個電視節目

**189** 王先生為什麼會要求修改他上節目時的說法？
(A) 他揭露了他客戶的敏感資訊。
(B) 他談到有關一名同仁的人事議題。
(C) 他提到公司未來的業務計畫。
(D) 他指出公司有財務困難。

**190** 特別節目和常態性節目將有何不同？
(A) 將從晚上 9 點開播。
(B) 將播出超過一小時。
(C) 將在星期日播出。
(D) 將在 16 頻道播出。

### 191-195 廣告與兩封電子郵件

#### 渥太華線上商務會議

十月時將舉辦年會，對我們渥太華線上商務會議的員工來說是最重要的月分。但對賓客來說，最重要的卻是六月。六月是早鳥登記參加第 27 屆渥太華線上商務會議（OOBC）的月分，亦即 7 月 1 日起價格會變貴。現在就是省下登記費的大好時機，尤其針對會有一群員工與會的公司。在這個月登記，每個人將省下 100 美元。我們不只有早鳥折扣，還會給您 50 美元的禮品卡，可在皇家、一流及新世代三家飯店使用。還有個超棒消息要給六月登記的所有人，其中一名幸運兒將贏得會議期間三晚的免費住宿。您必須在 6 月 30 日前註冊才有得獎機會。

我們迫不及待在渥太華線上商務會議見到您。這是學習長期發展網路事業實務的最佳機會。今天就註冊，馬上享受最優惠的價格。

---

收件者：Reservations@royalhotel.com
寄件者：richard.morris@estrada.com
日期：6 月 28 日
關於：預約

您好，我叫李察‧莫里斯，在星達企業工作。敝公司計劃在 10 月派一些員工參加第 27 屆渥太華線上商務會議。我們和 OOBC 的人談過，基於地點和貴飯店員工所提供的服務，他們向我們推薦了貴飯店。我想知道您們是否還有空房。我試過在您的網站上訂房，但沒找到團體預訂的選項。

11 名員工將從 10 月 12 日住到 14 日，需要三間單人房和四間雙人房。可能的話，他們偏好住在同一層樓。我也想確認他們能否使用 OOBC 的禮品卡。

如果還有空房，請和我聯繫並告知該如何訂房。

誠摯地，
李察‧莫里斯
總務部
星達企業

---

收件者：olga.carter@estrada.com
寄件者：james.stanley@royalhotel.com
日期：10 月 22 日
關於：預訂

敬愛的卡特女士，

感謝您聯繫渥太華的皇家飯店。這封信是回覆您在 10 月 20 日的電子郵件。就您要求，我們立即查看了您的帳戶並發現我們超收了費用。我們一名同仁沒有用到您所提供的 OOBC 禮品卡。由於我們最近找了新的支付服務公司合作，部分員工還沒習慣新系統。我們對於出錯深表歉意。您以 100 美元的價格在單人房住了三晚，使用禮品卡後，我們應該向您收取 250 美元。

我向您保證我們正盡力彌補錯誤。超收的金額將在兩個工作天內退還到您的信用卡帳戶。作為補償，我們也想提供給您一張免費住宿券，可在全球任何一家皇家飯店免費留宿一晚。

給您造成不便，我們再次抱歉。希望能再次為您服務。

詹姆斯・史丹利
總經理
皇家飯店，渥太華

**191** 關於渥太華線上商務會議，文中指出什麼？
(A) 員工六月最忙。
(B) 將在六月持續五天。
(C) 六月的登記費用最低。
(D) 全體與會者都有中獎機會。

**192** 廣告中第二段、第二行的「sustainable」，意思最接近下列何者？
(A) 可能發生的
(B) 存在現實的
(C) 可輕易移動的
(D) 能夠被持續下去的

**193** 關於星達公司的員工，文中沒有提到什麼？
(A) 11 名員工將出席會議。
(B) 他們需要飯店的七間房間。
(C) 他們想要住在同一層樓。
(D) 他們想要景觀好的房間。

**194** 關於問題的原因，史丹利先生說了什麼？
(A) 支付系統暫時故障。
(B) 一名員工不熟悉新系統。
(C) 禮品券在十月過期了。
(D) 在最後一刻修改了賓客姓名。

**195** 飯店收了卡特女士多少錢？
(A) 300 美金
(B) 350 美金
(C) 400 美金
(D) 500 美金

## 196-200　告示、報導與網頁

### 公聽會告示

　　此告示要通知您公聽會的資訊。里奇蒙市規畫局將在公聽會後決定是否採用預定計畫。歡迎感興趣的各方出席。您可以了解到預定計畫，並有機會對此發表意見。

**公聽會主題**：潘蜜拉大道計畫
道路改善提案，包括整治汙水系統、舖設路面和更新交通號誌

**地點**：里奇蒙市政廳
　　　西八街 523
　　　里奇蒙市，喬治亞州 30003

**公聽會日期**：9 月 9 日，星期四
**時間**：晚上 6:00 到 8:00
**更多相關消息請洽**：里奇蒙市規畫局 555-3217

### 潘蜜拉大道計畫獲准

　　里奇蒙市，喬治亞州──里奇蒙市通過了潘蜜拉大道的整治計畫，將斥資 120 萬美元整治這條當地居民的重要道路。市政官員表示，建設安排在明年初開始。有此建設需求是因這條道路在去年夏天下大雨時嚴重淹水導致關閉。里奇蒙老化的下水道非為大雨設計，汙水系統因此受損。計畫中也包括道路舖設和交通號誌更新。

　　「大雨使道路無法通行，住南區的人無法上到幾條主要道路。」市長詹姆斯・諾里斯表示：「道路升級計畫將改善雨季時通往重要交流道的交通狀況。」

　　市府 9 月 9 日舉行公聽會，200 多名市民參加並表達意見。他們表示，資金應該直接用在替換老舊的汙水系統。

　　市長表示：「我們聽取市民的意見，他們最關心的就是潘蜜拉路的整修。這是件大事，所以我們決定把注大部分的市政預算。」

www.RichmondCity.gov/notice

　　自 2 月 1 日至 10 月 31 日，以下道路維修可能導致交通路線減少或封閉。都市規畫局將竭盡所能盡快完成所需工程。俟完工，我們希望里奇蒙的市民能享受其便利性。

**潘蜜拉大道計畫**
● 時間：二月至六月
● 說明：潘蜜拉大道的汙水系統改善和交通號誌升級

**海曼路計畫**
● 時間：三月至九月
● 說明：海曼路增設自行車道，並升級行人穿越道

**西菲爾德橋計畫**
● 時間：五月至十月
● 說明：橋樑和橋樑圍欄的維修

**安納波利斯街計畫**
- 日期：六月至十月
- 說明：十字路口重建

　　市府官網將發布可能的交通混亂或分流相關資訊。請註冊我們的電子郵件或簡訊通知，以便自動收到所有的更新資訊。按這裡。

**字彙** public hearing 公聽會　adopt 採納
sewage 汙水下水道　critical 主要的
sewer 下水道　aging 老化的
impassable 無法通行的
pedestrian crossing 行人穿越道
railing 欄杆；圍欄　intersection 十字路口
disruption 混亂；擾亂
detour 繞道　alert 通知
disapprove 不贊成

**196** 潘蜜拉大道的計畫中沒有提議什麼？
(A) 鋪設道路
(B) 安裝道路號誌燈
(C) 更換汙水管線
(D) 維修人行道

**197** 關於公聽會，下列何者為真？
(A) 攸關橋樑維修計畫。
(B) 市長因為大雨沒有出席。
(C) 在市政廳舉行並有幾百人到場。
(D) 市民反對這項計畫。

**198** 根據文章報導，其中提及潘蜜拉大道的什麼問題？
(A) 太暗不易行駛。
(B) 夏天時淹水了。
(C) 太窄不易車流通行。
(D) 冬天時太滑。

**199** 文中第二段、第一行的「impassable」，意思最接近下列何者？
(A) 整修
(B) 封閉
(C) 骯髒
(D) 解除

**200** 該網頁的目的為何？
(A) 公告地方活動
(B) 發布即將來臨的風暴警告
(C) 提供交通受阻的資訊
(D) 招攬建設公司

| 1. (B) | 2. (A) | 3. (C) | 4. (A) | 5. (D) | 6. (D) | 7. (A) | 8. (A) | 9. (B) | 10. (C) |
|---|---|---|---|---|---|---|---|---|---|
| 11. (A) | 12. (B) | 13. (C) | 14. (B) | 15. (C) | 16. (B) | 17. (B) | 18. (A) | 19. (B) | 20. (A) |
| 21. (C) | 22. (B) | 23. (B) | 24. (B) | 25. (C) | 26. (A) | 27. (A) | 28. (A) | 29. (B) | 30. (A) |
| 31. (C) | 32. (B) | 33. (D) | 34. (D) | 35. (D) | 36. (A) | 37. (D) | 38. (D) | 39. (A) | 40. (C) |
| 41. (A) | 42. (D) | 43. (A) | 44. (B) | 45. (A) | 46. (B) | 47. (B) | 48. (D) | 49. (B) | 50. (C) |
| 51. (A) | 52. (B) | 53. (C) | 54. (C) | 55. (A) | 56. (D) | 57. (C) | 58. (C) | 59. (A) | 60. (D) |
| 61. (C) | 62. (D) | 63. (B) | 64. (A) | 65. (C) | 66. (C) | 67. (C) | 68. (A) | 69. (C) | 70. (D) |
| 71. (A) | 72. (D) | 73. (A) | 74. (A) | 75. (D) | 76. (B) | 77. (A) | 78. (C) | 79. (C) | 80. (A) |
| 81. (D) | 82. (A) | 83. (C) | 84. (A) | 85. (D) | 86. (A) | 87. (C) | 88. (B) | 89. (D) | 90. (D) |
| 91. (B) | 92. (B) | 93. (C) | 94. (C) | 95. (D) | 96. (D) | 97. (B) | 98. (D) | 99. (C) | 100. (C) |
| 101. (A) | 102. (B) | 103. (B) | 104. (A) | 105. (A) | 106. (D) | 107. (D) | 108. (D) | 109. (D) | 110. (D) |
| 111. (A) | 112. (D) | 113. (C) | 114. (D) | 115. (C) | 116. (A) | 117. (A) | 118. (C) | 119. (C) | 120. (B) |
| 121. (A) | 122. (C) | 123. (B) | 124. (D) | 125. (A) | 126. (A) | 127. (D) | 128. (D) | 129. (A) | 130. (B) |
| 131. (C) | 132. (C) | 133. (A) | 134. (D) | 135. (B) | 136. (C) | 137. (B) | 138. (C) | 139. (C) | 140. (A) |
| 141. (D) | 142. (C) | 143. (C) | 144. (B) | 145. (C) | 146. (D) | 147. (B) | 148. (D) | 149. (D) | 150. (C) |
| 151. (A) | 152. (B) | 153. (A) | 154. (D) | 155. (C) | 156. (D) | 157. (C) | 158. (D) | 159. (C) | 160. (C) |
| 161. (A) | 162. (A) | 163. (C) | 164. (A) | 165. (A) | 166. (D) | 167. (A) | 168. (C) | 169. (B) | 170. (A) |
| 171. (A) | 172. (D) | 173. (C) | 174. (A) | 175. (C) | 176. (B) | 177. (A) | 178. (A) | 179. (C) | 180. (C) |
| 181. (C) | 182. (D) | 183. (C) | 184. (C) | 185. (C) | 186. (A) | 187. (B) | 188. (C) | 189. (D) | 190. (A) |
| 191. (C) | 192. (B) | 193. (D) | 194. (C) | 195. (A) | 196. (C) | 197. (D) | 198. (A) | 199. (D) | 200. (C) |

**PART 1**

P. 188

**1** (A) A display case is being cleaned out.
美M (B) A woman is helping customers.
(C) Some people are looking out the window.
(D) Some people are entering a restaurant.

(A) 有人正在清理展示櫃。
(B) 一名女子正在服務客人。
(C) 有些人正看向窗外。
(D) 有些人正走進餐廳。

字彙 display case 展示櫃　clean out 清理

**2** (A) A wall borders a walking path.
英M (B) A walkway protrudes into the water.
(C) Some buildings overlook the train tracks.
(D) People are strolling through the tunnel.

(A) 步道外緣有堵牆擋著。
(B) 步道延伸到水上。
(C) 有幾棟建築能俯瞰鐵道。
(D) 人群正在慢慢穿過隧道。

字彙 border 形成……的邊；圍著
walking path 步道
walkway 走道；人行道
protrude 伸向；延伸往
overlook 俯瞰；眺望　train track 鐵道
stroll 散步；慢行

**3** (A) She is stretching out on the chair.
美W (B) She has her hand on the back of a bench.
(C) She is throwing away a piece of paper.
(D) She is raising the blinds.

(A) 她正坐著伸懶腰。
(B) 她坐在長椅上把手放在背後。
(C) 她正要丟紙屑。
(D) 她正把窗簾拉起來。

字彙 stretch out 伸展；伸懶腰
throw away 丟掉；扔掉
blind 窗簾；百葉窗

**4** (A) A lounge is divided by partitions.
澳M (B) Vases are arranged on the window ledges.
(C) There are plants near the steps.
(D) An awning has been stretched across the door.

(A) 休息室分成幾個隔間。
(B) 花瓶擺在窗台上。
(C) 樓梯旁有植物。
(D) 門外搭著遮雨篷。

字彙 lounge 休息室；候機室
partition 隔板　window ledge 床台
step 樓梯　awning （門窗等前面的）遮篷
stretch 伸出

**5** (A) A rider is removing a helmet.
美W (B) Some tires are being rolled up a ramp.
(C) A walkway is being resurfaced.
(D) A bicycle is casting a shadow.

(A) 自行車手正要脫下安全帽。
(B) 一些輪胎被推上斜坡。
(C) 正在重鋪人行道。
(D) 一台腳踏車的影子投射在地上。

字彙 rider （自行車；機車）騎士
roll up 滾上　ramp （人造）斜坡；坡道
resurface 重新鋪設
cast a shadow 投下影子

**6** (A) Some workers are trimming grass along a path.
英M (B) They are mowing a lawn in front of the house.
(C) A man is watering some trees.
(D) A man is securing the base of a ladder.

(A) 沿著步道有幾名工人正在除草。
(B) 他們正在屋前整修草坪。
(C) 一名男子正在幫樹木澆水。
(D) 一名男子正抓穩梯子底部。

字彙 trim 修剪；修整　path 步道
mow a lawn 修整草坪　water 澆灌
secure 固定　base 底部；基礎
ladder 梯子

184

## PART 2

P. 192

**7** Have you met the management consultant?
(美M) (A) Yes, she seemed friendly.
(美W) (B) Not yet, I don't have them.
(C) Online consultation is the best.

你見過管理顧問了嗎？
(A) 有，她感覺很友善。
(B) 還沒，我還沒有它們。
(C) 網路諮詢是最好的。

字彙 management 管理　consultant 顧問
consultation 諮詢

**8** Who's been assigned to do the editing of this
(美W) feature?
(英M) (A) Magda is going to do it.
(B) Use the business credit card.
(C) She had another appointment.

是誰被指派來編輯這次的專題？
(A) 瑪格達會做。
(B) 用公司信用卡。
(C) 她有其他約了。

字彙 assign 指派　edit 編輯
feature 專題
business credit card 公司信用卡
appointment 約會

**9** Do you have a room booked at our hotel?
(美W) (A) She told me her address.
(美M) (B) Yes, I just did it an hour ago.
(C) Three first-class tickets.

您在我們飯店有預約嗎？
(A) 她告訴我她的地址。
(B) 有，我一個小時前才做的。
(C) 三張頭等艙的票。

字彙 first-class 頭等艙

**10** The best place to purchase recycled
(英M) computers is Bytesize.
(美W) (A) No, I won't, thanks.
(B) A special discount.
(C) Yes, they have a great range.

買二手電腦的最好地點是 Bytesize。
(A) 不，我不會，謝謝。
(B) 有特價。
(C) 對，他們有各種商品。

字彙 special discount 特價
range（生產或出售的）某類產品；某系列產品

**11** Isn't Ali's office upstairs?
(美W) (A) No, he moved this week.
(美M) (B) Yes, in the basement.
(C) We've met before.

阿里的辦公室不是在樓上嗎？
(A) 不，他這週搬走了。
(B) 對，在地下室。
(C) 我們之前見過面。

字彙 upstairs 在樓上　basement 地下室

**12** Which vehicle is yours?
(美M) (A) Thanks for your proposal.
(美W) (B) The blue one parked in the car park.
(C) Yes, I just leased it.

哪一台是你的車？
(A) 感謝你的提議。
(B) 停在停車場那台藍色的。
(C) 對，我剛剛才租了它。

字彙 vehicle 交通工具；車輛　proposal 建議
lease（房屋、設備等）租賃

**13** Do you want to bring the glass or the plastic
(美W) samples?
(美M) (A) It costs three hundred dollars.
(B) That's our main priority.
(C) The glass is hard to transport.

你想要帶玻璃或塑膠製的樣品嗎？
(A) 要價 300 美元。
(B) 這是我們的首要任務。
(C) 玻璃的運送很麻煩。

字彙 main priority 主要任務；優先事項
transport 運送；運輸

**14** How much longer will you be using the
(美M) photocopier?
(美W) (A) At the end of each month.
(B) I'm almost finished.
(C) We used to be employed here.

185

你還會用影印機用多久?
(A) 每個月底。
(B) 我快好了。
(C) 我以前是這裡的員工。

字彙 photocopier 影印機　employ 僱用

**15** It's quite hot here in Orlando, don't you think?
(美W) (A) A stunning building.
(英M) (B) No, the flight left earlier.
(C) Yes, do you want to borrow a fan?

你不覺得奧蘭多的天氣很熱嗎?
(A) 一棟很美的建築。
(B) 不,班機提早飛了。
(C) 是啊,你想要借台電風扇嗎?

字彙 stunning 極漂亮的;極迷人的
　　 fan 電風扇;扇子

**16** Shall we take a lunch break before we
(英M) reconvene?
(美M) (A) It only took an hour.
(B) No, let's just keep going.
(C) Yes, it's faulty.

我們重新開會前要先午休嗎?
(A) 只花了一小時。
(B) 不,讓我們繼續開吧。
(C) 是的,這有錯。

字彙 lunch break 午餐休息;午休
　　 reconvene 重新召開會議
　　 faulty 有缺陷的;不完美的

**17** Why is the store already closed?
(美W) (A) You can travel there from here.
(美M) (B) The display units are being changed.
(C) In the hardware department.

商店怎麼關了?
(A) 你可以從這裡前往那裡。
(B) 正在更換顯示設備。
(C) 在五金區。

字彙 travel （通常指長途）旅行
　　 display unit 顯示設備
　　 hardware 五金;硬體

**18** Can you call someone to fix this problem?
(美M) (A) Actually, I think I can solve it.
(美W) (B) Who was at the door?
(C) Save it for lunch then.

你可以找誰來解決這個問題嗎?
(A) 事實上,我想我能解決它。
(B) 誰在門邊?
(C) 這樣的話,把它留到午餐。

字彙 fix 修正　solve 解決

**19** I'm leaving for Hawaii tomorrow.
(美W) (A) I prefer flying, too.
(美M) (B) Have a good journey.
(C) At the hotel in the suburbs.

我明天將出發前往夏威夷。
(A) 我也比較喜歡搭飛機。
(B) 旅途愉快。
(C) 在郊區的飯店。

字彙 flying 搭飛機　journey 旅行
　　 suburb 郊區

**20** Who's leading the training session next
(英M) month?
(美W) (A) Two consultants from Austria.
(B) Sustainable energy.
(C) Opening hours are nine to five.

由誰帶下個月的培訓課程?
(A) 兩位奧地利的顧問。
(B) 永續能源。
(C) 營業時間是九點到五點。

字彙 lead 帶領;領導
　　 training session 培訓課程
　　 sustainable 可持續的,能長期保持的
　　 opening hours 營業時間

**21** Did Andrea end up buying a property or is
(美W) she going to carry on leasing?
(美M) (A) It's an unfriendly environment.
(B) That price sounds practical.
(C) She's renting for now.

安德莉雅最後是要買房子還是打算繼續租屋?
(A) 那個環境不友善。
(B) 價格聽起來很實際。
(C) 她現階段要租房子。

字彙 end up 最後成為；以……告終
buy a property 買房
carry on 繼續做…… lease 租賃
practical 切合實際的

**22** Aren't you bringing your wife to the banquet?
(美M) (A) Let's leave it in the lobby.
(英M) (B) I'm considering it.
(C) A three-course meal.

你不帶妻子參加宴會嗎？
(A) 讓我們把它留在大廳就好。
(B) 我還在考慮。
(C) 一份有三道菜的套餐。

字彙 banquet 宴會 lobby 大廳
a three-course meal 三道菜的一份餐點

**23** Why did we order these lasers?
(美W) (A) When we have extra funding.
(英M) (B) They're more durable.
(C) Good, I'll set up the trial.

我們為什麼要訂這些雷射筆？
(A) 當我們得到額外資助的時候。
(B) 它們比較耐用。
(C) 好，我會準備測試。

字彙 laser 雷射筆 funding 資助
durable 耐用的 trial 測試

**24** Let's take the midday train into the financial
(美M) center.
(美W) (A) Yes, I think there is.
(B) I'd prefer to drive.
(C) The shopping center.

讓我們搭午班火車去金融中心吧。
(A) 是的，我想那裡會有。
(B) 我比較想開車。
(C) 購物中心。

字彙 midday 正午 financial center 金融中心

**25** What is the procedure for submitting an
(美W) application?
(英M) (A) Is it in your home?
(B) A lot of practice.
(C) You can post it.

遞出申請的流程是什麼？
(A) 它在你家嗎？
(B) 很多練習。
(C) 你可以用寄的。

字彙 procedure 流程；程序
application 申請；應徵 post 郵寄

**26** This financial application form is not user-
(美M) friendly, is it?
(美M) (A) I haven't used it yet.
(B) An accounting clerk.
(C) The software was not installed.

這份財務申請書不太好寫，對吧？
(A) 我還沒用過。
(B) 一位記帳人員。
(C) 還沒安裝軟體。

字彙 financial application 財務申請書
user-friendly 方便用戶的；易於使用的
accounting clerk 記帳員

**27** I heard the senior nursing officers are getting
(美W) a pay increase.
(英M) (A) How large will it be?
(B) Four new openings have appeared.
(C) He's not in the main hospital.

我聽說護理長要被加薪了。
(A) 加多少？
(B) 出現了四個新職缺。
(C) 他不在本院。

字彙 senior nursing officer 護理長
pay increase 加薪 opening 職缺

**28** When should the parcel be delivered?
(美M) (A) Once you confirm the details.
(美W) (B) 33 contemporary paintings.
(C) I'll pack an overnight bag.

包裹什麼時候送出？
(A) 等您確認好細節。
(B) 33 幅當代畫作。
(C) 我會收拾過夜用的行李。

字彙 parcel 包裹 contemporary 當代的
pack 收拾；打包
overnight bag （過夜用的）旅行袋

**29** I'm going to need the addresses of your 
(美W) clients.
(美M) (A) No more than twice a week.
(B) I'll email them to you by tomorrow.
(C) Yes, I'm hoping to leave immediately.

我會需要您客戶的地址。
(A) 一週不超過兩次。
(B) 我明天前寄電子郵件給您。
(C) 對，我想立即離開。

字彙 client 客戶

**30** Do you think I should take an umbrella on my 
(英M) trip next week?
(英W) (A) It's forecast to be sunny.
(B) You're right, I should do that.
(C) Is it quicker by plane?

你想我下週出遊需要帶傘嗎？
(A) 預報說會是晴天。
(B) 你是對的，我應該做那件事。
(C) 搭飛機會比較快嗎？

字彙 forecast （特定形勢或天氣的）預測，預報

**31** The blueprints for our designs have been 
(美W) scanned, haven't they?
(美M) (A) A signed invoice.
(B) In a blue tone.
(C) They have, every last one.

我們的設計草稿已經掃描了嗎，還是還沒？
(A) 已簽名的出貨單。
(B) 藍色調的。
(C) 好了，全部都好了。

字彙 blue print 藍圖；草稿　scan 掃描
invoice 發貨單　every last 全部；每一個

---

 19

<PART **3**                                    P. 193

**Questions 32-34 refer to the following conversation.**
(美M) (美W)

**M** Hello, my name is Liam Kavanagh. My department sent an order to this restaurant over an hour ago. Can you tell me if my order is ready?

**W** Let me check for you. Oh . . . **32** the order has only just been accepted. I apologize, but I have a number of other orders ahead of you. **33** So yours won't be available for at least a quarter of an hour.

**M** I see. Well, **34** I was planning to pick up some office supplies during lunch. I'll do that and pick up the order in 15 minutes.

對話

男：您好，我的名字是連恩·卡瓦納。我們部門一個多小時前和您們餐廳訂餐。請問我的餐點好了嗎？

女：讓我為您確認一下。喔，訂單才剛剛接下。我很抱歉，但您前面還有不少餐點。所以您的餐點至少要等15分鐘才會好。

男：了解。嗯，我想在午餐時間順道買些辦公用品。15分鐘後，我買完再過去取餐。

字彙 department 部門　apologize 道歉
ahead of 在……之前　quarter 四分之一
pick up 順道買　office supplies 辦公用品

**32** Who most likely is the woman?
(A) A supplier
(B) A restaurant worker
(C) A chef
(D) An office employee

女子最有可能是做什麼的？
(A) 供應商
(B) 餐廳員工
(C) 主廚
(D) 公司雇員

**33** Why does the woman apologize?
(A) She provided the wrong meal.
(B) There is a mistake in the order.
(C) A business is closing late.
(D) An order was not completed on time.

女子為何道歉？
(A) 她出錯餐。
(B) 訂單有錯。
(C) 店家很晚才關門。
(D) 訂單沒有準時完成。

**34** What will the man do next?
(A) Go to a neighbor
(B) Pay for an order
(C) Send an e-mail
(D) Do some shopping

男子接下來將會做什麼？
(A) 到附近去
(B) 為訂單付款
(C) 發電子郵件
(D) 買點東西

**Questions 35-37 refer to the following conversation.**
美W 美M

W 35 I had to work overtime for a fortnight to meet the demands on the Blundell account. I'm certainly looking forward to enjoying my weeklong vacation.

M I know. You've been putting in a lot of extra hours. So, do you have anything exciting to do during the week?

W Well, 36 I'm traveling with family on Monday on a ski trip to Gradia Mountain. We like to go up there when the weather's favorable.

M Oh, did you know 37 there will be a snow board gala on Gradia Mountain on Tuesday? You should check it out during your ski trip.

對話
女：為了滿足布倫德爾帳戶的要求，我加班了兩個星期。我真的很期待之後放一個星期的長假。
男：我知道，妳加了很多班。所以妳這週有打算做什麼好玩的事嗎？
女：嗯，我星期一要和家人去格蘭迪亞山參加雙板滑雪之旅。我們想在天氣好時去那裡看看。
男：哦？妳知道格蘭迪亞山星期二有單板滑雪節嗎？妳們行程期間可以去看看。

字彙 **work overtime** 超時工作；加班
**fortnight** 兩週
**meet the demand** 滿足要求
**account** 帳戶　**weeklong** 為期一週的
**favorable** 有利的；適合的
**gala** 節日；慶祝；盛會　**take a look** 看一下
**negotiate** 協商；談判

**35** What did the woman have to do this week?
(A) Go on a vacation
(B) Cancel her account
(C) Join a different department
(D) Work extra hours

女子這週必須得做什麼事？
(A) 度假
(B) 取消她的帳戶
(C) 加入別的部門
(D) 加班

**36** Where will the woman go on Monday?
(A) To a mountainous area
(B) To a station
(C) To a park
(D) To a concert

女子星期一將要去哪？
(A) 山區
(B) 車站
(C) 公園
(D) 音樂會

**37** What does the man suggest the woman do?
(A) Work from home
(B) Negotiate a pay raise
(C) Ride in a cable car
(D) Go to watch a sports event

男子建議女子做什麼？
(A) 在家工作
(B) 談加薪
(C) 搭纜車
(D) 去看體育活動

19

英M 美W

**M** Camila, ㊳ **I just received a message from a customer asking if we stock the Arnis brand's cameras. We don't sell them here, do we?**

**W** Actually, we generally do have Arnis cameras on display, but we're currently out of stock.

**M** Do you know when we'll receive a new supply? ㊴ **I'd like to call the customer back** and get him to reserve one.

**W** Let me place a request to the order department. ㊵ **It looks like we'll get them in two weeks.**

---

對話

男：卡蜜拉，我剛收到客人的訊息，詢問我們有沒有阿尼斯牌相機的存貨。我們這邊沒賣，對嗎？

女：我們其實蠻常展示阿尼斯的相機的，但我們現在缺貨。

男：妳知道我們哪時候會進新貨嗎？我想給客人打個電話並幫他訂一台。

女：讓我向採購部門提出需求，應該兩週內會到。

字彙 stock 庫存　on display 展示
obviously 顯然
out of stock 缺貨；沒有庫存
place a request 提出需求
agenda（待辦的）事項；（會議）議程
write up（正式）填寫
obsolete 過時的；淘汰的　release 發布
in stock 有現貨或存貨

**38** What are the speakers mainly discussing?
(A) A computer system
(B) A delivery charge
(C) A work agenda
(D) A piece of item

說話的人主要在討論什麼？
(A) 電腦系統
(B) 運費
(C) 工作交辦事項
(D) 某項商品

**39** What does the man plan to do?
(A) Talk to a customer
(B) Write up an order
(C) Make an appointment
(D) Send an invoice

男子打算做什麼？
(A) 和顧客談談
(B) 填寫訂單
(C) 敲定見面時間
(D) 寄出發貨單

**40** According to the woman, what will happen in two weeks?
(A) An order will be cancelled.
(B) A catalog will be released.
(C) Some products will be back in stock.
(D) A computer brand will become obsolete.

根據女子所述，兩週後會發生什麼事？
(A) 會取消一筆訂單。
(B) 會發表新型錄。
(C) 有些產品將有現貨。
(D) 某電腦品牌將會被淘汰。

美W 英M

**W** Hello, my name is Dai Davies. I'm calling because I was looking at the employment opportunities offered on your Web site. ㊶ **I noticed there was a position as an architectural technician. Is that job still open?**

**M** Yes, it is. Do you have any experience in an architectural practice?

**W** Yes, I do. ㊷ **I was employed as an architectural technician at Jones and Fabria in Wales** for two years before relocating back to England with my family.

**M** Oh, yes. I'm aware of that firm. ㊸ **Why don't you send me your résumé?** Once we have a look at it, I'll be back in touch.

---

對話

女：您好，我的名字是戴‧戴維斯。我看到您官網上正在徵人，所以打了這通電話。我有看到建築技術員的職位，這個職缺還有嗎？

男：有，還有缺。您有建築實務的任何經驗嗎？

女：有的。我和家人搬回英國前在威爾斯的瓊斯和法布里亞做過兩年的建築技術員。

男：喔，好的。我知道這間公司。不如您把履歷寄給我？等我們看過後再跟您聯繫。

**41** What type of position has been advertised?
(A) Architect
(B) Designer
(C) Legal clerk
(D) Lab Technician

哪一類工作正在對外徵才？
(A) 建築師
(B) 平面設計師
(C) 法務人員
(D) 研究技術人員

**42** Where did the woman work most recently?
(A) In Ireland
(B) In Scotland
(C) In England
(D) In Wales

女子近期的工作地點在哪？
(A) 愛爾蘭
(B) 蘇格蘭
(C) 英格蘭
(D) 威爾蘭

**43** What does the man ask the woman to do?
(A) Send in further information
(B) Fill out an online form
(C) Check for more details
(D) Submit a portfolio

男子請女子做什麼？
(A) 寄出更詳細的資訊
(B) 填寫網路表格
(C) 查看更多細節
(D) 提供作品集

**Questions 44-46 refer to the following conversation.**
美M 美W

**M** Hi, I saw your ad online for an office unit for rent on Main Street. ㊹ **I'm contacting you to find out when it is vacant.**

**W** We're looking for a tenant who can take up occupation on September 21. It's an excellent location. ㊺ **In fact, it's the only unit in the complex that faces the river. It's really stunning.** Would you like to come and see it?

**M** Yes, I would. I'm available on Thursday all day.

**W** ㊻ **Why don't you come to see the complex on Thursday at 11 A.M.?** I'll meet you in the reception area.

---

對話

男：您好，我看到了您在網路上出租緬因街的辦公室。我聯絡您是想知道它什麼時候會清空。

女：我們正在找可以在 9 月 21 號入住的住戶。它的位置非常好，事實上，它是整棟建築唯一向著河流的地點，非常漂亮。您想來看看嗎？

男：是的，我想要。我星期四整天都有空。

女：不如您星期四上午 11 點過來這棟大樓好嗎？我會在接待處等您。

**44** What does the man ask about the office?
(A) Where it is located
(B) When it is available
(C) How many other businesses are there
(D) How much is the rent

關於辦公室，男子問了什麼？
(A) 位於哪裡
(B) 何時可以用
(C) 有多少公司在那邊
(D) 租金多少

**45** What is unique about the unit?
(A) Its scenic view
(B) Its storage space
(C) Its historic site
(D) Its reduced price

這間空房有何獨到之處？
(A) 它的風景很好
(B) 它的庫存空間
(C) 它的古蹟
(D) 它的折扣

**46** When will the woman meet the man?
(A) At 10:00 A.M.
(B) At 11:00 A.M.
(C) At 1:00 P.M.
(D) At 11:00 P.M.

女子將會在何時和男子見面？
(A) 上午 10 點
(B) 上午 11 點
(C) 下午 1 點
(D) 晚上 11 點

**Questions 47-49 refer to the following conversation.**
英M 美W

**M** Ailey, I have to leave the office now. ㊼ I'm going to meet a client downtown.
**W** I see, Mr. Campbell. ㊼ Are you coming back this afternoon?
**M** ㊼ No, it's going to be a long discussion, so I won't be back today.
**W** ㊽ I wonder if you remember your 3 o'clock meeting with the marketing team today.
**M** Oh, I completely forgot about it. Can you call the team manager and reschedule it for some time next week?
**W** No problem. I'll contact him and let you know the rescheduled date.
**M** Wait a minute. Come to think of it, I'd better do it myself. ㊾ I need to discuss some issues with him anyway.

- - - - - - - - - - - - - - - - - - - - - -

對話
**男：**艾麗，我現在得離開辦公室了。我要去市中心見一位客戶。
**女：**坎貝爾先生，我了解了。您今天下午會回來嗎？
**男：**不，應該會討論很久，所以我今天不會回來。

**女：**我不確定您是否記得今天三點要和行銷團隊開會？
**男：**噢，我完全忘了。您可以打電話給行銷經理，看可以改到下星期的某個時間嗎？
**女：**沒問題。我會打給他並通知您重新安排的日期。
**男：**等等，想想還是我自己來比較好，我需要和他討論一些事。

字彙 issue 問題；議題

**47** What will the man probably do this afternoon?
(A) Have a meeting with coworkers
(B) Attend an appointment with a client
(C) Pick up a friend
(D) Go to a show downtown

男子今天下午可能會做什麼？
(A) 和同事開會
(B) 和一名客戶見面
(C) 接一位朋友
(D) 去市中心看展

**48** What was the man supposed to do at 3:00 P.M.?
(A) Attend a workshop
(B) Visit a branch office
(C) Meet with new employees
(D) Discuss issues with the marketing team

男子下午 3 點原來應該要做什麼？
(A) 參加工作坊
(B) 訪問分公司
(C) 見新進員工
(D) 和行銷團隊討論問題

**49** What does the man mean when he says, "Come to think of it, I'd better do it myself"?
(A) He will cancel a reservation.
(B) He will contact a coworker.
(C) He will attend a meeting.
(D) He will email some reports.

男子說：「想想還是我自己來比較好」時，其意思為何？
(A) 他會取消預約。
(B) 他會聯絡同事。
(C) 他會參加會議。
(D) 他會用電子郵件寄些報告。

**Questions 50-52 refer to the following conversation.**
美W 美M

**W** Rick, I need to go early this evening but there's an extra party of 20 people arriving at 8 P.M. and ⑤⓿ **I've been put down to prepare meals for them. Is there any chance you can help me with the preparations?**

**M** Sure, but I understood you were scheduled to work up till midnight tonight. ⑤❶ **If you are planning to leave early, we might not be able to cope.** It's one of our busiest nights.

**W** Oh, I thought the owner told you. I changed shifts with Alex so there'll be plenty of kitchen staff available. Now, ⑤❷ **the 8 o'clock customers want the fish menu as they are all vegetarians.** So let's prepare some salmon to be marinated.

---

對話

女：瑞克，我今晚得早點走，但晚上 8 點會加開一場 20 人的派對，我被點名為他們準備餐點，你有可能幫我準備嗎？

男：當然，但我知道妳今天排班到午夜。如果妳打算提早走，我們可能應付不來。今晚也會很忙。

女：哦，我以為店長告訴你了，我和阿歷克斯換班了，這樣子廚房人應該夠。那麼現在，因為八點鐘的客人吃素所以點了魚，讓我們準備一些鮭魚拿來醃吧。

---

字彙 **extra party** 加開的派對
**put down** 被寫在名單上
**Is there any chance . . . ?**
有機會可以……嗎？
**cope** 處理；應付　**shift** 輪班
**plenty of** 充足的；大量的
**salmon** 鮭魚　**marinate** 醃製
**short staffed** 人手不足的

**50** What does the woman ask the man to help her with?
(A) Serving drinks
(B) Moving some tables
(C) Preparing meals
(D) Changing his shifts

女子請男子幫她做什麼？
(A) 發放酒水
(B) 搬動一些桌子
(C) 準備餐點
(D) 改他的班表

**51** Why is the man concerned?
(A) They might be short staffed.
(B) The party might get out of hand.
(C) The kitchen will not be open.
(D) The ingredients may not be available.

男子為什麼擔心？
(A) 他們人手可能不夠。
(B) 派對可能會很難應付。
(C) 廚房將不會開。
(D) 食材可能沒辦法用。

**52** What did some customers request?
(A) More floor space
(B) A vegetarian menu
(C) A beachfront view
(D) An event calendar

有些客人要求什麼？
(A) 更大的樓層空間
(B) 素食餐點
(C) 看得到海景
(D) 活動日程表

**Questions 53-55 refer to the following conversation with three speakers.** 美M 澳M 美W

**M1** ❺❸ **Who do you think the new sales manager is going to be — Ms. Park or Mr. Tatum?**

**M2** I think both are outstanding candidates for the position.

**W** Neither of them. I heard the board of directors is looking for someone from outside the company.

**M1** Why does the board want to do that? They are talented sales representatives, and they have worked here for over 15 years.

**M2** ❺❹ **And internal promotions happen much faster than recruiting externally.**

**W** I couldn't agree more. ❺❺ **But the board members want someone who will be able to deliver a dramatic increase in sales.**

## 對話

男1：你覺得帕克女士和塔圖先生，誰會是新的業務經理呢？

男2：我認為兩位都是這個職位的出色人選。

女：兩人都不是，我聽說董事會要從外部找人。

男1：為什麼董事會要這樣做？兩人都是很有才能的業務員，也都工作超過 15 年了。

男2：而且內部晉升比外部招聘快多了。

女：我完全同意。不過，董事會想找一個可以帶動銷量暴增的人。

> **字彙** outstanding 傑出的；出色的
> representative 代表　internal 內部的
> externally 在（或從）外部
> deliver 給出（成果）　dramatic 戲劇性的
> restructure 重整；改組

**53** What is the conversation mainly about?
(A) A sales result
(B) A retiring employee
(C) Candidates for a position
(D) A company's anniversary

談話內容主要是關於什麼？
(A) 銷售成果
(B) 一位屆退同仁
(C) 一個職位的人選
(D) 一家公司的週年慶

**54** What does the woman mean when she says, "I couldn't agree more"?
(A) Now is the time for recruiting.
(B) 10 years' working experience is a requirement.
(C) An internal promotion is a fast way to fill a position.
(D) The company needs to contact a staffing agency.

女子說：「我完全同意」時，意思是什麼？
(A) 應該要徵才了。
(B) 十年工作經驗是必備條件。
(C) 內部晉升是很快的填補職缺方式。
(D) 公司需要聯繫人資公司。

**55** According to the woman, what do the board members want?
(A) Increased sales
(B) Relocation of one of their branches
(C) Adding new delivery locations
(D) Restructuring of the sales team

根據女子所述，董事會成員想要的是什麼？
(A) 增加的銷售量
(B) 搬遷一家分店
(C) 新增配送地點
(D) 重整業務團隊

**Questions 56-58 refer to the following conversation.**
美W 英M

**W** 56 Mr. Bloomberg just called to tell me that he wants quarry flooring for his office instead of carpeting.

**M** Oh, he's such a demanding client. 57 He keeps changing his mind. Is he allowing us to push back the deadline?

**W** No, he wants the remodeling to be completed by August 10th as scheduled.

**M** Hmm, we need another week to meet his request. 58 I think we should hire at least two more skilled workers to keep up with such a tight schedule.

**W** That is what I was going to propose, actually.

**M** I will contact Mr. Ferrell. He probably knows some contractors.

女：彭博先生剛剛打電話給我說，他的辦公室想用石子鋪面取代地毯。

男：哦，他是很棘手的客戶，不斷改變主意。他能讓我們延後期限嗎？

女：不，他希望改造如期在 8 月 10 日前完成。

男：嗯，為了滿足他的需求，我們還需要再一個星期，我想我們還得再找至少兩名的技術工，才能在這麼緊迫的時程裡趕工。

女：其實這正是我想提的。

男：我會聯繫法洛先生，他也許認識一些承包商。

> **字彙** quarry 採石場
> demanding 費時費力的；耗費精力的
> tight（時間、金錢）緊湊的，排滿的
> unpredictable 難以預測的
> floor plan 樓層平面圖
> contractor 承包商

**56** According to the woman, why did Mr. Bloomberg call her?
(A) To inquire about the status of the project
(B) To discuss costs
(C) To reschedule a deadline
(D) To change a flooring material

根據女子所述，為什麼彭博先生會打給她？
(A) 要詢問計畫進度
(B) 要討論成本
(C) 要更改期限
(D) 要更換地板材質

**57** What does the man mention about Mr. Bloomberg?
(A) He doesn't like changing plans.
(B) He asked for an additional discount.
(C) He is unpredictable.
(D) He is a frequent client.

關於彭博先生，男子提到什麼？
(A) 他不喜歡改變計畫。
(B) 他要求額外折扣。
(C) 他很難預測。
(D) 他是常客。

**58** What does the woman mean when she says, "That is what I was going to propose, actually"?
(A) A new floor plan is needed for the client.
(B) Mr. Bloomberg is a demanding client.
(C) Hiring workers will help meet the deadline.
(D) Mr. Ferrell is a popular contractor.

女子說：「其實這正是我想提的」時，意思是什麼？
(A) 客戶需要新的樓層平面設計。
(B) 彭博先生是個很棘手的客戶
(C) 招募工人有助趕上期限。
(D) 法洛先生是很受歡迎的承包商。

**Questions 59-61 refer to the following conversation.**
美M 美W

**M** Hi, my wife informed me that 59 60 your branch is offering a special deal on Trion car accessories. Can you give me more information?

**W** Sure, for one month, if you purchase a Trion handheld car vacuum, you'll get 30% off the Trion Car Jet Wash, too. It's an excellent deal if you consider the savings you make on buying both products.

**M** It certainly is. Do you deliver free of charge?

**W** Yes, we'll ship the products at no extra cost. If you wish to place an order, 61 you'll need the special code. Enter it when you're directed to the checkout page and you'll get 30% off.

---

**對話**

男：您好，我太太告訴我說，您分店的特萊昂汽車配件正在特價。可以請您給我更多資訊嗎？

女：當然可以，為期一個月的時間，如果您買了特萊昂的車用手持吸塵器，也將得到特萊昂洗車七折優惠。考慮到您同時買兩項產品省的錢，這筆買賣非常划算。

男：肯定是的。你們免運送費嗎？

女：對的，我們送貨並不會額外收費。您想訂購的話，將會需要特別的折扣碼。導向結帳頁面時輸入代碼，您將得到30％的折扣。

**字彙** branch 分店　handheld 手持
vacuum 吸塵器　savings 省下的錢
**at no extra cost** 不需額外花費
checkout 結帳

19

**59** Why is the man calling?
(A) To ask about a special deal
(B) To reply to a consumer survey
(C) To track a delivery
(D) To inquire about his savings

男子為何打這通電話？
(A) 要詢問特價
(B) 要答覆消費者調查
(C) 要追蹤配送進度
(D) 要詢問他儲蓄的事

**60** What products are the speakers discussing?
(A) Electronic products
(B) Gardening equipment
(C) Cooking appliances
(D) Vehicle accessories
說話的人討論的是什麼產品？
(A) 電子產品
(B) 園藝設備
(C) 廚具
(D) 汽車配件

**61** What information is the man told to submit on the Web site?
(A) A delivery schedule
(B) A shipping number
(C) A promotional code
(D) A credit card billing address
男子被告知要在官網上提供哪項資訊？
(A) 配送行程表
(B) 船運編號
(C) 促銷代碼
(D) 信用卡帳單地址

**Questions 62-64 refer to the following conversation.**
美W 美M

**W** Hello, my name is Mary Blake and (62) **I'm a marketing agent from 'Blooms Right – All Exotic Flowers.'** I'm visiting all shops in the region that we supply to and giving them the option to use our sales material and displays.
**M** Well, I do think having displays and marketing material is very helpful. I'm certain it would boost the sales of the Blooms Right products. But (63) **it'll be time-consuming to have my workers set it all up and have to monitor any detailed display.**
**W** Oh, actually Blooms Right would provide someone to do all that. So there's no extra work involved for you. (64) **This brochure has all the details about the point of sales service including a list of days** we are in your area.

**對話**
女：您好，我叫瑪麗·布萊克，是「花開正好——異國花卉大全」的行銷代理。我正在當地訪問我們供貨的所有店家，並帶著文宣品和展示品供他們選用。
男：嗯，我的確認為有展示品和文宣非常有幫助。我也有把握這能刺激花開正好產品的買氣。不過，為了把全部打點好、或顧好精緻的展品，會花我員工很多時間。
女：喔，其實那些花開正好都會找人來弄，所以您完全不須要再費工。這本小冊子有銷售服務的所有詳細資訊，包括我們會在您這個地區的日期。

**字彙** **marketing agent** 行銷代理人
**exotic** 異國的
**sales material** 行銷用品；文宣
**display** 展示品 **boost** 提振；刺激
**time-consuming** 費時的 **set up** 設置
**monitor** 監控；顧好 **representative** 代表
**timespan** （兩件事之間或事情發生的）期間
**timetable** 時程

**62** Who is the woman?
(A) A florist
(B) A shop owner
(C) A customer
(D) A sales representative
女子是誰？
(A) 花店店員
(B) 店長
(C) 顧客
(D) 業務代表

**63** What concern does the man mention about the display?
(A) The cost involved in the process
(B) The time consumption for his employees
(C) The amount of space required
(D) The timespan of delivery
提到展品時，男子表示他擔心什麼？
(A) 過程中產生的費用
(B) 他員工所花費的時間
(C) 需要的空間
(D) 到貨要等的時間

**64** What information does the brochure contain?
(A) A timetable
(B) Cost information
(C) A list of other stores
(D) A flower sample

小冊包含什麼資訊？
(A) 時程表
(B) 成本資訊
(C) 其他店面的一覽表
(D) 花卉樣品

**Questions 65-67 refer to the following conversation and floor directory.** 美W 英M

| Hubert Research Center - 3rd Floor | |
|---|---|
| Laboratory | Room 301 |
| Incubation Room | Room 302 |
| ❻❺ Low-Pressure Chamber | **Room 303** |
| High-Pressure Chamber | Room 304 |

**W** Gerald, why do you look so tired? Are you okay?

**M** You're not going to believe it. ❻❺ ❻❻ **I was locked inside the low-pressure chamber last night.** I didn't know that all the chamber doors lock automatically at midnight. ❻❼ **I barely slept because it was so stuffy.**

**W** Why didn't you call someone else?

**M** I tried to call the facility manager, but for some reason the phone didn't ring at the time. And it was already too late, so I decided to wait until someone opened the chamber this morning.

----

| 胡博研究中心——三樓 | |
|---|---|
| 實驗室 | 301 室 |
| 孵化室 | 302 室 |
| 低壓室 | 303 室 |
| 高壓室 | 304 室 |

女：杰拉德，為什麼你看起來很累？你還好嗎？

男：妳可能不會相信，我昨晚被鎖在低壓室裡了。我不知道所有房間的門會在半夜自動上鎖。太悶了，我幾乎都沒睡。

女：你怎麼沒打電話找人？

男：我試著打給大樓管理員，但電話因為某些原因當時沒有響。而且已經太晚了，所以我就決定等到早上開門的人來。

字彙 chamber 房間
stuffy 悶的；通風不順暢的

**65** Look at the graphic. Where did the man stay last night?
(A) Room 301
(B) Room 302
(C) Room 303
(D) Room 304

請看圖表，男子昨晚待在哪裡？
(A) 301 室
(B) 302 室
(C) 303 室
(D) 304 室

**66** What happened to the man?
(A) He lost a garage key.
(B) He left his house door open.
(C) He was locked inside a space.
(D) He was under pressure with his task.

男子遇到了什麼事？
(A) 他弄丟車庫鑰匙。
(B) 他沒關家門。
(C) 他被鎖在一個空間裡。
(D) 他的工作讓他壓力很大。

**67** According to the man, why didn't he sleep well?
(A) The space was cold.
(B) The space was scary.
(C) The space was stuffy.
(D) The space was too noisy.

根據男子所述，他為什麼睡不好？
(A) 該空間太冷了。
(B) 該空間太可怕了。
(C) 該空間太悶了。
(D) 該空間太吵了。

19

Questions 68-70 refer to the following conversation and schedule. 美M 美W

| Mr. Brooks' schedule | |
|---|---|
| Tuesday | Urban Kitchen |
| Wednesday | Polly's Restaurant |
| Thursday | Top Cloud (in Hotel Dublin) |
| 70 Friday | New York Diner |

M I think we're a bit behind schedule. 68 We haven't even started preparing properly for the employee appreciation banquet. I think we need to hurry up. Have you reserved the venue at least, Linda?

W Yes, Mr. Brooks. 69 I paid the deposit to the Oriental Hotel last night. The ballroom I reserved is the largest one in the hotel.

M That's wonderful. Did you find a catering service as well?

W Yes, I did. The company promised to provide high-quality food, drinks, and services to our guests. We have been offered some sample meals to help us decide on the menu items.

M I see. 70 Could you make an appointment to visit the company on Friday?

W Certainly.

------------------------------------------------

| 布魯克斯先生的行程 | |
|---|---|
| 星期二 | 都會廚房 |
| 星期三 | 波莉的餐廳 |
| 星期四 | 雲頂（都柏林飯店內） |
| 星期五 | 紐約小餐館 |

男：我想我們進度有點落後，我們甚至還沒開始準備員工感恩餐會。我想我們需要加快腳步，至少妳訂好場地了吧，琳達？

女：是的，布魯克斯先生。我昨晚付給了東方飯店訂金。我訂的宴會廳是飯店中最大的一間。

男：太棒了。妳找好外燴服務了嗎？

女：有的。業者承諾會提供我們賓客優質餐飲和服務。我們拿到一些試菜菜單，可以幫助我們決定菜色。

男：了解。妳可以約星期五去業者那嗎？

女：當然。

字彙 a bit 有點　behind schedule 進度落後　properly 恰當地；正確地　deposit 訂金　ballroom 宴會廳　catering 外燴

68 What are the speakers preparing for?
(A) An appreciation event
(B) A retirement party
(C) A grand opening
(D) An employee workshop

說話的人正在準備什麼？
(A) 感恩活動
(B) 退休歡送會
(C) 盛大開幕
(D) 員工工作坊

69 What does the woman say she did last night?
(A) Searched for a location
(B) Sampled some food
(C) Paid a deposit
(D) Picked up supplies

女子說她昨晚做了什麼？
(A) 找地點
(B) 試一些菜
(C) 付訂金
(D) 順便買用品

70 Look at the graphic. What is the name of the catering service that the woman contacted?
(A) Urban Kitchen
(B) Polly's Restaurant
(C) Top Cloud
(D) New York Diner

請看圖表，女子聯繫的外燴服務名稱為何？
(A) 都會廚房
(B) 波莉的餐廳
(C) 雲頂
(D) 紐約小餐館

🎧 20

## PART 4

P. 197

**Questions 71-73 refer to the following advertisement.**
美M

Looking for something appetizing and refreshing to gratify your craving? ❼ **Plusto-brand vegetable juice** has it all. It's filling yet 100% nutritious. You get nothing but pure vegetables, straight from the ground. ❼ **If you visit our Web site www.plusto.com, you will find a selection of money-off vouchers.** ❼ **And beginning next month, we'll be launching our latest flavor Tasty Potato.** Look for it at a store near you.

----

廣告

　　正在找開胃又清爽的東西，滿足您的口腹之慾嗎？「加把淨」品牌的蔬菜汁通通都有。充滿飽足感又有100%營養。只有產地現摘的純淨蔬菜，絕無其他添加物。若上我們的官網 www.plusto.com，您還會找到各種的折價券。而且自下個月起，我們將開賣新口味的好好吃馬鈴薯。在您附近的商店就能找到。

字彙 **appetizing** 開胃的　**refreshing** 使人涼爽的；消除疲勞的；提神的
**gratify** 滿足　**craving** 渴望；渴求
**filling** 容易填飽肚子的
**nutritious** 有營養的
**a selection of** 可供挑選的
**money-off voucher** 折價券
**launch** 開賣；推出　**flavor** 口味

**71** What is being advertised?
(A) A beverage
(B) A store
(C) A food bar
(D) A dessert
這在廣告什麼？
(A) 飲料
(B) 店家
(C) 美食吧
(D) 甜點

**72** According to the speaker, what can be found at the Plusto Web site?
(A) Details of ingredients
(B) A list of vegetable growers
(C) A map of store locations
(D) Discount coupons

根據說話的人所言，「加把淨」官網上能找到什麼？
(A) 詳細的食材資訊
(B) 菜農的名單
(C) 店鋪位置的地圖
(D) 折價券

**73** What will happen next month?
(A) A new flavor will be launched.
(B) Different-colored packaging will be offered.
(C) Prices will be reduced.
(D) A company name will change.
下個月將有什麼事？
(A) 將推出新口味。
(B) 將提供不同顏色的包裝。
(C) 價格將調降。
(D) 公司將換名稱。

**Questions 74-76 refer to the following recorded message.** 英W

You have reached ❼ **the Coverall Parcel tracking service.** ❼ **Starting tomorrow, you can track the transit of all items sent through Coverall on the Internet.** Just visit our Web site at www.coverall.com. And enter your tracking number where prompted by the online instructions. This facility will pinpoint exactly where your package is on its route. If you would like to hear this message again, please press the hash key. ❼ **To return to the main menu, please press star.**

----

留言錄音

　　這裡是「無所不在」包裹追蹤服務。自明天開始，您可以在線上追蹤任何由無所不在運送的物品，只需訪問我們官網 www.coverall.com，並於網頁指示處輸入您的追蹤號碼。此功能將精確定位出您的包裹運送時的所在位置。如果您想再次收聽此留言，請按＃字鍵；返回主選單，請按＊字鍵。

字彙 **parcel** 包裹　**tracking service** 追蹤服務
**transit** 運輸；輸送　**prompt** 引發；促發
**instruction** 指示；說明　**facility** 功能
**pinpoint** 準確指出，確定（位置或時間）
**hash** 電話（或電腦鍵盤）上的＃號
**alert** 推播；警報　**operator** 接線生

🎧 20

**74** What type of business created the message?
(A) A delivery service
(B) A bus company
(C) A telephone exchange
(D) A travel agency
哪一類型的公司留了這則留言？
(A) 配送服務
(B) 巴士業者
(C) 電話交換局
(D) 旅行社

**75** What new service does the business offer?
(A) A web-based payment option
(B) Mobile message alerts
(C) Priority delivery options
(D) An online tracking system
該公司提供哪種新服務？
(A) 線上付款
(B) 行動簡訊通知
(C) 優先快遞方案
(D) 線上追蹤系統

**76** Why would a listener press star?
(A) To speak to an operator
(B) To return to the main menu
(C) To have this message repeated
(D) To hear the message again
聽話的人為何需要按＊字鍵？
(A) 和接線生說話
(B) 回到主選單
(C) 使留言複誦
(D) 重複聽留言

**Questions 77-79 refer to the following talk.** 英M

Welcome to Birmingham Armed Forces Training Ground. My name is Stephen and (77) **I will be in charge of today's endurance test.** Our aim is to get you (78) **prepared for the overseas tour of Kosovo in two months' time.** And I want every one of you to increase your stamina levels. Today, we'll be undergoing extensive body fitness training for four hours and will increase this time by 30 minutes every day. Before we begin training, please let the medical staff check your body mass. (79) **They will check you at every session to record your progress.**

**談話**

歡迎來到白金漢軍隊訓練場。我叫史蒂夫，將負責今天的耐力測試。我們的目標是在兩個月的時間內，做好您到科索沃海外旅行的準備。我希望你們全體體能都能提升。今天，我們將進行四個小時大範圍的體適能訓練，之後的訓練時間每天將增加 30 分鐘。訓練開始前，請讓醫療人員測量您的身高體重。他們在每一次訓練時都會為您做檢查、追蹤您的表現。

**字彙** armed forces 軍隊；武裝部隊
training ground 訓練場；訓練場
be in charge of 負責……
endurance test 耐力測試
overseas 海外的　stamina 體力
undergo 經歷
extensive 大範圍的；廣泛的
body fitness 體適能
medical staff 醫療人員
body mass 身體質量　progress 進展
take part in 參加
log（工程、試驗等的）工作記錄簿

**77** Who most likely is the speaker?
(A) A fitness trainer
(B) An army doctor
(C) A sports journalist
(D) A medical expert
說話的人最有可能是誰？
(A) 健身教練
(B) 軍醫
(C) 體育記者
(D) 醫學專家

**78** What are the listeners preparing to do in two months?
(A) Run a race
(B) Take part in an endurance test
(C) Travel overseas
(D) Participate in a fitness program
聽眾於兩個月後將準備做什麼？
(A) 參加賽跑
(B) 參加耐力測試
(C) 到海外旅遊
(D) 參加體適能課程

**79** What does the speaker encourage the listeners to do?
(A) Take weekly breaks
(B) Purchase appropriate weapons
(C) Consult a medical professional daily
(D) Keep a personal log

說話的人鼓勵聽眾做什麼？
(A) 每週休息
(B) 買適當的武器
(C) 每天諮詢醫療專業人員
(D) 持續做個人紀錄

**Questions 80-82 refer to the following talk.** 美W

Welcome to Gringo's Gourmet, the home of Andalusia's favorite frozen meals. In half an hour, we'll commence the tour. ❽⓪ **You'll be taken through all the stages of manufacture of frozen desserts and savouries.** We have only one request. Please do not approach any of the factory machinery. This is both for your own protection and the wellbeing of Gringo's operatives. When we finish the tour, ❽① **we'll offer you the chance to make your own frozen snack.** Now, ❽② **before we depart from the reception, please take a look at this image of the original factory** from 1967. As you can see, our contemporary factory looks very different. The modernization will be explained in the informational booklet I'll hand out.

----

談話

　　歡迎來到老外老饕，安達魯西亞超人氣冷凍食品的發源地。接下來半小時將開始導覽參觀，帶您認識冷凍甜點和鹹品的不同生產階段。我們只有一個請求，請勿碰觸工廠的任何機器，這是為了保護您以及老外員工的安全。我們結束參觀後，您有機會製作自己的冷凍小點心。從接待處出發前，現在請您看一下 1967 年工廠最初的照片，您可以看出現代工廠很不一樣，我現在要發的資訊冊裡將解釋它的現代化過程。

字彙　gourmet 美食家；老饕　frozen 冷凍的
commence 開始
take A through B 帶 A 認識或了解 B
manufacture （通常指工廠機械大量）製造
frozen dessert 冷凍甜點
savoury 鹹味小吃　machinery 機器
wellbeing 安全；福利
operative 技工，工人　depart 出發
contemporary 現代的；當代的
modernization 現代化
informational 含有資訊或資料的
booklet 小冊子　hand out 發送

**80** Where does the talk most likely take place?
(A) At a factory
(B) At a restaurant
(C) At a photographic studio
(D) At a museum

這段談話最有可能發生在哪裡？
(A) 工廠
(B) 餐廳
(C) 攝影棚
(D) 博物館

**81** What does the speaker say listeners will receive?
(A) Food samples
(B) A choice of desserts
(C) A photograph
(D) A cookery opportunity

說話的人表示聽眾將得到什麼？
(A) 試吃品
(B) 某種甜點
(C) 一張照片
(D) 料理機會

**82** What does the speaker ask the listeners to do in the reception?
(A) Check out a picture
(B) Leave their possessions
(C) Form a line
(D) Listen to an audio message

在接待處，說話的人要求聽眾做什麼？
(A) 看一下照片
(B) 留下個人物品
(C) 排隊
(D) 聽語音訊息

**Questions 83-85 refer to the following news report.** 澳M

And now for the Jinny Ring Fitness Community latest news. This Saturday will be an opportunity for you to join in **㉓ our first annual sports day**. Come along to Runnings Park to sign up for a number of events from wrestling competition, 5-a-side soccer games to athletics for athletes of all ages. **㉔ There is a possibility of storms for the morning** but the afternoon should be clear. Whichever event you want to participate in, **㉕ I advise you to wear suitable sports clothing.** Sports equipment is free to borrow, but we cannot provide clothing or running shoes.

新聞報導

現在是有關金妮・鈴健身中心的最新消息。本週六您將有機會參加我們第一屆的年度運動日。活動很多,快到賽跑公園報名登記,從角力競技到五人制足球,還有適合各年齡層運動員的田徑運動。早上可能會有暴風雨,但下午應該就會放晴。無論您參加的活動為何,建議您穿著合適的運動服裝。運動器材供免費借用,不過我們不會提供服裝和慢跑鞋。

字彙 **fitness** 健身 **join in** 參加;加入
**come along** 到達;出現;一起來
**sign up** 登記
**wrestling competition** 角力競技
**5-a-side soccer games** 五人制足球
**athletics** 田徑運動 **athlete** 運動員
**of all ages** 各年齡層的
**be meant to be** 必須要……;一定要……
**participate in** 參加
**sports equipment** 運動器材
**running shoes** 慢跑鞋 **municipal** 市政的
**fair** 展覽會

**83** What is the main topic of the report?
(A) A concert opening
(B) A community
(C) A sports competition
(D) A municipal fair
這篇報導的主旨為何?
(A) 音樂會開幕活動
(B) 社團
(C) 體育比賽
(D) 市辦展覽會

**84** What problem does the speaker mention?
(A) Bad weather is forecast.
(B) Traffic is expected to be heavy.
(C) Parking is limited.
(D) Some events have been cancelled.
說話的人提到什麼問題?
(A) 預告說有壞天氣。
(B) 預期交通會很塞。
(C) 停車空間有限。
(D) 有些活動取消了。

**85** What does the speaker suggest listeners do?
(A) Bring a packed lunch
(B) Use public transport
(C) Run in the park
(D) Wear suitable clothing
說話的人建議聽眾做什麼?
(A) 自備午餐
(B) 搭乘公共運輸工具
(C) 在公園裡跑步
(D) 穿著合適的服裝

**Questions 86-88 refer to the following announcement.**
英W

**㉖ Attention, library users. ㉗ In 30 minutes, we will start a painting class.** Professional painter Jay Colman will teach you how to simply draw paintings with your limited painting supplies at home. You can learn some practical tips and techniques. We'd like to invite everyone, whether you are a brand-new painter or have been practicing for years. If you're interested, please come to the community room on the second floor of the library. **㉘ Once the class starts, there will be no further admittance.** This is to avoid interruptions. Thank you.

宣告

請圖書館使用者注意,我們的繪畫課將在30分鐘後開始。專業畫家傑・科爾曼將教您如何用家中有限的繪畫材料進行簡易繪畫。您可以學到一些實用技巧和技法。我們想邀請所有人參加,不論您是繪畫新手還是已經畫了好幾年。您感興趣的話,請到圖書館二樓的社區教室。課程一旦開始將不再開放進場,這是為了避免干擾課程進行,感謝您。

字彙 **practical** 實用的 **admittance** 入場許可
**interruption** 打擾;干擾 **punctual** 準時的

**86** Who most likely are the listeners?
(A) Library users
(B) Librarians
(C) Shoppers
(D) Seminar participants

聽眾最有可能是誰？
(A) 圖書館使用者
(B) 圖書館員
(C) 購物的人
(D) 參加研討會的人

**87** What is being announced?
(A) An art exhibition
(B) A community fair
(C) An art class
(D) A painting action

正在宣告什麼？
(A) 藝術展
(B) 社區展覽會
(C) 藝術課程
(D) 行動繪畫

**88** What does the speaker imply when she says, "This is to avoid interruptions"?
(A) The listeners should register for the event.
(B) The listeners should be punctual for the event.
(C) The listeners should wait in a line.
(D) The listeners should hold their questions for a while.

說話的人說：「這是為了避免干擾到課程進行」時，意思為何？
(A) 聽眾須登記參加活動。
(B) 聽眾準時參加活動。
(C) 聽眾須排隊等候。
(D) 聽眾須稍後再提問。

**Questions 89-91 refer to the following advertisement.**
(澳M)

**❽❾** Fresh Groceries is having a big sale on all products for a week from today.
**❾⓿** Buy a 20-pound bag of tomatoes for $2. The regular price is $3. Save one dollar on every pound of carrots, onions, and ginger that you purchase. You can also buy fresh blueberries for only 50 cents per pound, which is 50 cents off the regular price.
**❾❶** Fresh Groceries' produce is grown locally. That means they travel very little from the farm to your table. So, all our fruits and vegetables are super fresh. That's our trick of the trade. Come and try some samples. You'll realize why Fresh Groceries produce is the best.

**廣告**

　　新鮮雜貨店今天將展開各種農產品的大拍賣，為期一個星期。20磅的番茄，平常要價3美元，只要2美元就能買到。胡蘿蔔、洋蔥和生薑，每買1磅您就能省下1美元。您還可以用每磅50分的價格購買新鮮藍莓，比平常省50分。新鮮雜貨店只賣在地農產品，這代表從產地到餐桌的路程很短，所以我們的蔬菜水果全都超級新鮮，這是我們的生意之道。請您過來試吃，就會了解到為什麼新鮮雜貨店的農產品最棒。

**字彙** produce 農產　trick 花招；竅門
trade 商業　publicize 宣傳
organic 有機的

**89** What is the purpose of the advertisement?
(A) To publicize a grand opening
(B) To advertise job openings
(C) To inform the customers of the origin of the produce
(D) To promote a sale

這則廣告的目的為何？
(A) 宣傳盛大開幕活動
(B) 宣傳職缺
(C) 告知顧客農產品的產地
(D) 宣傳拍賣活動

**90** What is Fresh Groceries mainly selling?
(A) Meat
(B) Dairy products
(C) Bakery
(D) Fruits and vegetables

新鮮雜貨店主要賣什麼？
(A) 肉
(B) 乳製品
(C) 西點麵包
(D) 蔬菜水果

**91** What does the speaker mean when he says, "That's our trick of the trade"?
(A) Their products are cheap.
(B) Their products are grown locally.
(C) They import products.
(D) The products are all organic.

說話者說：「這是我們的生意之道」，意思為何？
(A) 他們的產品很便宜。
(B) 他們的產品是在地種植的。
(C) 他們進口產品。
(D) 產品全都是有機的。

**Questions 92-94 refer to the following talk and receiving log.** 美M

| Received | Vendor | Item | Quantity |
|---|---|---|---|
| 12/14 | Ralph | Blazer | 25 |
| 12/15 | Dash | Sweater | 30 |
| 12/16 | Custom | 93 Trousers | 40 |
| 12/17 | Hiller | Accessory | 120 |

92 93 Okay, everyone, we just received the shipment of pants we were expecting. What I need you to do is to bring the boxes to the front area of the store. When you remove the pants from the boxes, be careful not to remove the price tags that are attached to them. After unpacking, you will have to fold the pants and arrange them in the displays that I have set up between the shirts and the sweaters. They need to be organized by size and color. Large go on the right, medium in the middle, and small on the left. 93 I'll be in my office adding the new shipment to the inventory. 94 When I come back, I'll check the displays. Alright?

---

談話與取貨記錄簿

| 取貨時間 | 廠商 | 物品 | 數量 |
|---|---|---|---|
| 12/14 | 雷夫 | 西裝外套 | 25 |
| 12/15 | 達許 | 毛衣 | 30 |
| 12/16 | 訂製 | 長褲 | 40 |
| 12/17 | 希勒 | 配件 | 120 |

好的，大家，我們剛剛總算等到褲子到貨了。我需要你們做的是把盒子搬到店內前方的空間來，從盒子中拿出褲子時，請注意不要拿掉它附的價格標籤。打開包裝盒後，請把褲子摺好，並放在襯衫和毛衣之間、我裝好的展示架上。褲子照尺寸和顏色整理，尺寸大的在右邊、中的在中間、小的在左邊。我會在辦公室內把新貨加到庫存單上，等我回來就會檢查展示狀況，沒問題吧？

字彙 **shipment** 運輸的貨物；運輸；裝運
**inventory** 庫存單；存貨單
**alter** 改變

**92** What most likely is the speaker's job?
(A) Clothing designer
(B) Store manager
(C) Delivery person
(D) Inspector

說話的人的職業最有可能為何？
(A) 服裝設計師
(B) 店鋪經理
(C) 送貨員
(D) 督察員

**93** Look at the graphic. What quantity will the speaker add to the inventory?
(A) 25
(B) 30
(C) 40
(D) 120

請看圖表，說話的人將加到庫存單的數量為何？
(A) 25
(B) 30
(C) 40
(D) 120

**94** What does the speaker say he will do when he returns?
(A) Change the price tags
(B) Send back arrivals
(C) Inspect the displays
(D) Alter some pants

說話的人說他回來時將做什麼？
(A) 換價格標籤
(B) 退貨
(C) 檢查陳列情形
(D) 修改幾件褲子

**Questions 95-97 refer to the following talk and map.**

英W

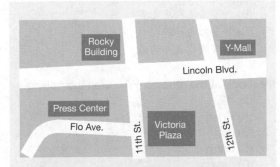

Tom & Stephany is reopening after two months of renovations. We are now proud to serve you in a gorgeously remodeled space. Come and check out our updated store and jewelry selection. To celebrate the reopening, ⑨⑤ **all visitors can enter a drawing to win a gift card valued at $200.** You will find the finest rings, watches, necklaces, and earrings in our renovated showroom. ⑨⑥ **Our jewelry is all of the finest quality and made by top designers.** If you are thinking of buying a magical gift for one of your loved ones, visit Tom & Stephany today. ⑨⑦ **We are located on the corner of Lincoln Boulevard and 12th Street.**

**談話與地圖**

「湯姆與史蒂芬妮」經過兩個月整修將重新開幕，我們現在很榮幸能在裝潢華麗的空間為您服務，歡迎來參觀整修後的店面和精選珠寶。為了慶祝重新開幕，到店的所有人均可參加 200 美元禮品卡的抽獎。您在我們翻修後的展示廳中可找到最精緻的戒指、手錶、項鍊和耳環。我們的珠寶都是最高品質、且由頂尖設計師製作。如果您想向所愛之人送上魔幻大禮，今天就來湯姆與史蒂芬妮。我們位於林肯大道和 12 街的路口。

字彙 gorgeously 華麗地；輝煌地
**selection** 精選品　**value** 價值
**fine** 精緻的；極好的
**complimentary** 贈送的
**drawing** 抽獎　**voucher** 禮券

🎧20

**95** What will visitors receive?
(A) A complimentary gift
(B) A voucher for a meal
(C) A discount coupon
(D) A gift certificate

到店的人可以獲得什麼？
(A) 贈品
(B) 餐券
(C) 折價券
(D) 禮券

**96** What does the speaker mention about Tom & Stephany's products?
(A) They are shipped at no charge.
(B) They are custom made.
(C) They are popular.
(D) They are made by top designers.

關於湯姆與史蒂芬妮的產品，說話的人提到什麼？
(A) 寄送免運費。
(B) 為客製商品。
(C) 很受歡迎。
(D) 由頂尖設計師製作。

**97** Look at the graphic. Where is Tom & Stephany most likely located?
(A) At the Press Center
(B) At Y-Mall
(C) At Victoria Plaza
(D) At the Rocky Building

請看圖表，湯姆與史蒂芬妮最可能位於哪裡？
(A) 新聞中心
(B) Y 賣場
(C) 維多利亞廣場
(D) 岩石大樓

## Questions 98-100 refer to the following report and table. 澳M

| Winner | Trumpet Shell Weight (Pound) |
|--------|------------------------------|
| Brian  | 5   |
| Jim    | 4.5 |
| John   | 3   |
| Jason  | 4   |

**98** To mark the opening of trumpet shell season, many divers participate in the trumpet shell contest. This annual contest was founded in 1970. This year, about 400 divers competed. Surprisingly enough, a 5-pound trumpet shell was caught. Brian was the diver who caught the giant trumpet shell. Jim placed second with a 4.5 pounder. **99** A 13-year-old boy caught a 3 pounder and won a special prize. What happened to these massive trumpet shells? They were served as the main course at the divers' family dinners. **100** I'll be back with more local news after this commercial break.

報導與表格

| 優勝者 | 海螺重量（磅） |
|--------|----------------|
| 布萊恩 | 5   |
| 吉姆   | 4.5 |
| 約翰   | 3   |
| 強生   | 4   |

為慶祝海螺產季開始，不少潛水者前來參加海螺比賽。這場年度賽事創立於 1970 年。今年大約有 400 名潛水者參賽。令人驚訝的是，有人抓到五磅的海螺。布萊恩是抓到最大隻海螺的潛水者。吉姆以 4.5 磅居次。一名 13 歲的男孩抓到了 3 磅重的螺贏得特別獎。這些巨大的海螺會發生什麼事呢？它們會成為潛水者家庭晚餐的主菜。廣告時間過後，我將帶來更多的當地新聞。

字彙 mark 慶祝；紀念　found 創立
contest 比賽
pounder （重量）……磅的東西
trumpet shell 海螺
revitalize 使復興；使再次活絡

**98** According to the speaker, what is the purpose of the event?
(A) To raise trumpet shells
(B) To revitalize local business
(C) To honor a person
(D) To celebrate the opening of a season

根據說話的人所述，活動的目的為何？
(A) 為了捕撈海螺
(B) 為了活絡在地產業
(C) 為了紀念一個人
(D) 為了慶祝產季開始

**99** Look at the graphic. Who won the special prize?
(A) Brian
(B) Jim
(C) John
(D) Jason

請看圖表，誰得到了特別獎？
(A) 布萊恩
(B) 吉姆
(C) 約翰
(D) 強生

**100** What will listeners probably hear next?
(A) Music
(B) Local news
(C) Advertisements
(D) A traffic report

聽眾接下來可能會聽到什麼？
(A) 音樂
(B) 地方新聞
(C) 廣告
(D) 路況報導

**101**

委員們將在心巷大廳召開股東會。

(A) convene 召開
(B) implement 實施
(C) nominate 提名
(D) initiate 開始

解析 空格後方沒有連接受詞，因此要填入不及物動詞。(A) convene（聚集）是選項中唯一的不及物動詞，故為正確答案。implement（執行）、nominate（提名）、initiate（開始）皆為及物動詞，因此並非答案。

字彙 committee 委員會　shareholder 股東

**102**

員工被要求更新他們的工時。

(A) theirs 他們的東西
(B) their 他們的
(C) them 他們
(D) they 他們

解析 名詞前方要填入代名詞的所有格，因此答案為 (B)。theirs 為所有代名詞，不能放在名詞前方；them 要置於受詞的位置；they 則要置於主詞的位置。

另外補充一點，〈be 動詞＋ p.p.〉後方連接 to 不定詞屬於「主詞＋動詞＋受詞＋受詞補語」的句型結構，適用該句型的動詞有 be requested、be required、be asked、be advised、be reminded、be encouraged、be expected、be told、be urged、be forced、be intended 等。

字彙 update 更新；為……補充最新資訊

**103**

帕姆‧艾斯禮先生簡要說明了這間公司的雙月預算報告。

(A) brief 簡報；作……的提要
(B) briefly 簡要地
(C) briefness 簡單；（時間）短促
(D) briefing 簡報；作戰指示

解析 空格置於應相連在一起的動詞片語之間，要填入副詞，因此答案為 (B) briefly。

字彙 bimonthly 兩月一次；一個月兩次

**104**

所有遺留在休息室的個人物品都會保留 30 天才丟棄。

(A) left 被遺留
(B) leave 離開
(C) leaving 正在離開
(D) leaves 離開

解析 句中已經有一個主要動詞 are kept，因此空格不能再填入動詞，請先刪去 (B) 和 (D)。空格用來修飾前方的名詞（items），要填入形容詞片語。(A) 和 (C) 為分詞，皆可扮演形容詞的角色。而空格後方並未連接受詞，因此答案要選 (A) left。

字彙 discard 丟棄

**105**

喬伊斯電器因應傳出缺陷零件的消息，召回了今年度的微波爐系列產品。

(A) response 回應；反應
(B) responsibility 責任
(C) responsible 有責任的
(D) responsive 反應積極的；反應敏捷的

解析 空格位在介系詞 in 的受詞位置，因此答案為名詞 (A) response。另外，建議一併熟記 in response to（對……回答、反應），將有助於作答。

字彙 recall 召回　component 零件

**106**

所有人員操作電力設備時都應戴安全帽。

(A) are operated 被操作
(B) operates 操作
(C) to operate 操作
(D) operate 操作

解析 主詞為 All workers，動詞為 must wear，「who . . . equipment」為形容詞子句，用來修飾前方的名詞 workers，因此空格為子句中的動詞。空格後方連接受詞（electrical equipment），根據題意，表達「操作電子設備的工人」較為適當，因此答案要選 (D)，表示主動。

字彙 electrical equipment 電力設備　hard hat（工地用的）安全帽

**107**

在莎頂管理顧問公司，我們盡量簡潔地向客戶解釋我們的意見。

(A) believe 相信
(B) insert 插入
(C) decide 決定
(D) explain 解釋；說明

解析 本題考的是動詞詞彙。根據題意，表達「簡潔地說明」最為適當，因此答案為 (D)。

字彙 management consultant 管理顧問
concisely 簡潔地

**108**

這棟建築的結構被保存了下來，但內部已徹底改建。

(A) preserving 正在保護
(B) preserved 保存了
(C) had been preserving 正在保存
(D) has been preserved 已被保存

解析 but 前方的子句中需要一個動詞，選項中的 preserving 並非動詞，因此請優先刪去該選項。接著再從其他選項中，根據單複數、主被動語態和時態選出適當的動詞。空格後方沒有受詞，應填入被動語態，因此答案為 (D) has been preserved。

字彙 structure 結構

**109**

報告一開始好像有些資訊遺失，但很快就找到了。

(A) little 少的
(B) few of 一些
(C) few 很少；幾乎沒有
(D) little of 一些；幾個

解析 冠詞 the 前方不能填入形容詞，因此請先刪去 little 和 few；A few of 後方要連接複數可數名詞，因此也不適合填入。(D) little of 後方可以連接不可數名詞（information），故為正確答案。

**110**

哈勒克工業目前正在設法提高空調設備的產能。

(A) produce 製造
(B) production 製造
(C) productive 多產的；有成效的
(D) productively 多產地；有成效地

解析 空格置於 to 不定詞（to manufacture）的中間，應填入副詞，修飾原形動詞，因此答案為 (D)。另外補充一點，more 後方可以連接名詞、形容詞、或副詞，千萬不能只靠 more 來解題，請特別留意。

字彙 explore 探索；探究

**111**

為了利用較低的利率，現在有越來越多的屋主為抵押貸款再融資。

(A) number 數量
(B) amount 數量
(C) type 種類
(D) supply 供應品

解析 建議背下 An increasing number of（越來越多的……），有助於作答，因此答案為 (A)。另外補充一點，A(n) (increasing) number of 後方只能連接複數可數名詞，請特別熟記。

字彙 refinance 再融資
mortgage 抵押；抵押借款
interest rate 利率

**112**

科崔軟體公布了一款音樂播放器，它可以容納任何類型的聲音檔。

(A) dispose 配置；布置
(B) contain 包含
(C) reconcile 調停；調解
(D) accommodate 容納；為……提供空間

解析 dispose（丟棄、處理）當作不及物動詞使用時，要搭配介系詞 of 一起使用；contain（包含）和 reconcile（調解）不適合搭配受詞 sound file 使用。(D) accommodate 的意思為「容納」，最符合題意，故為正確答案。

字彙 unveil 揭曉；使公諸於眾

**113**

除非董事會今天做出結論，否則投票將需延到下個月的會議舉行。

(A) Whereas 鑑於；反之
(B) If 如果
(C) Unless 除非
(D) Even 甚至

解析 空格要填入從屬連接詞，(D) Even 為副詞，因此並非答案。根據題意，表達「除非得出結論，否則將會延期」最為適當，因此答案為 (C) Unless。

字彙 postpone 延遲

**114**

預測人員預期，蘭斯鎮在未來三年公共支出將會增加。

(A) between 在……之間
(B) upon 在……上
(C) against 反對；與…相反
(D) over 在……期間

解析 本題要選出適當的介系詞。只有 (D) 可以搭配後方的一段時間（three years）一起使用。另外補充一點，介系詞 for、during、over、through、within、in、throughout 皆能放在一段時間的前方使用。

字彙 forecaster 預測人員
anticipate 預期；期望
public spending 公共支出

**115**

動物園的主管們預測，稀有白虎出生後遊客的數量會增加。

(A) insert 插入物
(B) effort 努力
(C) increase 增加
(D) array （軍隊等）列陣

解析 本題考的是名詞詞彙。根據題意，表達「預估來客數增加」最為適當，因此答案為 (C)。increase、decrease、rise、fall、drop 等表示增加或減少的名詞，後方會搭配介系詞 in 一起使用，因此便能由空格後方的 in 選出答案。

字彙 cub（獅、熊、狼等的）幼崽，幼獸
insert 插入物
array（軍隊等）列陣；（排列整齊的）一批

**116**

格蘭瑟姆彩妝在時尚雜誌登廣告，但熟悉它系列產品的消費者不多。

(A) whose ……的
(B) what 什麼
(C) which 那一個；那一些
(D) who ……的人

解析 空格至 magazines 為形容詞子句，用來修飾前方的名詞，因此答案可能是 which, whose 或 who。(A) 為關係代名詞所有格，可以與空格後方的名詞（advertisement）結合，作為形容詞子句的主詞。who 為關係代名詞主格，後方要連接動詞開頭的子句才行；which 為關係代名詞主格或受格，後方要連接沒有主詞或受詞的子句。

字彙 be familiar with 熟悉；精通
product line 系列產品
manufacture（大量）製造，加工
cosmetic 化妝品
glossy magazine（通常指內容為名人、時尚或美容的）高級亮光紙印刷的雜誌

**117**

價格金融服務的劉先生將使用第一會議室彙整公司的年度報告。

(A) compiles 彙編
(B) responds 作答；回答
(C) proceeds 繼續進行
(D) realizes 領悟；了解

解析 本題考的是動詞詞彙。根據題意，表達「在他彙整公司年度報告的期間」最為適當，因此答案為 (A)。

字彙 financial service 金融服務　annual report 年報
compile 彙編；編輯
respond 作答；回答
proceed 繼續進行

**118**

「健體人生」促銷的 DVD 標榜各種有益健康的各種運動，特別著重上半身的肌力。

(A) emphasize 強調
(B) emphasized 被強調的
(C) emphasis 重視；強調
(D) emphasizes 強調

209

**解析** 空格位在冠詞（an）的後方，且空格後方並未連接名詞，因此空格應填入名詞，答案為 (C)。另外補充一點，feature 當作名詞使用時，意思為「特色」；當作動詞使用時，意思則為「以……為特色」，請特別熟記。

**字彙** feature 以……為特色
upper body 上半身　strength 力氣

**119**

哈里斯超市堅持更好的顧客服務，目標是吸引更多人到店裡購物。
(A) inquiry 詢問；調查
(B) structure 結構
(C) objective 目標
(D) transfer 轉移；調動

**解析** 本題考的是名詞詞彙。空格後方內容為超市的「目的」，因此最符合題意的選項為 (C)。

**字彙** inquiry 詢問；調查　objective 目標
transfer 轉移；調動

**120**

桑托斯鎮因野火燒往尼瑟曼瀑布，已進行疏散。
(A) provided that 如果；只要
(B) owing to 因為；由於
(C) instead of 作為…的替代
(D) even if 即使

**解析**「The town . . . evacuated」為一個結構完整的句子，因此空格至 towards Netherman Falls 具有修飾的作用。而空格後方連接名詞（a bush fire），因此空格應填入介系詞，搭配該名詞一起扮演修飾的角色。owing to（因為）和 instead of（代替）皆為介系詞，使用表示原因的介系詞較符合題意，因此答案為 (B)。

provided that（倘若）和 even if（即使）為從屬連接詞，後方要連接子句才行，因此並非答案。另外補充一點，表示原因的介系詞有 because of、due to、owing to、on account of、thanks to，請一併熟記。

**字彙** evacuate 撤離；疏散
bush fire （灌木林的）野火
head（向特定方向）出發

**121**

勇勝電機除了廚房家電的銷售小幅下滑外，其他產業均大幅成長。
(A) Aside from 除……外
(B) Compared to 和……相比
(C) Although 雖然
(D) For instance 舉例來說

**解析** 空格後方為名詞片語加上修飾語，因此空格應填入介系詞。選項中的介系詞有 Aside from（除此之外）和 Compared to（比較），需從中選出符合題意的選項。根據題意，表達「除了單一品項的銷售量減少之外，整體而言為上升」因此答案為 (A) Aside from。另外，Although 為從屬連接詞；For instance 為副詞。

**字彙** minor 輕微的　surge 激增；劇烈上升

**122**

和工會的討論開始後，福斯通工業同意提高工資並減少全體員工的工時。
(A) permitted 允許
(B) included 包含
(C) consented 同意
(D) complied 彙整

**解析** 動詞 permitted 要先連接受詞後，才能連接 to 不定詞，當作受詞補語，因此並非答案；included 不符合題意；complied（遵守）為不及物動詞，後方要搭配介系詞 with 一起使用，因此並不適當。綜合前述，答案要選 (C) consented（同意）。

**字彙** labor union 工會

**123**

購買第三代光榮咖啡機的顧客被鼓勵填寫並寄回顧客調查表。
(A) circulated 被散布
(B) encouraged 被鼓勵
(C) conducted 被進行；被處理
(D) considered 被認為

**解析** 請熟記 be encouraged to 不定詞（鼓勵、慫恿……）的用法。句子的主詞為人（Customers），因此空格填入 circulated（循環）或 conducted（實施）皆不適當。considered（視為）適用「主詞＋動詞＋受詞＋受詞補語」的句型結構，若使用被動語態，後方要保留名詞或形容詞才行，因此並非答案。綜合前述，答案要選 (B) encouraged。

**字彙** edition 版本

**124**

氣象預報員預測未來接連五天將是晴天，應有助緩解近來空前的雨勢。

(A) refreshed 精神振作的
(B) atmospheric 富有情調的
(C) deliberate 蓄意的
(D) consecutive 連續的

**解析** 本題考的是形容詞詞彙。根據題意，表達「連續五天的晴天」最為適當，因此答案為 (D)。

**字彙** weather forecaster 氣象預報員
reprieve 暫時緩解
unprecedented 史無前例的，空前的
rainfall 降雨　refreshed 精神振作的
atmospheric 富有情調的
deliberate 蓄意的
consecutive 連續的；無間斷的

**125**

年度盛事格拉斯頓柏立音樂節再兩週就要開始了，主辦方尚未決定主力演出為何。

(A) yet 至今尚未
(B) not 沒有
(C) finally 終於
(D) already 已經

**解析** have 和 to 不定詞之間加上 yet，可以表示「尚未去……」。請務必熟記 have yet to do 的用法，意思為「尚未去做……」，因此答案為 (A)。

**字彙** organizer 主辦單位　act 演出
headline（在娛樂活動中）扮演主角，充當主角

**126**

當地的石油業者佩德羅公司，計劃開始生產新一系列的石油產品。

(A) production 生產；製造
(B) producing 生產；出產
(C) product 產品
(D) productivity 生產力；產能

**解析** 空格要填入及物動詞 start 的受詞，producing 並非名詞，因此不適合填入。product 的意思為「產品」，為可數名詞，不能單獨使用。因為是新開始的東西，比起「產能」（productivity），填入「生產」（production）更為適當，因此答案為 (A)。

**字彙** corporation 公司
plan to 計劃做……

**127**

魯斯·海斯克爾出任執行長，將鞏固馬貝克公司在埃及製藥業界的領先地位。

(A) incline （使）傾向於
(B) accomplish 完成；實現
(C) administer 管理；治理
(D) solidify （使）穩固；鞏固

**解析** 本題考的是動詞詞彙。根據題意，表達「將鞏固其地位、成為埃及具領導地位的製藥機構之一」最為適當，因此答案為 (D)。

**字彙** appointment 任命
leading 主要的；頂級的
pharmaceutical 製藥的
institution 機構
incline （使）傾向於
accomplish 完成；實現
administer 管理；治理
solidify （使）穩固；鞏固

**128**

坎特羅斯公司自從採用奇文製法後，產品缺陷便減少了。

(A) That 那個
(B) Because 因為
(C) For 因為
(D) Since 自從

**解析** That 和 Because 為連接詞，後方要連接子句（主詞＋動詞），因此不適合填入；For 為介系詞，雖然後方可以連接動名詞，但是它的意思是「為了」，並不符合題意；(D) Since 為從屬連接詞，可以用來引導分詞構句（adopting . . .），故為正確答案。

另外，請特別熟記當主要子句為現在完成式（has experienced）時，最適合搭配使用的從屬連接詞為 Since。

**字彙** adopt 採用　defect 缺陷

**129**

修訂後的退換貨條款將於 6 月 1 日生效，但不適用於 5 月 15 日前購買的顧客。
(A) effect 效力
(B) effective 有效的
(C) effectively 有效地
(D) effectiveness 有效性

**解析** 空格位在介系詞 into 的受詞位置，因此應填入名詞，答案要選 (A) effect。另外，go into effect 的意思為「開始生效、實施」。

**字彙** be exempt from 免於；被排除於

**130**

優強建設在世界各地建造節能住宅，因此需要技術熟練、經驗豐富的工人。
(A) because 因為
(B) therefore 因此
(C) however 然而
(D) rather 有點

**解析** 該句話的主詞為 Ucham Construction，同時以連接詞 and 連接兩個動詞 builds 和 requires，屬於一個結構完整的句子，因此空格應填入副詞。除了 (A) 之外，其餘選項皆有可能是答案。根據題意，空格前方內容為空格後方內容的根據，因此填入 (B) 較為適當。

**字彙** energy efficient 節能的
residential 住宅的　structure 建築物
worldwide 在世界各地

**131-134 文章**

5 月 1 日——英特靈和皇勝兩家信用合作社昨天宣布了它們的合併計畫。新公司名為勝利信用合作社。它將是當地最大的金融公司，擁有 12 萬名會員和逾 50 億美元的資產。

兩家信用合作社的董事會數個月前召開會議考慮合併，於上週無異議投票通過合併案，詳情昨天才首度對外公開。

新的合資公司需數週時間組成。該期間內，建議會員繼續使用各別公司所提供的服務。不過，會員也能使用其新合作夥伴的服務。

**字彙** unveil 使公諸於眾；揭露
merge 合併　entity 實體；企業；公司
convene 召開，召集（會議）
credit union 信用合作社
unanimously 無異議地
joint entity 合資公司；合資企業
respective 各自的；分別的
be compliant with 遵守
federal 聯邦的

**131**

(A) its 它的
(B) our 我們的
(C) their 它們的
(D) his 他的

**解析** 四個選項皆為所有格，都能用來修飾名詞。空格應用來代替 Interling Credit Union 和 Royalwin Credit Union 兩間公司，表示「他們的」計畫，因此答案為 (C) their。

**132**

(A) finance 金融
(B) financed 受資助的
(C) financial 金融的
(D) financially 金融上

**解析** 空格用來修飾名詞，應填入形容詞，而選項中的形容詞有 financed（受到融資的）和 financial（金融的）。文中並未提到新公司受到融資，因此答案要選 (C) financial。

**133**

(A) 詳情昨天才首度對外公開。
(B) 官方紀錄顯示該企業完全遵守聯邦法規。
(C) 銀行業是門快速發展的行業。
(D) 特定對象得成為會員。

解析 此段落的內容為兩家公司合併一事。空格前方提到已進行匿名投票，因此空格填入「昨天首次公開細節」最符合文意，答案為 (A)。

**134**

(A) distinction 區別
(B) assessment 評估
(C) estimate 估計
(D) formation 組成；成形

解析 本題要選出符合文意的名詞。(D) formation 的意思為「組成、構成」，適合表示成為新的合營公司的狀況，故為正確答案。

### 135-138 電子郵件

收件者：sanrao@kignet.com
寄件者：accounts@osn.com
日期：11 月 15 日
主旨：您的電話帳單
────────────────────────
敬愛的拉奧女士：

您現在已能上網查詢您 ONS 門號結尾為 5110 的電話帳單，應付總額為美金 25.80 元。

目前無需任何動作，您已申辦我們的自動扣繳服務。因此，您的信用卡將於 11 月 25 日扣繳當期額度的款項。

如欲查看帳單，請登入您於 www. osntelecom.net 的帳戶。您也可下載或列印當期或前期帳單。

帳單內可能有您帳戶重大變更的資訊。因此，我們建議您每個月徹底檢查您的帳單。

誠摯地，
會員服務部

字彙 autopay 自動付款；自動扣繳
balance 額度；欠款　thoroughly 徹底地

**135**

(A) obtained 獲得的
(B) due 應付款的
(C) kept 保有的
(D) returned 退還的

解析 由下一段內容可以得知顧客尚未付款，因此應該先告知對方「應支付的」（due）總額較為適當，答案為 (B)。

**136**

(A) In fact 事實上
(B) Otherwise 否則
(C) Hence 因此
(D) However 然而

解析 本題要選出適當的連接副詞，連接前後兩句話。前句話提到對方已申請自動繳費方案，後句話則表示將從信用卡扣款，由此可以看出兩句話為因果關係，因此答案為 (C) Hence（因此）。

**137**

(A) Check 查看
(B) To check 查看
(C) Checking 正在查看
(D) Having checked 已查看

解析 空格用來修飾主要子句，應填入副詞。雖然分詞構句和 to 不定詞皆可扮演副詞的角色，但是 to 不定詞的意思為「為了……」更符合文意，因此答案為 (B)。

**138**

(A) 此信附件為特別提供給忠實用戶的折價券。
(B) 感謝您和 OSN 電信有商業往來。
(C) 帳單內可能有您帳戶重大變更的資訊。
(D) 逾期繳款將收取額外費用。

解析 空格後方建議對方仔細確認帳單，因此空格表示「當中包含重要的變更事項」較為適當，答案為 (C)。

## 139-142 電子郵件

收件者：harvey@koln.com
寄件者：kyra@koln.com
主旨：面試
日期：9 月 2 日
附件：contact_list.doc

敬愛的哈維：

您可能還記得，我工作的招聘委員會計劃在未來幾週面試幾名應徵者。我想請您聯繫每一位應徵者，並安排他們個別面試。隨信附上有其姓名及聯絡資訊的檔案。其中也列出他們偏好的面試日期和時間。請您安排好面試時立即向我回報。

感謝您處理這件要事。如果您有進一步的疑問，儘管告訴我。我到明天以前都不在鎮上，但我會查看我的電子郵件和簡訊。

祝好，
凱拉

**字彙** candidate 應徵者　following 接著的
preferred 偏好的；優先的
patronage 贊助；惠顧

### 139
(A) employees 員工
(B) acquaintances 認識的人
(C) applicants 應徵者
(D) residents 住戶

**解析** 第一句話提到打算面試求職者，接著請對方聯絡「申請者們」最符合文意，因答案為 (C) applicants。

### 140
(A) lists 列有
(B) would have listed 應列有
(C) will list 將列有
(D) listed 列有了

**解析** 本題要選出適當的動詞時態。表達清單上的內容要用現在簡單式，因此答案為 (A) lists。另外，〈would have p.p.〉用於與過去事實相反的假設語氣。

### 141
(A) 我們可以明天見面討論細節。
(B) 感謝您的經常惠顧。
(C) 您只需要訓練新進員工。
(D) 感謝您處理這件要事。

**解析** 前方請對方敲定面試時間，(D) 針對對方處理重要的計畫表達感謝，故為正確答案。

### 142
(A) whereas 反之
(B) although 雖然
(C) but 但
(D) unless 除非

**解析** 四個選項皆為連接詞，因此要選出最符合文意的選項。空格前方提到明天不會進公司，後方則表示會確認電子郵件和簡訊，最適合連接這兩句話的連接詞為 (C) but。

## 143-146 備忘錄

公告人：楊・格雷迪
致：包裝部門
日期：12 月 2 日

我們部門規畫團隊的一個目標是於明年度削減成本。我們確定了可能減少成本的三個方向：人力、材料和流程。我們已有效分配員工工時，因此將聚焦另外兩個方面。材料方面，我們部門將啟用較為便宜的新盒子。有關這類以及其他新包裝材料的詳細資訊很快就會確定。至於流程方面，我們仍在評估現有的包裝流程，以找出潛在的效率問題，一旦發現便會做出調整。我們應讓員工熟悉新流程。如果您對這些變動有任何疑問，請向您的主管反映。

**字彙** objective 目標　identify 確定；發現
potential 潛在的；可能的
cost-cutting 減少成本的
evaluate 評估
ineffectiveness 低效率的問題
familiarize 使……熟悉　forward 轉達
allocate 分配　cutting-edge 最先進的

**143**
(A) evaluate 評估
(B) promote 推廣
(C) curtail 削減
(D) calculate 計算

解析 下句話提到已確認刪減成本（cost-cutting）的部分，表示目標為「縮減」（curtail）費用，因此答案為 (C)。

**144**
(A) 鼓勵新進員工參加訓練課程。
(B) 我們已有效分配員工工時。
(C) 接下來幾週將安裝最先進的設備。
(D) 我們的成功歸功於你們的貢獻。

解析 空格前方提到要在人力、材料和流程三方面上縮減費用，而空格後方提及材料和流程的部分，因此答案要選 (B)，為針對人力的內容。

**145**
(A) regards 問候
(B) regarded 被認為
(C) regarding 關於；至於
(D) to regard 注重

解析 空格連接名詞，應填入介系詞，組合成修飾語。選項中只有 (C) regarding（關於）為介系詞。另外補充一點，介系詞 concerning、pertaining to、about、as to、as for 皆屬於同義詞，建議一併熟記。

**146**
(A) promotions 促銷
(B) transactions 交易
(C) installments 分期付款
(D) adjustments 調整

解析 本文大致上是在探討部門為刪減成本所做的「改變」，因此一旦發現無效率的程序，便會進行「調整」（adjustment），答案為 (D)。

---

**147-148 廣告**

> **卡倫海產**
> 海洋大道 235 號
> 星期一至星期六：早上 8 點—晚上 7 點
> 星期日：早上 10 點—下午 5 點
> 339-555-4481
>
> 當地最好的新鮮海產批發商，產品包括：
> 魷魚、鮮魚和貝類
> 鱈魚和黑線鱈
> 比目魚和鰻魚
>
> 每週特價！以七五折購買牡蠣、淡菜、螃蟹和龍蝦，折扣到 2 月 2 日結束。

字彙 wholesaler 批發商　squid 魷魚
shellfish 貝類　cod 鱈魚
haddock 黑線鱈　halibut 比目魚
eel 鰻魚　oyster 牡蠣　mussel 淡菜
crab 螃蟹　lobster 龍蝦　frozen 冷凍的
overseas 海外的　specialize in 專門（於）
exotic 外來的；異國情調的

**147** 關於卡倫海產，文中提到什麼？
(A) 販賣冷凍食品。
(B) 每天都營業。
(C) 接受海外訂單。
(D) 專賣外來魚類。

**148** 根據廣告，什麼東西有折扣？
(A) 白肉魚
(B) 划船用品
(C) 深海魚
(D) 貝類及甲殼類

## 149-150 收據

**歡迎來到路易的汽車服務與維修**

營業時間：週一至週六
上午 8:30 至下午 5:00

客戶：艾力克斯·張
訂單號碼：20201187
10 月 8 日，星期三，上午 8:37

| 項目 | 服務 | 收送日期／時間 | 支出 |
|---|---|---|---|
| 廂型車 | 輪胎定位 | 10 月 8 日，星期三，下午 4 點 | 8 美元 |
| 掀背車 | 車內清潔 | 10 月 10 日，星期五，下午 6 點 | 20 美元 |
| 打檔車 | 服務 | 10 月 13 日，星期一，上午 10 點 | 30 美元 |
| 機車 | 服務 | 10 月 13 日，星期一，上午 10 點 | 30 美元 |

總支出：88 美元
已付款項：88 美元
應付餘額：0 美元

感謝您選擇路易
我們有星期一車內清潔服務可供洽詢

字彙 wheel alignment 輪胎定位
hatchback 掀背車
balance due 應付餘額
same-day service 當日服務
invoice 提供費用清單　bill 給……開立帳單

**149** 張女士為了哪一台車使用了當日服務？
(A) 打檔車
(B) 掀背車
(C) 機車
(D) 廂型車

**150** 關於張女士使用的服務，收據中指出了什麼？
(A) 將提供費用清單。
(B) 已在 10 月 10 日開立帳單。
(C) 已支付全額。
(D) 其中有幾台廂型車。

## 151-153 圖表

http://www.appliancereviewer.com

**不到 200 美元的微波爐**

| 型號 | 詳細資料 | 專家評論 |
|---|---|---|
| Access T-L | 重量：3 公斤<br>烤箱功能：有<br>建議零售價格：199 美元 | 只有不鏽鋼製<br>解凍很快 |
| Vista 4 | 重量：3 公斤<br>烤箱功能：無<br>建議零售價格：49 美元 | 簡單易操作的控制面板<br>替換零件很貴 |
| Caterham Special | 重量：5 公斤<br>烤箱功能：無<br>建議零售價格：99 美元 | 馬達有十年保固<br>烘烤設備很強 |
| Plasma 700 | 重量：6 公斤<br>烤箱功能：有<br>建議零售價格：99 美元 | 很笨重<br>高效率節能 |

字彙 microwave 微波　appliance 家用電器
weight 重量　retail price 零售價格
defrost 解凍
easy-to-use 易使用的；易操作的
replacement 替換　part 零件
guarantee 保固　roast 烘烤
facility 設備　cumbersome 笨重的
energy-efficiency 節能效率　rating 等級
component 零件　warranty 保固單
capacity 能力；容量

**151** 為何有些人會參考這張圖表？
(A) 以得知價格在特定範圍內的微波爐
(B) 以尋找每台微波爐的零件
(C) 以查出一家店每週賣出幾台微波爐
(D) 以比較微波爐的節能效率

**152** 提及了機型 Access T-L 的哪個優點？
(A) 有多種顏色可供選擇。
(B) 能迅速解凍食品。
(C) 有十年保固。
(D) 使用能源有效率。

**153** 機型 Caterham Special 和 Plasma 700 哪裡相似？
(A) 價格一樣。
(B) 都有烤箱功能。
(C) 重量相同。
(D) 都有負評。

## 154- 155 訊息串

**佛瑞德 · 蒙達雷 [下午 1:14]：** 花，十月的機器人會議，妳幫我們登記好了嗎？

**阮氏花 [下午 1:15]：** 我上網填好申請表了，既然你提到了，我想我並沒有收到回覆確認。

**佛瑞德 · 蒙達雷 [下午 1:18]：** 妳能確認一下嗎？

**阮氏花 [下午 1:25]：** 當然。

**阮氏花 [下午 1:26]：** 我剛打過電話，他們的清單上沒有我們。他們伺服器出了問題，我們現在登記好了。

**佛瑞德 · 蒙達雷 [下午 1:27]：** 太好了！那麼現在我們需要找個人幫忙，在我們去波士頓時監督實驗室的員工。

**阮氏花 [下午 1:27]：** 我認為麥克會做得不錯。

**佛瑞德 · 蒙達雷 [下午 1:28]：** 他不是也要去參加會議嗎？

**阮氏花 [下午 1:29]：** 他本來會，但米奇請他留下來把提案做完。

**佛瑞德 · 蒙達雷 [下午 1:30]：** 沒問題，我再問他。

**字彙** confirmation 確認　proposal 提案
embarrassed 感到尷尬的

**154** 關於麥克，文中提到什麼？
(A) 他不能監督實驗室。
(B) 他是新進員工。
(C) 他將出席會議。
(D) 他不會去波士頓。

**155** 下午1:15時，阮女士寫道：「既然你提到了」，是什麼意思？
(A) 她為自己忘記確認註冊狀況感到尷尬。
(B) 她意識到自己不應該忘記細節。
(C) 因為蒙達雷先生提醒，她才想到某件事。
(D) 她認為蒙達雷先生會填好登記表。

## 156-158 文章

### 愛米龍正失去市占率

朱奈德 · 卡西姆　報導

香港，4 月 11 日——據近期客戶滿意度的市調結果，愛米龍能源在最便利的能源供應業者中排名第 10，有 60％ 的用戶表示滿意。這項調查由奧斯頓研究中心在上個月進行，結果顯示愛米龍的排名雖比勁敵提瓦電力高，但較去年的第四名仍是慘跌。

「我們雖然落後其他競爭對手，但目標還是放在客戶需求上。」愛米龍發言人亞當 · 羅林並表示：「至於明年，我們會做出改變以改善我們的客戶服務。例如，將全體技術服務人員整合到一棟大樓內，便於加強培訓和品質控管。這將在明年 3 月前完成。」他們希望這些改變能使愛米龍更受客戶青睞。

**字彙** market share 市占率
following 根據……結果；在……之後
rank 把……評級
customer-friendly 方便客戶的
supplier 供應業者　claim 表示；聲稱
conduct 進行；實施　reveal 顯示；揭露
dramatically 明顯地；誇張地
fall behind 落後於　competitor 競爭對手
aim 目標　concentrate on 專注於
spokesperson 發言人
put . . . in place 實施
consolidate 合併；整併
short-staffed 人力短缺的
inconsistent 不一致的；易變的；不穩定的
merge 併購　carry out 實行

**156** 關於愛米龍，客戶最有可能說什麼？
(A) 能源供應太慢。
(B) 價格太高。
(C) 客服中心人手不足。
(D) 技術服務不穩定。

**157** 愛米龍明年將會做什麼？
(A) 將使用新科技。
(B) 將和其他競爭對手合併。
(C) 將把全體技術人員放在同一地點。
(D) 將進行更多市場研究。

**158** 在文中標記處，下列句子最適合放在哪裡？
「他們希望這些改變能使愛米龍更受客戶青睞。」
(A) [1]
(B) [2]
(C) [3]
(D) [4]

**159** 曼塞爾女士為何寫這封電子郵件？
(A) 要詢問出貨單
(B) 要推薦某台家電
(C) 要解決某個問題
(D) 要回應客戶

**160** 曼塞爾女士請鮑登先生做什麼？
(A) 解釋怎麼使用機器
(B) 幫忙促銷該洗／烘衣機
(C) 補償某些零件
(D) 催訂單

**161** 直基公司做了什麼決定？
(A) 將暫緩訂購某樣產品。
(B) 將販售更多款式的洗衣機。
(C) 將向客戶收取螺絲的費用。
(D) 將退回一些令人不甚滿意的商品。

## 159-161 電子郵件

收件者：cbowden@washngo.com
寄件者：rmansell@plumbbase.com
日期：6 月 30 日
回覆：菁英洗衣烘乾兩用機

敬愛的鮑登先生，

　　我是為了貴公司所生產的菁英洗衣烘乾兩用機聯絡您的。為數眾多的顧客購買產品後投訴，內部水箱少了根螺絲鎖不緊。幸虧我們庫存裡還有該尺寸的螺絲可提供給顧客。

　　您如能歸還我們提供給顧客的螺絲，使我們庫存不至於損失，我們將不勝感激。

　　我們考量機器的這項缺失，決定在問題解決前暫時不再訂購更多洗衣烘乾兩用機。一旦您確定問題已解決，我們非常樂意繼續和您訂購。

　　感謝您協助我處理這件事。

誠摯地，
雷恩・曼塞爾
經理
直基公司

**字彙** **washer-dryer** 洗衣烘乾兩用機
**manufacture**（通常指工廠利用機械大量）製造　**significant** 顯著的；值得注意的
**internal** 內部的　**liquid** 液體的
**holder** 容器　**loose** 鬆動的
**in stock** 在庫存　**supply** 提供；供應
**grateful**（對他人）感激的，表示感謝的
**profit** 利潤　**fault** 過錯；缺失
**additional** 額外的；另外的
**matter**（正在處理或考慮的）問題
**rectify** 改正；矯正　**assurance** 確定；確保
**resolve** 解決　**resume** 繼續
**address** 處理；解決　**postpone** 延後
**particular** 特定的　**charge** 收費
**unsatisfactory** 讓人不滿意的
**merchandise** 商品

## 162-165 文章報導

### 每週餐飲新聞

　　莎樂美夜店週五已同意收購三家嘉蘭特賭場的條件，其中一家賭場位於安特里姆，另兩家則在貝爾法斯特，收購價還沒對外宣布。

　　賭場並未宣布改名，可預見的未來將繼續以嘉蘭特的品牌名稱經營。莎樂美執行長安薩爾・基達在記者會宣布：「我很高興以沙樂美品牌之名收購這幾家賭場。我們的目標是成為安特里姆和貝爾法斯特地區娛樂事業的領導品牌，長久之道是要提供當地好玩又負擔得起的休閒娛樂。」基達先生也強調任何工作職務都不會受威脅。

　　沙樂美夜總會是基達先生的曾祖父的智慧結晶，他在一個世紀多前開了奧馬格的第一家酒吧。基達先生在其父親七年前去世後接手經營。目前在愛爾蘭的多個城鎮都有沙樂美酒吧。

**字彙** **terms** 條件；條款
**foreseeable future** 可預見的未來
**venue** 場所；地點　**press release** 記者會
**incorporate** 把……合併
**leading** 主要的；領先的；領導的
**long-term** 長期的
**affordable** 負擔得起的　**leisure** 休閒
**be under threat** 受到威脅
**brainchild** 智慧結晶
**take over ownership** 接下所有權
**acquisition** 收購　**recruit** 招聘
**relocation** 搬遷　**headquarters** 總部
**entry** 入場　**retain** 保持；保留
**performance-based bonus** 績效獎勵

**162** 此篇報導的目的為何？
(A) 要宣布一項收購
(B) 要報導博奕市場
(C) 要招聘酒吧員工
(D) 要評論一家公司的搬遷

**163** 關於安特里姆和貝爾法斯特分店的員工，基達先生說了什麼？
(A) 他想試試新的招聘方式。
(B) 他預期能在當地獲得支持。
(C) 他打算留下現有員工。
(D) 他計劃提供績效獎勵。

**164** 關於沙樂美夜店，文中提到什麼？
(A) 是家族企業。
(B) 是國際夜總會。
(C) 很快就會到蘇格蘭展店。
(D) 提供免費賭博。

**165** 在文中標記處，下列句子最適合放在哪裡？
「收購價還沒有對外宣布。」
(A) [1]
(B) [2]
(C) [3]
(D) [4]

**166-168 線上討論**

艾兒瑪·維加 [上午 10:08]：早安，我剛做完我們上一季的銷售報告，銷售額和去年同期相比下降了 20%，我們需要扭轉這個局面。

榮·庫盧瓦爾 [上午 10:09]：我們何不做個大促銷吸引人們光顧呢？像買一送一。

艾兒瑪·維加 [上午 10:10]：這想法先緩緩，我想知道我們第一時間還能想到什麼辦法。

凱瑟琳·貝克 [上午 10:11]：何不增加廣告？說不定因為開了新的購物中心，大家已經把我們忘了。

榮·庫盧瓦爾 [上午 10:12]：真的，但廣告很貴。

凱瑟琳·貝克 [上午 10:13]：廣播廣告就不貴，不用多花錢我們也可以做到。

艾兒瑪·維加 [上午 10:14]：好，繼續說。

凱瑟琳·貝克 [上午 10:15]：你看看，我們現在每個月花 1,500 美元在地方報買廣告。同樣的價格，我們能每天在三、四家電台買廣告。

艾兒瑪·維加 [上午 10:16]：這樣會有很多廣告。

榮·庫盧瓦爾 [上午 10:17]：這個我喜歡，也比較容易打中年輕人，他們也是喜歡潮鞋的族群。

艾兒瑪·維加 [上午 10:18]：試試看吧。凱瑟琳，妳能打幾家電台詢問報價嗎？

凱瑟琳·貝克 [上午 10:19]：當然。

艾兒瑪·維加 [上午 10:20]：榮恩，我想請你先記下幾個廣告腳本要用的點子。我們賣的鞋子和購物中心的一樣，我們需要讓消費者知道我們的比較便宜。

榮·庫盧瓦爾 [上午 10:20]：了解。

> **字彙** reverse 徹底改變；推翻
> hold off 延期；保持距離
> come up with 想出；提出（主意或計畫）
> estimate 估價
> jot down 匆匆記下，草草記下
> generate 產生；造成
> skeptical 懷疑的

**166** 傳訊息的人最有可能在哪裡工作？
(A) 廣播電台
(B) 服飾店
(C) 購物中心
(D) 鞋店

**167** 庫盧瓦爾先生同意做什麼？
(A) 想出廣告點子
(B) 確認部分同業的價位
(C) 設計促銷方案
(D) 和商場顧客聊聊

**168** 上午 10:14 時，維加女士寫道：「好，繼續說」，是什麼意思？
(A) 她想結束討論並開始實行。
(B) 她在重新考慮庫盧瓦爾先生所提出的點子。
(C) 她想讓貝克女士解釋她想法的內容。
(D) 她不確定廣播廣告是否會有用。

## 169-171 電子郵件

寄件者：winble@stein.com
收件者：brinkov@nomak.com
日期：8月1日
主旨：您的詢問

敬愛的布林科夫先生：

感謝您的詢問，我今天收到信了。現在和您說明一下，我們可以如何重新設計您的網站，幫諾馬克印刷增加流量。

斯坦設計在五年前成立。很多大企業、特別是海外公司，都委託我們當它們的網路顧問。我們幾個主要客戶包括蒙巴薩的 KKS 服裝、紐約的稀印設計和香港的法拉絲企業。這些公司在諮詢後，官網的訪客人數均大增，很多訪客也成為業務往來的客戶。

如您想和我們合作，我們保證給您最高規格工作品質。斯坦設計能在預算內準時完成專案，合作紀錄讓人印象深刻。我很肯定貴公司的利潤將有所成長。

歡迎直接透過 901-555-1232 聯繫我安排會議，以進一步分析您的需求。我期待收到您的答覆。

蕾娜‧溫布
高級銷售經理
斯坦設計

> **字彙** traffic（網站的）流量
> appoint 任命；委託
> as a result of 作為……的結果
> dramatic 急遽的；戲劇化的
> assure 向…保證；使確信  on time 準時
> profitability 收益性；利益率
> analyze 分析
> pursue 追求；（投入長時間）達成
> secure 取得  convince 說服

**169** 溫布女士為何寫這封信？
(A) 以確認隨後在諾馬克印刷召開的會議
(B) 以促進某間公司與其發展合作關係
(C) 以提供設計論壇的資訊
(D) 以說明建立新官網的方式

**170** 關於斯坦設計，文中提到什麼？
(A) 和海外有商業往來。
(B) 它的收費比其他顧問公司來得低。
(C) 近期聘了好幾名設計師。
(D) 總部位於蒙巴薩。

**171** 文中第三段、第一行的「assure」，意思最接近下列何者？
(A) 承諾
(B) 告知
(C) 說服
(D) 推廣

## 172-175 文章

西雅圖（3月3日）——總部位於西雅圖的瑪琳斯彩妝，近期宣布了一項計畫，將再打造一家研發機構。瑪琳斯彩妝目前唯一的研發機構坐落於緬因州，距西雅圖總部兩百多公里。新機構的成本據稱為 400 萬美元，是擴展到歐洲市場新策略的重要起步。

高層希望這次大膽邁向德國柏林的行動，能提升公司在歐洲彩妝業界的聲望。計畫一完成，兩個研發機構將能夠輕鬆滿足美國和歐洲市場的需求。該公司總裁史蒂夫‧貝克表示：「關鍵優勢在於，我們將能夠取得先前須透過供應商進口的歐洲產品和原料，在這之前很花時間、也提高了成本。」

貝克的父親大衛‧貝克自加州大學畢業後，於 1981 年創立瑪琳斯彩妝。他回到西雅圖後開始兼職向當地的學生兜售進口化妝品。他的兼職事業在六個月內賺了很多錢，隔年轉為全職後賺得更多。瑪琳斯彩妝在超過 20 個國家設有直營店，已被視為一家高品質的製造商，享譽全球。最近在貝克先生率領下，新的研發團隊正積極求新求變，但銷售量卻下滑了。

研發總監安娜‧波特蘭姆稱，瑪琳斯彩妝現有的所有產品，今年底前大多會在歐洲國家販售。波特蘭姆女士的長期規畫是補充現有產品線的不足，以高齡人士為目標推出抗老化面霜。她說：「我們的目標是公司成長，並開發客戶賞識的新產品。」

**字彙** based 以……為基地；立基於
initiative 新措施
be situated in 坐落於；位於
forefront 最顯要的位置；最重要的地位
executive（公司或組織的）執行委員會；
領導階層　bold 勇敢的；無畏的
boost 改善；提升　reputation 聲譽
accommodate 使適應；滿足
access to （有管道）取得……
source 從（某地）獲取
import 進口　margin 利潤
found 建立；創立
manage 成功完成；設法
outlet 直營零售店；經銷點
fall off （數量）減少；（比率）下降；（品質）降低
aggressively 主動積極地
angle 角度；立場　range 範圍
existing 現有的　majority 大多數
anti-aging 抗老化
complement 補充；補足
appreciate 賞識；欣賞；重視
operation 經營；運作
oblige 強迫；討好

**172** 瑪琳斯彩妝為何要蓋新機構？
(A) 因為生產部門距離總部太遠
(B) 因為現址的營運成本增加了
(C) 因為需要引進現代化的設備
(D) 因為高層想要到新地點銷售產品

**173** 新機構位於何處？
(A) 西雅圖
(B) 緬因州
(C) 柏林
(D) 加州

**174** 關於瑪琳斯彩妝，文中提到什麼？
(A) 產品的銷售近來停止成長。
(B) 在海外賣的產品較多。
(C) 顧客目前只能在西雅圖買到它的產品。
(D) 計劃開除多名高層。

**175** 瑪琳斯彩妝打算研發哪一類的產品？
(A) 口紅
(B) 乳液
(C) 面霜
(D) 粉餅

## 176-180 電子郵件與網路文章

收件者：安卓亞・高汀
寄件者：托亞・拉蓬
主旨：英格頓
日期：6 月 14 日，下午 2:44
附件：網球插圖 .zip

安卓亞好：

　　我今天稍早接到拉爾斯・英格頓來電，談他新書《世紀網球選手》封面的事。這系列書和現代體育英雄有關，預計將有三冊。他不同意我們想採用的中性色調照片，希望封面和他前作《美國足球》的設計相仿。所以我可否請妳儘速提出一些初步設計，讓我們徵詢英格頓先生的同意？我在信中附上網球插圖供妳參考。

　　英格爾頓先生和我交談並非只提出這項設計問題，所以我想讓設計部門中、和此專案有關的所有人員聽聽他的說法，這將會很有幫助。因此，我安排星期二正午致電他在奧地利阿爾卑斯山區的家，和他召開電話會議。我會再用電子郵件給妳開會人員的名單。如妳有任何疑問，請讓我知道。

托亞

---

### 封面藝術
8 月 11 日，星期二

　　《奧地利評論》每年都會請傑出藝術家票選最喜愛的書籍封面。本週，比利時阿爾特雷希特大學藝術設計主任伊利亞那・德羅布維克揭曉了他的最愛。

　　伊利亞那・德羅布維克：我很愛看到書封上有和書本身內容有關的多張圖片；且書封要能認出書中提及的人物才能讓我感興趣。因此，我偶然看到安卓亞・高汀設計的《世紀網球選手》封面便留下非常深刻的印象。這本書由奧地利作家拉爾斯・英格頓所寫、順序出版社出版。封面上有過去與當代網球明星的插畫，但沒有標題和作者名稱。取而代之的是，封面只利用黑白插畫和紅色背景表現。這封面的設計，和拉爾斯・英格頓先生計劃的三部曲中第一本書明顯相似；第一本書的封面也是利用黑白插畫，背景則是藍色。高汀顯然是位繪製線稿的專家，其設計讓我讚賞。

**176** 下列何者為電子郵件的目的之一？
(A) 請一名同仁歸還她借閱的書籍
(B) 告知同仁須做調整
(C) 為一項計畫增加的工作設定期限
(D) 公告某位作者新書的出版日

**177** 關於托亞・拉蓬，文中指出什麼？
(A) 她邀請拉爾斯・英格頓先生參加會議。
(B) 她是結構工程的專家。
(C) 她下週會造訪奧地利阿爾卑斯山區。
(D) 她是五本書的作者。

**178** 關於《美國足球》的封面，文中提到什麼？
(A) 僅以三個顏色為主。
(B) 由伊利亞那・德羅布維克設計。
(C) 拉爾斯・英格頓對其感到不滿意。
(D) 貼滿了照片。

**179** 網路文章中第二段、第五行的「bears」，意思最接近下列何者？
(A) 接受
(B) 需要
(C) 呈現
(D) 適合

**180** 關於安卓亞・高汀，文中沒有提到什麼？
(A) 她的作品在順序出版社所出版的書籍上。
(B) 她設計了三部曲中的其中一本。
(C) 她的作品用色豐富。
(D) 一名藝評家稱她的作品是他的最愛。

## 181-185 新聞稿與電子郵件

**9 月 13 日**　　　　　　　　　　　　　　新聞稿

路易茲企業很榮幸宣布，9 月 13 日星期六將揭幕潘帕和科瓦瓦的新工廠。此外，我們也要宣布，這週終於通過和圖庫曼省中央的拉蘇爾工業的合併案。路易茲董事長阿曼德・瑞索克表示，這筆買賣更加鞏固這家公司要在阿根廷擴大影響力的決心。

路易茲是約阿希姆・菲蘭五年前被波麗露工業解僱後成立。在那裡工作了十年的他已準備好返回家鄉巴拉拿，在那裡和家人朋友合夥開始批發水果。菲蘭先生的規畫是利用當地的供應鏈，以國產作物為主力。此策略利潤相當豐厚，菲蘭的概念很快就被全國各地類似的批發商採納，因此該公司備受同業的尊敬和好評。

儘管該公司在市場上成長驚人，五年前專門打造的辦公室，至今仍是公司的重要基地且業務不斷創新。其資訊科技團隊最近引進了一套揀貨系統，處理訂單的速度幾乎是早前機型的兩倍快。

---

寄件者：阿曼德・瑞索克
收件者：提姆・詹克
日期：9 月 21 日
標題：好消息

---

敬愛的詹克先生：

我很高興通知您人力資源部的決定，您是今年終身服務獎的得主。該獎項肯定您加入路易茲以來對公司的投入及貢獻。您從那時起便不斷協助路易茲公司，從地方企業轉型到成為南美洲批發業務的領先企業。此外，您作為團隊領導人的職業操守，尤其是擔任運輸部經理一職堪稱典範。

為了慶祝年度獎項，訂於 9 月 25 日週二下午 5 點在公司總部舉行盛大晚宴，晚宴後我將進行頒獎。再次感謝您的辛勞和貢獻，我很期待屆時可以看到您。

阿曼德・瑞索克
執行長

**181** 根據新聞稿，路易茲企業為何成功？
(A) 它很快擴展海外市場。
(B) 它提供比對手更低的價格。
(C) 它建立了一套廣為使用的批發系統。
(D) 它和波麗露有合夥關係。

**182** 文中沒有提到哪項路易茲企業參與的行動？
(A) 和一家公司合併
(B) 設立新辦事處
(C) 引進一套升級的系統
(D) 提供訓練機會

**183** 菲蘭先生在波麗露工業做了多久？
(A) 2 年
(B) 5 年
(C) 10 年
(D) 15 年

**184** 路易茲企業為什麼將主辦餐會？
(A) 要慶祝簽成一筆交易
(B) 要在阿根廷吸引更多商機
(C) 要公開表揚多名員工的服務
(D) 要紀念公司創立週年的日子

**185** 詹克先生 9 月 25 日最可能會在哪裡？
(A) 圖庫曼
(B) 潘帕
(C) 巴拉拿
(D) 哥多華

**186-190 廣告、資訊與電子郵件**

**辦公室便利店**

840 號商店－聖佩德羅
555-8203

每週特價（3 月 2 日－3 月 9 日）
報稅軟體：25 美金
筆電均享 10％折扣——最低僅需 300 美元（平常價格：330 美元）
得速達品牌印表機均享 20％折扣——最低僅需 100 美元（平常價格：120 美元）
辦公用品折扣 5％至 50％
購買 75 美元以上將獲得免費 USB 硬碟（價值 5 美元）

登錄取得我們的獎勵卡，到店內或透過 officeexpress.com 購物均能積點。您每消費一美元積一點。購買特定商品將獲得額外積點，但不包含折扣商品。

　　感謝您購買得速達 T950 印表機。您的印表機內含一組三色墨水匣和一組黑色墨水匣。在印表機內安裝墨水匣時，請遵守卡背上的說明。建議您初次使用前先試印一頁，這有助確保印表機噴頭已正確對齊。

　　不少店面均有販賣替換用的墨水匣，此外也能在我們的官網 www.dextra.com 購買。在官網上訂購的墨水匣將在 48 小時內免運費送達。您首次訂購時可使用優惠碼 DT2000 取得額外 10％的折扣，這僅適用於我們官網上購買的商品。

　　如您對新購買的印表機有任何疑問，我們全年度全天候待命，歡迎隨時聯繫。

客戶支援：1-800-555-1818 /
　　　　　customersupport@dextra.com
技術支援：1-800-555-0909 /
　　　　　techsupport@dextra.com

寄件者：丹・法默
收件者：得速達企業
主旨：訂單號 8945
日期：3 月 25 日

此致相關人士：

　　我 3 月 2 日拜訪聖保羅的朋友時，在辦公室便利店購買了一台 T950 印表機。印表機很棒，正是我列印事業用的高品質傳單所需，我用得太勤幾乎把墨水用完了。由於在我的居住地區並沒有辦公室便利店，所以我用代碼 DT2000 從貴公司官網訂購了四組替換用的墨水匣（訂單號 8945）。遺憾的是，寄來給我的貨物尺寸有誤。我想換成正確尺寸的，請您建議我該怎麼做。

誠摯地，
丹・法默

**字彙** office supply 辦公用品
redeem 彌補；補救
complimentary 免費的；附贈的
awesome 很好的；了不起的

**186** 根據廣告，關於獎勵卡下述何者為真？
(A) 網購可以積點。
(B) 有折扣可以補發。
(C) 折扣商品可以積點。
(D) 只有常客才有。

**187** 關於法墨先生，文中提到什麼？
(A) 他經常在 840 號商店購物。
(B) 他得到免費的 USB 硬碟。
(C) 他登記領取獎勵卡。
(D) 他買印表機花不到 100 美元。

**188** 關於訂單號 8945，下述何者最可能為真？
(A) 花了四天才送到。
(B) 有運費。
(C) 折扣了 10%。
(D) 地址有錯。

**189** 在資訊中第一段、第五行的「ensure」，意思最接近下列何者？
(A) 調整
(B) 傳遞
(C) 測量
(D) 確認

**190** 關於得速達的客戶支援，文中提到什麼？
(A) 週末打電話也能聯繫到。
(B) 他們處理得速達官網上的訂單。
(C) 其會員偏好用電子郵件聯絡。
(D) 他們可以協助解決安裝問題。

### 191-195 通知、電子郵件與帳單

寄件者：莎朗・威爾森醫師辦公室
野馬路 27 號，比靈斯，蒙大拿州 61520
(894) 555-0128
office@doctorwilson.com

敬愛的森寶莉女士：

　　我們很關心您的健康，因此想通知您，您預約了一門門診於：

　　10 月 5 日，星期二，上午 8:30

　　如果您是初次到診，請在預約前十分鐘到達，以填寫病歷資料表和支付授權書。

　　如您因故想取消或更改門診，請至少提前 24 小時與我們聯繫，以避免衍生取消費用。我們期待看到您！

---

寄件者：ms2002@netmail.com
收件者：office@doctorwilson.com
日期：10 月 3 日 下午 3:45

---

　　感謝您提醒，我差點忘記預訂了門診。我這幾週一直很忙，但我知道年度體檢很重要。請問有可能把我的預訂改到 10 月 8 日星期五嗎？任何時間都行。我會確保提早十分鐘到並填妥相關文件。

　　另外，同事一直建議我順便注射流感疫苗，我不知道是不是真的有效。在同意注射前，我想和威爾遜醫師討論一下這件事。

謝謝，

瑪莎・森寶莉

## 醫療費明細

| | |
|---|---|
| 瑪莎・森寶莉 | 莎朗・威爾森醫師 |
| 賈斯珀峽谷巷 1898 號 | 野馬路 27 號 |
| 比靈斯，蒙大拿州 | 比靈斯，蒙大拿州 |
| 61520 | 61520 |

**服務內容**

| | |
|---|---|
| 體檢 | 250 美元 |
| 注射，流感 | 25 美元 |

**帳戶內容**

帳號：8093-034
服務日期：10 月 8 號
收費：$ 150
付款方式：保險
提供者名稱：第一健康

注意：向提供服務之保險業者開具的所有費用，均須取得其批准。倘提供者拒絕繳費，款項則由病患全額負擔。授權服務前，請和您的保險公司確認。

**191** 通知中沒有提到什麼？
(A) 門診時間
(B) 門診地點
(C) 門診原因
(D) 取消門診的時限

**192** 關於森寶莉女士，文中提到什麼？
(A) 她的健康近期出了問題。
(B) 她是威爾森醫師的新病人。
(C) 她工作時經常生病。
(D) 她須支付取消費用。

**193** 森寶莉女士為何寫此封電子郵件？
(A) 以詢問更多資訊
(B) 以預約門診
(C) 以提交文件
(D) 以更改預約

**194** 關於森寶莉女士的來訪，下述何者最可能為真？
(A) 發生在早上。
(B) 她比預計的晚到。
(C) 是在她想要的日期。
(D) 她決定不要打流感疫苗。

**195** 帳單上第四段、第三行的「authorizing」，意思最接近下列何者？
(A) 允許
(B) 考慮
(C) 拒絕
(D) 支付

## 196-200 電子郵件、文章與資訊

| | |
|---|---|
| 寄件者： | 馬克斯・歐文 |
| 收件者： | 湯姆・基特里居 |
| 日期： | 9 月 8 日 |
| 主旨： | 建議 |

湯姆，

我有個想法想和你討論，我店面附近蓋了間新公寓，我發現現在有很多研究生使用我們的服務，他們經常來這邊複印和寄包裹。我想我們應考慮在大學旁再開一家店，生意應該會很好。我們準備開店前可以再請一次「大班研究」做市場分析。在我決定要開現在負責的這間店時，這家公司的數據很有幫助。

不知你怎麼想？

馬克斯

伯靈頓—（5 月 8 日）全國連鎖的列複印中心「快捷列印」宣布，下個月將在大學校園南方鄰近社區開設新分店。

該公司同時也提供郵政服務，並表示希望能提供學生比圖書館更快、更實惠的列印服務。

區域分店長湯姆・基特里居解釋：「我們的市調資料顯示，這個市區對我們服務的需求非常大。」

新店面將全天候營業，位於惠勒街上、鄰近爪哇滿滿咖啡廳。

這家快捷和伯靈頓的其他店面不同，學生可以在此建立預付帳戶，能預先加值並獲得一組學生密碼。該系統能避免攜帶現金或信用卡的麻煩，學生可以很容易地在店裡確認帳戶並加值。

## 自助列印／複印

**指示**

1. 插入您的信用卡／簽證金融卡或輸入學生證號。

2. 選擇服務類型：列印／複印
   a. 如需列印，請插入您的 USB 硬碟，<u>並導照螢幕上指示列印該儲存裝置上的檔案</u>。
   b. 如需複印，請選擇複印類型和紙張尺寸。

3. 輸入所需的頁數。

4. 按開始鍵。

5. 工作完成後，將詢問您是否要保留紙本或電子收據。如果您使用信用卡／簽證金融卡，則需提供電子郵件地址以接收電子收據。

需要協助嗎？請詢問服務台處和善的同仁。

**196** 這封電子郵件的目的為何？
(A) 要報告銷售情形
(B) 要提出客訴
(C) 要提出建議
(D) 要要求數據資料

**197** 關於基特里居先生，何者最有可能為真？
(A) 他將管理快捷列印的新店面。
(B) 他是歐文先生的員工之一。
(C) 他是柏靈頓的居民。
(D) 他再次委託了某家市調公司。

**198** 文中第五段、第五行的「hassle」，意思最接近下列何者？
(A) 不便
(B) 互動
(C) 花費
(D) 矛盾

**199** 指示中沒有提到什麼？
(A) 可用信用卡付款。
(B) 可從 USB 硬碟列印。
(C) 如有需求可獲得協助。
(D) 學生可以使用全彩列印。

**200** 關於自助複印機，文中提到什麼？
(A) 只有這家大學分店才能使用。
(B) 學生可從手機傳送檔案。
(C) 有預付帳戶的學生可使用。
(D) 和圖書館內的機款一樣。

| | | | | | | | | | |
|---|---|---|---|---|---|---|---|---|---|
| 1. (D) | 2. (A) | 3. (B) | 4. (C) | 5. (B) | 6. (C) | 07. (A) | 08. (A) | 09. (A) | 10. (C) |
| 11. (B) | 12. (C) | 13. (A) | 14. (C) | 15. (C) | 16. (B) | 17. (A) | 18. (A) | 19. (B) | 20. (C) |
| 21. (B) | 22. (B) | 23. (C) | 24. (A) | 25. (C) | 26. (B) | 27. (B) | 28. (B) | 29. (C) | 30. (A) |
| 31. (B) | 32. (B) | 33. (A) | 34. (D) | 35. (A) | 36. (D) | 37. (A) | 38. (B) | 39. (D) | 40. (A) |
| 41. (D) | 42. (A) | 43. (A) | 44. (D) | 45. (A) | 46. (A) | 47. (D) | 48. (C) | 49. (A) | 50. (A) |
| 51. (D) | 52. (D) | 53. (C) | 54. (C) | 55. (A) | 56. (D) | 57. (C) | 58. (A) | 59. (B) | 60. (C) |
| 61. (A) | 62. (B) | 63. (D) | 64. (A) | 65. (A) | 66. (D) | 67. (D) | 68. (B) | 69. (B) | 70. (C) |
| 71. (A) | 72. (C) | 73. (B) | 74. (D) | 75. (A) | 76. (B) | 77. (D) | 78. (A) | 79. (C) | 80. (D) |
| 81. (C) | 82. (C) | 83. (D) | 84. (B) | 85. (A) | 86. (B) | 87. (A) | 88. (C) | 89. (D) | 90. (B) |
| 91. (C) | 92. (A) | 93. (C) | 94. (D) | 95. (B) | 96. (B) | 97. (B) | 98. (B) | 99. (B) | 100. (C) |
| 101. (B) | 102. (A) | 103. (B) | 104. (D) | 105. (B) | 106. (A) | 107. (B) | 108. (A) | 109. (A) | 110. (A) |
| 111. (A) | 112. (C) | 113. (A) | 114. (A) | 115. (B) | 116. (B) | 117. (B) | 118. (B) | 119. (C) | 120. (C) |
| 121. (B) | 122. (D) | 123. (C) | 124. (A) | 125. (D) | 126. (A) | 127. (C) | 128. (B) | 129. (B) | 130. (A) |
| 131. (C) | 132. (C) | 133. (B) | 134. (A) | 135. (C) | 136. (B) | 137. (D) | 138. (D) | 139. (C) | 140. (D) |
| 141. (B) | 142. (C) | 143. (C) | 144. (A) | 145. (C) | 146. (A) | 147. (A) | 148. (B) | 149. (C) | 150. (A) |
| 151. (A) | 152. (B) | 153. (D) | 154. (B) | 155. (C) | 156. (C) | 157. (A) | 158. (A) | 159. (A) | 160. (D) |
| 161. (D) | 162. (A) | 163. (D) | 164. (A) | 165. (B) | 166. (C) | 167. (A) | 168. (B) | 169. (A) | 170. (D) |
| 171. (C) | 172. (A) | 173. (B) | 174. (D) | 175. (B) | 176. (D) | 177. (A) | 178. (D) | 179. (A) | 180. (C) |
| 181. (B) | 182. (A) | 183. (A) | 184. (A) | 185. (C) | 186. (B) | 187. (D) | 188. (A) | 189. (A) | 190. (D) |
| 191. (A) | 192. (D) | 193. (D) | 194. (B) | 195. (C) | 196. (D) | 197. (C) | 198. (B) | 199. (A) | 200. (D) |

## 21

**PART 1**  P. 230

**1** (A) Meals have been brought to a table.
英M (B) The women are greeting each other.
(C) One woman is carrying some bottles.
(D) One woman is handing the other an item.

(A) 有人送餐到桌子上。
(B) 女子們正互相問候。
(C) 一名女子正拿著幾個瓶子。
(D) 一名女子正在把東西遞給另一人。

字彙 greet 問候；招呼　hand 將……遞給

**2** (A) Some clothes are hanging outside.
美W (B) Some ropes are being tied up.
(C) Some flags are fastened to the poles.
(D) The windows of a building are being polished.

(A) 幾件衣服晾在外面。
(B) 正在繫上幾條繩子。
(C) 幾面旗幟綁在桿子上。
(D) 正在擦洗大樓的窗戶。

字彙 tie up 綁緊　fasten 繫牢　pole 桿子
polish 擦亮

**3** (A) Baskets have been filled with food.
美M (B) Baked goods are being removed from an oven.
(C) A chef is scrubbing a tray.
(D) A diner is sampling some dessert.

(A) 籃裡盛滿食物。
(B) 正從烤箱中拿出烤過的點心。
(C) 一名廚師正在擦洗托盤。
(D) 一名顧客正在品嚐甜點。

字彙 baked 烘烤的
scrub（尤指用硬刷、肥皂和水）擦洗
tray 托盤
diner（餐廳裡的）食客；進食的人
sample 品嚐

**4** (A) Some people are loading some cargo.
美W (B) Luggage has been stored in the corner.
(C) Passengers are approaching a plane.
(D) Travelers are waiting inside the terminal.

(A) 有些人正在裝貨。
(B) 行李放在角落。
(C) 乘客們正在接近一輛飛機。
(D) 旅客們正在航廈內等待。

字彙 load 裝載　cargo 貨物　store 存放

**5** (A) The man is leaving a construction site.
澳M (B) The man is bending over to draw a line.
(C) Pipes are laid in the trench.
(D) Earth is being shoveled into bags.

(A) 男子正離開工地。
(B) 男子正彎著腰畫線。
(C) 壕溝裡鋪設有管線。
(D) 土正被剷入袋子裡。

字彙 construction site 工地；施工現場
bend over 彎腰　draw a line 畫線
trench 壕溝；溝渠　earth 土壤
shovel 用鏟子鏟起

**6** (A) A man is writing on a chart.
美W (B) A man is pointing at something on the board.
(C) They are reviewing the content of a book.
(D) They are concentrating on their own game.

(A) 一名男人正在圖表上寫東西。
(B) 一名男子正指著板上的某個東西。
(C) 他們正在查看書本的內容。
(D) 他們正專心玩自己的遊戲。

字彙 chart 圖表；示意圖；曲線圖
point 指；指向　content 內容

**PART 2**  P. 234

**7** Who ordered the steak?
美M (A) No one did yet.
美W (B) Yes, I am.
(C) It's almost complete.

牛排是誰點的？
(A) 還沒有人做。
(B) 對的，我是。
(C) 快完成了。

**8** Where do you need my signature?
(美W) (A) At the end of this page.
(美M) (B) At ROTA Hotel.
(C) Sit over here.

我需要在哪裡簽名？
(A) 在這一頁的最後。
(B) 在羅塔飯店。
(C) 坐這裡。

字彙 signature 簽名

**9** Do you have the number for the deli?
(美W) (A) No, but I can hunt it out for you.
(美M) (B) A liter of milk, please.
(C) It's working well.

你有小吃店的電話號碼嗎？
(A) 沒有，但我可以幫你找出來。
(B) 麻煩一公升的牛奶。
(C) 運作良好。

字彙 deli (=delicatessen) 熟食店；小吃店
hunt out 找出（尤指閒置或不復使用之物）

**10** Are you attending any of the sporting events?
(美M) (A) Soccer field 4.
(美W) (B) No, I am an assistant coach.
(C) Yes, the one in which Alan's playing.

你會參加任何的運動活動嗎？
(A) 四號足球場。
(B) 不，我是個助理教練。
(C) 會，就艾倫參賽的那場。

字彙 soccer field 足球場　assistant 助理

**11** You wrote these articles, didn't you?
(美W) (A) Oh, that's very good news.
(美M) (B) Paloma worked on them.
(C) Yes, we're hiring three reporters.

這些文章是你們寫的，不是嗎？
(A) 哦，那真是個好消息。
(B) 鴿子牌對他們有用。
(C) 是，我們聘了三位記者。

字彙 article 文章　reporter 記者

**12** Why don't you inform the landlord that we
(美W) won't be taking the lease?
(美M) (A) A month's notice.
(B) The booking agent.
(C) Sure, I will tell him.

你何不跟房東說我們沒有要租房子？
(A) 提前一個月通知。
(B) 售票員。
(C) 當然，我再跟他說。

字彙 landlord 房東　lease 租借；租約
a month's notice 提前一個月通知
booking agent 售票員；（演員等的）經紀人

**13** Where is the nearest restroom facility?
(英M) (A) On the adjacent road.
(美M) (B) They're behind schedule.
(C) Just one room, please.

最近的廁所在哪裡？
(A) 在隔壁條路上。
(B) 他們進度落後。
(C) 只要一個房間，謝謝。

字彙 adjacent 鄰近的
behind schedule 落後進度

**14** Would you prefer I book by phone or via the
(美W) Web site?
(英M) (A) Yes, I have them.
(B) No, he will do it himself.
(C) Via the Internet is better.

你希望我用電話還是官網預訂？
(A) 是的，我有。
(B) 不，他會自己來。
(C) 用網路比較好。

字彙 book 預訂　via 透過

**15** You went to the doctor's yesterday, didn't
(美M) you?
(美W) (A) Isn't it time?
(B) Let's take the elevator.
(C) No, I'm going on Friday.

你昨天去了醫院，不是嗎？
(A) 時間還沒到嗎？
(B) 我們搭電梯吧。
(C) 不，我星期五才要去。

字彙 go to the doctor's 去醫院；去醫療中心

**16** Who is in charge of the sales drive?
(美W) (A) We're going to visit her.
(美M) (B) Mr. Alverez is overseeing that.
(C) I think he is too busy to do that.

負責這次促銷的是誰？
(A) 我們會去拜訪她。
(B) 那個歸阿勒瓦雷茲管。
(C) 我覺得他太忙了，沒辦法做那個。

字彙 **in charge of** 負責；掌管
**sales drive** 促銷活動　**section** 部分；部門
**oversee** 監督

**17** What type of wallcovering did you select for
(英M) your office?
(美W) (A) I'm still deliberating.
(B) It's a beautiful texture.
(C) The fourth office on the left.

你為你的辦公室挑了哪一種壁紙？
(A) 我還在考慮。
(B) 這個質感很漂亮。
(C) 左邊數來第四間辦公室。

字彙 **wallcovering** 壁紙　**deliberate** 慎重考慮
**texture** 質感；質地

**18** Why did Jules move to the Alexandria area?
(美W) (A) To be nearer to his office.
(美M) (B) From the top to the bottom floor.
(C) Because it's still working.

朱爾斯為什麼搬到亞歷山卓區？
(A) 較靠近他的辦公室。
(B) 從頂樓到一樓。
(C) 因為它還能用。

字彙 **nearer to** 較接近　**bottom floor** 一樓

**19** The inauguration ball will be held next week.
(美M) (A) It improved steadily.
(英M) (B) Where will it be?
(C) A group of seven.

就職典禮的舞會訂於下週舉行。
(A) 已經逐漸改善。
(B) 會在哪？
(C) 七個人。

字彙 **inauguration** 就職典禮　**ball** 舞會
**hold** 舉辦　**steadily** 穩定地

**20** How do I find out if we've been awarded the
(英M) pay rise?
(英M) (A) Two or three pages.
(B) The launch was very successful.
(C) Try asking Ms. Piemont.

我們要怎麼知道是否被加薪？
(A) 兩到三頁。
(B) 新品上市非常成功。
(C) 試著問看看皮埃蒙特女士。

字彙 **find out** 得知；找出
**award** 給予；頒獎　**pay rise** 加薪
**launch** 推出；發射

**21** Why do you need training to control that
(美W) machinery?
(美M) (A) I haven't noticed her.
(B) Because it's hazardous.
(C) The instruction manual.

你為什麼需要訓練才能操作機械？
(A) 我還沒注意到她。
(B) 因為很危險。
(C) 使用說明書。

字彙 **machinery** （大型的）機器；機械
**hazardous** 危險的
**instruction manual** 使用說明書

**22** Isn't the highway still being repaired?
(英M) (A) Some overdue programs.
(美M) (B) Yes, for a long time now.
(C) Over five hundred vehicles.

公路不是還在維修嗎？
(A) 延誤的幾個計畫。
(B) 是的，已經很久了。
(C) 超過五百輛車。

字彙 **highway** 公路　**overdue** 過期的；延誤的

**23** How was your first week lecturing here?
(美W) (A) I'm coming out soon.
(美M) (B) Yes, behind the office.
(C) The students were very interactive.

你在這裡講課的第一個星期怎麼樣？
(A) 我很快就出去了。
(B) 是的，在辦公室後面。
(C) 學生的互動變好的。

字彙 **lecturing**（常指在大學裡）講課，講授
**interactive** 互動的；相互交流的

**24** Is the buffet being delivered or do we have to 美M collect?
美W (A) It's supposed to be here in an hour.
  (B) No, I don't like that taste.
  (C) Over by the dining room.

餐點會送過來，還是我們得自己去拿？
(A) 應該會在一個小時內送到。
(B) 不，我不喜歡那個味道。
(C) 在餐廳旁邊。

字彙 collect 取；領取　dining room 餐廳

**25** I will print out a picture of our latest clothing 美W range for you.
美M (A) Yes, I will purchase this printer.
  (B) It doesn't fit at all.
  (C) Thanks for your assistance.

我會把我們最新系列服裝的照片印給你。
(A) 是的，我會買這台印表機。
(B) 一點都不合身。
(C) 感謝你的幫忙。

字彙 print out 印出　clothing 衣服；服裝
  assistance 幫忙

**26** Isn't Peter Varlet on the judging panel?
美M (A) He didn't know she was.
美W (B) I think he is.
  (C) It's bigger than usual.

彼得‧瓦勒不是在評審團裡嗎？
(A) 他不知道她是。
(B) 我想他是。
(C) 比平常大。

字彙 judging panel 評審團

**27** You included the attachment with the e-mail, 美W didn't you?
英M (A) Mail is much quicker.
  (B) Yes, I sent it yesterday.
  (C) An extra amount.

你在電子郵件附檔了，沒有嗎？
(A) 用郵寄的比較快。
(B) 有，我昨天寄了。
(C) 額外的量。

字彙 attachment 附件
  amount （不可數名詞的）數量

**28** Who'd be the head of marketing?
美M (A) The headlines are condemning.
美W (B) Haven't they already selected someone?
  (C) Chris agreed to attend.

會當上行銷經理的是誰？
(A) 標題罵得很兇。
(B) 他們不是已經選出人選了嗎？
(C) 克里斯同意要出席。

字彙 headline 標題　condemn 譴責
  select 選擇；挑選

**29** Why don't we take a stroll by the lake this 美W afternoon?
英M (A) Because I ran out of time.
  (B) No, I don't have any.
  (C) Let's meet after work.

我們今天下午不如去湖邊散步怎麼樣？
(A) 因為我沒時間了。
(B) 不，我什麼都沒有。
(C) 下班後見吧。

字彙 take a stroll 散步
  run out of time 沒時間

**30** Which hall can we practice in?
美M (A) Is the gymnasium large enough?
美W (B) Yes, you should.
  (C) I have a plan of my own.

哪個館可以讓我們練習？
(A) 那間體育館夠大嗎？
(B) 對，你應該。
(C) 我有自己的計畫。

字彙 practice 練習
  gymnasium 體育館；健身房

**31** Would you like to book a translator for the 美W conference in Korea?
美M (A) Because I went there last month.
  (B) I don't think we need one.
  (C) No, I haven't heard about that facility.

你想預約韓國會議上的翻譯嗎？
(A) 因為我上個月去過了。
(B) 我覺得我們不需要。
(C) 沒有，我沒有聽過那個場所。

字彙 translator 翻譯；譯者

22

23

# PART 3

P.235

**Questions 32-34 refer to the following conversation.**

美W 美M

**W** Hi, this is Rica Dante. ㉜ **I ordered a coffee maker from your store** more than three days ago, but it still hasn't been delivered. Do you know how much longer I will have to wait?

**M** Sorry for the inconvenience, Ms. Dante. ㉝ **One of our conveyor belt lines has broken down**, so we're delivering behind the planned schedules. If you are prepared to wait, it should be there within 48 hours.

**W** On second thought, ㉞ **why don't I drive over to the store to collect the coffee maker myself**? I only live three blocks away.

**對話**

女：您好，我是莉卡．丹特。我在您店裡訂了一台咖啡機，已經超過三天了，但我還沒收到貨。請問您知道還要等多久嗎？

男：丹特女士，很抱歉造成您的不便。我們有條輸送帶壞了，所以送貨情況不如預期。如果您還願意等的話，它會在 48 小時內送達。

女：我想想，不如我自己開車過去你們店拿咖啡機？我就住在相隔三條街遠的地方。

**字彙** break down（機器或車輛）故障
behind the schedule 進度落後
on second thought 我再想想；轉念
drive over to 開車到　collect 取；領取
appliance 家電　distribution 分發；分配
alternative 可替代的

**32** Where does the man work?
(A) At a café
(B) At an appliance store
(C) At a repair shop
(D) At a distribution center

男子的工作地點是？
(A) 咖啡廳
(B) 家電賣場
(C) 維修店
(D) 物流中心

**33** Why is the woman's order delayed?
(A) A fault has occurred in the factory.
(B) A delivery van has broken down.
(C) A payment was refused.
(D) Her appliance is out of stock.

女子的訂單為何耽擱了？
(A) 工廠出了問題。
(B) 貨運卡車壞了。
(C) 付款遭拒。
(D) 她的電器缺貨了。

**34** What does the woman say she will do?
(A) Select an alternative appliance
(B) Cancel the order
(C) Use a different credit card
(D) Collect her own order

女子說她將會做什麼？
(A) 選擇替代產品
(B) 取消訂單
(C) 用另一張信用卡
(D) 自取訂貨商品

**Questions 35-37 refer to the following conversation.**

美W 英M

**W** Hello, ㉟ **I'm calling to inquire about the theater's new winter schedule.** I understand that you'll be closing early some days.

**M** Yes, from November until the end of February we'll be open only until 5 every Tuesday afternoon. But ㊱ **we will be open on Sundays for special children's shows.**

**W** That sounds good. Does it cost extra to see these new shows?

**M** No, the cost is included in the 5 dollar admission fee. We expect the theater will be busy though. So ㊲ **we advise that you buy tickets online**. Then you will be able to steer clear of the long ticket line.

**對話**

女：嗨，我打電話是想詢問劇院這個冬天的日程。我知道有幾天會提早結束營業。

男：是的，從 11 月到 2 月底，我們每個星期二只會開到下午 5 點。不過，星期天會有給兒童的特別表演，都會開。

女：聽起來很不錯，看這些新表演需要另外花錢嗎？

男：不用，相關費用已包含在 5 美元的入場費裡了。劇院預計會很擁擠，所以我們建議您透過網路購票，這樣您就能避掉長長的買票隊伍。

**35** Why is the woman calling?
(A) To ask about a theater schedule
(B) To find out the cost for children
(C) To sign up for membership
(D) To arrange a show

女子為何打這通電話？
(A) 要詢問劇院的日程
(B) 要釐清兒童的花費
(C) 要註冊會員
(D) 要安排演出

**36** What is the theater going to offer during the winter?
(A) Membership packages
(B) Discounted tickets
(C) Free admission
(D) Special shows

劇院冬天時會提供什麼？
(A) 會員套票
(B) 折扣票
(C) 免費入場
(D) 特別演出

**37** What does the man recommend?
(A) Purchasing from the Web site
(B) Checking the times of the shows
(C) Arriving early for tickets
(D) Signing up for discounts

男子建議了什麼？
(A) 用官網購買
(B) 確認演出時間
(C) 提前來買票
(D) 登錄折扣活動

**Questions 38-40 refer to the following conversation.**
美W 美M

**W** ㉛ Is this where I can borrow a security pass for laboratory equipment? I'm a worker here.
**M** You've come to the right department. Only, we don't give out temporary cards. You can renew your security card for £150. ㉝ I just have to check your employee badge and passport.
**W** But I can't find any of my identification because I left my wallet in a taxi. Is there anyone who can lend me a security card?
**M** ㊵ You can always try asking human resources on the third floor. It won't take as long.

---

**對話**
女：我可以在這裡借一張實驗室設備的門禁卡嗎？我是這裡的員工。
男：您來對地方了，只是我們不提供臨時卡，您可以花 150 英鎊更新您的門禁卡，我只需要核對您的員工證和護照。
女：不過我找不到任何的身分證件，因為我的錢包掉在計程車上了。有人可以借我門禁卡嗎？
男：您隨時都能去三樓的人力資源部問問看，應該不會花太多時間。

**38** What does the woman request?
(A) A lab coat
(B) A temporary security pass
(C) An alternative entrance
(D) Directions to a department

女子要求的是什麼？
(A) 實驗室外套
(B) 臨時門禁卡
(C) 其他入口
(D) 到某個部門的方向

**39** What does the man ask to see?
(A) A registration form
(B) A driver's license
(C) A safety certificate
(D) A form of identification

男子要求要看什麼？
(A) 登記表
(B) 駕照
(C) 安全證書
(D) 某種身分證明

**40** What does the man suggest?
(A) Contacting a different department
(B) Paying with cash
(C) Changing her ID details
(D) Searching for her wallet

男子建議什麼？
(A) 聯絡其他部門
(B) 用現金支付
(C) 修改她的識別資訊
(D) 去找她的錢包

**Questions 41-43 refer to the following conversation.**
美M 美W

**M** Excuse me, I sent off my application to register for the free seminar on archeology but ㊶ **I can't see my name tag on the table.** There was a small fee for the practical sessions, so I just want to make sure I am on the list.
**W** Oh, there was a problem with the registration process at the head office and some names were left out of the system. ㊷ **Can you give me your letter of confirmation?**
**M** Yes, but it's back in my office. I can fetch it.
**W** That'll be helpful. And when you return, ㊸ **I'll make sure you get a free pass to our local archeology exhibition.** The event coordinators are giving them to people whose registrations were left out. I apologize for the inconvenience.

- - - - - - - - - - - - - - - - - - - - - - - -

對話

男：不好意思，我有寄考古學研討會的申請書給您，但我在桌上沒看到我的名牌。校外教學會花一點錢，所以我只是想確認自己在名單上。

女：喔，我們中心的註冊過程有狀況，系統上漏了幾個名字。可以給我看您的確認信嗎？

男：可以，但我放在我的辦公室，我可以拿過來。

女：那樣就太好了。您回來時，我會給您當地考古學展覽的免費入場券。這些是承辦人準備給沒有成功註冊到的人，造成您的不便還請原諒。

**字彙** send off 發出；郵寄　archeology 考古學
name tag 姓名標籤；名牌
practical 實際的；實做的
registration 登記　head office 總部
be left out 被忽略；被排除
letter of confirmation 確認信
fetch 帶來
event coordinator 活動承辦人
entry 入場　voucher 禮券；優惠券

**41** What is the man's problem?
(A) He left his confirmation at home.
(B) He cannot attend the exhibition.
(C) He forgot to register.
(D) His name is missing from a list.

男子的問題是什麼？
(A) 他把確認信放在家裡。
(B) 他不能去看展覽。
(C) 他忘記註冊了。
(D) 他的名字沒在名單上。

**42** What does the woman ask to see?
(A) A letter of confirmation
(B) A payment receipt
(C) A form of identification
(D) A coordinators badge

女子要求看什麼？
(A) 確認信
(B) 付款收據
(C) 某種身分證明
(D) 承辦人的徽章

**43** What is being offered to some conference participants?
(A) Free entry to an exhibition
(B) A voucher for a meal
(C) Access to a conference
(D) A gift shop coupon

部分會議參與者會得到什麼？
(A) 某場展覽的免費入場
(B) 一張餐券
(C) 參加會議的機會
(D) 禮品店禮券

## Questions 44-46 refer to the following conversation.
美W 美M

**W** Novak, **44** I requested the food for the charity event tonight. But I can't find the meat.

**M** Oh, **45** our delivery was delayed this morning so we don't have any in the freezer.

**W** Well, **44** they asked for chicken and beef and I really wanted to begin preparing the meals now.

**M** Don't worry. **46** I'll call the butchers in Birmingham and see if they can supply us with the meat we need.

---

對話

女：諾瓦克，我有叫今晚慈善活動要用的食材，但我找不到肉。

男：喔，今天早上送貨延誤了，所以我們冰箱裡什麼都沒有。

女：好喔，他們點了雞和牛，而我現在真的很想開始做準備。

男：別擔心，我會打給伯明罕的肉店打電話，看看他們能不能提供我們需要的肉。

字彙 **charity event** 慈善活動　**freezer** 冰箱
**beef** 牛肉　**butcher** 肉店；屠夫
**alternative** 可替代的

**44** Where most likely do the speakers work?
(A) At an office
(B) At a jewelry shop
(C) At a supermarket
(D) At a catering business

談話的人最有可能在哪裡工作？
(A) 辦公室
(B) 珠寶店
(C) 超市
(D) 餐飲業

**45** What problem does the man mention?
(A) A delivery did not arrive.
(B) A colleague was late.
(C) A dinner was postponed.
(D) A freezer was faulty.

男子提到了什麼問題？
(A) 貨沒有送到。
(B) 同事遲到了。
(C) 晚飯延後了。
(D) 冰箱有問題

**46** Why will the man make a telephone call?
(A) To find an alternative supplier
(B) To ask for more time
(C) To confirm the status of an order
(D) To check on a client's booking

男子為什麼要打電話？
(A) 以找到替代的供應商
(B) 以要求更多時間
(C) 以確認訂單狀態
(D) 以確認顧客的訂單

## Questions 47-49 refer to the following conversation.
美W 英M

**W** Martin, **47** I saw the living room set you designed in this season's catalog!
I loved it so much that I got the entire set, including the shelves and the table.

**M** Really? Thank you so much! I spent a lot of time thinking about the design.

**W** Actually, I'm setting up four model office spaces for my work this week. I'd like it very much if you would join the team.

**M** You know I really want to be a part of it, but I'm in the middle of several other projects. I'll have to talk to my supervisor about this.

**W** I completely understand. **49** Why don't I stop by later today and ask if I can borrow you for this project?

**M** That would be better. Thank you.

---

對話

女：馬丁，我在這一季的型錄上看到你設計的整套客廳傢俱！我好喜歡，整套傢俱包括櫃子桌子我全都買了。

男：真的嗎？太感謝了！我為了這次設計想很久。

女：我這星期其實忙著打造四間樣品辦公室。我想，如果你可以加入團隊，那就太好了。

23

男：妳懂的，我真的很想參與，但我現在還有好幾個案子在做。這件事我得和我的主管談談。

女：我完全懂的。不如我今天稍晚過去一趟，問問看能不能為了這個案子借用你一下？

男：那樣不錯，謝啦。

> **字彙** entire 全部的；完整的
> stop by 順路造訪　permission 允許；許可

**47** Where do the speakers most likely work?
(A) At a printing company
(B) At a financial institute
(C) At a construction firm
(D) At an office furniture design firm

談話的人最有可能在哪裡工作？
(A) 印刷公司
(B) 金融機構
(C) 建築公司
(D) 辦公傢俱設計公司

**48** What does the man mean when he says, "You know I really want to be a part of it"?
(A) He needs some part for repairs.
(B) His supervisor didn't give him permission.
(C) He is interested in joining the team.
(D) He will go on a business trip soon.

男子說：「我真的很想參與」，其意思為何？
(A) 他需要一些維修用的零件。
(B) 他主管沒有答應。
(C) 他想加入團隊。
(D) 他快要出差。

**49** What does the woman suggest?
(A) Talking to a supervisor
(B) Checking schedules
(C) Postponing a deadline
(D) Borrowing some equipment

女子建議了什麼？
(A) 和老闆談
(B) 確定行程
(C) 延後期限
(D) 借一些設備

**Questions 50-52 refer to the following conversation.**
英M 美W

**M** Hello, Sarah. This is Rafael Figaro calling from Market Force Lawyers. **50 I really want to express thanks for hosting the seminar at the convention center last week**, detailing the benefits of online marketing.

**W** I was happy to do so. The subject's quite complex but your team are very good listeners.

**M** I'm glad to hear that. They commented that the information was very useful. However, some of our employees couldn't make it due to a client visit. I was hoping you could come to our headquarters soon and **51 repeat the lecture** for those who missed it the first time.

**W** Well, I'd be delighted to visit you but **52 I am on vacation for two weeks**. Let's fix a date when I return.

---

男：哈囉，莎拉。我是市場原力律師事務所的拉斐爾·費加洛。您上星期在會議中心主講的研討會，詳細地介紹了網路行銷的優勢，我真的很感謝。

女：我很開心能做到。主題很複雜，不過您的團隊是很棒的聽眾。

男：很高興聽您這麼說。他們反映說資訊很實用，不過有些員工因為客戶來訪沒辦法參加。我希望您能盡快再來我們總部，幫這次沒上到課的同仁再上一次。

女：嗯，可以訪問的話我很開心，不過我目前休假兩週。等我回來我們再敲個時間。

> **字彙** host 主講；主持；主辦　complex 複雜的
> comment 評論　make it 成功；即時趕到
> headquarters 總部
> be delighted to 高興做……
> inspect 視導；檢查；審視
> superior 高於平均的；優越的
> fortnight 兩週

**50** What did the woman do last week?
(A) She spoke at a seminar.
(B) She inspected a college.
(C) She went on a vacation.
(D) She visited a headquarters.

女子上週做了什麼？
(A) 她在研討會上演講。
(B) 她督察了某間大學。
(C) 她去度假了。
(D) 她參觀了總部。

**51** What does the man ask the woman to do?
(A) Talk to a superior
(B) Go on a vacation
(C) Attend a workshop
(D) Repeat a seminar

男子請女子做什麼？
(A) 和上級交談
(B) 去度假
(C) 參加工作坊
(D) 再辦研討會

**52** What problem does the woman mention?
(A) She cannot travel to the office.
(B) She has forgotten her notes.
(C) She has not received her fee.
(D) She is away for a fortnight.

女子提到了什麼問題？
(A) 她到不了辦公室。
(B) 她忘了筆記。
(C) 她沒收到講師費
(D) 她有兩週不在。

**Questions 53-55 refer to the following conversation with three speakers.** 美W 美M 英W

**W1** Hi, Mark and Jessica. **53 You worked here in the marketing division for several months before your first performance review, right?**
**M** Yes, that's right.
**W2** It was four months before I had my first evaluation. Why?
**W1** I've already been with the company for four months, **53 but nobody's said anything to me about a performance review yet. 54 I wonder if I should bring it up.**
**M** Well, we don't have any specific procedure for this.
**W2** That's right. It's possible that your supervisor forgot. You know she's been away on business for the last month. **55 She's meeting with some new clients in Thailand.**

**W1** Well, as soon as she gets back, I'll ask her about it.

--------

三人對話

女1：嗨，馬克、潔西卡。你們來行銷部工作了幾個月以後，才拿到第一次考績的，對嗎？

男：是的，沒錯。

女2：我來四個月時拿到第一次考績，怎麼了嗎？

女1：我來公司四個月了，不過沒人跟我談到任何有關考績的事。我在想要不要主動提這件事。

男：嗯，針對這個，我們並沒有特定的程序。

女2：對啊，妳主管可能忘了吧。妳也知道她這個月都在出差，她正在泰國和一些客戶開會。

女1：好吧，這件事等她一回來我再問她。

字彙 performance review 考績；績效評量
evaluation 評量　procedure 過程
put off 延遲；拖延　clarify 澄清；得到澄清

**53** What are the speakers mainly discussing?
(A) A new contract
(B) A marketing report
(C) An employee evaluation
(D) A travel itinerary

談話的人主要在討論什麼？
(A) 新合約
(B) 行銷報告
(C) 員工評鑑
(D) 差旅行程

**54** Why does the man say, "we don't have any specific procedure for this"?
(A) To put off an announcement
(B) To give the woman an approval
(C) To clarify an issue
(D) To suggest a policy change

為什麼男子說：「針對這個，我們並沒有特定的程序」？
(A) 要延後宣布
(B) 要給予女子許可
(C) 要釐清問題
(D) 要建議修改政策

**55** Why is the supervisor unavailable?
(A) She is meeting some clients.
(B) She is training new employees.
(C) She is finalizing a contract.
(D) She is speaking at a convention.

為什麼找不到主管？
(A) 她正和一些客戶在開會。
(B) 她正在訓練新進同仁。
(C) 她正在幫合約收尾。
(D) 她正在某場會議演講。

Questions 56-58 refer to the following conversation.
(美W) (英M)

W Hi, my name is Nitasha Lark. I took one of your taxis yesterday. I believe **56 I may have left my briefcase on the seat** when I arrived at my destination. Has anyone handed it in?

M Yes, we have it, Ms. Lark. It's secured in the lost-and-found section. We are closed for now but we'll be open in an hour.

W What a relief! Thank you! **57 I'll drop by and collect it in an hour or so.**

M You're welcome. Please remember to **58 bring identification with you** such as a passport or ID card. We have to check that before we can hand over the item.

- - - - - - - - - - - - - - - - - - - - - - - - - -

女：您好，我的名字是尼塔莎‧拉克。我昨天搭乘貴公司的計程車，到目的地時，我想我可能把公事包放在座位上了，有人拿過去嗎？

男：是的，拉克女士，我們這邊有。它保留在失物招領區。我們目前還沒有上班，但一個小時後會開始工作。

女：太好了！謝謝你！我一個小時左右再順道過去拿。

男：歡迎您來。請記得帶上身分證或護照等身分證件。因為交還東西前，我們得先對過證件。

字彙 briefcase 公事包　destination 目的地
hand in 提交　secure 使安全；保護
lost and found 失物招領
relief 寬慰；輕鬆
identification 身分證明；識別
hand over 把……交給
arrangement 安排　description 描述

**56** Why is the woman calling?
(A) To discuss travel arrangements
(B) To complain about a service
(C) To request a taxi
(D) To inquire about a missing item

女子為何打這通電話？
(A) 要討論旅程安排
(B) 要抱怨某項服務
(C) 要叫計程車
(D) 要詢問一件遺失物品

**57** Where will the woman most likely go in an hour?
(A) To a client's office
(B) To a restaurant
(C) To a taxi firm
(D) To a department store

女子一小時後最有可能去哪？
(A) 客戶辦公室
(B) 餐廳
(C) 計程車公司
(D) 百貨公司

**58** What does the man tell the woman to bring?
(A) A form of identification
(B) An application form
(C) A description of the item
(D) Her car

男子提醒女子帶什麼？
(A) 身分證件
(B) 申請表
(C) 物品描述
(D) 她的車

Questions 59-61 refer to the following conversation.
(美W) (美M)

W Oh, look at those cakes! They look delicious!

M Yes, I was thinking of buying something like this for my cousin for his birthday.

W Really? What's special about that package?

M The fruits are hand-dipped in a dark chocolate infused with espresso. Since they're made by hand, they all look slightly different. **59 The problem is that they're only available for a few days, so I don't know if I can order them in time.**

**W** I wish I could buy them for my parents' anniversary that's coming up soon, but I'm actually short of cash now.

**M** That's fine. ⑥ I can order for both of us, and you can pay me back later.

--------------------------------------------------------

對話

女：噢，你看那些蛋糕！看起來好好吃！

男：對啊，我想在表哥生日那天買個像這樣的蛋糕。

女：真的假的？這組合有什麼特別的嗎？

男：水果上淋的是摻有濃縮咖啡的黑巧克力。因為是手工製作，每個看起來都不太一樣。問題在於這只有賣幾天，不知道我訂不訂得到。

女：我爸媽的結婚紀念日快到了，我希望可以買給他們，但我其實缺現金。

男：還好啦，我可以訂我們兩人份的，妳之後再還我錢。

字彙 infuse 充滿；浸泡
slightly 輕微地；些許地
anniversary 週年

**59** What is mentioned about the products?
(A) They are all the same design.
(B) They can be ordered for a limited time.
(C) They are only available online.
(D) They will not be delivered on time.

關於產品，對話中提到什麼？
(A) 設計都一樣。
(B) 限期訂購。
(C) 只能上網買。
(D) 無法準時交貨。

**60** What does the woman imply when she says, "I'm actually short of cash now"?
(A) She only has credit cards.
(B) She left some money in her car.
(C) She does not have enough money.
(D) She can lend some cash to the man.

女子說：「我其實缺現金」，其意思為何？
(A) 她只有信用卡。
(B) 她把錢留在車上。
(C) 她錢不夠。
(D) 她可以借給男子一些現金。

**61** What will the man probably do next?
(A) Place an order
(B) Borrow some money from the woman
(C) Give the woman a lift
(D) Show the woman around the facility

男子接下來可能會做什麼？
(A) 訂購。
(B) 向女子借錢。
(C) 載女子一程。
(D) 帶女子逛設施。

**Questions 62-64 refer to the following conversation.**
英M 美W

**M** Susan, I've been checking the outcome of the research group we arranged to get reaction to ⑥ our new toddler seat and we might have a problem. Most of the feedback reported that the seat is too large and complicated to fit.

**W** Oh! I see. Well, perhaps, ⑥ we should focus more on the ergonomics to ensure the seat is less complicated.

**M** Um maybe, but we've already allocated the majority of our design funding. We will really require more money ⑥ if we are proposing to redesign the seat to alter the complexity. At tomorrow's meeting, ⑥ I can inquire about increasing the funds.

--------------------------------------------------------

對話

男：蘇珊，我一直試著了解我們安排的研究小組做出來的結果，針對新嬰兒座椅的市場反應，我們或許有個問題。多數的回饋意見都說椅子太大了很難裝。

女：喔！我了解了。也許我們應該更著重人體工學，讓椅子沒那麼複雜。

男：嗯，或許吧，但我們已投入大部分的設計經費。如果提議重新設計來解決複雜問題，我們真的需要更多錢。明天開會時我可以問問看投入更多資金的事。

字彙 outcome 結果；成果
research group 研究小組
get reaction 得到反應 toddler 幼童
complicated 複雜的 focus on 專注於
ergonomics 人體工學 allocate 配置
majority of 大部分的；大多數的
funding 資金 redesign 重新設計
alter 改變 complexity 複雜程度；複雜性
inquire 詢問；打聽

解答&中譯解析 Actual Test 6 PART 3

23

**62** What item are the speakers discussing?
(A) A mobile phone
(B) A child seat
(C) A television
(D) A watch

談話的人在討論什麼產品？
(A) 手機
(B) 嬰兒座椅
(C) 電視
(D) 手錶

**63** What does the woman suggest?
(A) Reviewing an advertising strategy
(B) Canceling production
(C) Delaying a consumer survey
(D) Altering a product design

女子建議什麼？
(A) 檢討廣告策略
(B) 取消生產
(C) 延後消費者調查
(D) 變更產品設計

**64** What topic does the man say he will bring up at the meeting?
(A) A request for funding
(B) More time for research
(C) A changed schedule
(D) An alternative product

男子說他開會時將談到什麼議題？
(A) 要求資金
(B) 增加研究時間
(C) 修改後的行程
(D) 替代用品

**Questions 65-67 refer to the following conversation and chart.** 美M 美W

| Vacation Packages | Price (per person) |
|---|---|
| Single ticket | $700 |
| Couple ticket | $500 |
| Family member | $450 |
| ⑥⑥ Group of 6 or more | $400 |

**M** ⑥⑤ **Melanie, there's going to be a company trip to Poland.** A couple of us from the office are planning to go together. Do you want to join us?

**W** Oh, I don't know if I have enough money for an overseas vacation.

**M** It's not that expensive! ⑥⑥ **There are different travel packages, and if we form a group of six or more, we can get a group discount.**

**W** Sure, why not? What should I do?

**M** Here's a brochure with all of the packages explained. ⑥⑦ **You should also call Karl from accounting and tell him that you want to be part of our group.**

**W** That sounds good! When do we leave?

**M** Our flight leaves early on Friday morning!

---

對話與圖表

| 套裝行程 | 價格（每人） |
|---|---|
| 單程票 | 700 美元 |
| 來回票 | 500 美元 |
| 家庭式 | 450 美元 |
| 六人以上團體 | 400 美元 |

**男：** 梅蘭妮，員工旅遊快到了，要去波蘭。我們辦公室裡幾個人打算一起去，妳要加入嗎？

**女：** 喔，我不知道我的錢夠不夠出國玩。

**男：** 沒那麼貴啦！有不同的套裝行程，如果我們六人以上同行還能得到團體折扣。

**女：** 那沒什麼好拒絕的。我該做什麼嗎？

**男：** 這本冊子有解釋所有的套裝行程。妳也得打電話給會計部門的卡爾，告訴他妳想跟我們的團。

**女：** 聽起來很棒！我們什麼時候出發？

**男：** 我們的班機星期五凌晨飛！

字彙 overseas 海外的　accounting 會計

**65** What are the speakers talking about?
(A) A vacation
(B) An overseas business trip
(C) A package delivery
(D) An accounting staff

談話的人在談什麼？
(A) 休假
(B) 海外出差
(C) 包裹遞送
(D) 一名會計同仁

**66** Look at the graphic. What ticket price will the speakers most likely pay?
(A) $700
(B) $500
(C) $450
(D) $400

請看圖表，談話的人買票最有可能付多少錢？
(A) 700 美元
(B) 500 美元
(C) 450 美元
(D) 400 美元

**67** What does the man suggest the woman do?
(A) Go to an accounting office
(B) Buy tickets as soon as possible
(C) Work overtime
(D) Call a colleague

男子建議女人做什麼？
(A) 去會計室
(B) 趕快買票
(C) 加班
(D) 打電話給同事

**Questions 68-70 refer to the following conversation and schedule.** 英M 美W

| Conference Room A | |
|---|---|
| Accounting | 11:00 A.M. |
| ❻❾ Marketing | 2:00 P.M. |
| Sales | 3:00 P.M. |
| Advertising | 4:00 P.M. |

**M** Mrs. Park, have you reserved Conference Room A? ❻❽ **We need to make a sales presentation about our new probiotic pill.** And it is the only room where we can make conference calls.

**W** ❻❾ **Ron's team specifically asked for Conference Room A for two o'clock to train the new staff.** Audrey is in charge of arranging a meeting room, but she is on vacation.

**M** I don't think that they need the conference call option. ❼⓿ **Could you call and ask them if they can use Conference Room B?** Be sure to mention that it's a newly renovated room.

**W** ❼⓿ **Understood. I'll get right on it.**

---

**對話與時程表**

| 一號會議室 | |
|---|---|
| 會計 | 早上 11:00 |
| 行銷 | 下午 2:00 |
| 銷售 | 下午 3:00 |
| 廣告 | 下午 4:00 |

男：朴女士，妳預約一號會議室了嗎？我們要做新益生菌藥丸的銷售簡報，那裡是我們唯一可以開視訊會議的地點。

女：榮恩的團隊指定兩點要在第一會議室培訓新進員工。奧黛麗負責安排會議室，但她現在正在休假。

男：我認為他們不需要開視訊會議。妳能不能打電話問他們可不可以用第二會議室？別忘了跟他們提到，那間才剛整修完。

女：了解，我馬上辦。

字彙 probiotic 益生菌　pill 藥丸
specifically 特別地　in charge of 負責做
arrange 安排　pharmaceutical 製藥的

**68** Where do the speakers most likely work?
(A) At a shipping company
(B) At a pharmaceutical company
(C) At a real estate agency
(D) At a software manufacturer

談話的人最有可能在哪裡工作？
(A) 貨運公司
(B) 藥廠
(C) 房仲業
(D) 軟體製造商

**69** Look at the graphic. In which department does Ron most likely work?
(A) Accounting
(B) Marketing
(C) Sales
(D) Advertising

請看圖表，榮恩最有可能在哪個部門工作？
(A) 會計
(B) 行銷
(C) 銷售
(D) 廣告

23

**70** What will the woman probably do next?
(A) Bring some presentation materials
(B) Conduct an online survey
(C) Ask a coworker to change rooms
(D) Reschedule a meeting

女子接下來可能會做什麼？
(A) 帶簡報素材來
(B) 上網發問卷
(C) 請同事換房間
(D) 重新安排會議

## PART 4

P. 239

**Questions 71-73 refer to the following advertisement.**
美M

Are you searching for a substitute to television and books? Then come to **71** **Ziggy's, the area's largest retailer of computer games and apps.** Our customers keep returning because we stock the most extensive selection of games available, including award winning fantasy, war, sport and adventure games. **72** **We also have a children's games arena for them to try out games under adult supervision.** So you can look around while we look after them. And if you are unable to visit the store, you can order any of our games straight from our warehouse. **73** **We assure overnight delivery.** You'll receive your order the next day.

------

廣告

您是不是正在找取代電視和書本的娛樂呢？那就來齊集市吧！它是當地最大的電腦遊戲和應用程式零售商店。擁有市面上最廣泛的遊戲類型，得獎的幻想、戰爭、運動和冒險遊戲通通有，難怪客人會一直回購。我們還設有兒童遊戲區，讓他們在大人陪同下試玩遊戲。我們幫您顧孩子時，您也能到處逛逛。而且，如果您沒辦法親自前來，也能直接從庫存訂購我們的任何遊戲。我們保證隔天到貨。訂完隔天您就會收到。

**71** What kind of business is Ziggy's?
(A) A gaming store
(B) A bookstore
(C) A video store
(D) A music store

齊集市是什麼業者？
(A) 遊戲店
(B) 書店
(C) 影視出租販賣店
(D) 樂器或唱片行

**72** What does Ziggy's offer for families with children?
(A) Free drinks in the evenings
(B) A parental list of safe games
(C) A supervised gaming area
(D) A monthly free workshop

齊集市為有小孩的家庭提供什麼？
(A) 傍晚的免費飲料
(B) 家長的安全遊戲清單
(C) 被看管的遊戲區
(D) 每個月的免費工作坊

**73** What does the advertisement say about online orders?
(A) They are shipped at a small cost.
(B) They are delivered overnight.
(C) They will come with special discounts.
(D) They can be gift wrapped.

關於線上訂購，這則廣告說了什麼？
(A) 運費低廉。
(B) 隔天交貨。
(C) 有特別折扣。
(D) 可包裝禮品。

**Questions 74-76 refer to the following announcement.**
美W

❼❹ Attention, all Vanquis Bank customers. We'll be ❼❺ closing the Rianta branch earlier than normal. We apologize for any inconvenience this may cause you. Customers who are paying a bill due today, please make your way to the front desk where you will be dealt with immediately. Please note that ❼❻ any money paid in today will be immediately transmitted without delay. Again, we apologize for the inconvenience at Vanquis Bank.

宣告

　　范克希銀行全體客戶請注意。里安達分行將比平常提早結束營業，我們對此帶來的任何不便深表歉意。客戶如有今日到期的帳單請至櫃檯，行員將即刻為您辦理。也請您留意，今日支付的所有款項都將立即轉帳。我們再次為造成您在范克希銀行的任何不便深表歉意。

字彙　normal 平常的　pay a bill 繳帳單；結帳
　　　due 到期　make one's way to 前往……
　　　deal with 前往　note 留意；注意
　　　pay in 把……存入銀行　account 帳戶

**74** Where most likely is the announcement being made?
(A) On a tour bus
(B) On an airplane
(C) In a hotel
(D) In a bank
此廣播最可能在哪裡聽到？
(A) 觀光巴士上
(B) 飛機上
(C) 飯店內
(D) 銀行內

**75** What does the speaker apologize for?
(A) Early closure
(B) A cancelled service
(C) Delayed payments
(D) A bomb alert
說話的人為何道歉？
(A) 提早關門
(B) 取消服務
(C) 延後撥款
(D) 炸彈警報

**76** What are customers paying bills assured of?
(A) Their payments will not be accepted.
(B) Their bills will be paid at once.
(C) Another option will be offered.
(D) Refunds will be issued.
繳款帳單的客戶得到什麼保障？
(A) 他們的繳款將不被接受。
(B) 他們的帳單將即刻處理。
(C) 將有別的選擇。
(D) 將得到退款。

**Questions 77-79 refer to the following excerpt from a speech.** 澳M

And the next matter to discuss, the closing date for submissions for the Picoult Awards is July 23rd. You know these are the most influential awards in dance and performance arts. ❼❽ For the last two years, we came second overall in the contemporary dance category. And our management trustees would like to better that this year. So they've requested that we select the best performances from the past twelve months ❼❼ to put forward for the competition. ❼❾ Does anyone have any memorable performances we should choose from?

發言摘錄

　　接下來要討論的是皮考特獎，它的收件截止日是 7 月 23 日。如眾所知，這是舞蹈和表演藝術領域最具影響力的獎項。過去兩年，我們在現代舞蹈類排名第二，而我們的董事希望今年可以更好。所以，他們要求我們挑出十二個月以來最好的表演去參賽。有誰要推薦難忘的演出嗎？

字彙　closing date 截止日期
　　　influential 有影響力的
　　　performance arts 表演藝術
　　　contemporary 現代的；當代的
　　　trustee（學校、社團等的）理事會理事；董事
　　　put forward 推薦；推出
　　　competition 競爭；競賽
　　　memorable 難忘的；值得紀念的
　　　appoint 指派
　　　routine（舞蹈）動作；慣例；例行公事

**77** What is the speaker discussing?
(A) A television program
(B) A theater production
(C) An advertising campaign
(D) A performance competition

談話的人在討論什麼？
(A) 電視節目
(B) 劇場作品
(C) 廣告宣傳活動
(D) 表演競賽

**78** What does the speaker say happened two years ago?
(A) The company won an award.
(B) A new director was appointed.
(C) The company changed its dance routine.
(D) An alternative schedule was introduced.

談話的人說兩年前發生了什麼事？
(A) 公司獲獎。
(B) 任命了新董事。
(C) 公司修改了舞蹈動作。
(D) 彈性工時上路。

**79** What are listeners asked to do?
(A) Appoint a trustee
(B) Contact an audience
(C) Make recommendations
(D) Plan a new routine

聽話者被要求做什麼？
(A) 指派一名董事
(B) 聯絡觀眾
(C) 推薦
(D) 設計新的舞蹈動作

**Questions 80-82 refer to the following telephone message.** 美W

Hello, this message is for Okambe Kwan. My name is Rosalind Laker and ⑧⓪ I'm ringing from the Holiday Club Tour on Lister Street. Last month, you entered a photographic competition and I'm delighted to inform you that you have won the first prize of a weekend city break for two worth £300. ⑧① We have your prize waiting for you in the store. Please ⑧② remember to bring your passport when you come in to claim your prize. Thank you for entering the Holiday Club Tour competition and we look forward to meeting you soon.

-----

電話留言

您好，這是給岡本‧關的留言。我是羅莎琳德‧雷克，從李斯特街的假日俱樂部之旅打給您。您上個月參加了攝影比賽，我很高興通知您您贏得首獎，價值三百英鎊的雙人週末城市之旅。獎品保留在我們店裡等您來領取。領獎時，請記得攜帶您的護照。感謝您參加假日俱樂部的比賽，我們期待很快能與您相見。

字彙 **photographic competition** 攝影競賽
**city break** 城市之旅；城市遊
**claim** 要求（擁有）；認領；索取
**retrieve** 獲得
**identification** 識別；身分證明

**80** Where most likely does the speaker work?
(A) At a photographic store
(B) At a supermarket
(C) At an art gallery
(D) At a travel agency

說話的人最可能在哪裡工作？
(A) 相館
(B) 超市
(C) 美術館
(D) 旅行社

**81** Why does the speaker ask the listener to come to the business?
(A) To refund a holiday
(B) To enter a competition
(C) To pick up a prize
(D) To retrieve a lost item

說話的人為何要求聽話者來店裡？
(A) 補假
(B) 參賽
(C) 領獎
(D) 領取遺失物

**82** What does the speaker ask the listener to bring?
(A) An invoice
(B) Holiday brochures
(C) Passport identification
(D) Account details

說話的人要求聽話者帶什麼？
(A) 發貨單
(B) 旅遊手冊
(C) 護照
(D) 帳戶資訊

## Questions 83-85 refer to the following telephone message. 澳M

Hello, this message is for Mr. Desi Landau. **83 I'm calling from the Frenhill Surgery to confirm your attendance** for a mandatory eye examination at 10:30 this Friday morning. As the test requires you to see at long and short distances, please ensure that you **84 bring any glasses or contact lenses with you.** If not, it may affect the outcome of the test. Could you give me a call when you receive this voicemail? Also **85 I need the address of your workplace.** We'll see you on Friday.

----

電話留言

您好，這是給德西·藍道的留言。這裡是法蘭丘診所，想確認這星期五早上十點半的強制性視力檢查您是否會到場。檢查時需要您從近距離和遠距離觀看，請確保隨身攜帶您的眼鏡或隱形眼鏡，否則可能會影響檢查結果。您收到這則語音留言後可以回電給我嗎？另外，我也需要您工作地點的地址。我們星期五見。

字彙 surgery（醫生或牙醫的）診所
attendance 出席
mandatory 強制的；必須履行的；法定的
eye examination 視力檢查
long and short distance 遠近距離
ensure 確保　outcome 結果
voicemail 語音留言
workplace 工作地點　referral 轉診

**83** What is the purpose of the message?
(A) To provide a referral
(B) To change a date
(C) To provide a driving test
(D) To confirm an appointment
這則留言的主旨為何？
(A) 協助轉診
(B) 改期
(C) 提供路考
(D) 確認門診

**84** What does the speaker remind Mr. Landau to do on Friday morning?
(A) Submit an insurance claim
(B) Bring eye glasses if necessary
(C) Call back for examination results
(D) Arrive half an hour early
說話的人提醒藍道先生週五早上要做什麼？
(A) 要求保險理賠
(B) 必要時攜帶眼鏡
(C) 回電詢問檢查結果
(D) 提前半小時到

**85** What information does the speaker need from Mr. Laundau?
(A) The address of his workplace
(B) An alternative contact number
(C) An identification number
(D) A date for a repeat visit
說話的人需要藍道先生提供什麼資訊？
(A) 他工作地點的地址
(B) 備用電話號碼
(C) 身分證字號
(D) 回診日期

## Questions 86-88 refer to the following telephone message. 英W

Hi, Jim. It's Lisa, your next-door neighbor. I was supposed to come back from a business trip early this evening, but the subway's currently shut down, and buses are really slow because of all the heavy rain. **86 I've been trying to get a taxi**, but it isn't easy thus far. I have a huge favor to ask of you. **88 Could you possibly go to my apartment and feed my cat?** She tends to get cranky and scratches the furniture when she is hungry. There's a bag of cat food on the counter that you can open and put into her bowl. Thanks.

----

電話留言

嗨，吉姆。我是你的鄰居麗莎。我本來今晚會出差回來，但現在地鐵關了、公車也因為大雨開得很慢。我試著叫計程車，可是到現在還是很難叫到。我可以麻煩你一件很重要的事嗎？你有沒有可能到我的公寓幫我餵貓呢？她要是餓了很容易抓狂、還會抓家具。吧台上有袋貓飼料，你可以打開來把飼料倒進她的碗裡嗎？謝謝。

字彙 shut down 關閉；停止運作
thus far 迄今　tend to 傾向；易於
cranky 暴躁不安的；脾氣壞的

86 Where is the speaker most likely calling from?
(A) An airport
(B) A taxi stand
(C) A bus stop
(D) A pet shop

說話的人最有可能從哪裡打電話？
(A) 機場
(B) 計程車站
(C) 公車站
(D) 寵物店

87 What does the speaker imply when she says, "but it isn't easy thus far"?
(A) She cannot get a taxi.
(B) She is stuck in traffic.
(C) She doesn't know where the taxi stand is.
(D) She thinks the destination is too far away.

說話的人說：「可是到現在還是很難叫到」時，意思為何？
(A) 她叫不到車。
(B) 她塞車了。
(C) 她不知道計程車站在哪裡。
(D) 她覺得目的地太遠了。

88 What does the speaker ask the listener to do?
(A) Call back
(B) Walk the pet
(C) Feed her pet
(D) Close the bedroom door

說話的人希望聽話者做什麼？
(A) 回電
(B) 帶寵物散步
(C) 餵她的寵物
(D) 關臥室的門

Questions 89-91 refer to the following announcement.
美W

Hello, and ❽❾ welcome to the annual conference on building harmony in the office. This conference was originally scheduled to end at 3:30 P.M., but I'm going to need you for a little more time ❾⓿ as we have a lot of material to cover and many activities to do. ❾❶ What we are handing out right now are questionnaires that we would like for you to fill out as a show of participation and also evidence that you attended this conference. Once you complete the questionnaire, please drop it in the white plastic box right by the door at the end of the day.

宣告

您好，歡迎參加營造融洽辦公室的年會。會議原定下午三點半結束，但因為還有很多資料需要處理、很多活動要做，得再耽誤你們一點時間。我們現在正在發放的問卷，希望您能填完，代表您有出席並留下證明。等您寫完問卷，請在今天結束前放進門邊的白色塑膠盒裡面。

字彙 harmony 融洽；和諧　cover 處理
questionnaire 問卷
evidence 證明；證據　goer 參加者；來賓

89 Who most likely are the listeners?
(A) Competition participants
(B) Festival goers
(C) Security guards
(D) Conference attendees

聽眾最有可能是誰？
(A) 參賽者
(B) 慶典來賓
(C) 維安人員
(D) 會議來賓

90 What does the speaker imply when she says, "I'm going to need you for a little more time"?
(A) The listeners are in a hurry to leave.
(B) The event will go longer than expected.
(C) The speaker is busy with other projects.
(D) The audience wants the event to end soon.

說話的人說：「我得再耽誤你們一點時間」時，意思為何？

(A) 聽話的人得快點離開。
(B) 活動比預計時間更長。
(C) 說話的人正忙著趕別的案子。
(D) 聽眾希望活動盡快結束。

**91** What is the speaker distributing to the listeners?
(A) Brochures
(B) Greeting cards
(C) Survey forms
(D) Vouchers

說話的人正在發什麼東西給聽眾？

(A) 小冊子
(B) 賀卡
(C) 調查表
(D) 優待券

**Questions 92-94 refer to the following excerpt from a meeting and table.** 英M

| Types of services | Fastshipping | BSS |
|---|---|---|
| Additional charge for an international shipping | O | O |
| Arrival notification service | O | O |
| Package pickup | O | O |
| ❾❹ Breakage insurance | | O |

❾❷ **Before we get started, we should congratulate ourselves on how much Fastshipping, our online business, has grown in the last ten months.** When we first started, we were in the red because we were getting maybe a couple of orders a month. Because the number of orders is rising rapidly, ❾❸ **we need to improve our services.** The table you see on the screen compares our company with our competitor, BSS. ❾❹ **I'd like to discuss how we can improve our service to keep up with BSS.**

---

| 服務類型 | 快速到貨 | BSS |
|---|---|---|
| 國際運輸之附加費用 | O | O |
| 到貨通知 | O | O |
| 包裹領取 | O | O |
| 貨損保險 | | O |

開始前，首先先恭喜我們的網路業務「快速到貨」十個月來大幅成長。因為每個月的訂單可能只有個位數，起初都是赤字。由於訂單增加得很快，我們必須改善服務。你在螢幕上看到的表格，比較了我們公司和競爭對手 BSS。我想討論我們服務的改善方法，才能趕上 BSS。

字彙 **in the red** 有赤字；虧損　**rapidly** 很快地　**compare** 比較　**keep up with** 跟上（形勢）　**notification** 通知　**breakage** 損壞　**insurance** 保險

24

**92** Who most likely is the speaker?
(A) A business owner
(B) A retiring employee
(C) A technician
(D) A professor in a college

說話的人最有可能是誰？

(A) 企業老闆
(B) 退休員工
(C) 技術員
(D) 大學教授

**93** What is the main purpose of the meeting?
(A) To recruit more employees
(B) To open a new branch
(C) To improve the service
(D) To analyze a rival company

會議的主要目的為何？

(A) 要招聘更多員工
(B) 要設立分公司
(C) 要改善服務
(D) 要分析競爭對手

**94** Look at the graphic. What will the speaker most likely discuss next?
(A) Additional charge for international shipping
(B) Arrival notification service
(C) Package pickup
(D) Breakage insurance

請看圖表，說話的人接下來最可能討論
什麼事？
(A) 國際運輸之附加費用
(B) 到貨通知
(C) 包裹領取
(D) 貨損保險

## Questions 95-97 refer to the following announcement and chart. 澳M

| Survey Results | |
|---|---|
| Waste treatment system | 35% |
| ⑨⑥ Enlarging Parking Lot | 30% |
| Fitness Facility | 25% |
| Repainting work | 10% |

I'd like to share the results of the residents' survey taken the last month to start this meeting. As you can see on the screen, ⑨⑤ the question we focused on from the survey was "Which of the following improvements would you like to see in your residence?" The top four results are on the next slide. Although the most popular answer was waste treatment system, I'm afraid to say that this is not a possible option for now considering we have to get it approved by the city, which may take more than 6 months. ⑨⑥ The second most popular option would be best to address first. ⑨⑦ By the end of this meeting, I want an outline of possible layouts and a calculation of the costs of two new parking lots for the complex.

宣告與圖表

| 調查結果 | |
|---|---|
| 廢棄物處理設施 | 35% |
| 停車場擴建 | 30% |
| 健身房 | 25% |
| 塗裝工程 | 10% |

　　會議一開始，我想分享上個月的住戶調查結果。在螢幕上能看到，我們調查所聚焦的問題是「您希望在居住環境中看到哪一項改善？」。前四名在下一張投影片上。雖然得到最多響應的是廢棄物處理設施，但考慮到我們必須取得市府批准，可能需要超過六個月的時間，我恐怕得說它現階段不可行。響應第二高的選項看起來最好率先處理。會議結束前，我想看到平面配置圖的簡圖，以及該建築內兩處新停車場的報價。

字彙 resident 住戶；居民
improvement 改善；改進；修繕
residence 住宅；居住環境
treatment 處理
considering 考慮到；就……而言
address 處理　outline 簡圖；草圖；輪廓
layout 配置　enlarge 擴建；擴大
tentative 臨時的　floor plan 樓層平面圖

**95** What is the focus on the meeting?
(A) Improving the community center
(B) Meeting residents' requests
(C) Raising money
(D) Remodeling commercial facilities
會議的重點是什麼？
(A) 改善社區中心
(B) 滿足居民需求
(C) 募資
(D) 改造商家

**96** Look at the graphic. What does the speaker want to focus on?
(A) Waste treatment system
(B) Enlarging parking lot
(C) Fitness facility
(D) Repainting work
請看圖表，說話的人想要聚焦的是什麼？
(A) 廢棄物處理設施
(B) 停車場擴建
(C) 健身房
(D) 塗裝工程

**97** What does the speaker want from the listeners?
(A) A decision on whether to increase rent
(B) A suggestion for a new parking lot
(C) A tentative contract
(D) A new floor plan
說話的人想從聽眾那裡得到什麼？
(A) 是否增加租金的決定
(B) 對新停車場的建議
(C) 臨時契約
(D) 新的樓層平面圖

Questions 98-100 refer to the following announcement and timetable. 英W

| Departing Flight | Destination | Departure Time |
|---|---|---|
| 742 | London | 2:00 P.M. |
| 707 | 99 Seattle | 3:15 P.M. |
| 747 | Los Angeles | 3:30 P.M. |
| 778 | Hawaii | 5:30 P.M. |

Attention, 99 all passengers waiting for the flight bound for Seattle. 98 As announced earlier, the flight has been grounded for the time being due to several mechanical issues of the aircraft. I am more than glad to announce that repairs are now successfully underway. Since the flight will not take off until these concerns are fully addressed, 100 please follow the airport staff members to the lounge to enjoy some refreshments. 99 The updated departure time has been posted on the screen. We apologize for any inconveniences and thank you for your patience.

-------

**宣告與時間表**

| 離站航班 | 目的地 | 起飛時間 |
|---|---|---|
| 742 | 倫敦 | 下午 2:00 |
| 707 | 西雅圖 | 下午 3:15 |
| 747 | 洛杉磯 | 下午 3:30 |
| 778 | 夏威夷 | 下午 5:30 |

　　前往西雅圖班機的候機旅客請注意。如先前所廣播的，班機由於多項機械問題，目前暫時停飛。我很高興通知您，維修進展得很順利。由於班機在問題徹底解決前無法起飛，請您跟隨機場人員前往貴賓室享用小點心。更新後的起飛時間已顯示在螢幕上。有任何不便之處請您見諒，並感謝您的耐心等候。

**字彙** bound for 前往……　ground 使停飛
underway 在進行中的　take off 起飛
refreshments 點心；茶點
inconvenience 不便　patience 耐心
inclement 天氣惡劣的　flaw 缺陷
routine 例行公事

**98** What is the cause of the delay?
(A) Inclement weather
(B) A mechanical flaw
(C) A human error
(D) A routine maintenance

延誤的原因為何？
(A) 天氣惡劣
(B) 機械缺陷
(C) 人為錯誤
(D) 例行檢查

**99** Look at the graphic. What is the updated time for the flight?
(A) 2:00 P.M.
(B) 3:15 P.M.
(C) 3:30 P.M.
(D) 5:30 P.M.

請看圖表，該班機更新後的起飛時間為何？
(A) 下午 2:00
(B) 下午 3:15
(C) 下午 3:30
(D) 下午 5:30

**100** What are the listeners asked to do?
(A) Board the airplane in advance
(B) Wait for the announcement
(C) Follow the staff members
(D) Buy some food

聽眾被要求做什麼？
(A) 提前登機
(B) 等待廣播
(C) 跟隨工作人員
(D) 買些食物

**101**

馬克成功把新的廚房家電打進市場。

(A) successes 成功
(B) successfully 成功地
(C) successful 成功的
(D) success 成功

解析 空格位在 has 和 p.p. 之間，應填入副詞，用來修飾動詞，因此答案為 (B)。success 為名詞、successful 為形容詞，都不能修飾動詞。

字彙 appliance 家電

**102**

寬頻連結可能是馬諾特通訊或服務供應商切斷的。

(A) either（兩者中）任何一個
(B) both 兩者
(C) however 然而
(D) plus 並且

解析 本題考的是相關連接詞。空格與後方的 or 搭配使用，either A or B 的意思為 A 或者 B 其中一個，因此答案要選 (A)。neither A nor B、both A and B、not only A but (also) B 皆為相關連接詞，請特別熟記。

字彙 broadband 寬頻
access 連結；通道　cut off 切斷
service provider 服務供應商

**103**

知名環保人士卡門‧桑切斯因拯救北極熊的運動受到表揚。

(A) environmental 環保的
(B) environmentalist 環保人士
(C) environmentally 有關環境方面
(D) environments 環境

解析 在冠詞（a）和形容詞（well-known）後方的空格，應填入名詞。environmentalist 和 environments 皆為名詞，但是空格前方的主詞為人，填入同位語較為適當，因此答案為人物名詞 (B)。

字彙 environmentalist 環保人士
environmentally 有關環境方面的

**104**

阿蘭西有機食品促銷得到很正面的迴響，行銷團隊打算在未來六個月內增產四成。

(A) increase 增加
(B) increasing　增加中的
(C) increases 增加
(D) to increase 增加

解析 空格置於動詞 plan 的受詞位置，而 plan 要使用 to 不定詞作為受詞，因此答案為 (D)。後方連接 to 不定詞使用的動詞有 need、wish、hope、desire、expect、plan、aim、decide、propose、offer、ask、promise、agree、refuse、fail、serve、pretend、afford、manage、prefer 等，請特別熟記。

字彙 positive 正面的　response 迴響
promotion 促銷　production 生產

**105**

高效率的團隊合作能帶來卓越的成果，我們在宣傳活動時的夥伴關係就是一例。

(A) excellently 極好地
(B) excellent 卓越的
(C) excel 擅長
(D) excellence 卓越

解析 空格後方連接名詞，應填入形容詞，用來修飾後方名詞，因此答案為 (B)。excellently 為副詞、excel 為動詞、excellence 為名詞，都不適合填入空格中。另外補充一點，how 的後方可以直接連接形容詞或副詞。

字彙 partnership 夥伴關係
publicity 宣傳　drive（宣傳）活動
lead to 帶來；導致　excel 擅長

**106**

朗客歷險軟體是專門設計給當主管不在辦公室時仍想監控員工的公司。

(A) designed 被設計
(B) appointed 被任命
(C) accomplished 被完成
(D) informed 被告知

解析 本題考的是動詞詞彙。根據題意，表達「為他們專門設計」最為適當，因此答案為 (A)。

字彙　monitor 監控　away from 離開
appoint 任命；約定
accomplish 完成

**107**

兩天前，海耶斯女士告訴大家角落裡的幾堆文件是她的。

(A) she 她
(B) hers 她的（東西）
(C) her 她的
(D) herself 她自己

解析　空格位在 be 動詞後方，扮演補語的角色。根據題意，表達「告知人們那一疊文書是她的」較為適當，因此答案為 (B)。

字彙　pile 堆　paperwork 文書工作

**108**

管線重新鋪設的工程原定 2 月 11 日前完成。

(A) originally 原本
(B) extremely 極其
(C) strongly 強烈地
(D) highly 非常

解析　本題考的是副詞詞彙。根據題意，表達「原本計劃於 2 月 11 日完成」最為適當，因此答案為 (A)。

字彙　reconstruction 重建；改造
pipeline 管線　originally 原本；起先
highly 非常；極其

**109**

因應員工的建議，我們的辦公室早上會提前開。

(A) suggestions 建議
(B) suggest 建議
(C) suggests 建議
(D) suggested 被建議的

解析　本題考的是名詞詞彙。空格與前方的 employee 一同放在介系詞後方，作為受詞使用。因此答案為 (A)，與前方名詞組合成複合名詞。suggested 當作過去分詞使用時，雖然可以用來修飾前方名詞，但是 employee 屬於可數名詞，不能單獨使用，因此該選項不能作為答案。

字彙　response 回應；因應

**110**

新進人員訓練課程上不只提供無酒精飲料，也將有各種開胃菜。

(A) during 在……時候
(B) along 沿著
(C) onto 到……之上
(D) about 關於

解析　本題考的是介系詞。根據題意，表達「在新進人員培訓期間」最為適當，因此答案為 (A)。另外補充一點，on、over、as to/for、regarding、concerning、pertaining to、in reference to、with/in respect to、in/with regard to、when it comes to 等皆為 about 的同義字，請特別熟記。

字彙　soft drink 無酒精飲料
a selection of 各種

**111**

員工因為近期在產線上的努力付出，獲得麥克布萊德先生的讚賞。

(A) their 他們的
(B) them 他們
(C) theirs 他們的（東西）
(D) they 他們

解析　介系詞（for）和名詞（dedication）之間的空格，應填入代名詞的所有格，因此答案為 (A)。

字彙　applaud 稱讚
dedication 努力付出；貢獻
run 運行；運作

**112**

雷蒙 DVD 因其客戶服務贏得民間好評。

(A) impact 影響
(B) access 管道
(C) feedback 回饋意見
(D) experience 經驗

解析　本題考的是名詞詞彙。根據題意，表達「針對客戶服務收到正面的反饋」最為適當，因此答案為 (C)。

字彙　impact 影響

**113**

請在宣布得獎者前，確保所有得獎人均已
抵達宴會廳。

(A) announcing 宣布
(B) announced 被宣布
(C) announcement 公告
(D) announcer 主持人

**解析** announcing, announcement,
announcer 皆能放在 before 的後方，但是
空格後方連接了名詞（the winners）。當中
只有動名詞後方可以連接受詞，因此答案為
(A)。

**字彙** in attendance 出席；到場
dining hall 宴會廳

**114**

為了緩解主幹道的交通壅塞做了很多努
力，只是沒半個能解決問題。

(A) none 全無
(B) nothing 沒有東西
(C) nobody 無人
(D) neither 兩者皆非

**解析** of 後方的 which 為關係代名詞，用來
代替前方出現的先行詞 efforts。空格位在
形容詞子句中的主詞位置，根據題意，表達
「皆無法解決問題」最為適當，因此答案為
(A)。

**字彙** ease 減輕；緩解
main highway 主幹道；主要公路

**115**

鄧祿普縣歷史博物館由在地歷史研究協會
維護。

(A) maintained 維護了
(B) is maintained 被維護
(C) is maintaining 正在維護
(D) can maintain 可維護

**解析** 空格後方並未連接受詞，應填入動詞
的被動語態，故答案為 (B) is maintained。

**字彙** maintain 維護

**116**

由於低稅率和豐沛的勞動力，阿馬澤縣吸
引了為數眾多的新企業。

(A) as a result 作為……的結果
(B) owing to 由於
(C) now that 既然
(D) because 因為

**解析** 空格連接後方的名詞片語，組合成
修飾語，因此空格應填入介系詞。as a
result（結果）為副詞、now that（既然）
和 because（因為）為連接詞、(B) owing
to（因為）為選項中唯一的介系詞，故為
正確答案。另外補充一點，due to 和 on
account of 皆為表示原因的介系詞，請一併
熟記。

**字彙** bountiful 量大的；豐沛的
workforce 勞動力；工人

**117**

我們將在 11 月 1 日或之後給您錄取通知。

(A) to 去
(B) of 關於
(C) for 為了
(D) from 從

**解析** 請熟記常用片語 notify A of B（將 B
通知 A），因此答案要選 (B)。另外補充一
點，動詞 notify（通知）後方要直接連接通
知的「對象」當作受詞，其後方再連接通
知的「內容」；有時也會使用句型 notify A
that . . .，請一併記下此用法。

**118**

採購最新設備對公司整體獲利能力有重大
影響。

(A) profitable 有盈利的
(B) profitability 獲利能力
(C) profitably 有利地
(D) profited 受益的

**解析** 空格受到所有格（a company's）和
形容詞（overall）的修飾，應填入名詞，因
此答案為 (B) profitability（收益性）。

**字彙** acquisition 收購

**119**

我們的人力指派會定期調整，以確保所有人都有機會直接與客戶合作。

(A) previously 先前地
(B) accordingly 相應地
(C) periodically 定期地
(D) extremely 極其

解析 previously（以前）要搭配動詞的過去式一起使用，因此不能作為答案；accordingly（因此）不符合題意；extremely（非常）雖為副詞，卻不能用來修飾動詞，因此也不正確。綜合前述，答案為 (C) periodically。另外補充一點，frequently、usually、periodically、often 這類頻率副詞經常搭配動詞的現在簡單式一起使用，請特別熟記。

字彙 adjust 調整

**120**

雖然飯店的接待櫃檯全天開放，但往返機場的免費接駁車只有在上午 6 點到晚上 10 點間服務。

(A) Despite 雖然
(B) However 然而
(C) Although 雖然
(D) Nevertheless 然而

解析 空格用來引導後方的子句（主詞＋動詞），因此應填入連接詞。選項中，However（無論如何）和 Although（儘管）皆能當作連接詞使用，但是填入 (C) Although 較符合題意，故為正確答案。Despite（儘管）為介系詞、Nevertheless（不過）為副詞，都無法填入空格中。另外補充一點，However 當作連接詞使用時，意思為「無論如何」；當作副詞使用時，意思為「然而」，請特別熟記。

字彙 around the clock 全天的；24 小時的
to and from 往返

**121**

擔心近期的惡劣天氣將衝擊日邊島的觀光，當地多家飯店業者已宣布特別優惠。

(A) Concerning 關於
(B) Concerned 擔心
(C) Been concerned 擔心過
(D) To have been concerning 已擔心許久

解析 空格至逗點扮演副詞的角色，用來修飾整句話。分詞構句和 to 不定詞片語皆能扮演副詞的角色，但是 be 動詞本身屬於不及物動詞，無法省略，因此 (C) Been concerned 不能作為答案，請先刪去（若為 Being concerned，則能省略 Being）。

其餘選項分成主動、和被動語態，需從此差異判斷答案。動詞 concern（影響、使擔心）後方要連接一個對象當作受詞（通常是人），但空格後方直接連接 that 子句，並未連接受詞，因此答案要選被動語態 (B) concerned。

字彙 inclement 天氣惡劣的

**122**

依照公司政策，銷售人員須獲得上級許可才能自己使用公司設備。

(A) Instead of 代替
(B) As well as 也
(C) On behalf of 代表
(D) In accordance with 依照

解析 空格連接後方的名詞片語，組合成修飾語，因此空格應填入介系詞。As well as 兩邊要放置相同的詞性，屬於對等連接詞，並不適合填入空格中；Instead of（代替）、On behalf of（代表）、In accordance with（按照）皆為介系詞，當中 (D) 最符合題意，故為正確答案。

字彙 associate 同事

**123**

在卑爾根國家公園，你能盡情爬山也能在湖邊散步。

(A) persistent 持續的
(B) conclusive 決定性的
(C) leisurely 悠閒的
(D) tolerant 寬容的

解析 本題考的是形容詞詞彙。根據題意，表達「能夠享受悠閒的散步」最為適當，因此答案為 (C)。

字彙 trek （徒步）長途跋涉
mountainside 山腰；山邊
persistent 持續的
conclusive 決定性的
leisurely 悠閒的　tolerant 寬容的

**124**

金融區位於史坦堡市中心,搭乘公共交通工具可輕鬆抵達。

(A) accessible 可到達的
(B) active 積極的
(C) necessary 需要的
(D) transportable 可運輸的

解析 本題考的是形容詞詞彙。根據題意,表達「鄰近大眾運輸」最為適當,因此答案為 (A)。

字彙 financial district 金融區
accessible 可到達的
transportable 可運輸的

**125**

韋斯勒的任何員工要是將公司機密洩露給他人,都將面臨解僱。

(A) All 所有
(B) Several 幾個
(C) Few 一些
(D) Any 任何

解析 本題要選出最適合填入空格的限定詞。(D) 用於肯定句中表示「任何」的意思,最符合題意,故為正確答案。

字彙 reveal 洩漏 confidential 機密的
terminate 解僱

**126**

史塔克蘭的官員和索羅嫩的工程師正忙著磋商新環狀道路的建案。

(A) negotiations 磋商
(B) receipts 收據
(C) construction 建設
(D) increase 增加

解析 本題考的是名詞詞彙。根據題意,表達「現在忙於協商」最為適當,因此答案為 (A)。

字彙 official 官員 currently 目前
be engaged in 忙著做
proposal 提案 ring road 環狀道路
negotiation 磋商;協商

**127**

湯林森市長為改善公路實施了新措施,包括切割部分 22 號公路,僅供公共運輸使用。

(A) implementing 正在實施
(B) implement 實施
(C) implemented 實施了
(D) implements 實施

解析 本句主詞 initiative、動詞 involved,主詞和動詞之間的 that . . . highways 為形容詞子句,用來修飾 initiative。空格置於形容詞子句中的動詞位置,而 implementing 並非動詞、implement 不符合單複數的一致性,因此請刪去這兩個選項。剩下的選項為現在式和過去式,根據題意,填入過去式 (C) 較為適當。

字彙 initiative 新措施 mayor 市長
section off 切割出
public transport 公共運輸
implement 實施

**128**

員工須受僱一年以上才符合公司退休金制度的資格。

(A) compatible 相容的
(B) eligible 合乎資格的
(C) responsive 反應積極的
(D) flexible 靈活的

解析 本題考的是形容詞詞彙。根據題意,表達「合乎適用退休金制度的資格」最為適當,因此答案為 (B)。compatible 要搭配介系詞 with 一起使用,意思為「與……和睦相處的」;responsive 要搭配介系詞 to 一起使用,意思為「對……的反應」。

字彙 employ 僱用
pension scheme 退休金制度
compatible 相容的
be eligible for 合乎……的資格

**129**

哈立德先生表示,為了公司前景,他隨時都願意出國。

(A) somewhere 某處
(B) whenever 無論何時
(C) himself 他自己
(D) whether 不管

解析 空格前後皆為結構完整的句子，因此空格可以填入從屬連接詞、或是對等連接詞。somewhere 為副詞、himself 為代名詞，請先刪去這兩個選項。whether 和 whenever 當中，表達「只要是對他的機構有幫助，隨時都可以」最符合題意，因此答案為 (B)。whether 當作從屬連接詞使用時，意思為「不管是……或是……」。

字彙 indicate 表示；表明　abroad 到國外
prospect 前景；展望

**130**

減少營業成本是在工作場所投資新技術的一項正當理由。

(A) justification 正當理由
(B) condolence 弔唁、哀悼
(C) translation 翻譯
(D) diagnosis 診斷

解析 選項中表達「為正當的理由之一」的最符合題意，因此答案為 (A) justification。

字彙 reduction 減少；降低

## PART 6

P. 245

### 131-134 傳單

**表演工作者注意！**

　　您對在我們劇場舞台上表演的獨家機會感興趣嗎？如是，請把握 6 月 23 日報名「約克露天藝術節」展現才華的機會，儘速報名。

　　申請表請上 www.yorkopen.org 取得，您的表演將由多名當地劇場演出的人士評審。填好申請表上傳時，也請附上您專業領域的詳細資訊，這將有助評審將您正確分類。

　　申請至 5 月 1 日截止，當天評審也將做出決議。受邀的申請人將有權使用演出設施，且須全程參與活動。

字彙 performing artist 表演工作者；表演藝術家
exclusive 獨家的；排外的
perform 表演　sign up 報名；註冊
display 展示　talent 才華
entry form 申請表；報名表　judge 評審
specialist area 專業領域
application 申請　duration 期間

**131**

(A) Instead 代替
(B) Even so 儘管如此
(C) If so 如是
(D) After that 在這之後

解析 先掌握空格前後句子的意思後，再找出適當連接副詞。根據文意，將 If you interested in it 改寫成 (C) If so（要是這樣的話）最為適當。

**132**

(A) developments 發展
(B) instructions 指示
(C) details 詳細資訊
(D) requirements 要求；必需品

解析 本題問的是欲參加活動的表演藝術家，需要將參加申請書和什麼東西一起上傳。空格後方的 of your specialist area 為答題線索，選擇 (C) 最為適當，表示「詳細說明擅長的領域」。

**133**

(A) 我們已審查所有申請表。
(B) 這將有助評審將您正確分類。
(C) 您得在接待處領取必要的表格。
(D) 舞台表演需要勇氣和隨機應變的能力。

解析 空格前方要求上傳詳細內容，表示這有助於判斷適合分到哪個類別中，因此答案為 (B)。

**134**

(A) Invited 受邀的
(B) Invites 邀請
(C) Invitation 邀請
(D) Inviting 正在邀請

解析 空格用來修飾名詞 applicants（申請者），應填入形容詞，因此請先刪去 (B) 和 (C)。而根據文意，並非申請者主動邀請，而是受到邀請，因此空格要填入過去分詞形容詞 (A) 較為適當。

## 135-138 文章

　　蒙大拿州（3 月 15 日）──國內知名的連鎖加油站馬克斯天然氣，即將在蒙大拿州首度開設兩家加油站。該公司加油站的特色是 24 小時服務的大型便利商店，提供各式小吃、飲料和其他日常必需品。此外，馬克斯加油站也以高效管理和友善員工聞名，並以安全且乾淨的設施為傲。

　　蒙大拿州的第一座馬克斯天然氣，將蓋在勞埃德街和第十大道的轉角。第二座將位於基斯可街和二十大道，這間馬克斯天然氣將為特殊站點，設有小廚房。和其他特殊站點一樣，這裡也將有桌椅供顧客用餐。

字彙 gas stations 加油站
feature 以……為特色
a wide array of 各式各樣的；多樣的
necessity 必需品
friendly 友善的　patron 顧客
amenity 設施　consumer goods 消費品

**135**
(A) Nonetheless 然而
(B) After all 畢竟
(C) Besides 此外
(D) Namely 也就是說

解析 本題要選出適合連接前後句子的連接副詞。空格前方提到加油站的特色，後方則說明加油站有名的原因，因此最適合填入的連接副詞為 (C) Besides（此外）。

**136**
(A) 公路的改善歸功於政府的努力
(B) 他們也以安全且乾淨的設施為傲。
(C) 隨著油價上漲，通勤族愈來愈少開自家車。
(D) 消費品近來將會更容易取得。

解析 空格前方提到 Max-Gas 加油站的特色，接著應表示令他們感到自豪的部分，因此答案為 (B)。

**137**
(A) similar 類似的
(B) former 先前地
(C) rival 競爭的
(D) second 第二的

解析 第一句話提到將在這個地方開兩間新的加油站，而本段開頭針對第一間加油站進行說明，接著對「第二間」加油站說明較為適當，因此答案為 (D)。

**138**
(A) there 那裡
(B) whose 某人的
(C) which 某物的
(D) where 在那裡

解析 空格用來引導後方的子句，應填入連接詞。there 為副詞，因此請先刪去該選項。其餘選項皆為連接詞，可以用來引導形容詞子句，同時修飾前方的名詞（先行詞）。先行詞為 tables and chairs，是顧客可以坐下來用餐的「地方」，因此答案為 (D) where。

## 139-142 電子郵件

收件者：dcarlton@jetmail.net
寄件者：jdelphi@houndban.com
日期：4 月 5 日
主旨：您的面試

敬愛的卡爾頓先生：

　　我代表獵犬邦公司的徵才團隊寫這封信。您週四面試時讓我們團隊印象深刻，實際上也是最被看好的應徵者之一。很遺憾的是，我們目前並沒有適合您的職缺。然而，我們想邀請您把履歷寄到我們位於芬維爾的辦公室。那裡正在徵求資深會計專員。考量您的經驗和知識，您將是獵犬邦公司的一大資產。如果您願意考慮搬到芬維爾，我們很樂意向該職缺推薦您。

誠摯地，
瓊安娜・德爾菲

字彙 on behalf of 作為……的代表
promising 前途看好的
be willing to 願意；有意
recommend 推薦
reference letter 推薦信

**139**

(A) Otherwise 否則
(B) Meanwhile 於此同時
(C) In fact 實際上
(D) As always 如常

**解析** 本題要選出適合連接前後句子的連接副詞。空格前方提到對先前的面試感到印象深刻，後方又提到對方是最有望被選上的人之一，因此填入表示「事實上」的連接副詞最為適當，針對前方內容進一步說明。

**140**

(A) 我們從未收到您的推薦信。
(B) 我們認為您的經驗不足
(C) 我們希望您到我們公司實習。
(D) 很遺憾的是，我們目前並沒有適合您的職缺。

**解析** 雖然空格前方提到對面試感到印象深刻，但是後方卻建議對方至另一個地方工作，因此答案要選 (D)，告知無法提供對方本次的職缺。

**141**

(A) Now that 既然
(B) Given 考量；鑑於
(C) Unlike 不像
(D) Also 也

**解析** 空格用來引導名詞子句，應填入介系詞。Now that（既然）為連接詞、Also（還有）為副詞，皆不適合填入。Given（若考慮到……）和 Unlike（不同於……）當中，填入 (B) Given 較符合文意。另外補充一點，Given 既可以當作連接詞，也可當作介系詞使用。

**142**

(A) program 計畫
(B) lodging 寄宿的地方
(C) vacancy 職缺
(D) training 訓練

**解析** 本文為徵才部門寫給應徵者的郵件，因此表示願意推薦分公司的「職缺」給應徵者較為適當，答案要選 (C)。

**143-146 文章**

### 新圖書館開幕

9 月 10 日——新市立圖書分館位於勝利中心，兩天前開始為訪客提供服務。市長出席了開幕式，且多個社區團體的成員和學童也共襄盛舉。

這間新圖書館佔地 1,200 平方公尺，配合環境設計，館內保暖全仰賴日照，屋頂太陽能板更供應建築用電的六成之多。

圖書館的一大目標是讓民眾使用到尖端科技。不只有豐富參考資料，也備有多台電腦終端機，訪客還可以攜帶自己的設備使用館內的免費高速網路。

**字彙** solar panel 太陽能板
cutting-edge 尖端的；最新的
reference material 參考資料
computer terminal 電腦終端機

**143**

(A) presented 被呈現
(B) presenting 呈現
(C) present 出席的
(D) presently 現在

**解析** 空格位在 be 動詞後方，應填入補語，因此答案有可能是一般形容詞、現在分詞、或是過去分詞。現在分詞後方要連接受詞，因此不能作為答案，答案要選一般形容詞 (C) present（出席的）。

**144**

(A) participated 參加
(B) participating 正在參加
(C) will participate 將參加
(D) would have participated
　　假使當時有參加

**解析** 本題考的是動詞的時態。第一句話提到圖書館從兩天前開始營運，接著也使用過去式，表示市長有出席（was present），因此答案要選 (A) participated。

**145**
(A) 有五台大型空調設備。
(B) 它由著名建築師設計。
(C) 暖內保暖全仰賴日照。
(D) 地點靠近地鐵站。

**解析** 空格後方提到與太陽能板有關的內容，因此答案為 (C)。

**146**
(A) technology 科技
(B) vehicles 交通工具
(C) education 教育
(D) appliance 家電

**解析** 後方句子提到有多台電腦終端機，還能在此使用超高速網路，表示圖書館提供了最新「科技」，因此答案為 (A) technology。

## PART 7

P. 249

## 147-148 廣告

### 紐黑文退休村

紐黑文退休村出租中！

- 一或兩臥的公寓
- 位於紐黑文市中心，有 48 間房的住宅區，適合退休人士。
- 現場設施包括兩間交誼廳、一座游泳池、健身房以及充足的停車位，收費已包含在每月租金內。
- 村莊俯瞰水下橋，靠近商店和公共設施，地點極其理想。
- 參觀樣品屋並了解現有空房，我們的房仲隨時都能帶未來住戶到村裡逛逛。

紐黑文退休村
樹頂路 32 號
紐黑文

**字彙** retirement village 退休村；銀髮村
lease 出租 unit 房間；單位
residential 居住的
cater to 適合；迎合 on-site 現場的
amenities 設施
communal 公共的；共有的

ample 充足的；足夠的 rental 租用的
charge 花費 overlook 俯瞰
showroom 樣品屋 on hand 在手邊；在場
prospective 潛在的
deposit payment 保證金

**147** 廣告上描述了什麼？
(A) 養老院出租
(B) 公司搬遷服務
(C) 當地遊客的景點
(D) 度假小屋出售

**148** 讀者被鼓勵做什麼？
(A) 加入會員
(B) 參觀
(C) 簽合約
(D) 交保證金

## 149-150 電子郵件

收件者：凱爾默工業員工
寄件者：莎莉・阿諾
日期：2 月 12 日
主旨：公司資訊

最近，我們寄給全體員工新員工手冊的複本，同時也附上獨立的簽收單。

該手冊內有凱爾默工業公司政策和程序的完整資訊，也有職務和員工福利的詳細資訊。請仔細閱讀該手冊，確認讀畢且了解手冊所述之規則和流程，承諾遵守公司規則並簽署附件的簽收單。

請將簽名的表單寄給人力資源部的約翰・菲瑟斯，感謝您的配合。

莎莉・阿諾
人力資源部董事總經理

**字彙** employee manual 員工手冊
separate 分開的；單獨的
acknowledgement 確認
manual 手冊 regarding 關於
procedure 程序 job descriptions 職務
employee benefits 員工福利
enclosed 附件的 undertake 承擔
cooperation 合作；配合
publication 出版品

**149** 阿諾女士在電子郵件中討論了什麼？
(A) 訓練課程
(B) 就業機會
(C) 公司出版品
(D) 就職程序的變動

**150** 阿諾女士要求員工做什麼？
(A) 簽署並寄出表單
(B) 檢討工作福利
(C) 出席會議
(D) 還書

## 151-153 資訊

　　感謝您購買 Mission B-452 筆記型電腦，消費即附贈防毒軟體。由於這只是入門版，推薦您盡快購買完整版，您可直接在 www.missioncomputers.com 訂購。我們保證您能馬上下載，並於 5 個工作日內收到軟體包。如您未在期間內收到，將獲得全額退款。由於您是重要客戶，首次購買軟體將獲得 15% 的折扣，只需在訂購時輸入代碼 41230。如果您偏好在實體店面購買軟體包，各大電腦用品店都有庫存。但請留意，大多數零售業者不讓客人使用我們公司的折扣。

　　請洽 800-555-3412，24 小時均能洽詢技術支援，或於週一至週五上午 8 點至晚上 9 點間，致電表達您對購買商品的疑問和意見。

字彙　anti-virus 防毒
introductory 入門的；初步的
guarantee 保證　type in 輸入
place an order 訂購；下訂單
retail outlet 零售店　stock 庫存
leading 主要的　aware 得知　query 詢問
promptly 立即的；迅速的
24/7 全年全天候　voucher 優惠券

**151** 這則公告是寫給誰看的？
(A) 新筆電的主人
(B) 銷售顧問
(C) 技術支援專家
(D) 軟體開發者

**152** 訂購軟體時，店家承諾了什麼？
(A) 入門版三個月效期。
(B) 如太晚到貨，買方將免費獲得軟體。
(C) 技術部門將立即答覆詢問。
(D) 客服全年全天候提供服務。

**153** 買家能如何取得折扣？
(A) 在電腦店購物
(B) 郵寄優惠券
(C) 打給客服
(D) 網路訂購時輸入號碼

## 154-155 訊息串

**班·查爾茲 [上午 9:19]**：內特，我正在店裡，我找不到你要我帶的投影機燈泡。有其他型號，但不是我們要的。

**內特·萊特 [上午 9:20]**：你問過客服櫃檯了嗎？經理跟我說他庫存有一顆，會留給我們。

**班·查爾茲 [上午 9:22]**：喔，了解。我馬上和他確認。

**班·查爾茲 [上午 9:25]**：有了，我再次確認過型號了，正是我們要的。

**內特·萊特 [上午 9:26]**：太好了。你能趕回辦公室嗎？會議一小時後開始，我們需要裝燈泡和事先測試投影機。

**班·查爾茲 [上午 9:27]**：我在路上了。

字彙　beforehand 事先；提早

**154** 關於萊特先生，下列何者最可能為真？
(A) 他給查爾茲先生的型號錯誤。
(B) 他為了投影機燈泡聯絡過商家。
(C) 他打算馬上回到辦公室。
(D) 他將進行簡報。

**155** 上午 9:22 時，查爾斯先生寫道：「喔，了解」，意思為何？
(A) 他找到了僅剩的投影機燈泡。
(B) 他還在商店裡逛。
(C) 他現在了解狀況了。
(D) 他能看到客服櫃檯。

## 156-158 案語

### 編者按

《泰美味》九月號恰逢本雜誌發行兩週年。我們出版第一期至今兩年,已成為當地大受歡迎的風味菜雜誌。近期發行量達到 22,000 冊並持續增長。

我們的刊物得到在地美食家讚賞,上個月拿下世界美食節最佳新食品雜誌的殊榮。作為總編輯,我想感謝盡責的同仁、作者群、廣告主和愈來愈多的讀者群,因為你們才成就了我們。

史黛拉‧摩根

> **字彙** cuisine 烹飪
> coincide 適逢;(幾乎)同時發生
> ethnic 民族的;種族的
> circulation(報紙雜誌的)發行量,銷售量
> accolade 嘉獎;讚賞
> dedicated 盡責的;盡心盡力的
> advertiser 廣告商
> contribute 貢獻;(給報紙、雜誌或書)投稿;撰稿
> contribution 貢獻;投稿;捐款
> distribute 分發;分配
> contributor 貢獻人;投稿人

**156** 摩根女士的案語目的為何?
(A) 要出價
(B) 要徵稿
(C) 要表達感謝
(D) 要介紹作者

**157** 關於《泰美味》,文中提到什麼?
(A) 愈來愈受歡迎。
(B) 它提高了廣告的價碼。
(C) 很快就會發行全球。
(D) 正在找其他撰稿人。

**158** 摩根女士為何提到世界美食節?
(A) 因為雜誌在該活動獲獎
(B) 因為出版商贊助了該活動
(C) 因為她在那裡招到志工
(D) 因為她示範烹飪

## 159-161 備忘錄

寄件者:傑拉爾丁‧康普頓
收件者:比克福行銷員工
主旨:史丹利‧海恩斯

我們很高興宣布,新加坡分公司董事總經理史丹利‧海恩斯,預計兩週後訪問我們華盛頓特區辦公室。海恩斯先生轉調亞洲前,曾在比克福行銷擔任研究分析師及網頁設計師五年。

海恩斯先生花了兩年,成立並整頓好新加坡分公司的網路部門。此舉帶動銷售額大幅成長,比克福也在亞洲打響名號。

海恩斯先生將聚焦社交媒體行銷帶討論,簡報討論將會很詳細,並會於結束後進行問答。會議進行時,建議與會同仁做筆記。

全體員工均須參加,如因工作安排不克前來,請聯繫沃克女士或您辦公室經理。

期待很快與您相會。

誠摯地,
比克福行銷

> **字彙** managing director 董事總經理
> analyst 分析師  transfer 轉調
> set up 成立;建立  sales figures 銷售額
> significantly 顯著地
> established(因為優秀而)被認可的,著名的
> in the case of 至於;就……而言
> scheduling conflict(工作;行程)安排衝突;撞期

**159** 這則備忘錄通知了什麼?
(A) 即將舉行的業務簡報
(B) 公司五週年慶活動
(C) 新加坡辦公室的工作機會
(D) 新公司董事的任命案

**160** 關於海恩斯先生,文中提了什麼?
(A) 最近被比克福聘僱。
(B) 轉介客戶給比克福營銷。
(C) 他將管理華盛頓辦公室。
(D) 他有拓展網路行銷的經驗。

**161** 根據備忘錄,與會同仁應攜帶什麼?
(A) 預備的問題單
(B) 行銷主題的清單
(C) 履歷複本
(D) 記筆記的東西

## 162-164 信件

沙爾姆拉飯店
美麗諾街 50 號
開羅，埃及
8 月 7 日

致有意申請者：

　　感謝您向沙爾姆拉飯店徵詢培訓機會，我們將提供有意從事旅宿業的合格申請者少量給薪的夏季培訓課程。獲選參與培訓計畫的申請人，將在實際工作環境中習得實務經驗，並和導師共同完成與個人職涯規畫有關的專案。

　　請參考附件的申請資料及各部門的職務內容。請在詳細閱讀後，直接向您感興趣的部門提出申請。完整申請資料應於本月底前提交，通過初選後的面試將於 9 月第一週進行。培訓課程預計於 2 月 1 日起至 3 月 10 日，期待很快能收到您的申請。

誠摯地，
塞爾瑪銀行
培訓規畫
附件

> **字彙** traineeship 培訓；教育訓練
> qualified 符合資格的　scheme 計畫
> hands-on 實務　tutor 導師
> aspiration 志向；抱負　enclosed 附件
> thoroughly 詳細地；仔細地
> shortly 很快；不久

**162** 關於這封信的收件者，文中提到什麼？
(A) 他們已聯繫沙爾姆拉飯店。
(B) 他們將由塞爾瑪銀行面試。
(C) 他們正在規劃假期。
(D) 他們在旅行社工作。

**163** 收信的人被要求查看什麼？
(A) 飯店資訊的冊子
(B) 公司財務程序
(C) 計畫內容異動的清單
(D) 有關培訓計畫的資訊

**164** 申請何時截止？
(A) 8 月 31 日
(B) 9 月 4 日
(C) 2 月 1 日
(D) 3 月 10 日

## 165-168 線上討論

**山姆・詹金斯 [上午 10:15]：** 既然我們正在準備下一財政年度的預算，應該來討論更換我們銷售部門用的筆電，他們為此抱怨好一段時間了。

**路易斯・帕克 [上午 10:17]：** 有什麼問題嗎？我以為我們給過他們新筆電了。

**艾笛・斯旺森 [上午 10:22]：** 那已是五年前的事了。筆電速度越來越慢，但更大的問題是無法應付下一次軟體升級，它們跑不動。

**傑夫・隆 [上午 10:25]：** 我們規劃在幾個月後安裝新的盤點資料庫，這樣沒有太多時間做決定。

**艾笛・斯旺森 [上午 10:28]：** 沒錯，我也建議這次買比較耐用的。

**傑夫・隆 [上午 10:29]：** 這樣的話，我推薦金斯頓。該公司剛發布了 XM 系列的新型號，迴響非常好。

**路易斯・帕克 [上午 10:30]：** 價格怎麼樣？

**傑夫・隆 [上午 10:31]：** 都是 1,000 美元起跳，配給 22 名同仁並不便宜。

**路易斯・帕克 [上午 10:32]：** 是啊，不過放長遠看，能省錢就值得。

**山姆・詹金斯 [上午 10:33]：** 好吧，但做決定前，我想我們應該比較至少三、四個選擇。

**傑夫・隆 [上午 10:36]：** 我再來查。

> **字彙** budget 預算　fiscal year 財政年度
> inventory 盤點；清點存貨
> withstand 承受　wear and tear 磨損
> in the long run 長期來看　obsolete 不敷
> 使用的；過時的；可淘汰；老化的

**165** 關於銷售部門，文中提到什麼？
(A) 他們最近更新庫存軟體。
(B) 他們已用同樣設備好幾年了。
(C) 他們最近提出請購筆電的預算。
(D) 他們有處理銷售訂單的問題。

**166** 關於目前的筆電，文中提到什麼？
(A) 價值超過 1,000 美元。
(B) 電源出現問題。
(C) 快不敷使用了。
(D) 當時以折扣價購買。

**167** 關於金斯頓，文中提到什麼？

(A) 其筆電堅固耐用。

(B) 公司負擔不起。

(C) 只出一款機型。

(D) 是評價最好的品牌。

**168** 上午 10:36 時，隆先生寫道：「我再來查」，意思是？

(A) 他將查出可省多少錢。

(B) 他將收集其他機型的資訊。

(C) 他會問員工偏好哪台筆電。

(D) 他將確認金斯頓的價格。

## 169-171 職缺公告

### 巴西的綜合灌溉法和蔬菜生產（IIVPB）

三街 54 號

格拉瓦塔，巴西

職缺

IIVPB 十年來致力教育小農有機農法，目標是利用灌溉法的最新研究提高產量並同時維持有機農法的高品質。我們是一家受到獨立資助的公司，總部位於聖保羅，並在巴西各州設有分部，如帕拉伊巴、巴伊亞，伯南布哥和北大河州。

我們正在尋找帕拉伊巴分部的專案經理，錄取者將率領研究團隊，並擔任團隊和小農的聯絡窗口。合適的應徵者應具備可靠的學術背景，農業相關為佳，且有至少四年的專業管理經驗。

請於 11 月 10 日前，由個人、電子郵件、一般郵件或上官網 www.iivpb.br/careers 應徵，申請時請一併附上應徵函和履歷。錄取者預計於 12 月 10 日就職。

> **字彙** integrate 使合併　irrigation 灌溉
> vacant 職缺的　small holder 小農
> method 方法
> successful candidate 合適的應徵者
> liaison 聯絡人　smallholding 小塊耕地
> solid 可靠的;扎實的　preferably ……為佳
> agricultural 農業的　managerial 管理的
> accompanied by 伴隨著
> cover letter 應徵函;求職信
> revise 修改;訂正

**169** 關於 IIVPB，文中提到什麼？

(A) 致力使用現代灌溉方法。

(B) 正在調整企業使命。

(C) 販賣灌溉設備。

(D) 取得政府資助。

**170** 關於該職位，文中沒有提到什麼？

(A) 職缺將在今年底前補上。

(B) 須與多方溝通。

(C) 須有專案管理經驗。

(D) 限巴西國民。

**171** 在文中標記處，下列句子最適合放在哪裡？
「我們正在尋找帕拉伊巴分部的專案經理。」

(A) [1]

(B) [2]

(C) [3]

(D) [4]

## 172-175　文章

### 焦點員工：史黛西‧梅伊

史黛西‧梅伊擬於 3 月卸下資深保險經紀人職務，她在特拉福德保險服務 25 年、做過許多職務。保險公司董事長傑弗里‧馬克斯表示：「在特拉福德保險公司，要找到像史黛西一樣經驗廣泛的人很難。」

梅伊女士因在哈洛威的辛普森保險仲介公司擔任臨時行政助理，而踏入保險業。她在這份工作得到成就感，合約結束後找起全職工作，隨後在特拉福德保險的安德頓分部找到行政職。梅伊女士經過 18 個月的接線和例行行政庶務後，她受聘為特拉福德愛金頓分部的儲備保險經紀人，並在六個月內升上保險經紀人。

梅伊並未停止向上爬。她解釋：「我熱愛鑽研保單，也想成為資深保險經紀人。對此，愛金頓的經理克雷格‧林給了我建議，我便決定像他五年前一樣申請安德頓的巴特里克學院的保險學程。我申請學貸付課程費，並繼續兼職作保險經紀人。我花了六年完成學業。」

她從巴特里克學院畢業，隨即進到特拉福德保險總部的保險部門。兩年後，她被任命為資深保險經紀人霍普‧班奈特的助理，當班奈特女士轉調至重大理賠部門，梅伊接下她的位子。梅伊女士說：「想想我可是從歸檔開始，做到公司總部的資深專員。」

> **字彙** step down 卸下;辭職;下台
> underwriter 保險經紀人;保險業務員
> range 範圍;幅度　temporary 臨時的
> administrative 行政的
> insurance broker 保險仲介業者
> permanent position 全職工作

routine 例行　trainee 儲備人員
climb 攀爬　upwards 向上　rank 職級
finance 向……提供資金；資助
appoint 任命
take one's place 接替某人的職位
filing 歸檔；整理檔案
varied 各種各樣的；形形色色的

**172** 本文的目的為何？
(A) 要介紹工作多年準備退休的員工
(B) 要提供申請培訓課程的資訊
(C) 要描述保險公司的所有職缺
(D) 要報告員工不同的職責

**173** 關於林先生，文中提到什麼？
(A) 他接受該篇報導的採訪。
(B) 他讀過保險學。
(C) 他有教學經驗。
(D) 他是保險公司的兼職經紀人。

**174** 關於特拉福德保險，文中提到什麼？
(A) 補助員工大學進修學費。
(B) 最近和辛普森保險仲介公司合併。
(C) 總公司位於愛金頓。
(D) 有重大理賠部門。

**175** 在文中標記處，下列句子最適合放在哪裡？
「她受聘為特拉福德愛金頓分部的儲備保險經紀人。」
(A) [1]
(B) [2]
(C) [3]
(D) [4]

**176-180 傳單與電子郵件**

### 第十屆曼斯菲爾德藝術戲劇節
#### 10 月 10 日至 12 日

曼斯菲爾德藝術戲劇節精采報你知。活動由曼斯菲爾德文化協會贊助，為期三天，將呈現藝術家的特展、當地音樂家和演員的表演。現場可購買小吃和手工藝品，並安排各類兒童活動。

部分活動如下：
**10 月 10 日，週五，下午 4 點，畢卡索博物館**
伊蓮娜·馬丁《我的家族肖像》開幕。展至 11 月 17 日。週一至週五，上午 10:30 至晚上 8:00，週六日中午至下午 6 點。免費入場。

10 月 11 日至 12 日，週六日，
上午 11 點至下午 7 點，聖瑪麗天主教堂
兒童美術、手工藝與遊戲活動。

10 月 11 日，週六，
下午 3:00 瑞斯戴爾戶外劇場
（雨備：維爾博里劇院）眾所期待的秘魯青年合唱團音樂會。入口購票。

10 月 11 日至 12 日，週六日，
下午 1 點至晚間 7 點，麥克連恩紀念館
民俗美食和手工市集。

10 月 12 日，週日，
下午 6：00 至晚間 8:00，芬尼莫爾劇院
斯托布里奇劇團演出斯特爾·高瑟的劇作《田園夏日》。入口購票。

10 月 1 日起預售。欲了解詳情或活動完整列表，請上 www.madf.org。

收件者：諾亞·穆拉尼
寄件者：瑪麗亞·羅薩多
主旨：資訊
日期：10 月 15 日

敬愛的穆拉尼：

再次感謝您邀請我們到曼斯菲爾德藝術戲劇節，表演我們的秘魯音樂。很不巧下了大雨，迫使我們轉往室內，也代表享受我們演出的聽眾少了很多。但我們還是很高興聽到觀眾的熱烈掌聲。有很多人買了我們的 CD，或詢問可否從流行音樂網站上下載我們的音樂。

我們希望未來也有榮幸再到藝術節演出。

瑪麗亞·羅薩多
秘魯青年合唱團活動經理

**字彙** prominent 著名的；重要的
refreshments 茶點；小點心　craft 手工藝
admission 入場
open air theater 戶外劇場
Peruvian 祕魯的　choir 合唱團
memorial 紀念館　ethnic 民族的；種族的
theater company 劇團
playwright 劇作家
pre-booing 預購；預訂
heavily 劇烈地　indoors 室內
ovation 熱烈掌聲　privilege 榮幸
duration 期間

**176** 週日下午 6 點沒有安排哪項活動？
(A) 手工藝創作
(B) 藝術展
(C) 民俗美食市集
(D) 芭蕾舞表演

**177** 關於藝術節，文中提到什麼？
(A) 有在網路上行銷。
(B) 每天早上 11 點開始。
(C) 每年舉行三次。
(D) 為期一週。

**178** 戲劇何時演出？
(A) 10 月 1 日
(B) 10 月 9 日
(C) 10 月 10 日
(D) 10 月 12 日

**179** 羅薩多女士為什麼寫電子郵件給穆拉尼先生？
(A) 要表示感謝
(B) 要索取演出票券
(C) 要取消預訂
(D) 要取消演出

**180** 關於秘魯青年合唱團，文中提到什麼？
(A) 官網的訪客愈來愈多。
(B) 正在南美洲巡演。
(C) 曾在維爾博里劇院演出。
(D) 是首次參與音樂節。

### 181-185 特色表與官網

---

**歐馬克 2 雙層瓦斯烤箱**
**EM-3189 型**

**特色：**
－加大雙層烤箱，比標準烤箱更多的烹飪空間。
－熱處理鋼表層提供絕佳的防鏽保護且便於清潔。
－內建自動定時器，提醒您料理完成。操作面板指示燈顯示最佳烹飪溫度。
－新節能技術能多段控溫，瓦斯用量比多款機型都少。
－大中小型各類烤盤
－三隔層設計，可同時烘烤、烹飪和加熱食物，讓您的料理完美協調。

---

| 評價 | 產品 | 合約條款 | 店鋪位置 |
|------|------|---------|---------|

「錢花得超值得的。」
由 阿比蓋爾・戴維斯 發布
發表於 9 月 14 日
地點 英國伯克夏

　　我家前一台他牌烤箱只撐了三年。很高興歐馬克設計出這台先進又實惠的機型。我不覺得比前一台便宜卻感到很驚喜。這台能完美烹飪各種食物。內部分為三層（烘烤、烹飪、加熱），並有四種烤盤（小、中、兩個大的），適合各種尺寸的鍋具。讓我特別印象深刻的是我能放著烤便外出，因為料理完成會自動關機。有多種鮮豔的顏色可以選。最棒的是，歐馬克把它設計得很耐用。我唯一的不滿是功能太多，我花了較長時間才搞清楚。為了遵循說明，我得很詳細閱讀手冊。

> **字彙** gas cooker 瓦斯爐　extra-large 加大
> heat-treated steel 熱處理鋼
> exterior 表層；外觀　rust 鏽
> integral 內建的　optimum 最佳的
> cooking pan 烤盤　roast 烤
> coordinate 使協調；使一致
> terms and conditions 合約條款
> advanced 先進的　inexpensive 不貴的
> economical 省錢的　appliance 家電
> tier 一層　internally 內部地　suit 適合
> long lasting 耐用的　durability 耐久性

**181** 特色表內寫了什麼？
(A) 一套食譜的指示
(B) 產品的優點
(C) 不同類型瓦斯烤箱的資訊
(D) 各種歐馬克 2 雙層瓦斯烤箱可料理的食物

**182** 根據特色表，節能技術的優點為何？
(A) 用較少的能源。
(B) 節省用戶時間。
(C) 使家電更耐用。
(D) 使產品更易清潔。

**183** 官網上第一段、第六行的「suit」，意思最接近下列何者？
(A) 適合
(B) 穿上
(C) 取得資格
(D) 呼籲

**184** 戴維斯女士對產品有何批評？

(A) 很複雜。

(B) 太重。

(C) 太吵。

(D) 很貴。

**185** 產品描述中，沒有提到戴維斯女士喜歡的哪一項特色？

(A) 碗的數量

(B) 加大烤箱尺寸

(C) 多種外觀

(D) 烹飪設置

## 186-190 傳單、電子郵件與明信片

**在新科技校園精進你的電腦技能**
**秋季課程（第一學期）**

使用資料庫（初階課程）　　　　975 美元
8 節課（上午 9:30 至上午 11:45）
開始：9 月 3 日

文書處理訓練營（中階課程）　　825 美元
6 節課（上午 8:30 至上午 11:30）
開始：9 月 10 日

完美簡報軟體（高階課程）　　　775 美元
5 節課（下午 1:00 至下午 5:30）
開始：9 月 17 日

試算表的秘密（中階課程）　　　450 美元
4 節課（上午 9:00 －下午 12:15）
開始：9 月 24 日

所有課程都在週六
羅曼進修教育大樓
萊特福特大道 8904 號，弗農
(818) 555-9303
請上 www.newtechnologycampus.com 註冊。
註冊時須支付不予退還的訂金
（學費的 10%）。

寄件者：湯姆・巴頓
收件者：布蘭達・藍
日期：8 月 20 日
主旨：秋季課程

敬愛的藍女士：

　　我寫這封信給您反應我上網註冊時遇到的問題。我想登記您下個月的初學者課程，請告訴我該如何付款。我準備提前全額支付學費，再向我的公司報銷。

因此，我需要收據。

誠摯地，
湯姆・巴頓

敬愛的巴頓：

　　您的課程將於下週開始。請注意教室尚未分配，我們因此請您提早在表定課前 15 分鐘抵達。到達時請在大樓東入口旁的保全櫃檯登記，您將取得臨時停車證和出入證，到時將有人引導您教室位置。

　　如您尚未繳清學費，須在開學日繳納。將有註冊組的人員在大廳待命。

　　您如有任何問題，歡迎透過 (818) 555-8787 與我們聯繫。

**字彙** nonrefundable 不予退還的
deposit 訂金　tuition 註冊費
up front 提前　reimbursement 報銷
balance 餘款　in-person 當面

**186** 關於新技術校園的課程，文中提到什麼？

(A) 允許現場註冊。

(B) 要求預付款項。

(C) 只有早上有課。

(D) 限制上課人數。

**187** 有關巴頓先生想上的課程，下列何者為真？

(A) 總共會上六次。

(B) 下午上課。

(C) 將花他的公司 450 美元。

(D) 上課時間少於三小時。

**188** 電子郵件第一段、第二行的「full」，意思最接近下列何者？

(A) 全部

(B) 額外的

(C) 重要的

(D) 逾期的

**189** 根據明信片，巴頓先生應該做什麼？

(A) 第一堂課前提早到。

(B) 帶身分證件。

(C) 在特區停車。

(D) 發放停車許可證。

**190** 關於明信片，文中提到什麼？
(A) 寄到巴頓先生的工作場所。
(B) 是藍女士寫的。
(C) 需巴頓先生的回信。
(D) 於 9 月 3 日前寄出。

## 191-195 網站、文章與電子郵件訊息

| 關於我們 | 產品 | 分部 | 網路銷售 | 聯絡我們 |
|---|---|---|---|---|

**我們的故事**

「極好食」於 1920 年開業，起先是紐約西部小鎮的極好烘焙坊。店長暨創始人大衛·赫克特使用獨門家族食譜烤麵包和甜點。公司 1950 年代開始製作洋芋片和其他點心。1958 年，赫克特決定將公司出售給一群投資人，並由他們改名為「極好食」。新的所有權人出售了烘焙坊的經營權，僅專注於開發和生產洋芋片、玉米片、爆米花和其他美味點心，包括受歡迎的低脂食品系列產品，主打注重健康的客群。極好食至今向全美 50 個州、加拿大和墨西哥的零售商店供應產品。

水牛城（7 月 16 日）──為了健康教育募款，系列路跑賽事將於 7 月 21 日週日，在市區的伯靈頓公園舉行。「為健康而跑」有 15、10 和 5 公里的賽事，最早於早上 7:30 開跑。參賽者據年齡和性別分為六種不同組別，每個組別前三名都將獲獎。另有兩公里長非競賽的趣味健走，各年齡都能參加。活動由伯靈頓運動飲料和極好食等多家當地廠商及聖詹姆斯醫院贊助。報名請上 www.racehealth.org。趣味健走報名費為 25 美元，賽跑則為 45 美元。參加者將獲得贊助商提供的 T 恤、免費飲料和贈品。

**收件者：**肯·斯坦頓
**寄件者：**榮恩·托比雅斯
**日期：**7 月 22 日

敬愛的斯坦頓：

真的很感謝您告訴我這次新賽跑的消息。我和一群同事昨天參加了最長的賽事。大家離勝利遠得很，但還是很好玩。我希望您明年也能辦活動。我和工作團隊裡其他人說了，他們都有興趣參加。

再次感謝您的辛勞。

誠摯地，
榮恩·托比雅斯

**字彙** founder 創始人　exclusively 專門地
health-conscious 注重健康的
feature 以……為特色　sponsor 贊助
nonetheless 但是；仍然
put together 組織；安排

**191** 官網第一段、第五行的「operation」，意思最接近下列何者？
(A) 經營
(B) 設備
(C) 程序
(D) 手術

**192** 關於極好食，文中指出什麼？
(A) 他們定期贊助活動。
(B) 他們捐錢給學校。
(C) 他們在加拿大有一家工廠。
(D) 他們位於水牛城。

**193** 關於活動，文章沒有提到什麼？
(A) 兒童有資格參加。
(B) 需要報名費。
(C) 將頒發 18 個獎項。
(D) 所有比賽將在中午前結束。

**194** 斯坦頓先生最有可能是誰？
(A) 15 公里競賽的得獎者
(B) 為健康而跑的主辦者
(C) 聖詹姆斯醫院的醫療照護工作者
(D) 托比亞斯先生公司的員工

**195** 關於托比雅斯先生，文中提到什麼？
(A) 他跑了 10 公里的賽事。
(B) 他付了 25 美元參加。
(C) 他收到免費食物。
(D) 他獲頒獎項。

## 196-200 廣告與兩封電子郵件

### 吉姆老大的夏末促銷
本月限定
8 月 1 日（週日）開跑，一起來買
為兒童發放氣球

| 精選配件包括所有魔術牌耳機及黑人牌相機包均享 20％折扣 | G5 牌、李文斯頓和華德牌小家電享 15％折扣 |
|---|---|
| 提圖斯、李文斯頓和華德牌大家電享 10％折扣 | 電視、立體聲音響和 LCD 投影機均享 5％的折扣 |

加入會員俱樂部，每次購物賺取積分。

積分可兌換贈品或折扣。

詳查 www.bigjims.com。

以下吉姆老大店面可見特價產品：

瑞斯路 88 號，馬斯頓 555-0340

老鷹路 7816 號，林肯 555-2149

賈斯珀大街 908 號，溫斯頓 555-3873

部分產品免運，詳洽店鋪經理。

---

**收件者**：山姆・隆
**寄件者**：唐娜・金斯利
**主旨**：運送
**日期**：9 月 2 日上午 8:29

---

敬愛的隆先生：

　　我上次在您店裡購買華德牌洗碗機，原本是要求您 3 號出貨，但發生了一些事，這項提議和我的行程會衝突。可否請您在 6 號下午 4 點或 7 號早上 10 點出貨？請讓我知道日期和時間您是否方便。賈斯珀大街上的店面離我家不遠，希望您能通融。我很抱歉沒儘早聯繫您。

謝謝，
唐娜・金斯利

---

**收件者**：唐娜・金斯利
**寄件者**：山姆・隆
**主旨**：運送
**日期**：9 月 2 日上午 8:29

---

親愛的金斯利女士：

　　很高興能顧及您的需求，於您建議的早上時間出貨。我們的一名駕駛將與您聯繫，並確認您的地址和取貨時間。於此同時，如您有任何疑問或顧慮，請隨時與我們聯絡。

感謝您選擇購買我們的商品。

誠摯地，
山姆・隆

> **字彙** kickoff 開始　redeem 將（點數）兌換
> accommodate 顧及
> multiple 多樣的　carry 運送

**196** 關於吉姆老大，文中沒有提到什麼？
(A) 地點很多。
(B) 有販售電子產品。
(C) 給忠實買家回饋獎勵。
(D) 在網路販賣產品。

**197** 金斯利女士為什麼聯繫隆先生？
(A) 要確認最近的訂單
(B) 要詢問折扣
(C) 要更改約定的時間
(D) 要提供取貨地址

**198** 關於金斯利女士，下列何者最有可能為真？
(A) 她付了運費。
(B) 她獲得 10％的折扣。
(C) 她住在林肯。
(D) 她賺到回饋點數。

**199** 第二封電子郵件中，第一段、第一行的
「accommodate」，意思最接近下列何者？
(A) 答應
(B) 調整
(C) 複查
(D) 保護

**200** 金斯利女士何時會收到購買的商品？
(A) 9 月 2 日
(B) 9 月 3 日
(C) 9 月 6 日
(D) 9 月 7 日